THE YEAR'S BEST SCIENCE FICTION

**FOURTEENTH
ANNUAL
COLLECTION**

ALSO BY GARDNER DOZOIS

ANTHOLOGIES

A Day in the Life
Another World
Best Science Fiction Stories of the Year #6–10
The Best of Isaac Asimov's Science Fiction Magazine
Time-Travellers from Isaac Asimov's Science Fiction Magazine
Transcendental Tales from Isaac Asimov's Science Fiction Magazine
Isaac Asimov's Aliens   *Isaac Asimov's Mars*
Isaac Asimov's SF Lite   *Isaac Asimov's War*
Isaac Asimov's Planet Earth (with Sheila Williams)
Isaac Asimov's Robots (with Sheila Williams)
Isaac Asimov's Cyberdreams (with Sheila Williams)
Isaac Asimov's Skin Deep (with Sheila Williams)
Isaac Asimov's Ghosts (with Sheila Williams)
Isaac Asimov's Vampires (with Sheila Williams)
The Year's Best Science Fiction, #1–13
Future Earths: Under African Skies (with Mike Resnick)
Future Earths: Under South American Skies (with Mike Resnick)
Future Power (with Jack Dann)   *Aliens!* (with Jack Dann)
Unicorns! (with Jack Dann)   *Magicats!* (with Jack Dann)
Magicats 2 (with Jack Dann)   *Bestiary!* (with Jack Dann)
Mermaids! (with Jack Dann)   *Sorcerers!* (with Jack Dann)
Demons! (with Jack Dann)   *Dogtales!* (with Jack Dann)
Ripper! (with Susan Casper)   *Seaserpents!* (with Jack Dann)
Dinosaurs! (with Jack Dann)   *Little People!* (with Jack Dann)
Dragons! (with Jack Dann)   *Horses!* (with Jack Dann)
Unicorns 2 (with Jack Dann)   *Invaders!* (with Jack Dann)
Angels! (with Jack Dann)   *Dinosaurs II* (with Jack Dann)
Hackers (with Jack Dann)   *Timegates* (with Jack Dann)
Modern Classics of Science Fiction
Modern Classic Short Novels of Science Fiction
Modern Classics of Fantasy
Killing Me Softly

FICTION

Strangers
The Visible Man (collection)
Nightmare Blue (with George Alec Effinger)
Slow Dancing Through Time (with Jack Dann, Michael Swanwick,
    Susan Casper, and Jack C. Haldeman II)
The Peacemaker
Geodesic Dreams (collection)

NONFICTION

The Fiction of James Tiptree, Jr.

THE YEAR'S BEST SCIENCE FICTION

**FOURTEENTH
ANNUAL
COLLECTION**

Gardner Dozois, Editor

ST. MARTIN'S GRIFFIN 🜍 **NEW YORK**

For Gordon Van Gelder

Edited by Gordon Van Gelder

ISBN 0-312-15703-7

First St. Martin's Griffin Edition: June 1997

10 9 8 7 6 5 4 3 2 1

CONTENTS

Acknowledgments		viii
Summation: 1996		ix
IMMERSION	Gregory Benford	1
THE DEAD	Michael Swanwick	47
THE FLOWERS OF AULIT PRISON	Nancy Kress	56
A DRY, QUIET WAR	Tony Daniel	82
THIRTEEN PHANTASMS	James P. Blaylock	99
PRIMROSE AND THORN	Bud Sparhawk	109
THE MIRACLE OF IVAR AVENUE	John Kessel	142
THE LAST HOMOSEXUAL	Paul Park	167
RECORDING ANGEL	Ian McDonald	178
DEATH DO US PART	Robert Silverberg	188
THE SPADE OF REASON	Jim Cowan	203
THE COST TO BE WISE	Maureen F. McHugh	218
BICYCLE REPAIRMAN	Bruce Sterling	254
THE WEIGHING OF AYRE	Gregory Feeley	279
THE LONGER VOYAGE	Michael Cassutt	311
THE LAND OF NOD	Mike Resnick	330
RED SONJA AND LESSINGHAM IN DREAMLAND	Gwyneth Jones	350
THE LADY VANISHES	Charles Sheffield	362
CHRYSALIS	Robert Reed	373
THE WIND OVER THE WORLD	Steven Utley	407
CHANGES	William Barton	430
COUNTING CATS IN ZANZIBAR	Gene Wolfe	445
HOW WE GOT IN TOWN AND OUT AGAIN	Jonathan Lethem	457
DR. TILMANN'S CONSULTANT: A SCIENTIFIC ROMANCE	Cherry Wilder	475
SCHRÖDINGER'S DOG	Damien Broderick	492
FOREIGN DEVILS	Walter Jon Williams	518
IN THE MSOB	Stephen Baxter	535
THE ROBOT'S TWILIGHT COMPANION	Tony Daniel	539
HONORABLE MENTIONS: 1996		590

ACKNOWLEDGMENTS

The editor would like to thank the following people for their help and support: first and foremost, Susan Casper, for doing much of the thankless scut work involved in producing this anthology; Michael Swanwick, Ellen Datlow, Virginia Kidd, Sheila Williams, Tina Lee, David Pringle, Kristine Kathryn Rusch, Pat Cadigan, Charles C. Ryan, Harlan Ellison, David G. Hartwell, Craig Engler, Leslie What, Torsten Scheihagen, Warren Lapine, Ed McFadden, Tom Piccirilli, Dave Truesdale, Lawrence Person, Dwight Brown, Darrell Schweitzer, Robert Killheffer, Corin See, and special thanks to my own editor, Gordon Van Gelder.

Thanks are also due to Charles N. Brown, whose magazine *Locus* (Locus Publications, P.O. Box 13305, Oakland, CA 94661, $43.00 for a one-year subscription [twelve issues] via second class; credit card orders [510] 339-9198) was used as a reference source throughout the Summation, and to Andrew Porter, whose magazine *Science Fiction Chronicle* (Science Fiction Chronicle, P.O. Box 022730, Brooklyn, NY 11202-0056, $35.00 for a one-year subscription [twelve issues]; $42.00 first class) was also used as a reference source throughout.

SUMMATION: 1996

Nineteen ninety-six was a year when some of the birds that have been hovering ominously over the genre for a number of years came home to roost. It would be premature to say that the recession/bust/slump that some pessimistic genre pundits have been predicting for more than a decade has finally arrived—science fiction and the related fields of fantasy and horror are still large and varied genres, with over 1,100 "books of interest" to the three fields published in 1996, according to the newsmagazine *Locus,* some of which sold very well indeed. There are still many contradictory omens out there to be read (the number of science fiction books published this year actually *increased* for instance, from 239 to 253, although there were declines in fantasy and horror, working out to a 6 percent drop overall), with new publishing lines being launched even as some of the old ones dwindle, and it is still possible to read the same signs and make either pessimistic or optimistic predictions about the future, depending on what evidence you look at and what weight you arbitrarily decide to give it.

Nevertheless, SF has had better years than 1996, which saw an extremely bad year in the magazine market, and saw the sale of mass market paperbacks plummet dramatically (although some hardcovers and trade paperbacks continued to sell well), with record returns, to the point where many industry insiders were saying that mass market was no longer a viable publishing category. Domestic distribution networks, responsible for getting books and magazines to newsstands and bookstores, underwent major upheavals this year and last, with some disappearing and others merging or swallowing up smaller independent distributors, all with very significant consequences, particularly in the precarious magazine market. There were some major changes at the very top levels of publishing houses, and some big mergers, the consequences of which may take years to work themselves out. And the dream of electronic publishing remained still largely a promise for the future, although its prophets are still vocal (and there were interesting developments here and there—this anthology, for instance, features three stories that have never been published in print form before, existing before then only as phosphor dots on a screen, an indication that the electronic market is becoming a more viable and more important place to search for quality SF).

So, the long-predicted Big Bust has not come *yet* (the comics and gaming industries were hit much harder last year than SF has been to date), and SF remains a big genre, but of course all of the above omens make publishers nervous. The poor sales of mass-market originals that aren't media tie-ins are particularly worrisome, and there's likely to be some belt-tightening and line-trimming going on next year, as publishers either react to poor sales or try to dodge the bullet. Some publishers seem to think that they can boost the reliability of performance by shifting their emphasis away from adult SF to media tie-in books of various sorts, which are considered a "safe sale," and this may work for a while—until they glut and oversell the market with such items, and readers abruptly get tired of media tie-ins . . . and then the shit will *really* hit the fan. (Something similar seems to be happening in early 1997 with the once-booming *Goose-*

bumps Young Adult Horror empire, where sales seem to have suddenly and dramatically fallen off, probably because the ever-increasing flood of *Goosebumps* titles and related tie-in products over-saturated the audience.) These publishers are certainly not going to listen to *me,* though, so you're likely to see media tie-in books continue to proliferate at the expense of adult SF books—swallowing monthly slots and rack space that might once have gone to core SF instead—for at least the next few years. Some publishers also seem to be flirting with the idea that fantasy sells much better than science fiction (and so you should publish *nothing but* fantasy); this idea has infected the British publishing world to the extent that it is now almost impossible to sell an SF book to a British publisher, even for Big Name Writers. At this year's Worldcon, many top agents and editors were buzzing excitedly about the sales potential of fantasy, and the talk of the convention was the fact that a fantasy anthology featuring new stories set in various famous fantasy series had just sold for an enormous six-figure advance, the highest ever paid for an anthology—while the corresponding science fiction anthology, new stories set in various famous science fiction series, could not be sold at all; the publishers weren't interested. So what's happened to the British publishing world *could* happen here as well—in which case, non-media-oriented science fiction would effectively vanish, driven off the shelves by a self-fulfilling prophecy imposed on the publishing world by itself.

I don't really think that this is going to happen; this scenario is probably much too bleak. Regular adult non-media-oriented SF still makes too much money for too many different publishers—the inclination, in fact (in some places at least), seems to be to publish *more* science fiction. Avon, for instance, is planning an ambitious new and expanded line for 1998. And even if the worse came to the absolute worst, with the bleak scenario above coming true in every particular, that *still* wouldn't mean that science fiction was dead—small presses and smaller non-corporate imprints would take up the slack and continue to publish core SF, and eventually some of those small presses would start to grow, and other publishers would notice their success and imitate it— and the cycle would start all over again. A very similar sort of thing happened with Western novels, which for about a decade were almost driven out of the trade publishing industry, but which are now making something of a comeback, with bookstores putting in shelves of Westerns once again. Historical novels went through a similar dry spell, and are now flourishing again as well.

So would it be with science fiction, I think—but we are still a long, long way away from that scenario, and, with luck, the cycle of bust-and-eventual-resurgence will never start in the first place.

Meanwhile, whether there are storms ahead or not, there was a fair amount of activity in the SF publishing world this year. Putnam Berkley were sold to the Penguin Publishing Group, which plans to merge the operations of the two giant companies, although management is claiming that editorial structures will remain essentially the same, with imprints and smaller publishing units (such as the Ace and Putnam SF lines) left intact. Avon, with a new editorial team under the direction of Lou Aronica now in place, announced a five-month hiatus in publishing, from September 1997 to January 1998 (although books bought under the old regime will continue to be published during this period); in 1998, they plan to launch a new SF line and imprint, dropping the old AvoNova name. Several CEOs of major publishing houses departed this year, which could have big impact down the line: Peter Mayer, longtime CEO of the Penguin Group, stepped down to run his own small publishing house, Overlook Press; Thomas McCormack, longtime CEO and editorial director of St Martin's Press, retired; and Charlie Haywood, president and CEO of Little, Brown, resigned. Other changes at the top included Nancy Neiman-Legette being named senior vice-president of the Putnam Berkley group; Ken Fun, CEO and president of Harper San Francisco, being named senior vice-president and deputy publisher of the entire HarperCollins adult trade group, replacing Geoff Hannell; and Judith Curr joining the Ballantine Publishing Group as senior vice-president and editor-in-chief of the Group's mass-market and hardcover publishing. John Silbersack was promoted from vice-president, editor-in-chief of HarperPrism to Publishing Director, in charge of marketing and merchandising as well as editorial. White Wolf underwent a number of upheavals, with Publisher Stewart Wieck becoming Senior Editor of their Borealis Science Fiction imprint (although he will still oversee the White Wolf publishing program as a whole) and the rest of the editorial staff still not settled enough for me to report anything accurately. And Zebra Books announced that they were dropping their horror imprint, one of the last existing genre horror lines.

The usual game of Editorial Musical Chairs continued in full vigor this year. Laura Anne Gilman moved from Ace to Penguin/NAL, where she became executive editor of Roc Books, replacing Amy Stout, who, later in the year, became a consulting acquisitions editor at Del Rey. James Turner, longtime editor of Arkham House, was discharged, and later became an editor for Golden Gryphon Press. Pamela Weintraub replaced Keith Ferrell as editor of Omni Internet. And early in 1997, Tom Dupree left Bantam, following other former Bantam colleagues to Avon; he was replaced at Bantam by Pat Lo Brutto, who had at one time been the editor of the Doubleday SF line.

So, what's ahead for the science fiction field, as we hurtle toward the last few years of the century?

Well, I've said this before, but, since several gloomy notes have been sounded in this summation so far (with several more yet to come), perhaps it's worth saying again: A recession or bust in the SF publishing industry is by no means a sure thing, but, even if one does come along . . . well, SF has gone through boom-and-bust cycles before, ever since there was such a thing as SF as a distinct publishing category, and every such boom-and-bust cycle has left the habitual SF-reading audience *larger than it was before the boom began.* SF is so large a genre at this point that I find it unlikely that any recession will be capable of reducing SF to pre-1974 levels of readership or sales, unless most of the publishing industry at large collapses with it. Even with a lot of the fat trimmed away—and there's a lot of fat out there to be trimmed—there will still be a good deal of solid red meat left behind.

To switch metaphors with a sickening swoop, there may be storm clouds on the horizon—but storms have been weathered before. And will be again this time, I think.

It was a terrible year in the magazine market, even worse than last year—one of the worst years, in fact, since the collapse of the post–war SF boom wiped out magazines by the dozen in the fifties.

The circulations of all the professional SF magazines were down this year, with the digest-sized magazines particularly hard-hit, several of them registering the lowest circulation figures in their histories. Last year saw skyrocketing paper and production costs, and a dramatic industry-wide drop-off in "stamp" subscription sales from places like Publisher's Clearing House, which, responding to an overall slump in sales, "tightened their belts" by dropping many SF magazines and other small "marginal" magazines from their stamp subscription mailings altogether; this, plus 1994's massive postal rate hike, killed some magazines outright in 1995, or forced them to give up print publication for "online electronic magazine" formats (another print SF magazine, *Tomorrow,* made that decision this year, see below), and also caused big cuts in the number of pages and the frequency of publication for many of the digests. In 1996, the chaos in the domestic distribution networks, with bigger distributors swallowing up

many of the small independent distributors, further hurt the ailing SF magazine scene—
the few distributors left often charging fees for carrying titles or asking for greatly
increased "discounts" higher than many SF magazines can easily afford to pay, and
with some distributors setting "subscription caps," refusing to even handle magazines
with a circulation below a certain set figure, usually a higher circulation figure than
most genre magazines can boast. Logistical problems generated by the takeover of
smaller firms by larger ones also resulted in lots of inefficiency—a distributor who had
previously serviced outlets in a hundred-mile area might now be expected to cover a
territory two or three times as large—so that sometimes, even when a distributor was
theoretically willing to handle them, magazines just didn't physically even *get to* those
newsstands that wanted to display them, because of breakdowns in the delivery systems.
And many newsstands themselves became pickier, sometimes refusing to display magazines that fell below a certain circulation figure—again, a figure usually higher than
that of most genre magazines.

The net result of all this was that it was harder to find genre magazines, particularly
the digest-sized titles, on the newsstands in 1996. Some outlets that had carried such magazines for years dropped them altogether, either by choice or because the distributor had
refused to carry them, or because the genre magazines just got lost in the welter of confusion over which distributor was responsible for serving which newsstand with *what.*

There were a few bright spots this year—the latest postal hike was not as bad as had
been anticipated, and the price of paper even went down; *Aboriginal SF,* which had
been reported to be dead in 1995, returned from the grave; and there was increased
activity in the area of online electronic publication—but you had to look long and hard
to find them.

It was a bad year for the three major digest magazines, *Analog, Asimov's Science
Fiction,* and *The Magazine of Fantasy & Science Fiction,* which all continued to lose
circulation to one degree or another.

Analog and *Asimov's Science Fiction* both dropped to their lowest circulation figures
ever. *Analog* lost about 9,000 in subscriptions and another 1,900 in newsstand sales,
for a 14.8 percent loss in overall circulation. *Asimov's Science Fiction* lost over 10,000
in subscriptions and about another 2,300 in newsstand sales, for a 22.2 percent loss in
overall circulation. Both magazines lost a signature (sixteen pages) per issue and
dropped one of their double issues this year, going to an eleven-issue-per-year schedule,
one of those issues being a double issue on sale for two months—the same schedule
that *F&SF* has been on for a few years now. *Analog* and *Asimov's* also changed owners
in 1996, being bought—along with the rest of the Dell Magazines chain, including
mystery magazines, crossword-puzzle magazines, and horoscope magazines—from
Bantam Doubleday Dell by Penny Press, a family-owned Connecticut-based publisher.
The Magazine of Fantasy & Science Fiction lost about 5,300 in subscriptions and about
another 600 in newsstand sales, for an 11.6 percent loss in overall circulation. *F&SF*
also lost its longtime distributor in 1996, and by year's end several readers were reporting that it seemed to be missing from a number of newsstands that had previously
carried it for years, a worrisome development. Longtime editor Kristine Kathryn Rusch
stepped down to pursue a full-time writing career, and was replaced at the beginning
of 1997 by Gordon Van Gelder.

It's hard to put too hopeful a spin on these declining circulation figures, although it
should probably also be said that things are perhaps a little less bleak than they would
at first appear. Most of the digest magazines have always been subscription-driven
anyway; where declining newsstand sales hurt the digests the most is by cutting them
off from attracting new readers who will eventually, with luck, become subscribers.
Eventually, if cut off from newsstand distribution altogether, the subscription list would

dwindle through natural attrition to the point where the magazine was no longer viable, although this might take years. So, with decreasing availability on the newsstands, one of the biggest problems facing the digests is to find ways to attract new subscribers—perhaps an increased presence on the Internet will be a way around the newsstand crunch, and most of the digests are looking into this. In spite of declining circulation, most of the digests are probably still profitable, because digest magazines are so *cheap* to produce in the first place, one of the traditional advantages that has always helped the digest magazines to survive. The publishers of *Analog* and *Asimov's* were also busy adjusting their "draw" this year—sending fewer issues to newsstands that habitually sell less, so that fewer issues overall need to be printed and distributed in order to sell one issue, so that the "efficiency" of both magazines actually *increased,* increasing their profitability—and probably similar efforts are underway at *The Magazine of Fantasy & Science Fiction* as well.

So the digest magazines may not be in quite as much danger of imminent death as the circulation figures might at first suggest—but no publication can afford to lose circulation steadily, and there's no doubt that the digest magazines will have to find ways to turn the decline around and increase circulation again if they want to survive in the long term. And I continue to think—although you can of course discount this opinion, since I am, after all, the editor of *Asimov's Science Fiction*—that the survival of the SF magazines, particularly the three digest titles, is vital to the continued health of the field. Such magazines, as well as being by far the best showcase for emerging writers, provide what little continuity and cohesive sense of community there is in the genre these days.

The British magazine *Interzone* completed its sixth full year as a monthly publication. Circulation went down slightly again this year, in spite of last year's Hugo win, which I had been hoping would translate into increased support for the magazine, particularly in the British fannish community, who largely seem unsupportive of, or even hostile to, *Interzone.* The literary quality of the stories in *Interzone* remains high; *Interzone,* in fact, is one of the most reliable places to find first-rate fiction in the entire magazine market, and it deserves your support in that most practical of forms: money sent in for a subscription. There are still relatively few American subscribers to *Interzone*—although it's flat-out impossible to find it on newsstands here, or even in most SF specialty bookstores—and the magazine deserves to have a lot more.

Science Fiction Age successfully completed their fourth full year of publication. The overall circulation of *Science Fiction Age* dropped in 1996 as well, with them losing over 4,400 subscription sales and over 2,600 newsstand sales, for a 12.5 percent loss in overall circulation. Editor Scott Edelman attributes most of this loss to readers switching subscriptions to *Science Fiction Age*'s companion magazine, *Realms of Fantasy,* and to the publisher's newly launched SF-media magazine *Sci-Fi Entertainment* (also edited by Edelman), both of which made extensive use of *Science Fiction Age*'s subscription list in their start-ups; Edelman points out that Sovereign Media, the parent company, now has *three* successful genre-oriented magazines in place, where a few years before there had been only one, and that this is worth some siphoning of the original subscription base for *Science Fiction Age.* This is a good argument, and will hold up as long as the circulation of *Science Fiction Age* doesn't *continue* to slip in years to come, at which point it will be hard to blame it on the launching of *Realms of Fantasy* and *Sci-Fi Entertainment.* For the moment, though, the Sovereign Media magazines look like success stories, rare bright spots in the gloom of the magazine market. In terms of literary quality, *Science Fiction Age* had perhaps its best year ever, in part because its increased number of pages allows it now to run long novelettes and novellas, the categories in which the highest number of first-rate stories probably appear.

For the first time ever, I found *Science Fiction Age* to be a more reliable source for good core science fiction overall than was *The Magazine of Fantasy & Science Fiction,* where the ratio of fantasy and soft horror stories to SF stories swung way out of balance this year.

Tomorrow Speculative Fiction, which has struggled with undercapitalization since its beginning, published five bimonthly print issues this year, and then abandoned its print incarnation in the face of rising costs, announcing instead that it would reinvent itself as an "online electronic magazine" (see below). The more cynical industry insiders seem to think that this is tantamount to *Tomorrow* having died, but I'm not so sure—in fact, it may do well in its new electronic format; only time will tell. Another severely undercapitalized magazine, *Aboriginal Science Fiction,* suspended publication in 1995 and was widely reported to have died, but came back to life in 1996, publishing three issues this year; a welcome return, in a market that can use all the short fiction outlets it can get.

Realms of Fantasy, a slick, large-size, full-color magazine similar in format to its companion magazine *Science Fiction Age,* except devoted to fantasy rather than science fiction, completed their second full year of publication. They were the only genre magazine whose overall circulation actually *increased* in 1996, rising in subscription sales by about 4,500, although they decreased in newsstand sales (perhaps because of regular readers converting to subscription) by 3,473, for an overall gain in circulation of 2.4 percent—not a lot, perhaps, but much better than any *other* magazine was doing. In terms of literary quality, *Realms of Fantasy* is now easily the best of the all-fantasy magazines, with editor Shawna McCarthy delivering a diverse mix of first-rate fantasy stories, rivaled for sophistication and literary excellence only by the best of the fantasy stories published by *The Magazine of Fantasy & Science Fiction* and *Asimov's Science Fiction.* Among the other fantasy magazines, *Worlds of Fantasy and Horror* also publishes some good work, but continues to have trouble meeting its publication schedule, publishing only two issues in 1996; let's hope they can improve this record next year. *Marion Zimmer Bradley's Fantasy Magazine,* on the other hand, is one of the most reliably produced of all genre magazines, now in its ninth year of publication, but the fiction here remains largely not to my taste, light-years away from the stuff in *Realms of Fantasy* or *F&SF* in terms of depth and literary sophistication.

(Subscription addresses follow for those magazines hardest to find on the newsstands: *The Magazine of Fantasy & Science Fiction,* Mercury Press, Inc., 143 Cream Hill Road, West Cornwall, CT, 06796, annual subscription, $29.90 in U.S.; *Asimov's Science Fiction,* Dell Magazines, P.O. Box 5130, Harlan, IA, 51593-5130, $33.97 for annual subscription; *Interzone,* 217 Preston Drove, Brighton BN1 6FL, United Kingdom, $60 for an airmail one year—twelve issues—subscription; *Analog,* Dell Magazines, P.O. Box 5133, Harlan, IA, 51593-5133, $33.97 for annual subscription; *Worlds of Fantasy and Horror,* Terminus Publishing Company, 123 Crooked Lane, King of Prussia, PA 19406-2570, $16 for four issues in U.S.; *Aboriginal Science Fiction,* P.O. Box 2449, Woburn, MA 01888-0849, $21.50 for four issues; *Marion Zimmer Bradley's Fantasy Magazine,* P.O. Box 249, Berkeley, CA 94701, $16 for four issues in U.S.)

Since an increasing number of genre magazines are abandoning the print world for the still largely unexplored territory of "online electronic publication," it's probably time to take a closer look at this developing market. The most famous story of this type is that of *Omni,* a high-visibility, big-budget magazine that fled the print world early in 1995 to establish an "electronic magazine" version of itself, largely because production costs were becoming prohibitive in spite of the fact that they had a circulation base of more than 700,000. (Discouraging news for *other* magazines, who are struggling to survive with circulations only a fraction of that; if *Omni* couldn't make it with a circulation of 700,000 . . . although production costs at *Omni* were unusually high, and many of their subscriptions were cut-rate PCH "stamp card" subscriptions, which cost more to fulfill than they bring in.)

So, how is *Omni* faring, now that it's an "online magazine?"

Thus far, signals are mixed. In 1995, *Omni Online* "published" a new novella every month through most of the year, and those novellas included some of the best stories available anywhere that year, but the novella program sputtered into silence early in 1996, and so far has not been reinstituted, alas, a big loss to the genre. The original *Omni* site itself, on AOL, seemed to fall quiescent for several months, and has been more or less abandoned. Then Pamela Weintraub took over from Keith Ferrell as editor of Omni Internet, and *Omni Online* was relaunched in September, with a brand-new site on the Internet. Ellen Datlow, longtime fiction editor of the print *Omni,* is still acting as fiction editor for the online version, and has "published" several of the best stories of the year on *Omni Online* since the new site went up, including stories by Robert Silverberg, Harlan Ellison, James P. Blaylock, Cherry Wilder, and Kathleen Ann Goonan. In fact, the best online-only science fiction stories published only in electronic format, that I've been able to find on the Internet are to be found at *Omni Online* (http://www.omnimag.com), and that's where I'd advise you to look first for high-quality SF.

Is anybody actually *reading* these stories, though? Again, signals are mixed. The *Omni* site seems to be popular, claiming thousands of "hits" every day, but I get the uneasy feeling that many genre readers are just not *seeing* the *Omni Online* stories, based on admittedly subjective factors such as how often the stories are showing up on award ballots and being mentioned in Year End wrap-up lists (which is not as often as you would think they would, especially as they are high-quality stories by big names), and on how many core SF fans I talk to have ever heard of them. To date—ironically, considering that SF is supposed to be a forward-looking literature—much of the core SF reading audience doesn't seem to be surfing the net, and stuff that's published there seems to be going largely unnoticed by the genre audience. I suspect that this situation will change rapidly over the next few years, though, as the Internet itself continues to expand.

So where else can you look for good SF stories online? Well, at the moment, genre electronic publishing remains a largely unfulfilled promise—although there *are* other promising sites out there, and signs that things may get more interesting in the near future.

Other than *Omni Online,* your best bet for finding good professional-level SF online would seem to be the online reincarnation of *Tomorrow Speculative Fiction,* now called *Tomorrow SF,* which can be found on the Internet at http://www.tomorrowsf.com. Although only put up in January of 1997, this is already proving itself to be a lively and very promising site, with good fiction already available there by Geoffrey A. Landis, Rob Chilson, Sheila Finch, and others. It'll also be an experiment that those interested in the electronic publishing of fiction should keep a close eye on, as editor Algis Budrys's idea is to "publish" the first three online issues of *Tomorrow SF* for free, and then to begin charging for access to the Web site. Most other current sites, like the *Omni Online* site, don't charge for access (*Omni Online* seems to be being supported mostly by Web advertising from some fairly substantial companies), and it will be very interesting to see if *Tomorrow* can actually make the online audience pay for access to their site in any sort of reliable fashion, and in numbers large enough to be profitable. If they *can,* then the face of electronic genre publishing could change very rapidly.

Quality of the fiction falls off quickly after the *Omni Online* and *Tomorrow SF* sites—there's oceans worth of amateur-level, slushpile-quality stuff out there, more than you could wade through in a year, but, for the moment, not a lot of professional-quality SF. There are some longer-established sites that are worth keeping an eye on, though, such as *InterText* (http://www.etext.org/Zines/InterText/), which, although uneven, does occasionally publish some good material, including several good stories by Jim Cowan, and *E-Scape* (http://www.interink.com/escape.html), which has published good stuff by K. D. Wentworth, James Gunn, C. J. Cherryh, and others. At *Mind's Eye Fiction* (http://tale.com/genres.htm), you can check out the first half of stories by writers such as Spider Robinson, Bud Sparhawk, David Brin, and other professionals, and then decide whether or not you want to pay to read the second half—it'll also be very interesting to see how well this experiment works. *Talebones* (http://www.nventure.com/) is oriented toward horror and dark fantasy rather than SF, but is a lively site that seems worth checking out as well. If you're really a glutton for punishment, you can find *lots* of other genre "electronic magazines," most of them extremely bad, by doing a search of http://www.yahoo.com/arts/humanities/literature/genres/science_fiction_fantasy_horror/magazines/.

As long as you're surfing the Net, you might want to also check out some of the genre-related sites that *don't* publish fiction. *Science Fiction Weekly* (http://www.scifiweekly.com) is a good, lively general-interest site, with interviews and book and media reviews (and with plans to begin publishing fiction as well next year), and, as it has links to many genre-related sites, a good place to start. As is *SFF NET* (http//www.sff.net), which features dozens of home pages for SF writers, genre-oriented "live chats," and, among other lists of data, the *Locus* Magazine Index 1984–1996, which is an extremely valuable research tool; you can also link to the Science Fiction Writers of America page from here, where valuable research data and reading lists are to be found as well, or you can link directly to the SFFWA Web Page at http://www.sfwa.org/sfw. *HotWired* does weekly live interactive interviews with genre figures, Tuesday at nine P.M. EST in their HeadSpace area (http://www.hotwired.com), and *Omni Online* regularly features live interactive interviews as well. Many Bulletin Board Services, such as *GEnie, Delphi, Compuserve,* and *AOL,* have large online communities of SF writers and fans, with *GEnie* having perhaps the largest and most active such community, and also feature live interactive real-time "chats" or conferences, as does *SFF NET*—the SF-oriented chat on *Delphi* starts every Wednesday at about 10 P.M. EST (*Delphi* has also just opened a Web site, at http://www.delphi.com/sflit/).

Emerging back into the print world with a shock and a shiver, we should also mention in passing that, as usual, short SF and fantasy also appeared in many magazines outside genre boundaries, from *Alfred Hitchcock's Mystery Magazine* to *Playboy. Playboy* in particular, under Fiction Editor Alice K. Turner, continues to run some important SF stories every year. On the downside, *VB Tech,* which had been publishing at least one SF story per issue, dropped the fiction this year, and if the promised "*Playboy* rival," *Rage,* which was supposed to use a good deal of short SF, ever hit the newsstands this year, I was unable to find it.

It was not a particularly good year in the semiprozine market either, although new fiction semiprozines continue to proliferate in spite of the very long odds against them even surviving, let alone increasing their circulation to the point where they would be considered professional magazines.

One of the newish fiction semiprozines that seemed last year to have a pretty good shot at establishing itself was *Century,* perhaps the best fiction semiprozine to be launched in the last ten years or more. *Century* received more positive reviews and widespread acclaim than any other newly-launched fiction semiprozine I can think of, with stories from it reaching major award ballots and being frequently mentioned in Year End wrap-up lists, and seemed poised on the brink of success. And the one issue they did manage to publish in 1996, *Century 4,* lived up to the magazine's reputation or bettered it, featuring one of the year's best stories, Jim Cowan's "The Spade of Reason," as well as first-rate SF by Kathleen Ann Goonan and Marc Laidlaw, and interesting, quirky, harder-to-classify stuff by Jack Cady, Jessica Amanda Salmonson, Karen Jordan Allen, Karawynn Long, and others. Unfortunately, *Century* only published one of its scheduled four issues in 1996 (they'd only published two out of four in 1995), and, worse, fell into a long silence that lasted for most of the year, not responding to letters or phone calls, something that spawned widespread rumors that *Century* had died, and spread panic among the ranks of authors who still had unpublished stories in inventory there. Both Publisher Meg Hamel and Editor Robert K. J. Killheffer assured me at the end of the year that *Century* was *not* dead (in spite of the rumors), that the magazine was going to continue, and that they would make every effort to stick to a more reliable publication schedule in 1997. You have to wonder, though, if these problems will scare off potential subscribers; at the very least, they've cost *Century* much of the momentum, good will, and critical "buzz" it had been generating in the genre audience in 1995. Let's hope that this very promising magazine can get its act together in 1997 and build some trust in its reliability again, as it has the potential to be one of the most important magazines of the nineties.

A semiprozine similar in quality and the eclecticism of the material (although with perhaps a rawer in-your-face attitude) is Bryan Cholfin's *Crank!,* which also struggled with keeping to its publication schedule this year, although it did manage to produce two issues, featuring quirky stuff (although little—if any—real science fiction) from Karen Joy Fowler, Carter Scholz, Michael Kandel, Jonathan Lethem, Eliot Fintushel, R. A. Lafferty, A. M. Dellamonica, and others.

There was a special one-shot revival of *New Worlds* magazine, edited by Michael Moorcock in honor of the magazine's 50th Anniversary (oddly, it only now exists as an anthology series of the same name), and featuring good work by Brian W. Aldiss, Harvey Jacobs, and others.

Turning to the more science fiction–oriented of the newer semiprozines, your best bets remain *Absolute Magnitude: The Magazine of Science Fiction Adventures* and *Pirate Writings: Tales of Fantasy, Mystery & Science Fiction,* two slick, professional-looking, full-size magazines with full-color covers, both of them hovering just under professional status, which they might be able to reach if they could increase their circulations (and, in the case of *Absolute Magnitude,* which only published two issues out of their scheduled four, stabilize its production schedule—although they claim they'll be "back on schedule" in 1997). *Pirate Writings* continues to have a slight edge in the quality of the fiction, featuring worthwhile stuff this year by Allen Steele, Paul Di Filippo, Sue Storm, Esther M. Friesner, Jessica Amanda Salmonson, and others. *Absolute Magnitude* has had the better cover art of the two, although it also published worthwhile stuff by Geoffrey A. Landis, Denise Lopes Heald, Barry B. Longyear, and others. Both *Absolute Magnitude* and *Pirate Writings* publish a lot of reprints, and I still don't understand the rationale for this, especially when many of the reprints are of relatively recent material that is still fairly accessible elsewhere; you'd think that they'd want to save their limited space for their own original material instead. I also think that *Pirate Writings* is making a mistake (the same mistake that *Tomorrow* made) by publishing so many short-short stories. It's very hard to find really *good* short-shorts, harder than it is to find good longer stories. Most of the short-shorts I see during the year strike me as undistinguished at best; and that's the case here, as well. (I also notice, with amusement, that in spite of similar polemic stances about how they were going to use nothing but Good Old-Fashioned SF, both *Absolute Magnitude* and *Tomorrow* have ended up using a good deal of fantasy as well.)

Of the long-established fiction semiprozines, your best bets remain the two Australian magazines, *Aurealis* and *Eidolon,* and the Canadian magazine *On Spec. Eidolon* had a particularly strong year in 1996, producing by far the best fiction of the three, including one of the year's best stories, by Damien Broderick, first-rate work by Jack Dann, Terry Dowling, and Andrew Whitmore, and good work by Lucy Sussex, Simon Brown, Sara Douglass, Sean Williams, Avram Davidson and Ethan Davidson, and others, as well as good reprint material by Harlan Ellison—an impressive performance. We saw three issues of *Eidolon* this year, out of a scheduled four. *Aurealis,* the other Australian semiprozine, didn't quite make it up to the level of *Eidolon* as far as the overall quality of the fiction was concerned, although they did publish good work by Stephen Dedman, Dirk Strasser, and others; they had better and more evocative covers than *Eidolon* did, though, and more critical material. We saw two issues of *Aurealis. On Spec* seemed weaker than usual in terms of overall literary quality this year, perhaps because the average was dragged down by their unfortunate "XF/SF Cross-Genre" Special Theme Issue, which mostly contained pretty weak stuff; their covers this year were inferior to their usually high standard of cover art, too. We saw three issues of *On Spec,* although one of them, dated Winter 1996, arrived in late February of 1997, and so we'll save consideration of that issue for next year. *Eidolon* may be demonstrating itself as the one here most worth keeping your eye on, but all three of these magazines merit your support, they have all been around long enough to be considered fairly established and reliable, and all have good track records for delivering interesting and unusual fiction.

Of the other fiction semiprozines, there were, as far as I could tell, several issues of the newish *Plot Magazine,* one issue of *Tales of the Unanticipated* (which featured professional-level work by L. Timmel Duchamp, Eleanor Arnason, and others); one issue of *Xizquil;* and three issues of a promising new Canadian magazine called *TransVersions* (which featured professional-level work by Jeff VanderMeer, Derryl Murphy, Michael Payne, and others). There were either fewer semiprozines published this year or they were harder to find, and it's often difficult to find reliable information about them—I believe that the British semiprozines *Back Brain Recluse* and *REM* still exist, for instance, but I don't really know for sure. I saw no issues of *Argonaut Science Fiction, Next Phase,* or *Space & Time.*

New fiction semiprozines included the promising *Terra Incognita* (although its self-imposed restriction of publishing only stories that take place on Earth seems somewhat limiting), which had one issue this year, featuring interesting professional-level work by L. Timmel Duchamp, Kandis Elliot, W. Gregory Stewart, and others; *Keen Science Fiction,* which seems well-intentioned and enthusiastic, producing eight issues this year, although the quality of the fiction in it is not yet reliably up to professional levels; *The Thirteenth Moon Magazine,* somewhat more literary/metafictional in orientation, which featured hard-to-classify stories this year by Ursula K. Le Guin, Michael Bishop, and others; and *Adventures of Sword & Sorcery,* which, not surprisingly, was mostly pretty pulpish stuff.

I follow the horror semiprozine market as little as I can these days, but *Talebones: Fiction on the Dark Edge* seems to be a lively and ambitious little magazine, and the highly respected *Cemetery Dance* began publishing again after a hiatus caused by the ill health of the editor. *Aberrations* seemed to be improving somewhat in literary quality as the year progressed, concentrating less on hardcore stuff. There were two issues of *The Urbanite,* which is well subtitled "Surreal & Lively & Bizarre," with work perhaps a bit more intellectual than the usual horror semiprozine stuff. There were issues of *Grue* and *Deathrealm,* although I didn't see them. There were probably other horror semiprozines published this year, too, but I didn't see them either.

Turning to the critical magazines, Charles N. Brown's *Locus* and Andy Porter's *SF*

Chronicle, as always, remain your best bet among that sub-class of semiprozines known as "newszines," invaluable if you are looking for news and/or an overview of what's happening in the genre. (Unusually, *SF Chronicle* failed to publish several issues this year; let's hope that this long-running, valuable, and usually reliable magazine gets back on schedule in 1997.) *The New York Review of Science Fiction,* edited by David G. Hartwell, completed its eighth full year of publication and remains by far the most reliably published and probably the most interesting and accessible of the more scholarly oriented "criticalzines"—its "Read This" lists of recommended books by various authors is a valuable feature, and its letter column is interesting and frequently acerbic. There was one issue of Steve Brown's *SF Eye* in 1996, and one issue of Lawrence Person's *Nova Express,* both magazines that contain a lot of intriguing and interesting material—when you can find them, which isn't often. *Tangent,* edited by David A. Truesdale, has already become something of an institution in the field after only a few years, and performs an invaluable service for the genre by extensively reviewing the year's short fiction, almost the only source that does, except for Mark Kelly's *Locus* column. *Tangent* occasionally annoys me by running the kind of reviews that criticize *Asimov's* for not being *Analog* and criticize *Analog* for not being *Asimov's* or *F&SF,* but on the whole the level of the criticism is pretty good here—especially considering that it's the work of largely unpaid or underpaid volunteers—and seems to have improved since the magazine's launch a few years back. On the whole, *Tangent* is doing a good job of filling a nearly vacant ecological niche, and if it disappeared the field would be much the poorer for it. In the last couple of years, *Tangent* has made itself even more valuable by becoming deeply involved in helping to assemble a recommended reading list for the yearly Sturgeon Award, a list that rivals the Locus Recommended List for usefulness. *Speculations* is more of a magazine of writing advice for young or would-be authors than a criticalzine, but many will find its extensive section of market reports and market news to be useful. I saw no issues of *Non-Stop Magazine* this year.

(*Locus, The Newspaper of the Science Fiction Field,* Locus Publications, Inc., P.O. Box 13305, Oakland, CA 94661, $53 for a one-year first-class subscription, twelve issues; *Science Fiction Chronicle,* Algol Press, P.O. Box 022730, Brooklyn, NY 11202-0056, $42 for one-year first-class subscription, twelve issues; *The New York Review of Science Fiction,* Dragon Press, P.O. Box 78, Pleasantville, NY, 10570, $31 per year, twelve issues; *SF Eye,* P.O. Box 18539, Asheville, NC 28814, $12.50 for one year; *Nova Express,* P.O. Box 27231, Austin, TX 78755-2231, $10 for a one-year (four issues) subscription; *Tangent,* 5779 Norfleet, Raytown, MO 64133, $20 for one year, four issues; *Speculations,* 111 West El Camino Real, Suite 109-400, Sunnyvale, CA 94087-1057, a first-class subscription, six issues, $25; *On Spec,* the Canadian Magazine of Speculative Writing, P.O. Box 4727, Edmonton, AB, Canada T6E 5G6, $18 for a one-year subscription; *Crank!,* Broken Mirrors Press, P.O. Box 1110, New York, NY 10159, $12 for four issues; *Century,* P.O. Box 259270, Madison, WI 53715-0270, $27 for a one-year subscription; *Aurealis: the Australian Magazine of Fantasy and Science Fiction,* Chimaera Publications, P.O. Box 2164, Mt. Waverley, Victoria 3149, Australia, $43 for a four-issue overseas airmail subscription, "all cheques and money orders must be made out to Chimaera Publications in Australian dollars"; *Eidolon: the Journal of Australian Science Fiction and Fantasy,* Eidolon Publications, P.O. Box 225, North Perth, Western Australia 6006, $45 (Australian) for a four-issue overseas airmail subscription, payable to Eidolon Publications; *Back Brain Recluse,* P.O. Box 625, Sheffield S1 3GY, United Kingdom, $18 for four issues; *REM,* REM Publications, 19 Sandringham Road, Willesden, London NW2 5EP, United Kingdom, 7.50 pounds sterling for four issues; *Xizquil,* order from Uncle River/*Xizquil,* Blue, Arizona, 85922, $11 for a three-issue subscription; *Pirate Writings: Tales of Fantasy, Mystery & Science Fiction,*

Pirate Writings Publishing, Subscriptions, P.O. Box 329, Brightwaters, NY 11718-0329, $15 for one year (four issues), all checks payable to "Pirate Writings Publishing"; *Absolute Magnitude: The Magazine of Science Fiction Adventures,* P.O Box 13, Greenfield, MA 01302, four issues for $14, all checks payable to "D.N.A. Publications"; *TransVersions,* Island Specialty Reports, 1019 Colville Rd., Victoria, BC, Canada, V9A 4P5, four-issue subscription, $18 Can. or U.S., "make cheques payable to Island Specialty Reports"; *Terra Incognita,* Terra Incognita, 52 Windermere Avenue #3, Lansdowne, PA 19050-1812, $15 for four issues; *Thirteenth Moon Magazine,* 1459 18th Street #139, San Francisco, CA 94107, $24 for four issues; *PLOT Magazine,* Calypso Publishing, P.O. Box 1351, Sugar Land, TX 77487-1351, four issues for $14, "make checks payable to Calypso Publishing"; *The Urbanite: Surreal & Lively & Bizarre,* Urban Legend Press, P.O. Box 4737, Davenport, IA 52808, $13.50 for three issues, "all checks or money orders payable to Urban Legend Press"; *Keen Science Fiction,* Teresa Keene, P.O. Box 9067, Spokane, WA 99209-0067, $36 for twelve issues; *Talebones: Fiction on the Dark Edge,* Fairwood Press, 12205 1st Avenue S., Seattle, WA 98168, $16 for four issues; *Cemetery Dance,* CD Publications, Box 18433, Baltimore, MD 21237; Grue Magazine, Hell's Kitchen Productions, Box 370, Times Square Stn., New York, NY 10108, $14 for three issues; *Aberrations,* P.O. Box 460430, San Francisco, CA 94146, $31 for twelve issues; *Deathrealm,* 2210 Wilcox Drive, Greensboro, NC 27405, $15.95 for four issues; *Adventures of Sword & Sorcery,* Double Star Press, P.O. Box 285, Xenia, OH 45385, $15.95 for four issues.)

Nineteen ninety-six was another mixed year in the original anthology market, a year that saw the reputed death of one of the most prominent anthology series of recent years, but also the launching of a highly promising new anthology series, and a supposed new lease on life granted to two older anthology series that had widely been reported to be dead. There were one or two worthwhile one-shot anthologies this year, although there seemed to be fewer original anthologies overall than there had been in 1995 (the number of reprint anthologies was down as well, so that fewer anthologies of any type saw print this year), and many of them that did appear were, at best, mediocre. There was no anthology easily identifiable as a "hard science" anthology this year, unlike last year, which saw the publication of anthologies such as *New Legends* and *Far Futures;* a few of the year's anthologies *did* feature core science fiction, but it was usually mixed in with fantasy and literary surrealism of one sort or another. There was a "tribute" anthology and a "regional" anthology, both rather rare and specialized types. The once-torrential tide of shared-world anthologies seems to have mostly dried up, except in the media-related, gaming-related, and comics-related areas. And after an influx of strong fantasy anthologies in 1995, there seemed to be fewer fantasy anthologies, and fewer prominent ones, in 1996. Almost all of the year's most prominent anthologies were issued in hardback or trade paperback; those few original mass-market paperback anthologies that *were* issued were mostly rather minor.

The worse news in this market this year was the reputed death of the *Full Spectrum* anthology series; this doesn't really surprise me, since the last member of the editorial team that worked on the series, Tom Dupree, moved this year from Bantam to another publishing house, as all of the series's founding editors had before him, but it's a major blow to the original anthology market; *Full Spectrum* was probably the most widely acclaimed and prominent (and widely promoted) anthology series of the nineties, and if *it* can't make it (sales were reputed to be poor), then that could be taken as an indicator that it'll be difficult for *any* original anthology series to succeed in the current market.

Original anthology series are, in fact, something of a literary endangered species these days. At one time, there were at least five or six major SF anthology series, including *Orbit, New Dimensions, Nova, Universe,* and others, but they have vanished one by one over the years, and none of the newer series created to replace them has survived. The news isn't entirely negative: Two anthology series formerly rumored to be dead, David Garnett's *New Worlds* series and George Zebrowski's *Synergy* series, are being revived by White Wolf, and will reportedly have issues in the bookstores in 1997. In 1996, though, original anthology series had almost vanished from the scene— only one was still in the bookstores, the first volume in the newly launched *Starlight* series . . . but that was one of the most promising such series to come along in a long while, and we should all keep our fingers crossed that this one manages to survive, because it's a series that could be very important to the field.

In fact, *Starlight 1* (Tor), edited by Patrick Nielsen Hayden, was the best original anthology of the year, of any type, with little real competition, and one of the best *in* some years as well. It wasn't as firmly centered on SF as last year's *New Legends,* featuring a good deal of fantasy as well, in addition to a number of harder-to-classify literary experiments of one sort or another, but it did publish several of the best core-SF stories of the year, as well as a number of other worthwhile ones, and even the fantasy stories here are good examples of *that* genre. Even the ambitious failures, of which there are several here, are more interesting and valuable to check out than the usual run-of-the-mill stuff; they may not be able to chew everything that they bite off, but they bite off a good deal more than most routine stories do, and so should be admired for their audacity and ambition.

The best work here, in my opinion (and it's probably a clear demonstration of my own tastes that most of them are center-SF), are the stories by Michael Swanwick, Maureen F. McHugh, Gregory Feeley, and Robert Reed, with the story by Andy Duncan a half step down only because of some shakiness in his core assumption, and the story by Susan Palwick a full step down *because* of its unfortunate core assumption. The ambitious failures are John M. Ford's "Erase/Record/Play" and Carter Scholz's "Mengele's Jew." Everything else in the book ranges itself between those two poles— although nothing here, flawed or not, is really *bad,* and almost everything in the volume would make a worthwhile addition to an average issue of an average magazine.

Michael Swanwick's "The Dead" is so bleak at points as to be almost stylized, but it does paint a creepy and effective picture, with typical Swanwickian inventiveness, of a society where the living are being replaced by reanimated corpses at every level of society and in every possible role. I found it especially appropriate to be reading this story, as it happened that I was, while waiting for a plane at Dallas/Ft. Worth airport; watching crowds of empty-eyed people shuffling by down endless corridors and along "moving sidewalks" under the pitiless glare of airport lighting adding a certain frisson, although I'm sure you'll find the story sufficiently grim if you're sitting cozily at home in your favorite armchair. Robert Reed manages to be even more inventive than Swanwick—a difficult task—in his "Killing the Morrow," which has enough conceptualization packed into it for a much longer story, but which somehow manages to gain impact from being told in a small number of pages rather than feeling fragmented or sketchy. Reed also comes up with an ingenious new twist on the time-travel story, a relentlessly logical viewpoint that makes time-travel seem even more unlikely than it already does—or more unlikely that it could take place without profound effects, anyway; if you thought that Bradbury having everything change because someone steps on a *butterfly* was something, you'll find that Reed takes this idea a good deal further! Maureen F. McHugh's novella "The Cost to Be Wise" is probably the most wrenching, emotionally powerful story in the book, and if it's clearly reminiscent in tone of Le Guin's Hanish stories—and it is—McHugh does manage to work in some ingenious gracenotes that are all her own, and some interesting points of view; it's also somewhat more bleak than Le Guin usually is (the overall tone of the anthology, in fact, is somewhat bleak, with only one or two stories, notably the Duncan, striking more upbeat notes). Gregory Feeley's "The Weighing of Ayre" could be taken for a straight historical story for most of its length, but it's actually a sort of stealth hard science fiction, centrally concerned with technology, and by the end has turned into a neat and effective parable, obviously still applicable to our own times, as to the uses and misuses to which any new technology can be put, and the moral choices involved.

On the next tier down, Andy Duncan makes a very successful foray into Howard Waldrop/Terry Bisson territory in "Lisa and the Crazy Water Man," which is wry, funny, sweetly eccentric, and unexpectedly lyrical in places—I'd place it, in fact, in among the anthology's top stories if the underlying Fantastic Element—which the story doesn't really need anyway—made more sense, but, alas, it doesn't: Why does this affliction come to *Lisa*? And how come her voice can be broadcast over the radio, but can't be recorded? No real explanation for any of this, or even a hint of one, is given, and I'm not sure that the author has really worked the implications out logically, either. The story is good enough, though, that judging by it and by a few other Duncan stories I've seen in manuscript, I think that Duncan could turn out to be a major talent in the making. Susan Palwick's "GI Jesus" is another fundamentally sweet and moving story, with some very good writing and character stuff, but the core idea is so silly—not only blasphemous, which wouldn't in itself bother me all that much, but *dumb,* like something from a bad *Saturday Night Live* sketch—that it spoiled most of the impact of the story for me; everything here *except* the core idea itself is brilliant, but that idea trivializes and drags down what could have been a substantial story.

It would take more space than I have left here to explain in detail why I think that John M. Ford's "Erase/Record/Play: A Drama for Print," although vaultingly ambitious and certainly unique, wonderfully written and full of inventiveness and dry wit, is, in the final analysis, an interesting failure. For one thing, the situation is entirely artificial, set up for the author's purposes to enable the author to make the points he wants to make, and nothing that would ever arise in the real world. Perhaps most damning for me, though, is the fact that I don't believe that the psychological game that they're playing in the story would actually have even a remote chance of actually *producing* the psychological results they claim that it will produce. (For the sake of fairness, I should probably say that at least one other critic is on record as thinking that the Ford is the best story in the book—so your millage may vary dramatically here.) Carter Scholz's "Mengele's Jew" has similar strengths and similar weaknesses, with some wonderful writing and some audacious conceptualization, but with the overall effect ultimately rather bloodless and abstract, it is more an interesting technical exercise than a story that most readers are going to find involving.

The rest of the stories in *Starlight 1* are worth reading, but not in the same league as the stuff mentioned above, even the "ambitious failures." It's interesting to compare the treatment that Emily Dickinson gets in Jane Yolen's "Sister Emily's Lightship" with the pitiless mocking she gets in the year's *other* Emily Dickinson story, Connie Willis's "The Soul Selects Her Own Society." Yolen, by contrast, treats Dickinson reverentially—perhaps *too* reverentially; by the end, when space aliens come down and take Emily on a tour of the planet because they respect the sincerity of her poetry so much, I was beginning to find the solemnly reverential tone unintentionally amusing, and I'm afraid that the story pretty much lost me after that. Martha Soukup's "Waking Beauty" is a reworking of a fairy tale in a modern setting, nicely done, but perhaps too long and too plotty to be completely convincing in the end; in this kind of story, you need to keep it short enough to keep the reader from having time to think about how unlikely this all is. Mark Kreighbaum contributes a Rashmon-like story with some ingenious touches, but one that wasn't terribly emotionally involving, another interesting technical exercise. The story I liked the least here (although there's not really anything *wrong* with it; just the story furthest from my taste) is Susanna Clarke's slow and intricate mannerist fantasy, "The Ladies of Grace Adieu."

At any rate, *Starlight 1* is one of the most promising debuts of an original anthology series since the high days of *Orbit* and *New Dimensions*—and, tastes varying as much as they do, you may like some of what I considered to be the lesser stories better than the stories I liked best. It's all honest work, and there's almost nothing here that isn't, at the very least, worth reading.

Runner-up for the title of year's best original anthology would be *Intersections: The Sycamore Hill Anthology* (Tor), edited by John Kessel, Mark L. Van Name, and Richard Butner, a collection of stories, with commentary from the participants, from the yearly session of the well-known Sycamore Hill Writers' Workshop. This is one of several anthologies this year that serves double-duty as both a critical study and a collection of stories—the insight into the writing workshop process here, complete with comments from the workshoppers on the stories contained in the book, will be of great interest to anyone who wants to learn how to write (although the book as a whole would have been more useful if it could have printed the individual stories as they were both before *and* after the workshop, so you could better see the effect that the critique sessions had on the text; I suppose that considerations of the book's length ruled that out, though). Most readers, however, will be more interested in how the anthology holds up as a *fiction* collection—in fact, it holds up quite well; the mix is similar to that of *Starlight 1,* with fantasy and a number of hard-to-classify literary experiments sharing pages with some of the year's best SF stories.

The best stories here, in my opinion, are Bruce Sterling's "Bicycle Repairman," John Kessel's "The Miracle of Ivar Avenue," James Patrick Kelly's "The First Law of Thermodynamics," and Karen Joy Fowler's "The Marianas Islands." The first three are all science fiction to one degree or another—fairly centrally in the case of the Sterling and the Kessel, more marginally in the case of the Kelly; the Fowler, which is beautifully crafted, skates somewhere between fantasy and a nostalgic literary story, working much the same sort of territory that James Thurber was working in his *My Life and Hard Times . . .* the story reminds me a lot of Thurber, in fact, soaked through with the same sort of nostalgic, bittersweet whimsy.

Everything else in the book would have to be ranked somewhere below those top four stories, for one reason or another. The story that comes the closest to their level in quality is Maureen F. McHugh's "Homesick," another beautifully crafted story, but one that ultimately seemed disappointing to me. I'm not quite sure why I reacted to the McHugh that way, but somehow it seemed as though there was something *missing* from the story that should have been there, even though I'm not entirely sure *what* it should have been, as if the story was somehow missing its own point. This was the one story in the anthology where I would have most liked to have gotten to read the *original* version of the story, rather than the story as it appears after having been revised to satisfy criticisms from the workshop; I can't help but wonder if it would have worked better *without* the changes inspired by the workshop criticism, since I'm puzzled as to just why the current version *doesn't* work for me—it doesn't, though, although the writing and scene-setting are very fine indeed. A step or two down from there, were Nancy Kress's slight and melodramatic "Sex Education," Richard Butner's muted and hip "Horses Blow Up Dog City," Gregory Frost's earnest "That Blissful Height," and Alexander Jablokov's "The Fury at Colonus," which features the most audacious and outrageous story idea in the book, but which can't sustain the metaphor throughout a story as long and plotty as this one is without it all crumbling under its own weight. Much the same could be said of Jonathan Lethem's "The Hardened Criminals," which becomes downright silly the moment the story slows up enough to actually let you think about the central idea; this is one of the pieces here that works better as a dark, surrealistic literary joke than it does as a science fiction story. Michaela Roessner's "The Escape Artist" has a good setting and setup—Houdini comes to the Winchester Mystery House—and then wastes it by sidestepping its own story, which obviously should have pitted Houdini against the Mystery House in some sort of contest or duel, but which instead, unsatisfyingly, swerves off in another direction.

War of the Worlds: Global Dispatches (Bantam), edited by Kevin J. Anderson, an anthology written in honor of the 100th anniversary of the release of H. G. Wells's famous novel *War of the Worlds,* although very uneven in quality, is probably your next best bet in this year's original anthology market. These updated "War of the Worlds" stories have been appearing here and there throughout the year in the science fiction magazines, and that's probably the best way to read them, in fact: spaced as widely as possible. Taken together, the stories actually become negatively effective, since the same scenes—most notably, the scene in which the top of a Martian capsule slowly unscrews itself, the Martians emerge, heat-ray the crowd, rear up in a tripod fighting machine, and so on—occur in story after story, which becomes annoying if you're reading the book cover to cover in one sitting. I also think that the anthology might have worked better overall if they'd stuck just to the idea of showing what happened in other places around the world during Wells's Martian invasion. The idea that the stories *also* had to be told from the perspective of a Famous Nineteenth Century Author, and written in his literary *style* as well, was one elaboration too many; many of these stories would be less artificial if that frame hadn't been imposed on them— and, frankly, many of the authors here just aren't *up* to an accurate pastiche of the style of the authors they've chosen. The only reprint here, and the admitted inspiration for the anthology, is Howard Waldrop's "Night of the Cooters," which gives a sharp satirical spin to the material—Martians invading Texas are no match for *rednecks,* who just grab up guns and shoot them to pieces—that is sadly missing from most of the stories here. Some of the authors are also not really all *that* familiar with Wells's original story, as is shown by a number of internal inconsistencies, which really should have been caught by the editor (who makes one mistake in chronology himself).

Still, keeping all these caveats in mind, there are a fairly high number of entertaining stories here, especially if you clear your palate between stories with some other kind of reading. The best stories here are Walter Jon Williams's exotic "Foreign Devils," Connie Willis's tart, disrespectful, and funny "study" of Emily Dickinson, "The Soul Selects Her Own Society, etc.," and Dave Wolverton's "After a Lean Winter," which does a good job of capturing the mood and atmosphere of Jack London, in a story that manages at the same time to be valid as SF and believable as something London might have actually written.

Also near the top would be Robert Silverberg's "The Martian Invasion Journals of Henry James," M. Shayne Bell's "To See the World End," which, unlike most of the stories in the book, actually packs some emotional punch, and George Alec Effinger's "Mars: The Home Front," which does a hilarious job of capturing the atmosphere of an Edgar Rice Burroughs novel (although it doesn't end so much as stop—which is too bad, since I actually found myself wanting to read the *rest* of this silly adventure, which in its way is high praise indeed!).

Everything below there is flawed to one extent or another, including a number of stories that just feel pointless. The worst story in the book by far, though, is Gregory

Benford and David Brin's monumentally silly "Paris Conquers All," in which two of the Martian tripod fighting machines destroying Paris decide that the Eiffel Tower is a *female* Martian fighting machine and have sex with it. While they're circling the tower, hooting lustfully, Jules Verne wires it up and connects it to a series of quickly assembled batteries, and when the Martian fighting machines crawl onto the tower to copulate, he throws the switch, frying them. This, of course, totally ignores the fact that the tripods are machines run by organic creatures *inside* them, and is rather like a Ford deciding to have sex with a Volkswagen on the freeway, or perhaps like two cars deciding to hump a gas station, ignoring the wishes of their drivers.

In the end, what seems to be demonstrated here is that the Wells's Martian invasion images and archetypes still have a good deal of juice when they are handled by writers of talent; when they are handled by less talented writers, or at least by writers less genuinely excited by the material, writers just fulfilling an anthology assignment, then those images and archetypes become cartoons, devoid of the power to move us. I suppose none of this is surprising. (Which brings up an interesting point: Are the stories in *War of the Worlds: Global Dispatches* still science fiction, even though the writers *know* in advance that the premise is based upon obsolete science, the now-outdated premise that Mars has a climate that could support a technologically advanced alien race? Certainly most of them are written as if they are science fiction, obsolete initial premise or not. Retro science fiction? Alternate world science fiction, from a universe where Mars proved to be a more welcoming abode for life? (Whatever, the stories here seem similar somehow to the Victorian science fiction and the alternate space program stories that I discuss later, in the novel section.)

Off Limits: More Tales of Alien Sex (St. Martin's Press), edited by Ellen Datlow, a follow-up to 1990's popular *Alien Sex,* a mixed reprint and original anthology (mostly original), might be more fairly reviewed as a horror anthology, but since it seems to be being marketed as a science fiction anthology, I'll talk about it here. I was a fan of Datlow's previous *Alien Sex* anthology, but I found myself mildly disapped by this one.

Although there are some science fiction stories here, including one first-rate one— Gwyneth Jones's "Red Sonja and Lessingham in Dreamland"—most of the stuff in *Off Limits* is either horror or dark literary surrealism of various sorts, or mixtures of both. Even considering just the science fiction stories here, there's a real sameness to the future worlds and the takes on the future of sex that are portrayed: all the futures are bleak and depressing, often narrated by a prostitute or featuring a prostitute as the main character, some sort of AIDS-like disease is slowly killing everybody off, the sexes are totally estranged and only touch each other in negative and sometimes horrifyingly abusive ways, there's no valid family life, all you see is betrayal and murder and people who have become deadly monsters of perversion. Gee. I guess there's not much future for sex. I guess there's not much hope for relationships between men and women. I guess that the future is going to be a pretty grim and depressing place. I guess that the human race has pretty much *had* it. There's very little relief from this mood here, and the horror stories are even more extreme. (There are also more original horror stories here than there are original science fiction stories—adding the reprints, all SF, ups the overall percentage of science fiction some, but ultimately, most of the stuff here would probably appeal more to the average horror reader than to the average SF reader.)

Worse than the sameness of tone is that there's very little imagination shown in the thinking about future or alien sex in most of the stories—the most imagination here by far shows up in the exchange of joke poems between Joe Haldeman and Jane Yolen, "Sextraterrestrials," and I couldn't help but feel it as a lack that the kind of science-fictional thinking that turns up in a jokey way there couldn't have been utilized more seriously in more of the stories themselves. Of the original SF stories here, the best by far is the Gwyneth Jones. Martha Soukup's "Fetish" manages to generate a good deal of intensity with one simple SF idea, and says what it has to say and then stops with admirable restraint and efficiency. Brian Stableford's "The House of Mourning" is set in the same AIDS-analogue ravaged future as several of the others, and is also narrated by a prostitute, but he manages to handle the material with a bit more interest and ingenuity than some of the others do—this is far from major Stableford, however, suffering badly from one of Stableford's big problems as a writer, the inability to smoothly and believably integrate big jagged infodumps into the story. Bruce McAllister's "Captain China" is one of the horror stories rather than one of the SF stories, but deserves mention because of the emotional impact it generates, as an abused and dying male child prostitute in a crib in an American Chinatown dreams of rescue by the superhero whose exploits he watches from his dirt-streaked window, Captain China. There is, alas, really no fantastic element at all here, since it's pretty clear that Captain China exists only in the child's own mind, but it's a strong story on its own terms, although not at all a pleasant read—rather a queasy one, in fact, all the more so because the horrors here, unlike some of the more floridly described horrors in other stories, are narrated in an understated, matter-of-fact voice: They're just part of everyday life for the kid, and that's where the real horror lies. The anthology also features original stories by Susan Wade, Sherry Coldsmith, Scott Bradfield, Mike O'Driscoll, Lisa Tuttle, Roberta Lannes, Neil Gaiman, Kathe Koja and Barry N. Malzberg, Joyce Carol Oates, and others, as well as several reprint stories.

I'm left with two general impressions of *Off Limits:* One, that in spite of this being supposedly an anthology of erotic tales, I found almost none of the stories to actually *be* erotic at all (a problem I have with most erotic horror anthologies, in fact), as the sex that is described in them is so negative and bleakly depressing and grotesque . . . and I'm not sure I'd want to date a person who *did* find them really erotic. Two, that as far as the science fiction stories here are concerned, anyway, the reprint stories— Robert Silverberg's "The Reality Trip," Elizabeth Hand's "In the Month of Athyr," Simon Ings's "Grand Prix," Samuel R. Delany's "Aye, and Gomorrah . . ."—are for the most part stronger than the original stories; the best story in the book, "Aye, and Gomorrah . . . ," remains head and shoulders above almost anything else here in spite of being more than twenty years old. (There was another mixed horror/SF original anthology edited by Ellen Datlow this year, *Lethal Kisses,* but it came out only in the United Kingdom, so late in the year that I was unable to obtain a copy in time; I'll save consideration of it for next year.)

Those were the year's top four anthologies, in the SF anthology market, anyway. Almost everything below this point is weaker than the four anthologies reviewed above, to one extent or another, although there were a few worthwhile stories to be found in almost all of them (whether there's *enough* worthwhile stuff in each to make them worth their cover prices is a question that individuals will have to decide for themselves).

The best of the remaining SF anthologies is probably Roger Zelazny's last book, *The Williamson Effect* (Tor), edited by Roger Zelazny. This is a "tribute" anthology, made up of stories written in honor of Jack Williamson, with most of the authors contributing Williamson pastiches or writing new stories in various old Williamson series, a few authors writing stories that feature Williamson himself as the main character, exploring fanciful paths that his life could have taken in an Alternate Reality—all in very similar fashion to other "tribute" anthologies we've seen in the last few years, honoring writers such as Isaac Asimov and Ray Bradbury. Hardcore Jack Williamson fans, of course, will unquestionably want to have this book; how many general readers will get enough entertainment out of it to justify the $23.95 cover price is another question. Like most such "tribute" anthologies, the quality here varies widely from story to story, with some of the authors just not having the right touch or the sympathy for the Williamson material required for an effective pastiche, and the anthology as a whole is somewhat less vigorous and entertaining than Zelazny's two major 1995 anthologies, *Warriors of Blood and Dream* and *Wheel of Fortune* (which were also much better buys—mass-market paperbacks instead of an expensive hardcover). The best stories here are by Connie Willis, Frederik Pohl, and the late John Brunner, though there's also worthwhile stuff here by Poul Anderson, Mike Resnick, Ben Bova, and others.

Space Opera (DAW), edited by Anne McCaffrey and Elizabeth Ann Scarborough, an original anthology of stories about music in its various forms, is an odd book, ostensibly a science fiction anthology ("symphonies of the starways by the modern-day maestros of science fiction"), although many if not most of the stories actually turn out to be fantasy instead. (I wonder if they decided to publish it as SF because of the title? The joke wouldn't work if it had been published as fantasy.... Although several anthologies in recent years have given me the uneasy feeling that the distinction between fantasy and science fiction is disappearing, and that perhaps no one even really knows what that distinction is anymore.) At any rate, in spite of the misleading classification, this is a pretty good anthology, with several worthwhile stories, and a good buy as a mass-market paperback. The kingpiece here, Peter S. Beagle's wonderfully evocative fantasy novella "The Last Song of Sirit Byar," is worth the cover price all by itself. *Space Opera* also features good work by Gene Wolfe, Elizabeth Ann Scarborough, Suzette Haden Elgin, Charles de Lint, Robin Wayne Bailey, and others.

High Fantastic: Colorado's Fantasy, Dark Fantasy and Science Fiction (Ocean View Books), edited by Steve Rasnic Tem (technically a late 1995 release, although we didn't catch up with it until 1996), is an example of that curious subcategory of anthology, the "regional" anthology, collecting stories ostensibly written by writers who all come from one particular region of the country, or written *about* one particular region of the country. *High Fantastic* is a handsome book, a mixed reprint and original anthology that also contains regional-themed poetry, critical essays, cartoon strips, and art in addition to the fiction; the fiction itself is a mixture of (mostly) fantasy and horror, science fiction, and mainstream historical fiction. As usual with "regional" anthologies, the rationale for including some of these writers as Colorado authors is slender—they once lived briefly in the state, before moving elsewhere—but *High Fantastic* scores points by reprinting stories from long-dead Coloradians as well as by current residents, and actually manages to deliver more of a distinct "regional" flavor and feeling than most such anthologies do. The best of the fiction, both reprint and original, is by Dan Simmons, Connie Willis, Ed Bryant, Don Webb, Wil McCarthy, Michael Bishop, Melanie Tem, Steve Rasnic Tem himself, and others. On the whole, it's an interesting and worthwhile package—although the steep cover price may daunt some readers. (Ocean View Books, P.O. Box 102650, Denver, CO 80250, $29.95 for *High Fantastic*.)

Another odd small-press item is *Buried Treasures: An Anthology of Unpublished Pulphouse Stories* (Eugene Professional Writers Workshops, Inc), edited by Jerry Oltion, which is exactly what the subtitle *says* that it is: thirty-eight stories left unpublished in inventory when *Pulphouse* magazine went out of business, collected in a hardcover anthology made to look as much like the old Pulphouse "Hardback Magazines" as possible. Not surprisingly, many of the stories here are minor, and many of them are quite short, only a page or two long, mostly the kind of weird black-humored vignettes (often on the far edge of horror, pun stories, and gross-out jokes, although some of them are surreal enough to be hard to classify) that *Pulphouse: The Magazine* itself was known for publishing. Nevertheless, there is some interesting stuff here, including a substantial story by Kate Wilhelm that you're not going to find anywhere else, and worthwhile stuff by Kij Johnson, Leslie What, Robert J. Howe, and others. (Eugene Professional Writers Workshops, Inc., P.O. Box 50395, Eugene, OR 97405, $25 plus $3 shipping and handling for *Buried Treasures.*)

Future Net (DAW), edited by Martin H. Greenberg and Larry Segriff, an original anthology about computer networks and virtual reality, has an interesting theme, although the actual stories are mostly rather weak—there is worthwhile work here by Gregory Benford, Josepha Sherman, and others. *Virtually Now: Stories of Science, Technology and the Future* (Persea), a mixed original and reprint anthology edited by Jeanne Schinto, covered much the same sort of territory, as did two of the year's reprint anthologies. *Don't Forget Your Spacesuit, Dear* (Baen), edited by Jody Lynn Nye, is one of those one-joke anthologies, like last year's *Chicks in Chainmail;* this time, the joke is that these are stories about nagging mothers in space (although a few stories are set in fantasy worlds as well), and, as usual, the joke quickly wears thin, and even becomes a bit tiresome as the authors relentlessly drag out every you'll-poke-your-eye-out-clean-up-your-room-don't-put-that-in-your-mouth-you-don't-know-where-it's-been Mother cliche you've ever heard, weakly rationalized in SF and fantasy settings; it would help to read these one at a time instead of all at once, widely spaced. Other SF anthologies included *L. Ron Hubbard Presents Writers of the Future, Volume XII* (Bridge), edited by Dave Wolverton, which, as usual, presented novice work by beginning writers, some of whom may later turn out to be important talents; *The Resurrected Holmes* (St. Martin's Press), edited by Marvin Kaye, Sherlock Holmes pastiches by various hands, many with fantastic elements; and *Swords of the Rainbow* (Alyson), edited by Eric Garber and Jewelle Gomez, an original (mostly) anthology of gay-themed SF and fantasy.

There was an anthology of Australian feminist stories, *She's Fantastical,* which I was unable to find; I'll try to catch up with it next year.

The year's few shared-world anthologies included: *Star Wars: Tales from Jabba's Palace* (Bantam), edited by Kevin J. Anderson; *Star Wars: Tales of the Bounty Hunters* (Bantam), edited by Kevin J. Anderson; *Sandman: Book of Dreams* (HarperPrism), edited by Neil Gaiman and Edward E. Kramer; *The Ultimate Spiderman* (Berkley/Boulevard), edited by Stan Lee; *The Ultimate Super-Villians* (Berkley/Boulevard), edited by Stan Lee; and *In Celebration of Lammas Night* (Baen), edited by Josepha Sherman.

There were fewer important fantasy anthologies this year than there were last year. The big fantasy anthology of the year would probably be *The Shimmering Door* (HarperPrism), edited by Katharine Kerr, but it didn't strike me as being as strong overall as last year's preeminent fantasy anthology, *Immortal Unicorn,* although it did still feature a good deal of strong work; the best story here is M. John Harrison's elliptical but evocative "Seven Guesses of the Heart," although the anthology also features good work by Gregory Feeley, Esther M. Friesner, Susan Shwartz, Richard Parks, Connie Hirsch, Charles de Lint, and others. I was unable to obtain a copy of the year's other big fantasy anthology from HarperPrism, *David Copperfield's Beyond Imagination* (HarperPrism), edited by David Copperfield and Janet Berliner. I'll save it for consideration for next year's anthology. *Otherwere: Stories of Transformation* (Ace), edited by Laura Anne Gilman and Keith R. A. DeCandido, plays the shapeshifter theme mostly for laughs, with stories about were-guppies and were-hamsters and so forth, and the stories *do* manage to generate a few good laughs, most notably in the stories by Esther M. Friesner and Josepha Sherman—but the aesthetic slant of the anthology kills the *power* of the theme as well, which makes this another of those anthologies that is like eating a gallon of caramel popcorn at one sitting. *Warrior*

Enchantresses (DAW), edited by Kathleen M. Massie-Ferch and Martin H. Greenberg, takes its theme a good deal more seriously (perhaps even a bit too seriously, since the overall tone here is rather solemn), but the theme is specialized enough that many of the stories here seem too much alike; there are good stories here, though, by Pamela Sargent, Deborah Wheeler, Tanith Lee, Rebecca Ore, and others. *Castle Fantastic* (DAW), edited by John DeChancie and Martin H. Greenberg, also suffered from an overly restrictive theme, but featured interesting work by S. N. Dyer, Pamela Sargent, Mike Resnick and Linda Dunn, and others. *Sisters in Fantasy 2* (Roc), edited by Susan Shwartz and Martin H. Greenberg, a more generalized fantasy anthology, features good work by Tanith Lee, Beth Meacham, Jane Yolen, Susan Casper, Rebecca Ore, Valerie J. Freireich, and others. Other fantasy anthologies included *CatFantastic IV* (DAW), edited by Andre Norton and Martin H. Greenberg and *Sword and Sorceress XIII* (DAW), edited by Marion Zimmer Bradley.

I haven't been following the horror field closely for some time now, but it seemed to me that the most prominent original horror anthologies of the year probably included *Dante's Disciples* (White Wolf), edited by Peter Crowther and Edward E. Kramer, *Darkside: Horror for the Next Millennium* (Darkside Press), edited by John Pelan, and *Touch Wood* (Warner Aspect), edited by Peter Crowther, the first US publication of an anthology that came out in the UK a few years ago. Ellen Datlow's *Off Limits,* if considered as a horror anthology rather than a science fiction anthology, would probably rank right up there too. *Diagnosis: Terminal: An Anthology of Medical Terror* (Tor), edited by F. Paul Wilson, is being marketed as a horror anthology, but the best stories in it, by Ed Gorman, Karl Edward Wagner, and F. Paul Wilson himself, are actually science fiction; the book also has interesting work by Steven Spruill, Chet Williamson, and others. *Twists of the Tale: An Anthology of Cat Horror* (Dell), edited by Ellen Datlow, a mixed original (mostly) and reprint anthology of horror stories about cats, features good work by Nancy Kress, Susan Wade, Harvey Jacobs, Sarah Clemens, Tanith Lee, Nina Kiriki Hoffman, and others (cats are the *villains* in many of the stories here, though, unlike most of the other fantasy cat anthologies, and I wonder if cat lovers—who, after all, love their cats—are going to respond well to that. It'll be interesting to find out.).

Other horror anthologies this year included: *Phantoms of the Night* (DAW), edited by Richard Gilliam and Martin H. Greenberg; *Night Screams* (Roc), edited by Ed Gorman and Martin H. Greenberg; *The Time of the Vampires* (DAW), edited by P. N. Elrod and Martin H. Greenberg; *Fear the Fever: Hot Blood #4* (Pocket), edited by Jeff Gelb and Michael Garrett; *White House Horrors* (DAW), edited by Martin H. Greenberg; and *It Came From the Drive-In* (DAW), edited by Norman Partridge and Martin H. Greenberg.

Last year I speculated that someone would surely soon combine 1995's two trends in horror anthologies and give us an anthology called *Arthurian Vampires* or *Vampire Arthurs!*. Well, it hasn't showed up yet . . . but there actually was a King Arthur-is-a-vampire story this year, so can the anthology be far behind? Maybe next year.

An associational small-press anthology of surreal slipstream stories, the supposed beginning of an anthology series, is *Leviathan, Volume No. I, Into The Gray* (Mule Press and the Ministry of Whimsy), edited by Jeff VanderMeer and Luke O'Grady; this will probably be too far out on the edge for most genre readers, but it does contain interesting work by Kathryn Kulpa, Stepan Chapman, Mark Rich, and others. (Mule Press and The Ministry of Whimsy, P.O. Box 4248, Tallahassee, FL 32315, $8.50 postpaid for *Leviathan.*)

It was a bad year in the novel market, in terms of overall sales (although some individual books sold very well indeed), something that doesn't show up much (yet) in the number totals of new books published; those totals may well drop a lot more *next* year when publishers, pinched by losses, begin to tighten their belts. In some ways, the news was almost as bad here as it was in the magazine market, with sales down and returns up dramatically, with the chaos in the independent distribution system affecting the book market as well. The *kind* of books that sells continues to drift from one end of the spectrum to the other. It was a very bad year for mass market original paperbacks, with at least one major editor unequivocally saying "Mass market is dead." More and more, genre books—once almost exclusively a mass-market paperback phenomenon— are being published as hardcover originals or as trade paperbacks, a trend that is likely to continue for the foreseeable future, as book prices continue to climb and consumers figure that they might as well shell out a few bucks more to get a hardcover or a trade paperback rather than spend nearly the same sort of money for a mass-market paper- back. It'll be interesting to see what the long-term effect of the upheavals in the dis- tribution systems will be, as well as of the increase in returns—*Publishers Weekly* reported one rumor that a major bookstore chain was preparing several *railroad box- cars* full of returns to ship back to a publisher—but it's unlikely to be good.

The statistics themselves only reflect some of this turmoil. According to the news- magazine *Locus,* there were 1,121 original books "of interest to the SF field" published in 1996, as opposed to 1,250 such books in 1995, a 6 percent drop—not good, but there's probably worse news to come. The number of new SF novels published actually went *up* slightly, with 253 novels published as opposed to 239 in 1995, fantasy was down some, with 224 fantasy novels published instead of the 227 novels that were published in 1995, and horror was down substantially, with only 122 horror novels published as compared to last year's total of 193. (It should be noted that although the number of adult horror novels was shrinking, the Young Adult and children's horror markets, which practically didn't exist a few years ago, are booming, with R. L. Stine's megaselling *Goosebumps* series only part of the flood—and that many of those books, particularly the ones without an overt supernatural element, are not reflected in these totals.)

In spite of the decline in new titles released, there are still a lot of science fiction/ fantasy/horror books coming out every year. Even if you count only the science fiction novels, it's obviously just about impossible for any one individual to read and review 253 new novels, or even a significant *fraction* of them—let alone somebody like me, who has enormous amounts of short material to read, both for *Asimov*'s and for this anthology.

As usual, therefore, I haven't read a lot of novels this year; of those I have read, I would recommend: *Holy Fire* (Bantam Spectra), Bruce Sterling; *Idoru* (Putnam) Wil- liam Gibson; *Blue Mars* (Bantam Spectra), Kim Stanley Robinson; *Whiteout* (Tor), Sage Walker; *River of Dust* (AvoNova), Alexander Jablokov; *The Bones of Time* (Tor), Kathleen Ann Goonan; *A Game of Thrones* (Bantam Spectra), George R.R. Martin; *Humpty Dumpty: An Oval* (Tor), Damon Knight; *Nadya: The Wolf Chronicles* (Tor), Pat Murphy; *Distress* (Millennium), Greg Egan; and a special mention of Jack Vance's best novel in years, *Night Lamp* (Tor), Jack Vance.

Other novels that have received a lot of attention and acclaim in 1996 include: *The Ringworld Throne* (Del Rey), Larry Niven; *Beggars Ride* (Tor), Nancy Kress; *Endym- ion* (Bantam Spectra), Dan Simmons; *Voyage* (HarperPrism), Stephen Baxter; *The Other End of Time* (Tor), Frederik Pohl; *Starplex* (Ace) Robert J. Sawyer; *North Wind* (Tor), Gwyneth Jones; *Widowmaker* (Bantam Spectra), Mike Resnick; *Clouds End* (Ace), Sean Stewart; *Wildside* (Tor), Steven Gould; *Excession* (Bantam Spectra), Iain M. Banks; *Pirates of the Universe* (Tor), Terry Bisson; *Bellwether* (Bantam Spectra), Connie Willis; *The Tranquillity Alternative* (Ace), Allen Steele; *Lunatics* (St. Martin's

Press), Bradley Denton; *Exodus from the Long Sun* (Tor), Gene Wolfe; *Ancient Shores* (HarperPrism), Jack McDevitt; *Gibbon's Decline and Fall* (Bantam Spectra), Sheri S. Tepper; *The Two Georges* (Tor), Harry Turtledove & Richard Dreyfuss; *The Transmigration of Souls* (Warner), William Barton; *Remnant Population* (Baen), Elizabeth Moon; *Expiration Date* (Tor), Tim Powers; *Dreamfall* (Warner Aspect), Joan D. Vinge; *Godmother Night* (St. Martin's Press), Rachel Pollack; *Walking the Labyrinth* (Tor), Lisa Goldstein; *Oaths and Miracles* (Forge), Nancy Kress; *Automated Alice* (Crown), Jeff Noon; *Blameless in Abaddon* (Harcourt Brace), James Morrow; *The Unicorn Sonata* (Turner), Peter S. Beagle; *The Hunger and Ecstasy of Vampires* (Ziesing), Brian M. Stableford; *The Pillow Friend* (White Wolf), Lisa Tuttle; *Ancient Echoes* (Roc), Robert Holdstock; *Night Sky Mine* (Tor), Melissa Scott; *Firestar* (Tor) Michael F. Flynn; *Shards of Empire* (Tor), Susan Shwartz; *Fisherman's Hope* (Warner Aspect), David Feintuch; *The Gap into Ruin: This Day All Gods Die* (Bantam Spectra), Stephen Donaldson; *One for the Morning Glory* (Tor), John Barnes; *The Prestige* (St. Martin's Press), Christopher Priest; *Pastwatch: The Redemption of Christopher Columbus* (Tor), Orson Scott Card; *Inheritor,* (DAW) C. J. Cherryh; *The Dragon and the Unicorn* (HarperPrism), A. A. Attanasio; *Murder in the Solid State* (Tor), Wil McCarthy; *Cetaganda* (Baen), Lois McMaster Bujold; *The Time Ships* (HarperPrism), Stephen Baxter; *The Shift* (Bantam) George Foy; *The Virgin and the Dinosaur* (Avon) R. García y Robertson; *Winter Rose* (Ace) Patricia A. McKillip; *Panda Ray* (St. Martin's Press), Michael Kandel, *The Wild* (Bantam Spectra), David Zindell; *Paris in the Twentieth Century* (Random House), Jules Verne; and *The 37th Mandala* (St. Martin's Press), Marc Laidlaw.

It was another pretty good year for first novels, a good deal stronger than 1995. The first novel that received the most attention and acclaim this year was Sage Walker's *Whiteout* (Tor), mentioned above, which showed up on several year's-end wrap-up lists, and which was touted as best first novel of the year by *Locus* reviewer Farren Miller. The next most frequently reviewed first novels would probably be *Celestial Matters* (Tor), Richard Garfinkle, and *Top Dog* (Ace), Jerry Jay Carroll. Other first novels included: *Looking for the Mahdi* (Ace), N. Lee Wood; *Reclamation* (Warner Aspect), Sarah Zettel; *Mordred's Curse* (AvoNova), Ian McDowell; *The Jigsaw Woman* (Roc), Kim Antieau; *The Sparrow* (Villard), Mary Doria Russell; *Anvil of the Sun* (Roc), Anne Lesley Groell; *The Nature of Smoke* (Tor), Anne Harris; *First Dawn* (Ace), Mike Moscoe; *The Fortunate Fall* (Tor), Raphael Carter; *Luck in the Shadows* (Bantam Spectra), Lynn Flewelling; *Door Number Three* (Tor), Patrick O'Leary; and *The Wood Wife* (Tor), Terri Windling. In spite of recessionary talk, first novelists don't seem to be having much trouble getting into print (although, the way the field works now, they may find it considerably *more* difficult to sell their third or fourth novels, ironically enough, if the sales figures on the earlier books have not been impressive); there were a *lot* of first novels published this year—more of them by women than by men, for whatever that's worth. Come to think of it, it seems as though most of the most impressive first novels of the last few years (by writers such as Maureen F. McHugh, Nicola Griffith, Mary Rosenblum, Patricia Anthony, Kathleen Ann Goonan, Valerie J. Freireich, Linda Nagata, Tricia Sullivan, Catherine Asaro, and others) have been written by women. Does this represent an ongoing (and largely unnoticed) demographic shift in the ranks of science fiction writers? Up until now, the perception has been that male SF writers outnumber female SF writers by a large margin. Judging from all these new women writers coming along, though, that may no longer be true in a few years. Tor, Ace, and Roc in particular seem to be publishing a lot of first novels these days, and they are to be commended for it, as are all imprints that take a chance on new talent—without a steady influx of new writers growing and developing, SF wouldn't have much of a future, and if the market was hard enough that first novelists couldn't break into print, things would look considerably bleaker than they do.

It seemed like a pretty strong year for novels to me. As can be seen from the lists above, Tor had a very strong year, as did Bantam Spectra. I don't see any clear favorite here for the Nebula and Hugo Awards; one of Robinson's Mars books has already won the Hugo, *Idoru* is not as strong as *Neuromancer* was, Sterling has to date not been popular enough with the electorate to win, and so on down the line. George R. R. Martin's *A Game of Thrones* is clearly the year's Big Fantasy Novel, reviewed everywhere, and may end up a favorite for the World Fantasy Award, but it remains to be seen how it will do with the Hugo voters, who traditionally are somewhat more resistant to fantasy than the Nebula electorate has been in recent years. And, thanks to SFWA's bizarre "rolling eligibility" rule, many of the books up against the 1996 books for the Nebula Award are holdovers from 1995 (the majority of the novels which made this year's Preliminary Nebula Ballot, in fact, are from 1995, 15 to 8), which muddies the waters even more. So it's anybody's guess who'll end up walking off with the major awards this year.

One interesting trend, showing up both in the novels and even more heavily in the short fiction this year, is what might be called the alternate space program story. Clearly fueled by nostalgia for the good old days of the Apollo program, this kind of story rewrites history to show us how we could have done the space program right and had colonies on the Moon or on Mars by now, if things had only worked out *differently*. It's an interesting specialization of the alternate history story, and clearly also related to the Victorian SF (as I guess you'd have to call it) that's been popular in Britain in the past few years, wherein various Victorian-era figures develop working space programs—although usually by cheating and using some variant of that convenient anti-gravity mineral, first refined by H. G. Wells, Cavorite—all the way back in the nineteenth century (which leads to the usually unvoiced assumption that of course by *now* the solar system would be up to its ass in astronauts—the triumph of the space program done *right* once again). A bit sad that the Space Age is now widely considered to be *over*, a bit of pastel nostalgia receding into the past (I feel, to the contrary, that the Space Age is just on the verge of really *beginning*—but that's an argument for some other place) . . . but then again, perhaps this is just an example, and a rather benign one at that, of end-of-the-millennium chilistic panic. I've been waiting for this to show up in the form of lots of end of the world stories, but so far they don't seem to have materialized (the apocalyptic end of the world stuff has mostly been showing up in nonfiction books such as *The Hot Zone* and in speculations about how we could be wiped out at any second by the impact of a dinosaur-killer asteroid). Given a choice, I'd much rather have the alternate space program stories, so I'm not complaining—but it is an interesting, and interestingly timed, phenomenon.

An associational mainstream novel (with occasional traces of a fantastic element) that would probably appeal to many genre readers was *The Sweetheart Season* (Henry Holt), by Karen Joy Fowler. Paul Park's *The Gospel of Corax* (Soho Books), a sort of alternate history of Jesus, also balances right on the edge of the genre. Mystery novels by SF writers this year, which may perhaps be of interest to their fans, included *Skinny Annie Blues* (Kensington Books), Neal Barrett, Jr., *Draconian New York* (Forge), Robert Sheckley; *The Silver Chariot Killer* (St. Martin's Press), Richard A. Lupoff; and *Malice Prepense* (St. Martin's Press), Kate Wilhelm. A series of historical mysteries that seem to be enjoyed by a lot of SF and fantasy fans, perhaps because of her strong and sometimes quirky (the books are often quite funny) feel for the historic milieu, are Lindsey Davis's mysteries set in ancient Rome, the most recent of which is this year's *Last Act in Palmyra* (Mysterious Press).

Once again this year there were several reissues of classic novels; small presses have been struggling to make this kind of stuff available for years now, but this year, like last year, surprisingly, and very commendably, a lot of the reissuing is being done by trade houses such as AvoNova, Tor, Baen, and Ace, bucking a well-established trend. That's very encouraging, as over the last decade or so this has been a field where books tend to go out of print fast and *stay* out of print. Often things are nearly impossible to find once they are out of print, so my advice is to buy copies of these books now, while you have the chance. It may be years before you get another opportunity. Re-issued this year were: two of the best SF novels ever written, *The Stars My Destination* and *The Demolished Man,* both by Alfred Bester, both from Vintage; *The Moon Is a Harsh Mistress* (Tor), by Robert A. Heinlein, his best novel by a considerable margin (including the more famous *Stranger in a Strange Land*); *Lest Darkness Fall,* by L. Sprague de Camp, still perhaps the best Alternate History novel ever written, bound in a package with David Drake's *To Bring the Light,* from Baen; three novels by the Grandmaster of Australian SF, George Turner, all of them largely unknown on this side of the world, *Beloved Son, The Drowning Towers,* and *Yesterday's Men,* all from AvoNova; Jack Williamson's classic *The Humanoids* (Tor Orb); Greg Bear's landmark *Blood Music* (Ace); Jack Vance's pioneering early study of immortality, still as fresh as ever, *To Live Forever* (Charles F. Miller); Samuel R. Delany's controversial SF novel *Trouble on Triton* (Wesleyan/New England); a package of three long out-of-print and nearly forgotten fantasies by Thomas Burnett Swann, *The Minotaur Trilogy* (Mathew D. Hargreaves); a package of several long-out-of-print novels by Philip José Farmer, *The World of Tiers* (Tor), and Michael Moorcock's famous shocker, *Behold the Man,* now in a special thirtieth anniversary edition from Mojo Press. Get 'em while you can.

(Addresses follow for the small-press items that may be hard to find in bookstores: Mark V. Ziesing, P.O. Box 76, Shingletown, CA, 96088, $25 for *The Hunger and Ecstasy of Vampires,* by Brian Stableford; Charles F. Miller, 708 Westover Drive, Lancaster, PA 17601, $60 for *To Live Forever,* by Jack Vance; University Press of New England, 23 South Main St., Hanover, NH 03755, $14.95 for *Trouble on Triton,* by Samuel R. Delany; Mathew D. Hargreaves, P.O. Box 66099, Seattle, WA 98166-0099, $50 plus $5 for shipping for *The Minotaur Trilogy,* by Thomas Burnett Swann; Mojo Press, P.O. Box 14005, Austin, TX 78714, $12.95 for *Behold the Man: The Thirtieth Anniversary Edition,* by Michael Moorcock.)

Although 1996 was perhaps not quite as strong a year for short-story collections overall as last year was, there were still some excellent collections published, including a number of good retrospective collections that offer capsule glimpses of a writer's career in short fiction, and which ought to be in every home library.

The best collections of the year included: *None So Blind* (Morrow/AvoNova), Joe Haldeman; *The Invisible Country* (Gollancz), Paul J. McAuley; *Synthesis and Other Virtual Realities* (Arkham House), Mary Rosenblum; *Unlocking the Air and Other Stories* (HarperCollins), Ursula K. LeGuin; and *The Wall of the Sky, the Wall of the Eye* (Harcourt Brace), Jonathan Lethem. Among the year's other top collections were: *Standard Candles* (Tachyon Publications), Jack McDevitt; *At the City Limits of Fate* (Edgewood), Michael Bishop; *All-American Alien Boy* (Old Earth Books), Allen Steele; *Before . . . 12:01 . . . and After* (Fedogan & Bremer), Richard A. Lupoff; *Blue Apes* (Tesseract), Phyllis Gotlieb; and *Bible Stories for Adults* (Harcourt Brace), James Morrow. Paul Di Filippo's *Ribofunk* (Four Walls Eight Windows), is a collection of "linked stories" tracing the development of one of Di Filippo's stylized and deliberately outrageous future history scenarios; Di Filippo occasionally loses control of his material here, but that is made up for by the exuberance and energy of the writing, and the wild audacity of the conceptualization. Ray Bradbury's most recent collection, *Quicker Than the Eye* (Avon), is, disappointingly, filled mostly with weak or minor stories, although here and there you can still hear the echo of the master's voice as it sounded in his prime, when it sang with a beauty and a passion that had never been heard in the genre before.

There were many excellent retrospective omnibus collections published this year, collections that ought to be foundation stones in your library: *Lean Times in Lankhmar* (White Wolf Borealis), by the late Fritz Leiber, is the second volume in White Wolf's laudable attempt to return to print all of Leiber's marvelous Gray Mouser stories, one of the indispensable works of modern fantasy. *Microcosmic God: Volume II: The Complete Stories* of Theodore Sturgeon (North Atlantic Books) and *Killdozer!: Volume III: The Complete Stories of Theodore Sturgeon* (North Atlantic Books), both by the late Theodore Sturgeon, are the second and third volumes in this publisher's epic attempt to return to print everything ever written by Theodore Sturgeon, a project of staggering dimensions, and one that may be the thing that rescues this once-famous author from the undeserved oblivion that seems to be creeping upon him. Another writer who deserves to be rescued from being forgotten, in these days of almost zero historical memory in the field, is the late Clifford D. Simak, and a small press named Tachyon has made a good start at doing that with the retrospective collection, *Over the River and Through the Woods* (Tachyon Publications). The feisty and controversial Harlan Ellison is still very much with us, but a good idea of his importance to the development of several genres (most notably the modern horror genre, where he has obviously been an ancestral figure of immense influence), can be gotten by the retrospective *Edgeworks* (White Wolf Borealis), by Harlan Ellison, part of a project by White Wolf to bring all of Ellison's stories and essays back into print in omnibus volumes. Bruce Sterling is still a relatively young writer by any reasonable standard, in spite of being one of the big names of the nineties. but if you're not familiar with his work, *Schismatrix Plus* (Ace), makes a convenient place to start, a tasty package made up of Sterling's well-known Shaper/Mechanist stories as well as a reprint of his novel *Schismatrix,* one of the prime works of SF's Cyberpunk Revolution, which is set in the same baroque and fascinating future. And *All One Universe* (Tor), gives us a look back over the amazing fifty-year career of Poul Anderson, who's still writing stuff today that's every bit as vigorous, compelling, and imaginative as the stuff he was writing back in the 1950s.

Although trade publishers continued to put out an encouraging number of collections this year, notably HarperCollins and Harcourt Brace, small presses were even more important in getting collections to the reading public, as has been true more often than not over the past decade; small presses such as White Wolf, Tachyon Publishing, Arkham House, Edgewood, North Atlantic Books, Old Earth Books, Edgewood, Tesseracts, and Four Walls Eight Windows all contributed important collections this year. Arkham House, which had been for some years now one of the prime publishers of first-rate science fiction collections, parted ways with James Turner, and presumably will now abandon science fiction and return to being an imprint primarily of interest to fans of H. P. Lovecraft and similar occult writers, a major blow to the SF short-story collection market. (Fortunately, Turner has started up Golden Gryphon Press, and has already announced an upcoming major collection from them by James Patrick Kelly, so perhaps the loss will be minimized.) And all those publishers who bucked the trend of recent publishing wisdom by bringing old material back into print are to be especially commended, including Tachyon Publishing (who are becoming very active lately in publishing collections, in spite of being a very small press indeed), White Wolf, and North Atlantic Books.

With the exception of books by White Wolf and Four Walls Eight Windows, very few small-press titles will be findable in the average bookstore, or even in the average chain store, which means that mail-order is your best bet, and so I'm going to list the addresses of the small-press publishers mentioned above: Arkham House, Arkham House Publishers, Inc., Sauk City, WI 53583, $21.95 for *Synthesis and Other Virtual Realities,* by Mary Rosenblum; North Atlantic Books, P.O. Box 12327, Berkeley, CA, 94701, $25 for *Microcosmic God: Volume II: The Complete Stories of Theodore Sturgeon,* $25 for *Killdozer!: Volume III: The Complete Stories of Theodore Sturgeon;* Tachyon Publications, 1459 18th Street #139, San Francisco, CA, 94107, $25 for *Standard Candles,* by Jack McDevitt, $25 for *Over the River and Through the Woods,* by Clifford D. Simak; Edgewood Press, P.O. Box 380264, Cambridge, MA, 02238, $14 for *At the City Limits of Fate,* by Michael Bishop; Fedogan & Bremer, 603 Washington Avenue, SE #77, Minneapolis MN 55415, $27 for *Before . . . 12:01 . . . and After,* by Richard A. Lupoff; Tesseract Books, 214-21 10405 Jasper Avenue, Edmonton, Alberta, Canada T5J 352, $21.95 for *Blue Apes,* by Phyllis Gotlieb.

There didn't seem to be as many reprint anthologies this year as last year, and many of the ones that did appear were rather weak, but there were still a few good values in this market.

As usual, unsurprisingly, some of the best bets for your money in this category were the various "Best of the Year" anthologies, and the annual Nebula Award anthology, *Nebula Awards 30* (Harcourt Brace), edited by Pamela Sargent. After a number of years of being covered by only one "Best of the Year" volume, science fiction is now covered by *two* such anthology series, the one you are holding in your hand, and the *Year's Best SF* series (HarperPrism), edited by David G. Hartwell, up to its second volume. I won't presume to review Hartwell's Best of the Year anthology, that would be inappropriate, since it's in direct competition with *this* volume, but the field is wide and various enough for there to be a number of best volumes, each representing a different aesthetic slant and perspective; you could produce five different Best of the Year volumes by five different editors, and, tastes varying as radically as they do, I'm sure that they wouldn't overlap to any significant degree. So a bit of variety in this market is certainly a healthy thing for the genre at large, giving a larger number of authors—since Hartwell will almost certainly like stories that I didn't, and vice versa—a chance to be showcased every year. There were two Best of the Year anthologies covering horror in 1996: the latest edition in a now slightly retitled British series (last year it was just *The Best New Horror*), *The Mammoth Book of Best New Horror Volume 7* (Robinson/Raven Carroll & Graf), edited by Stephen Jones, and the Ellen Datlow half of a huge volume covering both horror and fantasy, *The Year's Best Fantasy and Horror* (St. Martin's Press), edited by Ellen Datlow and Terri Windling, this year up to its Ninth Annual Collection. Fantasy, as opposed to horror, is still only covered by the Windling half of the Datlow/Windling anthology.

Turning away from the anthology series, your best buy among the year's singleton reprint anthologies was probably the big retrospective anthology *Visions of Wonder: The Science Fiction Research Association Anthology* (Tor), edited by David G. Hartwell and Milton T. Wolf. This is another of those big academically oriented retrospectives, such as *The Norton Book of Science Fiction* or Hartwell's own *The Ascent of Wonder,* that have been kicking up a lot of controversy among critics and scholars for the last few years. This one is no exception to the rule—critics are already arguing with the polemical opinions expressed in the book, or saying that it doesn't make an effective teaching anthology for actual classroom use (something too far out of my area of expertise for me to judge), or complaining about the stories that the editors have chosen, or speculating on what stories they *should* have chosen instead. . . . I must admit that it's true that some of the selections here, are, to put the best spin possible on it, eclectic, if not downright *peculiar.* None of this controversy will really matter to the average reader, however, nor should it. What will be important to the average reader is that this is a big fat anthology stuffed full of first-rate stories, a very good buy for the money. Although there are a few minor stories here that make me scratch my head in puzzlement and wonder why *they* were used—and some other critic might come up with a different list of just which stories those are, which, of course, is always the rub. Any anthology that brings together under the same covers stories such as Greg Bear's "Blood Music," James Patrick Kelly's "Mr. Boy," Joanna Russ's "Souls," James Tiptree, Jr.'s "The Girl Who Was Plugged In," and William Gibson's "Burning Chrome," as well as more than a dozen other first-rate stories, is a valuable anthology to have on your bookshelves, and an anthology that ought to be read. It's also good to see some of the critical essays that are included here, stuff like Damon Knight's "Critics" and Algis Budrys's "Paradise Charted," and a number of others, back in print (although again, the selection of essays used is . . . eclectic).

Much the same sort of thing could be said about *Paragons: Twelve Master Science Fiction Writers Ply Their Craft* (St. Martin's Press), edited by Robin Wilson. The primary purpose of this book is to act as a how-to-write-SF teaching guide, to which end it contains critical essays on various areas of craftsmanship from well-known SF writers . . . but, since stories by those authors are also reproduced here, as examples of the craft, the book can also legitimately be viewed solely as a reprint fiction anthology. And considered as a reprint anthology, it's quite a good one, one of the year's best, in fact, containing as it does first-rate stories such as Nancy Kress's "The Price of Oranges," Kim Stanley Robinson's "Glacier," Joe Haldeman's "Feedback," Pat Cadigan's "Pretty Boy Crossover," and eight other stories by top authors. The same kind of remarks also apply to reissues of two academically oriented retrospective anthologies, *The Road to Science Fiction: Volume 3* (White Wolf), edited by James Gunn, and *Those Who Can* (St. Martin's Press), edited by Robin Wilson. All of these books do double-duty as teaching artifacts *and* as enjoyable fiction anthologies, and they can be appreciated even by someone who doesn't give a fig about the history of science fiction or about how to craft a saleable story.

Other reprint SF anthologies this year included *Cybersex* (Carroll & Graf), edited by Richard Glyn Jones, an anthology of (mostly) reprint erotic SF stories that included good work by writers such as Kathe Koja, Greg Egan, and others; *The Way It Wasn't* (Citadel), edited by Martin H. Greenberg; and *Monster Brigade 3000* (Ace), edited by Charles Waugh and Martin H. Greenberg. Noted without comment is *Hackers* (Ace), edited by Jack Dann and Gardner Dozois.

Reprint fantasy and horror anthologies this year (which also seemed to be fewer in number) included: *The Oxford Book of Twentieth-Century Ghost Stories* (Oxford), edited by Michael Cox; *Supernatural Detectives* (DAW), edited by Charles Waugh and Martin H. Greenberg; and *Tarot Tales* (Ace), edited by Rachel Pollack and Caitlín Matthews. Noted without comment is *Isaac Asimov's Vampires* (Ace), edited by Gardner Dozois and Sheila Williams.

It was an unspectacular year in the SF-oriented nonfiction and reference book field, although some solid items did appear, with the most interesting book for the non-specialist probably being L. Sprague de Camp's literary autobiography *Time & Chance,* which gives us a fascinating retrospective of de Camp's almost sixty-year career. There were fewer important reference books this year, and most of them were oriented toward fantasy rather than science fiction—an exception was *Outside the Human Aquarium:*

Masters of Science Fiction, 2nd Edition (Borgo Press), by Brian Stableford—with the best of them probably being the *St. James Guide to Fantasy Writers* (St. James Press), edited by David Pringle, and *The Tough Guide to Fantasyland* (Vista), by Diana Wynne Jones; a bit more technical was *Fiction and Fantasy* (University of Georgia Press), edited by George Slusser, Gary Westfahl, & Eric S. Rabkin. As interesting as these or perhaps even *more* interesting for the casual reader is a compilation of photographs of famous fantasy writers, *The Faces of Fantasy* (Tor), photographs by Patti Perret, a follow-up to 1985's well-known *The Faces of Science Fiction*. The best of the year's critical books was undoubtedly *Look at the Evidence* (Serconia Press), by John Clute, a collection of Clute's strongly opinionated but literate and intelligent essays about science fiction. There was also *Ash of Stars: On the Writing of Samuel R. Delany* (University Press of Mississippi), edited by James Sallis; *Dreams and Wishes* (Simon & Schuster), by Susan Cooper; *Shadows of the Future* (Syracuse), by Patrick Parrinder; *Inventing Wonderland* (Free Press), Jackie Wullschläger; and *Immortal Engines: Life Extension and Immortality in Science Fiction and Fantasy* (University of Georgia Press), edited by George Slussar, Gary Westfahl, & Eric S. Rabkin. *Paragons: Twelve Master Science Fiction Writers Ply Their Craft* (St. Martin's Press), edited by Robin Wilson, which I mentioned above for its value as a reprint fiction anthology, should also be mentioned here for its value as a how-to-write book, with excellent essays on one aspect or another of the craft of writing by "Masters" such as Pat Cadigan, John Kessel, Howard Waldrop, Nancy Kress, Joe Haldeman, Kim Stanley Robinson, James Patrick Kelly, Lucius Shepard, Karen Joy Fowler, Greg Bear, Pat Murphy, and Bruce Sterling.

There were several literary biographies/studies of well-known authors, including *H. P. Lovecraft: A Life* (Necronomicon Press), S. T. Joshi; *James Blish: Author Mirabilis* (Galactic Central), Phil Stephensen-Payne; *Welcome to the Revolution: the Literary Legacy of Mack Reynolds* (Borgo Press), by Curtis C. Smith; *Bram Stoker* (Knopf), Barbara Belford; and *The Jules Verne Encyclopedia* (Scarecrow Press), Brian Taves & Stephen Michaluk Jr.

There seemed to be fewer art books this year than last year, when we saw major art collections from Bob Eggleton, Barclay Shaw, James Gurney, Stephen E. Fabian, and others, probably because of the bankruptcy of Paper Tiger, the imprint that had produced most of them. Among the best values in the art book field this year were *Barlowe's Guide to Fantasy* (HarperPrism), Wayne Barlowe; *Even Weirder* (Forge), Gahan Wilson; *The World of Edward Gorey* (Abrams), illustrations by Edward Gorey (who is clearly one of Wilson's artistic ancestors), text by Clifford Ross & Karen Wilkin; and the latest edition of a sort of "Best of the Year" series that compiles the year's fantastic art, *Spectrum III: The Best in Contemporary Fantastic Art* (Underwood Books), edited by Cathy Burnett, Arnie Fenner, and Jim Loehr. Maxfield Parrish is not technically a genre artist, but a look into *Maxfield Parrish: A Retrospective* (Pomegranate), edited by Laurence S. Cutler and Judy Goffman Cutler, will clearly demonstrate his strong influence on many of today's top genre artists; the book is also worth having for its own sake, for Parrish's lushly imagined and gorgeously colored visualizations of exotic landscapes—obviously Parrish *could* have made it as a top genre artist if he had been so inclined, and he has left his mark on those who came after him. Also out on the fringes of fantasy art, somewhere on its elusive border with illustrated children's books, and also well worth owning, are *The Voyage of the Basset* (Artisan), with quirky and evocative illustrations by James C. Christensen, text by Renwick St. James and Alan Dean Foster, and *Ship of Dreams* (Abrams) written and magnificently illustrated by Dean Morrissey; Christensen and Morrissey may be two of the most underrated artists in the whole area of fantastic art, never showing up on Hugo ballots, and the Morrissey

paintings here in particular are as rich and lush and imaginative and painterly as anything you're ever going to see, fully the equal of more famous children's book illus-
trations by artists such as N. C. Wyeth. Fantasy art fans will probably also like *The
Wanderings of Odysseus* (Delacorte), with text by Rosemary Sutcliff, and painterly
illustrations by Alan Lee. Horror fans will probably want to check out *Neurotica: The
Darkest Art of J. K. Potter* (Overlook Press), J. K. Potter, and *Species Design* (Morpheus
International), and *H. R. Giger's Film Design* (Morpheus International), both by H. R.
Giger, but be warned that these images are disturbing, particularly Giger's dark and
psychologically unsettling work, and not for the faint of heart.

The best general genre-related nonfiction book of the year was probably the late Carl
Sagan's last book, *The Demon-Haunted World: Science as a Candle in the Dark* in
which Sagan concentrates on one of the areas that obsessed him throughout his life,
the war on pseudoscience, here turning a sharp and skeptical eye on psychics, astrology,
"channeling," and a host of other fashionable New Age beliefs—all of which is more
welcome, and more appropriate, than ever, as the millennium approaches, with all the
attendant supernatural dread that traditionally whips up, and in a time when even SF
readers—and even some SF *writers*—are far more credulous, unquestioning, and non-
skeptical than they really ought to be. A handsome reissue of *The Realm of Prester
John* (Ohio University Press), by Robert Silverberg, a nonfiction study of the roots of
the legend of Prester John and his fabulous lost kingdom, should also be of interest to
many genre readers, especially fantasy fans, who can use this erudite, elegant, and well-
researched volume to trace the historical origins of many of the themes, tropes, and
images that are being used in fantasy writing to this day. *A User's Guide to the Millennium* (Picador USA), by J. G. Ballard, a collection of Ballard's outspoken and sometimes deliberately provocative reviews and essays, spanning a thirty-year period and a
wide variety of subjects, will not be to everyone's taste (I disagree with almost everything Ballard has to say about contemporary science fiction, for instance), but is wide-
ranging and eclectic enough that there's sure to be *some*thing here to interest almost
anyone; Ballard's wartime autobiographical piece is especially fascinating.

This seemed to be a halfway-decent year for genre films for a change, with at least one
artistically ambitious and successful movie, a couple of solid popular entertainments,
and one major box-office blockbuster. The best science fiction movie of the year (it
actually opened in a limited number of theaters very late in 1995, but we didn't catch
up with it until 1996) was Terry Gilliam's *Twelve Monkeys,* a stylish, engrossing, and
imaginative film that featured Gilliam's usual stunningly creative set-dressing and vis-
uals, and some very good performances from actors you don't usually think of as all
that good, such as Bruce Willis and Brad Pitt. It will come as no surprise to anyone
who has seen Gilliam's other films that it is a very *dark* movie, too relentlessly depressing for some viewers, and complex enough that people I know are *still* arguing
months later about what *really* was supposed to have happened in one scene or another.
Still, it's an ambitious and serious-minded film, a rarity in the genre market these days,
and one that I would consider, on balance, a success.

The big genre box office success of the year, of course, was *Independence Day,*
whose profits become especially impressive when you realize that it really was not very
expensive to produce, by the standards of big effects-heavy lots-of-stuff-blowing-up
spectaculars anyway. Many SF fans were very grumpy about *Independence Day,* considering it an insulting farrago of the dumbest sci-fi cliches, and it's true that it's riddled
with logical inconsistencies and holes in the plot logic that you could fly a mile-wide
Mother Ship through, but it's all done with such cheerful *élan,* and so many broad we-
know-this-is-a-hoary-cliche-but-isn't-it-*fun*? winks into the wings (it may well contain

a postmodern wink-wink reference to every other science fiction movie and TV show ever made, or at least to a preponderance of them), that I find it hard to be annoyed by it. I watched it with enjoyment with an audience that was clearly having a great deal of fun, and the serious objections only really sank in on the way home, when the logical part of my mind began to pick holes in what passes here for a plot—at which point the movie unraveled swiftly in retrospect, like the gossamer construction it is. I had fun *watching* it, though, especially Will Smith's hugely enjoyable tongue-in-cheek performance as a swaggering macho action hero, a performance that has almost certainly established him as a bankable megastar. The scene in which a cigar-chomping, totally unflappable Smith puts down a menacing, chittering alien by casually punching it in the ''nose'' is a moment that typifies the whole film: silly, when you stop to think about it, and the more you do think about it the sillier it gets (these aliens are later shown to be physically formidable enough to toss a half dozen men around like paper dolls, and yet Smith can knock one cold with one punch) . . . and yet this moment was greeted by the audience with a roar of laughter and a spontaneous outbreak of applause that shook the whole theater, and I found myself laughing right along with them. So it's a film well worth seeing if you can leave your critical faculties at home; if you can't, as many fannish critics have been unable to, then you're going to find it an experience far more annoying than entertaining, I fear. Whatever the strengths and weaknesses of *Independence Day,* I found it more palatable than the year's other big-budget alien invasion movie, the self-consciously arch, much more obviously played-for-laughs *Mars Attacks!,* inspired by a series of comic trading cards from the sixties, a one-joke movie in which really dumb-looking and obviously phony aliens (the special effects are clearly *intended* to be bad, as part of the joke) mow down a horde of Big Hollywood Stars in cameo roles; there are a few good laughs here, but the material can't really support a full-length movie, and becomes tiresome by the end. *The Arrival,* which could be considered the year's third alien invasion movie, leaned heavily on the paranoia key—it's actually an aliens-are-*already*-among-us-as-secret-rulers movie as opposed to an alien invasion movie—and played everything very earnestly indeed, probably too earnestly, with none of the redeeming humor of *Independence Day* or *Mars Attacks!.*

After 1994's muddled and disappointing *Star Trek Generations,* expectations were low for the new *Star Trek* movie, the first to feature the *Star Trek: The Next Generation* cast exclusively. *Star Trek: First Contact* was much more successful than the previous movie, both artistically and at the box office, and probably has revived the *Star Trek* franchise yet again, at a point where, after *Generations,* there had been a lot of talk about it having run out of steam. This time, the moviemakers were smart enough to stick with a straight action film, pitting the TNG crew against their most fearsome enemy, the Borg, and if the time-travel sequences were riddled with temporal paradoxes and didn't make a whole lot of logical sense, that was at least no *more* true here than it usually was in similar story lines on *Star Trek: The Next Generation* itself. Some critics protested that you could only really appreciate the movie if you were *already* a big *Star Trek* fan, but people went to see it in large enough numbers to encourage the speculation that its appeal as a fast-moving big screen adventure movie must have outweighed any problems produced by the lack of prior expertise, even among non-Trekkers. Among the *Star Trek* fans themselves, *First Contact* seemed to generate widespread acclaim, where the response to *Generation* had ranged from—at best—lukewarm all the way to downright negative, so *First Contact* seems to have rekindled the wanning enthusiasm of the franchise's core fans as well—all of which almost certainly means that there will be more *Star Trek* movies coming up in years to come.

Of the year's other box-office successes, *Twister*—which seems to be accepted by everyone as a genre movie, although the rationalization for that (testing a new invention) is slim—offered a lot of mind-blowing special effects, and little else. The success of *Twister* has inspired a wave of big disaster movies that'll be washing over theaters in 1997, including at least two movies about erupting volcanoes and one about catastrophic floods, but, alas, the fact that tornadoes have already been ''done'' probably means that nobody will film Bruce Sterling's tornado-chaser SF novel *Heavy Weather,* although if it were executed correctly, with the same kind of awesome special effects, it would be much more interesting than *Twister* was. Some people would consider *Mission: Impossible, The Rock, Eraser,* and *Chain Reaction* to be genre films as well, but, although each does contain some SF-ish elements, I think that a film has to be able to offer more than just the extreme improbability of its physical action, which borders on Roadrunner cartoon–impossible in some cases—in order to be justified as a science fiction movie. *Space Jam,* which didn't seem to generate *quite* the level of enthusiasm the producers were hoping for (although it was hard to walk into a shopping mall anywhere without seeing tons of merchandising tie-ins for it), is a feature-length animated film that features Bugs Bunny, Michael Jordan, and a team of Toons playing basketball against a team of evil space monsters. *The Relic* was a predictable *Alien* clone set in a natural history museum. *Phenomenon* was a well-meaning ''little'' film that was a bit too woo-woo and New Age–credulous for my taste. And *The Nutty Professor* was commercially successful enough to revive Eddie Murphy's career, something that I would have thought impossible after last year's *A Vampire in Brooklyn.*

Turning to the things that *weren't* big box-office smashes, *The Island of Dr. Moreau* was a heavyhanded remake that added a lot of explosions and physical action to the mix, without adding much of real value. *Multiplicity* was an amiable one-joke movie that ran out of steam long before it was over. *Escape From L.A.* was a sequel to 1981's cult success *Escape From New York* that did little but recycle all the tropes from the earlier movie, with less energy this time around. *The Phantom* generated a lot of enthusiasm among fans of the original serial, but never caught on with the wider movie audience. And *Jack* was sort of a depressing version of *Big,* with Robin Williams as a kid inhabiting a man's body, except this time he's the victim of a disease which makes him age prematurely, *not* exactly a feel-good concept.

There's a movie called *The Whole Wide World* making the rounds of the small art houses, a film about the life of fantasy writer Robert E. Howard, the creator of Conan, but I haven't been able to catch it; sounds interesting, though.

There were fewer good fantasy movies this year than there had been in 1995. Best of them may have been the quirky and imaginative animated film *James and the Giant Peach* (from the same strange crew who brought you *The Nightmare Before Christmas,* a film with which it shares a similar twisted aesthetic). Other fans would pump for *Dragonheart,* which brought an extremely sophisticated CGI special-effects dragon (voiced, somewhat improbably, by Sean Connery) and some good-natured humor to a plot that is a simple reversal of an old fairy tale formula, where the knight and the dragon join forces rather than fighting each other, an idea that goes back in the genre at least as far as Gordon Dickson's ''St. Dragon and the George'' (although it occurs to me that *The Reluctant Dragon* had a similar plotline even before *that,* come to think of it). There were several angel movies, including *Michael* and *The Preacher's Wife*—a remake of the old movie *The Bishop's Wife*—neither of which seemed to do terrific business. *The Frighteners* also had some intelligent touches, but also seemed unable to find an audience. *The Craft* was a movie about teenage high-school girls discovering the power of witchcraft. *101 Dalmatians* was a live-action remake of the classic 1961 Disney animated feature, something that to me seems so pointless a thing to do that I never bothered to catch it; most critics were underwhelmed, although it seemed to do okay at the box office and in the sale of merchandising rights (which is what many movies today are actually *for* anyway: generating merchandising rights, which usually earn considerably more than even the most successful movies earn in upfront ticket sales). There was another live-action remake of an animated film, or a live-action version of an old folk story, anyway, *The Adventures of Pinocchio,* but few people seem to have caught that one. And I refused to see the animated Disney version of *The Hunchback of Notre Dame,* the one with the cute singing gargoyles and the cute singing Hunchback, out of a sense of moral indignation. Pfui.

Turning to television, some of the new genre shows that had been introduced in 1995 died, and were replaced by a raft of even *newer* genre shows—most of them unimpressive too.

Among the longer-established shows, I've pretty much given up on "Star Trek: Voyager," which just seems to get sillier and sillier. Many of the core *Star Trek* fans seem to have given up on it too, and its ratings have continued to drop. The latest attempt to shore the ratings up is to have the Voyager crew battle the Borg, but I'm not convinced that this is going to work either. Adding Lt. Worf, one of the most popular members of the old "Star Trek: The Next Generation" cast to the cast of "Star Trek: Deep Space Nine" *has* made that show a bit more interesting to watch, but it's still nowhere near as good a show as "Star Trek: The Next Generation" was during its best seasons, and I wonder how long "DS9" is going to be able to hold the attention and loyalty of the immense audience originally attracted to the franchise in the first place by "Star Trek: TNG" and the original "Star Trek." Many of even the stone, hardcore *Star Trek* fans I talk to are growing restive with "DS9"—and most of them have already given up on "Star Trek: Voyager."

Meanwhile, the dreaded rival of "Star Trek: Deep Space Nine," a show called "Babylon 5," has become a cult item in some circles, whipping up a depth of loyalty and devotion and intense emotional excitement among the core "B5" fans unlike anything I've seen since the original "Star Trek" left the air, and any "B5" panel or function at an SF convention (let alone at a *media* convention) is likely to be standing-room-only. I must admit that I don't really understand what all the shouting is about, since to me most "B5" episodes still seem woodenly acted and leadenly directed, with mediocre-to-awful dialog, but an impressive number of SF writers and professionals seem to be closet "B5" fans, so there must be something there that I'm missing. Unfortunately, although the hardcore fans are intensely loyal, the ratings among the *general* television-viewing audience have reputedly been not all that good, and reportedly the producer is under heavy pressure from the network to scrap the projected fifth season of "Babylon 5" in favor of a more action-oriented spinoff series called "Babylon 5: Crusaders." Only time will tell how this one is going to go.

"The X-Files," another cult show, is still quite popular, although I myself wonder how many seasons you can go on finding one unresolved cosmic conspiracy after another, even with your tongue as firmly in cheek as it often is here. "The X-Files" has a spin-off show this season, "Millennium," which is sort of like an "X-Files" that concentrates mostly on the doings of serial killers, and without the tongue-in-cheek humor, played much more solemnly instead—somewhat disappointing, like an "X-Files" that takes itself *seriously.* There are also a number of "X-Files" clones, such as "Dark Skies," most of them derivative and lacking the panache of the original. "Mystery Science Theater 3000" seems to be back, although I haven't caught any of the new episodes. "Lois and Clark," which was almost canceled last year, seems to be doing very well this season. "Third Rock from the Sun" is another big hit, and another case where I don't understand what the shouting is about, since it still seems like an "Alf" retread to me. "Sliders" is a lame show that wastes a promising concept—travel among alternate worlds—by giving us alternate worlds that are mostly pretty silly and unbelievable. The quirky and interesting ''StrangeLuck'' died, and a new show with a somewhat similar kind of feel, ''Early Edition,'' is probably too limited in concept to survive; they're already running low on new things to do with the basic gimmick, which is the old chestnut about the man who get's tomorrow's newspaper today (an idea that in the print genre goes back to at least 1939). I suppose that the new ''The Outer Limits'' is still on the air, but I've given up on that show too. The new the-puppets-are-really-aliens comedy, ''Lost on Earth,'' is, in a word, dumb.

I consider ''Highlander: The Series'' to be a fantasy show rather than a science fiction one—surely it's hard to take the initial premise seriously as anything *other* than fantasy—but whether you consider it to be fantasy or SF, it's probably the best, or at least the most entertaining, genre show on television (with the possible exception of ''Babylon 5''). The initial premise behind the show is as silly and as riddled with logical inconsistencies as that of the original *Highlander* movie, but, once you grant it that initial premise, the show itself is a fairly intelligent, stylish, and even reasonably sophisticated bit of junk food gothic, with some welcome lighter touches here and there to leaven things, and an effective lead in Adrian Paul, who plays the Byronic action hero with a nice combination of brooding dark intensity and self-depreciating humor, believable in a comic scene but able to suddenly seem menacing and formidable when the script calls for it. If nothing else, ''Highlander'' ought to be given credit for having been able to come up with interesting new variants on the same basic plot—MacLeod has a sword fight with another immortal, and cuts his head off just before the end titles—for four seasons now. Let's hope they can keep it up for a while longer. ''Hercules: The Legendary Journeys'' has also become immensely popular, as has its successful spin-off, ''Xena: Warrior Princess.'' ''Hercules'' is good cheesy fun, often deliberately silly and self-mocking, with likable performers, but its plotlines are even more limited than those of ''Highlander'' are, and after watching a few episodes, they all begin to seem a bit familiar; still, the deliberate anachronisms here, such as having Aphrodite look and talk like a surfer girl, usually provide a few good laughs (although the purist in me occasionally wonders, grumpily, how many kids are going to grow up believing that the Punic Wars took place in ancient Greece), and you certainly can't complain that the show takes itself too seriously. Oddly, ''Xena,'' although just as absurd in concept, *does* seem to take itself a bit more seriously, or at least is a bit more solemn in tone, which is one reason why I like it less than ''Hercules.'' One unfortunate result of the success of ''Hercules,'' though, is that by the beginning of 1997 it was spanning a whole host of cloned imitations, such as ''The New Adventures of Robin Hood,'' ''Tarzan: The Epic Adventures,'' and ''The Adventures of Sinbad,'' most of which look pretty lame even by comparison to ''Hercules,'' which is itself hardly high art. And there are more such shows in the pipeline behind *these*.

Again this year, with a few partial exceptions, the boob tube pretty much lives up to its nickname.

The 54th World Science Fiction Convention, LACon III, was held in Anaheim, California, from August 29 to September 2, and drew an estimated attendance of 6,700—a good deal fewer than the 8,000–10,000 attendees who had been expected, but still enough to make it the fourth largest worldcon in history. The 1996 Hugo Awards, presented at LACon III, were: Best Novel, *The Diamond Age,* Neal Stephenson; Best Novella, ''The Death of Captain Future,'' Allen Steele; Best Novelette, ''Think Like a Dinosaur,'' James Patrick Kelly; Best Short Story, ''The Lincoln Train,'' Maureen F. McHugh; Best Nonfiction, *Science Fiction: The Illustrated Encyclopedia,* John Clute;

Best Professional Editor, Gardner Dozois; Best Professional Artist, Bob Eggleton; Best Original Artwork, *Dinotopia: The World Beneath,* James Gurney; Best Dramatic Presentation, "The Coming of Shadows," from *Babylon 5*; Best Semiprozine, *Locus,* edited by Charles N. Brown; Best Fanzine, *Ansible,* edited by David Langford; Best Fan Writer, David Langford; Best Fan Artist, William Rotsler; plus the John W. Campbell Award for Best New Writer to David Feintuch.

The 1995 Nebula Awards, presented at a banquet aboard the floating hotel the Queen Mary in Long Beach, California, on April 27, 1996, were: Best Novel, *The Terminal Experiment,* Robert J. Sawyer; Best Novella, "Last Summer at Mars Hill," Elizabeth Hand; Best Novelette, "Solitude," Ursula K. Le Guin; Best Short Story, "Death and the Librarian," Esther M. Friesner; plus a Grand Master award to A. E. van Vogt.

The World Fantasy Awards, presented at the Twenty-Second Annual World Fantasy Convention in Schaumburg, Illinois, on November 3, 1996, were: Best Novel, *The Prestige,* Christopher Priest; Best Novella, "Radio Waves," Michael Swanwick; Best Short Fiction, "The Grass Princess," Gwyneth Jones; Best Collection, *Seven Tales and a Fable,* Gwyneth Jones; Best Anthology, *The Penguin Book of Modern Fantasy by Women,* edited by A. Susan Williams and Richard Glyn Jones; Best Artist, Gahan Wilson; Special Award (Professional), to Richard Evans; Special Award (Non-Professional), to Marc Michaud for Necronomicon Press; plus a Life Achievement Award to Gene Wolfe.

The 1996 Bram Stoker Awards, presented by the Horror Writers of America during a banquet at the Warwick Hotel in New York City on June 8, were: Best Novel, *Zombie,* Joyce Carol Oates; Best First Novel, *The Safety of Unknown Cities,* Lucy Taylor; Best Collection, *The Panic Hand,* Jonathan Carroll; Best Long Fiction, "Lunch at the Gotham Café," Stephen King; Best Short Story, "Chatting With Anubis," Harlan Ellison; plus a Life Achievement Award to Harlan Ellison.

The 1995 John W. Campbell Memorial Award was won by *The Time Ships,* by Stephen Baxter.

The 1995 Theodore Sturgeon Award for Best Short Story was won by "Jigoku no Mokushiroku (The Symbolic Revelation of the Apocalypse)," by John G. McDaid.

The 1995 Philip K. Dick Memorial Award went to *Headcrash,* by Bruce Bethke.

The 1995 Arthur C. Clarke Award was won by *Fairyland,* by Paul J. McAuley.

The 1995 James Tiptree, Jr. Memorial Award was won by *Waking the Moon,* by Elizabeth Hand and *The Memoirs of Elizabeth Frankenstein,* by Theodore Roszak (tie).

Dead in 1996 or early 1997 were: **Horace L. Gold,** 81, founding editor of *Galaxy* (he also edited *Beyond* and *Worlds of If*), one of the most important and influential editors in the history of science fiction, also known as the author of the classic fantasy story "Trouble with Water," as well as other works collected in *The Old Die Rich and Other Science Fiction Stories*; **Carl Sagan,** 62, writer and scientist, one of the most influential science popularizers of the century, author of nonfiction books such as *The Dragons of Eden, Broca's Brain,* and *Cosmos,* which was also a popular television series; **Sam Merwin, Jr.,** 85, editor of *Thrilling Wonder Stories* and *Startling Stories,* in which capacity he discovered Jack Vance and published the first of Ray Bradbury's "Martian Chronicles" stories, as well as publishing classic work such as Philip José Farmer's "The Lovers"; **Richard Evans,** 46, acclaimed British editor, Editorial Director of Science Fiction at Gollancz, formerly Editorial Director of Science Fiction at MacDonald and Orbit; **David Lasser,** 94, editor of *Science Wonder Stories,* first president of The Interplanetary Society, author of one of the first popular books about space travel, 1931's *The Conquest of Space*; **Evangeline Walton,** 88, author of the well-known fantasies *The Island of the Mighty, The Children of Llyr, The Song of Rhiannon, Prince* *of Annwn,* and other fantasy novels, winner of the World Fantasy Convention's prestigious Life Achievement Award; **Richard Powers,** 75, perhaps the dominant and most frequently used SF cover artist of the fifties and early sixties, and one of the most popular SF artists of all time; **Walter Sullivan,** 78, longtime science reporter for *The New York Times,* author of an influential book about the search for alien intelligence, *We Are Not Alone;* **Brian Daley,** 48, SF writer, author of *The Doomfarers of Coramonde* and *The Starfollowers of Coramonde,* among others; **Vera Chapman,** 98, author of a trilogy of well-known Arthurian fantasies collected in a single volume as *The Three Damosels,* as well as of other fantasy novels; **Richard Condon,** 81, author of the classic paranoid thriller *The Manchurian Candidate,* which was made into a movie of the same name, as well as of such novels as *The Final Addiction* and *Prizzi's Honor;* **Leigh Richmond,** 84, author, in collaboration with her husband, the late Walt Richmond, of such SF novels as *Shock Wave, Phase Two,* and *The Lost Millennium;* **Frank Riley,** 80, co-winner with collaborator Mark Clifton of the 1955 Best Novel Hugo for a magazine serial later published in book form as *They'd Rather Be Right;* **Claudia Peck,** 43, SF writer, author of *Spirit Crossings;* **L. A. Taylor,** 57, SF and mystery writer, author of *The Blossom of Erda* and *Catspaw;* **Eleanor Butler Cameron,** 84, children's book author best known to genre readers for her book *The Wonderful Flight to the Mushroom Planet;* **P. L. Travers,** 96, author of the long-running "Mary Poppins" series of children's fantasy novels, as well as of other fantasy books; **Jerry Siegel,** 81, cocreator, along with the late Joe Schuster, of the original *Superman* comic book; **Burne Hogarth,** 84, comic-strip artist who worked for many years on the *Tarzan* newspaper comic strip, and on many other comics; **Shamus Culhane,** 87, pioneering animator who worked on Disney's *Snow White* as well as on many other animated features and cartoons; **Jon Pertwee,** 76, actor, probably best known to the genre audience as the third actor to portray Doctor Who in the BBC television series; **Ed Wood,** 70, co-founder of the small press line *Advent: Publishers,* which produced many important early works of SF criticism, such as Damon Knight's *In Search of Wonder,* also a well-known fan; **Willis Conover,** 75, early fan and correspondent with H. P. Lovecraft, author of the critical study *Lovecraft At Last,* also known for his broadcasting work with the Voice of America; **Charles Burbee,** 81, well-known fan and fanzine editor; **Redd Boggs,** 75, well-known fan, fannish humorist, and fanzine editor; **Ethel Lindsay,** 75, longtime fan and fanzine editor, prominent in British fannish circles, another fan who, along with her friend Ella Parker, went out of her way to be kind to me when I was a totally unknown new fan at his first science fiction convention; **Joni Stopa,** long-time Chicago-area fan, a friend; **David R. Friesner,** father of SF writer Esther M. Friesner; **Neil Hudner,** 55, half-brother of the late Philip K. Dick; **Christopher Robin Milne,** 75, son of the late children's fantasy writer A. A. Milne, and the "Christopher Robin" about whose adventures the "Winnie the Pooh" books were written; **Raymond Dozois,** 80, father of SF editor Gardner Dozois.

IMMERSION

Gregory Benford

▼

Gregory Benford is one of the modern giants of the field. His 1980 novel Timescape *won the Nebula Award, the John W. Campbell Memorial Award, the British Science Fiction Association Award, and the Australian Ditmar Award, and is widely considered one of the classic novels of the last two decades. His other novels include* The Stars in Shroud, In the Ocean of Night, Against Infinity, Artifact, Across the Sea of Suns, Great Sky River, *and* Tides of Light. *His most recent books are the two concluding volumes of his Galactic Cluster series,* Furious Gulf *and* Sailing Bright Eternity, *a new novel in Isaac Asimov's Foundation series,* Foundation's Fear, *and a collection of stories,* Matter's End. *He has recently become one of the regular science columnists for* The Magazine of Fantasy & Science Fiction. *His short fiction has appeared in our Seventh and Ninth Annual Collections. Benford is a professor of physics at the University of California, Irvine.*

Here he takes us to Africa for a suspenseful and unsettling look at what it really means to be human—and how it came to be *that way.*

Africa came to them in air thick with smells. In the dry, prickly heat was a promise of the primitive, of ancient themes beyond knowing.

Warily Kelly gazed out at the view beyond the formidable walls. ''We're safe here from the animals?''

''I imagine so. Those walls are high and there are guard canines. Wirehounds, I believe.''

''Good.'' She smiled in a way that he knew implied a secret was about to emerge. ''I really urged you to come here to get you away from Helsinki.''

''Not to study chimpanzees?''

''Oh, that might be useful—or better still, fun,'' she said with wifely nonchalance. ''My main consideration was that if you had stayed in Helsinki you might be dead.''

He stopped looking at the striking scenery. She was serious. ''You think they would . . . ?''

''They *could*, which is a better guide to action than trying to guess *woulds*.''

''I see.'' He didn't, but he had learned to trust her judgment in matters of the world. ''You think Imperial Industrie would . . . ?''

''Knock you off for undermining their case? Sure. But they'd be careful.''

"But the case is over. Settled."

He had made a successful sociometric prediction of political and economic trends in central Europe. His reputation was powerful enough to cause a fall in certain product markets. Economics increasingly resembled fashion: Commodities racheted like hemlines.

Imperial Industrie had lost considerably—a fortune, even for a world-wrapping corporation. They had accused him of manipulating the markets, but he had in all honesty merely tried to test his new model of sociohistory. His reputation among econometric circles was enough to circulate the predictions. Imperial Industrie, he thought, was simply being childish. Reason would prevail there soon enough.

"You intend to make more predictions, don't you?" she asked.

"Well, once I get some better parameter fixes—"

"There. Then they can lose again. Imperial doesn't like losing."

"You exaggerate." He dismissed the subject with a wave of his hand.

Then too, he thought, perhaps he did need a vacation. To be on a rough, natural world—he had forgotten, in the years buried in Helsinki, how vivid wild things could be. Greens and yellows leaped out, after decades amid steel and glitter.

Here the sky yawned impossibly deep, unmarked by the graffiti of aircraft, wholly alive to the flapping wonder of birds. Bluffs and ridges looked like they had been shaped hastily with a putty knife. Beyond the station walls he could see a sole tree thrashed by an angry wind. Its topknot finally blew off in a pocket of wind, fluttering and fraying over somber flats like a fragmenting bird. Distant, eroded mesas had yellow streaks down their shanks which, as they met the forest, turned a burnt orange tinge that suggested the rot of rust. Across the valley, where the chimps ranged, lay a dusky canopy hidden behind low gray clouds and raked by winds. A thin, cold rain fell there and Leon wondered what it was like to cower beneath the sheets of moisture, without hope of shelter or warmth. Perhaps Helsinki's utter predictability was better, but he wondered, breathing in the tangy air.

He pointed to the distant forest. "We're going there?" He liked this fresh place, though the jungle was foreboding. It had been a long time since he had even worked with his hands, alongside his father, back on the farm.

"Don't start judging."

"I'm anticipating."

She grinned. "You always have a longer word for it, no matter what I say."

"The treks look a little, well—touristy."

"Of course. We're tourists."

The land here rose up into peaks as sharp as torn tin. In the thick trees beyond, mist broke on gray, smooth rocks. Even here, high up the slope of an imposing ridge, the Excursion Station was hemmed in by slimy, thick-barked trees standing in deep drifts of dead, dark leaves. With rotting logs half buried in the wet layers, the air swarmed so close it was like breathing damp opium.

Kelly stood, her drink finished. "Let's go in, socialize."

He followed dutifully and right away knew it was a mistake. Most of the indoor stim-party crowd was dressed in rugged safari-style gear. They were ruddy folk, faces flushed with excitement or perhaps just enhancers. Leon waved away the bubbleglass-bearing waiter; he disliked the way it dulled his wits. Still, he smiled and tried to make small talk.

This turned out to be not merely small, but microscopic. "Where are you from? Oh, *Helsinki*—what's it like? We're from (fill in the city)—have you ever heard of it?" Of course he had not.

Most were Primitivists, drawn by the unique experience available here. It seemed to him that every third word in their conversation was *natural* or *vital*, delivered like a mantra.

"What a *relief*, to be away from straight lines," a thin man said.

"Um, how so?" Leon said, trying to seem interested.

"Well, of course straight lines don't exist in nature. They have to be put there by humans." He sighed. "I love to be free of straightness!"

Leon instantly thought of pine needles; strata of metamorphic rock; the inside edge of a half-moon; spider-woven silk strands; the line along the top of a breaking ocean wave; crystal patterns; white quartz lines on granite slabs; the far horizon of a vast calm lake; the legs of birds; spikes of cactus; the arrow dive of a raptor; trunks of young, fast-growing trees; wisps of high windblown clouds; ice cracks; the two sides of the V of migrating birds; icicles.

"Not so," he said, but no more.

His habit of laconic implication was trampled in the headlong talk, of course; the enhancers were taking hold. They all chattered on, excited by the prospect of immersing themselves in the lives of the creatures roaming the valleys below. He listened, not commenting, intrigued. Some wanted to share the world view of herd animals, others of hunters, some of birds. They spoke as though they were entering some athletic event, and that was not his view at all. Still, he stayed silent.

He finally escaped with Kelly into the small park beside the Excursion Station, designed to make guests familiar with local conditions before their treks or immersions. There were whole kraals of domestic stock. The unique assets, the genetically altered and enhanced animals, were nowhere near, of course.

He stopped and stared at the kraals and thought again about sociohistory. His mind kept diving at it from many angles. He had learned to just stand aside and let his thoughts run.

Animals. Was there a clue here? Despite millennia of trying, humans had domesticated few animals. To be domesticated, wild beasts had to have an entire suite of traits. Most had to be herd animals, with instinctive submission patterns which humans could co-opt. They had to be placid; herds that bolt at a strange sound and can't tolerate intruders are hard to keep. Finally, they had to be willing to breed in captivity. Most humans didn't want to court and copulate under the watchful gaze of others, and neither did most animals.

So here there were sheep and goats and cows, slightly adapted by biotechnology but otherwise unremarkable. Except for the chimps. They were unique artifacts of this preservation deep in the rugged laboratory of central Africa. A wirehound came sniffing, checking them out, muttering an unintelligible apology. "Interesting," he remarked to Kelly, "that Primitivists still want to be protected from the wild, by the domesticated."

"Well, of course. This fellow is *big*."

"Not sentimental about the natural state? We were once just another type of large mammal."

"The natural state might be a pleasant place to visit, but . . ."

"Right, wouldn't want to live there. Still, I want to try the chimps."

"What? An immersion?" Her eyebrows lifted in mild alarm.

"As long as we're here, why not?"

"I don't . . . well, I'll think about it."

"You can bail out at any time, they say."

She nodded, pursed her lips. "Um."

"We'll *feel* at home—the way chimps do."

"You believe everything you read in a brochure?"

"I did some research. It's a well-developed tech."

Her lips had a skeptical tilt. "Um."

He knew by now better than to press her. Let time do his work.

The canine, quite large and alert, snuffled at his hand and slurred, "Goood naaaght, suuur." He stroked it. In its eyes he saw a kinship, an instant rapport that he did not need to think about. For one who dwelled in his head so much, this was a welcome rub of reality.

Significant evidence, he thought. *We have a deep past together.* Perhaps that was why he wanted to immerse in a chimp. To go far back, peering beyond the vexing state of being human.

"We're certainly closely related, yes," Expert Specialist Ruben said. He was a big man, tanned and muscular and casually confident. He was both a safari guide and immersion specialist, with a biology background. He did research using immersion techniques, but keeping the Station going soaked up most of his time, he said. "Chimp-riding is the best immersion available."

Leon looked skeptical. *Pan troglodytes* had hands with thumbs, the same number of teeth as humans, no tails, but he had never felt great empathy for them, seen behind bars in a zoo.

Ruben waved a big hand at the landscape below the Station. "We hope to make them more useful. We haven't tried training them much, beyond research purposes. Remember, they're supposed to be kept wild. The original UN grant stipulated that."

"Tell me about your research," Leon said. In his experience, no scientist ever passed up a chance to sing his own song. He was right.

They had taken human DNA and chimp DNA—Ruben said, waxing enthusiastically on—then unzipped the double-helix strands in both. Linking one human strand with a chimp strand made a hybrid.

Where the strands complemented, the two then tightly bound in a partial, new double helix. Where they differed, bonding between the strands was weak, intermittent, with whole sections flapping free.

Then they spun the watery solutions in a centrifuge, so the weak sections ripped apart. Closely linked DNA was 98.2 percent of the total. Chimps were startlingly like humans. Less than 2 percent different—yet they lived in forests and invented nothing.

The typical difference between individual people's DNA was a tenth of a percentage point, Ruben said. Roughly, then, chimps were twenty times more different from humans than particular people differed among themselves—genetically. But genes were like levers, supporting vast weights by pivoting about a small fulcrum.

"But we don't *come* from them. We parted company, genetically, six million years ago."

"Do they think like us?" Leon asked.

"Best way to tell is an immersion," Ruben said. "Very best way."

He smiled invitingly, and Leon wondered if Ruben got a commission on immersions. His sales pitch was subtle, shaped for an academic's interest—but still a sales pitch.

Ruben had already made the vast stores of data on chimp movements, population dynamics, and behaviors available to Leon. It was a rich source and with some math modeling might be fertile ground for a simple description, using a truncated version of sociohistory.

"Describing the life history of a species mathematically is one thing," Kelly said. "But *living in* it . . ."

"Come now," Leon said. Even though he knew the entire Excursion Station was geared to sell the guests safaris and immersions, he was intrigued. " 'I need a change,' you said. 'Get out of stuffy old Helsinki,' you said."

Ruben said warmly, "It's completely safe."

Kelly smiled at Leon tolerantly. "Oh, all right."

He spent morning studying the chimp data banks. The mathematician in him pondered how to represent their dynamics with a trimmed-down sociohistory. The marble of fate rattling down a cracked slope. So many paths, variables. . . .

In the afternoons they took several treks. Kelly did not like the dust and heat and they saw few animals. "What self-respecting beast would want to be seen with these overdressed Primitivists?" she said. The others could never stop talking; that kept the animals away.

He liked the atmosphere and relaxed into it as his mind kept on working. He thought about this as he stood on the sweeping veranda, drinking pungent fruit juice as he watched a sunset. Kelly stood beside him silently. Raw Africa made it clear that the Earth was an energy funnel, he thought. At the bottom of the gravitational well, Earth captured for use barely a tenth of a percent of the sunlight that fell. Nature built organic molecules with a star's energy. In turn, plants were prey for animals, who could harvest roughly a tenth of the plant's stored energy. Grazers were themselves prey to meat-eaters, who could use about a tenth of the flesh-stored energy. So, he estimated, only about one part in a hundred thousand of a star's lancing energy wound up in the predators.

Wasteful! Yet nowhere had a more efficient engine evolved. Why not? Predators were invariably more intelligent than their prey, and they sat atop a pyramid of very steep slopes. Omnivores had a similar balancing act. Out of that rugged landscape had come humanity.

That fact *had* to matter greatly in any sociohistory. The chimps, then, were essential to finding the ancient keys to the human psyche.

Kelly said, "I hope immersion isn't, well, so hot and sticky."

"Remember, you'll see the world through different eyes."

She snorted. "Just so I can come back whenever I want and have a nice hot bath."

· · ·

"Compartments"? Kelly shied back. "They look more like caskets."

"They have to be snug, Madam."

ExSpec Ruben smiled amiably—which, Leon sensed, probably meant he wasn't feeling amiable at all. Their conversation had been friendly, the staff here was respectful of the noted Dr. Mattick, but, after all, basically he and Kelly were just more tourists. Paying for a bit of primitive fun, all couched in proper scholarly terms, but—tourists.

"You're kept in fixed status, all body systems running slow but normal," the ExSpec said, popping out the padded networks for inspection. He ran through the controls, emergency procedures, safeguards.

"Looks comfortable enough," Kelly observed begrudgingly.

"Come on," Leon chided. "You promised we would do it."

"You'll be meshed into our systems at all times," Ruben said.

"Even your data library?" Leon asked.

"Sure thing."

The team of ExSpecs booted them into the stasis compartments with deft, sure efficiency. Tabs, pressors, magnetic pickups plated onto his skull to pick up thoughts directly. The very latest tech.

"Ready? Feeling good?" Ruben asked with his professional smile.

Leon was not feeling good (as opposed to feeling well) and he realized part of it was this ExSpec. He had always distrusted bland, assured people. Something about this one bothered him, but he could not say why. Oh well; Kelly was probably right. He needed a vacation. What better way to get out of yourself?

"Good, yes. Ready, yes."

The suspension tech suppressed neuromuscular responses. The customer lay dormant, only his mind engaged with the chimp.

Magnetic webs capped over his cerebrum. Through electromagnetic inductance they interwove into layers of the brain. They routed signals along tiny thread-paths, suppressing many brain functions and blocking physiological processes. All this, so that the massively parallel circuitry of the brain could be inductively linked out, thought by thought. Then it was transmitted to chips embedded in the chimp subject. Immersion.

The technology had ramified throughout the world, quite famously. The ability to distantly manage minds had myriad uses. The suspension tech, however, found its own odd applications.

In certain European classes, women were wedded, then suspended for all but a few hours of the day. Their wealthy husbands awoke them from freeze-frame states only for social and sexual purposes. For more than a half century, the wives experienced a heady whirlwind of places, friends, parties, vacations, passionate hours—but their total accumulated time was only a few years. Their husbands died in what seemed to the wives like short order indeed. They left a wealthy widow of perhaps thirty. Such women were highly sought, and not only for their money. They were uniquely sophisticated, seasoned by a long "marriage." Often, these widows returned the favor, wedding freeze-frame husbands whom they revived for similar uses.

All this Leon had taken with the sophisticated veneer he had cultivated in Helsinki. So he thought his immersion would be comfortable, interesting, the stuff of stim-party talk.

He had thought that he would in some sense *visit* another, simpler, mind.

He did not expect to be swallowed whole.

A good day. Plenty of grubs to eat in a big moist log. Dig them out with my nails, fresh tangy sharp crunchy.

Biggest, he shoves me aside. Scoops out plenty rich grubs. Grunts. Glowers.

My belly rumbles. I back off and eye Biggest. He's got pinched-up face, so I know not to fool with him.

I walk away, I squat down. Get some picking from a fem. She finds some fleas, cracks them in her teeth.

Biggest rolls the log around some to knock a few grubs loose, finishes up. He's strong. Fems watch him. Over by the trees a bunch of fems chatter, suck their teeth. Everybody's sleepy now in early afternoon, lying in the shade. Biggest, though, he waves at me and Hunker and off we go.

Patrol. Strut tall, step out proud. I like it fine. Better than humping even.

Down past the creek and along to where the hoof smells are. That's the shallow spot. We cross and go into the trees sniff-sniffing and there are two Strangers.

They don't see us yet. We move smooth, quiet. Biggest picks up a branch and we do too. Hunker is sniffing to see who these Strangers are and he points off to the hill. Just like I thought, they're Hillies. The worst. Smell bad.

Hillies come onto our turf. Make trouble. We make it back.

We spread out. Biggest, he grunts and they hear him. I'm already moving, branch held up. I can run pretty far without going all-four. The Strangers cry out, big-eyed. We go fast and then we're on them.

They have no branches. We hit them and kick and they grab at us. They are tall and quick. Biggest slams one to the ground. I hit that one so Biggest knows real well I'm with him. Hammer hard, I do. Then I go quick to help Hunker.

His Stranger has taken his branch away. I club the Stranger. He sprawls. I whack him good and Hunker jumps on him and it is wonderful.

The Stranger tries to get up and I kick him solid. Hunker grabs back his branch and hits again and again with me helping hard.

Biggest, his Stranger gets up and starts to run. Biggest whacks his ass with the branch, roaring and laughing.

Me, I got my skill. Special. I pick up rocks. I'm the best thrower, better than Biggest even.

Rocks are for Strangers. My buddies, them I'll scrap with, but never use rocks. Strangers, though, they deserve to get rocks in the face. I love to bust a Stranger that way.

I throw one clean and smooth and catch the Stranger on the leg. He stumbles and I smack him good with a sharp-edged rock, in the back. He runs fast then and I can see he's bleeding. Stranger leaves drops in the dust.

Biggest laughs and slaps me and I know I'm in good with him.

Hunker is clubbing his Stranger. Biggest takes my club and joins in. The blood all over the Stranger sings warm in my nose and I jump up and down on him. We keep at it like that a long time. Not worried about the other Stranger coming back. Strangers are brave sometime but they know when they have lost.

The Stranger stops moving. I give him one more kick.

No reaction. Dead maybe.

We scream and dance and holler out our joy.

Leon shook his head to clear it. That helped a little.

"You were that big one?" Kelly asked. "I was the female, over by the trees."

"Sorry, I couldn't tell."

"It was . . . different, wasn't it?"

He laughed dryly. "Murder usually is."

"When you went off with the, well, leader—"

"My chimp thinks of him as 'Biggest.' We killed another chimp."

They were in the plush reception room of the immersion facility. Leon stood and felt the world tilt a little and then right itself. "I think I'll stick to historical research for a while."

Kelly smiled sheepishly. "I . . . I rather liked it." He thought a moment, blinked. "So did I," he said, surprisingly himself.

"Not the murder—"

"No, of course not. But . . . the *feel*."

She grinned. "Can't get that in Helsinki, Professor."

He spent two days coasting through cool lattices of data in the formidable Station library. It was well-equipped and allowed interfaces with several senses. He patrolled through cool, digital labyrinths.

In the vector spaces portrayed on huge screens, the research data was covered with thick, bulky protocols and scabs of security precautions. All were easily broken or averted, of course, but the chunky abstracts, reports, summaries, and crudely processed statistics still resisted easy interpretation. Occasionally some facets of chimp behavior were carefully hidden away in appendices and sidebar notes, as though the biologists in the lonely outpost were embarrassed by it. Some *was* embarrassing: mating behavior, especially. How could he use this?

He navigated through the 3-D maze and cobbled together his ideas. Could he follow a strategy of analogy?

Chimps shared nearly all their genes with humans, so chimp dynamics should be a simpler version of human dynamics. Could he then analyze chimp troop interactions as a reduced case of sociohistory?

At sunset of the next day he sat with Kelly watching blood-red shafts spike through orange-tinged clouds. Africa was gaudy beyond good taste and he liked it. The food was tangy, too. His stomach rumbled in anticipation of dinner.

He remarked to Kelly, "It's tempting, using chimps to build a sort of toy model of sociohistory."

"But you have doubts."

"They're like us in . . . only they have, well, uh . . ."

"Base, animalistic ways?" She smirked, then kissed him. "My prudish Leon."

"We have our share of beastly behaviors, I know. But we're a lot smarter too."

Her eyelids dipped in a manner he knew by now suggested polite doubt. "They live intensely, you'll have to give them that."

"Maybe we're smarter than we need to be anyway."

"What?" This surprised her.

"I've been reading up on evolution. Plainly, the human brain was an evolutionary overshoot—far more capable than a competent hunter-gatherer needed. To get the better of animals, it would have been enough to master fire and simple stone tools. Such talents alone would have made people the lords of creation, removing selection pressure to change. Instead, all evidence from the brain itself said that change accelerated. The human cerebral cortex added mass, stacking new circuitry atop older wiring. That mass spread over the lesser areas like a thick new skin."

"Considering the state of the world, I'd say we need all the brains we can get," she said skeptically.

"From that layer came musicians and engineers, saints and savants," he finished with a flourish. One of Kelly's best points was her willingness to sit still while he waxed professorially long-winded, even on vacation. "And all this evolutionary selection happened in just a few million years."

Kelly snorted prettily. "Look at it from the woman's point of view. It happened, despite putting mothers in desperate danger in childbirth."

"Uh, how?"

"From those huge baby heads. They're hard to get out. We women are still paying the price for your brains—and for ours."

He chuckled. She always had a special spin on a subject that made him see it fresh. "Then why was it selected for, back then?"

Kelly smiled enigmatically. "Maybe men and women alike found intelligence sexy in each other."

"Really?"

Her sly smile. "How about us?"

"Have you ever watched very many 3-D stars? They don't feature brains, my dear."

"Remember the animals we saw in the Madrid Senso-Zoo? The mating exhibit? It could be that for early humans, brains were like peacock tails, or moose horns—display items, to attract the females. Runaway sexual selection."

"I see, an overplayed hand of otherwise perfectly good cards." He laughed. "So being smart is just a bright ornament."

"Works for me," she said, giving him a wink.

He watched the sunset turn to glowering, ominous crimson, oddly happy. Sheets of light worked across the sky among curious, layered clouds. "Ummm . . . ," Kelly murmured.

"Yes?"

"Maybe this is a way to use the research the ExSpecs are doing too. Learn who we were—and therefore who we are."

"Intellectually, it's a jump. In social ways, though, the gap could be less."

Kelly looked skeptical. "You think chimps are only a bit further back in a social sense?"

"Ummm. I wonder if in logarithmic time we might scale from chimps to us, now?"

"A big leap. To do anything you'll need more experience with them." She eyed him. "You like immersion, don't you?"

"Well, yes. It's just . . ."

"What?"

"That ExSpec Ruben, he keeps pushing immersions—"

"That's his job."

"—and he knew who I was."

"So?" She spread her hands and shrugged.

"You're normally the suspicious one. Why should an ExSpec know an obscure mathematician?"

"He looked you up. Data dumps on incoming guests are standard. And in some circles you're hardly obscure. Plenty of people back in Helsinki line up to see you."

"And some would like to see me dead. Say, you're supposed to be the ever-vigilant one." He grinned. "Shouldn't you be encouraging my caution?"

"Paranoia isn't caution. Time spent on nonthreats subtracts from vigilance."

By the time they went in for dinner she had talked him into more immersions.

Hot day in the sun. Dust makes me snort.

That Biggest, he walks by, gets respect right away. Fems and guys alike, they stick out their hands.

Biggest touches them, taking time with each, letting them know he is there. The world is all right.

I reach out to him too. Makes me feel good. I want to be like Biggest, to be big, be as big as him, be *him*.

Fems don't give him any trouble. He wants one, she goes. Hump right away. He's Biggest.

Most males, they don't get much respect. Fems don't want to do with them as much as they do with Biggest. The little males, they huff and throw sand and all that but everybody knows they're not going to be much. No chance they could ever be like Biggest. They don't like that but they are stuck with it.

Me, I'm pretty big. I get respect. Some, anyway.

All the guys like stroking. Petting. Grooming. Fems give it to them and they give it back.

Guys get more though. After it, they're not so gruff.

I'm sitting getting groomed and all of a sudden I smell something. I don't like it. I jump up, cry out. Biggest, he takes notice. Smells it too.

Strangers. Everybody starts hugging each other. Strong smell, plenty of it. Lots of Strangers. The wind says they are near, getting nearer.

They come running down on us from the ridge. Looking for fems, looking for trouble.

I run for my rocks. I always have some handy. I fling one at them, miss. Then they are in among us. It's hard to hit them, they go so fast.

Four Strangers, they grab two fems. Drag them away.

Everybody howling, crying. Dust everywhere.

I throw rocks. Biggest leads the guys against the Strangers.

They turn and run off. Just like that. Got the two fems though and that's bad.

Biggest mad. He pushes around some of the guys, makes noise. He not looking so good now, he let the Strangers in.

Those Strangers bad. We all hunker down, groom each other, pet, make nice sounds.

Biggest, he come by, slap some of the fems. Hump some. Make sure everybody know he's still Biggest.

He don't slap me. He know better than to try. I growl at him when he come close and he pretend not to hear.

Maybe he not so Big any more, I'm thinking.

He stayed with it this time. After the first crisis, when the Stranger chimps came running through, he sat and let himself get groomed for a long time. It really did calm him.

Him? Who was he?

This time he could fully sense the chimp mind. Not below him—that was an evolutionary metaphor—*but around* him. A swarming scattershot of senses, thoughts, fragments like leaves blowing by him in a wind.

And the wind was *emotion*. Blustering gales, howling and whipping in gusts, raining thoughts like soft hammer blows.

These chimps thought poorly, in the sense that he could get only shards, like human musings chopped by a nervous editor. But chimps *felt* intensely.

Of course, he thought—and he could think, nestled in the hard kernel of himself, wrapped in the chimp mind. *Emotions told it what to do, without thinking. Quick reactions demanded that. Strong feeling amplified subtle clues into strong imperatives. Blunt orders from Mother Evolution.*

He saw now that the belief that high order mental experiences like emotion were unique to people was . . . simply conceited. These chimps shared much of the human world view. A theory of chimp sociohistory could be valuable.

He gingerly separated himself from the dense, pressing chimp mind. He wondered if the chimp knew he was here. Yes, it did—dimly. But somehow this did not bother the chimp. He integrated it into his blurred, blunt world. Leon was somewhat like an emotion, just one of many fluttering by and staying a while, then wafting away.

Could he be more than that? He tried getting the chimp to lift its right arm—and it was like lead. He struggled for a while that way with no success. Then he realized his error. He could not overpower this chimp, not as a kernel in a much larger mind.

He thought about this as the chimp groomed a female, picking carefully through coarse hair. The strands smelled good, the air was sweet, the sun stroked him with blades of generous warmth. . . .

Emotion. Chimps didn't follow instructions because that simply lay beyond them. They could not understand directions in the human sense. Emotions—those they knew. He had to be an emotion, not a little general giving orders.

He sat for a while simply *being* this chimp. He learned—or rather, he felt. The troop groomed and scavenged food, males eyeing the perimeter, females keeping close to the young. A lazy calm descended over him, carrying him effortlessly through warm moments of the day. Not since he was a boy had he felt anything like this. A slow, graceful easing, as though there were no time at all, only slices of eternity.

In this mood, he could concentrate on a simple movement—raising an arm, scratching—and create the desire to do it. His chimp responded. To make it happen, he had to *feel* his way toward a goal. Sail before the emotion wind.

Catching a sweet scent on the air, Leon thought about what food that might signal. His chimp meandered upwind, sniffed, discarded the clue as uninteresting. Leon could now smell the reason why: fruit, true, sweet, yes—but inedible for a chimp.

Good. He was learning. And he was integrating himself into the deep recesses of this chimp-mind.

Watching the troop, he decided to name the prominent chimps, to keep them straight: Agile the quick one, Sheelah the sexy one, Grubber the hungry one. . . . But what was his own name? His he dubbed Ipan. Not very original, but that was its main characteristic, *I as Pan troglodytes.*

Grubber found some bulb-shaped fruit and the others drifted over to scavenge. The hard fruit smelled a little too young (how did he know that?) but some ate it anyway.

And which of these was Kelly? They had asked to be immersed in the same troop, so one of these—he forced himself to count, though somehow the exercise was like moving heavy weights in his mind—these twenty-two was her. How could he tell? He ambled over to several females who were using sharp-edged stones to cut leaves from branches. They tied the strands together so they could carry food.

Leon peered into their faces. Mild interest, a few hands held out for stroking, an invitation to groom. No glint of recognition in their eyes.

He watched a big fem, Sheelah, carefully wash sand-covered fruit in a creek. The troop followed suit; Sheelah was a leader of sorts, a female lieutenant to Biggest.

She ate with relish, looked around. There was grain growing nearby, past maturity, ripe tan kernels already scattered in the sandy soil. Concentrating, Leon could tell from the faint bouquet that this was a delicacy. A few chimps squatted and picked grains from the sand, slow work. Sheelah did the same, and then stopped, gazing off at the creek. Time passed, insects buzzed. After a while she scooped up sand and kernels and walked to the brook's edge. She tossed it all in. The sand sank, the kernels floated. She skimmed them off and gulped them down, grinning widely.

An impressive trick. The other chimps did not pick up on her kernel-skimming method. Fruit washing was conceptually easier, he supposed, since the chimp could keep the fruit the whole time. Kernel-skimming demanded throwing away the food first, then rescuing it—a harder mental jump.

He thought about her and in response Ipan sauntered over her way. He peered into Sheelah's eyes—and she winked at him. Kelly! He wrapped hairy arms around her in a burst of sweaty love.

"Pure animal love," she said over Dinner. "Refreshing."

Leon nodded. "I like being there, living that way."

"I can *smell* so much more."

"Fruit tastes differently when they bite into it." He held up a purple bulb, sliced into it, forked it into his mouth. "To me, this is almost unbearably sweet. To Ipan, it's pleasant, a little peppery. I suppose chimps have been selected for a sweet tooth. It gets them more fast calories."

"I can't think of a more thorough vacation. Not just getting away from home, but getting away from your species."

He eyed the fruit. "And they're so, so . . ."

"Horny?"

"Insatiable."

"You didn't seem to mind."

"My chimp, Ipan? I bail out when he gets into his hump-them-all mood."

She eyed him. "Really?"

"Don't you bail out?"

"Yes, but I don't expect men to be like women."

"Oh?" he said stiffly.

"I've been reading in the ExSpec's research library, while you toy with chimp social movements. Women invest heavily in their children. Men can use two strategies—parental investment, plus 'sow the oats.' " She lifted an eyebrow. "Both must have been selected for in our evolution, because they're both common."

"Not with *me*."

To his surprise, she laughed. "I'm talking in general. My point is: The chimps are much more promiscuous than we are. The males run everything. They help out the females who are carrying their children, I gather, but then they shop around elsewhere *all* the time."

Leon switched into his professional mode; it was decidedly more comfortable, when dealing with such issues. "As the specialists say, they are pursuing a mixed reproductive strategy."

"How polite."

"Polite plus precise."

Of course, he couldn't really be sure Kelly bailed out of Sheelah when a male came by for a quick one. (They were always quick too—thirty seconds or less.) *Could* she exit the chimp mind that quickly? He required a few moments to extricate himself. Of course, if she saw the male coming, guessed his intentions . . .

He was surprised at himself. What role did jealousy have when they were inhabiting other bodies? Did the usual moral code make any sense? Yet to talk this over with her was . . . embarrassing.

He was still the country boy, like it or not.

Ruefully he concentrated on his meal of local "roamer-fleisch," which turned out to be an earthy, dark meat in a stew of tangy vegetables. He ate heartily and in response to Kelly's rather obviously amused silence said, "I'd point out that chimps understood commerce too. Food for sex, betrayal of the leader for sex, spare my child for sex, grooming for sex, just about anything for sex."

"It does seem to be their social currency. Short and decidedly not sweet. Just quick lunges, strong sensations, then boom—it's over."

He nodded. "The males need it, the females use it."

"Ummm, you've been taking notes."

"If I'm going to model chimps as a sort of simplified people, then I must."

"Model chimps?" came the assured tones of ExSpec Ruben. "They're not model citizens, if that's what you mean.'' He gave them a sunny smile and Leon guessed this was more of the obligatory friendliness of this place.

Leon smiled mechanically. "I'm trying to find the variables that could describe chimp behavior."

"You should spend a lot of time with them," Ruben said, sitting at the table and holding up a finger to a waiter for a drink. "They're subtle creatures."

"I agree," said Kelly. "Do you ride them very much?"

"Some, but most of our research is done differently now." Ruben's mouth twisted ruefully. "Statistical models, that sort of thing. I got this touring idea started, using the immersion tech we had developed earlier, to make money for the project. Otherwise, we'd have had to close."

"I'm happy to contribute," Leon said.

"Admit it—you like it," Kelly said, amused.

"Well, yes. It's . . . different."

"And good for the staid Professor Mattick to get out of his shell," she said.

Ruben beamed. "Be sure you don't take chances out there. Some of our customers think they're superchimps or something."

Kelly's eyes flickered. "What danger is there? Our bodies are in slowtime, back here."

Ruben said, "You're strongly linked. A big shock to a chimp can drive a back-shock in your own neurological systems."

"What sort of shock?" Leon asked.

"Death, major injury."

"In that case," Kelly said to Leon, "I really do not think you should immerse."

Leon felt irked. "Come on! I'm on vacation, not in prison."

"Any threat to you—"

"Just a minute ago you were rhapsodizing about how good for me it was."

"You're too important to—"

"There's really very little danger," Ruben came in smoothly. "Chimps don't die suddenly, usually."

"And I can bail out when I see danger coming," Leon added.

"But *will* you? I think you're getting a taste for adventure."

She was right, but he wasn't going to concede the point. If he wanted a little escape from his humdrum mathematician's routine, so much the better. "I like being out of Helsinki's endless corridors."

Ruben gave Kelly a confident smile. "And we haven't lost a tourist yet."

"How about research staff?" she shot back.

"Well, that was a most unusual—"

"What happened?"

"A chimp fell off a ledge. The human operator couldn't bail out in time and she came out of it paralyzed. The shock of experiencing death through immersion is known from other incidents to prove fatal. But we have systems in place to short-circuit—"

"What else?" she persisted.

"Well, there was one difficult episode. In the early days, when we had simple wire fences." The ExSpec shifted uneasily. "Some predators got in."

"What sort of predators?"

"A primate-pack hunter, *Carnopapio grandis*. We call them raboons, genetically derived in an experiment two decades ago. They took baboon DNA—"

"How did they get in?" Kelly insisted.

"They're somewhat like a wild hog, with hooves that double as diggers. Carnivores, though. They smelled game—our corralled animals. Dug under the fences."

Kelly eyed the high, solid walls. "These are adequate?"

"Certainly. They're from a genetic experiment. Someone tried to make a predator by raising the earlier baboon stock up onto two legs."

Kelly said dryly, "Evolutionary gambling."

Ruben didn't catch the edge in her voice. "Like most bipedal predators, the forelimbs are shortened and the head carries forward, balanced by a thick tail they use for signaling to each other. They prey on the biggest herd animals, the gigantelope—another experiment—and eat only the richest meat."

"Why attack humans, then?" she asked.

"They take targets of opportunity too. Chimps, even. When they got into the compound, they went for adult humans, not children—a very selective strategy."

Kelly shivered. "You look at this very . . . objectively."

"I'm a biologist."

"I never knew it could be so interesting," Leon said to defuse her apprehension.

Ruben beamed. "Not as involving as higher mathematics, I'm sure."

Kelly's mouth twisted with wry skepticism. "Do you mind if guests carry weapons inside the compound?"

He had a glimmering of an idea about the chimps, a way to use their behaviors in building a simple toy model of sociohistory. He might be able to use the statistics of chimp troop movements, the ups and downs of their shifting fortunes.

He talked it over with Kelly and she nodded, but beneath it she seemed worried. Since Ruben's remark she was always tut-tutting about safety. He reminded her that she had earlier urged him to do more immersions. "This is a vacation, remember?" he said more than once.

Her amused sidewise glances told him that she also didn't buy his talk about the toy modeling. She thought he just liked romping in the woods. "A country boy at heart," she chuckled.

So the next morning he skipped a planned trek to view the vast gigantelope herds. He immediately went to the immersion chambers and slipped under. To get some solid work done, he told himself.

The chimps slept in trees and spent plenty of time grooming each other. For the lucky groomer a tick or louse was a treat. With enough, they could get high on some peppery-tasting alkaloid. He suspected the careful stroking and combing of his hair by Kelly was a behavior selected because it improved chimp hygiene. It certainly calmed Ipan, also.

Then it struck him: Chimps groomed rather than vocalizing. Only in crises and when agitated did they call and cry, mostly about breeding, feeding, or self-defense.

They were like people who could not release themselves through the comfort of talk.

And they needed comfort. The core of their social life resembled human societies under stress—in tyrannies, in prisons, in city gangs. Nature red in tooth and claw, yet strikingly like troubled people.

But there were "civilized" behaviors here too. Friendships, grief, sharing, buddies-in-arms who hunted and guarded turf together. Their old got wrinkled, bald, and toothless, yet were still cared for.

Their instinctive knowledge was prodigious. They knew how to make a bed of leaves as dusk fell, high up in trees. They could climb with grasping feet. They felt, cried, mourned—without being able to parse these into neat grammatical packages, so the emotions could be managed, subdued. Instead, emotions drove them.

Hunger was the strongest. They found and ate leaves, fruit, insects, even fair-sized animals. They loved caterpillars.

Each moment, each small enlightenment, sank him deeper into Ipan. He began to sense the subtle nooks and crannies of the chimp mind. Slowly, he gained more cooperative control.

That morning a female found a big tree and began banging it. The hollow trunk boomed like a drum and all the foraging party rushed forward to beat it too, grinning wildly at the noise. Ipan joined in and Leon felt the burst of joy, seethed in it.

Later, coming on a waterfall after a heavy rain, they seized vines and swung among trees—out over the foaming water, screeching with joy as they performed twists and leaps from vine to vine. Like children in a new playground. Leon got Ipan to make impossible moves, wild tumbles and dives, propelling him forward with abandon—to the astonishment of the other chimps.

They were violent in their sudden, peevish moments—in hustling available females, in working out their perpetual dominance hierarchy, and especially in hunting. A successful hunt brought enormous excitement—hugging, kissing, pats. As the troop descended to feed the forest rang with barks, screeches, hoots, and pants. Leon joined the tumult, sang, danced with Sheelah/Kelly.

In some matters he had to restrain his feelings. Rats they ate head first. Larger game they smashed against rocks. They devoured the brains first, a steaming delicacy. Leon gulped—metaphorically, but with Ipan echoing the impulse—and watched, screening his reluctance. Ipan had to eat, after all.

At the scent of predators, he felt Ipan's hair stand on end. Another tangy bouquet made Ipan's mouth water. He gave no mercy to food, even if it was still walking. Evolution in action; those chimps who had showed mercy in the past ate less and left fewer descendants. Those weren't represented here anymore.

For all its excesses, he found the chimps' behavior hauntingly familiar. Males gathered often for combat, for pitching rocks, for blood sports, to work out their hierarchy. Females networked and formed alliances. There were trades of favors for loyalty, alliances, kinship bonds, turf wars, threats and displays, protection rackets, a hunger for "respect," scheming subordinates, revenge—a social world enjoyed by many people that history had judged "great." Much like an emperor's court, in fact.

Did people long to strip away their clothing and conventions, bursting forth as chimps?

Leon felt a flush of revulsion, so strong Ipan shook and fidgeted. Humanity's lot *had* to be different, not this primitive horror.

He could use this, certainly, as a test bed for a full theory. Learn from our nearest genetic neighbors. *Then* humankind would be self-knowing, captains of themselves. He would build in the imperatives of the chimps, but go far beyond—to true, deep sociohistory.

"I don't see it," Kelly said at dinner.

"But they're so much like us!" He put down his spoon. "We're a brainy chimp—that's a valuable insight. We can probably train them to work for us, do housekeeping."

"I wouldn't have them messing up *my* house."

Adult humans weighed little more than chimps, but were far weaker. A chimp could lift five times more than a well-conditioned man. Human brains were three or four times more massive than a chimp's. A human baby a few months old already had a brain larger than a grown chimp. People had different brain architecture, as well.

But was that the whole story? Give chimps bigger brains and speech, ease off on the testosterone, saddle them with more inhibitions, spruce them up with a shave and a haircut, teach them to stand securely on hind legs—and you had deluxe-model chimps that would look and act rather human. They might pass in a crowd without attracting notice.

Leon said curtly, "Look, my point is that they're close enough to us to make a sociohistory model work."

"To make anybody believe that, you'll have to show that they're intelligent enough to have intricate interactions."

"What about their foraging, their hunting?" he persisted.

"Ruben says they couldn't even be trained to do work around this Excursion Station."

"I'll show you what I mean. Let's master their methods together."

"What method?"

"The basic one. Getting enough to eat."

She bit into a steak of a meaty local grazer, suitably processed and "fat-flensed for the fastidious urban palate," as the brochure had it. Chewing with unusual ferocity, she eyed him. "You're on. Anything a *chimp can do,* I can do better."

Kelly waved at him from within Sheelah. *Let the contest begin.*

The troop was foraging. He let Ipan meander and did not try to harness the emotional ripples that lapped through the chimp mind. He had gotten better at it, but at a sudden smell or sound he could lose his grip. And guiding the blunt chimp mind through anything complicated was like moving a puppet with rubber strings.

Sheelah/Kelly waved and signed to him. *This way.*

They had worked out a code of a few hundred words, using finger and facial gestures, and their chimps seemed to go along with these fairly well. Chimps had a rough language, mixing grunts and shrugs and finger displays. These conveyed immediate meanings, but not in the usual sense of sentences. Mostly they just set up associations.

Tree, fruit, go, Kelly sent. They ambled their chimps over to a clump of promising spindly trunks, but the bark was too slick to climb.

The rest of the troop had not even bothered. *They have forest smarts we lack,* Leon thought ruefully.

What there? he signed to Sheelah/Kelly.

Chimps ambled up to mounds, gave them the once-over, and reached out to brush aside some mud, revealing a tiny tunnel. *Termites*, Kelly signed.

Leon analyzed the situation as chimps drifted in. Nobody seemed in much of a hurry. Sheelah winked at him and waddled over to a distant mound.

Apparently termites worked outside at night, then blocked the entrances at dawn. Leon let his chimp shuffle over to a large tan mound, but he was riding it so well now that the chimp's responses were weak. Leon/Ipan looked for cracks, knobs, slight hollows—and yet when he brushed away some mud, found nothing. Other chimps readily unmasked tunnels. Had they memorized the hundred or more tunnels in each mound?

He finally uncovered one. Ipan was no help. Leon could control, but that blocked up the wellsprings of deep knowledge within the chimp.

The chimps deftly tore off twigs or grass stalks near their mounds. Leon carefully followed their lead. His twigs and grass didn't work. The first lot was too pliant, and when he tried to work them into a twisting tunnel, they collapsed and buckled. He switched to stiffer ones, but those caught on the tunnel walls, or snapped off. From Ipan came little help. Leon had managed him a bit too well.

He was getting embarrassed. Even the younger chimps had no trouble picking just the right stems or sticks. Leon watched a chimp nearby drop a stick that seemed to work. He then picked it up when the chimp moved on. He felt welling up from Ipan a blunt anxiety, mixing frustration and hunger. He could *taste* the anticipation of luscious, juicy termites.

He set to work, plucking the emotional strings of Ipan. This job went even worse. Vague thoughts drifted up from Ipan, but Leon was in control of the muscles now, and that was the bad part.

He quickly found that the stick had to be stuck in about ten centimeters, turning his wrist to navigate it down the twisty channel. Then he had to gently vibrate it. Through Ipan he sensed that this was to attract termites to bite into the stick.

At first he did it too long and when he drew the stick out it was half gone. Termites had bitten cleanly through it. So he had to search out another stick and that made Ipan's stomach growl.

The other chimps were through termite-snacking while Leon was still fumbling for his first taste. The nuances irked him. He pulled the stick out too fast, not turning it enough to ease it past the tunnel's curves. Time and again he fetched forth the stick, only to find that he had scraped the luscious termites off on the walls. Their bites punctured his stick, until it was so shredded he had to get another. The termites were dining better than he.

He finally caught the knack, a fluid slow twist of the wrist, gracefully extracting termites, clinging like bumps. Ipan licked them off eagerly. Leon liked the morsels, filtered through chimp taste buds.

Not many, though. Others of the troop were watching his skimpy harvest, heads tilted in curiosity, and he felt humiliated.

The hell with this, he thought.

He made Ipan turn and walk into the woods. Ipan resisted, dragging his feet. Leon found a thick limb, snapped it off to carrying size, and went back to the mound.

No more fooling with sticks. He whacked the mound solidly. Five more and he had punched a big hole. Escaping termites he scooped up by the delicious handful.

So much for subtlety! he wanted to shout. He tried writing a note for her in the dust but it was hard, forcing the letters out through his suddenly awkward hands. Chimps could handle a stick to fetch forth grubs, but marking a surface was somehow not a ready talent. He gave up.

Sheelah/Kelly came into view, proudly carrying a reed swarming with white-bellied termites. These were the best, a chimp gourmet delicacy. I *better*, she signed.

He made Ipan shrug and signed, *I got more.*

So it was a draw.

Later Kelly reported to him that among the troop he was known now as Big Stick. The name pleased him immensely.

At dinner he felt elated, exhausted, and not in the mood for conversation. Being a chimp seemed to suppress his speech centers. It took some effort to ask ExSpec Ruben about immersion technology. Usually he accepted the routine technomiracles, but understanding chimps meant understanding how he experienced them.

"The immersion hardware puts you in the middle of a chimp's posterior cingulate gyrus," Ruben said over dessert. "Just 'gyrus' for short. That's the brain's center for mediating emotions and expressing them through action."

"*The* brain?" Kelly asked. "What about ours."

Ruben shrugged. "Same general layout. Chimps' are smaller, without a big cerebrum."

Leon leaned forward, ignoring his steaming cup of Kaf. "This 'gyrus,' it doesn't give direct motor control?"

"No, we tried that. It disorients the chimp so much, when you leave, it can't get itself back together."

"So we're more subtle," Kelly said.

"We have to be. In chimp males, the pilot light is always on in neurons that control action and aggression—"

"That's why they're more violence-prone?" she asked.

"We think so. It parallels structures in our own brains."

"Really? Men's neurons?" Kelly looked doubtful.

"Human males have higher activity levels in their temporal limbic systems, deeper down in the brain—evolutionarily older structures."

"So why not put me into that level?" Leon asked.

"We place the immersion chips into the gyrus area because we can reach it from the top, surgically. The temporal limbic is way far down, impossible to implant a chip and net.''

Kelly frowned. ''So chimp males—''

''Are harder to control. Professor Mattick here is running his chimp from the backseat, so to speak.''

''Whereas Kelly is running hers from a control center that, for female chimps, is more central?'' Leon peered into the distance. ''I was handicapped!''

Kelly grinned. ''You have to play the hand you're dealt.''

''It's not fair.''

''Big Stick, biology is destiny.''

The troop came upon rotting fruit. Fevered excitement ran through them.

The smell was repugnant and enticing at the same time and at first he did not understand why. The chimps rushed to the overripe bulbs of blue and sickly green, popping open the skins, sucking out the juice.

Tentatively, Leon tried one. The hit was immediate. A warm feeling of well-being kindled up in him. Of course—the fruity esters had converted into—alcohol! The chimps were quite deliberately setting about getting drunk.

He ''let'' his chimp follow suit. He hadn't much choice in the matter.

Ipan grunted and thrashed his arms whenever Leon tried to turn him away from the teardrop fruit. And after a while, Leon didn't want to turn away either. He gave himself up to a good, solid drunk. He had been worrying a lot lately, agitated in his chimp, and . . . this was completely natural, wasn't it?

Then a pack of raboons appeared, and he lost control of Ipan.

They come fast. Running two-legs, no sound. Their tails twitch, talking to each other.

Five circle left. They cut off Esa.

Biggest thunder at them. Hunker runs to nearest and it spikes him with its fore-puncher.

I throw rocks. Hit one. It yelps and scurries back. But others take its place. I throw again and they come and the dust and yowling are thick and the others of them have Esa. They cut her with their punch-claws. Kick her with sharp hooves.

Three of them carry her off.

Our fems run, afraid. We warriors stay.

We fight them. Shrieking, throwing, biting when they get close. But we cannot reach Esa.

Then they go. Fast, running on their two hoofed legs. Furling their tails in victory. Taunting us.

We feel bad. Esa was old and we loved her.

Fems come back, nervous. We groom ourselves and know that the two-legs are eating Esa somewhere.

Biggest come by, try to pat me. I snarl.

He Biggest! This thing he should have stopped.

His eyes get big and he slap me. I slap back at him. He slam into me. We roll around in dust. Biting, yowling. Biggest strong, strong and pound my head on ground.

Other warriors, they watch us, not join in.

He beat me. I hurt. I go away.

Biggest starts calming down the warriors. Fems come by and pay their respects to Biggest. Touch him, groom him, feel him the way he likes. He mounts three of them real quick. He feeling Biggest all right.

Me, I lick myself. Sheelah come groom me. After a while I feel better. Already forgotten Esa.

I not forget Biggest beat me though. In front of everybody. Now I hurt, Biggest get grooming.

He let them come and take Esa. He Biggest, he should stop them.

Someday I be all over him. On his back.

Someday I be Bigger.

"When did you bail out?" Kelly asked.

"After Biggest stopped pounding on me . . . uh, on Ipan."

They were relaxing in brilliant sun beside a swimming pool. The heady smells of the forest seemed to awaken in Leon the urge to be down there again, in the valleys of dust and blood. He trembled, took a deep breath. The fighting had been so involving he hadn't wanted to leave, despite the pain. Immersion had a hypnotic quality.

"I know how you feel," she said. "It's easy to totally identify with them. I left Sheelah when those raboons came close. Pretty scary."

"Why did anybody develop them?"

"Plans for using raboons as game, to hunt, Ruben said. Something new and challenging."

"*Hunting?* Business will exploit any throwback primitivism to—" He had been about to launch into a little lecture on how far humanity had come, when he realized that he didn't believe it anymore. "Um."

"You've always thought of people as cerebral. No sociohistory could work if it didn't take into account our animal selves."

"Our worst sins are all our own, I fear." He had not expected that his experiences here would shake him so. This was sobering.

"Not at all." Kelly gave him a lofty look. "I've been reading some of the Station background data on our room computer. Genocide occurs in wolves and chimps alike. Murder is widespread. Ducks and orangutans rape. Even *ants* have organized warfare and slave raids. Chimps have at least as good a chance of being murdered as do humans, Ruben says. Of all the hallowed hallmarks—speech, art, technology, and the rest—the one which comes most obviously from animal ancestors was genocide."

"You've been learning from Ruben."

"It was a good way to keep an eye on him."

"Better to be suspicious than sorry?"

"Of course," she said blandly. "Can't let Africa soften our brains."

"Well, luckily, even if we are superchimps, throughout human society, communication blurs distinctions between Us and Them."

"So?"

"That blunts the deep impulse to genocide."

She laughed again, this time rather to his annoyance. "You haven't understood history very well. Smaller groups still kill each other off with great relish. In Bosnia, during the reign of Omar the Impaler—''

''I concede, there are small-scale tragedies by the dozens. But on the scale where sociohistory might work, averaging over populations of many millions—''

''What makes you so sure numbers are any protection?'' she asked pointedly.

''Well—without further work, I have nothing to say.''

She smiled. ''How uncharacteristic.''

''Until I have a real, working theory.''

''One that can allow for widespread genocide?''

He saw her point then. ''You're saying I really need this 'animal nature' part of humans.''

''I'm afraid so. 'Civilized man' is a contradiction in terms. Scheming, plots, Sheelah grabbing more meat for her young, Ipan wanting to do in Biggest—those things happen in fancy urban nations. They're just better disguised.''

''I don't follow.''

''People use their intelligence to hide motives. Consider ExSpec Ruben. He made a comment about your working on a 'theory of history' the other evening.''

''So?''

''Who told him you were?''

''I don't think I—ah, you think he's checking up on us?''

''He already knows.''

''We're just tourists here.''

She graced him with an unreadable smile. ''I do love your endless, naive way of seeing the world.''

Later, he couldn't decide whether she had meant that as a compliment.

Ruben invited him to try a combat sport the Station offered, and Leon accepted. It was an enhanced swordplay using levitation through electrostatic lifters. Leon was slow and inept. Using his own body against Ruben's swift moves made him long for the sureness and grace of Ipan.

Ruben always opened with a traditional posture: one foot forward, his prod-sword making little circles in the air. Leon poked through Ruben's defense sometimes, but usually spent all his lifter energy eluding Ruben's thrusts. He did not enjoy it nearly as much as Ruben. The dry African air seemed to steal energy from him too, whereas Ipan reveled in it.

He did learn bits and pieces about chimps from Ruben, and from trolling through the vast Station library. The man seemed a bit uneasy when Leon probed the data arrays, as though Ruben somehow owned them and any reader was a thief. Or at least that was what Leon took to be the origin of the unease.

He had never thought about animals very much, though he had grown up among them on the farm. Yet he came to feel that they, too, had to be understood.

Catching sight of itself in a mirror, a dog sees the image as another dog. So did cats, fish, or birds. After a while they get used to the harmless image, silent and smell-free, but they did not see it as themselves.

Human children had to be about two years old to do better.

Chimps took a few days to figure out that they were looking at themselves. Then they preened before it shamelessly, studied their backs, and generally tried to see themselves differently, even putting leaves on their backs like hats and laughing at the result.

So they could do something other animals could not—get outside themselves, and look back.

They plainly lived in a world charged with echoes and reminiscences. Their dominance hierarchy was a frozen record of past coercion. They remembered termite mounds, trees to drum, useful spots where large water-sponge leaves fell, or grain matured.

All this fed into the toy model he had begun building in his notes—a chimp sociohistory. It used their movements, rivalries, hierarchies, patterns of eating, and mating and dying. Territory, resources, and troop competition for them. He found a way to factor into his equations the biological baggage of dark behaviors. Even the worst, like delight in torture and easy exterminations of other species for short-term gain. All these the chimps had. Just like today's newspaper.

At a dance that evening he watched the crowd with fresh vision.

Flirting was practice mating. He could see it in the sparkle of eyes, the rhythms of the dance. The warm breeze wafting up from the valley brought smells of dust, rot, life. An animal restlessness moved in the room.

He quite liked dancing and Kelly was a lush companion tonight. Yet he could not stop his mind from sifting, analyzing, taking the world before him apart into mechanisms.

The nonverbal template humans used for attract/approach strategies apparently descended from a shared mammalian heritage, Kelly had pointed out. He thought of that, watching the crowd at the bar.

A woman crosses a crowded room, hips swaying, eyes resting momentarily on a likely man, then coyly looking away just as she apparently notices his regard. A standard opening move: *Notice me.*

The second is *I am harmless.* A hand placed palm up on a table or knee. A shoulder shrug, derived from an ancient vertebrate reflex, signifying helplessness. Combine that with a tilted head, which displays the vulnerability of the neck. These commonly appeared when two people drawn to each other have their first conversation—all quite unconsciously.

Such moves and gestures are subcortical, emerging far below in a swamp of primordial circuitry . . . which had survived until now, because it worked.

Did such forces shape history more than trade balances, alliances, treaties? He looked at his own kind and tried to see it through chimp eyes.

Though human females matured earlier, they did not go on to acquire coarse body hair, bony eye ridges, deep voices, or tough skin. Males did. And women everywhere strove to stay young-looking. Cosmetics makers freely admitted their basic role: *We don't sell products; we sell hope.*

Competition for mates was incessant. Male chimps sometimes took turns with females in estrus. They had huge testicles, implying that reproductive advantage had come to those males who produced enough to overwhelm their rivals' contributions. Human males had proportionally smaller testicles.

But humans got their revenge where it mattered. Of all primates, humans had the largest penises.

All primates had separated out as species many millions of years ago. In DNA-measured time, chimps lay six million years from humans. He mentioned to Kelly that only 4 percent of mammals formed pair bonds, were monogamous. Primates rated a bit higher, but not much. Birds were much better at it.

She sniffed. "Don't let all this biology go to your head."

"Oh no, I won't let it get that far."

"You mean it belongs in lower places?"

"Madam, you'll have to be the judge of that."

"Ah, you and your single-entendre humor."

Later that evening, with her, he had ample opportunity to reflect upon the truth that, while it was not always great to be human, it was tremendous fun being a mammal.

They spent a last day immersed in their chimps, sunning themselves beside a gushing stream. The plane would pick them up early the next morning; Helsinki waited. They packed and entered the immersion capsule and sank into a last reverie. Sun, sweet air, the lassitude of the primitive . . .

Until Biggest started to mount Sheelah.

Leon/Ipan sat up, his head foggy. Sheelah was shrieking at Biggest. She slapped him.

Biggest had mounted Sheelah before. Kelly had bailed out, her mind returning to her body in the capsule.

Something was different now. Ipan hurried over and signed to Sheelah, who was throwing pebbles at Biggest. *What?*

She moved her hands rapidly, signing, *No go.*

She could not bail out. Something was wrong back at the capsule. He could go back himself, tell them.

Leon made the little mental flip that would bail him out.

Nothing happened.

He tried again. Sheelah threw dust and pebbles, backing away from Biggest. Nothing.

No time to think. He stepped between Sheelah and Biggest.

The massive chimp frowned. Here was Ipan, buddy Ipan, getting in the way. Denying him a fem. Biggest seemed to have forgotten the challenge and beating of the day before.

First he tried bellowing, eyes big and white. Then Biggest shook his arms, fists balled.

Leon made his chimp stand still. It took every calming impulse he could muster.

Biggest swung his fist like a club.

Ipan ducked. Biggest missed.

Leon was having trouble controlling Ipan, who wanted to flee. Sheets of fear shot up through the chimp mind, hot yellows in the blue-black depths.

Biggest charged forward, slamming Ipan back. Leon felt the jolt, a stabbing pain in his chest. He toppled backward. Hit hard.

Biggest yowled his triumph. Waved his arms at the sky.

Biggest would get on top, he saw. Beat him again.

Suddenly he felt a deep, raw hatred.

From that red seethe he felt his grip on Ipan tighten. He was riding both with and within the chimp, feeling its raw red fear, overrunning that with an iron rage. Ipan's own wrath fed back into Leon. The two formed a concert, anger building as if reflected from hard walls.

He might not be the same kind of primate, but he knew Ipan. Neither of them was going to get beaten again. And Biggest was not going to get Sheelah/Kelly.

He rolled to the side. Biggest hit the ground where he had been.

Ipan leaped up and kicked Biggest. Hard, in the ribs. Once, twice. Then in the head.

Whoops, cries, dust, pebbles—Sheelah was still bombarding them both. Ipan shivered with boiling energy and backed away.

Biggest shook his dusty head. Then he curled and rolled easily up to his feet, full of muscular grace, face a constricted mask. The chimp's eyes widened, showing white and red.

Ipan yearned to run. Only Leon's rage held him in place.

But it was a static balance of forces. Ipan blinked as Biggest shuffled warily forward, the big chimp's caution a tribute to the damage Ipan had inflicted.

I need some advantage, Leon thought, looking around. He could call for allies. Hunker paced nervously nearby.

Something told Leon that would be a losing strategy. Hunker was still a lieutenant to Biggest. Sheelah was too small to make a decisive difference. He looked at the other chimps, all chattering anxiously—and decided. He picked up a rock.

Biggest grunted in surprise. Chimps didn't use rocks against each other. Rocks were only for repelling invaders. He was violating a social code.

Biggest yelled, waved to the others, pounded the ground, huffed angrily. Then he charged.

Leon threw the rock hard. It hit Biggest in the chest, knocked him down.

Biggest came up fast, madder than before. Ipan scurried back, wanting desperately to run. Leon felt control slipping from him—and saw another rock. Suitable size, two paces back. He let Ipan turn to flee, then stopped and looked at the stone. Ipan didn't want to hold it. Panic ran through him.

Leon poured his rage into the chimp, forced the long arms down. Hands grabbed at the stone, fumbled, got it. Sheer anger made Ipan turn to face Biggest, who was thundering after him. To Leon, Ipan's arm came up in achingly slow motion. He leaned heavily into the pitch. The rock smacked Biggest in the face.

Biggest staggered. Blood ran into his eyes. Ipan caught the iron scent of it, riding on a prickly stench of outrage.

Leon made his trembling Ipan stoop down. There were some shaped stones nearby, made by the fems to trim leaves from branches. He picked up one with a chipped edge.

Biggest waved his head, dizzy.

Ipan glanced at the sober, still faces of his troop. No one had used a rock against a troop member, much less Biggest. Rocks were for Strangers.

A long, shocked silence stretched. The chimps stood rooted, Biggest grunted and peered in disbelief at the blood that spattered into his upturned hand.

Ipan stepped forward and raised the jagged stone, edge held outward. Crude, but a cutting edge.

Biggest flared his nostrils and came at Ipan. Ipan swept the rock through the air, barely missing Biggest's jaw.

Biggest's eyes widened. He huffed and puffed, threw dust, howled. Ipan simply stood with the rock and held his ground. Biggest kept up his anger-display for a long while, but he did not attack.

The troop watched with intense interest. Sheelah came and stood beside Ipan. It would have been against protocols for a female to take part in male-dominance rituals.

Her movement signaled that the confrontation was over. But Hunker was having none of that. He abruptly howled, pounded the ground, and scooted over to Ipan's side.

Leon was surprised. With Hunker maybe he could hold the line against Biggest. He was not fool enough to think that this one standoff would put Biggest to rest. There would be other challenges and he would have to fight them. Hunker would be a useful ally.

He realized that he was thinking in the slow, muted logic of Ipan himself. He *assumed* that the pursuit of chimp status-markers was a given, the great goal of his life.

This revelation startled him. He had known that he was diffusing into Ipan's mind, taking control of some functions from the bottom up, seeping through the deeply buried, walnut-sized gyrus. It had not occurred to him that the chimp would diffuse into *him*. Were they now married to each other in an interlocked web that dispersed mind and self?

Hunker stood beside him, eyes glaring at the other chimps, chest heaving. Ipan felt the same way, madly pinned to the moment. Leon realized that he would have to do something, break this cycle of dominance and submission which ruled Ipan at the deep, neurological level.

He turned to Sheelah. *Get out?* he signed.

No. No. Her chimp face wrinkled with anxiety.

Leave. He waved toward the trees, pointed to her, then him.

She spread her hands in a gesture of helplessness.

It was infuriating. He had so much to say to her and he had to funnel it through a few hundred signs. He chippered in a high-pitched voice, trying vainly to force the chimp lips and palate to do the work of shaping words.

It was no use. He had tried before, idly, but now he wanted to badly and none of the equipment worked. It couldn't. Evolution had shaped brain and vocal chords in parallel. Chimps groomed, people talked.

He turned back and realized that he had forgotten entirely about the status-setting. Biggest was glowering at him. Hunker stood guard, confused at his new leader's sudden loss of interest in the confrontation—and to gesture at a mere fem too.

Leon reared up as tall as he could and waved the stone. This produced the desired effect. Biggest inched back a bit and the rest of the troop edged closer. Leon made Ipan stalk forward boldly. By this time it did not take much effort, for Ipan was enjoying this enormously.

Biggest retreated. Fems inched around Biggest and approached Ipan.

If only I could leave him to the fems' delights, Leon thought.

He tried to bail out again. Nothing. The mechanism wasn't working back at the Excursion Station. And something told him that it wasn't going to get fixed.

He gave the edged stone to Hunker. The chimp seemed surprised but took it. Leon hoped the symbolism of the gesture would penetrate in some fashion because he had no time left to spend on chimp politics. Hunker hefted the rock and looked at Ipan. Then he cried in a rolling, powerful voice, tones rich in joy and triumph.

Leon was quite happy to let Hunker distract the troop. He took Sheelah by the arm and led her into the trees. No one followed.

He was relieved. If another chimp had tagged along, it would have confirmed his suspicions. Ruben might be keeping track.

Still, he reminded himself, absence of evidence is not evidence of absence.

The humans came swiftly, with clatter and booms.

He and Sheelah had been in the trees a while. At Leon's urging they had worked their way a few klicks away from the troop. Ipan and Sheelah showed rising anxiety at being separated from their troop. His teeth chattered and eyes jerked anxiously at every suspicious movement. This was natural, for isolated chimps were far more vulnerable.

The humans landing did not help.

Danger, Leon signed, cupping an ear to indicate the noise of fliers landing nearby.

Sheelah signed, *Where go?*

Away.

She shook her head vehemently. *Stay here. They get us.*

They would indeed, but not in the sense she meant. Leon cut her off curtly, shaking his head. *Danger*. They had never intended to convey complicated ideas with their signs and now he felt bottled up, unable to tell her his suspicions.

Leon made a knife-across-throat gesture. Sheelah frowned.

He bent down and made Ipan take a stick. In soft loam he wrote:

IMPERIAL INDUSTRIE AGENTS. WANT US DEAD.

Sheelah looked dumbfounded. Kelly had probably been operating under the assumption that the failure to bail out was a temporary error. It had lasted too long for that. The landing of people in noisy, intrusive fashion confirmed his hunch. No ordinary team would disturb the animals so much. And nobody would come after them directly. They would fix the immersion apparatus, where the real problem was.

THEY KEEP US HERE, KILL US, BLAME ON ANIMALS.

He had better arguments to back up his case, the slow accumulation of small details in Ruben's behavior. That, and the guess that letting them die in an "accident" while immersed in a chimp was plausible enough to escape an investigation.

The humans went about their noisy business. They were enough, though, to make his case. Sheelah's eyes narrowed, the big brow scowled. *Where?* she signed.

He had no sign for so abstract an idea, so he scribbled with the stick, AWAY. Indeed, he had no plan.

I'LL CHECK, she wrote in the dirt. She set off toward the noise of humans deploying on the valley floor below. To a chimp the din was a dreadful clanking irritation. Leon was not going to let her out of his sight. He followed her. She waved him back but he shook his head and stuck behind her. She gave up and let him follow.

They stayed in bushes until they could get a view of the landing party below. A skirmish line was forming up a few hundred meters away. They were encircling the area where the troop had been. Leon squinted. Chimp eyesight was not good for distance. Humans had been hunters once, and one could tell by the eyes alone.

He thought abstractly about the fact that nearly everybody needed eye aids by the age of forty. Either civilization was hard on eyes, or maybe humans in prehistory had not lived long enough for eye trouble to rob them of game. Either conclusion was sobering.

The two chimps watched the humans calling to one another and in the middle of them Leon saw Ruben. That confirmed it. That, and that each man and woman carried a weapon.

Beneath his fear he felt something strong, dark.

Ipan trembled, watching humans, a strange awe swelling in his mind. Humans seemed impossibly tall in the shimmering distance, moving with stately, swaying elegance.

Leon floated above the surge of emotion, fending off its powerful effects. The reverence for those distant, tall figures came out of the chimp's dim past.

That surprised him until he thought it over. After all, animals were reared and taught by adults much smarter and stronger. Most species were like chimps, spring-loaded by evolution to work in a dominance hierarchy. Awe was adaptive.

When they met lofty humans with overwhelming power, able to mete out punishment and rewards—literally life and death—something like religious fervor arose in them. Dim, fuzzy, but strong.

Atop that warm, tropical emotion floated a sense of satisfaction at simply *being*. His chimp was happy to be a chimp, even when seeing a being of clearly superior power and thought.

Ironic, Leon thought. His chimp had just disproved another supposedly human earmark: their self-congratulatory distinction of being the only animal that congratulated itself.

He jerked himself out of his abstractions. How human, to ruminate even when in mortal danger.

CAN'T FIND US ELECTRONICALLY, he scratched in the sand.

MAYBE RANGE IS SHORT, she wrote.

RUBEN SABOTAGED LINK, he printed. She bit her lip, nodded.

Go. We go, he signed.

Sheelah nodded and they crept quickly away. Ipan was reluctant to leave the presence of the revered humans, his steps dragging.

They used chimp modes of patrolling. He and Kelly let their chimps take over, experts at silent movement, careful of every twig. Once they had left the humans behind the chimps grew even more cautious. Chimps had few enemies but the faint scent of a single predator could change the feel of every moment in the wild.

Ipan climbed tall trees and sat for hours surveying open land ahead before venturing forth. He weighed the evidence of pungent droppings, faint prints, bent branches.

They angled down the long slope of the valley and kept in the forest. Leon had only glanced at the big color-coded map of the area all guests received and had trouble recalling much of it. Once he recognized one of the distant, beak-shaped peaks he got his bearings. Kelly spotted a stream snaking down into the main river and that gave them further help, but still they did not know which way lay the Excursion Station. Or how far.

That way? Leon signed, pointing over the distant ridge.

No. That, Kelly insisted.

Far, not

Why?

The worst part of it all was that they could not talk. He could not say clearly that the technology of immersion worked best at reasonably short range, less than a hundred klicks, say. And it made sense to keep the subject chimps within easy flier distance. Certainly Ruben and the others had gotten to the troop quickly.

Is. He persisted.

Not. She pointed down the valley. *Maybe there.*

He could only hope Kelly got the general idea. Their signs were scanty and he began to feel a broad, rising irritation. Chimps felt and sensed strongly, but they were so *limited.*

Ipan expressed this by tossing limbs and stones, banging on tree trunks. It didn't help much. The need to speak was like a pressure he could not relieve and Kelly felt it too. Sheelah chippered and grunted in frustration.

Beneath his mind he felt the smoldering presence of Ipan. They had never been together this long before and urgency welled up between the two canted systems of mind. Their uneasy marriage was showing greater strains.

Sit. Quiet. She did. He cupped a hand to his ear.

Bad come?

No. Listen—In frustration Leon pointed to Sheelah herself. Blank incomprehension in the chimp's face. He scribbled in the dust, LEARN FROM CHIMPS. Sheelah's mouth opened and she nodded.

They squatted in the shelter of prickly bushes and listened to the sounds of the forest. Scurryings and murmurs came through strongly as Leon relaxed his grip on the chimp. Dust hung in slanted cathedral light, pouring down from the forest canopy in rich yellow shafts. Scents purled up from the forest floor, chemical messengers telling Ipan of potential foods, soft loam for resting, bark to be chewed. Leon gently lifted Ipan's head to gaze across the valley at the peaks . . . musing . . . and felt a faint tremor of resonance.

To Ipan the valley came weighted with significance beyond words. His troop had imbued it with blunt emotions, attached to clefts where a friend fell and died, where the troop found a hoard of fruits, where they met and fought two big cats. It was an intricate landscape suffused with feeling, the chimp mechanism of memory.

Leon faintly urged Ipan to think beyond the ridgeline and felt in response a diffuse anxiety. He bore in on that kernel—and an image burst into Ipan's mind, fringed in fear. A rectangular bulk framed against a cool sky. The Excursion Station.

There. He pointed for Kelly.

Ipan had simple, strong, apprehensive memories of the place. His troop had been taken there, outfitted with the implants which allowed them to be ridden, then deposited back in their territory.

Far, Kelly signed.

We go?

Hard. Slow.

No stay here. They catch.

Kelly looked as skeptical as a chimp could look. *Fight?*

Did she mean fight Ruben here? Or fight once they reached the Excursion Station? *No here. There.*

Kelly frowned but accepted this. He had no real plan, only the idea that Ruben was ready for chimps out here, and might not be so prepared for them at the Station. There he and Kelly might gain the element of surprise. How, he had no idea.

They studied each other, each trying to catch a glimmer of the other in an alien face. She stroked his earlobe, Kelly's fond calming gesture. Sure enough, it made him tingle. But he could say so little. . . . The moment crystallized for him the hopelessness of their situation.

Ruben plainly was trying to kill Leon and Kelly through Ipan and Sheelah. What would become of their own bodies? The shock of experiencing death through immersion was known to prove fatal. Their bodies would fail from neurological shock, without ever regaining consciousness.

He saw a tear run down Sheelah's cheek. She knew how hopeless matters were too. He swept her up in his arms and, looking at the distant mountains, was surprised to find tears in his own eyes as well.

He had not counted on the river. Men, animals—these problems he had considered. They ventured down to the surging waters where the forest gave the nearest protection and the stream broadened, making the best place to ford.

But the hearty river that chuckled and frothed down the valley was impossible to swim.

Or rather, for Ipan to swim. Leon had been coaxing his chimp onward, carefully pausing when his muscles shook or when he wet himself from anxiety. Kelly was having similar trouble and it slowed them. A night spent up in high branches soothed both chimps, but now at midmorning all the stressful symptoms returned, as Ipan put one foot into the river. Cool, swift currents.

Ipan danced back onto the narrow beach, yelping in dread.

Go? Kelly/Sheelah signed.

Leon calmed his chimp and they tried to get it to attempt swimming. Sheelah displayed only minor anxiety. Leon plumbed the swampy depths of Ipan's memory and found a cluster of distress, centered around a dim remembrance of nearly drowning when a child. When Sheelah helped him he fidgeted, then bolted from the water again.

Go! Sheelah waved long arms upstream and downstream and shook her head angrily.

Leon guessed that she had reasonably clear chimp-memories of the river, which had no easier crossings than this. He shrugged, lifted his hands palm up.

A big herd of gigantelope grazed nearby and some were crossing the river for better grass beyond. They tossed their great heads, as if mocking the chimps. The river was not deep, but to Ipan it was a wall. Leon, trapped by Ipan's solid fear, seethed and could do nothing.

Sheelah paced the shore. She huffed in frustration and looked at the sky, squinting. Her head snapped around in surprise. Leon followed her gaze. A flier was swooping down the valley, coming this way.

Ipan beat Sheelah to the shelter of trees, but not by much. Luckily the gigantelope herd provided a distraction for the flyer. They cowered in bushes as the machine hummed overhead in a circular search pattern. Leon had to quell Ipan's mounting apprehension by envisioning scenes of quiet and peace and food while he and Sheelah groomed each other.

The flier finally went away. They would have to minimize their exposure on open grasslands now.

They foraged for fruit. His mind revolved uselessly and a sour depression settled over him. He was quite neatly caught in a trap, a pawn in politics. Worse, Kelly was in it too. He was no man of action. *Nor a chimp of action, either*, he thought dourly.

As he brought a few overripe bunches of fruit back to their bushes overlooking the river, he heard cracking noises. He crouched down and worked his way uphill and around the splintering sounds. Sheelah was stripping branches from the trees. When he approached she waved him on impatiently, a common chimp gesture remarkably like a human one.

She had a dozen thick branches lined up on the ground. She went to a nearby spindly tree and peeled bark from it in long strips. The noise made Ipan uneasy. Predators would be curious at this unusual sound. He scanned the forest for danger.

Sheelah came over to him, slapped him in the face. She wrote with a stick on the ground, RAFT.

Leon felt particularly stupid as he pitched in. Of course. Had his chimp immersion made him more stupid? Did the effect worsen with time? Even if he got out of this, would he be the same? Many questions, no answers. He forgot about them and worked.

They lashed branches together with bark, crude but serviceable. They found two small fallen trees and used them to anchor the edge of the raft. *I*, Sheelah pointed, and demonstrated pulling the raft.

First, a warm-up. Ipan liked sitting on the raft in the bushes. Apparently the chimp could not see the purpose of the raft yet. Ipan stretched out on the deck of saplings and gazed up into the trees as they swished in the warm winds.

They carried the awkward plane of branches down to the river after another mutual grooming session. The sky was filled with birds but he could see no fliers.

They hurried. Ipan was skeptical about stepping onto the raft when it was halfway into the water, but Leon called up memories filled with warm feeling, and this calmed the quick-tripping heart he could feel knocking in the chimp veins.

Ipan sat gingerly on the branches. Sheelah cast off.

She pushed hard but the river swept them quickly downstream. Alarm spurted in Ipan.

Leon made Ipan close his eyes. That slowed the breathing, but anxiety skittered across the chimp mind like heat lightning forking before a storm. The raft's rocking motion actually helped, making Ipan concentrate on his queasy stomach. Once his eyes flew open when a floating log smacked into the raft, but the dizzying sight of water all around made him squeeze them tight immediately.

Leon wanted to help her, but he knew from the trip-hammer beating of Ipan's heart that panic hovered near. He could not even see how she was doing. He had to sit blind and feel her shoving the raft along.

She panted noisily, struggling to keep it pointed against the river's tug. Spray splashed onto him. Ipan jerked, yelped, pawed anxiously with his feet, as if to run.

A sudden lurch. Sheelah's grunt cut off with a gurgle and he felt the raft spin away on rising currents. A sickening spin . . .

Ipan jerked clumsily to his feet. Eyes jumped open.

Swirling water, the raft unsteady. He looked down and the branches were coming apart. Panic consumed him. Leon tried to promote soothing images but they blew away before winds of fright.

Sheelah came paddling after the raft but it was picking up speed. Leon made Ipan gaze at the far shore but that was all he could do before the chimp started yelping and scampering on the raft, trying to find a steady place.

It was no use. The branches broke free of their bindings and chilly water swept over the deck. Ipan screamed. He leaped, fell, rolled, jumped up again.

Leon gave up any idea of control. The only hope lay in seizing just the right moment. The raft split down the middle and his half veered heavily to the left. Ipan started away from the edge and Leon fed that, made the chimp step further. In two bounds he took the chimp off the deck and into the water—toward the far shore.

Ipan gave way then to pure blind panic. Leon let the legs and arms thrash—but to each he gave a push at the right moment. He could swim, Ipan couldn't.

The near-aimless flailing held Ipan's head out of water most of the time. It even gained a little headway. Leon kept focused on the convulsive movements, ignoring the cold water—and then Sheelah was there, her jaws agape.

She grabbed him by the scruff of the neck and shoved him toward shore. Ipan tried to grapple with her, climb up her. Sheelah socked him in the jaw. He gasped. She pulled him toward shore.

Ipan was stunned. This gave Leon a chance to get the legs moving in a thrusting stroke. He worked at it, single-minded among the rush and gurgle, chest heaving . . . and after a seeming eternity, felt pebbles beneath his feet. Ipan scrambled up onto the rocky beach on his own.

He let the chimp slap himself and dance to warm up. Sheelah emerged dripping and bedraggled and Ipan swept her up in his thankful arms.

Walking was work and Ipan wasn't having any.

Leon tried to make the chimp cover ground, but now they had to ascend difficult gullies, some mossy and rough. They stumbled, waded, climbed, and sometimes just crawled up the slopes of the valley. The chimps found animal trails, which helped a bit.

Ipan stopped often for food or just to gaze idly into the distance. Soft thoughts flitted like moths through the foggy mind, buoyant on liquid emotional flows which eddied to their own pulse.

Chimps were not made for extended projects. They made slow progress. Night came and they had to climb trees, snagging fruit on the way.

Ipan slept, but Leon did not. Could not.

Their lives were just as much at risk here as the chimps', but the slumbering minds he and Kelly attended had always lived this way. To the chimps, the forest night seeped through as a quiet rain of information, processed as they slept. Their minds keyed vagrant sounds to known nonthreats, leaving slumber intact.

Leon did not know the subtle signs of danger and so mistook every rustle and tremor in the branches as danger approaching on soft feet. Sleep came against his will.

In dawn's first pale glow Leon awoke with a snake beside him. It coiled like a green rope around a descending branch, getting itself into striking position. It eyed him and Leon tensed.

Ipan drifted up from his own profound slumber. He saw the snake but did not react with a startled jerk, as Leon feared he might.

A long moment passed between them and Ipan blinked just once. The snake became utterly motionless and Ipan's heart quickened but he did not move. Then the snake uncoiled and glided away, and the unspoken transaction was done. Ipan was unlikely prey, this green snake did not taste good, and chimps were smart enough to be about other business.

When Sheelah awoke they went down to a nearby chuckling stream for a drink, scavenging leaves and a few crunchy insects on the way. Both chimps nonchalantly peeled away fat black land leeches which had attached to them in the night. The thick, engorged worms sickened Leon, but Ipan pulled them off with the same casualness Leon would have retying loosened shoelaces.

Ipan drank and Leon reflected that the chimp felt no need to clean himself. Normally Leon showered twice a day, before breakfast and before dinner, and felt ill at ease if he sweated, but here he wore the shaggy body comfortably. Had his frequent cleansings been a health measure, like the chimps' grooming? Or a rarified, civilized habit? He dimly remembered that as a boy he had gone for days in happy, sweaty pleasure, and had disliked baths and showers. Somehow Ipan returned him to a simpler sense of self, at ease in the grubby world.

His comfort did not last long. They sighted raboons uphill.

Ipan had picked up the scent, but Leon did not have access to the part of the chimp brain that made scent-picture associations. He had only known that something disturbed Ipan, wrinkling the knobby nose. The sight at short range jolted him.

Thick hindquarters, propelling them in brisk steps. Short forelimbs, ending in sharp claws. Their large heads seemed to be mostly teeth, sharp and white above slitted, wary eyes. A thick brown pelt covered them, growing bushy in the heavy tail they used for balance.

Days before, from the safety of a high tree, Ipan had watched some rip and devour the soft tissues of a gigantelope out on the grasslands. These came sniffing, working downslope in a skirmish line, five of them. Sheelah and Ipan trembled at the sight. They were downwind of the raboons and so beat a retreat in silence.

There were no tall trees here, just brush and saplings. Leon and Sheelah angled away downhill and got some distance, and then saw ahead a clearing. Ipan picked up the faint tang of other chimps, wafting from across the clearing.

He waved to her: *Go.* At the same moment chorus rose behind them. The raboons had smelled them.

Their wheezing grunts came echoing through the thick bushes. Down the slope there was even less cover, but bigger trees lay beyond. They could climb those.

Ipan and Sheelah hurried across the broad tan clearing on all fours but they were not quick. Snarling raboons burst into the grass behind them. Leon scampered into the trees—and directly into the midst of a chimp troop.

There were several dozen, startled and blinking. He yelled incoherently, wondering how Ipan would signal to them.

The nearest large male turned, bared teeth, and shrieked angrily. The entire pack took up the call, whooping and snatching up sticks and rocks, throwing them—at Ipan. A pebble hit him on the chin, a branch on the thigh. He fled, Sheelah already a few steps ahead of him.

The raboons came charging across the clearing. In their claws they held small, sharp stones. They looked big and solid but they slowed at the barrage of screeches and squawks coming from the trees.

Ipan and Sheelah burst out into the grass of the clearing and the chimps came right after them. The raboons skidded to a halt.

The chimps saw the raboons but they did not stop or even slow. They still came after Ipan and Sheelah with murderous glee.

The raboons stood frozen, their claws working uneasily.

Leon realized what was happening and picked up a branch as he ran, calling hoarsely to Sheelah. She saw and copied him. He ran straight at the raboons, waving the branch. It was an awkward, twisted old limb, useless, but it looked big. Leon wanted to seem like the advance guard of some bad business.

In the rising cloud of dust and general chaos the raboons saw a large party of enraged chimps emerging from the forest. They bolted.

Squealing, they ran at full stride into the far trees.

Ipan and Sheelah followed, running with the last of their strength. By the time Ipan reached the first trees, he looked back and the chimps had stopped halfway, still screeching their vehemence.

He signed to Sheelah, *Go,* and they cut away at a steep angle, heading uphill.

Ipan needed food and rest to stop his heart from lurching at every minor sound. Sheelah and Ipan clutched each other, high in a tree, and crooned and petted.

Leon needed time to think. Who was keeping their bodies alive at the Station? It would be smart to let them stay out here, in danger, saying to the rest of the staff that the two odd tourists wanted a really long immersion.

His thinking triggered jitters in Ipan, so he dropped that mode. Better to think abstractly. And there was plenty out here that needed understanding.

The biotechnicians who planted chimps and gigantelope and the rest here had tinkered with the raboons. The wild days of explosive biotech, in the first years of the twencen, had allowed just about anything. Capabilities soon thereafter, in the twentens, had allowed the biotech tinkerers to see if they could turn a more distant primate relative, the baboon, into something like humans. A perverse goal, it seemed to Leon, but believable. Scientists loved to monkey with matters.

The work had gotten as far as pack-hunting behavior. But raboons had no tools beyond crudely edged stones, occasionally used to cut meat once they had brought it down.

In another few million years, under evolution's raw rub, they might be as smart as chimps. Who would go extinct then?

At the moment he didn't much care. He had felt real rage when the chimps—*his own kind!*—had turned against them, even when the raboons came within view. Why?

He worried at the issue, sure there was something here he had to understand. Sociohistory had to deal with such basic, fundamental impulses. The chimps' reaction had been uncomfortably close to myriad incidents in human history. *Hate the Stranger.*

He had to fathom that murky truth.

Chimps moved in small groups, disliking outsiders, breeding mostly within their modest circle of a few dozen. This meant that any genetic trait that emerged could pass swiftly into all the members, through inbreeding. If it helped the band survive, the rough rub of chance would select for that band's survival. Fair enough.

But the trait had to be undiluted. A troop of especially good rock throwers would get swallowed up if they joined a company of several hundred. Contact would make them breed outside the original small clan. Outbreeding: Their genetic heritage would get watered down.

Striking a balance between the accidents of genetics in small groups, and the stability of large groups—that was the trick. Some lucky troop might have fortunate genes, conferring traits that fit the next challenge handed out by the ever-altering world. They would do well. But if those genes never passed to many chimps, what did it matter?

With some small amount of outbreeding, that trait got spread into other bands. Down through the strainer of time, others picked up the trait. It spread.

This meant it was actually *helpful* to develop smoldering animosity to outsiders, an immediate sense of their wrongness. *Don't breed with them.*

So small bands held fast to their eccentric traits, and some prospered. Those lived on; most perished. Evolutionary jumps happened faster in small, semi-isolated bands which outbred slightly. They kept their genetic assets in one small basket, the troop. Only occasionally did they mate with another troop—often, through rape.

The price was steep: a strong preference for their own tiny lot.

They hated crowds, strangers, noise. Bands of less than ten were too vulnerable to disease or predators; a few losses and the group failed. Too many, and they lost the concentration of close breeding. They were intensely loyal to their group, easily identifying each other in the dark by smell, even at great distances. Because they had many common genes, altruistic actions were common.

They even honored heroism—for even if the hero died, his shared genes were passed on through his relatives.

Even if strangers could pass the tests of difference in appearances, manner, smell, grooming—even then, culture could amplify the effects. Newcomers with different language or habits and posture would seem repulsive. Anything that served to distinguish a band would help keep hatreds high.

Each small genetic ensemble would then be driven by natural selection to stress the noninherited differences—even arbitrary ones, dimly connected to survival fitness . . . and so they could evolve culture. As humans had.

Diversity in their tribal intricacies avoided genetic watering down. They heeded the ancient call of aloof, wary tribalism.

Leon/Ipan shifted uneasily. Midway through his thinking, the word *they* had come in Leon's thinking to mean humans as well as chimps. The description fit both.

That was the key. Humans fit into civilization *despite* their innate tribalism, their chimplike heritage. It was a miracle!

But even miracles called out for explanation. How could civilization possibly have kept itself stable, using such crude creatures as humans?

Leon had never seen the issue before in such glaring, and humbling, light.

And he had no answer.

They moved on against the blunt, deep unease of their chimps.

Ipan smelled something that sent his eyes darting left and right. With the full tool kit of soothing thoughts and the subtle tricks he had learned, Leon kept him going.

Sheelah was having more trouble. The female chimp did not like laboring up the long, steep gullies that approached the ridgeline. Gnarled bushes blocked their way and it took time to work their way around. Fruit was harder to find at these altitudes.

Ipan's shoulders and arms ached constantly. Chimps walked on all fours because their immensely strong arms carried a punishing weight penalty. To navigate both trees and ground meant you could optimize neither. Sheelah and Ipan groaned and whined at the soreness that never left feet, legs, wrists, and arms. Chimps would never be far-ranging explorers.

Together they let their chimps pause often to crumble leaves and soak up water from tree holes, a routine, simple tool use. They kept sniffing the air, apprehensive.

The smell that disturbed both chimps got stronger, darker.

Sheelah went ahead and was the first over the ridgeline. Far below in the valley they could make out the rectangular rigidities of the Excursion Station. A flier lifted from the roof and whispered away down the valley, no danger to them.

He recalled a century ago sitting on the veranda there with drinks in hand and Kelly saying, *If you stayed in Helsinki you might be dead.* Also if you didn't stay in Helsinki . . .

They started down the steep slope. Their chimps' eyes jerked at every unexpected movement. A chilly breeze stirred the few low bushes and twisted trees. Some had a feathered look, burnt and shattered by lightning. Air masses driven up from the valleys fought along here, the brute clash of pressures. This rocky ridge was far from the comfortable province of chimps. They hurried.

Ahead, Sheelah stopped.

Without a sound, five raboons rose from concealment, forming a neat half-circle around them.

Leon could not tell if it was the same pack as before. If so, they were quite considerable pack hunters, able to hold memory and purpose over time. They had waited ahead, where there were no trees to climb.

The raboons were eerily quiet as they strode forward, their claws clicking softly.

He called to Sheelah and made some utterly fake ferocious noises as he moved, arms high in the air, fists shaking, showing a big profile. He let Ipan take over while he thought.

A raboon band could certainly take two isolated chimps. To survive this they had to surprise the raboons, frighten them.

He looked around. Throwing rocks wasn't going to do the trick here. With only a vague notion of what he was doing he shuffled left, toward a tree that had been splintered by lightning.

Sheelah saw his move and got there first, striding energetically. Ipan picked up two stones and flung them at the nearest raboon. One caught him on the flank but did no real harm.

The raboons began to trot, circling. They called to each other in wheezing grunts.

Sheelah leaped on a dried-out shard of the tree. It snapped. She snatched it up and Leon saw her point. It was as tall as she was and she cradled it.

The largest raboon grunted and they all looked at each other.

The raboons charged.

The nearest one came at Sheelah. She caught it on the shoulder with the blunt point and it squealed.

Leon grabbed a stalk of the shattered tree trunk. He could not wrench it free. Another squeal from behind him and Sheelah was gibbering in a high, frightened voice.

It was best to let the chimps release tension vocally, but he could feel the fear and desperation in the tones and knew it came from Kelly too.

He carefully selected a smaller shard of the tree. With both hands he twisted it free, using his weight and big shoulder muscles, cracking it so that it came away with a point.

Lances. That was the only way to stay away from the raboon claws. Chimps never used such advanced weapons. Evolution hadn't gotten around to that lesson yet.

The raboons were all around them now. He and Sheelah stood back-to-back. He barely got his feet placed when he had to take the rush of a big, swarthy raboon.

They had not gotten the idea of the lance yet. It slammed into the point, jerked back. A fearsome bellow. Ipan wet himself with fear but something in Leon kept him in control.

The raboon backed off, whimpering. It turned to run. In midstride it stopped. For a long, suspended moment the raboon hesitated—then turned back toward Leon.

It trotted forward with new confidence. The other raboons watched. It went to the same tree Leon had used and with a single heave broke off a long, slender spike of wood. Then it came toward Leon, stopped, and with one claw held the stick forward. With a toss of its big head it looked at him and half-turned, putting one foot forward.

With a shock Leon recognized the swordplay position. Ruben had used it. Ruben was riding this raboon.

It made perfect sense. This way the chimps' deaths would be quite natural. Ruben could say that he was developing raboon-riding as a new commercial application of the same hardware that worked for chimp-riding.

Ruben came forward a careful step at a time, holding the long lance between two claws now. He made the end move in a circle. Movement was jerky; claws were crude, compared with chimp hands. But the raboon was stronger.

It came at him with a quick feint, then a thrust. Leon barely managed to dodge sideways while he brushed the lance aside with his stick. Ruben recovered quickly and came from Leon's left. Jab, feint, jab, feint. Leon caught each with a swoop of his stick.

Their wooden swords smacked against each other and Leon hoped his didn't snap. Ruben had good control of his raboon. It did not try to flee as it had before.

Leon was kept busy slapping aside Ruben's thrusts. He had to have some other advantage or the superior strength of the raboon would eventually tell. Leon circled, drawing Ruben away from Sheelah. The other raboons were keeping her trapped, but not attacking. All attention riveted on the two figures as they poked and parried.

Leon drew Ruben toward an outcropping. The raboon was having trouble holding its lance straight and had to keep looking down at its claws to get them right. This meant it paid less attention to where its two hooves found their footing. Leon slapped and jabbed and kept moving, making the raboon step sideways. It put a big hoof down among some angular stones, teetered, then recovered.

Leon moved left. It stepped again and its hoof turned and it stumbled. Leon was on it in an instant. He thrust forward as the raboon looked down, feet scrambling for purchase. Leon caught the raboon full with his point.

He pushed hard. The other raboons let out a moaning.

Snorting in rage, the raboon tried to get off the point. Leon made Ipan step forward and thrust the tip into the raboon. The thing wailed hoarsely. Ipan plunged again. Blood spurted from it, spattering the dust. Its knees buckled and it sprawled.

Leon shot a glance over his shoulder. The others had surged into action. Sheelah was holding off three, screeching at them so loudly it unnerved even him. She had already wounded one. Blood dripped down its brown coat.

But the others did not charge. They circled and growled and stamped their feet, but came no closer. They were confused. Learning too. He could see the quick, bright eyes studying the situation, this fresh move in the perpetual war.

Sheelah stepped out and poked the nearest raboon. It launched itself at her in a snarling fit and she stuck it again, deeper. It yelped and turned—and ran.

That did it for the others. They all trotted off, leaving their fellow bleating on the ground. Its dazed eyes watched its blood trickle out. Its eyes flickered and Ruben was gone. The animal slumped.

With deliberation Leon picked up a rock and bashed in the skull. It was messy work and he sat back inside Ipan and let the dark, smoldering chimp anger come out.

He bent over and studied the raboon brain. A fine silvery webbing capped the rubbery, convoluted ball. Immersion circuitry.

He turned away from the sight and only then saw that Sheelah was hurt.

The station crowned a rugged hill. Steep Gullies gave the hillside the look of a weary, lined face. Wiry bushes thronged the lower reaches.

Ipan puffed as he worked his way through the raw land cut by erosion. In chimp vision the night was eerie, a shimmering vista of pale greens and blue-tinged shadows. The hill was a nuance in the greater slope of a grand mountain, but chimp vision could not make out the distant features. Chimps lived in a close, immediate world.

Ahead he could see clearly the glowing blank wall ringing the Station. Massive, five meters tall. And, he remembered from his tourist tour of the place, rimmed with broken glass.

Behind him came gasps as Sheelah labored up the slope. The wound in her side made her gait stiff, face rigid. She refused to hide below. They were both near exhaustion and their chimps were balky, despite two stops for fruit and grubs and rest.

Through their feeble vocabulary, their facial grimacing and writing in the dust, they had "discussed" the possibilities. Two chimps were vulnerable out here. They could not expect to be as lucky as with the raboons, not tired out and in strange territory.

The best time to approach the Station was at night. And whoever had engineered this would not wait forever. They had hidden from fliers twice more this last day. Resting through the next day was an inviting option, but Leon felt a foreboding press him onward.

He angled up the hillside, watching for electronic trip wires. Of such technical matters he knew nothing. He would have to keep a lookout for the obvious and hope that the Station was not wired for thinking trespassers. Chimp vision was sharp and clear in dim light for nearby objects, but he could find nothing.

He chose a spot by the wall shadowed by trees. Sheelah panted in shallow gasps as she approached. Looking up, the wall seemed immense. Impossible. . . .

Slowly he surveyed the land around them. No sign of any movement. The place smelled peculiar to Ipan, somehow *wrong*. Maybe animals stayed away from the alien compound. Good; that would make security inside less alert.

The wall was polished concrete. A thick lip jutted out at the top, making climbing it harder.

Sheelah gestured where trees grew near the wall. Stumps nearer showed that the builders had thought about animals leaping across from branches. But some were tall enough and had branches within a few meters of the top.

Could a chimp make the distance? Not likely, especially when tired. Sheelah pointed to him and back to her, then held hands and made a swinging motion. Could they *swing* across the distance?

He studied her face. The designer would not anticipate two chimps cooperating that way. He squinted up at the top. Too high to climb, even if Sheelah stood on his shoulders.

Yes, he signed.

A few moments later, her hands holding his feet, about to let go of his branch, he had second thoughts.

Ipan didn't mind this bit of calisthenics, and in fact was happy to be back in a tree. But Leon's human judgment still kept shouting that he could not possibly do it. Natural chimp talent conflicted with human caution.

Luckily, he did not have much time to indulge in self-doubt. Sheelah yanked him off the branch. He fell, held only through her hands.

She had wrapped her feet securely around a thick branch, and now began to oscillate him like a weight on a string. She swung him back and forth, increasing the amplitude. Back, forth, up, down, centrifugal pressure in his head. To Ipan it was unremarkable. To Leon it was a wheeling world of heart-stopping whirls.

Small branches brushed him and he worried about noise and then forgot about that because his head was coming up level with the top of the wall.

The concrete lip was rounded off on the inside, so no hook could find a grip.

He swung back down, head plunging toward ground. Then up into the lower branches, twigs slapping his face.

On the next swing he was higher. All along the top of the wall thick glass glinted. Very professional.

He barely had time to realize all this when she let him go.

He arced up, hands stretched out—and barely caught the lip. If it had not protectively protruded out, he would have missed.

He let his body slam against the side. His feet scrabbled for purchase against the sheer face. A few toes got hold. He heaved up, muscles bunching—and over. Never before had he appreciated how much stronger a chimp could be. No man could have made it here.

He scrambled up, cutting his arm and haunch on glass. It was a delicate business, getting to his feet and finding a place to stand.

A surge of triumph. He waved to Sheelah, invisible in the tree.

From here on it was up to him. He realized suddenly that they could have fashioned some sort of rope, tying together vines. Then he could lift her up here. *Good idea, too late.*

No point in delaying. The compound was partly visible through the trees, a few lights burning. Utterly silent. They had waited until the night was about half over, he had nothing but Ipan's gut feelings to tell him when.

He looked down. Just beyond his toes razor wire gleamed, set into the concrete. Carefully he stepped between the shiny lines. There was room among the sharp glass teeth to stand. A tree blocked his vision and he could see little below him in the dim glow from the Station. At least that meant they couldn't see him, either.

Should he jump? too high. The tree that hid him was close, but he could not see into it.

He stood and thought, but nothing came to him. Meanwhile Sheelah was behind him, alone, and he hated leaving her where dangers waited that he did not even know.

He was thinking like a man and forgetting that he had the capability of a chimp.

Go. He leaped. Twigs snapped and he plunged heavily in shadows. Branches stabbed his face. He saw a dark shape to his right and so curled his legs, rotated, hands out—and snagged a branch. His hands closed easily around it and he realized it was too thin, *too thin*—

It snapped. The *crack* came like a thunderbolt to his ears. He fell, letting go of the branch. His back hit something hard and he rolled, grappling for a hold. His fingers closed around a thick branch and he swung from it. Finally he let out a gasp.

Leaves rustled, branches swayed. Nothing more.

He was halfway up the tree. Aches sprouted in his joints, a galaxy of small pains.

Leon relaxed and let Ipan master the descent. He had made far too much noise falling in the tree but there was no sign of any movement across the broad lawns between him and the big, luminous Station.

He thought of Sheelah and wished there were some way he could let her know he was inside now. Thinking of her, he measured with his eye the distances from nearby trees, memorizing the pattern so that he could find the way back at a dead run if he had to.

Now what? He didn't have a plan. That, and suspicions.

Leon gently urged Ipan—who was nervous and tired, barely controllable—into a triangular pattern of bushes. Ipan's mind was like a stormy sky split by skittering lightning. Not thoughts precisely; more like knots of emotion, forming and flashing around crisp kernels of anxiety. Patiently Leon summoned up soothing images, getting Ipan's breathing slowed, and he almost missed the whispery sound.

Nails scrabbling on a stone walkway. Something running fast.

They came around the triangle peak of bushes. Bunched muscles, sleek skin, stubby legs eating up the remaining distance. They were well trained to seek and kill soundlessly, without warning.

To Ipan the monsters were alien, terrifying. Ipan stepped back in panic before the two onrushing bullets of muscle and bone. Black gums peeled back from white teeth, bared beneath mad eyes.

Then Leon felt something shift in Ipan. Primeval, instinctive responses stopped his retreat, tensed the body. No time to flee, so *fight.*

Ipan set himself, balanced. The two might go for his arms so he drew them back, crouching to bring his face down.

Ipan had dealt with four-legged pack hunters before, somewhere far back in ancestral memory, and knew innately that they lined up on a victim's outstretched limb, would go for the throat. The canines wanted to bowl him over, slash open the jugular, rip and shred in the vital seconds of surprise.

They gathered themselves, bundles of swift sinew, running nearly shoulder to shoulder, big heads up—and leaped.

In air, they were committed, Ipan knew. And open.

Ipan brought both hands up to grasp the canines' forelegs.

He threw himself backward, holding the legs tight, his hands barely beneath the jaws. The wirehounds' own momentum carried them over his head as he rolled backward.

Ipan rolled onto his back, yanking hard. The sudden snap slammed the canines forward. They could not get their heads turned around and down to close on his hand.

The leap, the catch, the quick pivot and swing, the heave—all combined in a centrifugal whirl that slung the wirehounds over Ipan as he himself went down, rolling. He felt the canines' legs snap and let go. They sailed over him with pained yelps.

Ipan rolled over completely, head tucked in, and came off his shoulders with a bound. He heard a solid thud, clacks as jaws snapped shut. A thump as the canines hit the grass, broken legs unable to cushion them.

He scrambled after them, his breath whistling. They were trying to get up, turning on snapped legs to confront their quarry. Still no barks, only faint whimpers of pain, sullen growls. One swore vehemently and quite obscenely. The other chanted, "Baaas'ard . . . baaas'ard . . ."

Animals turning in their vast, sorrowful night.

He jumped high and came down on both. His feet drove their necks into the ground and he felt bone give way. Before he stepped back to look he knew they were gone.

Ipan's blood surged with joy. Leon had never felt this tingling thrill, not even in the first immersion, when Ipan had killed a Stranger. Victory over these alien things with teeth and claws that come at you out of the night was a profound, inflaming pleasure.

Leon had done nothing. The victory was wholly Ipan's.

For a long moment Leon basked in it in the cool night air, felt the tremors of ecstasy.

Slowly, reason returned. There were other wirehounds. Ipan had caught these just right. Such luck did not strike twice.

The wirehounds were easy to see on the lawn. Would attract attention.

Ipan did not like touching them. Their bowels had emptied and the smell cut the air. They left a smear on the grass as he dragged them into the bushes.

Time, time. Someone would miss the canines, come to see.

Ipan was still pumped up from his victory. Leon used that to get him trotting across the broad lawn, taking advantage of shadows. Energy popped in Ipan's veins. Leon knew it was a mere momentary glandular joy, overlaying a deep fatigue. When it faded, Ipan would become dazed, hard to govern.

Every time he stopped he looked back and memorized landmarks. He might have to return this way on the run.

It was late and most of the Station was dark. In the technical area, though, a cluster of windows blossomed with what Ipan saw as impossibly rich, strange, superheated light.

He loped over to them and flattened himself against the wall. It helped that Ipan was fascinated by this strange citadel of the godlike humans. Out of his own curiosity he peeked in a window. Under enamel light a big assembly room sprawled, one that Leon recognized. There, centuries ago, he had formed up with the other brightly dressed tourists to go out on a trek.

Leon let the chimp's curiosity propel him around to the side, where he knew a door led into a long corridor. The door opened freely, to Leon's surprise. Ipan strolled down the slick tiles of the hallway, quizzically studying the phosphor-paint designs on the ceiling and walls, which emitted a soothing ivory glow.

An office doorway was open. Leon made Ipan squat and bob his head around the edge. Nobody there. It was a sumptuous den with shelves soaring into a vaulted ceiling. Leon remembered sitting there discussing the immersion process. That meant the immersion vessels were just a few doors away down—

The squeak of shoes on tiles made him turn.

ExSpec Ruben was behind him, leveling a weapon. In the cool light the man's face looked odd to Ipan's eyes, mysteriously bony.

Leon felt the rush of reverence in Ipan and let it carry the chimp forward, chippering softly. Ipan felt awe, not fear.

Leon wondered why Ruben said nothing and then realized that of course he could not reply.

Ruben tensed up, waving the snout of his ugly weapon. A metallic click. Ipan brought his hands up in a ritual chimp greeting and Ruben shot him.

The impact spun Ipan around. He went down, sprawling.

Ruben's mouth curled in derision. "Smart prof, huh? Didn't figure the alarm on the door, huh?"

The pain from Ipan's side was sharp, startling. Leon rode the hurt and gathering anger in Ipan, helping it build. Ipan felt his side and his hand came away sticky, smelling like warm iron in the chimp's nostrils.

Ruben circled around, weapon weaving. "You *killed* me, you weak little dope. Ruined a good experimental animal too. Now I got to figure what to do with you."

Leon threw his own anger atop Ipan's seethe. He felt the big muscles in the shoulders bunch. The pain in the side jabbed suddenly. Ipan groaned and rolled on the floor, pressing one hand to the wound.

Leon kept the head down so that Ipan could not see the blood that was running down now across the legs. Energy was running out of the chimp body. A seeping weakness came up the legs.

He pricked his ears to the shuffle of Ruben's feet. Another agonized roll, this time bringing the legs up in a curl.

"Guess there's really only one solution—"

Leon heard the metallic click.

Now, yes. He let his anger spill.

Ipan pressed up with his forearms and got his feet under him. No time to get all the way up. Ipan sprang at Ruben, keeping low.

A tinny shot whisked by his head. Then he hit Ruben in the hip and slammed the man against the wall. The man's scent was sour, salty.

Leon lost all control. Ipan bounced Ruben off the wall and instantly slammed arms into the man with full force.

Ruben tried to deflect the impact. Ipan pushed the puny human arms aside. Ruben's pathetic attempts at defense were like spiderwebs brushed away.

He butted Ruben and pounded massive shoulders into the man's chest. The weapon clattered on the tiles.

Ipan slammed himself into the man's body again and again.

Strength, power, joy.

Bones snapped. Ruben's head snapped back, smacked the wall, and he went limp.

Ipan stepped back and Ruben sagged to the tiles. *Joy.*

Blue-white flies buzzed at the rim of his vision.

Must move. That was all Leon could get through the curtain of emotions that shrouded the chimp mind.

The corridor lurched. Leon got Ipan to walk in a sidewise teeter.

Down the corridor, painful steps. Two doors, three. Here? Locked. Next door. World moving slower somehow.

The door snicked open. An antechamber that he recognized. Ipan blundered into a chair and almost fell. Leon made the lungs work hard. The gasping cleared his vision of the dark edges that had crept in but the blue-white flies were there, fluttering impatiently, and thicker.

He tried the far door. Locked. Leon summoned what he could from Ipan. *Strength, power, joy.* Ipan slammed his shoulder into the solid door. It held. Again. And again, sharp pain—and it popped open.

Right, this was it. The immersion bay. Ipan staggered into the array of vessels. The walk down the line, between banks of control panels, took an eternity. Leon concentrated on each step, placing each foot. Ipan's field of view bobbed as the head seemed to slip around on the liquid shoulders.

Here. His own vessel.

He fumbled with the latches. Popped it open.

There lay Leon Mattick, peaceful, eyes closed.

Emergency controls, yes. He knew them from the briefing.

He searched the polished steel surface and found the panel on the side. Ipan stared woozily at the meaningless lettering and Leon himself had trouble reading. The letters jumped and fused together.

He found several buttons and servo controls. Ipan's hands were stubby, wrong. It took three tries to get the reviving program activated. Lights cycled from green to amber.

Ipan abruptly sat down on the cool floor. The blue-white flies were buzzing all around his head now and they wanted to bite him. He sucked in the cool dry air but there was no substance in it, no help. . . .

Then, without any transition, he was looking at the ceiling. On his back. The lamps up there were getting dark, fading. Then they went out.

Leon's eyes snapped open.

The recovery program was still sending electrostims through his muscles. He let them jump and tingle and ache while he thought. He felt fine. Not even hungry, as he usually did after an immersion. How long had he been in the wilderness? At least five days.

He sat up. There was no one in the vessel room. Evidently Ruben had gotten some silent alarm, but had not alerted anyone else. That pointed, again, to a tight little conspiracy.

He got out shakily. To get free he had to detach some feeders and probes but they seemed simple enough.

Ipan. The big body filled the walkway. He knelt and felt for a pulse. Rickety.

But first, Kelly. Her vessel was next to his and he started the revival. She looked well.

Ruben must have put some transmission block on the system, so that none of the staff could tell by looking at the panel that anything was wrong. A simple cover story, a couple who wanted a really long immersion. Ruben had warned them, but no, they wanted it so. . . . A perfectly plausible story.

Kelly's eyes fluttered. He kissed her. She gasped.

He made a chimp sign, *quiet*, and went back to Ipan.

Blood came steadily. Leon was surprised to find that he could not pick up the rich, pungent elements in the blood from smell alone. A human missed so much!

He took off his shirt and made a crude tourniquet. At least Ipan's breathing was regular. Kelly was ready to get out by then and he helped her disconnect.

"I was hiding in a tree and then—poof!" she said. "What a relief. How did you—"

"Let's get moving," he said.

As they left the room she said, "Who can we trust? Whoever did this—" She stopped when she saw Ruben. "Oh."

Somehow her expression made him laugh. She was very rarely surprised.

"*You* did this?"

"Ipan."

"I never would have believed a chimp could, could . . ."

"I doubt anyone's been immersed this long. Not under such stress, anyway. It all just, well, it came out."

He picked up Ruben's weapon and studied the mechanism. A standard pistol, silenced. Ruben had not wanted to awaken the rest of the Station. That was promising. There should be people here who would spring to their aid. He started toward the building where the Station personnel lived.

"Wait, what about Ruben?"

"I'm going to wake up a doctor."

They did—but Leon took him into the vessel room first, to work on Ipan. Some patchwork and injections and the doctor said Ipan would be all right. Only then did he show the man Ruben's body.

The doctor got angry about that, but Leon had a gun. All he had to do was point it. He didn't say anything, just gestured with the gun. He did not feel like talking and wondered if he ever would again. When you couldn't talk you concentrated more, entered into things. Immersed.

And in any case, Ruben had been dead for some time.

Ipan had done a good job. The doctor shook his head at the severe damage.

Kelly looked at him oddly throughout the whole time. He did not understand why, until he realized that he had not even thought about helping Ruben first. Ipan was *himself*, in a sense he could not explain.

But he understood immediately when Kelly wanted to go to the Station wall and call to Sheelah. They brought her, too, in from the wild darkness.

A year later, when the industrial conspiracy had been uncovered and dozens brought to trial, they returned to the Excursion Station.

Leon longed to lounge in the sun, after a year of facing news cameras and attorneys. Kelly was equally exhausted with the rub of events.

But they both immediately booked time in the immersion chambers and spent long hours there. Ipan and Sheelah seemed to greet their return with something approximating joy.

Each year they would return and live inside the minds. Each year they would come away calmer, somehow fuller.

Leon's analysis of sociohistory appeared in a ground-breaking series of papers, modeling all of civilization as a "complex adaptive system." Fundamental to the intricately structured equations were terms allowing for primordial motivations, for group behavior in tension with individual longings, for deep motivations kindled in the veldt, over a thousand millennia ago. This was exact, complex, and original; his papers resounded through the social sciences, which had finally been made quantitative.

Fifteen years later the work received a Nobel prize, then worth 2.3 million New Dollars. Leon and Kelly spent a lot of it on travel, particularly to Africa.

When questioned in interviews, he never spoke of the long trek he and Kelly had undergone. Still, in his technical papers and public forums, he did give chimpanzees as examples of complex, adaptive behavior. As he spoke, he gave a long, slow smile, eyes glittering enigmatically, but would discuss the subject no further.

THE DEAD

Michael Swanwick

▼

We've been worried about technological unemployment for decades, but, as the bleak and elegant story that follows suggests, now there may be another threat to your job security: dead people. They're back from the grave and looking for work. . . .

Michael Swanwick made his debut in 1980, and has gone on to become one of the most popular and respected of all that decade's new writers. He has several times been a finalist for the Nebula Award, as well as for the World Fantasy Award and for the John W. Campbell Award, and has won the Theodore Sturgeon Memorial Award and the Asimov's *Readers Award poll. In 1991, his novel* Stations of the Tide *won him a Nebula Award as well, and last year he won the World Fantasy Award for his story "Radio Waves." His other books include his first novel,* In the Drift, *which was published in 1985, a novella-length book,* Griffin's Egg, *and 1987's popular novel* Vacuum Flowers. *His critically acclaimed short fiction has been assembled in* Gravity's Angels *and in a collection of his collaborative short work with other writers,* Slow Dancing Through Time. *His most recent book is a new novel,* The Iron Dragon's Daughter, *which was a finalist for the World Fantasy Award and the Arthur C. Clarke Award. He's just completed a new novel,* Jack Faust. *He's had stories in our Second, Third, Fourth, Sixth, Seventh, Tenth, and Thirteenth Annual Collections. Swanwick lives in Philadelphia with his wife, Marianne Porter, and their son Sean.*

Three boy zombies in matching red jackets bused our table, bringing water, lighting candles, brushing away the crumbs between courses. Their eyes were dark, attentive, lifeless; their hands and faces so white as to be faintly luminous in the hushed light. I thought it in bad taste, but "This is Manhattan," Courtney said. "A certain studied offensiveness is fashionable here."

The blond brought menus and waited for our order.

We both ordered pheasant. "An excellent choice," the boy said in a clear, emotionless voice. He went away and came back a minute later with the freshly strangled birds, holding them up for our approval. He couldn't have been more than eleven when he died and his skin was of that sort connoisseurs call "milk-glass," smooth, without blemish, and all but translucent. He must have cost a fortune.

As the boy was turning away, I impulsively touched his shoulder. He turned back. "What's your name, son?" I asked.

"Timothy." He might have been telling me the *specialité de maison*. The boy waited a breath to see if more was expected of him, then left.

Courtney gazed after him. "How lovely he would look," she murmured, "nude. Standing in the moonlight by a cliff. Definitely a cliff. Perhaps the very one where he met his death."

"He wouldn't look very lovely if he'd fallen off a cliff."

"Oh, don't be unpleasant."

The wine steward brought our bottle. "Château Latour '17." I raised an eyebrow. The steward had the sort of old and complex face that Rembrandt would have enjoyed painting. He poured with pulseless ease and then dissolved into the gloom. "Good lord, Courtney, you *seduced* me on cheaper."

She flushed, not happily. Courtney had a better career going than I. She outpowered me. We both knew who was smarter, better connected, more likely to end up in a corner office with the historically significant antique desk. The only edge I had was that I was a male in a seller's market. It was enough.

"This is a business dinner, Donald," she said, "nothing more."

I favored her with an expression of polite disbelief I knew from experience she'd find infuriating. And, digging into my pheasant, murmured, "Of course." We didn't say much of consequence until dessert, when I finally asked, "So what's Loeb-Soffner up to these days?"

"Structuring a corporate expansion. Jim's putting together the financial side of the package, and I'm doing personnel. You're being headhunted, Donald." She favored me with that feral little flash of teeth she made when she saw something she wanted. Courtney wasn't a beautiful woman, far from it. But there was that fierceness to her, that sense of something primal being held under tight and precarious control that made her hot as hot to me. "You're talented, you're thuggish, and you're not too tightly nailed to your present position. Those are all qualities we're looking for."

She dumped her purse on the table, took out a single-folded sheet of paper. "These are the terms I'm offering." She placed it by my plate, attacked her torte with gusto.

I unfolded the paper. "This is a lateral transfer."

"Unlimited opportunity for advancement," she said with her mouth full, "if you've got the stuff."

"Mmm." I did a line-by-line of the benefits, all comparable to what I was getting now. My current salary to the dollar—Ms. Soffner was showing off. And the stock options. "This can't be right. Not for a lateral."

There was that grin again, like a glimpse of shark in murky waters. "I knew you'd like it. We're going over the top with the options because we need your answer right away—tonight preferably. Tomorrow at the latest. No negotiations. We have to put the package together fast. There's going to be a shitstorm of publicity when this comes out. We want to have everything nailed down, present the fundies and bleeding hearts with a *fait accompli*."

"My God, Courtney, what kind of monster do you have hold of now?"

"The biggest one in the world. Bigger than Apple. Bigger than Home Virtual. Bigger than HIVac-IV," she said with relish. "Have you ever heard of Koestler Biological?"

I put my fork down.

"Koestler? You're peddling corpses now?"

"Please. Postanthropic biological resources." She said it lightly, with just the right touch of irony. Still, I thought I detected a certain discomfort with the nature of her client's product.

"There's no money in it." I waved a hand toward our attentive waitstaff. "These guys must be—what—maybe two percent of the annual turnover? Zombies are luxury goods: servants, reactor cleanups, Hollywood stunt deaths, exotic services"—we both knew what I meant—"a few hundred a year, maybe, tops. There's not the demand. The revulsion factor is too great."

"There's been a technological breakthrough." Courtney leaned forward. "They can install the infrasystem and controllers and offer the product for the factory-floor cost of a new subcompact. That's way below the economic threshold for blue-collar labor.

"Look at it from the viewpoint of a typical factory owner. He's already down-sized to the bone and labor costs are bleeding him dry. How can he compete in a dwindling consumer market? Now let's imagine he buys into the program." She took out her Mont Blanc and began scribbling figures on the tablecloth. "No benefits. No liability suits. No sick pay. No pilferage. We're talking about cutting labor costs by at least two thirds. Minimum! That's irresistible, I don't care how big your revulsion factor is. We project we can move five hundred thousand units in the first year."

"Five hundred thousand," I said. "That's crazy. Where the hell are you going to get the raw material for—?"

"Africa."

"Oh, God, Courtney." I was struck wordless by the cynicism it took to even consider turning the sub-Saharan tragedy to a profit, by the sheer, raw evil of channeling hard currency to the pocket Hitlers who ran the camps. Courtney only smiled and gave that quick little flip of her head that meant she was accessing the time on an optic chip.

"I think you're ready," she said, "to talk with Koestler."

At her gesture, the zombie boys erected projector lamps about us, fussed with the settings, turned them on. Interference patterns moiréd, clashed, meshed. Walls of darkness erected themselves about us. Courtney took out her flat and set it up on the table. Three taps of her nailed fingers and the round and hairless face of Marvin Koestler appeared on the screen. "Ah, Courtney!" he said in a pleased voice. "You're in—New York, yes? The San Moritz. With Donald." The slightest pause with each accessed bit of information. "Did you have the antelope medallions?" When we shook our heads, he kissed his fingertips. "Magnificent! They're ever so lightly braised and then smothered in buffalo mozzarella. Nobody makes them better. I had the same dish in Florence the other day, and there was simply no comparison."

I cleared my throat. "Is that where you are? Italy?"

"Let's leave out where I am." He made a dismissive gesture, as if it were a trifle. But Courtney's face darkened. Corporate kidnapping being the growth industry it is, I'd gaffed badly. "The question is—what do you think of my offer?"

"It's . . . interesting. For a lateral."

"It's the start-up costs. We're leveraged up to our asses as it is. You'll make out better this way in the long run." He favored me with a sudden grin that went mean around the edges. Very much the financial buccaneer. Then he leaned forward, lowered his voice, maintained firm eye contact. Classic people-handling techniques. "You're not sold. You know you can trust Courtney to have checked out the finances. Still, you think: It won't work. To work the product has to be irresistible, and it's not. It can't be."

"Yes, sir," I said. "Succinctly put."

He nodded to Courtney. "Let's sell this young man." And to me, "My stretch is downstairs."

He winked out.

Koestler was waiting for us in the limo, a ghostly pink presence. His holo, rather, a genial if somewhat coarse-grained ghost afloat in golden light. He waved an expansive and insubstantial arm to take in the interior of the car and said, "Make yourselves at home."

The chauffeur wore combat-grade photomultipliers. They gave him a buggish, inhuman look. I wasn't sure if he was dead or not. "Take us to Heaven," Koestler said.

The doorman stepped out into the street, looked both ways, nodded to the chauffeur. Robot guns tracked our progress down the block.

"Courtney tells me you're getting the raw materials from Africa."

"Distasteful, but necessary. To begin with. We have to sell the idea first—no reason to make things rough on ourselves. Down the line, though, I don't see why we can't go domestic. Something along the lines of a reverse mortgage, perhaps, life insurance that pays off while you're still alive. It'd be a step toward getting the poor off our backs at last. Fuck 'em. They've been getting a goddamn free ride for too long; the least they can do is to die and provide us with servants."

I was pretty sure Koestler was joking. But I smiled and ducked my head, so I'd be covered in either case. "What's Heaven?" I asked, to move the conversation onto safer territory.

"A proving ground," Koestler said with great satisfaction, "for the future. Have you ever witnessed bare-knuckles fisticuffs?"

"No."

"Ah, now there's a sport for gentlemen! The sweet science at its sweetest. No rounds, no rules, no holds barred. It gives you the real measure of a man—not just of his strength but his character. How he handles himself, whether he keeps cool under pressure—how he stands up to pain. Security won't let me go to the clubs in person, but I've made arrangements."

Heaven was a converted movie theater in a run-down neighborhood in Queens. The chauffeur got out, disappeared briefly around the back, and returned with two zombie bodyguards. It was like a conjurer's trick. "You had these guys stashed in the *trunk*?" I asked as he opened the door for us.

"It's a new world," Courtney said. "Get used to it."

The place was mobbed. Two, maybe three hundred seats, standing room only.

A mixed crowd, blacks and Irish and Koreans mostly, but with a smattering of uptown customers as well. You didn't have to be poor to need the occasional taste of vicarious potency. Nobody paid us any particular notice. We'd come in just as the fighters were being presented.

"Weighing two-five-oh, in black trunks with a red stripe," the ref was bawling, "tha gang-bang *gang*sta, the bare-knuckle *brawla*, the man with tha—"

Courtney and I went up a scummy set of back stairs. Bodyguard-us-bodyguard, as if we were a combat patrol out of some twentieth-century jungle war. A scrawny, potbellied old geezer with a damp cigar in his mouth unlocked the door to our box. Sticky floor, bad seats, a good view down on the ring. Gray plastic matting, billowing smoke.

Koestler was there, in a shiny new hologram shell. It reminded me of those plaster Madonnas in painted bathtubs that Catholics set out in their yards. "Your permanent box?" I asked.

"All of this is for your sake, Donald—you and a few others. We're pitting our product one-on-one against some of the local talent. By arrangement with the management. What you're going to see will settle your doubts once and for all."

"You'll like this," Courtney said. "I've been here five nights straight. Counting tonight." The bell rang, starting the fight. She leaned forward avidly, hooking her elbows on the railing.

The zombie was gray-skinned and modestly muscled, for a fighter. But it held up its hands alertly, was light on its feet, and had strangely calm and knowing eyes.

Its opponent was a real bruiser, a big black guy with classic African features twisted slightly out of true, so that his mouth curled up in a kind of sneer on one side. He had gang scars on his chest and even uglier marks on his back that didn't look deliberate but like something he'd earned on the streets. His eyes burned with an intensity just this side of madness.

He came forward cautiously but not fearfully, and made a couple of quick jabs to get the measure of his opponent. They were blocked and countered.

They circled each other, looking for an opening.

For a minute or so, nothing much happened. Then the gangster feinted at the zombie's head, drawing up its guard. He drove through that opening with a slam to the zombie's nuts that made me wince.

No reaction.

The dead fighter responded with a flurry of punches, and got in a glancing blow to its opponent's cheek. They separated, engaged, circled around.

Then the big guy exploded in a combination of killer blows, connecting so solidly it seemed they would splinter every rib in the dead fighter's body. It brought the crowd to their feet, roaring their approval.

The zombie didn't even stagger.

A strange look came into the gangster's eyes, then, as the zombie counterattacked, driving him back into the ropes. I could only imagine what it must be like for a man who had always lived by his strength and his ability to absorb punishment to realize that he was facing an opponent to whom pain meant nothing. Fights were lost and won by flinches and hesitations. You won by keeping your head. You lost by getting rattled.

Despite his best blows, the zombie stayed methodical, serene, calm, relentless. That was its nature.

It must have been devastating.

The fight went on and on. It was a strange and alienating experience for me. After a while I couldn't stay focused on it. My thoughts kept slipping into a zone where I found myself studying the line of Courtney's jaw, thinking about later tonight. She liked her sex just a little bit sick. There was always a feeling, fucking her, that there was something truly repulsive that she *really* wanted to do but lacked the courage to bring up on her own.

So there was always this urge to get her to do something she didn't like. She was resistant; I never dared try more than one new thing per date. But I could always talk her into that one thing. Because when she was aroused, she got pliant. She could be talked into anything. She could be made to beg for it.

Courtney would've been amazed to learn that I was not proud of what I did with her—quite the opposite, in fact. But I was as obsessed with her as she was with whatever it was that obsessed her.

Suddenly Courtney was on her feet, yelling. The hologram showed Koestler on his feet as well. The big guy was on the ropes, being pummeled. Blood and spittle flew from his face with each blow. Then he was down; he'd never even had a chance. He must've known early on that it was hopeless, that he wasn't going to win, but he'd refused to take a fall. He had to be pounded into the ground. He went down raging, proud and uncomplaining. I had to admire that.

But he lost anyway.

That, I realized, was the message I was meant to take away from this. Not just that the product was robust. But that only those who backed it were going to win. I could see, even if the audience couldn't, that it was the end of an era. A man's body wasn't worth a damn anymore. There wasn't anything it could do that technology couldn't handle better. The number of losers in the world had just doubled, tripled, reached maximum. What the fools below were cheering for was the death of their futures.

I got up and cheered too.

In the stretch afterward, Koestler said, "You've seen the light. You're a believer now."

"I haven't necessarily decided yet."

"Don't bullshit me," Koestler said. "I've done my homework, Mr. Nichols. Your current position is not exactly secure. Morton-Western is going down the tubes. The entire service sector is going down the tubes. Face it, the old economic order is as good as fucking gone. Of course you're going to take my offer. You don't have any other choice."

The fax outed sets of contracts. "A Certain Product," it said here and there. Corpses were never mentioned.

But when I opened my jacket to get a pen Koestler said, "Wait, I've got a factory. Three thousand positions under me. I've got a motivated workforce. They'd walk through fire to keep their jobs. Pilferage is at zero. Sick time practically the same. Give me one advantage your product has over my current workforce. Sell me on it. I'll give you thirty seconds."

I wasn't in sales and the job had been explicitly promised me already. But by reaching for the pen, I had admitted I wanted the position. And we all knew whose hand carried the whip.

"They can be catheterized," I said—"no toilet breaks."

For a long instant Koestler just stared at me blankly. Then he exploded with laughter. "By God, that's a new one! You have a great future ahead of you, Donald. Welcome aboard."

He winked out.

We drove on in silence for a while, aimless, directionless. At last Courtney leaned forward and touched the chauffeur's shoulder.

"Take me home," she said.

Riding through Manhattan I suffered from a waking hallucination that we were driving through a city of corpses. Gray faces, listless motions. Everyone looked dead in the headlights and sodium-vapor streetlamps. Passing by the Children's Museum I saw a mother with a stroller through the glass doors. Two small children by her side. They all three stood motionless, gazing forward at nothing. We passed by a stop-and-go where zombies stood out on the sidewalk drinking forties in paper bags. Through upper-story windows I could see the sad rainbow trace of virtuals playing to empty eyes. There were zombies in the park, zombies smoking blunts, zombies driving taxies, zombies sitting on stoops and hanging out on street corners, all of them waiting for the years to pass and the flesh to fall from their bones.

I felt like the last man alive.

Courtney was still wired and sweaty from the fight. The pheromones came off her in great waves as I followed her down the hall to her apartment. She stank of lust. I found myself thinking of how she got just before orgasm, so desperate, so desirable. It was different after she came, she would fall into a state of calm assurance; the same sort of calm assurance she showed in her business life, the aplomb she sought so wildly during the act itself.

And when that desperation left her, so would I. Because even I could recognize that it was her desperation that drew me to her, that made me do the things she needed me to do. In all the years I'd known her, we'd never once had breakfast together.

I wished there was some way I could deal her out of the equation. I wished that her desperation were a liquid that I could drink down to the dregs. I wished I could drop her in a winepress and squeeze her dry.

At her apartment, Courtney unlocked her door and in one complicated movement twisted through and stood facing me from the inside. "Well," she said. "All in all, a productive evening. Good night, Donald."

"Good night? Aren't you going to invite me inside?"

"No."

"What do you mean, no?" She was beginning to piss me off. A blind man could've told she was in heat from across the street. A chimpanzee could've talked his way into her pants. "What kind of idiot game are you playing now?"

"You know what no means, Donald. You're not stupid."

"No I'm not, and neither are you. We both know the score. Now let me in, goddamnit."

"Enjoy your present," she said, and closed the door.

I found Courtney's present back in my suite. I was still seething from her treatment of me and stalked into the room, letting the door slam behind me so that I was standing in near-total darkness. The only light was what little seeped through the draped windows at the far end of the room. I was just reaching for the light switch when there was a motion in the darkness.

Jackers! I thought, and all in panic lurched for the light switch, hoping to achieve I don't know what. Credit-jackers always work in trios, one to torture the security codes out of you, one to phone the numbers out of your accounts and into a fiscal trapdoor, a third to stand guard. Was turning the lights on supposed to make them scurry for darkness, like roaches? Nevertheless, I almost tripped over my own feet in my haste to reach the switch. But of course it was nothing like what I'd feared.

It was a woman.

She stood by the window in a white silk dress that could neither compete with nor distract from her ethereal beauty, her porcelain skin. When the lights came on, she turned toward me, eyes widening, lips parting slightly. Her breasts swayed ever so slightly as she gracefully raised a bare arm to offer me a lily. "Hello, Donald," she said huskily. "I'm yours for the night." She was absolutely beautiful.

And dead, of course.

Not twenty minutes later I was hammering on Courtney's door. She came to the door in a Pierre Cardin dressing gown and from the way she was still cinching the sash and the disarray of her hair I gathered she hadn't been expecting me.

"I'm not alone," she said.

"I didn't come here for the dubious pleasures of your fair white body." I pushed my way into the room. (But couldn't help remembering that beautiful body of hers, not so exquisite as the dead whore's, and now the thoughts were inextricably mingled in my head: death and Courtney, sex and corpses, a Gordian knot I might never be able to untangle.)

"You didn't like my surprise?" She was smiling openly now, amused.

"No, I fucking did not!"

I took a step toward her. I was shaking. I couldn't stop fisting and unfisting my hands.

She fell back a step. But that confident, oddly expectant look didn't leave her face. "Bruno," she said lightly. "Would you come in here?"

A motion at the periphery of vision. Bruno stepped out of the shadows of her bedroom. He was a muscular brute, pumped, ripped, and as black as the fighter I'd seen go down earlier that night. He stood behind Courtney, totally naked, with slim hips and wide shoulders and the finest skin I'd ever seen.

And dead.

I saw it all in a flash.

"Oh, for God's sake, Courtney!" I said, disgusted. "I can't believe you. That you'd actually . . . That thing's just an obedient body. There's nothing there—no passion, no connection, just . . . physical presence."

Courtney made a kind of chewing motion through her smile, weighing the implications of what she was about to say. Nastiness won.

"We have equity now," she said.

I lost it then. I stepped forward, raising a hand, and I swear to God I intended to bounce the bitch's head off the back wall. But she didn't flinch—she didn't even look afraid. She merely moved aside, saying, "In the body, Bruno. He has to look good in a business suit."

A dead fist smashed into my ribs so hard I thought for an instant my heart had stopped. Then Bruno punched me in my stomach. I doubled over, gasping. Two, three, four more blows. I was on the ground now, rolling over, helpless and weeping with rage.

"That's enough, baby. Now put out the trash."

Bruno dumped me in the hallway.

I glared up at Courtney through my tears. She was not at all beautiful now. Not in the least. You're getting older, I wanted to tell her. But instead I heard my voice, angry and astonished, saying, "You . . . you goddamn, fucking necrophile!"

"Cultivate a taste for it," Courtney said. Oh, she was purring! I doubted she'd ever find life quite this good again. "Half a million Brunos are about to come on the market. You're going to find it a lot more difficult to pick up *living* women in not so very long."

I sent away the dead whore. Then I took a long shower that didn't really make me feel any better. Naked, I walked into my unlit suite and opened the curtains. For a long time I stared out over the glory and darkness that was Manhattan.

I was afraid, more afraid than I'd ever been in my life.

The slums below me stretched to infinity. They were a vast necropolis, a never-ending city of the dead. I thought of the millions out there who were never going to hold down a job again. I thought of how they must hate me—me and my kind—and how helpless they were before us. And yet. There were so many of them and so few of us. If they were to all rise up at once, they'd be like a tsunami, irresistible. And if there was so much as a spark of life left in them, then that was exactly what they would do.

That was one possibility. There was one other, and that was that nothing would happen. Nothing at all.

God help me, but I didn't know which one scared me more.

THE FLOWERS OF AULIT PRISON

Nancy Kress

▼

Born in Buffalo, New York, Nancy Kress now lives in Brockport, New York. She began selling her elegant and incisive stories in the mid-seventies, and has since become a frequent contributor to Asimov's Science Fiction, The Magazine of Fantasy & Science Fiction, Omni, *and elsewhere. Her books include the novels* The Prince of Morning Bells, The Golden Grove, The White Pipes, An Alien Light, *and* Brain Rose, *and the collections* Trinity and Other Stories *and* The Aliens of Earth. *Her most recent books are the novel version of her Hugo- and Nebula-winning story,* Beggars in Spain; *a sequel,* Beggars and Choosers; *a new novel,* Oaths & Miracles; *and most recently, the third "Beggars" volume,* Beggars Ride. *She has also won a Nebula Award for her story "Out of All Them Bright Stars." She has had stories in our Second, Third, Sixth, Seventh, Eighth, Ninth, Tenth, Eleventh, Twelfth, and Thirteenth Annual Collections.*

Here she transports us to a distant alien world for a troubling study of loyalty, duty, compulsion, and the way things change depending on how you look at them. . . .

My sister lies sweetly on the bed across the room from mine. She lies on her back, fingers lightly curled, her legs stretched straight as elindel trees. Her pert little nose, much prettier than my own, pokes delicately into the air. Her skin glows like a fresh flower. But not with health. She is, of course, dead.

I slip out of my bed and stand swaying a moment, with morning dizziness. A Terran healer once told me my blood pressure was too low, which is the sort of nonsensical thing Terrans will sometimes say—like announcing the air is too moist. The air is what it is, and so am I.

What I am is a murderer.

I kneel in front of my sister's glass coffin. My mouth has that awful morning taste, even though last night I drank nothing stronger than water. Almost I yawn, but at the last moment I turn it into a narrow-lipped ringing in my ears that somehow leaves my mouth tasting worse than ever. But at least I haven't disrespected Ano. She was my only sibling and closest friend, until I replaced her with illusion.

"Two more years, Ano," I say, "less forty-two days. Then you will be free. And so will I."

Ano, of course, says nothing. There is no need. She knows as well as I the time until her burial, when she can be released from the chemicals and glass that bind her dead body and can rejoin our ancestors. Others I have known whose relatives were under atonement bondage said the bodies complained and recriminated, especially in dreams, making the house a misery. Ano is more considerate. Her corpse never troubles me at all. I do that to myself.

I finish the morning prayers, leap up, and stagger dizzily to the piss closet. I may not have drunk pel last night, but my bladder is nonetheless bursting.

At noon a messenger rides into my yard on a Terran bicycle. The bicycle is an attractive design, sloping, with interesting curves. Adapted for our market, undoubtedly. The messenger is less attractive, a surly boy probably in his first year of government service. When I smile at him, he looks away. He would rather be someplace else. Well, if he doesn't perform his messenger duties with more courteous cheer, he will be.

"Letter for Uli Pek Bengarin."

"I am Uli Pek Bengarin."

Scowling, he hands me the letter and pedals away. I don't take the scowl personally. The boy does not, of course, know what I am, any more than my neighbors do. That would defeat the whole point. I am supposed to pass as fully real, until I can earn the right to resume being so.

The letter is shaped into a utilitarian circle, very business-like, with a generic government seal. It could have come from the Tax Section, or Community Relief, or Processions and Rituals. But of course it hasn't; none of those sections would write to me until I am real again. The sealed letter is from Reality and Atonement. It's a summons; they have a job for me.

And about time. I have been home nearly six weeks since the last job, shaping my flower beds and polishing dishes and trying to paint a skyscape of last month's synchrony, when all six moons were visible at once. I paint badly. It is time for another job.

I pack my shoulder sack, kiss the glass of my sister's coffin, and lock the house. Then I wheel my bicycle—not, alas, as interestingly curved as the messenger's—out of its shed and pedal down the dusty road toward the city.

Frablit Pek Brimmidin is nervous. This interests me; Pek Brimmidin is usually a calm, controlled man, the sort who never replaces reality with illusion. He's given me my previous jobs with no fuss. But now he actually can't sit still; he fidgets back and forth across his small office, which is cluttered with papers, stone sculptures in an exaggerated style I don't like at all, and plates of half-eaten food. I don't comment on either the food or the pacing. I am fond of Pek Brimmidin, quite apart from my gratitude to him, which is profound. He was the official in R&A who voted to give me a chance to become real again. The other two judges voted for perpetual death, no chance of atonement. I'm not supposed to know this much detail about my own case, but I do. Pek Brimmidin is middle-aged, a stocky man whose neck fur has just begun to yellow. His eyes are gray, and kind.

"Pek Bengarin," he says, finally, and then stops.

"I stand ready to serve," I say softly, so as not to make him even more nervous. But something is growing heavy in my stomach. This does not look good.

"Pek Bengarin." Another pause. "You are an informer."

"I stand ready to serve our shared reality," I repeat, despite my astonishment. Of course I'm an informer. I've been an informer for two years and eighty-two days. I killed my sister, and I will be an informer until my atonement is over, I can be fully real again, and Ano can be released from death to join our ancestors. Pek Brimmidin knows this. He's assigned me every one of my previous informing jobs, from the first easy one in currency counterfeiting right through the last one, in baby stealing. I'm a very good informer, as Pek Brimmidin also knows. What's wrong with the man?

Suddenly Pek Brimmidin straightens. But he doesn't look me in the eye. "You are an informer, and the Section for Reality and Atonement has an informing job for you. In Aulit Prison."

So that's it. I go still. Aulit Prison holds criminals. Not just those who have tried to get away with stealing or cheating or child-snatching, which are, after all, normal. Aulit Prison holds those who are unreal, who have succumbed to the illusion that they are not part of shared common reality and so may do violence to the most concrete reality of others: their physical bodies. Maimers. Rapists. Murderers.

Like me.

I feel my left hand tremble, and I strive to control it and to not show how hurt I am. I thought Pek Brimmidin thought better of me. There is of course no such thing as partial atonement—one is either real or one is not—but a part of my mind nonetheless thought that Pek Brimmidin had recognized two years and eighty-two days of effort in regaining my reality. I have worked so hard.

He must see some of this on my face because he says quickly, "I am sorry to assign this job to you, Pek. I wish I had a better one. But you've been requested specifically by Rafkit Sarloe." Requested by the capital; my spirits lift slightly. "They've added a note to the request. I am authorized to tell you the informant job carries additional compensation. If you succeed, your debt will be considered immediately paid, and you can be restored at once to reality."

Restored at once to reality. I would again be a full member of World, without shame. Entitled to live in the real world of shared humanity, and to hold my head up with pride. And Ano could be buried, the artificial chemicals washed from her body, so that it could return to World and her sweet spirit could join our ancestors. Ano, too, would be restored to reality.

"I'll do it," I tell Pek Brimmidin. And then, formally, "I stand ready to serve our shared reality."

"One more thing, before you agree, Pek Bengarin." Pek Brimmidin is fidgeting again. "The suspect is a Terran."

I have never before informed on a Terran. Aulit Prison, of course, holds those aliens who have been judged unreal: Terrans, Fallers, the weird little Huhuhubs. The problem is that even after thirty years of ships coming to World, there is still considerable debate about whether *any* aliens are real at all. Clearly their bodies exist; after all, here they are. But their thinking is so disordered they might almost qualify as all being unable to recognize shared social reality, and so just as unreal as those poor empty children who never attain reason and must be destroyed.

Usually we on World just leave the aliens alone, except of course for trading with them. The Terrans in particular offer interesting objects, such as bicycles, and ask in return worthless items, mostly perfectly obvious information. But do any of the aliens have souls, capable of recognizing and honoring a shared reality with the souls of others? At the universities, the argument goes on. Also in market squares and pel shops, which is where I hear it. Personally, I think aliens may well be real. I try not to be a bigot.

I say to Pek Brimmidin, "I am willing to inform on a Terran."

He wiggles his hand in pleasure. "Good, good. You will enter Aulit Prison a Capmonth before the suspect is brought there. You will use your primary cover, please."

I nod, although Pek Brimmidin knows this is not easy for me. My primary cover is the truth: I killed my sister Ano Pek Bengarin two years and eighty-two days ago and was judged unreal enough for perpetual death, never able to join my ancestors. The only untrue part of the cover is that I escaped and have been hiding from the Section police ever since.

"You have just been captured," Pek Brimmidin continues, "and assigned to the first part of your death in Aulit. The Section records will show this."

Again I nod, not looking at him. The first part of my death in Aulit, the second, when the time came, in the kind of chemical bondage that holds Ano. And never ever to be freed—*ever*. What if it were true? I should go mad. Many do.

"The suspect is named 'Carryl Walters.' He is a Terran healer. He murdered a World child, in an experiment to discover how real people's brains function. His sentence is perpetual death. But the Section believes that Carryl Walters was working with a group of World people in these experiments. That somewhere on World there is a group that's so lost its hold on reality that it would murder children to investigate science."

For a moment the room wavers, including the exaggerated swooping curves of Pek Brimmidin's ugly sculptures. But then I get hold of myself. I am an informer, and a good one. I can do this. I am redeeming myself, and releasing Ano. I am an informer.

"I'll find out who this group is," I say. "And what they're doing, and where they are."

Pek Brimmidin smiles at me. "Good." His trust is a dose of shared reality: two people acknowledging their common perceptions together, without lies or violence. I need this dose. It is probably the last one I will have for a long time.

How do people manage in perpetual death, fed on only solitary illusion?

Aulit Prison must be full of the mad.

Traveling to Aulit takes two days of hard riding. Somewhere my bicycle loses a bolt and I wheel it to the next village. The woman who runs the bicycle shop is competent but mean, the sort who gazes at shared reality mostly to pick out the ugly parts.

"At least it's not a *Terran* bicycle."

"At least," I say, but she is incapable of recognizing sarcasm.

"Sneaky soulless criminals, taking us over bit by bit. We should never have allowed them in. And the government is supposed to protect us from unreal slime, ha, what a joke. Your bolt is a nonstandard size."

"Is it?" I say.

"Yes. Costs you extra."

I nod. Behind the open rear door of the shop, two little girls play in a thick stand of moonweed.

"We should kill all the aliens," the repairer says. "No shame in destroying them before they corrupt us."

"Eurummmn," I say. Informers are not supposed to make themselves conspicuous with political debate. Above the two children's heads, the moonweed bends gracefully in the wind. One of the little girls has long brown neck fur, very pretty. The other does not.

"There, that bolt will hold fine. Where you from?"

"Rafkit Sarloe." Informers never name their villages.

She gives an exaggerated shudder. "I would never visit the capital. Too many aliens. They destroy *our* participation in shared reality without a moment's thought! Three and eight, please."

I want to say, *No one but you can destroy your own participation in shared reality*, but I don't. Silently I pay her the money.

She glares at me, at the world. "You don't believe me about the Terrans. But I know what I know!"

I ride away, through the flowered countryside. In the sky, only Cap is visible, rising on the horizon opposite the sun. Cap glows with a clear white smoothness, like Ano's skin.

The Terrans, I am told, have only one moon. Shared reality on their world is, perhaps, skimpier than ours: less curved, less rich, less warm.

Are they ever jealous?

Aulit Prison sits on a flat plain inland from the South Coast. I know that other islands on World have their own prisons, just as they have their own governments, but only Aulit is used for the alien unreal, as well as our own. A special agreement among the governments of World makes this possible. The alien governments protest, but of course it does them no good. The unreal is the unreal, and far too painful and dangerous to have running around loose. Besides, the alien governments are far away on other stars.

Aulit is huge and ugly, a straight-lined monolith of dull red stone, with no curves anywhere. An official from R&A meets me and turns me over to two prison guards. We enter through a barred gate, my bicycle chained to the guards', and I to my bicycle. I am led across a wide dusty yard toward a stone wall. The guards of course don't speak to me; I am unreal.

My cell is square, twice my length on a side. There is a bed, a piss pot, a table, and a single chair. The door is without a window, and all the other doors in the row of cells are closed.

"When will the prisoners be allowed to be all together?" I ask, but of course the guard doesn't answer me. I am not real.

I sit in my chair and wait. Without a clock, it's difficult to judge time, but I think a few hours pass totally without event. Then a gong sounds and my door slides up into the ceiling. Ropes and pulleys, controlled from above, inaccessible from inside the cell.

The corridor fills with illusionary people. Men and women, some with yellowed neck fur and sunken eyes, walking with the shuffle of old age. Some young, striding along with that dangerous mixture of anger and desperation. And the aliens.

I have seen aliens before, but not so many together. Fallers, about our size but very dark, as if burned crisp by their distant star. They wear their neck fur very long and dye it strange bright colors, although not in prison. Terrans, who don't even have neck fur but instead fur on their heads, which they sometimes cut into fanciful curves—rather pretty. Terrans are a little intimidating because of their size. They move slowly. Ano, who had one year at the university before I killed her, once told me that the Terrans' world makes them feel lighter than ours does. I don't understand this, but Ano was very intelligent and so it's probably true. She also explained that Fallers, Terrans, and World people are somehow related far back in time, but this is harder to believe. Perhaps Ano was mistaken.

Nobody ever thinks Huhuhubs could be related to us. Tiny, scuttling, ugly, dangerous, they walk on all fours. They're covered with warts. They smell bad. I was glad to see only a few of them, sticking close together, in the corridor at Aulit.

We all move toward a large room filled with rough tables and chairs and, in the corner, a trough for the Huhuhubs. The food is already on the tables. Cereal, flatbread, elindel fruit—very basic, but nutritious. What surprises me most is the total absence of guards. Apparently prisoners are allowed to do whatever they wish to the food, the room, or each other, without interference. Well, why not? We aren't real.

I need protection, quickly.

I choose a group of two women and three men. They sit at a table with their backs to the wall, and others have left a respectful distance around them. From the way they group themselves, the oldest woman is the leader. I plant myself in front of her and look directly into her face. A long scar ridges her left cheek to disappear into grizzled neck fur.

"I am Uli Pek Bengarin," I say, my voice even but too low to be heard beyond this group. "In Aulit for the murder of my sister. I can be useful to you."

She doesn't speak, and her flat dark eyes don't waver, but I have her attention. Other prisoners watch furtively.

"I know an informer among the guards. He knows I know. He brings things into Aulit for me, in return for not sharing his name."

Still her eyes don't waver. But I see she believes me; the sheer outrage of my statement has convinced her. A guard who had already forfeited reality by informing—by violating shared reality—might easily turn it to less pernicious material advantage. Once reality is torn, the rents grow. For the same reason, she easily believes that I might violate my supposed agreement with the guard.

"What sort of things?" she says, carelessly. Her voice is raspy and thick, like some hairy root.

"Letters. Candy. Pel." Intoxicants are forbidden in prison; they promote shared conviviality, to which the unreal have no right.

"Weapons?"

"Perhaps," I say.

"And why shouldn't I beat this guard's name out of you and set up my own arrangement with him?"

"He will not. He is my cousin." This is the trickiest part of the cover provided to me by R&A Section; it requires that my would-be protector believe in a person who has kept enough sense of reality to honor family ties but will nonetheless violate a larger shared reality. I told Pek Brimmidin that I doubted that such a twisted state of mind would be very stable, and so a seasoned prisoner would not believe in it. But Pek Brimmidin was right and I was wrong. The woman nods.

''All right. Sit down.''

She does not ask what I wish in return for the favors of my supposed cousin. She knows. I sit beside her, and from now on I am physically safe in Aulit Prison from all but her.

Next, I must somehow befriend a Terran.

This proves harder than I expect. The Terrans keep to themselves, and so do we. They are just as violent toward their own as all the mad doomed souls in Aulit; the place is every horror whispered by children trying to shock each other. Within a tenday, I see two World men hold down and rape a woman. No one interferes. I see a Terran gang beat a Faller. I see a World woman knife another woman, who bleeds to death on the stone floor. This is the only time guards appear, heavily armored. A priest is with them. He wheels in a coffin of chemicals and immediately immerses the body so that it cannot decay to release the prisoner from her sentence of perpetual death.

At night, isolated in my cell, I dream that Frablit Pek Brimmidin appears and rescinds my provisional reality. The knifed, doomed corpse becomes Ano; her attacker becomes me. I wake from the dream moaning and weeping. The tears are not grief but terror. My life, and Ano's, hang from the splintery branch of a criminal alien I have not yet even met.

I know who he is, though. I skulk as close as I dare to the Terran groups, listening. I don't speak their language, of course, but Pek Brimmidin taught me to recognize the cadences of ''Carryl Walters'' in several of their dialects. Carryl Walters is an old Terran, with gray head fur cut in boring straight lines, wrinkled brownish skin, and sunken eyes. But his ten fingers—how do they keep the extra ones from tangling them up?—are long and quick.

It takes me only a day to realize that Carryl Walters's own people leave him alone, surrounding him with the same nonviolent respect that my protector gets. It takes me much longer to figure out why. Carryl Walters is not dangerous, neither a protector nor a punisher. I don't think he has any private shared realities with the guards. I don't understand until the World woman is knifed.

It happens in the courtyard, on a cool day in which I am gazing hungrily at the one patch of bright sky overhead. The knifed woman screams. The murderer pulls the knife from her belly and blood shoots out. In seconds the ground is drenched. The woman doubles over. Everyone looks the other way except me. And Carryl Walters runs over with his old-man stagger and kneels over the body, trying uselessly to save the life of a woman already dead anyway.

Of course. He is a healer. The Terrans don't bother him because they know that, next time, it might be they who have need of him.

I feel stupid for not realizing this right away. I am supposed to be *good* at informing. Now I'll have to make it up by immediate action. The problem, of course, is that no one will attack me while I'm under Afa Pek Fakar's protection, and provoking Pek Fakar herself is far too dangerous.

I can see only one way to do this.

I wait a few days. Outside in the courtyard, I sit quietly against the prison wall and breathe shallowly. After a few minutes I leap up. The dizziness takes me; I worsen it by holding my breath. Then I ram as hard as I can into the rough stone wall and slide down it. Pain tears through my arm and forehead. One of Pek Fakar's men shouts something.

Pek Fakar is there in a minute. I hear her—hear all of them—through a curtain of dizziness and pain.

"—just *ran* into the wall, I saw it—"

"—told me she gets these dizzy attacks—"

"—head broken in—"

I gasp, through sudden real nausea, "The healer. The Terran—"

"The Terran?" Pek Fakar's voice, hard with sudden suspicion. But I gasp out more words, ". . . disease . . . a Terran told me . . . since childhood . . . without help I . . ." My vomit, unplanned but useful, spews over her boots.

"Get the Terran," Pek Fakar rasps to somebody. "And a towel!"

Then Carryl Walters bends over me. I clutch his arm, try to smile, and pass out.

When I come to, I am lying inside, on the floor of the eating hall, the Terran cross-legged beside me. A few World people hover near the far wall, scowling. Carryl Walters says, "How many fingers you see?"

"Four. Aren't you supposed to have five?"

He unbends the fifth from behind his palm and says, "You fine."

"No, I'm not," I say. He speaks childishly, and with an odd accent, but he's understandable. "I have a disease. Another Terran healer told me so."

"Who?"

"Her name was Anna Pek Rakov."

"What disease?"

"I don't remember. Something in the head. I get spells."

"What spells? You fall, flop on floor?"

"No. Yes. Sometimes. Sometimes it takes me differently." I look directly into his eyes. Strange eyes, smaller than mine, and that improbable blue. "Pek Rakov told me I could die during a spell, without help."

He does not react to the lie. Or maybe he does, and I don't know how to read it. I have never informed on a Terran before. Instead he says something grossly obscene, even for Aulit Prison: "Why you unreal? What you do?"

I move my gaze from his. "I murdered my sister." If he asks for details, I will cry. My head aches too hard.

He says, "I sorry."

Is he sorry that he asked, or that I killed Ano? Pek Rakov was not like this; she had some manners. I say, "The other Terran healer said I should be watched carefully by someone who knows what to do if I get a spell. Do you know what to do, Pek Walters?"

"Yes."

"Will you watch me?"

"Yes." He is, in fact, watching me closely now. I touch my head; there is a cloth tied around it where I bashed myself. The headache is worse. My hand comes away sticky with blood.

I say, "In return for what?"

"What you give Pek Fakar for protection?"

He is smarter than I thought. "Nothing I can also share with you." She would punish me hard.

"Then I watch you, you give me information about World."

I nod; this is what Terrans usually request. And where information is given, it can also be extracted. "I will explain your presence to Pek Fakar," I say, before the pain in my head swamps me without warning, and everything in the dining hall blurs and sears together.

Pek Fakar doesn't like it. But I have just given her a gun, smuggled in by my "cousin." I leave notes for the prison administration in my cell, under my bed. While the prisoners are in the courtyard—which we are every day, no matter what the weather—the notes are replaced by whatever I ask for. Pek Fakar had demanded a "weapon"; neither of us expected a Terran gun. She is the only person in the prison to have such a thing. It is to me a stark reminder that no one would care if all we unreal killed each other off completely. There is no one else to shoot; we never see anyone not already in perpetual death.

"Without Pek Walters, I might have another spell and die," I say to the scowling Pek Fakar. "He knows a special Terran method of flexing the brain to bring me out of a spell."

"He can teach this special method to me."

"So far, no World person has been able to learn it. Their brains are different from ours."

She glares at me. But no one, even those lost to reality, can deny that alien brains are weird. And my injuries are certainly real: bloody head cloth, left eye closed from swelling, skin scraped raw the length of my left cheek, bruised arm. She strokes the Terran gun, a boringly straight-lined cylinder of dull metal. "All right. You may keep the Terran near you—if he agrees. Why should he?"

I smile at her slowly. Pek Fakar never shows a response to flattery; to do so would be to show weakness. But she understands. Or thinks she does. I have threatened the Terran with her power, and the whole prison now knows that her power extends among the aliens as well as her own people. She goes on glaring, but she is not displeased. In her hand, the gun gleams.

And so begin my conversations with a Terran.

Talking with Carryl Pek Walters is embarrassing and frustrating. He sits beside me in the eating hall or the courtyard and publicly scratches his head. When he is cheerful, he makes shrill horrible whistling noises between his teeth. He mentions topics that belong only among kin: the state of his skin (which has odd brown lumps on it) and his lungs (clogged with fluid, apparently). He does not know enough to begin conversations with ritual comments on flowers. It is like talking to a child, but a child who suddenly begins discussing bicycle engineering or university law.

"You think individual means very little, group means everything," he says.

We are sitting in the courtyard, against a stone wall, a little apart from the other prisoners. Some watch us furtively, some openly. I am angry. I am often angry with Pek Walters. This is not going as I'd planned.

"How can you say that? The individual is very important on World! We care for each other so that no individual is left out of our common reality, except by his own acts!"

"Exactly," Pek Walters says. He has just learned this word from me. "You care for others so no one left alone. Alone is bad. Act alone is bad. Only together is real."

"Of course," I say. Could he be stupid after all? "Reality is always shared. Is a star really there if only one eye can perceive its light?"

He smiles and says something in his own language, which makes no sense to me. He repeats it in real words. "When tree falls in forest, is sound if no person hears?"

"But—do you mean to say that on your star, people believe they . . ." What? I can't find the words.

He says, "People believe they always real, alone or together. Real even when other people say they dead. Real even when they do something very bad. Even when they murder."

"But they're not real! How could they be? They've violated shared reality! If I don't acknowledge you, the reality of your soul, if I send you to your ancestors without your consent, that is proof that I don't understand reality and so am not seeing it! Only the unreal could do that!"

"Baby not see shared reality. Is baby unreal?"

"Of course. Until the age when children attain reason, they are unreal."

"Then when I kill baby, is all right, because I not kill real person?"

"Of course it's not all right! When one kills a baby, one kills its chance to become real, before it could even join its ancestors! And also all the chances of the babies to which it might become ancestor. No one would kill a baby on World, not even these dead souls in Aulit! Are you saying that on Terra, people would kill babies?"

He looks at something I cannot see. "Yes."

My chance has arrived, although not in a form I relish. Still, I have a job to do. I say, "I have heard that Terrans will kill people for science. Even babies. To find out the kinds of things that Anna Pek Rakov knew about my brain. Is that true?"

"Yes and no."

"How can it be yes *and* no? Are children ever used for science experiments?"

"Yes."

"What kinds of experiments?"

"You should ask, what kind children? Dying children. Children not born yet. Children born . . . wrong. With no brain, or broken brain."

I struggle with all this. Dying children . . . he must mean not children who are really dead, but those in the transition to join their ancestors. Well, that would not be so bad, provided the bodies were then allowed to decay properly and release the souls. Children without brains or with broken brains . . . not bad, either. Such poor unreal things would be destroyed anyway. But children not born yet . . . in or out of the mother's womb? I push this away, to discuss another time. I am on a different path.

"And you never use living, real children for science?"

He gives me a look I cannot read. So much of Terran expression is still strange. "Yes. We use. In some experiments. Experiments who not hurt children."

"Like what?" I say. We are staring directly at each other now. Suddenly I wonder if this old Terran suspects that I am an informer seeking information, and that is why he accepted my skimpy story about having spells. That would not necessarily be bad. There are ways to bargain with the unreal once everyone admits that bargaining is what is taking place. But I'm not sure whether Pek Walters knows that.

He says, "Experiments who study how brain work. Such as, how memory work. Including shared memory."

"Memory? Memory doesn't 'work.' It just is."

"No. Memory work. By memory-building pro-teenz." He uses a Terran word, then adds, "Tiny little pieces of food," which makes no sense. What does food have to do with memory? You don't eat memories, or obtain them from food. But I am further down the path, and I use his words to go further still.

"Does memory in World people work with the same . . . 'pro-teenz' as Terran memory?"

"Yes and no. Some same or almost same. Some different." He is watching me very closely.

"How do you know that memory works the same or different in World people? Have Terrans done brain experiments on World?"

"Yes."

"With World children?"

"Yes."

I watch a group of Huhuhubs across the courtyard. The smelly little aliens are clustered together in some kind of ritual or game. "And have you, personally, participated in these science experiments on children, Pek Walters?"

He doesn't answer me. Instead he smiles, and if I didn't know better, I'd swear the smile was sad. He says, "Pek Bengarin, why you kill your sister?"

The unexpectedness of it—now, so close to almost learning something useful—outrages me. Not even Pek Fakar had asked me that. I stare at him angrily. He says, "I know, I not should ask. Wrong for ask. But I tell you much, and answer is important—"

"But the question is obscene. You should not ask. World people are not so cruel to each other."

"Even people damned in Aulit Prison?" he says, and even though I don't know one of the words he uses, I see that yes, he recognizes that I am an informer. And that I have been seeking information. All right, so much the better. But I need time to set my questions on a different path.

To gain time, I repeat my previous point. "World people are not so cruel."

"Then you—"

The air suddenly sizzles, smelling of burning. People shout. I look up. Aka Pek Fakar stands in the middle of the courtyard with the Terran gun, firing it at the Huhuhubs. One by one they drop as the beam of light hits them and makes a sizzling hole. The aliens pass into the second stage of their perpetual death.

I stand and tug on Pek Walters's arm. "Come on. We must clear the area immediately or the guards will release poison gas."

"Why?"

"So they can get the bodies into bondage chemicals, of course!" Does this alien think the prison officials would let the unreal get even a little bit decayed? I thought that after our several conversations, Pek Walters understood more than that.

He rises slowly, haltingly, to his feet. Pek Fakar, laughing, strolls toward the door, the gun still in her hand.

Pek Walters says, "World people not cruel?"

Behind us, the bodies of the Huhuhubs lie sprawled across each other, smoking.

The next time we are herded from our cells into the dining hall and then the courtyard, the Huhuhub corpses are of course gone. Pek Walters has developed a cough. He walks more slowly, and once, on the way to our usual spot against the far wall, he puts a hand on my arm to steady himself.

"Are you sick, Pek?"

"Exactly," he says.

"But you are a healer. Make the cough disappear."

He smiles, and sinks gratefully against the wall. " 'Healer, heal own self.' "

"What?"

"Nothing. So you are informer, Pek Bengarin, and you hope I tell you something about science experiments on children on World."

I take a deep breath. Pek Fakar passes us, carrying her gun. Two of her own people now stay close beside her at all times, in case another prisoner tries to take the gun away from her. I cannot believe anyone would try, but maybe I'm wrong. There's no telling what the unreal will do. Pek Walters watches her pass, and his smile is gone. Yesterday Pek Fakar shot another person, this time not even an alien. There is a note under my bed requesting more guns.

I say, "*You* say I am an informer. I do not say it."

"Exactly," Pek Walters says. He has another coughing spell, then closes his eyes wearily. "I have not an-tee-by-otics."

Another Terran word. Carefully I repeat it. " 'An-tee-by-otics'?"

"Pro-teenz for heal."

Again that word for very small bits of food. I make use of it. "Tell me about the pro-teenz in the science experiments."

"I tell you everything about experiments. But only if you answer questions first."

He will ask about my sister. For no reason other than rudeness and cruelty. I feel my face turn to stone.

He says, "Tell me why steal baby not so bad for make person unreal always."

I blink. Isn't this obvious? "To steal a baby doesn't damage the baby's reality. It just grows up somewhere else, with some other people. But all real people of World share the same reality, and anyway after the transition, the child will rejoin its blood ancestors. Baby stealing is wrong, of course, but it isn't a really serious crime.''

''And make false coins?''

''The same. False, true—coins are still shared.''

He coughs again, this time much harder. I wait. Finally he says, ''So when I steal your bicycle, I not violate shared reality too much, because bicycle still somewhere with people of World.''

''Of course.''

''But when I steal bicycle, I violate shared reality a little?''

''Yes.'' After a minute I add, ''Because the bicycle is, after all, *mine*. You . . . made my reality shift a little without sharing the decision with me.'' I peer at him; how can all this not be obvious to such an intelligent man?

He says, ''You are too trusting for be informer, Pek Bengarin.''

I feel my throat swell with indignation. I am a *very good* informer. Haven't I just bound this Terran to me with a private shared reality in order to create an exchange of information? I am about to demand his share of the bargain when he says abruptly, ''So why you kill your sister?''

Two of Pek Fakar's people swagger past. They carry the new guns. Across the courtyard a Faller turns slowly to look at them, and even I can read fear on that alien face.

I say, as evenly as I can manage, ''I fell prey to an illusion. I thought that Ano was copulating with my lover. She was younger, more intelligent, prettier. I am not very pretty, as you can see. I didn't share the reality with her, or him, and my illusion grew. Finally it exploded in my head, and I . . . did it.'' I am breathing hard, and Pek Fakar's people look blurry.

''You remember clear Ano's murder?''

I turn to him in astonishment. ''How could I forget it?''

''You cannot. You cannot because of memory-building pro-teenz. Memory is strong in your brain. Memory-building pro-teenz are strong in your brain. Scientific research on World children for discover what is structure of pro-teenz, where is pro-teenz, how pro-teenz work. But we discover different thing instead.''

''What different thing?'' I say, but Pek Walters only shakes his head and begins coughing again. I wonder if the coughing spell is an excuse to violate our bargain. He is, after all, unreal.

Pek Fakar's people have gone inside the prison. The Faller slumps against the far wall. They have not shot him. For this moment, at least, he is not entering the second stage of his perpetual death.

But beside me, Pek Walters coughs blood.

He is dying. I am sure of it, although of course no World healer comes to him. He is dead anyway. Also, his fellow Terrans keep away, looking fearful, which makes me wonder if his disease is catching. This leaves only me. I walk him to his cell, and then wonder why I can't just stay when the door closes. No one will check. Or, if they do, will care. And this may be my last chance to gain the needed information, before either Pek Walters is coffined or Pek Fakar orders me away from him because he is too weak to watch over my supposed blood sickness.

His body has become very hot. During the long night he tosses on his bunk, muttering in his own language, and sometimes those strange alien eyes roll in their sockets. But other times he is clearer, and he looks at me as if he recognizes who I am. Those times, I question him. But the lucid times and unlucid ones blur together. His mind is no longer his own.

"Pek Walters. Where are the memory experiments being conducted? In what place?"

"Memory . . . memories . . ." More in his own language. It has the cadences of poetry.

"Pek Walters. In what place are the memory experiments being done?"

"At Rafkit Sarloe," he says, which makes no sense. Rafkit Sarloe is the government center, where no one lives. It is not large. People flow in every day, running the Sections, and out to their villages again at night. There is no square measure of Rafkit Sarloe that is not constantly shared physical reality.

He coughs, more bloody spume, and his eyes roll in his head. I make him sip some water. "Pek Walters. In what place are the memory experiments being done?"

"At Rafkit Sarloe. In the Cloud. At Aulit Prison."

It goes on and on like that. And in the early morning, Pek Walters dies.

There is one moment of greater clarity, somewhere near the end. He looks at me, out of his old, ravaged face gone gaunt with his transition. The disturbing look is back in his eyes, sad and kind, not a look for the unreal to wear. It is too much sharing. He says, so low I must bend over him to hear, "Sick brain talks to itself. You not kill your sister."

"Hush, don't try to talk. . . ."

"Find . . . Brifjis. Maldon Pek Brifjis, in Rafkit Haddon. Find . . ." He relapses again into fever.

A few moments after he dies, the armored guards enter the cell, wheeling the coffin full of bondage chemicals. With them is the priest. I want to say, *Wait, he is a good man, he doesn't deserve perpetual death*—but of course I do not. I am astonished at myself for even thinking it. A guard edges me into the corridor and the door closes.

That same day, I am sent away from Aulit Prison.

"Tell me again. Everything," Pek Brimmidin says.

Pek Brimmidin is just the same: stocky, yellowing, slightly stooped. His cluttered office is just the same. Food dishes, papers, overelaborated sculptures. I stare hungrily at the ugly things. I hadn't realized how much I'd longed, in prison, for the natural sight of curves. I keep my eyes on the sculptures, partly to hold back my question until the proper time to ask it.

"Pek Walters said he would tell me everything about the experiments that are, yes, going on with World children. In the name of science. But all he had time to tell me was that the experiments involve 'memory-building pro-teenz,' which are tiny pieces of food from which the brain constructs memory. He also said the experiments were going on in Rafkit Sarloe and Aulit Prison."

"And that is all, Pek Bengarin?"

"That is all."

Pek Brimmidin nods curtly. He is trying to appear dangerous, to scare out of me any piece of information I might have forgotten. But Frablit Pek Brimmidin can't appear dangerous to me. I have seen the real thing.

Pek Brimmidin has not changed. But I have.

I ask my question. "I have brought to you all the information I could obtain before the Terran died. Is it sufficient to release me and Ano?"

He runs a hand through his neck fur. "I'm sorry I can't answer that, Pek. I will need to consult my superiors. But I promise to send you word as soon as I can."

"Thank you," I say, and lower my eyes. *You are too trusting for be informer, Pek Bengarin.*

Why didn't I tell Frablit Pek Brimmidin the rest of it, about "Maldon Pek Brifjis" and "Rafkit Haddon" and not really killing my sister? Because it is most likely nonsense, the ravings of a fevered brain. Because this "Maldon Pek Brifjis" might be an innocent World man, who does not deserve trouble brought to him by an unreal alien. Because Pek Walters's words were personal, addressed to me alone, on his deathbed. Because I do not want to discuss Ano with Pek Brimmidin's superiors one more useless painful time.

Because, despite myself, I trust Carryl Pek Walters.

"You may go," Pek Brimmidin says, and I ride my bicycle along the dusty road home.

I make a bargain with Ano's corpse, still lying in curled-finger grace on the bed across from mine. Her beautiful brown hair floats in the chemicals of the coffin. I used to covet that hair desperately, when we were very young. Once I even cut it all off while she slept. But other times I would weave it for her, or braid it with flowers. She was so pretty. At one point, when she was still a child, she wore eight bid rings, one on each finger. Two of the bids were in negotiation between the boys' fathers and ours. Although older, I have never had a single bid.

Did I murder her?

My bargain with her corpse is this: If the Reality and Atonement Section releases me and Ano because of my work in Aulit Prison, I will seek no further. Ano will be free to join our ancestors; I will be fully real. It will no longer matter whether or not I killed my sister, because both of us will again be sharing in the same reality as if I had not. But if Reality and Atonement holds me unreal still longer, after all I have given them, I will try to find this "Maldon Pek Brifjis."

I say none of this aloud. The guards at Aulit Prison knew immediately when Pek Walters died, inside a closed and windowless room. They could be watching me here, now. World has no devices to do this, but how did Pek Walters know so much about a World man working with a Terran science experiment? Somewhere there are World people and Terrans in partnership. Terrans, as everyone knows, have all sorts of listening devices we do not.

I kiss Ano's coffin. I don't say it aloud, but I hope desperately that Reality and Atonement releases us. I want to return to shared reality, to the daily warmth and sweetness of belonging, now and forever, to the living and dead of World. I do not want to be an informer anymore.

Not for anyone, even myself.

• • •

The message comes three days later. The afternoon is warm and I sit outside on my stone bench, watching my neighbor's milkbeasts eye her sturdily fenced flower beds. She has new flowers that I don't recognize, with blooms that are entrancing but somehow foreign—could they be Terran? It doesn't seem likely. During my time in Aulit Prison, more people seem to have made up their minds that the Terrans are unreal. I have heard more mutterings, more anger against those who buy from alien traders.

Frablit Pek Brimmidin himself brings the letter from Reality and Atonement, laboring up the road on his ancient bicycle. He has removed his uniform, so as not to embarrass me in front of my neighbors. I watch him ride up, his neck fur damp with unaccustomed exertion, his gray eyes abashed, and I know already what the sealed message must say. Pek Brimmidin is too kind for his job. That is why he is only a low-level messenger boy all the time, not just today.

These are things I never saw before.

You are too trusting for be informer, Pek Bengarin.

"Thank you, Pek Brimmidin," I say. "Would you like a glass of water? Or pel?"

"No, thank you, Pek," he says. He does not meet my eyes. He waves to my other neighbor, fetching water from the village well, and fumbles meaninglessly with the handle of his bicycle. "I can't stay."

"Then ride safely," I say, and go back in my house. I stand beside Ano and break the seal on the government letter. After I read it, I gaze at her a long time. So beautiful, so sweet-natured. So loved.

Then I start to clean. I scrub every inch of my house, for hours and hours, climbing on a ladder to wash the ceiling, sloshing thick soapsuds in the cracks, scrubbing every surface of every object and carrying the more intricately shaped outside into the sun to dry. Despite my most intense scrutiny, I find nothing that I can imagine being a listening device. Nothing that looks alien, nothing unreal.

But I no longer know what is real.

Only Bata is up; the other moons have not risen. The sky is clear and starry, the air cool. I wheel my bicycle inside and try to remember everything I need.

Whatever kind of glass Ano's coffin is made of, it is very tough. I have to swing my garden shovel three times, each time with all my strength, before I can break it. On the third blow the glass cracks, then falls leisurely apart into large pieces that bounce slightly when they hit the floor. Chemicals cascade off the bed, a waterfall of clear liquid that smells only slightly acrid.

In my high boots I wade close to the bed and throw containers of water over Ano to wash off chemical residue. The containers are waiting in a neat row by the wall, everything from my largest washbasin to the kitchen bowls. Ano smiles sweetly.

I reach onto the soggy bed and lift her clear.

In the kitchen, I lay her body—limp, soft-limbed—on the floor and strip off her chemical-soaked clothing. I dry her, move her to the waiting blanket, take a last look, and wrap her tightly. The bundle of her and the shovel balances across the handles of my bicycle. I pull off my boots and open the door.

The night smells of my neighbor's foreign flowers. Ano seems weightless. I feel as if I can ride for hours. And I do.

I bury her, weighted with stones, in marshy ground well off a deserted road. The wet dirt will speed the decay, and it is easy to cover the grave with reeds and toglif branches. When I've finished, I bury my clothes and dress in clean ones from my pack. Another few hours of riding and I can find an inn to sleep in. Or a field, if need be.

The morning dawns pearly, with three moons in the sky. Everywhere I ride are flowers, first wild and then cultivated. Although exhausted, I sing softly to the curving blooms, to the sky, to the pale moonlit road. Ano is real, and free.

Go sweetly, sweet sister, to our waiting ancestors.

Two days later I reach Rafkit Haddon.

It is an old city, sloping down the side of a mountain to the sea. The homes of the rich either stand on the shore or perch on the mountain, looking in both cases like rounded great white birds. In between lie a jumble of houses, market squares, government buildings, inns, pel shops, slums, and parks, the latter with magnificent old trees and shabby old shrines. The manufacturing shops and warehouses lie to the north, with the docks.

I have experience in finding people. I start with Rituals and Processions. The clerk behind the counter, a preinitiate of the priesthood, is young and eager to help. "Yes?"

"I am Ajma Pek Goranalit, attached to the household of Menanlin. I have been sent to inquire about the ritual activity of a citizen, Maldon Pek Brifjis. Can you help me?"

"Of course," she beams. An inquiry about ritual activity is never written; discretion is necessary when a great house is considering honoring a citizen by allowing him to honor their ancestors. A person so chosen gains great prestige—and considerable material wealth. I picked the name "Menanlin" after an hour's judicious listening in a crowded pel shop. The family is old, numerous, and discreet.

"Let me see," she says, browsing among her public records. "Brifjis . . . Brifjis . . . it's a common name, of course . . . which citizen, Pek?"

"Maldon."

"Oh, yes . . . here. He paid for two musical tributes to his ancestors last year, made a donation to the Rafkit Haddon Priest House . . . Oh! And he was chosen to honor the ancestors of the house of Choulalait!"

She sounds awestruck. I nod. "We know about that, of course. But is there anything else?"

"No, I don't think so . . . wait. He paid for a charity tribute for the ancestors of his clu merchant, Lam Pek Flanoe, a poor man. Quite a lavish tribute too. Music, and three priests."

"Kind," I said.

"Very! Three priests!" Her young eyes shine. "Isn't it wonderful how many truly kind people share reality?"

"Yes," I say. "It is."

I find the clu merchant by the simple method of asking for him in several market squares. Sales of all fuels are of course slow in the summer; the young relatives left in charge of the clu stalls are happy to chat with strangers. Lam Pek Flanoe lives in a run-down neighborhood just behind the great houses by the sea. The neighborhood is home to servants and merchants who provide for the rich. Four more glasses of pel in three more pel shops, and I know that Maldon Pek Brifjis is currently a guest in the home of a rich widow. I know the widow's address. I know that Pek Brifjis is a healer.

A healer.

Sick brain talks to itself. You not kill your sister.

I am dizzy from four glasses of pel. Enough. I find an inn, the kind where no one asks questions, and sleep without the shared reality of dreams.

It takes me a day, disguised as a street cleaner, to decide which of the men coming and going from the rich widow's house is Pek Brifjis. Then I spend three days following him, in various guises. He goes a lot of places and talks to a lot of people, but none of them seem unusual for a rich healer with a personal pleasure in collecting antique water carafes. On the fourth day I look for a good opportunity to approach him, but this turns out to be unnecessary.

"Pek," a man says to me as I loiter, dressed as a vendor of sweet flatbreads, outside the baths on Elindel Street. I have stolen the sweets before dawn from the open kitchen of a bakeshop. I know at once that the man approaching me is a bodyguard, and that he is very good. It's in the way he walks, looks at me, places his hand on my arm. He is also very handsome, but that thought barely registers. Handsome men are never for such as me. They are for Ano.

Were for Ano.

"Come with me, please," the bodyguard says, and I don't argue. He leads me to the back of the baths, through a private entrance, to a small room apparently used for private grooming of some sort. The only furniture is two small stone tables. He checks me, expertly but gently, for weapons, looking even in my mouth. Satisfied, he indicates where I am to stand, and opens a second door.

Maldon Pek Brifjis enters, wrapped in a bathing robe of rich imported cloth. He is younger than Carryl Walters, a vigorous man in a vigorous prime. His eyes are striking, a deep purple with long gold lines radiating from their centers. He says immediately, "Why have you been following me for three days?"

"Someone told me to," I say. I have nothing to lose by an honest shared reality, although I still don't fully believe I have anything to gain.

"Who? You may say anything in front of my guard."

"Carryl Pek Walters."

The purple eyes deepen even more. "Pek Walters is dead."

"Yes," I say. "Perpetually. I was with him when he entered the second stage of death."

"And where was that?" He is testing me.

"In Aulit Prison. His last words instructed me to find you. To . . . ask you something."

"What do you wish to ask me?"

"Not what I thought I would ask," I say, and realize that I have made the decision to tell him everything. Until I saw him up close, I wasn't completely sure what I would do. I can no longer share reality with World, not even if I went to

Frablit Pek Brimmidin with exactly the knowledge he wants about the scientific experiments on children. That would not atone for releasing Ano before the Section agreed. And Pek Brimmidin is only a messenger, anyway. No, less than a messenger: a tool, like a garden shovel, or a bicycle. He does not share the reality of his users. He only thinks he does.

As I had thought I did.

I say, "I want to know if I killed my sister. Pek Walters said I did not. He said 'sick brain talks to itself,' and that I had not killed Ano. And to ask *you*. Did I kill my sister?"

Pek Brifjis sits down on one of the stone tables. "I don't know," he says, and I see his neck fur quiver. "Perhaps you did. Perhaps you did not."

"How can I discover which?"

"You cannot."

"Ever?"

"Ever." And then, "I am sorry."

Dizziness takes me. The "low blood pressure." The next thing I know, I lie on the floor of the small room, with Pek Brifjis's fingers on my elbow pulse. I struggle to sit up.

"No, wait," he says. "Wait a moment. Have you eaten today?"

"Yes."

"Well, wait a moment anyway. I need to think."

He does, the purple eyes turning inward, his fingers absently pressing the inside of my elbow. Finally he says, "You are an informer. That's why you were released from Aulit Prison after Pek Walters died. You inform for the government."

I don't answer. It no longer matters.

"But you have left informing. Because of what Pek Walters told you. Because he told you that the skits-oh-free-nia experiments might have . . . no. It can't be."

He, too, has used a word I don't know. It sounds Terran. Again I struggle to sit up, to leave. There is no hope for me here. This healer can tell me nothing.

He pushes me back down on the floor and says swiftly, "When did your sister die?" His eyes have changed once again; the long golden flecks are brighter, radiating from the center like glowing spokes. "Please, Pek, this is immensely important. To both of us."

"Two years ago, and one hundred fifty-two days."

"Where? In what city?"

"Village. Our village. Gofkit Ilo."

"Yes," he says. "*Yes*. Tell me everything you remember of her death. Everything."

This time I push him aside and sit up. Blood rushes from my head, but anger overcomes the dizziness. "I will tell you nothing. Who do you people think you are, ancestors? To tell me I killed Ano, then tell me I didn't, then say you don't know—to destroy the hope of atonement I had as an informer, then to tell me there is no other hope—no, there might be hope—no, there's *not*—how can you live with yourself? How can you twist people's brains away from shared reality and offer *nothing to replace it!*" I am screaming. The bodyguard glances at the door. I don't care; I go on screaming.

"You are doing experiments on children, wrecking their reality as you have wrecked mine! You are a murderer—'' But I don't get to scream all that. Maybe I don't get to scream any of it. For a needle slides into my elbow, at the inner pulse where Maldon Brifjis has been holding it, and the room slides away as easily as Ano into her grave.

A bed, soft and silky, beneath me. Rich wall hangings. The room is very warm. A scented breeze whispers across my bare stomach. Bare? I sit up and discover I am dressed in the gauzy skirt, skimpy bandeau, and flirting veil of a prostitute.

At my first movement, Pek Brifjis crosses from the fireplace to my bed. "Pek. This room does not allow sound to escape. Do not resume screaming. Do you understand?"

I nod. His bodyguard stands across the room. I pull the flirting veil from my face.

"I am sorry about that," Pek Brifjis says. "It was necessary to dress you in a way that accounts for a bodyguard carrying a drugged woman into a private home without raising questions."

A private home. I guess that this is the rich widow's house by the sea. A room that does not allow sound to escape. A needle unlike ours: sharp and sure. Brain experiments. "Skits-oh-free-nia."

I say, "You work with the Terrans."

"No," he says. "I do not."

"But Pek Walters . . ." It doesn't matter. "What are you going to do with me?"

He says, "I am going to offer you a trade."

"What sort of trade?"

"Information in return for your freedom."

And he says he does not work with Terrans. I say, "What use is freedom to me?" although of course I don't expect him to understand that. I can never be free.

"Not that kind of freedom," he says. "I won't just let you go from this room. I will let you rejoin your ancestors, and Ano."

I gape at him.

"Yes, Pek. I will kill you and bury you myself, where your body can decay."

"You would violate shared reality like that? For *me*?"

His purple eyes deepen again. For a moment, something in those eyes looks almost like Pek Walters's blue ones. "Please understand. I think there is a strong chance you did not kill Ano. Your village was one where . . . subjects were used for experimentation. I think that is the true shared reality here."

I say nothing. A little of his assurance disappears. "Or so I believe. Will you agree to the trade?"

"Perhaps," I say. Will he actually do what he promises? I can't be sure. But there is no other way for me. I cannot hide from the government all the years until I die. I am too young. And when they find me, they will send me back to Aulit, and when I die there they will put me in a coffin of preservative chemicals. . . .

I would never see Ano again.

The healer watches me closely. Again I see the Pek Walters look in his eyes: sadness and pity.

"Perhaps I will agree to the trade," I say, and wait for him to speak again about the night Ano died. But instead he says, "I want to show you something."

He nods at the bodyguard who leaves the room, returning a few moments later. By the hand he leads a child, a little girl, clean and well-dressed. One look makes my neck fur bristle. The girl's eyes are flat and unseeing. She mutters to herself. I offer a quick appeal for protection to my ancestors. The girl is unreal, without the capacity to perceive shared reality, even though she is well over the age of reason. She is not human. She should have been destroyed.

"This is Ori," Pek Brifjis says. The girl suddenly laughs, a wild demented laugh, and peers at something only she can see.

"Why is it here?" I listen to the harshness in my own voice.

"Ori was born real. She was made this way by the scientific brain experiments of the government."

"Of the government! That is a lie!"

"Is it? Do you still, Pek, have such trust in your government?"

"No, but . . ." To make me continue to earn Ano's freedom, even after I had met their terms . . . to lie to Pek Brimmidin . . . those offenses against shared reality are one thing. The destruction of a real person's physical body, as I had done with Ano's (had I?) is another, far far worse. To destroy a *mind*, the instrument of perceiving shared reality . . . Pek Brifjis lies.

He says, "Pek, tell me about the night Ano died."

"Tell me about this . . . thing!"

"All right." He sits down in a chair beside my luxurious bed. The thing wanders around the room, muttering. It seems unable to stay still.

"She was born Ori Malfisit, in a small village in the far north—"

"What village?" I need desperately to see if he falters on details.

He does not. "Gofkit Ramloe. Of real parents, simple people, an old and established family. At six years old, Ori was playing in the forest with some other children when she disappeared. The other children said they heard something thrashing toward the marshes. The family decided she had been carried off by a wild kilfreit—there are still some left, you know, that far north—and held a procession in honor of Ori's joining their ancestors.

"But that's not what happened to Ori. She was stolen by two men, unreal prisoners promised atonement and restoration to full reality, just as you were. Ori was carried off to Rafkit Sarloe, with eight other children from all over World. There they were given to the Terrans, who were told that they were orphans who could be used for experiments. The experiments were ones that would not hurt or damage the children in any way."

I look at Ori, now tearing a table scarf into shreds and muttering. Her empty eyes turn to mine, and I have to look away.

"This part is difficult," Pek Brifjis says. "Listen hard, Pek. The Terrans truly did not hurt the children. They put ee-lek-trodes on their heads . . . you don't know what that means. They found ways to see which parts of their brains worked the same as Terran brains and which did not. They used a number of tests and machines and drugs. None of it hurt the children, who lived at the Terran scientific compound and were cared for by World childwatchers. At first the children missed their parents, but they were young, and after a while they were happy."

I glance again at Ori. The unreal, not sharing in common reality, are isolated and therefore dangerous. A person with no world in common with others will violate those others as easily as cutting flowers. Under such conditions, pleasure is possible, but not happiness.

Pek Brifjis runs his hand through his neck fur. "The Terrans worked with World healers, of course, teaching them. It was the usual trade, only this time we received the information and they the physical reality: children and watchers. There was no other way World could permit Terrans to handle our children. Our healers were there every moment."

He looks at me. I say, "Yes," just because something must be said.

"Do you know, Pek, what it is like to realize you have lived your whole life according to beliefs that are not true?"

"No!" I say, so loudly that Ori looks up with her mad, unreal gaze. She smiles. I don't know why I spoke so loud. What Pek Brifjis said has nothing to do with me. Nothing at all.

"Well, Pek Walters knew. He realized that the experiments he participated in, harmless to the subjects and in aid of biological understanding of species differences, were being used for something else. The roots of skits-oh-free-nia, misfiring brain sir-kits—" He is off on a long explanation that means nothing to me. Too many Terran words, too much strangeness. Pek Brifjis is no longer talking to me. He is talking to himself, in some sort of pain I don't understand.

Suddenly the purple eyes snap back to mine. "What all that means, Pek, is that a few of the healers—our own healers, from World—found out how to manipulate the Terran science. They took it and used it to put into minds memories that did not happen."

"Not possible!"

"It is possible. The brain is made very excited, with Terran devices, while the false memory is recited over and over. Then different parts of the brain are made to . . . to recirculate memories and emotions over and over. Like water recirculated through millraces. The water gets all scrambled together. . . . No. Think of it this way: Different parts of the brain send signals to each other. The signals are forced to loop together, and every loop makes the unreal memories stronger. It is apparently in common use on Terra, although tightly controlled."

Sick brain talks to itself.

"But—"

"There are no objections possible, Pek. It is real. It happened. It happened to Ori. The World scientists made her brain remember things that had not happened. Small things, at first. That worked. When they tried larger memories, something went wrong. It left her like this. They were still learning; that was five years ago. They got better, much better. Good enough to experiment on adult subjects who could then be returned to shared reality."

"One can't plant memories like flowers, or uproot them like weeds!"

"These people could. And did."

"But—*why?*"

"Because the World healers who did this—and they were only a few—saw a different reality."

"I don't—"

"They saw the Terrans able to do everything. Make better machines than we can, from windmills to bicycles. Fly to the stars. Cure disease. Control nature. Many World people are afraid of Terrans, Pek. And of Fallers and Huhuhubs. Because their reality is superior to ours."

"There is only one common reality," I said. "The Terrans just know more about it than we do!"

"Perhaps. But Terran knowledge makes people uneasy. And afraid. And jealous."

Jealous. Ano saying to me in the kitchen, with Bata and Cap bright at the window, "I will too go out tonight to see him! You can't stop me! You're just jealous, a jealous ugly shriveled thing that not even your lover wants, so you don't wish me to have any—" And the red flood swamping my brain, the kitchen knife, the blood—

"Pek?" the healer says. "Pek?"

"I'm . . . all right. The jealous healers, they hurt their own people, World people, for revenge on the Terrans—that makes no sense!"

"The healers acted with great sorrow. They knew what they were doing to people. But they needed to perfect the technique of inducing controlled skits-oh-free-nia . . . they *needed* to do it. To make people angry at Terrans. Angry enough to forget the attractive trade goods and rise up against the aliens. To cause war. The healers are mistaken, Pek. We have not had a war on World in a thousand years; our people cannot understand how hard the Terrans would strike back. But you must understand: The outlaw scientists thought they were doing the right thing. They thought they were creating anger in order to save World.

"And another thing—with the help of the government, they were careful not to make any World man or woman permanently unreal. The adults manipulated into murder were all offered atonement as informers. The children are all cared for. The mistakes, like Ori, will be allowed to decay someday, to return to her ancestors. I will see to that myself."

Ori tears the last of the scarf into pieces, smiling horribly, her flat eyes empty. What unreal memories fill her head?

I say bitterly, "Doing the right thing . . . letting me believe I killed my sister!"

"When you rejoin your ancestors, you will find it isn't so. And the means of rejoining them was made available to you: the completion of your informing atonement."

But now that atonement never will be completed. I stole Ano and buried her without Section consent. Maldon Brifjis, of course, does not know this.

Through my pain and anger I blurt, "And what of *you*, Pek Brifjis? You work with these criminal healers, aiding them in emptying children like Ori of reality—"

"I don't work with them. I thought you were smarter, Pek. I work against them. And so did Carryl Walters, which is why he died in Aulit Prison."

"Against them?"

"Many of us do. Carryl Walters among them. He was an informer. And my friend."

Neither of us says anything. Pek Brifjis stares into the fire. I stare at Ori, who has begun to grimace horribly. She squats on an intricately woven curved rug that looks very old. A reek suddenly fills the room. Ori does not share with the rest of us the reality of piss closets. She throws back her head and laughs, a horrible sound like splintering metal.

"Take her away," Pek Brifjis says wearily to the guard, who looks unhappy. "I'll clean up here." To me he adds, "We can't allow any servants in here with you."

The guard leads away the grimacing child. Pek Brifjis kneels and scrubs at the rug with chimney rags dipped in water from my carafe. I remember that he collects antique water carafes. What a long way that must seem from scrubbing shit, from Ori, from Carryl Walters coughing out his lungs in Aulit Prison, among aliens.

"Pek Brifjis—did I kill my sister?"

He looks up. There is shit on his hands. "There is no way to be absolutely sure. It is possible you were one of the experiment subjects from your village. You would have been drugged in your house, to awake with your sister murdered and your mind altered."

I say, more quietly than I have said anything else in this room, "You will really kill me, let me decay, and enable me to rejoin my ancestors?"

Pek Brifjis stands and wipes the shit from his hands. "I will."

"But what will you do if I refuse? If instead I ask to return home?"

"If you do that, the government will arrest you and once more promise you atonement—if you inform on those of us working to oppose them."

"Not if I go first to whatever part of the government is truly working to end the experiments. Surely you aren't saying the *entire* government is doing this . . . thing."

"Of course not. But do you know for certain which Sections, and which officials in those Sections, wish for war with the Terrans, and which do not? *We* can't be sure. How can you?"

Frablit Pek Brimmidin is innocent, I think. But the thought is useless. Pek Brimmidin is innocent, but powerless.

It tears my soul to think that the two might be the same thing.

Pek Brifjis rubs at the damp carpet with the toe of his boot. He puts the rags in a lidded jar and washes his hands at the washstand. A faint stench still hangs in the air. He comes to stand beside my bed.

"Is that what you want, Uli Pek Bengarin? That I let you leave this house, not knowing what you will do, whom you will inform on? That I endanger everything we have done in order to convince you of its truth?"

"Or you can kill me and let me rejoin my ancestors. Which is what you think I will choose, isn't it? That choice would let you keep faith with the reality you have decided is true, and still keep yourself secret from the criminals. Killing me would be easiest for you. But only if I consent to my murder. Otherwise, you will violate even the reality you have decided to perceive."

He stares down at me, a muscular man with beautiful purple eyes. A healer who would kill. A patriot defying his government to prevent a violent war. A sinner who does all he can to minimize his sin and keep it from denying him the chance to rejoin his own ancestors. A believer in shared reality who is trying to bend the reality without breaking the belief.

I keep quiet. The silence stretches on. Finally it is Pek Brifjis that breaks it. "I wish Carryl Walters had never sent you to me."

"But he did. And I choose to return to my village. Will you let me go, or keep me prisoner here, or murder me without my consent?"

"Damn you," he says, and I recognize the word as one Carryl Walters used, about the unreal souls in Aulit Prison.

"Exactly," I say. "What will you do, Pek? Which of your supposed multiple realities will you choose now?"

It is a hot night, and I cannot sleep.

I lie in my tent on the wide empty plain and listen to the night noises. Rude laughter from the pel tent, where a group of miners drinks far too late at night for men who must bore into hard rock at dawn. Snoring from the tent to my right. Muffled lovemaking from a tent farther down the row, I'm not sure whose. The woman giggles, high and sweet.

I have been a miner for half a year now. After I left the northern village of Gofkit Ramloe, Ori's village, I just kept heading north. Here on the equator, where World harvests its tin and diamonds and pel berries and salt, life is both simpler and less organized. Papers are not necessary. Many of the miners are young, evading their government service for one reason or another. Reasons that must seem valid to them. Here government Sections rule weakly, compared to the rule of the mining and farming companies. There are no messengers on Terran bicycles. There is no Terran science. There are no Terrans.

There are shrines, of course, and rituals and processions, and tributes to one's ancestors. But these things actually receive less attention than in the cities, because they are more taken for granted. Do you pay attention to air?

The woman giggles again, and this time I recognize the sound. Awi Pek Crafmal, the young runaway from another island. She is a pretty thing, and a hard worker. Sometimes she reminds me of Ano.

I asked a great many questions in Gofkit Ramloe. *Ori Malfisit*, Pek Brifjis said her name was. *An old and established family.* But I asked and asked, and no such family had ever lived in Gofkit Ramloe. Wherever Ori came from, and however she had been made into that unreal and empty vessel shitting on a rich carpet, she had not started her poor little life in Gofkit Ramloe.

Did Maldon Brifjis know I would discover that, when he released me from the rich widow's house overlooking the sea? He must have. Or maybe, despite knowing I was an informer, he didn't understand that I would actually go to Gofkit Ramloe and check. You can't understand everything.

Sometimes, in the darkest part of the night, I wish I had taken Pek Brifjis's offer to return me to my ancestors.

I work on the rock piles of the mine during the day, among miners who lift sledges and shatter solid stone. They talk, and curse, and revile the Terrans, although few miners have as much as seen one. After work the miners sit in camp and drink pel, lifting huge mugs with dirty hands, and laugh at obscene jokes. They all share the same reality, and it binds them together, in simple and happy strength.

I have strength too. I have the strength to swing my sledge with the other women, many of whom have the same rough plain looks as I, and who are happy to accept me as one of them. I had the strength to shatter Ano's coffin, and to bury her even when I thought the price to me was perpetual death. I had the strength to follow

Carryl Walters's words about the brain experiments and seek Maldon Brifjis. I had the strength to twist Pek Brifjis's divided mind to make him let me go.

But do I have the strength to go where all of that leads me? Do I have the strength to look at Frablit Brimmidin's reality, and Carryl Walters's reality, and Ano's, and Maldon Brifjis's, and Ori's—and try to find the places that match and the places that don't? Do I have the strength to live on, never knowing if I killed my sister, or if I did not? Do I have the strength to doubt everything, and live with doubt, and sort through the millions of separate realities on World, searching for the true pieces of each—assuming that I can even recognize them?

Should anyone have to live like that? In uncertainty, in doubt, in loneliness. Alone in one's mind, in an isolated and unshared reality.

I would like to return to the days when Ano was alive. Or even to the days when I was an informer. To the days when I shared in World's reality, and knew it to be solid beneath me, like the ground itself. To the days when I knew what to think, and so did not have to.

To the days before I became—unwillingly—as terrifyingly real as I am now.

A DRY, QUIET WAR

Tony Daniel

▼

One of the fastest-rising stars of the 1990s, Tony Daniel grew up in Alabama, lived for a while on Vashon Island in Washington State, and in recent years, in the best tradition of the young bohemian artist, has been restlessly on the move, from Vashon Island to Europe, from Europe to New York City, from New York City to Alabama; at last report, he has just moved back to New York City again. He attended the Clarion West Writers' Workshop in 1989, and since then has become a frequent contributor to Asimov's Science Fiction, *as well as to markets such as* The Magazine of Fantasy & Science Fiction, Amazing, SF Age, Universe, Full Spectrum, *and elsewhere. His first novel,* Warpath, *was released simultaneously in America and England in 1993, and he subsequently won $2000 and the T. Morris Hackney Award for his inexplicably as-yet-unsold novel* Ascension. *His story "Life on the Moon" was a finalist for the Hugo Award in 1996. He is currently at work on a new science fiction novel,* Earthling.

Here he spins a colorful and exotic story of a battle-weary veteran who returns from a bewilderingly strange high-tech future war only to face his greatest and most sinister challenge right at home. . . .

I cannot tell you what it meant to me to see the two suns of Ferro set behind the dry mountain east of my home. I had been away twelve billion years. I passed my cabin to the pump well, and taking a metal cup from where it hung from a set-pin, I worked the handle three times. At first it creaked, and I believed it was rusted tight, but then it loosened, and within fifteen pulls, I had a cup of water.

Someone had kept the pump up. Someone had seen to the house and the land while I was away at the war. For me, it had been fifteen years; I wasn't sure how long it had been for Ferro. The water was tinged red and tasted of iron. Good. I drank it down in a long draft, then put the cup back onto its hanger. When the big sun, Hemingway, set, a slight breeze kicked up. Then Fitzgerald went down and a cold, cloudless night spanked down onto the plateau. I shivered a little, adjusted my internals, and stood motionless, waiting for the last of twilight to pass, and the stars—my stars—to come out. Steiner, the planet that is Ferro's evening star, was the first to emerge, low in the west, methane blue. Then the constellations. Ngal. Gilgamesh. The Big Snake, half-coiled over the southwestern horizon. There was no moon tonight. There was never a moon on Ferro, and that was right.

After a time, I walked to the house, climbed up the porch, and the house recognized me and turned on the lights. I went inside. The place was dusty, the furniture covered with sheets, but there were no signs of rats or jinjas, and all seemed in repair. I sighed, blinked, tried to feel something. Too early, probably. I started to take a covering from a chair, then let it be. I went to the kitchen and checked the cupboard. An old malt-whiskey bottle, some dry cereal, some spices. The spices had been my mother's, and I seldom used them before I left for the end of time. I considered that the whiskey might be perfectly aged by now. But, as the saying goes on Ferro, we like a bit of food with our drink, so I left the house and took the road to town, to Heidel.

It was a five-mile walk, and though I could have enhanced and covered the ground in ten minutes or so, I walked at a regular pace under my homeworld stars. The road was dirt, of course, and my pant legs were dusted red when I stopped under the outside light of Thredmartin's Pub. I took a last breath of cold air, then went inside to the warm.

It was a good night at Thredmartin's. There were men and women gathered around the fire hearth, usas and splices in the cold corners. The regulars were at the bar, a couple of whom I recognized—so old now, wizened like stored apples in a barrel. I looked around for a particular face, but she was not there. A jukebox sputtered some core-cloud deak, and the air was thick with smoke and conversation. Or was, until I walked in. Nobody turned to face me. Most of them couldn't have seen me. But a signal passed and conversation fell to a quiet murmur. Somebody quickly killed the jukebox.

I blinked up an internals menu into my peripheral vision and adjusted to the room's temperature. Then I went to the edge of the bar. The room got even quieter. . . .

The bartender, old Thredmartin himself, reluctantly came over to me.

"What can I do for you, sir?" he asked me.

I looked over him, to the selection of bottles, tubes, and cans on display behind him. "I don't see it," I said.

"Eh?" He glanced back over his shoulder, then quickly returned to peering at me.

"Bone's Barley," I said.

"We don't have any more of that," Thredmartin said, with a suspicious tone.

"Why not?"

"The man who made it died."

"How long ago?"

"Twenty years, more or less. I don't see what business of—"

"What about his son?"

Thredmartin backed up a step. Then another. "Henry," he whispered. "Henry Bone."

"Just give me the best that you do have, Peter Thredmartin," I said. "In fact, I'd like to buy everybody a round on me."

"Henry Bone! Why, you looked to me like a bad 'un indeed when you walked in here. I took you for one of them glims, I did," Thredmartin said. I did not know what he was talking about. Then he smiled an old devil's crooked smile. "Your money's no good here, Henry Bone. I do happen to have a couple of bottles of your old dad's whiskey stowed away in back. Drinks are on the house."

And so I returned to my world, and for most of those I'd left behind it seemed as if I'd never really gone. My neighbors hadn't changed much in the twenty years local that had passed, and of course, they had no conception of what had happened to me. They knew only that I'd been to the war—the Big War at the End of Time— and evidently everything turned out okay, for here I was, back in my own time and my own place. I planted Ferro's desert barley, brought in peat from the mountain bogs, bred the biomass that would extract the minerals from my hard ground water, and got ready for making whiskey once again. Most of the inhabitants of Ferro were divided between whiskey families and beer families. Bones were distillers, never brewers, since the Settlement, ten generations before.

It wasn't until she called upon me that I heard the first hints of the troubles that had come. Her name was Alinda Bexter, but since we played together under the floorplanks of her father's hotel, I had always called her Bex. When I left for the war, she was twenty, and I twenty-one. I still recognized her at forty, five years older than I was now, as she came walking down the road to my house, a week after I'd returned. She was taller than most women on Ferro, and she might be mistaken for a usa-human splice anywhere else. She was rangy, and she wore a khaki dress that whipped in the dry wind as she came toward me. I stood on the porch, waiting for her, wondering what she would say.

"Well, this is a load off of me," she said. She was wearing a brimmed hat. It had ribbon to tie under her chin, but Bex had not done that. She held her hand on it to keep it from blowing from her head. "This damn ranch has been one big thankless task."

"So it was you who kept it up," I said.

"Just kept it from falling apart as fast as it would have otherwise," she replied. We stood and looked at one another for a moment. Her eyes were green. Now that I had seen an ocean, I could understand the kind of green they were.

"Well then," I finally said. "Come on in."

I offered her some sweetcake I'd fried up, and some beer that my neighbor, Shin, had brought by, both of which she declined. We sat in the living room, on furniture covered with the white sheets I had yet to remove. Bex and I took it slow, getting to know each other again. She ran her father's place now. For years, the only way to get to Heidel was by freighter, but we had finally gotten a node on the Flash, and even though Ferro was still a backwater planet, there were more strangers passing through than there ever had been—usually en route to other places. But they sometimes stayed a night or two in the Bexter Hotel. Its reputation was spreading, Bex claimed, and I believed her. Even when she was young, she had been shrewd but honest, a combination you don't often find in an innkeeper. She was a quiet woman—that is, until she got to know you well—and some most likely thought her conceited. I got the feeling that she hadn't let down her reserve for a long time. When I knew her before, Bex did not have many close friends, but for the ones she had, such as me, she poured out her thoughts, and her heart. I found that she hadn't changed much in that way.

"Did you marry?" I asked her, after hearing about the hotel and her father's bad health.

"No," she said. "No, I very nearly did, but then I did not. Did you?"

"No. Who was it?"

"Rall Kenton."

"Rall Kenton? Rall Kenton whose parents run the hops market?" He was a quarter-splice, a tall man on a world of tall men. Yet, when I knew him, his long shadow had been deceptive. There was no spark or force in him. "I can't see that, Bex."

"Tom Kenton died ten years ago," she said. "Marjorie retired, and Rall owned the business until just last year. Rall did all right; you'd be surprised. Something about his father's passing gave him a backbone. Too much of one, maybe."

"What happened?"

"He died," she said. "He died too, just as I thought you had." Now she told me she would like a beer after all, and I went to get her a bottle of Shin's ale. When I returned, I could tell that she'd been crying a little.

"The glims killed Rall," said Bex, before I could ask her about him. "That's their name for themselves, anyway. Humans, repons, kaliwaks, and I don't know what else. They passed through last year and stayed for a week in Heidel. Very bad. They made my father give over the whole hotel to them, and then they had a . . . trial, they called it. Every house was called and made to pay a tithe. The glims decided how much. Rall refused to pay. He brought along a pistol—Lord knows where he got it—and tried to shoot one of them. They just laughed and took it from him." Now the tears started again.

"And then they hauled him out into the street in front of the hotel." Bex took a moment and got control of herself. "They burnt him up with a p-gun. Burned his legs off first, then his arms, then the rest of him after they'd let him lie there a while. There wasn't a trace of him after that; we couldn't even bury him."

I couldn't take her to me, hold her, not after she'd told me about Rall. Needing something to do, I took some tangled banwood from the tinder box and struggled to get a fire going from the burnt-down coals in my hearth. I blew into the fireplace and only got a nose full of ashes for my trouble. "Didn't anybody fight?" I asked.

"Not after that. We just waited them out. Or they got bored. I don't know. It was bad for everybody, not just Rall." Bex shook her head, sighed, then saw the trouble I was having and bent down to help me. She was much better at it than I, and the fire was soon ablaze. We sat back down and watched it flicker.

"Sounds like war-ghosts," I said.

"The glims?"

"Soldiers who don't go home after the war. The fighting gets into them and they don't want to give it up, or can't. Sometimes they have . . . modifications that won't let them give it up. They wander the timeways—and since they don't belong to the time they show up in, they're hard to kill. In the early times, where people don't know about the war, or have only heard rumors of it, they had lots of names. Vampires. Hagamonsters. Zombies."

"What can you do?"

I put my arm around her. It had been so long. She tensed up, then breathed deeply, serenely.

"Hope they don't come back," I said. "They are bad ones. Not the worst, but bad."

We were quiet for a while, and the wind, blowing over the chimney's top, made the flue moan as if it were a big stone flute.

"Did you love him, Bex?" I asked. "Rall?"

She didn't even hesitate in her answer this time. "Of course not, Henry Bone. How could you ever think such a thing? I was waiting to catch up with you. Now tell me about the future."

And so I drew away from her for a while, and told her—part of it at least. About how there is not enough dark matter to pull the cosmos back together again, not enough mass to undulate in an eternal cycle. Instead, there *is* an end, and all the stars are either dead or dying, and all that there is is nothing but dim night. I told her about the twilight armies gathered there, culled from all times, all places. Creatures, presences, machines, weapons fighting galaxy-to-galaxy, system-to-system, fighting until the critical point is reached, when entropy flows no more, but pools, pools in endless, stagnant pools of nothing. No light. No heat. No effect. And the universe is dead, and so those who remain . . . inherit the dark field. They win.

"And did you win?" she asked me. "If that's the word for it."

The suns were going down. Instead of answering, I went outside to the woodpile and brought in enough banwood to fuel the fire for the night. I thought maybe she would forget what she'd asked me—but not Bex.

"How does the war end, Henry?"

"You must never ask me that." I spoke the words carefully, making sure I was giving away nothing in my reply. "Every time a returning soldier tells that answer, he changes everything. Then he has two choices. He can either go away, leave his own time, and go back to fight again. Or he can stay, and it will all mean nothing, what he did. Not just who won and who lost, but all the things he did in the war spin off into nothing."

Bex thought about this for a while. "What could it matter? What in God's name could be worth fighting *for*?" she finally asked. "Time ends. Nothing matters after that. What could it possibly matter who won . . . who wins?"

"It means you can go back home," I said. "After it's over."

"I don't understand."

I shook my head and was silent. I had said enough. There was no way to tell her more, in any case—not without changing things. And no way to *say* what it was that had brought those forces together at the end of everything. And what the hell do *I* know, even now? All I know is what I was told, and what I was trained to do. If we don't fight at the end, there won't be a beginning. For there to be people, there has to be a war to fight at the end of things. We live in that kind of universe, and not another, they told me. They told me, and then I told myself. And I did what I had to do so that it would be over and I could go home, come back.

"Bex, I never forgot you," I said. She came to sit with me by the fire. We didn't touch at first, but I felt her next to me, breathed the flush of her skin as the fire warmed her. Then she ran her hand along my arm, felt the bumps from the operational enhancements.

"What have they done to you?" she whispered.

Unbidden the old words of the skyfallers' scream, the words that were yet to be, surfaced in my mind.

They sucked down my heart
to a little black hole.
You cannot stab me.

They wrote down my brain
on a hard knot of space.
You cannot turn me.

Icicle spike
from the eye of a star.
I've come to kill you.

I almost spoke them, from sheer habit. But I did not. The war was over. Bex was here, and I knew it was over. I was going to *feel* something, once again, something besides guile, hate, and rage. I didn't yet, that was true, but I *could* feel the possibility.

"I don't really breathe anymore, Bex; I pretend to so I won't put people off," I told her. "It's been so long, I can't even remember what it was like to *have* to."

Bex kissed me then. At first, I didn't remember how to do that either. And then I did. I added wood to the fire, then ran my hand along Bex's neck and shoulder. Her skin had the health of youth still, but years in the sun and wind had made a supple leather of it, tanned and grained fine. We took the sheet from the couch and pulled it near to the warmth, and she drew me down to her on it, to her neck and breasts.

"Did they leave enough of you for me?" she whispered.

I had not known until now. "Yes," I answered, "there's enough." I found my way inside her, and we made love slowly, in a way that might seem sad to any others but us, for there were memories and years of longing that flowed from us, around us, like amber just at the melting point, and we were inside and there was nothing but this present with all of what was, and what would be, already passed. No time. Finally, only Bex and no time between us.

We fell asleep on the old couch, and it was dim half-morning when we awoke, with Fitzgerald yet to rise in the west and the fire a bed of coals as red as the sky.

Two months later, I was in Thredmartin's when Bex came in with an evil look on her face. We had taken getting back together slow and easy up till then, but the more time we spent around each other, the more we understood that nothing basic had changed. Bex kept coming to the ranch and I took to spending a couple of nights a week in a room her father made up for me at the hotel. Furly Bexter was an old-style McKinnonite. Men and women were to live separately and only meet for business and copulation. But he liked me well enough, and when I insisted on paying for my room, he found a loophole somewhere in the Tracts of McKinnon about cohabitation being all right in hotels and hostels.

"The glims are back," Bex said, sitting down at my table. I was in a dark corner of the pub. I left the fire for those who could not adjust their own internals to keep them warm. "They've taken over the top floor of the hotel. What should we do?"

I took a draw of beer—Thredmartin's own thick porter—and looked at her. She was visibly shivering, probably more from agitation than fright.

"How many of them are there?" I asked.

"Six. And something else, some splice I've never seen, however many that makes."

I took another sip of beer. "Let it be," I said. "They'll get tired, and they'll move on."

"What?" Bex's voice was full of astonishment. "What are you saying?"

"You don't want a war here, Bex," I replied. "You have no idea how bad it can get."

"They killed Rall. They took our *money*."

"Money." My voice sounded many years away, even to me.

"It's muscle and worry and care. You know how hard people work on Ferro. And for those . . . *things* . . . to come in and take it! We cannot let them—"

"—Bex," I said. "I am not going to do anything."

She said nothing; she put a hand on her forehead as if she had a sickening fever, stared at me for a moment, then looked away.

One of the glims chose that moment to come into Thredmartin's. It was a halandana, a splice—human and jan—from up-time and a couple of possible universes over. It was nearly seven feet tall, with a two-foot-long neck, and it stooped to enter Thredmartin's. Without stopping, it went to the bar and demanded morphine.

Thredmartin was at the bar. He pulled out a dusty rubber, little used, and before he could get out an injector, the halandana reached over, took the entire rubber and put it in the pocket of the long gray coat it wore. Thredmartin started to speak, then shook his head, and found a spray shooter. He slapped it on the bar, and started to walk away. The halandana's hand shot out and pushed the old man. Thredmartin stumbled to his knees.

I felt the fingers of my hands clawing, clenching. Let them loosen; let them go.

Thredmartin rose slowly to one knee. Bex was up, around the bar, and over to him, steadying his shoulder. The glim watched this for a moment, then took its drug and shooter to a table, where it got itself ready for an injection.

I looked at it closely now. It was female, but that did not mean much in halandana splices. I could see it phase around the edges with dead, gray flames. I clicked in wideband overspace, and I could see through the halandana to the chair it was sitting in and the unpainted wood of the wall behind it. And I saw more, in the spaces between spaces. The halandana was keyed in to a websquad; it wasn't really an individual anymore. Its fate was tied to that of its unit commander. So the war-ghosts—the glims—were a renegade squad, most likely, with a single leader calling the shots. For a moment, the halandana glanced in my direction, maybe feeling my gaze somewhere outside of local time, and I banded down to human normal. It quickly went back to what it was doing. Bex made sure Thredmartin was all right, then came back over to my table.

"We're not even in its timeline," I said. "It doesn't think of us as really being alive."

"Oh God," Bex said. "This is just like before."

I got up and walked out. It was the only solution. I could not say anything to Bex. She would not understand. I understood—not acting was the rational, the *only*, way, but not *my* way. Not until now.

I enhanced my legs and loped along the road to my house. But when I got there,

I kept running, running off into the red sands of Ferro's outback. The night came down, and as the planet turned, I ran along the length of the Big Snake, bright and hard to the southwest, and then under the blue glow of Steiner, when she rose in the moonless, trackless night. I ran for miles and miles, as fast as a jaguar, but never tiring. How could I tire when parts of me stretched off into dimensions of utter stillness, utter rest? Could Bex see me for what I *was*, she would not see a man, but a kind of colonial creature, a mash of life pressed into the niches and fault lines of existence like so much grit and lichen. A human is anchored with only his heart and his mind; sever those, and he floats away. Floats away. What was I? A medusa fish in an ocean of time? A tight clump of nothing, disguised as a man? Something else?

Something damned hard to kill, that was certain. And so were the glims. When I returned to my house in the star-bright night, I half expected to find Bex, but she was not there. And so I rattled about for a while, powered down for an hour at dawn and rested on a living-room chair, dreaming in one part of my mind, completely alert in another. The next day, Bex still did not come, and I began to fear something had happened to her. I walked partway into Heidel, then cut off the road and stole around the outskirts, to a mound of shattered, volcanic rocks—the tailings of some early prospector's pit—not far from the town's edge. There I stepped up my vision and hearing, and made a long sweep of Main Street. Nothing. Far, far too quiet, even for Heidel.

I worked out the parabolic to the Bexter Hotel, and after a small adjustment, heard Bex's voice, then her father's. I was too far away to make out the words, but my quantitatives gave it a positive ID. So Bex was all right, at least for the moment. I made my way back home, and put in a good day's work making whiskey.

The next morning—it was the quarteryear's double dawn, with both suns rising in the east nearly together—Bex came to me. I brought her inside, and in the moted sunlight of my family's living room, where I now took my rest, when I rested, Bex told me that the glims had taken her father.

"He held back some old Midnight Livet down in the cellar, and didn't deliver it when they called for room service." Bex rubbed her left fist with her right fingers, expertly, almost mechanically, as she'd kneaded a thousand balls of bread dough. "How do they know these things? How do they know, Henry?"

"They can see *around* things," I said. "Some of them can, anyway."

"So they read our thoughts? What do we have left?"

"No, no. They can't see in *there*, at least I'm sure they can't see in your old man's McKinnonite nut lump of a brain. But they probably saw the whiskey down in the cellar, all right. A door isn't a very solid thing for a war-ghost out of its own time and place."

Bex gave her hand a final squeeze, spread it out upon her lap. She stared down at the lines of her palm, then looked up at me. "If you won't fight, then you have to tell *me* how to fight them," she said. "I won't let them kill my father."

"Maybe they won't."

"I can't take that chance."

Her eyes were blazing green, as the suns came full through the window. Her face was bright-lit and shadowed, as if by the steady coals of a fire. You have loved this woman a long time, I thought. You have to tell her something that will be of use. But what could possibly be of use against a creature that had survived— *will* survive—that great and final war—and so must survive *now*? You can't kill the future. That's how the old sergeants would explain battle fate to the recruits. If you are meant to be there, they'd say, then nothing can hurt you. And if you're not, then you'll just fade, so you might as well go out fighting.

"You can only irritate them," I finally said to Bex. "There's a way to do it with the Flash. Talk to that technician, what's his name—"

"Jurven Dvorak."

"Tell Dvorak to strobe the local interrupt, fifty, sixty tetracycles. It'll cut off all traffic, but it will be like a wasp nest to them, and they won't want to get close enough to turn it off. Maybe they'll leave. Dvorak better stay near the node after that too."

"All right," Bex said. "Is that all?"

"Yes," I said. I rubbed my temples, felt the vague pain of a headache, which quickly receded as my internals rushed more blood to my scalp. "Yes, that's it."

Later that day, I heard the crackle of random quantum-tunnel spray, as split, unsieved particles decided their spin, charm, and color without guidance from the world of gravity and cause. It was an angry buzz, like the hum of an insect caught between screen and windowpane, tremendously irritating to listen to for hours on end, if you were unlucky enough to be sensitive to the effect. I put up with it, hoping against hope that it would be enough to drive off the glims.

Bex arrived in the early evening, leading her father, who was ragged and half-crazed from two days without light or water. The glims had locked him in a cleaning closet, in the hotel, where he'd sat cramped and doubled over. After the buzz started, Bex opened the lock and dragged the old man out. It was as if the glims had forgotten the whole affair.

"Maybe," I said. "We can hope."

She wanted me to put the old man up at my house, in case the glims suddenly remembered. Old Furly Bexter didn't like the idea. He rattled on about something in McKinnon's "Letter to the Canadians," but I said yes, he could stay. Bex left me with her father in the shrouds of my living room.

Some time that night, the quantum buzz stopped. And in the early morning, I saw them—five of them—stalking along the road, kicking before them the cowering, stumbling form of Jurven Dvorak. I waited for them on the porch. Furly Bexter was asleep in my parents' bedroom. He was exhausted from his ordeal, and I expected him to stay that way for a while.

When they came into the yard, Dvorak ran to the pump and held to the handle, as if it were a branch suspending him over a bottomless chasm. And for him it was. They'd broken his mind and given him a dream of dying. Soon to be replaced by reality, I suspected, and no pump-handle hope of salvation.

Their leader—or the one who did the talking—was human-looking. I'd have to band out to make a full ID, and I didn't want to give anything away for the moment. He saved me the trouble by telling me himself.

"My name's Marek," he said. "Come from a D-line, not far down-time from here."

I nodded, squinting into the red brightness reflected off my hardpan yard.

"We're just here for a good time," the human continued. "What you want to spoil that for?"

I didn't say anything for a moment. One of Marek's gang spat into the dryness of my dirt.

"Go ahead and have it," I said.

"All right," Marek said. He turned to Dvorak, then pulled out a weapon—not really a weapon though, for it is the tool of behind-the-lines enforcers, prison interrogators, confession extractors. It's called an algorithmic truncheon, a *trunch*, in the parlance. A trunch, used at full load, will strip the myelin sheath from axons and dendrites; it will burn up a man's nerves as if they were fuses. It is a way to kill with horrible pain. Marek walked over and touched the trunch to the leg of Dvorak, as if he were lighting a bonfire.

The Flash technician began to shiver, and then to seethe, like a teapot coming to boil. The motion traveled up his legs, into his chest, out his arms. His neck began to writhe, as if the corded muscles were so many snakes. Then Dvorak's brain burned, as a teapot will when all the water has run out and there is nothing but flame against hot metal. And then Dvorak screamed. He screamed for a long, long time. And then he died, crumpled and spent, on the ground in front of my house.

"I don't know you," Marek said, standing over Dvorak's body and looking up at me. "I know *what* you are, but I can't get a read on *who* you are, and that worries me," he said. He kicked at one of the Flash tech's twisted arms. "But now you know *me*."

"Get off my land," I said. I looked at him without heat. Maybe I felt nothing inside, either. That uncertainty had been my companion for a long time, my grim companion. Marek studied me for a moment. If I kept his attention, he might not look around me, look inside the house, to find his other fun, Furly Bexter, half-dead from Marck's amusements. Marek turned to the others.

"We're going," he said to them. "We've done what we came for." They turned around and left by the road on which they'd come, the only road there was. After a while, I took Dvorak's body to a low hill and dug him a grave there. I set up a sandstone marker, and since I knew Dvorak came from Catholic people, I scratched into the stone the sign of the cross. Jesus, from the Milky Way. Another glim. Hard to kill.

It took old-man Bexter only a week or so to fully recover; I should have known by knowing Bex that he was made of a tougher grit. He began to putter around the house, helping me out where he could, although I ran a tidy one-man operation, and he was more in the way than anything. Bex risked a trip out once that week. Her father again insisted he was going back into town, but Bex told him the glims were looking for him. So far, she'd managed to convince them that she had no idea where he'd gotten to.

I was running low on food and supplies, and had to go into town the following Firstday. I picked up a good backpack load at the mercantile and some chemicals for treating the peat at the druggist, then risked a quick look-in on Bex. A sign on the desk told all that they could find her at Thredmartin's, taking her lunch, should they want her. I walked across the street, set my load down just inside Thredmartin's door, in the cloakroom, then passed through the entrance into the afternoon dank of the pub.

I immediately sensed glims all around, and hunched myself in, both mentally and physically. I saw Bex in her usual corner, and walked toward her across the room. As I stepped beside a table in the pub's middle, a glim—it was the halandana—stuck out a long, hairy leg. Almost, I tripped—and in that instant, I almost did the natural thing and cast about for some hold that was not present in the three-dimensional world—but I did not. I caught myself, came to a dead stop, then carefully walked around the glim's outstretched leg.

"Mind if I sit down?" I said as I reached Bex's table. She nodded toward a free chair. She was finishing a beer, and an empty glass stood beside it. Thredmartin usually had the tables clear as soon as the last drop left a mug. Bex was drinking fast. Why? Working up her courage, perhaps.

I lowered myself into the chair, and for a long time, neither of us said anything to the other. Bex finished her beer. Thredmartin appeared, looked curiously at the two empty mugs. Bex signaled for another, and I ordered my own whiskey.

"How's the ranch," she finally asked me. Her face was flush and her lips trembled slightly. She was angry, I decided. At me, at the situation. It was understandable. Completely understandable.

"Fine," I said. "The ranch is fine."

"Good."

Again a long silence. Thredmartin returned with our drinks. Bex sighed, and for a moment, I thought she would speak, but she did not. Instead, she reached under the table and touched my hand. I opened my palm, and she put her hand into mine. I felt the tension in her, the bonework of her hand as she squeezed tightly. I felt her fear and worry. I felt her love.

And then Marek came into the pub looking for her. He stalked across the room and stood in front of our table. He looked hard at me, then at Bex, and then he swept an arm across the table and sent Bex's beer and my whiskey flying toward the wall. The beer mug broke, but I quickly reached out and caught my tumbler of scotch in midair without spilling a drop. Of course, no ordinary human could have done it.

Bex noticed Marek looking at me strangely and spoke with a loud voice that got his attention. "What do you want? You were looking for me at the hotel?"

"Your sign says you're open," Marek said in a reasonable, ugly voice. "I rang for room service. Repeatedly."

"Sorry," Bex said. "Just let me settle up and I'll be right there."

"Be right there *now*," Marek said, pushing the table from in front of her. Again, I caught my drink, held it on a knee while I remained sitting. Bex started up from her chair and stood facing Marek. She looked him in the eyes. "I'll *be* there directly," she said.

Without warning, Marek reached out and grabbed her by the chin. He didn't seem to be pressing hard, but I knew he must have her in a painful grip. He pulled Bex toward him. Still, she stared him in the eyes. Slowly, I rose from my chair, setting my tumbler of whiskey down on the warm seat where I had been.

Marek glanced over at me. Our eyes met, and at that close distance, he could plainly see the enhancements under my corneas. I could see his.

"Let go of her," I said.

He did not let go of Bex.

"Who the hell are you?" he asked. "That you tell *me* what to do?"

"I'm just a grunt, same as you," I said. "Let go of her."

The halandana had risen from its chair and was soon standing behind Marek. It-she growled mean and low. A combat schematic of how to handle the situation iconed up into the corner of my vision. The halandana was a green figure, Marek was red, Bex was a faded rose. I blinked once to enlarge it. Studied it in a fractional second. Blinked again to close it down. Marek let go of Bex.

She stumbled back, hurt and mad, rubbing her chin.

"I don't think we've got a grunt here," Marek said, perhaps to the halandana, or to himself, but looking at me. "I think we've got us a genuine skyfalling space marine."

The halandana's growl grew deeper and louder, filling ultra and subsonic frequencies.

"How many systems'd you take out, skyfaller?" Marek asked. "A couple of galaxies worth?" The halandana made to advance on me, but Marek put out his hand to stop it. "Where do you get off? This ain't nothing but small potatoes next to what *you've* done."

In that moment, I spread out, stretched a bit in ways that Bex could not see, but that Marek could—to some extent at least. I encompassed him, all of him, and did a thorough ID on both him and the halandana. I ran the data through some trans-d personnel files tucked into a swirl in n-space I'd never expected to access again. Marek Lambrois. Corporal of a back-line military-police platoon assigned to the local cluster in a couple of possible worlds, deserters all in a couple of others. He was aggression enhanced by trans-weblink anti-alg coding. The squad's fighting profile was notched to the top level at all times. They were bastards who were now *preprogrammed* bastards. Marek was right about them being small potatoes. He and his gang were nothing but mean-ass grunts, small-time goons for some of the nonaligned contingency troops.

"What the hell?" Marek said. He noticed my analytics, although it was too fast for him to get a good glimpse of me. But he did understand something in that moment, something it didn't take enhancement to figure out. And in that moment, everything was changed, had I but seen. Had I but seen.

"You're some bigwig, ain't you, skyfaller? Somebody that *matters* to the outcome," Marek said. "This is your actual, and you don't want to fuck yourself uptime, so you won't fight." He smiled crookedly. A diagonal of teeth, straight and narrow, showed whitely.

"Don't count on it," I said.

"You won't," he said, this time with more confidence. "I don't know what I was worrying about! I can do anything I want here."

"Well," I said. "Well." And then I said nothing.

"Get on over there and round me up some grub," Marek said to Bex. "I'll be waiting for it in room forty-five, little lady."

"I'd rather—"

"Do it," I said. The words were harsh and did not sound like my voice. But they were my words, and after a moment, I remembered the voice. It was mine. From far, far in the future. Bex gasped at their hardness, but took a step forward, moved to obey.

"Bex," I said, more softly. "Just get the man some food." I turned to Marek. "If you hurt her, I don't care about anything. Do you understand? Nothing will matter to me."

Marek's smile widened into a grin. He reached over, slowly, so that I could think about it, and patted my cheek. Then he deliberately slapped me, hard. Hard enough to turn my head. Hard enough to draw a trickle of blood from my lip. It didn't hurt very much, of course. Of course it didn't hurt.

"Don't you worry, skyfaller," he said. "I know exactly where I stand now." He turned and left, and the halandana, its drugs unfinished on the table where it had sat, trailed out after him.

Bex looked at me. I tried to meet her gaze, but did not. I did not look down, but stared off into Thredmartin's darkness. She reached over and wiped the blood from my chin with her little finger.

"I guess I'd better go," she said.

I did not reply. She shook her head sadly, and walked in front of me. I kept my eyes fixed, far away from this place, this time, and her passing was a swirl of air, a red-brown swish of hair, and Bex was gone. Gone.

They sucked down my heart
to a little black hole.
You cannot stab me.

"Colonel Bone, we've done the prelims on sector eleven sixty-eight, and there are fifty-six class-one civilizations along with two-hundred seventy rationals in stage-one or -two development."

"Fifty-six. Two hundred seventy. Ah. Me."

"Colonel, sir, we can evac over half of them within thirty-six hours local."

"And have to defend them in the transcendent. Chaos neutral. Guaranteed forty percent casualties for us."

"Yes, sir. But what about the civs at least. We can save a few."

They wrote down my brain
on a hard knot of space.
You cannot turn me.

"Unacceptable, soldier."

"Sir?"

"Unacceptable."

"Yes, sir."

• • •

All dead. All those millions of dead people. But it was the end of time, and they had to die, so that they—so that we *all*, all in time—could live. But they didn't know, those civilizations. Those people. It was the end of time, but you loved life all the same, and you died the same hard way as always. For nothing. It would be for nothing. Outside, the wind had kicked up. The sky was red with Ferro's dust, and a storm was brewing for the evening. I coated my sclera with a hard and glassy membrane, and unblinking, I stalked home with my supplies through a fierce and growing wind.

That night, on the curtains of dust and thin rain, on the heave of the storm, Bex came to my house. Her clothes were torn and her face was bruised. She said nothing, as I closed the door behind her, led her into the kitchen, and began to treat her wounds. She said nothing as her worried father sat at my kitchen table and watched, and wrung his hands, and watched because there wasn't anything he could do.

"Did that man . . . ," her father said. The old man's voice broke. "Did he?"

"I tried to take the thing, the trunch, from him. He'd left it lying on the table by the door." Bex spoke in a hollow voice. "I thought that nobody was going to do anything, not even Henry, so I had to. I had to." Her facial bruises were superficial. But she held her legs stiffly together, and clasped her hands to her stomach. There was vomit on her dress. "The trunch had some kind of alarm set on it," Bex said. "So he caught me."

"Bex, are you hurting?" I said to her. She looked down, then carefully spread her legs. "He caught me and then he used the trunch on me. Not full strength. Said he didn't want to do permanent damage. Said he wanted to save me for later." Her voice sounded far away. She covered her face with her hands. "He put it in me," she said.

Then she breathed deeply, raggedly, and made herself look at me. "Well," she said. "So."

I put her into my bed, and he sat in the chair beside it, standing watch for who knew what? He could not defend his daughter, but he must try, as surely as the suns rose, now growing farther apart, over the hard pack of my homeworld desert.

Everything was changed.

"Bex," I said to her, and touched her forehead. Touched her fine, brown skin. "Bex, in the future, we won. I won, my command won it. Really, really big. That's why we're here. That's why we're all here."

Bex's eyes were closed. I could not tell if she'd already fallen asleep. I hoped she had.

"I have to take care of some business, and then I'll do it again," I said in a whisper. "I'll just have to go back up-time and do it again."

Between the first and second rising, I'd reached Heidel, and as Hemingway burned red through the storm's dusty leavings, I stood in the shadows of the entrance foyer of the Bexter Hotel. There I waited.

The halandana was the first up—like me, they never really slept—and it came down from its room looking, no doubt, to go out and get another rubber of its drug. Instead, it found me. I didn't waste time with the creature. With a quick twist in n-space, I pulled it down to the present, down to a local concentration of hate and lust and stupidity that I could kill with a quick thrust into its throat. But I let it live; I showed it myself, all of me spread out and huge, and I let it fear.

"Go and get Marek Lambrois," I told it. "Tell him Colonel Bone wants to see him. Colonel Henry Bone of the Eighth Sky and Light."

"Bone," said the halandana. "I thought—"

I reached out and grabbed the creature's long neck. This was the halandana weak point, and this halandana had a ceramic implant as protection. I clicked up the power in my forearm a level and crushed the collar as I might a tea cup. The halandana's neck carapace shattered to platelets and shards, outlined in fine cracks under its skin.

"Don't think," I said. "Tell Marek Lambrois to come into the street and I will let him live."

This was untrue, of course, but hope never dies, I'd discovered, even in the hardest of soldiers. But perhaps I'd underestimated Marek. Sometimes I still wonder.

He stumbled out, still partly asleep, onto the street. Last night had evidently been a hard and long one. His eyes were a red no detox nano could fully clean up. His skin was the color of paste.

"You have something on me," I said. "I cannot abide that."

"Colonel Bone," he began. "If I'd knowed it was *you*—"

"Too late for that."

"It's never too late, that's what you taught us all when you turned that offensive around out on the Husk and gave the Chaos the what-for. I'll just be going. I'll take the gang with me. It's to no purpose, our staying now."

"You knew enough *yesterday*—enough to leave." I felt the rage, the old rage that was to be, once again. "Why did you do that to her?" I asked. "Why did you—"

And then I looked into his eyes and saw it there. The quiet desire—beaten down by synthesized emotions, but now triumphant, sadly triumphant. The desire to finally, finally *die*. Marek was not the unthinking brute I'd taken him for after all. Too bad for him.

I took a step toward Marek. His instincts made him reach down, go for the trunch. But it was a useless weapon on me. I don't have myelin sheaths on my nerves. I don't have nerves anymore; I have *wiring*. Marek realized this was so almost instantly. He dropped the trunch, then turned and ran. I caught him. He tried to fight, but there was never any question of him beating me. That would be absurd. I'm Colonel Bone of the Skyfalling 8th. I kill so that there might be life. *Nobody* beats me. It is my fate, and yours too.

I caught him by the shoulder, and I looped my other arm around his neck and reined him to me—not enough to snap anything. Just enough to calm him down. He was strong, but had no finesse.

Like I said, glims are hard to kill. They're the same as snails in shells in a way, and the trick is to draw them out—way out. Which is what I did with Marek. As I held him physically, I caught hold of him, all of him, *over there*, in the place I can't tell you about, can't describe. The way you do this is by holding a glim still and causing him great suffering, so that they can't withdraw into the deep places. That's what vampire stakes and Roman crosses are all about.

And, like I told Bex, glims are bad ones, all right. Bad, but not the worst. *I* am the worst.

Icicle spike
from the eye of a star.
I've come to kill you.

I sharpened my nails. Then I plunged them into Marek's stomach, through the skin, into the twist of his guts. I reached around there and caught hold of something, a piece of intestine. I pulled it out. This I tied to the porch of the Bexter Hotel.

Marek tried to untie himself and pull away. He was staring at his insides, rolled out, raw and exposed, and thinking—I don't know what. I haven't died. I don't know what it is like to die. He moaned sickly. His hands fumbled uselessly in the grease and phlegm that coated his very own self. There was no undoing the knots I'd tied, no pushing himself back in.

I picked him up, and as he whimpered, I walked down the street with him. His guts trailed out behind us, like a pink ribbon. After I'd gotten about twenty feet, I figured this was all he had in him. I dropped him into the street.

Hemingway was in the northeast and Fitzgerald directly east. They both shone at different angles on Marek's crumple, and cast crazy, mazy shadows down the length of the street.

"Colonel Bone," he said. I was tired of his talking. "Colonel—"

I reached into his mouth, past his gnashing teeth, and pulled out his tongue. He reached for it as I extracted it, so I handed it to him. Blood and drool flowed from his mouth and colored the red ground even redder about him. Then, one by one, I broke his arms and legs, then I broke each of the vertebrae in his backbone, moving up his spinal column with quick pinches. It didn't take long.

This is what I did in the world that people can see. In the twists of other times and spaces, I did similar things, horrible, irrevocable things, to the man. I killed him. I killed him in such a way that he would never come to life again, not in any possible place, not in any possible time. I wiped Marek Lambrois from existence. Thoroughly. And with his death the other glims died, like lights going out, lights ceasing to exist, bulb, filament and all. Or like the quick loss of all sensation after a brain is snuffed out.

Irrevocably gone from this timeline, and that was what mattered. Keeping this possible future uncertain, balanced on the fulcrum of chaos and necessity. Keeping it *free*, so that I could go back and do my work.

I left Marek lying there, in the main street of Heidel. Others could do the mopping up; that wasn't my job. As I left town, on the way back to my house and my life there, I saw that I wasn't alone in the dawn-lit town. Some had business out at this hour, and they had watched. Others had heard the commotion and come to windows and porches to see what it was. Now they knew. They knew what I was, what I was to be. I walked alone down the road, and found Bex and her father both sound asleep in my room.

I stroked her fine hair. She groaned, turned in her sleep. I pulled my covers up to her chin. Forty years old, and as beautiful as a child. Safe in my bed. Bex. Bex. I will miss you. Always, always, Bex.

I went to the living room, to the shroud-covered furniture. I sat down in what had been my father's chair. I sipped a cup of my father's best barley-malt whiskey. I sat, and as the suns of Ferro rose in the hard-iron sky, I faded into the distant, dying future.

THIRTEEN PHANTASMS

James P. Blaylock

▼

James P. Blaylock was born in Long Beach, California, and now lives in Orange, California. He made his first sale to the now-defunct semiprozine Unearth, *and subsequently became one of the most popular, literate, and wildly eclectic fantasists of the '80s and '90s. His story "Paper Dragons" won him a World Fantasy Award in 1986. His critically acclaimed novels—often quirky blends of different genres (SF, fantasy, nineteen-century mainstream novels, horror, romance, ghost stories, mystery, adventure) that would seem doomed to clash, but which, in Blaylock's whimsically affectionate hands somehow do not—include* The Last Coin, Land of Dreams, The Digging Leviathan, Homunculus, Lord Kelvin's Machine, The Elfin Ship, The Disappearing Dwarf, The Magic Spectacles, The Stone Giant, The Paper Grail, *and* Night Relics. *His most recent book is the novel* All the Bells on Earth. *His aforementioned "Paper Dragons" appeared in our Third Annual Collection.*

In the evocative and lushly nostalgic story that follows, he shows us that sometimes you can *Go Home Again—if you just* try *hard enough.*

There was a small window in the attic, six panes facing the street, the wood frame unpainted and without moldings. Leafy wisteria vines grew over the glass outside, filtering the sunlight and tinting it green. The attic was dim despite the window, and the vines outside shook in the autumn wind, rustling against the clapboards of the old house and casting leafy shadows on the age-darkened beams and rafters. Landers set his portable telephone next to the crawl-space hatch and shined a flashlight across the underside of the shingles, illuminating dusty cobwebs and the skeleton frame of the roof. The air smelled of dust and wood, and the attic was lonesome with silence and moving shadows, a place sheltered from time and change.

A car rolled past out on the street, and Landers heard a train whistle in the distance. Somewhere across town, church bells tolled the hour, and there was the faint sound of freeway noise off to the east like the drone of a perpetual-motion engine. It was easy to imagine that the wisteria vines had tangled themselves around the window frame for some secretive purpose of their own, obscuring the glass with leaves, muffling the sounds of the world.

He reached down and switched the portable phone off, regretting that he'd brought it with him at all. It struck him suddenly as something incongruous, an artifact from an alien planet. For a passing moment he considered dropping it through the open hatch just to watch it slam to the floor of the kitchen hallway below.

Years ago old Mr. Cummings had set pine planks across the two-by-six ceiling joists to make a boardwalk beneath the roof beam, apparently with the idea of using the attic for storage, although it must have been a struggle to haul things up through the shoulder-width attic hatch. At the end of this boardwalk, against the north wall, lay four, dust-covered cardboard cartons—full of ''junk magazines,'' or so Mrs. Cummings herself had told Landers this morning. The cartons were tied with twine, pulled tight and knotted, all the cartons the same. The word ASTOUND-ING was written on the side with a felt marker in neat, draftsmanlike letters. Landers wryly wondered what sort of things Mr. Cummings might have considered astounding, and after a moment, he decided that the man had been fortunate to find enough of it in one lifetime to fill four good-sized boxes.

Landers himself had come up empty in that regard, at least lately. For years he'd had a picture in his mind of himself whistling a cheerful out-of-key tune, walking along a country road, his hands in his pockets and with no particular destination, sunlight streaming through the trees and the limitless afternoon stretching toward the horizon. Somehow that picture had lost its focus in the past year or so, and as with an old friend separated by time and distance, he had nearly given up on seeing it again.

It had occurred to him this morning that he hadn't brewed real coffee for nearly a year now. The coffee pot sat under the counter instead of on top of it, and was something he hauled out for guests. There was a frozen brick of ground coffee in the freezer, but he never bothered with it anymore. Janet had been opposed to freezing coffee at all. Freezing it, she said, killed the aromatic oils. It was better to buy it a half pound at a time, so that it was always fresh. Lately, though, most of the magic had gone out of the morning coffee; it didn't matter how fresh it was.

The Cummingses had owned the house since it was built in 1924, and Mrs. Cummings, ninety years old now, had held on for twenty years after her husband's death, letting the place run down, and then had rented it to Landers and moved into the Palmyra Apartments beyond the Plaza. Occasionally he still got mail intended for her, and it was easier simply to take it to her than to give it back to the post office. This morning she had told him about the boxes in the attic: ''Just leave them there,'' she'd said. Then she had shown him her husband's old slide rule, slipping it out of its leather case and working the slide. She wasn't sure why she kept it, but she had kept a couple of old smoking pipes too, and a ring-shaped cut-crystal decanter with some whiskey still in it. Mrs. Cummings didn't have any use for the pipes or the decanter any more than she had a use for the slide rule, but Landers, who had himself kept almost nothing to remind him of his own past, understood that there was something about these souvenirs, sitting alongside a couple of old photographs on a small table, that recalled better days, easier living.

The arched window of the house on Rexroth Street in Glendale looked out onto a sloping front lawn with an overgrown carob tree at the curb, shading a dusty Land Rover with what looked like prospecting tools strapped to the rear bumper. There was a Hudson Wasp in the driveway, parked behind an Austin Healey. Across the street a man in shirtsleeves rubbed paste polish onto the fender of a Studebaker, and a woman in a sundress dug in a flower bed with a trowel, setting out pansies. A little boy rode a sort of sled on wheels up and down the sidewalk, and the sound of the solid-rubber wheels bumping over cracks sounded oddly loud in the still afternoon.

Russell Latzarel turned away from the window and took a cold bottle of beer from Roycroft Squires. In a few minutes the Newtonian Society would come to order, more or less, for the second time that day. Not that it made a lot of difference. For Latzarel's money they could recess until midnight if they wanted to, and the world would spin along through space for better or worse. He and Squires were both bachelors, and so unlike married men they had until hell froze over to come to order.

"India Pale Ale," Latzarel said approvingly, looking at the label on the squat green bottle. He gulped down an inch of beer. "Elixir of the gods, eh?" He set the bottle on a coaster. Then he filled his pipe with Balkan Sobranie tobacco and tamped it down, settling into an armchair in front of the chessboard, where there was a game laid out, half played. "Who's listed as guest of honor at West Coast Con? Edward tells me they're going to get Clifford Simak and van Vogt both."

"That's not what it says here in the newsletter," Squires told him, scrutinizing a printed pamphlet. "According to this it's TBA."

"To be announced," Latzarel said, then lit his pipe and puffed hard on it for a moment, his lips making little popping sounds. "Same son of a bitch as they advertised last time." He laughed out loud and then bent over to scan the titles of the chess books in the bookcase. He wasn't sure whether Squires read the damned things or whether he kept them there to gain some sort of psychological advantage, which he generally didn't need.

It was warm for November, and the casement windows along the west wall were wide open, the muslin curtains blowing inward on the breeze. Dust motes moved in the sunshine. The Newtonian Society had been meeting here every Saturday night since the war ended, and in that couple of years it had seldom broken up before two or three in the morning. Sometimes when there was a full house, all twelve of them would talk straight through until dawn and then go out after eggs and bacon, the thirty-nine-cent breakfast special down at Velma's Copper Pot on Western, although it wasn't often that the married men could get away with that kind of nonsense. Tonight they had scheduled a critical discussion of E. E. Smith's *Children of the Lens,* but it turned out that none of them liked the story much except Hastings, whose opinion was unreliable anyway, and so the meeting had lost all its substance after the first hour, and members had drifted away, into the kitchen and the library and out to the printing shed in the backyard, leaving Latzarel and Squires alone in the living room. Later on tonight, if the weather held up, they would be driving out to the observatory in Griffith Park.

There was a shuffling on the front walk, and Latzarel looked out in time to see the postman shut the mailbox and turn away, heading up the sidewalk. Squires went out through the front door and emptied the box, then came back in sorting letters. He took a puzzled second look at an envelope. "You're a stamp man," he said to Latzarel, handing it to him. "What do you make of that?"

• • •

Landers found that he could stand upright on the catwalk, although the roof sloped at such an angle that if he moved a couple of feet to either side, he had to duck to clear the roof rafters. He walked toward the boxes, but turned after a few steps to shine the light behind him, picking out his footprints in the otherwise-undisturbed dust. Beneath that dust, if a person could only brush away the successive years, lay Mr. Cummings's own footprints, coming and going along the wooden boards.

There was something almost wrong about opening the boxes at all, whatever they contained, like prying open a man's coffin. And somehow the neatly tied string suggested that their packing hadn't been temporary, that old Mr. Cummings had put them away forever, perhaps when he knew he was at the end of things.

Astounding . . . ? Well, Landers would be the judge of that.

Taking out his pocket knife, he started to cut the string on one of the top boxes, then decided against it and untied it instead, afterward pulling back the flaps. Inside were neatly stacked magazines, dozens of issues of a magazine called *Astounding Science-Fiction,* apparently organized according to date. He picked one up off the top, December of 1947, and opened it carefully. It was well-preserved, the pulp paper yellowed around the outside of the pages, but not brittle. The cover painting depicted a robot with a head like an egg, holding a bent stick in his hand and looking mournfully at a wolf with a rabbit beside it, the world behind them apparently in flames. There were book ads at the back of the magazine, including one from something called the Squires Press: an edition of Clark Ashton Smith's *Thirteen Phantasms,* printed with hand-set type in three volumes on Winnebago Eggshell paper and limited to a hundred copies. ''Remit one dollar in seven days,'' the ad said, ''and one dollar monthly until six dollars is paid.''

A dollar a month! This struck him as fantastic—stranger in its way, and even more wonderful, than the egg-headed robot on the front cover of the magazine. He sat down beside the boxes and leaned back against the wall so that the pages caught the sunlight through the window. He wished that he had brought along something to eat and drink instead of the worthless telephone. Settling in, he browsed through the contents page before starting in on the editorial, and then from there to the first of the several stories.

When the sunlight failed, Landers ran an extension cord into the attic and hooked up an old lamp in the rafters over the catwalk. Then he brought up a folding chair and a little smoking table to set a plate on. He would have liked something more comfortable, but there was no fitting an overstuffed chair up through the hatch. Near midnight he finished a story called ''Rain Check'' by Lewis Padgett, which featured a character named Tubby (apparently there had been a time when the world was happy with men named Tubby) and another character who drank highballs. . . .

He laid the book down and sat for a moment, listening to the rustling of leaves against the side of the house.

Highballs. What did people drink nowadays?—beer with all the color and flavor filtered out of it. Maybe that made a sad and frightening kind of sense. He looked at the back cover of the magazine, where perhaps coincidentally, there was an ad for Calvert whiskey: ''Just be sure your highball is made with Calvert,'' the ad counseled. He wondered if there was any such thing anymore, whether anywhere within a twenty-mile radius someone was mixing up a highball out of Calvert whiskey. Hell, a *hundred* miles . . .

Rod's Liquor Store down on the Plaza was open late, and he was suddenly possessed with the idea of mixing himself a highball. He took the magazine with him when he climbed down out of the attic, and before he left the house, he filled out the order blank for the *Thirteen Phantasms* and slipped it into an envelope along with a dollar bill. It seemed right to him, like the highball, or like old Mrs. Cummings keeping the slide rule.

He wrote out Squires's Glendale address, put one of the new interim *G* stamps on the envelope, and slid it into the mail slot for the postman to pick up tomorrow morning.

The canceled stamp depicted an American flag with the words "Old Glory" over the top. "A *G* stamp?" Latzarel said out loud. "What is that, exactly?"

Squires shook his head. "Something new?"

"*Very* damned new, I'd say. Look here." He pointed at the flag on the stamp. "I can't quite . . ." He looked over the top of his glasses, squinting hard. "I count too many stars on this flag. Take a look."

He handed the envelope back to Squires, who peered at the stamp, then dug a magnifying glass out of the drawer of the little desk in front of the window. He peered at the stamp through the glass. "Fifty," he said. "It must be a fake."

"Post office canceled it, too." Latzarel frowned and shook his head. "What kind of sense does that make? Counterfeiting stamps and getting the flag obviously wrong? A man wouldn't give himself away like that, unless he was playing some kind of game."

"Here's something else," Squires said. "Look at the edge. There's no perforations. This is apparently cut out of a solid sheet." He slit the envelope open and unfolded the letter inside. It was an order for the Smith collection, from an address in the city of Orange.

There was a dollar bill included with the order.

Landers flipped through the first volume of the *Thirteen Phantasms,* which had arrived postage-due from Glendale. There were four stories in each volume. Somehow he had expected thirteen altogether, and the first thing that came into his mind was that there was a phantasm missing. He nearly laughed out loud. But then he was sobered by the obvious impossibility of the arrival of any phantasms at all. They had come enclosed in a cardboard carton that was wrapped in brown paper and sealed with tape. He looked closely at the tape, half surprised that it wasn't yellowed with age, that the package hadn't been in transit through the ether for half a century.

He sipped from his highball and reread a note that had come with the books, written out by a man named Russell Latzarel, president of a group calling itself the Newtonian Society—apparently Squires's crowd. In the note, Latzarel wondered if Landers was perpetrating a hoax.

A hoax . . . The note was dated 1947. "Who are you *really*?" it asked. "What is the meaning of the G stamp?" For a time he stared out of the window, watching the vines shift against the glass, listening to the wind under the eaves. The house settled, creaking in its joints. He looked at Latzarel's message again. "The dollar bill was a work of art," it read. On the back there was a hand-drawn map and an invitation to the next meeting of the Newtonians. He folded the map and tucked it into his coat pocket. Then he finished his highball and laughed out loud. Maybe it was the whiskey that made this seem monumentally funny. A hoax! He'd show them a hoax.

Almost at once he found something that would do. It was a plastic lapel pin the size of a fifty-cent piece, a hologram of an eyeball. It was only an eighth of an inch thick, but when he turned it in the light it seemed deep as a well. It was a good clear hologram too, the eyeball hovering in the void, utterly three-dimensional. The pin on the back had been glued on sloppily and at a screwball angle, and excess glue had run down the back of the plastic and dried. It was a technological marvel of the late twentieth century, and it was an absolute, and evident, piece of junk. He addressed an envelope, dropped the hologram inside, and slid it into the mail slot.

The trip out to Glendale took over an hour because of a traffic jam at the 605 junction and bumper-to-bumper cars on the Golden State. There was nothing apparently wrong—no accident, no freeway construction, just a million toiling automobiles stretching all the way to heaven-knew-where, to the moon. He had forgotten Latzarel's map, and he fought off a feeling of superstitious dread as the cars in front of him inched along. At Los Feliz he pulled off the freeway, cutting down the offramp at the last possible moment. There was a hamburger joint called Tommy's Little Oasis on Los Feliz, just east of San Fernando Road, that he and Janet used to hit when they were on their way north. That had been a few years back; he had nearly forgotten, but the freeway sign at Los Feliz had jogged his memory. It was a tiny Airstream trailer in the parking lot of a motel shaded by big elm trees. You went there if you wanted a hamburger. That was it. There was no menu except a sign on the wall, and even the sign was nearly pointless, since the only question was did you want cheese or not. Landers wanted cheese.

He slowed down as he passed San Fernando, looking for the motel, for the big overarching elms, recalling a rainy Saturday afternoon when they'd eaten their burgers in the car because it was raining too hard to sit under the steel umbrella at the picnic table out front. Now there was no picnic table, no Airstream trailer, no motel—nothing but a run-down industrial park. Somehow the industrial park had sprung up and fallen into disrepair in—what?—less than twenty years!

He U-turned and headed the opposite direction up San Fernando, turning right on Western. It was better not to think about it, about the pace of things, about the cheeseburgers of days gone by. . . .

Farther up Western, the houses along the street were run-down, probably rentals. There was trash in the street, broken bottles, newspapers soaked in gutter water. Suddenly he was a foreigner. He had wandered into a part of the country that was alien to him. And, unless his instincts had betrayed him, it was clearly alien to Squires Press and the Newtonian Society and men named Tubby. At one time the mix of Spanish-style and Tudor houses had been elegant. Now they needed paint and the lawns were up in weeds, and there was graffiti on fences and garage walls.

Windows and doors were barred. He drove slowly, calculating addresses and thinking about turning around, getting back onto the freeway and heading south again, just fleeing home, ordering something else out of the magazines—personally autographed books by long-dead authors, "jar-proof" watches that could take a licking and go on ticking. He pictured the quiet shelter of his attic—his magazines, the makings of another highball. If ever a man needed a highball . . .

And just then he came upon the sign for Rexroth Street, so suddenly that he nearly drove right through the intersection. He braked abruptly, swinging around toward the west, and a car behind him honked its horn hard. He heard the driver shout something as the car flew past.

Landers started searching out addresses. The general tenor of the neighborhood hadn't improved at all, and he considered locking his doors. But then the idea struck him as superfluous, since he was about to park the car and get out anyway. He spotted the address on the curb, the paint faded and nearly unreadable. The house had a turreted entry hall in front, with an arched window in the wall that faced the street. A couple of the windowpanes were broken and filled with aluminum foil, and what looked like an old bed sheet was strung across as a curtain. Weeds grew up through the cracked concrete of the front walk, and there was black iron debris, apparently car parts, scattered on the lawn.

He drifted to the curb, reaching for the ignition key, but then saw, crouched next to a motorcycle up at the top of the driveway, an immense man, tattooed and bearded and dressed in black jeans and a greasy T-shirt, holding a wrench and looking down the driveway at him. Landers instantly stepped on the gas, angling away from the curb and gunning toward the corner.

He knew what he needed to know. He could go home now. Whoever this man was, living in what must have been Squires's old house, he didn't have anything to do with the *Thirteen Phantasms*. He wasn't a Newtonian. There was no conceivable chance that Squires himself was somewhere inside, working the crank of his mechanical printing press, stamping out fantastic stories on Winnebago Eggshell paper. Squires was gone; that was the truth of it. The Newtonians were gone. The *world they'd inhabited,* with its twenty-five-cent pulp magazines and egg-headed robots and Martian canals, its highballs and hand-set type and slide rules, was gone too. Probably it was all at the bottom of the tar pits, turning into puzzling fossils.

Out beyond the front window, Rexroth Street was dark and empty of anything but the wind. To the south, the Hollywood Hills were a black wall of shadow, as if there were nothing there at all, just a vacancy. The sky above the dark line of the hills was so closely scattered with bright stars in the wind-scoured night that Latzarel might have been dreaming, and the broad wash of the Milky Way spanned the heavens like a lamp-lit road. From up the hall, he could hear Cummings talking on the telephone. Cummings would be talking to his wife about now, asking permission to stay out late. Squires had phoned Rhineholdt at the observatory, and they were due up on the hill in an hour, with just time enough to stop for a late-night burger at the Copper Kettle on the way.

Latzarel took the three-dimensional picture of the eyeball out of his coat pocket and turned it under the lamp in the window, marveling again at the eyeball that hung impossibly in the miniature void, in its little nonexistent cube of frozen space.

There was a sudden glow in the Western sky now—a meteor shower, hundreds of shooting stars, flaming up for a moment before vanishing beyond the darkness of the hills. Latzarel shouted for Squires and the others, and when they all ran into the room the stars were still falling, and the southern sky was like a veil of fireflies.

The totality of Landers's savings account hadn't been worth much at the coin shop. Gold standard bills weren't cheap. Probably he'd have been better off simply buying gold, but somehow the idea wasn't appealing. He wanted folding money in his wallet, just like any other pedestrian—something he could pay for lunch with, a burger and a Coke or a BLT and a slice of apple pie.

He glued the last of the foam-rubber blocks onto the inside top of the wooden crate on his living-room floor, then stood back and looked at the pile of stuff that was ready to go into the box. He'd had a thousand choices, an impossible number of choices. Everywhere he had turned in the house there was something else, some fabulous relic of the late twentieth century: throwaway wristwatches and dimmer switches, cassette tapes and portable telephones, pictorial histories and horse-race results, wallet-size calculators and pop-top cans, Ziploc baggies and Velcro fasteners, power screw guns and bubble paper, a laptop computer, software, a Styrofoam cup . . .

And then it had occurred to him that there was something about the tiniest articles that appealed to him even more than the obvious marvels. Just three trifling little wonders shifted backward in time, barely discernible in his coat pocket, might imply huge, baffling changes in the world: a single green-tinted contact lens, perhaps, and the battery out of a watch, and a hologram bird clipped out of a credit card. He wandered from room to room again, looking around. A felt-tipped pen? A nylon zipper? Something more subtle . . .

But of course if it were *too* subtle, it would be useless, wouldn't it? What was he really planning to *do* with these things? Try to convince a nearsighted man to shove the contact lens into his eye? Would the Newtonians pry the battery apart? To what end? What was inside? Probably black paste of some kind or a lump of dull metal—hardly worth the bother. And the hologram bird—it was like something out of a box of Cracker Jacks. Besides, the Newtonians had already gotten the eyeball, hadn't they? He couldn't do better than the eyeball.

Abruptly he abandoned his search, changing his thinking entirely. Hurrying into the study he pulled books out of the case, selecting and rejecting titles, waiting for something to appeal to him, something . . . He couldn't quite define it. He might as well take nearly any of them, or simply rip out a random copyright page. The daily papers? Better to take along a sack of rotten fruit.

He went out of the study and into the kitchen hallway where he climbed the attic ladder. Untying the last of the boxes, he sorted through the *Astounding*s, settling on March of 1956—ten years in the future, more or less, for the Newtonians. Unlike the rest of the issues, this one was beat up, as if it had been read to pieces, or carried around in someone's coat pocket. He scanned the contents page, noting happily that there was a Heinlein novel serialized in the volume, and he dug through the box again to find April of the same year in order to have all of the story—something called *Double Star*. The torn cover of the April issue showed an ermine-robed king of some kind inspecting a toy locomotive, his forehead furrowed with thought and wonder.

Satisfied at last, Landers hurried back down the ladder and into the living room again. To hell with the trash on the floor, the bubble paper and the screw gun. He would leave all the Buck Rogers litter right here in a pile. Packing that kind of thing into the box was like loading up the Trojan Horse, wasn't it? It was a betrayal. And for what? Show-off value? Wealth? Fame? It was all beside the point; he saw that clearly now. It was very nearly the antithesis of the point.

He slid the *Astounding*s into a niche inside the box along with the *Thirteen Phantasms,* an army-surplus flashlight, a wooden-handled screwdriver, and his sandwiches and bottled water. Then he picked up the portable telephone and made two calls, one to his next-door neighbor and one to Federal Express. His neighbor would unlock the door for the post office, who would haul the crate away on a handcart and truck it to Glendale.

The thought clobbered him suddenly. By what route? he wondered. Along what arcane boulevards would he travel?

He imagined the crate being opened by the man he had seen working on the motorcycle in the neglected driveway. What would Landers do? Threaten the man with the screwdriver? Offer him the antique money? Scramble out of the crate and simply walk away down the street without a backward glance, forever changing the man's understanding of human behavior?

He stopped his mind from running and climbed into the crate, pulling the lid on after him. Carefully and deliberately, he started to set the screws—his last task before lunch. It was silent in the box, and he sat listening for one last moment in the darkness, the attic sitting empty above him, still sheltered by its vines and wooden shingles. He imagined the world revolving, out beyond the walls of the old house, imagined the noise and movement, and he thought briefly of Mrs. Cummings across town, arranging and rearranging a leather-encased slide rule and a couple of old smoking pipes and photographs.

The Saturday meeting of the Newtonian society had come to order right on time. Phillip Mays, the lepidopterist, was home from the Amazon with a collection of insects that included an immense dragonfly commonly thought to have died out in the Carboniferous period. Squires's living-room floor was covered with display boxes and jars, and the room smelled of camphor and pipe smoke. There was the patter of soft rain through the open casements, but the weather was warm and easy despite the rain, and in the dim distance, out over the hills, there was the low rumble of thunder.

The doorbell rang, and Squires, expecting another Newtonian, opened the heavy front door in the turreted entry hall. A large wooden crate sat on the porch, sheltered by the awning, and a post-office truck motored away north toward Kenneth Road, disappearing beyond a mist of rain. Latzarel looked over Squires's shoulder at the heavy crate, trying to figure out what was wrong with it, what was odd about it. Something . . .

"I'll be damned," he said. "The top's screwed on from the inside."

"I'll get a pry bar," Hastings said from behind him.

Latzarel heard a sound then, and he put his ear to the side of the box. There was the click of a screwdriver on metal, the squeak of the screw turning. ''Don't bother with the pry bar,'' Latzarel said, winking at Squires, and he lit a match and held it to his pipe, cupping his hand over the bowl to keep the raindrops from putting it out.

PRIMROSE AND THORN

Bud Sparhawk

▼

Here's a vivid and exciting wide-screen adventure in the Grand Tradition, as intrepid sailors race each other across the vast, boiling gas-and-cloud oceans of Jupiter, where immense, roaring, tremendously powerful storms many times the size of the Earth can blow up and swallow your fragile little ship in a heartbeat, and money and prestige and fame are the prizes that goad them on in the face of overwhelming danger and almost-certain death. But worse than the physical danger of the winds that howl outside the thin shell of the ship's hull, the race is going to take them to places where they never expected to venture, and bring them face-to-face with things they may not have ever wanted to know. . . .

New writer Bud Sparhawk has become a frequent contributor to Analog *in recent years. Born in Baltimore, he now lives with his family in Annapolis, Maryland, where he works as an information technology consultant.*

> *"Build me straight, O worthy Master!*
> *Staunch and strong, a goodly vessel,*
>   *That shall laugh at all disaster,*
>   *And with wave and whirlwind wrestle!"*
>
> —The Building of the Ship,
> *Henry Wadsworth Longfellow*

"Why did I ever listen to you about *this* race? I already spend a bunch right here on Earth," protested Jerome Blacker, president of JBI. "I've been having second thoughts about this Jupiter race."

The two tanned and muscular people facing him looked uneasy. A sales tag was still attached to the man's sleeve and flapped as he waved his hand while speaking. "You already made the commitment, JB—you just have to follow through. Come on, it doesn't cost you any real money."

"You sure as hell aren't much of a businessman if you think this won't cost me anything!" JB said nastily.

"Mr. Blacker," Pascal interrupted, "the publicity about this race will bring in more than enough to offset expenses."

Jerome leaned across the desk. "What about insurance, the cost of transport, the cost of the boats? Those things aren't cheap!"

Pascal sighed. "The funds from the Jovian ventures can't be spent on Earth. Thanks to the treaty of '54, you have to reinvest at least seventy-five percent of your profits."

Jerome winced. "Don't remind me about those damn pirates! If it hadn't been for my stations and hubs, the damned Jovians wouldn't have a pot to piss in," he grumbled.

Pascal continued his attack. "Geo-Global and the *Times* cartel are both outfitting ships for the race. No telling how many the Jovians are going to enter themselves. If we don't race, JBI will lose a lot—the publicity about our entry will bring in more than enough revenue to cover our expenses."

Jerome mused, half to himself, as he rubbed his chin. "I remember your numbers, I've read the reports. So be it. What do I have to do to finalize the financial arrangements?"

Pascal spoke slowly, not wishing to reveal how anxious he was to get JB's approval. "I've already reserved *Thorn*, a used barkentine. You just need to sign the commitment for outfitting her. Once that's done, the orbital factories will start fabricating the sails—we've already sent them our specs. We'll use the Jovian funds for both of those efforts. The only cash outlay you need to worry about will be our transport out to Jupiter."

"Which leaves only the human element," Jerome said. "Even now I find it hard to believe that we can win this race." He swiveled in his chair to face the woman who sat beside Pascal. She was the best captain in his fleet and winner of more sailboat races than he could count. She'd been unusually quiet since she came in the office.

"Do you think you can race one of those barques, Louella?" he asked her quietly. "Do you think you can sail a boat on the seas of Jupiter?"

Pascal held his breath as he awaited her answer. The success of their entire enterprise, and the payoff for the past year's worth of intense training, rested on her reply. The answer she gave would make or break the deal.

"I could sail a fucking bathtub on the sun if the price was right," she spat back. "Now how the hell do I get a drink around here?"

Rams had stopped at the station in the hopes that there would be an opportunity for business. That, and a chance to restock his supplies. In order to keep his ship, *Primrose*, he had to take advantage of every opportunity that came his way.

Jake, an irritable old scamp who knew everything there was to know about sailing the winds of Jupiter, had taught Rams how to sail. Rams learned that every ship had its own personality. He learned how to balance keel and ballast, how to adjust the ship's buoyancy to ride the turbulence.

After teaching him the basics of sail, rudder, keel, and line, Jake went on to show him how to heave to in the hurricane-force winds so that they would ride easily, neither making way nor being blown back. They'd used that technique to mine the edges of Jupiter's storms. The updrafts in these dangerous hurricanes often pulled metal-rich meteorites and icebergs—worth their weight in gold to the floating stations—from the lower depths of the atmosphere. Jake showed him how

to "cheat" the boat close to the edges of the turbulence, using jib and main to
close in on these bits of rock and harvest them.

Jake had shared all of his secrets of playing the winds of Jupiter's storms and
winning its rewards. Jake taught Rams to love the winds on the wine-red seas.

Rams's transition from crewman to ship's captain hadn't been easy. He'd
scrimped and saved every cent he could, and signed away nearly all of his future
profits—all to buy a fast, outdated clipper at one of JBI's auctions. Clippers had
been deemed too inefficient to achieve JBI's "acceptable" level of profitability.

Refitting the boat and replacing the instruments that *Primrose*'s former crew had
stripped put him even further in debt. In addition, there had been the outlay for
new sails and refitting the keel. Both cost more than he expected, and suddenly,
his debt for *Primrose* started to look like a financial black hole from which there
was no hope of escape.

His first year had been a disaster. The cargo he'd hauled hadn't generated enough
to pay the interest on his loans. To keep from losing her he borrowed even more.
If he wasn't careful he could lose *Primrose* and be thrown in jail—that was the
penalty for simultaneously using her as collateral for multiple loans. Since then it
had been nip and tuck, keeping one financial step ahead of bankruptcy.

The second year of operations had taught him where the good money could be
earned—carrying perishable goods on quick dashes. JBI's huge, lumbering cargo
ships could move things cheaply, but they were neither speedy nor very maneu-
verable. Like the old square-riggers of Earth, they flew with the wind, stolid as the
stations, and scarcely moving much faster. Sometimes their crew endured months
between station-falls.

Rams usually got the best return when he had to make a darting emergency run
from station to hub and back. Double charges both ways, and no hassle for it,
either! Best of all, the fees kept him out of prison.

"Wind one-thirty meters per second and rising, Cap'n. Satellite shows some deep
turbulence spinning off the edge about twelve thousand klicks upwind and heading
to intercept your destination. Weather advises you should try to stay within the
central laminar flows of subbands MM and KK until you're almost to Charlie Sierra
One. That should keep you out of the storm," the stationmaster said.

"Put it down that I acknowledge the limits on bands MM and KK," Rams
replied as the 'master logged his ship out. "How much margin does Weather give
me before that storm hits?"

"Best they can project is that you have about a sixteen-hour margin, give or
take six hours. Of course, if it swings south of CS-42 the edge winds might give
you a lift."

"When did I ever see one of those storms change course in a way that would
help me?" Rams asked rhetorically. "I'll plan on beating the weather the last leg
of the trip. I just hope that Weather's prediction is right."

"I agree with that," the 'master replied. "You'd better keep a watch for any
miners who might be prospecting on the periphery of the storm. Wouldn't want to
run into one of those crazies, would you?"

Rams grinned, remembering when he had been one of those crazies. "I'll watch
out for them," he promised.

"Well, it looks like you are all set to go, *Primrose*," the stationmaster said as he popped the record from the computer and handed it to Rams. "Fair winds and good passage, Cap'n."

Rams checked the ballast tank when he returned to the ship. According to the leveling mark on the wall of *Primrose*'s berth, she was riding low—just a little too heavy, probably from the extra cargo he'd taken on. He switched on the heaters in the ballast tank. That would create enough steam pressure to drive the excess ballast out, lightening the ship. When *Primrose*'s bull's-eye was almost up to the mark, he turned the heater off. In a few moments more she was floating level with the station.

"Ready to cast off!" Rams said over the intercom. He listened for the 'master to loose the clamps that held *Primrose* in the station's embrace. Four loud bangs resounded through the pressure hull as the clamps released. Rams immediately felt the ship list to starboard as she drifted backward into the fierce winds of Jupiter.

Primrose heeled as it caught the full force of the wind. Rams braced himself, checked the instruments, and then turned the ship downwind as it emerged from the lee of the station.

The station's infrared image quickly faded as they exceeded the viewer's range. A few seconds later the sonar return vanished as well. Only a fuzzy radar image, quickly dissolving into a cloud of electronic noise, told him where the station rode. Even that image would fade once he got more than a kilometer away. After that he'd be sailing blind.

Primrose ran with the wind as he lowered the keel. He pointedly ignored the keelmeter as the diamond-mesh ribbon uncoiled from its housing. The thousand-ton weight at the keel's end started its familiar swinging motion as the keel was unwrapped from its spindle. *Primrose* rocked in response to the motion. The pendulum's swing slowed as the ribbon paid out farther and farther into the thick soup of the atmosphere.

Finally the rocking motion dampened and Rams halted the winch, locking it in place. Only then did he check the keelmeter. Although he relied more on the feel of the ship's trim when setting the keel depth, he liked to assure himself of the setting.

A single glance told him that his instincts had been correct. He'd halted the keel at fourteen hundred meters, one hundred meters shy of the theoretical setting the station master had calculated. He let an additional fifty meters of the mesh keel pay out; it wouldn't hurt to have *Primrose* a little bottom-heavy on an upwind run.

Rams reached for the sail controls. *Primrose* was being blown downwind at thirty meters per second, relative to the station. The station he'd just left plodded along *slower* than the wind, held back only by her massive drogues—a fancy word for sea anchors. The drogues that swung beneath the station's bulbous form created drag and provided a measure of control. It was sailing, but using anchors to steer instead of sails.

Rams hit the switch to release his mainsail from its housing on the main mast and braced himself. The ship tilted even further to starboard as the wind bit the suddenly increased surface area. He immediately played out the traveler, letting the main find the angle that would allow the fierce wind to flow across the sail's face. He kept a careful eye on the pressure gauges from both sides of the wishbone that constrained the sail, adjusting the sail's angle to maximize the front-to-back pressure differential. He wanted to get as much lift as possible from the airfoil effect.

Primrose finally stopped rocking and curved into the wind as Rams adjusted the line. *Primrose* was running at about sixty degrees to the wind when she finally balanced out and was making an appreciable sixty meters per second.

"All right, girl, let's show old man Jupiter what we can really do," he said, deploying the jib from its housing at the prow. There was a hellacious rattling from forward as the chain hoist protested the way the wind whipped at the small jib and smashed it against the pressure hull. Rams winched the line back until the jib sheets were taut and the small forward sail was funneling the wind along the back of the mainsail, forming a venturi between them.

Primrose heeled even more as the force on her increased from the additional sail surface exposed to the wind and turned tighter into the face of the wind. She was now running at about a forty-degree angle. Rams grinned in satisfaction as her speed increased proportionally. He watched the knotmeter rise past seventy, seventy-five, and settle at nearly eighty meters per second.

He checked his location on the inertial-positioning display and made a minor adjustment to the rudder, then adjusted both the mainsail and jib to account for the new angle of attack.

"Clipper ship *Primrose* out at fourteen hundred hours, under way and on course for Charlie Sierra Four Two," he said into the radio. The stationmaster probably wouldn't be able to hear the formal sign-off, given the usual overwhelming amount of static in the atmosphere. Nevertheless, Rams was always careful to observe the formalities.

As *Primrose* pulled steadily away, Rams made a thorough examination of the ship. He wanted to ensure that everything on board was shipshape. He double-checked the straps and buckles on all of the cargo crates, just to make sure they'd been properly secured.

Next he checked the topside sail locker, taking care to see that the spare sails were properly stored and ready for deployment when the need arose. If all went well he wouldn't have to replace the sails on this trip, which would help his profit margin. Having them fabricated in orbit and brought down by elevator was bloody expensive.

He swung the power-lifters from their clamps and started working on the new sail. He strained against the resistance of the tough foil of the sail as he refolded it. Even so, he tried to keep from flexing the thin metal more than was necessary.

As soon as he had the sail properly folded and secured, he moved it into its canister. His arms ached as he struggled to get it into the correct position, cursing the financial situation that forced him to fire his crew three months before and the expediency that kept him from having the time in dock to do this sort of housekeeping. One person could barely cope with the bulky sails against the drag of Jupiter's heavy gravity. Even with the one hundred–to-one ratio of the lifters, he still had to depend on his own muscle to force the cumbersome rig into the canister.

Finally the sail was loaded. He stowed the lifters and rubbed his aching back before fastening the heavy chain lines at the head end of the sail; one line that would lift it into place on the mast and another to connect it to the traveler that limited a sail's movement across the top deck.

Whenever he had to blow the main its lines would go with it. The lines were another expense he wished that he could avoid. But the only way to save them was to suit up, climb out onto the deck, and try to disconnect them while fighting hurricane-force winds. Only a fool went outside without a backup crew, no matter how securely he was clamped to the deck! The lost money for lines wasn't as important to him as his life.

By the time Rams worked his way back to the cockpit, *Primrose* had moved far north of the station. From this position he could start to tack without the risk of running into it. Just to make certain of his clearance, he peered at the screen, cranking the radar to maximum sensitivity to check.

The screen showed a uniform blur of undifferentiated noise; not even a shadow that could be suspected of being something other than the swirling electronic mist of atmosphere.

Rams and *Primrose* were now completely on their own, and in five days, more or less, he hoped to see the faint, white heat signature of his destination. He hoped that the storm wouldn't spoil his plans—he needed the money to make the next payment!

"What a dump," Louella complained loudly. She threw her bag against the bare metal deck and watched as it lazily bounced back into the air. "Not even a bar on the place! To make matters worse I have to share the damned cabin with you. I can't even have some gods-be-damned decent privacy before the race!"

Pascal winced at the strident tone of her voice. He regretted accompanying her throughout the long voyage from Earth to the Jovian system. He should have come on another ship.

Louella's growing catalog of complaints had increased throughout the long transit from Earth. Thankfully, there'd been enough distractions on the transport to silence her complaints, once in the while. The transport had a bar to keep her amused, and enough willing young crew members to keep her bemused. But those diversions were short-lived. Too soon she came back to the fact that she wasn't racing, wasn't in control, wasn't at sea.

It made her bitchy.

"How the devil am I supposed to keep my sanity if they can't even provide civilized, *basic* amenities?" Louella continued in a rasping voice that cut across his nerves like fingernails on slate.

"Bad enough that I have to miss *three* seasons of the circuit for this fool race! Bad enough that we have to stay in this stupid can until the others get here! But that doesn't mean I have to live like some *freaking* Spartan in the meantime!"

She lifted the lid of the utilitarian toilet. "Jesus, we even have to share the damned can!"

"Perhaps you should complain to the hubmaster," Pascal said quietly as he floated across the tiny cabin and anchored himself with one hand. "Maybe he can provide whatever it is that you need."

Louella spun gracefully around on her hold and frowned at him. "What is that supposed to mean?"

Pascal winced again. What had he said *now*? It didn't matter; she'd be hell to live with if he just let it be. "Nothing," he said. "I just thought that maybe the captain has resources we don't know about. It wouldn't hurt to ask."

"Humph," Louella huffed, as if unsure of the meaning of his answer. She kicked her floating bag into some netting to secure it. "You've got the bunk beside the door, asshole. And don't get any ideas about us sleeping together."

"I wouldn't dream of it," Pascal replied dryly and turned to fiddle with the controls on the wall. Under his breath he added, "Nightmares, perhaps, but not dreams." He pressed the switch to open the viewport.

"What did you say?" Louella asked sharply. "Something I wasn't supposed to—oh my god! Would you look at that!" Pascal didn't answer, he was as awed by the sight as she.

Framed in the viewport was the entirety of Jupiter, half orange, rose, and umber, and half in darkness. The rim of the planet filled the 'port from top to bottom, leaving only a narrow circle of stars at the edges to show that anything else existed in the heavens.

The bright line of the elevator cable extended from somewhere beneath the window and ran straight toward the planet's equator, far below, just as it extended thousands of kilometers out into space from this geosynchronous station. The cable's silvery line narrowed as it diminished into perfect perspective toward the giant planet.

Jupiter's great red spot wasn't visible. Pascal assumed that it was either on the other side of the planet or somewhere within the semicircle of darkness that marked the night side of Jupiter. But there were enough other large features present to occupy the eye.

Wide bands of permanent lateral weather patterns ran across Jupiter's face. Each showed feathery turbulence whorls at the edges as they dragged on the slower bands toward the equator or were accelerated by faster ones toward the poles. From here he could easily see the separations between them.

In the center of one of the higher-latitude bands there was a dark smudge. Pascal thought it might be the persistent traces of the "string of pearls" comet, over a hundred years ago, but he wasn't sure. He couldn't remember if the marks would be on top or bottom from his viewpoint. He decided to ask the hubmaster about orientation.

"What a sight," Louella whispered as she moved beside him. "Gorgeous, just gorgeous," she said, with a touch of awe. "Where are the floating stations? Could we see them from here?" she asked quickly and pressed closer to the viewport.

Pascal dismissed her inquiry with a shrug. "The stations are too small to see from here. You're still thinking in terms of Earth. We're over six hundred times farther out than one of the orbiting stations would be at home. CS-6 would have to be the size of Australia for you to see it with your naked eye.

"You've got to remember that each one of those weather bands is several thousand miles across," Pascal continued as he backed away from the viewport and the terrifying precipice it represented. "We could put the entire Pacific inside any one of them and still have plenty of room left over."

Louella's face took on a rapt expression as she absorbed the scale of what she was observing. "You could sail forever in those seas," she breathed heavily. "Forever."

Rams encountered his first problem when he was thirty hours under way. *Primrose* had been beating steadily to windward since he left CS-15. By his projections they should have been slightly north of the projected track of CS-42, the next station in line. This leg of his upwind trip would be two thousand kilometers long before he came about and headed south on the shorter lee leg. That was as far as he could travel and stay within the limits Weather had advised. He couldn't go beyond the MM subband without risking excessive turbulence. No, he thought, it was better to keep to the smooth and dependable jets of air in the middle of the band.

It was no small effort to steer *Primrose* between the two stations. CS-15 had been moving westward at a steady twenty-six meters per second under the slower westward winds of the KK subband.

The two stations had been about eight thousand kilometers apart when he had departed. He had planned to tack about eight times across the face of the wind; four two thousand–kilometer legs to the north and four three thousand–kilometer legs to the south. The southern tacks would gain him the least progress but give him good position to intercept the station as it raced toward him.

It was a good sail plan. The only problem was that it wasn't working out. The inertial guidance system indicated that, instead, he was steadily bearing west of his projected course. Rams checked the set of the sails and the pressure readings. Using these numbers, he calculated that *Primrose* was still bearing forty degrees to the wind, just as he had planned. What could be wrong? Was he was being blown off course by an unexpected head wind?

An hour later he understood the situation. Something was disturbing the "smooth laminar flow" predictions of Weather. He just encountered a more northerly wind than expected. He decided to adjust his tacking strategy to adapt to the shift. He'd have to take a longer line on the southern tack. But the slower passage would put him at risk from the storm, which could mean big trouble.

He plotted his course for the next ninety hours with great care.

As they sped down toward the seas of Jupiter, Pascal sat as far from the port of the tiny cab of the elevator as he could and tried to ignore the pit of blackness, a hole in the sky at the center of an enormous emptiness. The thought of all the distance they had to fall terrified him.

"I still don't understand how you guys do it," the pink-faced elevator pilot said from his perch at the bow. "I mean, I can see how a sailboat can go with the wind. The hot-air balloons on Earth just go with the wind, right? Why wouldn't they do the same here?"

"It's the keel," John said. He and Al were their competitors from Geo-Global. They'd arrived a few days before, along with the third crew that would participate in the race. "A sailboat would be just like a balloon if it didn't have a keel."

"Oh, I see. That's why the Jupiter ships have that long ribbon under them," the pilot remarked. "But how does that help them move against the wind? And isn't it impossible to go faster than the wind?"

"Good question," Pascal said, glad of the distraction. "A sailboat goes faster into the wind, not slower. The slowest speed of all is when you run with the wind directly behind you."

Pascal let the kid think about that for a moment before he continued. "A sail is an airfoil. One side forms a pocket of relatively dead air. The opposite side is bent out so that the wind has a longer distance to travel. The pressure differential pulls the sailboat along."

"A foresail funnels the air across the main and accentuates the effect," Al injected. "The closer you haul to the direction of the wind the faster you go."

John spoke up. "It's just a matter of physics: The angle of force on the sail and the keel produces a vector of force that moves the boat forward. The steeper the angle the greater the forward thrust. The trick is to balance the force of the wind and the sails, adjusting your angle of attack to obtain the greatest forward momentum possible, maximizing the transfer of static air pressure to dynamic motive force."

"Oh, I understand," the operator said, screwing his face up in concentration. "It's like continuously solving a set of differential equations." He smiled at them as if he were proud of learning the lesson so well.

"Don't bust a gut trying to do that if you're ever in a sailboat, kid," Louella said. "It's all scientific bullshit."

Louella glared at the three of them; a fierce set to her eyes and mouth that brooked no interruption. "These guys want you to think that sailing's a science—that it's all application of mathematical rules and physics. Listening to them, you'd think that you're constantly thinking, calculating, and plotting. Well, that's all a pile of crap—sailing isn't some branch of engineering."

She leaned forward to look straight into the operator's eyes, her expression softening as she did so. "Sailing's a love affair between you, the boat, the water, and the wind. Every one of them has to be balanced, held in check; let any one of them dominate and you've lost it. A good sailor has to be conscious of wind and water and responsive to the boat's needs. You have to understand the language of wind and sea and ship—you have to feel that *edge* that means you're running a tight line with every nerve of your body. The boat'll tell you how she wants to behave; she'll fight you when you're wrong, and support you when you're right."

She brushed at her cheek, as if something had gotten in her eye, before she continued. "The point I'm trying so damn hard to get across to you is that sailing is an art, not a bloody damn science. That means you have to sail with your heart, as well as your mind. When you're on the sea, managing the sails and the wheel, the rest of the universe could disappear, for all that you care. When everything works right, there's a rhythm, a reverie that transforms you, that makes you one with the universe. If you put everything you have into it, mind and body, your ego disappears—it's just you, the boat, the wind, and the water."

She turned back to stare out the viewport at the advancing planet and slumped into her seat. "If it was just science, JBI wouldn't be paying the big bucks to haul my ass all the way out here. No, they'd get some double-dome Ph. and D. to build a little machine to do it, and the hell with the beauty of a good line and a strong wind.

"But the fact that I am here to sail on Jupiter's orange seas says that there's still a human element to sailing that's better than the most refined engineering approach. It says that a human being can still stand on a ship's deck and dare the wind and the seas to do their worst. It tells me that even some damn overgrown pig of a planet can't tame the human spirit!''

The silence prevailed for long minutes. ''Well,'' said Al, apropos of nothing. ''Well.''

Louella said nothing for the rest of the trip down into the thick atmosphere. Pascal tried to ignore the view as sunrise raced across Jupiter's face, too far below.

Rams's destination was floating along at twenty-odd meters per second to the east of his present position. Her track was so reliably managed that the station's precise location could be calculated to within a kilometer.

Somewhere on the other side of CS-42 a whirling hurricane was advancing. Given the right spin and direction these storms could grow beyond reasonable bounds, turning into blows that made Earth's hurricanes look like a faint puff of air. Ninety-nine times out of a hundred Jupiter's hurricanes dissipated quickly, within two or three of his ten-hour rotations. If Rams was lucky, this one would do the same.

Rams was dismayed to discover that *Primrose* fell even farther westward off of her planned track whenever he turned to the north. That meant two things: The winds were continuing to shift, and the storm was deeper than expected. It looked as if he'd hit the edges of a major storm.

For the thousandth time he wished that Jupiter wasn't so electronically active. The ambient white noise on the radio bands was so intense that even pulse-code modulation couldn't punch a signal through. Just one crummy satellite picture, one quick radar image, one short broadcast was all he'd need to find out what was happening with the storm.

Instead, all he knew about the storm was its rough starting position, Weather's predicted track, and the data the stationmaster provided about prevailing winds. He also had the data from his own inertial system. From those weak components he had to navigate through a dark eight thousand kilometers, face unknown winds, and find the tiny station that was his destination.

''A little bit cramped, isn't it?'' Pascal remarked as they inspected *Thorn*, their tiny, nine-hundred ton, double-masted barque. He sat with one leg extended into the cockpit and the other in the ''stateroom,'' which also served as kitchen, bath, and bedroom. A single bunk stretched for two meters across the overhead with a single small seat below, which when lifted, revealed the toilet. A tiny shelf with a built-in microwave oven and a recessed sink—hidden under the working surface— ran along the second bulkhead, to the right. Their food and medical supplies were stored in hanging bags, Velcroed to the bulkhead above the microwave.

On the opposite bulkhead was a fold-down table whose opened edge would be in the lap of whomever was sitting on the seat. The navigation instruments, computer, and the storage for charts and instruments were revealed when the table was down. Rams could reach out with his left arm and just about touch the edge of the helmsman's seat, it was that close. For a big boat *Thorn* had mighty small crew quarters.

"Maybe we shouldn't have picked a cargo hauler—it's a little cramped, isn't it?" Louella remarked as she ducked her head to peek into the compartment. "Place looked a lot roomier in the plans. I guess the crew wasn't supposed to stay aboard for more than a day or two."

Pascal looked around. "Why couldn't they convert some of that cargo hold? This is pretty tight. I don't relish spending a couple of weeks in here."

"Too much trouble just to give us a little bit of comfort. I don't think the expense would be worth it—might upset the boat's balance."

Pascal sighed and wiggled in the tiny seat, trying to find a way to stretch his legs full length, and failed. "The navigator's station on the Bermuda run was bigger than this," he complained. He tried to put his arms out and his right elbow hit the hanging bags. He sighed again—this was going to be damned uncomfortable.

"Yeah, but you weren't nearly as warm and dry," Louella reminded him. "I don't mind cramped spaces during a race. Hell, on most of our races, dry underwear's a luxury! Count your blessings, Pascal. Count your blessings."

While Pascal squeezed up the narrow tube to examine the sail locker, Louella sat in the helmsman's seat. She let her hands run over the controls. She loved the slightly sticky feel of the wrappings on the wheel. Here and there she noted the faint, oily marks *Thorn*'s captains' sweating hands had put there.

A bright, shining circle was worn into the dull metal beside the winch controls. She reached for a knob, as if to activate it, and noticed that the heel of her hand centered on the worn spot. How many hundreds of times had another hand briefly touched there to wear the finish like that, she wondered. How many captains had sat in this seat to guide the tiny craft across the dark seas of Jupiter? In her mind, those other captains were a palpable presence in the tiny cabin, a trace of the boat's memory.

Directly in front of the helmsman's seat were the screens that displayed the fore and aft camera views. Their controls were in easy reach, just below them. To her left were the inertial-display unit, the pressure gauges, and various station-keeping controls. The housekeeping controls were mounted beneath the seat, where they could be reached from the stateroom.

On a swing arm above the wheel were the primary control readouts: sail pressure gauges, wind indicator, barometer, and dead-reckoning display. Once they were under way she'd be completely dependent on them.

There was a clatter as Pascal wormed his way out of the tube. "Sail sets look okay," he said, as he slid across the deck and dropped into the stateroom's seat. "We've got spares for every sail, plus the extras that you ordered. All of them are marked and set for loading."

"Did you make sure that we have enough lines? I don't want to get caught short on tack once we get out of here."

Pascal snorted. "Of course I checked. My butt's going to be out there too, you know."

Louella nodded, all business. "I double-checked the inspection reports. Just the same we need to do a walkaround."

She'd said it so calmly that Pascal *almost* missed the implication of what she had said. When he did, he snapped erect, banging his head on the bottom of the bunk.

"Y . . . you mean . . . go outside?" he blurted.

Louella sneered at him. "Sure. We can get some pressure suits and hand lights to work with. As long as you stay in the dock you won't have any problems. It will be just like going for our training stroll at geosynch. You didn't have any problems there, did you?"

Pascal stuttered. He'd been scared out of his wits the whole time, worrying whether his lines were securely attached, worrying about the ability of his boots to hold fast to the deck, worrying about slipping, about the vast distance that he would fall should he become detached from the station.

"N . . . no," he lied.

They didn't need the hand lights after all. *Thorn* was still parked in the repair bay where there was plenty of external illumination. Louella held tight to her walker as she stumbled through the lock. The walker took most of the weight off her legs, which was a blessing. Even though she didn't have too much of a problem with the two g's, the additional weight of the heavy pressure suit made movement difficult.

Pascal stumbled along behind her, clutching his own walker so tightly that it looked as if he'd leave glove marks in the metal.

"What a pig," Louella remarked as she examined the bulbous skin of *Thorn*'s outer envelope. "Looks like a damned overgrown, pregnant guppy," she said as she walked along the side of the bulging hull, thinking of the sleek craft she had sailed in Earth's tame waters. Every few steps she stopped to examine a weld, a spot of suspicious discoloration, or one of the vents for the ballast hold.

"Let's take a look at her rigging," she demanded and followed the crew chief to the boat's deck.

Two stubby masts projected up from the centerline of *Thorn*'s upper surface. These were thick triangles of heavy metal, nearly six meters across at their thickest dimension. They certainly weren't the slender masts she'd known all her life.

The trailing edge of each mast was a pair of clamshells. These were double-locked doors that would open when they deployed the sails. A short track ran back from each mast, with a crosswise track at the end. "We extended the travelers on both sides, like you asked," the crew chief said. "You're goin' to have a bit of trouble handling her. Keep a tight hand on the wheel and don't run close to the wind, is my advice." Disapproval was evident in his voice. "Don't think you should have done that, though. These little boats ain't built to take much heel, y'know."

Louella bristled as she checked the workmanship on the track modifications, looking for any indication that the repair crew had scrimped on her specifications. "Did you think about adjusting the traveler's winches to take the extra line?"

The crew chief bristled. "Of course I did," he said gruffly. "I don't appreciate you sayin' that I don't know how to do my job."

"Really? Well, I don't like you telling me how to sail a boat either, asshole!" she shot back. She moved to examine the other mast as the crew chief licked his wounds.

While Louella and the crew chief were above deck, Pascal examined the hull. The keel had already been retracted from the meter-by-meter safety inspection. The huge weights at the ends of the double keel swung slowly from side to side as *Thorn* bobbed up and down. *Thorn* was just a balloon when she wasn't under way. The keels' slender foils hardly seemed strong enough to support the three hundred tons of droplet-shaped weights. The blunt nose of the forward weight was smooth and bright, as if it had been polished. There were several long gouges along the sides.

"Impact scars," the crewman said as she reached across the gap and shoved her glove inside one of the larger ones. "There's always some gravel being driven around the atmosphere, especially down deep, where the keel runs. Sometimes they're pretty big and movin' fast. That's what made these dings, y'see."

Pascal was still staring at the thin ribbons that supported the weights. Each was only a few centimeters thick, hardly the width of his hand. One rip from a rough piece of gravel, he thought, and the ribbon could be severed and the weight would be released, dropping down into the depths far, far below.

Suddenly he realized that he was only one step away from the edge of the inspection platform. One step away from a fall that wouldn't stop until he reached a pressure level that would crush and kill him, compressing his suit and body into a tiny mass. He would still fall until he hit the layer of metallic hydrogen, hundreds and hundreds of kilometers below the station. No, that wasn't really true; he wouldn't fall that far. His body would come to rest somewhere where his density was equal to the surrounding atmosphere.

But he'd still be dead.

A wave of vertigo overcame him. He stumbled back from the dangerous precipice. "I . . . I need to get back inside," he told his escort, clamping his hand on the safety line. "Now!" he shouted when the crewman didn't respond at once. He had to get away from that horrid drop.

Twelve hours later Rams realized that he was in serious trouble. Whenever he tried to head due north, he was forced farther west of his planned track. To be so affected at this distance meant that the storm was immense.

He prepared for the coming storm. The two things a sailor had to remember about surviving a storm, whether on Jupiter or on Earth, were either to be prepared, or be elsewhere. Rams began to go through *Primrose* and secure her. Even a small item flying about in a two-g field could do substantial damage.

The galley and his own cabin were easy. Rams made it a practice to stow everything until needed. Just the same, he went through every locker to make sure that nothing would fall out and surprise him. He poured hot tea into a thermos and stowed that, along with some bread, in the cockpit.

Securing the cargo hold occupied him for an hour. He put double lashings on all the containers, and tied them together, just to make sure. That done, he made certain that all loose lines were in the lockers, along with all of the deck gear. Nothing that could become a flying missile was left unsecured.

Since he wasn't carrying passengers this trip, the other four cabins were empty. Just the same, he checked them for loose gear or an open locker. He had to make absolutely certain they were secure.

Securing the sail locker presented a problem. Rams had to balance being able to hoist sail in a hurry—which meant he had to have one loose—against the risk of it breaking free. He secured the larger sails and kept the two small ones ready to hoist as a compromise. If the blow was as heavy as he expected, the small ones were more likely to be used.

That done, Rams brought the ship about to begin another long, southerly tack. That way he could use the peripheral winds to stay on the outer fringes of the storm. With a little bit of luck, *Primrose* wouldn't be drawn into its roaring core. Then he settled down to see what the long night would bring.

Thorn was six days out from the start and making way at a steady 150 mps. Pascal had already grown sick of the close quarters, the five-hours-on, five-hours-off schedule that matched Jupiter's rotational rate, Louella's lousy cooking (even if it was better than his own), the dragging load from Jupiter's gravity, and the lingering, stinking ammonia smell from the boat's slight atmospheric leakage.

They'd added their own contribution to the atmosphere. After nearly a week of confined quarters they had created a unique miasma. The cabin was redolent of recirculated air, collected flatulence, sweat, and the miscellaneous aromas that the human body produced. Only the ability of the human nose to filter out the worst of these protected him. Still, the smells remained, and unfortunately, Pascal's nose sometimes forgot to ignore them.

He fidgeted at the wheel, keeping a wary eye on the instruments. It was important to maintain the sail's pressure differential right on the edge; that way they could keep their speed up. All week Louella had beaten his time. Somehow she was able to wrest a few extra knots from the wind. No matter how much he pushed, Louella was always able to do better.

They'd been competing ever since he could remember, each trying to outdo the other. She dared him to become a better sailor, even as she relentlessly strove to beat him every time. He challenged her to become the better navigator, and laughed at her struggles with simple plotting problems. She'd succeeded better than he, even if he never was able to offset her intuition with his science. Their teamwork had won numerous races over the years. Their success gained them prime berths in JBI's commercial racing fleet. Louella had worked her way from an Olympic dinghy championship at age thirteen to finally being the helmsman on most of JBI's Cup winners as well as the number one competitor in most of the other commercial classes.

Pascal had been recruited by JBI as a navigator for Louella's first Whitbread. Since then he'd been with her for every race, alternatively as navigator, tactician, winch crank, or sail master. He'd been helmsman when she was captain and shared bunk with her on the *Times*'s double-around-the-world. They'd weathered hurricanes and drifted demasted for days with only a bottle of water to share between them. They'd broached a hundred-thousand-dollar racer in 'Frisco Bay, lost a two-million-dollar racer in the South Pacific, and survived to win the Bermuda in spite of a hurricane that destroyed half the fleet and shredded their mainsail to ribbons. It had been a thrill the whole time.

He just wished that she wasn't such a pain in the ass.

Louella came awake in an instant and checked her watch. She had managed to sleep for nearly five hours without being jarred awake. "Damn Pascal's eyes," she

complained to herself as she fastened her truss. "He must be running safe again."
That meant that she would have to make up for lost time during her watch, as
usual.

She rolled out of the bunk, stepped cautiously to the deck and used the toilet,
splashing a little water from the sink up her nose to counteract the dryness from
the ammonia fumes.

"Tea's hot," Pascal called down to her in a voice heavy with fatigue.

"Thanks," she replied, looking for the thermos. "How did you find time to
make it?"

"You mean how much progress did that cost us, don't you?" he replied sharply.
"Not a bit, I'm sure."

"Do you think that the competition's doing better? Damn, but I wish we had
some way of telling where the other boats are!"

A week before everyone had set off from Charlie Sierra Six on the first leg of the
Great Jupiter Race, as the press had been calling it. The first leg would take them
around CS-15 and then back to CS-27, where they would come to windward and
race downwind to CS-6, where they had begun.

Louella had watched the heat signature of their prime competitor fall to *Thorn's*
lee when they came out of the shelter of the starting station, indicating that they
had caught the vortex off *Thorn* and were spinning away to get good air. It was a
trick most sailors learned before they left their cribs.

They had watched the diminishing white dot that represented the station fade
into the background noise as *Thorn* pulled steadily westward, their speed climbing
the whole time under Jupiter's fierce winds. It was therefore a little disturbing
to discover a heat signature steadily increasing in definition on their aft screen.
Somehow one of the other boats had managed to catch a better wind cell than
theirs.

Louella jibed to port, hoping to create a pocket of dirty air behind *Thorn* that
would interfere with the other's progress. The white dot responded by immediately
moving to starboard, long before they could have felt the effects of Louella's
maneuver.

"Obviously they can see us better than we can see them," Pascal cursed as he
tried to crank up the gain. "It's probably the wind blowing our signature back-
wards. Should we jibe again?"

Louella dismissed the idea; *Thorn* lost some momentum each time they jibed.
"Let's concentrate on building up our speed," she replied, making some tiny adjustments to the set of the sails.

The image of the other boat faded to port and finally disappeared. They were
six hours out from the start.

"What are they doing now?" Louella wondered aloud. "Could they have caught
another favorable wind cell? Do you think they're starting their northward leg
already?"

Pascal checked the inertial. *Thorn* was still a few hours from their planned turning point. "Let them go," he said. "Concentrate on our own course while I grab
some sleep."

· · ·

Pascal was having difficulty staying awake during his shift at the wheel. The days of five-hour sleep cycles, bland food, and lack of exercise were taking their toll. On most of the long races on Earth he at least could stand on the deck, stretch, and get a breath of air to refresh himself. Down here, in Jupiter's atmosphere, he couldn't even stand upright, much less sniff the air blowing by outside the boat. Not that he'd want to, he hastily amended.

But it was dry, as Louella had said, and that was something. He recalled how he'd always hated the pervasive dampness, the clinging, sticky moisture that characterized every ocean race.

Thorn's trim felt wrong, as if she were lumbering in thick syrup, even though her speed was good. Perhaps, he thought, the boat would have a better feel if she rode a little higher, a little lighter.

He clicked on the heaters in the ballast hold. They had pumped nearly four tons of liquefied gas from the bottom of the keel into the ballast tank to set their present trim. The heaters would expand the liquid and force the ballast out. He turned them off after an hour, when the trim felt better.

On the seventh day of their run they rounded CS-15 on their port side and watched the vivid image displayed on their radar screen until it faded back into the ambient noise. Pascal had dutifully recorded the close passage, to prove that they had indeed rounded the mark, while Louella concentrated on keeping *Thorn* a safe distance away. To do so she maneuvered the winches to switch the sails from side to side, slipping a little to slew the craft about without losing momentum.

As much as they'd like to do so, there was no time to stop, and no way to find out whether the station knew that they had passed. They'd tried the radio, but the deafening noise of atmospheric static masked any reply.

"I wish we could find out which boats have already gone by," Pascal remarked as he stowed the log and climbed wearily into his bunk. He loosened the truss and breathed a sigh of relief.

"The hell with them," Louella answered weakly in a voice that revealed that she, too, was getting tired. "We just have to do the best we can and hope that the rest do worse. That's what racing is all about."

"Yeah, remember the last Whitbread—didn't see another boat the whole race. It was like we had the whole ocean to ourselves."

"Not much fun there. What I remember is sitting dead in the water for three days while the sun baked us to a crisp; no wind, no progress. It was only luck that we caught the edge of that storm and got a boost."

"Won the race, didn't we? Luck falls to those with the most skill," Pascal said encouragingly.

"Let's just hope it works this time as well," she said dryly. "Now get some shut-eye so you can relieve me in two hours."

The rest of her watch passed without incident as she tacked at a twenty-degree angle to the head wind. The new sails that they had deployed on day five were still serviceable and were probably good for another two days at least. There was a minor fluctuation in the barometer and Louella let the keel down a few hundred meters. She nearly fell asleep at one point, she was so tired.

•   •   •

Louella was the first to notice how their track was consistently deviating to the south. On the last two tacks they had strayed nearly fifty kilometers west of plan.

"Unless there are some different physics out there we can't possibly be heading like the inertial shows," she remarked with a nod at the instrument when Pascal crawled up to relieve her.

Pascal looked at the readout. "This thing's supposed to be foolproof. Maybe you're misreading it?"

Louella snorted in reply. "You check it yourself. I'm getting something to eat and then some shut-eye." She slid from the helmsman's perch, past Pascal, and into the stateroom. "See if you can figure out what's wrong."

Pascal kept an eye on the inertial throughout his shift. Sure enough, the southern legs showed the same deviation. If the machine was to be believed, then the winds were coming almost directly down from the north instead of following the westerly course that they had been told to expect.

He wished that he were thinking a little more clearly. Something kept itching at the edges of thought. Something someone had warned them about. What was it? He looked at the curving southerly trace that the inertial was showing and wondered. It almost looked like a smooth curve. . . . Then he had it! A turbulence eddy must have formed along the edge. If the readout was right then they were already being drawn into its grasp. "Louella!" he shouted. "Wake up! We have a bit of a problem."

Hours later the winds rocked *Thorn* from side to side as Louella fought to make way. Unlike the smooth air they had encountered thus far, the winds on the edges of the storm were rough, uneven gusts that quartered with little warning. In one stomach-wrenching instance, *Thorn* had turned completely about, while pitching nearly sixty degrees to leeward, reversing as the wind switched and slammed them in the opposite direction.

She knew that they'd lost the foresail, and suspected that the aft was in tatters. There was no possibility of hoisting new ones in these rough seas. Something in the sail locker had torn loose and was smashing around. Pascal would be taking his life in his hands if he tried to go into the locker. For good or ill, they had to use whatever sail they had and hope that their skill, and no small amount of luck, would see them through.

"Can't even put out a damned sea anchor to steady her," she complained at one point. "How the hell do the sailors up here survive these storms, anyhow?"

"I think they are wise enough not to do something stupid like racing in a small boat," Pascal said dryly from the bunk where he had secured himself. "How are we doing?"

Louella checked the instruments. "As far as I can see we are straightening out our track somewhat. At least we aren't curving more."

"I hope that means we aren't getting sucked in. How big do you think this storm is?"

"No telling. I don't know how they scale these storms up here. Back home this would be called a one-million-year storm, I'm certain. It's a monster!"

Another gust hit them on the side. Louella threw the switch to lower the keel, and their center of gravity, to give them some more stability. It was all that she could do.

The remnants of the aft sail blew away during Pascal's watch. The rocking of the boat stopped as it drifted with the wind. Since he now had no control over *Thorn*, he lashed the wheel in place and crawled into the sail locker. The only way they had of restoring some measure of control to the boat was to get another sail up.

The locker was a mess. The big specialty main that Louella had ordered for the finishing run had broken loose from its restraints and had swept the mountings clean off the deck. Bits of broken metal and plastic tie-downs were everywhere. A large dent on the bulkhead showed where the big sail had struck before it finally wedged itself behind the canisters.

Pascal stumbled over the wreckage and selected one of the smaller sails. He undid the lashings, trying to maintain his balance against the pitching motion of the boat. As he worked he kept a wary eye on the huge mainsail in case it began to roll his way.

Twice the boat moved unexpectedly and threw him against the stowed sails, smashing their blunt edges into his chest and back. He knew that he'd have massive bruises to show for it.

Finally, he secured the winch to the sail head and locked the cables in place. He braced himself between the sail and the bulkhead, using the pressure of his legs to hold himself in position and began the torturous process of ratcheting the sail into place. It took all of his energy to move it the last few centimeters.

Louella was awake and in the helmsman's seat when he poked his head out of the tube. "Sail ready?" she asked calmly, as if nothing were amiss.

Pascal nodded. "Aft mast, small set." he said quickly, thankful that she had not made an issue of his reckless actions. She was all cool control and professional when the race was on.

"Brace yourself," she warned as she reached for the controls. "Release!" She threw the hoist switches to raise the sail as Pascal tightened the straps to hold him in the bunk.

Louella spun the wheel to bring the boat directly into the wind. The wind caught the edge of the new sail and pulled it the rest of the way out.

Louella adjusted the traveler. The wind filled the sail, throwing *Thorn* at a sharp angle. The boat heeled precariously and then leaped forward with a force that snapped Louella's head back against the headrest. She managed the trim of the sail, a matter more of feel than science, until the boat was riding steadily downwind, making steady progress. *Thorn* rode safely and secure in the teeth of the storm.

"That's the right thing to do," she said softly to the exhausted Pascal. "Good going, partner."

The relative calm following the storm was a blessing. Rams had managed to be blown only a couple hundred kilometers south of his planned track through a combination of his skill and considerable luck. All he had to do now was intercept the CS-42 track and pray that the storm hadn't forced her too far from the projected track in his computer.

Rams checked the sail one more time and then prepared to come about. It was time to head on a northerly leg. He buckled himself to the deck and released the hold-downs on the wheel. He felt a throb reverberate through the deck as the rudder cut into the dense soup, far below. He imagined it to be *Primrose*'s heartbeat.

The hull began to sound a deep resonant note that echoed throughout the ship. "Damn harmonics," Rams swore. He retracted the keel until the sound disappeared. Left alone, the wind blowing across the keel would set up a destructive harmonic that could destroy the ship.

"Ready, girl," he whispered, turning the wheel ever so slightly to starboard. He put one hand on the port-side jib release and waited. *Primrose* rolled to the perpendicular and then shook as her prow came through the eye of the wind.

Rams hit the port-side release and switched on the starboard-side jib winch. In his mind's eye he could see the mainsail whipping across the deck, slamming the traveler to rest on the opposite side as it turned its port side to weather.

There was a clatter of chain against the pressure hull that stopped when the loose jib finally stretched taut. *Primrose* heeled and started to pick up speed on the downwind leg. Rams held the wheel loosely, searching for balance until he was confident that the ship had once more found her line. Only then did he lock the wheel into place and relax.

He unbuckled the restraints and started to pour the last cup of tea from his thermos when he stopped. Something was out of the ordinary, but he couldn't put his finger on it. Rams examined the instrument panel. Everything seemed to be in order; no red warning lights that would scream that the hull had been breached, no flashing indication that the rigging was damaged, no alarm telling him that some life-threatening life-support system was malfunctioning. What could it have been?

Then the infrared display flashed again. Rams started in surprise. There, on the screen, was a white blob—a heat indication where there should be nothing but empty sky. A glance at the camera indicator told him that the blob was off his starboard bow, just at the edge of the imager's range.

Quickly he released the wheel and spun *Primrose* about, pulling the jib tight and letting it backwind, just as Jake had taught him. The winds buffeted the ship for a few seconds, rocking it from side to side until, finally, the motion subsided. The ship was close-hauled into the wind, the pressure on the reversed jib equal to the pressure on the loose main, and both constrained by the kilometers of keel beneath him.

He carefully turned the aft camera around, trying to find another indication of that heat signature. Several times he thought that he had it, but was mistaken. Stare at a screen of random noise long enough and you are likely to see anything you want. He continued to search.

Then he had it. A definite heat source, and quite close too. The object was moving at about the same speed and direction as the wind.

They were so far off their planned track by watch change that neither of them could see how they could make up the lost time. "I don't see how the other competitors could have avoided the storm," Pascal remarked as he examined the charts and the trace on the inertial. "Surely they're in as bad shape as we are."

"Don't count on it," Louella snarled. "Most of them are tough sons of a bitch.

Somebody probably figured out how to use this storm's winds to their advantage. I wouldn't be surprised to find that at least two of them have a good day's advantage on us.''

"Oh, when did you become such an optimist?'' Pascal asked bitterly.

"When I got you as a partner,'' she snapped back.

Pascal checked the trim while Louella snored in her bunk. *Thorn* felt sluggish— probably Louella had taken on more ballast, he thought. He switched on the heater to vent some of it and lighten the boat.

A sudden gust blew *Thorn* to the side. She tilted nearly forty degrees as the wheel whipped from side to side.

"What the hell?'' Louella yelled from her bunk.

"I think the sail's gone again,'' Pascal yelled down at her. "Take the wheel while I get another one ready.''

Louella squirmed into the seat as Pascal dragged himself into the sail locker. *Thorn* was rocking steadily from side to side. She turned on the winch to let out more keel and steady the boat, letting out another hundred meters of mesh.

"Let's try the foresail this time,'' she yelled at Pascal's disappearing feet.

Pascal wiggled into the cramped space beside the sails and braced himself. He ached all over. No matter how he positioned himself, some bruised part of his body pressed painfully against something. He rigged the lines and gear until the red-tagged foresail was ready to be ratcheted into the loading compartment.

He carefully attached the pulley to the head end of the sail and began to crank it into place. With every turn of the winch his muscles ached. He banged his elbow on the bulkhead with each long stroke of the winch handle.

With a twenty-to-one ratio, it took a long time to finally get the sail into place— long enough for the forgotten heater to turn the entire ballast load into steam.

Back in the cabin Louella noticed the sideways motion of the boat. She immediately checked the pressure gauges, thinking the wind had switched unexpectedly. But that wasn't the problem; their heading was still good and the wind had settled down. Why then were they slipping sideways? She tried to clear her head and reason it out. She wished that she weren't so damn tired.

Then she noticed the blinking warning light above the heater switch. "Damn,'' she swore, "how did I miss that?'' and turned it off.

Pascal stuck his head out of the end of the tube. "Sail's all ready to go.''

"Right, brace yourself,'' she responded and hit the winches to raise the sail.

Before she could react the ship moved violently to one side, throwing her from the seat and smashing her against the bulkhead. She didn't even have time to scream.

Pascal came painfully to full consciousness. His head throbbed and his side was a mass of agony, as if his ribs had been crushed. The first thing that he saw was Louella slumped against the bulkhead of the cockpit, her arm at an awkward angle. "She must have forgotten to buckle herself in,'' he mumbled and crawled to her. The pain in his side stabbed each time he moved.

Louella's pulse was all right, but her breathing was labored. He turned her to one side to relieve the front-to-back pressure from the two-g gravity. She moaned as he shifted her.

He ran his hand down her arm, feeling for a break, a dislocated joint. The arm was all right, but there was a swelling at her wrist indicating a possible sprain or fracture. Since there was nothing more serious apparent, he climbed into the seat and buckled himself in. He could take care of Louella's medical problems later, after he found out what *Thorn*'s situation was. The boat always came first!

A quick glance at the instruments showed that there was no pressure differential on the sails. The wind-speed indicator read a fat zero, which meant that *Thorn* must be moving at the same speed as the wind. He noted that the ballast was zip. In an obvious contradiction, the pressure gauge showed them to still be on the boundary layer. Nevertheless *Thorn* was bobbing uncomfortably, as if she had lost some trim.

He clicked on the pumps that would bring more ballast up through the pipes. Once the boat had the proper trim he could turn her back into the wind. As he was waiting for that, he looked at the inertial. According to the readout they had lost most of their progress for the last day, at least. They were being blown back toward CS-15, but on a southward angle.

Since it would be a while until the pumps did their work he got the first-aid kit out of storage and put a splint on Louella's arm. He prepared a dose of painkiller for when she awoke. He'd only give it if she asked for it. Carefully he turned her head and waved a broken ampule under her nose.

"Wha . . . where . . . humph," she said and tried to sit up. "Wha . . . what happened?" she asked.

"Don't know. Was coming back down the tube when all hell broke loose. Threw me against the side and knocked me out. We're way off course now."

"Oh, your head," she said and reached out with her good hand to touch his forehead. "You're bleeding!"

He brushed her hand away. "Just a bump, I think—rotten headache, though. How do you feel? Do you need this?" He held up the dose he'd prepared.

"Can't take something that will knock me out. Help me get to the bunk so I can lie down. We need to figure out what we have to do. Maybe then I'll let you use it."

By the time he'd wrestled her into the bunk and fastened the straps to secure her in place, the pumps had been running for a good ten minutes. He dropped into the seat and checked the gauges. The stabbing pains in his side abated for a moment.

"That's strange," he remarked as he flicked the pump switches on and off. "There doesn't seem to be any ballast."

"Yeah," Louella said. "You left the heaters on. I flipped them off while you were messing with the sail."

"Shit, I forgot about them when the sail blew. But that doesn't explain why the pumps aren't working."

"Maybe we're floating too high. Maybe the keel isn't deep enough to find anything to pump."

"Can't be. Pressure gauge says we're right where we're supposed to be." He glanced at the keelmeter. "The keel's down as far as it will go, so we should be pumping ballast. Since we aren't that means that either the pumps have stopped working or something has damaged the lines leading to the ballast tanks."

"Either way we can't trim the boat," Louella mused. "Well, let's try using the sails anyway to see what sort of maneuverability we have. We have to be able to make one of the stations or we're royally screwed."

Pascal threw the switches to pull the foresail back from its fully extended position. As the winches brought the sail tight, *Thorn* heeled to lee instead of turning into the wind. He let the sail out, hoping to run downwind instead. Perhaps on that setting he'd be able to steer from side to side. But the boat wouldn't turn that way either.

"Unless you can think of any other things to try," he said after an hour of experimenting with various settings of sails and the immobile keel, "I think we're stuck. There aren't any rescue boats out here. It looks like you'll get your wish to 'sail Jupiter's seas forever.' According to my calculations, *Thorn* won't intersect a station's track for at least a thousand years."

"Well, Pascal," Louella said in a surprisingly soft voice, "if we're going to die, I can't think of anybody I'd rather do it with than you, and no better place than on a racing boat."

"I'm afraid that I can," he replied too quickly and watched the gray nothingness of the infrared display as he contemplated his own death.

At least he'd be free of this damn headache, he thought.

Rams was puzzled as he approached the strangely warm object that had suddenly appeared. *Primrose* was now matched to the speed of the object. He carefully headed downwind and slowly closed the gap between them. Rams kept one hand on the winch controls as he maneuvered the ship closer and closer to the object, tightening and loosening the sail controls to creep forward.

At a few hundred meters the infrared image resolved into a strange double blob. The large upper blob was one or two hundred meters above *Primrose*. The smaller one was about the same distance below. A barely discernible thin line, apparently just a few degrees above the ambient temperature, connected the two blobs. He'd never seen anything so strange in all of the time he'd spent on Jupiter's seas.

As he drew closer, the upper blob resolved itself into the familiar heat signature of a small craft, possibly a cargo barque or maybe a miner. Maybe the connecting line was its keel, he thought. But what was the blob at the bottom? It was far too large and irregular to be keel weights.

He pumped a little more ballast into *Primrose*'s tanks and sank lower. He wasn't going to get any closer to the pair until he figured out what was going on. "Hate to mess up some science folks, wouldn't we?" he remarked to *Primrose*.

The heat image resolved into two keel ribbons. They appeared to be tangled around some large shape that was *below* ambient temperature, as if it had come from deeper in the atmosphere. He flooded it with his sonar, watching as the display built up a ghostly image of the irregular shape.

On a hunch he pinged it with the docking sonar frequency and listened through the static for the reply: One, two, three pings came back, which indicated that he had made the lump ring. Either it was hollow, which made no sense, or it had a high metallic content. Somehow the other ship had been hit by a piece of rock brought up by the storm—a huge piece that could be worth a fortune.

He brought the ship back up until it was level with the other ship, carefully staying downwind to avoid smashing into her. With fine adjustments of the jib he allowed the other ship to come closer and closer until they almost kissed.

"Hello," he yelled over the radio link, hoping that they were close enough to overcome the static. "This is the clipper *Primrose*, four days out of CS-15. Do you need assistance?"

Louella started at the sudden and unexpected sound of a strange human voice coming over the static of the radio. Pascal tried to sit upright and looked around. Since the accident he had slept in the helmsman's seat, letting Louella have the more comfortable bunk where she could sleep. She'd relented after the second day and let him administer the painkiller. "Just make sure it isn't a lethal dose," she'd jokingly remarked. "I don't want to miss the end of this race."

"Nor I," Pascal had replied slowly, and thought about what she had just said. He'd never considered that possibility. An "accidental" mistake in dosage would certainly be something to think about as the air grew closer.

To pass the time they'd talked about things that they never seemed to have time to discuss earlier. Except for the long trip out from Earth, when she was still pissed after their big argument and wouldn't talk to him, the only time they'd had together was during the races, or while preparing for them. Under those circumstances it had been all business; winning the race, discussing the set of the sails, the movement of the currents and the wind, talking about the positions and strategies of their competition, and the endless details of reconciling her art of sailing with his science. After every race they went their separate ways, until the next race, the next challenge that threw them together.

"Always wanted to have a place on Chesapeake Bay," Louella confided during one of the times they were both awake. Since the accident they had abandoned their five-hours-on, five-hours-off schedule. "Some little marina where I could teach kids to race. Maybe have a dinghy school of my own. You know, take a shot at producing a batch of Olympic champions."

Pascal snorted at that: If he ever got out of this he wanted to live as far from the ocean as possible, maybe in Arizona or New Mexico. Someplace where wet clothing, must and mildew, and cold, sodden food were unheard of. Someplace where the damned footing was solid and the horizon always stayed level with your eyes. He yearned for some place that was dry, flat, and had no dangerous cliffs.

But neither could convince the other of the desirability of their dreams, even though the chances of achieving them were impossible. There was only a day or two left of the life-support system. The water had gone the day before. Both knew that they were doomed. They would become a Jovian version of the Flying Dutchman.

"I repeat, do . . . **crackle** . . . hisssss . . . need assistance?" the voice rattled from the speaker. Pascal fumbled around under the instrument panel and found the microphone.

"I hear you loud and clear," he yelled. "Thank God you found us. I mean, yes, yes we need help badly!"

"Are . . . **crackle** pop** . . . under sail?" the voice said with what sounded like a tone of impatience.

"No," Pascal said in response. "We cannot maneuver. We are without ballast and cannot control our craft."

"**Pop . . . ** . . . wish to . . . ," came the hissing reply. "Do you . . . **** . . . rescued?"

"Of course we do, you fucking idiot!" Louella screamed into the microphone. "Of course we want to be rescued!" Tears of happiness were streaming down her face even as she cursed the stupidity of the question.

"Tell him to give us instructions," Pascal said, wiping the moisture from his own face with one hand while he gently wiped at the tears on Louella's with the other as they hugged in the cramped cockpit.

Rams tried to understand what the woman was saying about the condition of their boat. The radio handled low frequencies better than high, and that made her voice difficult to understand. If only she'd stop and let the other guy talk!

"**** . . . Can't maneuver . . . ," she told him. "No food, no water . . . life support gone. We're afraid . . . **crackle** . . . ship . . . complete loss . . . abandon . . . **pop** . . ."

Rams wondered what sort of idiots they were to talk about abandoning their ship. Didn't they know the wealth that they'd discovered? Didn't they realize how valuable their own ship was? "I'll take her under tow if you want."

"Understand. **** . . . need medical . . . **tention."

"All right. I will bring you aboard and secure your ship. By the way," he said slyly, "will you give me salvage rights if I do so?"

It took him several repeats before he could make them understand just what he was asking. He made sure that he had their request to abandon ship on file. It had to be clear that it was their idea, not a threat by him. He really had no choice but to help them—that was how you survived on Jupiter.

Rams struggled into the heavy pressure suit and, once inside, hooked its safety line to the ring near the hatch. Attached to his belt were lengths of high-tensile-strength line. He could use them to string the two craft together. Checking to make certain that everything was ready, he opened the hatch and stepped directly out into the howling winds of Jupiter.

Rams had brought the far larger *Primrose* to within fifty meters of the smaller ship's hull, letting the venturi effect of the winds in the narrow channel hold them close.

His exterior lights just barely illuminated the upper surface of the other ship. Rams watched as two figures struggled awkwardly out of the hatch and clamped their lines onto the deck rings.

The two ships bucked and lurched, the gap between them widening and closing. The decks rose and sank relative to each other as they bobbed, side by side. Rams prayed that he'd set the ship's sails properly to hold station with the drifting ship. He clicked his suit light four times to attract their attention.

When he got a wave of acknowledgment, he readied one of the lines, whirling the pulley at its end over his head in ever-widening circles before releasing it upwind. The pulley sailed out and too-quickly down, drawn by the higher acceleration of Jupiter's gravity. It clanked onto the near side of *Thorn*'s hull and slipped away.

Rams retrieved the line and tried again, and a third time. On the fourth toss, the pulley finally cleared the deck. The line whipped around to catch against the two figures, making the smaller of them stagger back from the impact.

The other figure secured the pulley to their deck with one arm and waited. Rams carefully pulled the light line back as he paid out a heavier one that was tied to its end. It took nearly half an hour before he had a slack double line rigged between the two rocking-and-bobbing craft. The line moved up and down, tightening and then loosening as the two ships lurched in the wind. He wrapped the line around a deck winch and locked it in place.

Finally, Rams attached a cradle of ropes and clamps he had rigged to a hook on the heavier line. Slowly he winched the cradle to the other ship, hoping that they would use it properly. The last thing he wanted was for someone to take a plunge.

"You first," Pascal said nervously as he caught hold of the rig. "Let me hook you up."

"No fucking way. I'm the captain of this boat and I leave last," Louella replied. "Turn around so I can hook the clamps to your suit."

"Yeah, and how are you going to hook yourself up with a broken arm?" he shot back. "Now turn around. For once, don't be such a bitch!"

"Why, Pascal," she said in surprise, "that sounds like you actually care about me."

"Well, it looks like we'll have the Whitbread next year after all," he said as he checked the rig's fastenings a second time to make certain they were secure. "I wouldn't want to be with anyone else in that race."

"It's a date, lover," said Louella.

Once he saw that Louella had been dipped, jerked, and lurched to the other ship, Pascal had to face what would happen next. In a few moments the rig would return and he would have to hook himself to it so that his rescuer could winch him across the bottomless chasm of Jupiter's atmosphere. Instead of a nice solid deck beneath his feet there would be nothing but black nothingness that went down forever, down into the cold heart of this cruel planet. He'd be suspended by only a few thin filaments of braided cord and his trust in the skill of some unknown captain. For long minutes he would be swinging above the great void, helpless as the strong fingers of Jupiter drew him down, down, down.

He doubted that he really had the nerve. Could he really trust himself to that hopelessly thin cable? And even if he did, where would he then find the courage to step out, off the solid deck, and place himself at risk?

The moment of decision had come. The rig was swinging out of the bright lights of the other ship and coming toward him. His stomach hurt. He was either going to die on this crippled ship or drop to a certain death. He felt like crying, he was so afraid.

• • •

"What are you doing out here anyway?" Rams asked as he unhooked the woman from the rig, confident that the suit radios would work at this close range. "You sure don't look like miners."

"We're one of the teams in the Great Race," Louella replied.

"A race? On Jupiter? What sort of foolishness is that?"

"Don't tell me that you haven't heard about the race. Hell, it's been on every newscast for the last year. Crap, we're probably the biggest celebrities on the whole planet."

"Don't have much time for news," Rams replied. "Radio don't work down here. Have to depend on the media they send down the elevator to keep up with events. Besides, if it doesn't have to do with cargo or weather I don't pay much attention to it."

"We're in a race with some other barkentines—it's the first Jupiter sailboat race," Louella explained. "JBI sponsored and financed our boat."

Rams cursed softly to himself, and then said aloud, "Must be nice to be able to waste money like that. I can think of guys who could use that boat for something worthwhile; something better than some fancy trophy!" he added vehemently.

"Well, I'm certain that JBI will be grateful. They'll probably reward you for rescuing us."

"Well, that might be nice, but I'm going to get more than a little reward out of JBI, you can depend on that. Salvage alone ought to pay off the debt on *Primrose*— that's my ship," he added, pointing at the deck with one glove. "The other thing might pay for something more."

"What other thing?" Louella asked, but Rams ignored her.

"What's going on with your partner?" he wondered. "What the devil is he waiting for? Why isn't he hooking himself up to the rig?"

"I was afraid this would happen," Louella answered. "Pascal's afraid of heights. Probably shitting in his suit right now, just thinking about the drop in front of him." Louella waved her good arm vigorously over her head. "Come on Pascal, you asshole; hook up and get the hell over here!" she shouted, forgetting that the object of her scorn couldn't possibly hear her.

After long minutes of waiting with no sign of action by the small figure on the deck of *Thorn*, Rams swore. "Do you think that you can operate that winch with one hand? Looks like I need to go over there and kick your buddy in the ass."

When Louella signaled the affirmative, Rams connected a pair of heavy lines to his belt. One of them was tied to the stern docking ring. He activated the winch to bring the rig back.

He grabbed the rig as it swung back, hooked it to the rings of his suit, and signaled Louella to start the winch. "Keep those lines from tangling," he warned her as he stepped off the deck and began to swing across the gap.

As soon as Rams's boots hit *Thorn*'s deck, he secured his safety line. He detached the rig and quickly clamped it to Pascal's suit, brushing aside the other man's arms when Pascal fought him. He secured the last clamp, unclipped Pascal's safety line, and waved his arm for Louella to start the winch.

Pascal protested, stiff-legged, against the pull of the winch. The resistance was putting an extra load on the line, so Rams stiff-armed him in the middle of the back, forcing him forward. At that moment the two ships spread apart and pulled the line taut. With a scream, Pascal was yanked from the deck to hang above the inky blackness. As the ships bobbed and danced in the winds, he jerked on the line like a spastic marionette.

Rams headed aft to secure one of the heavy lines to the stern docking ring. The other end was tied to the docking winch on *Primrose* and could be used to pull *Thorn*.

After trying the line Rams dropped through the hatch and recovered *Thorn*'s log. The owners would probably want it if they couldn't get the ship back. He stowed the log in his hip pouch and emerged on deck just in time to catch the returning rig. He grabbed it and lashed it to the deck. It would stay until he was finished securing the other line to the bow.

Thorn lurched, dropping far below *Primrose*. She rocked violently from side to side, her motion the result of the enormous mass embedded in her keel. If that thin ribbon broke from the strain, it would release the weight, and *Thorn* would shoot up like a released cork, endangering both ships.

Quickly paying the safety line behind him, Rams struggled to the bow. Bracing himself against further moves of the deck, he clamped the second line to the ring. This way, after he connected the other end of this lead line to *Primrose*'s forward winch, he could adjust the two ships so they rode side by side.

Satisfied with his work, he took the free end and began his way back to the rig. When he managed a quick glance at *Primrose*, he noticed that her sails were shifting, which indicated that she might be drifting, changing her heading. He had to get back and trim her sails before she got out of control. He started walking faster.

He was halfway back when a sudden gust shot the two ships apart. The tow line he'd tied at the stern straightened and vibrated like a violin string. The safety line parted with a snap that whipped the rig out and back. In seconds it was flailing downwind, lashing the hide of *Thorn* like the whip of a deranged jockey.

Rams straightened as the *Thorn*'s bow swung away and the ship came sternwise to *Primrose*, where it jolted it to a stop. He stumbled backward, trying to regain his balance, just as the wishbone switched sides and slammed to the end of the extended traveler.

And against Rams's right leg.

The intense pain in his leg was the first thing Rams felt when he recovered consciousness. Then he tried to make sense of the upside-down view of the swaying side of the ship. He realized that he was hanging head down from his safety line, his left leg bent under him. First, he felt cold, and then hot as the pain from his leg shot through him. Waves of increasingly severe pain washed up from his leg until he could think of nothing else.

During a brief respite from the pain, he tried to move. Something was holding his arm immobile. He tried to reach across with the other arm, desperately seeking the safety line that lay somewhere out of sight. After a few fumbling tries he gave up. Hell, even if he could find it, he wouldn't be able to climb back to the deck, not in his condition.

He calmly assessed his situation before the pain returned. He obviously couldn't do anything for himself, and the only other help was a woman with a broken arm and a little fart who was too afraid to do anything. Neither one would be able to help him. He was going to die.

Without warning he lost his dinner, fouling the inside of his helmet and filling his nose with sour, burning fluid.

Then he passed out.

Pascal picked himself off of the deck and looked toward *Thorn*. She was gone! In a panic he looked to the other side, saw nothing, and then looked to the stern.

Very faintly he could see the dim reflection of the ship's lights off *Thorn*'s pointed stern. Glinting in the lights was the thin line that held the two together; it must be the line the captain had rigged before the wind hit them.

"Do you see him?" Louella's voice crackled in his ears. "I lost sight of him when the gust hit us."

"Was he blown away? I don't see the safety line he rigged."

"It broke when we separated. Do you think he fell?" Louella screamed.

A wave of nausea washed through Pascal; his worst nightmare: to fall endlessly into the heavy, empty blackness beneath them. That could have been him if the line had separated when he was coming across. Thank God he was safety tied to his deck when it happened, he thought.

Louella was pulling on his arm, pointing toward the hatch. He followed quickly, eager for the added security of the ship.

"I've got to bring the two ships alongside, so we can bring him back," were the first words he heard when he undid his helmet in the small air lock. "We've got to get the ships positioned like they were."

Pascal nodded his head in agreement. If they could turn this huge ship so that *Thorn* was once again flying alongside, they could toss another line across and pull the captain back to safety. He bit his lip; it would be hard, going out on deck again, but he felt that he could do it.

"I'll ready a new line," he said, and screwed his helmet and his courage into place.

Louella couldn't possibly toss the line across with only one good arm. On the other hand, he had no doubt of her ability to handle this, or any other ship, even with one arm in a sling.

None whatsoever.

Through the most disconcerting lurches and jumps, Louella managed to bring *Thorn* back alongside. *Primrose* was actually sailing backward, the wind on the reverse of her sails. This allowed her to drag *Thorn* by the single tow line back into the range of *Primrose*'s bright lights.

Pascal was dismayed when he saw the dangling figure of their rescuer. He waved furiously, hoping the captain would wave back. But his attempt was in vain—the far figure dangled lifelessly, swinging from side to side with every motion of the boat.

Pascal pondered his situation. How was he to get a safety line across if the other man couldn't secure it? He didn't know whether the captain was dead or alive, awake or unconscious. But he couldn't just leave him there, alone in the dark, waiting to fall should that single, thin thread holding him in place break. What could he do?

He looked at the flapping remains of the former safety line whipping back and forth against the side of the boat, somehow hoping to find it restored.

Louella certainly wouldn't be able to help, not with her arm out of commission. He stood there for long minutes as he considered his options. First, Rams might recover and climb back up to where he could catch a line. That would allow him to winch the captain back.

If that didn't happen then he could, he could . . . what? Leap across the space between the ships, pick Rams up in his arms and leap back? Pascal watched the motions of the two ships carefully as they rose and fell, closed and separated, shifted forward and back, the one with a little sideways motion and the other rolling precariously. Jumping would be impossible, not only because of the unpredictable movement of the ships but for the distance as well. He'd barely clear the edge of the deck before plunging down. . . . He let the thought stop there as he tightened his sphincters. He discarded that option quickly.

Maybe, he hoped, he could catch the line on something over there and pull Rams back. Four futile tries showed him the stupidity of that idea. Which left only one option—going over to the other ship and bringing the slumped figure to safety. But how? He certainly couldn't get near the edge and risk that long, long fall beneath them.

He went back to the hatch, where he plugged into the intercom and explained the situation to Louella. Surely she would understand, he thought.

"You're wasting time thinking about it, damn it! Get your ass over there and get him back!" Louella screamed. "I don't give a rat's ass how you feel; if you don't get started in ten minutes I'll make sure that it gets done myself."

The thought of Louella with her arm in a cast trying to rescue Rams was so ludicrous that Pascal began to laugh. "You couldn't even get your suit on by yourself," he wheezed.

"Exactly, but one hand is all I need to lock the damn hatch so you can't get back in without him."

Pascal was horrified, doubting her at first, and then realizing that she was entirely capable of carrying out her threat. "You wouldn't," he said.

"Just try me," she shot back.

Pascal climbed back on deck and winched the stern tow line as close as was safe. He thought that he could slide down the line, but then realized that he couldn't chance it—one slip and he'd drop into the ten- or fifteen-meter gap between the ships and plunge into the forever, below. What if he froze halfway across? He'd probably hang there until he gave in to vertigo and then he'd fall, fall, fall into the black maw that thirsted, that called out to him. He shook his head and stepped back further from the edge of the deck. How could he overcome this fear that left him incapable of action? There had to be some other way, some way to rescue Rams without having to risk a fall. There had to be!

He returned to the hatch and pleaded with Louella to think of something, some way that did not involve making him cross the deep chasm of his innermost fear. They reached the same conclusion as before; that he was the sole resource they had to save Rams.

"In case you think I was kidding, I've already locked the hatch," she muttered before cutting off the conversation.

Pascal debated testing the hatch to see if she had really carried out her threat, but decided against it. He really didn't care to find out.

He returned topside and worked his way carefully to the stern. He stood there and contemplated what he had to do; what he could not escape doing, no matter what his fear.

Louella had been doing a good job of keeping station. *Thorn* was still drifting off to the port side, slightly below *Primrose*'s level. Their positions gave the tow line a downward slope.

All that he had to do was tie himself to the line and slide down to *Thorn*'s deck. It sounded so easy, so terribly easy. But what if the line parted? No, he couldn't afford to think about that.

Pascal retreated to the winch at midships, tore the remnants of the safety line away and wrapped a new line, fastening the other end to his suit. *That* would give him some added security, and could be used to drag Rams back aboard.

He fashioned a short loop around the tow rope with a short length of line, and tied both ends to his suit. After a moment's hesitation, he attached a second loop— and a third. Just for safety's sake, he detached the line that held him to the deck and put that around the tow as well. Finally certain that he was quadruple redundantly safe, he lay under the tow and grasped the line with both hands.

Through the narrow visor of his helmet he could only see the tow rope and the spider's web of lines he had attached. He concentrated on the line and his gloves around it, trying to suppress any thoughts of what he was about to do. He tried to drive away all thoughts of the depths below him, drawing him so deathly down, down, down. . . .

Pascal shook himself. If he hesitated for one more second, thinking about it, he would be unable to move. Ignoring a shudder of stomach-wrenching fear that tore at his insides, he tugged at the tow with one hand, said a short prayer, and began to slide.

There was a snap, a millisecond of a fall, as the slack in his safety lines was taken up by his weight. The tow vibrated for a second more and then Pascal was falling, sliding, hitting the deck of *Thorn* with a bone-jarring impact. He clutched the tow tightly through his gloves as he tested the solid reality of the deck beneath his feet. He had made it, he had not fallen. He had conquered the depths of his fear. Nothing was beyond him now. Nothing!

The smell inside his suit told him that his body had not shared his courage.

Squirming around to pull himself upright, securing a new safety line to the rolling deck, untangling the many lines that held him to the tow line, and making his way forward to stand on the deck above Rams took only a few minutes. The captain was still hanging, just a few meters down the side. Pascal could see that he had the safety line wrapped around one arm, pinning it to his side.

"Captain?" he called when he thought he was within range of the other's radio. "Can you hear me?" Only silence answered him. He could expect no help from Rams.

But how was he to get Rams's unconscious body up on deck? It would be impossible to pull the man the short distance up the side with the safety line. At best, he couldn't lift his own weight under two g's. What chance did he have of pulling a larger man, and one enclosed in a heavy pressure suit, that far? It would be the equivalent of lifting 350 kilos on Earth! Even professional weightlifters had trouble with that kind of load. No, he couldn't do that.

Neither did he think he could maneuver the tangled safety line sideways to the winch and use that to pull him up. A lateral pull would be the same as lifting Rams a half a meter or more; out of the question.

There was no choice; he'd have to climb down and attach the safety line he'd brought with him. Easy to say—sure, just drop down and hang over the depths once again. Nothing to it, he told himself. After all, hadn't he come across the gap?

No, you can't, his mind replied as the edges of his innermost fear crept back in. He tried not to listen to it as he rigged two lines to the deck; one to support him and one more for additional security. His empty stomach clenched in a knot of sour fear the whole time. He fervently wished that he didn't have to do this, that there was some other way. Tears stung his eyes. The fear of falling was too great to bear. Why did it have to be him?

The line he'd tied to the *Primrose*'s winch was attached to his belt, ready to clamp onto Rams's suit. Not incidentally, it provided another layer of security for himself.

Screwing up all of the resolve he could muster, he turned his back on *Primrose* and forced himself to take one small step backward, out and down, paying a few centimeters of line out behind him. He froze. He could move no farther no matter how hard he forced his legs to move. His fear had taken control. He couldn't put himself in danger.

Thorn suddenly started to roll to starboard and Pascal watched the level deck in front of him start to tilt away. He rapidly stepped backward, trying to stay on the top of the rolling ship, letting out line as fast as he could.

Then, as *Thorn* heeled to a sixty-degree list, Pascal found himself beside Rams. There was a solid deck directly beneath his feet. "Piece of cake," he remarked and knelt to attach the safety line to Rams.

First, though, he had to disconnect the tangled line. The tension between that and the safety line to *Primrose* would break the captain's arm if he didn't. He freed the line and let the wind take it.

He disconnected the safety line from his suit to clip it to Rams's when *Thorn* began to roll the other way. Rams's body started to slide down the hull. Pascal extended the safety clamp but was stopped short by the limits of the other line. The ship continued to roll. The captain was sliding. In seconds he would plunge into the dark and fall.

Pascal fumbled to release his own line, trying to balance on the moving hull. His fingers didn't want to operate the clamp. He felt himself starting to slide on the steepening slope. With a final, desperate twist of his hand, Pascal released the restricting line, lunged forward, and clipped the clamp onto Rams's suit.

Both of them began to slide, faster and faster, down the increasingly steep side of the ship. In a panic Pascal threw both arms and one leg around Rams's body, clinging to him in desperation, as the hull beneath him changed to a vertical wall.

Pascal screamed in pure terror as he felt them fall from the ship and down into the dark. He *knew* that the thin line he had put on Rams wouldn't hold the weight of both of them. He screamed louder as their downward fall stopped and they swung to the top of their arc and began to fall the other way.

"I am going to die. I am going to die," he repeated in an unending string of fear-crazed babble. He could feel Jupiter pulling at him, trying to pry his hands apart so he would fall, fall, fall. It was very dark and the manic strength of his arms were all that stood between him and certain death. He clenched his eyes tight and prayed as he had never prayed before.

There are moments in a man's life when he faces the core of his being; a single defining moment when his true nature is revealed to him and all pretense, all bluff and bluster, are stripped away. This was Pascal's moment. He knew that he would never be able to conquer the fear that rested in his innermost being. He knew that he was, at heart, a coward.

Something clanged on the back of Pascal's suit as they slammed against something, hard! He felt them start to swing out, and then "CLANG!"—he hit again. He opened his eyes and saw a vast gray wall receding from him. In seconds, they reached the end of their arc and the wall advanced to smash against him once more. He threw his legs out to brace and absorbed the worst of the impact. Rams nearly twisted from his grasp as they hit.

It took him a second to realize that the "wall" was actually the side of *Primrose*. It took him another second to realize that it was moving steadily downward beneath his feet.

He risked a glance up and saw the taut line disappear around the curve of the ship. They were definitely being pulled up the side. He set his feet against the ship's side and walked up the wall, clutching tightly to Rams and frightfully aware of the depths behind him, beneath him.

As soon he came over the edge of the deck he saw Louella standing by the winch. Finally, he was to the point where he could walk more or less upright. From Louella's perspective it must look as if he were holding the unconscious form of Rams in his arms. He hoped that she wouldn't realize that he was hanging on to the man for dear life. He hoped that she had not heard him screaming in the dark.

"Secure the ship," Louella yelled as soon as the winch stopped. With shaking hands Pascal quickly clipped himself to a safety line. That done, he struggled forward to secure the heavy line to the forward docking winch. The slow progress forward and back gave him time to compose himself. Time for the acceptance of his true nature to sink in.

"Don't worry. Everything's under control," were the first words that Rams heard when he finally recovered consciousness. The pain in his leg had stopped, as had all other sensation below his waist. "We've got both ships secured and we're out of the storm."

"My legs . . . ," he began and then stopped. A woman stood over him like a welcoming angel. One of her arms was in a sling.

"Gave you a nice little spinal to hold off the pain from your broken leg," the woman said with a chuckle. "But don't worry, you'll be functioning below the waist in a few days. At least I hope so."

"I don't understand. All I remember is getting hit from behind and . . ."

The woman smiled. It was a nice smile, he thought. "Pascal went after you and dragged your ass back here." She grinned. "I think he'll stop shaking by the time we make station."

"But how, where, what . . . ?" Rams mumbled in confusion, feeling himself start to slip back into unconsciousness. "I thought that he was too afraid."

Louella shrugged. "I guess the sea's got a way of getting the most extraordinary things out of you."

"The sea . . . ?"

"Rest now. You've got JBI's most expensive and experienced captain and navigator looking after you. I would think we have a reasonable chance of finding a station with that combination."

". . . Station," Rams thought as he succumbed to the call of the drugs. She'd said both ships were secure. He thought of the riches that awaited him.

The storms really did provide the most amazing things.

THE MIRACLE OF IVAR AVENUE

John Kessel

▼

Born in Buffalo, New York, John Kessel now lives with his family in Raleigh, North Carolina, where he is a professor of American literature and creative writing at North Carolina State University. Kessel made his first sale in 1978. His first solo novel, Good News from Outer Space, *was released in 1989 to wide critical acclaim, but before that he had made his mark on the genre primarily as a writer of highly imaginative, finely crafted short stories, many of which have since been assembled in his collection* Meeting in Infinity. *He won a Nebula Award in 1983 for his superlative novella "Another Orphan," which was also a Hugo finalist that year, and has been released as an individual book. His story "Buffalo" won the Theodore Sturgeon Memorial Award in 1992. His other books include the novel* Freedom Beach, *written in collaboration with James Patrick Kelly. His most recent book is an anthology of stories from the famous Sycamore Hill Writers' Workshop (which he also helps to run), called* Intersections, *coedited by Mark L. Van Name and Richard Butner. His stories have appeared in our First, Second (in collaboration with James Patrick Kelly), Fourth, Sixth, Eighth, and Thirteenth Annual Collections. He has just published a new novel,* Corrupting Dr. Nice, *and a new story collection,* The Pure Product, *is in the works.*

In the eloquent and ironic story that follows, he takes us back to the Glory Days of Old Hollywood, where a stranger has hit town, and some odd things have begun happening, things too strange even for the movies. . . .

Inside the coat pocket of the dead man Corcoran found an eyepiece. "Looks like John Doe was a photographer," the pathologist said, gliding his rubber-gloved thumb over the lens. He handed it to Kinlaw.

While Corcoran continued to peel away the man's clothing, Kinlaw walked over to the morgue's only window, more to get away from the smell of the dissecting table than to examine the lens. He looked through the eyepiece at the parking lot. The device produced a rectangular frame around a man getting into a 1947 Packard. "This isn't from a camera," Kinlaw said. "It's a cinematographer's monocle."

"A what?"

"A movie cameraman uses it to frame a scene."

"You think our friend had something to do with the movies?"

Kinlaw thought about it. That morning a couple of sixth-graders playing hooky had found the body on the beach in San Pedro. A man about fifty, big, over two hundred pounds, mustache, thick brown hair going gray. Wearing a beat-up tan double-breasted suit, silk shirt, cordovan shoes. Carrying no identification.

Corcoran hummed "Don't Get Around Much Anymore" while he examined the dead man's fingers. "Heavy smoker," he said. He poked in the corpse's nostrils, then opened the man's mouth and shone a light down his throat. "This doesn't look much like a drowning."

Kinlaw turned around. "Why not?"

"A drowning man goes through spasms, clutches at anything within his grasp; if nothing's there, he'll usually have marks on his palms from his fingernails. Plus there's no foam in his trachea or nasal cavities."

"Don't you have to check for water in the lungs?"

"I'll cut him open, but that's not definitive anyway. Lots of drowning men don't get water in their lungs. It's the spasms, foam from mucus, and vomiting that does them in."

"You're saying this guy was murdered?"

"I'm saying he didn't drown. And he wasn't in the water more than twelve hours."

"Can you get some prints?"

Corcoran looked at the man's hand again. "No problem."

Kinlaw slipped the monocle into his pocket. "I'm going upstairs. Call me when you figure out the cause of death."

Corcoran began unbuttoning the dead man's shirt. "You know, he looks like that director, Sturges."

"Who?"

"Preston Sturges. He was pretty hot stuff a few years back. There was a big article in *Life*. Whoa. Got a major surgical scar here."

Kinlaw looked over Corcoran's shoulder. A long scar ran right to center across the dead man's abdomen. "Gunshot wound?"

Corcoran made a note on his clipboard. "Looks like appendectomy. Probably peritonitis too. A long time ago—ten, twenty years."

Kinlaw took another look at the dead man. "What makes you think this is Preston Sturges?"

"I'm a fan. Plus, this dame I know pointed him out to me at the fights one Friday night during the war. Didn't you ever see *The Miracle of Morgan's Creek*?"

"We didn't get many movies in the Pacific." He took another look at the dead man's face.

When Corcoran hauled out his chest saw, Kinlaw spared his stomach and went back up to the detectives' staff room. He checked missing-persons reports, occasionally stopping to roll the cameraman's monocle back and forth on his desk blotter. There was a sailor two weeks missing from the Long Beach Naval Shipyard. A Mrs. Potter from Santa Monica had reported her husband missing the previous Thursday.

The swivel chair creaked as he leaned back, steepled his fingers, and stared at the wall calendar from Free State Buick pinned up next to his desk. The weekend had brought a new month. Familiar April was a blonde in ski pants standing in front of a lodge in the snowy Sierras. He tore off the page: May's blonde wore white shorts and was climbing a ladder in an orange grove. He tried to remember what he had done over the weekend but it all seemed to dissolve into a series of moments connected only by the level of scotch in the glass by his reading chair. He found a pencil in his center drawer and drew a careful X through Sunday, May 1. Happy May Day. After the revolution they would do away with pinup calendars and anonymous dead men. Weekends would mean something and lives would have purpose.

An hour later the report came up from Corcoran: There was no water in the man's lungs. Probable cause of death: carbon-monoxide poisoning. But bruises on his ankles suggested he'd had weights tied to them.

There was no answer at Mrs. Potter's home. Kinlaw dug out the L.A. phone book. *Sturges, Preston* was listed at 1917 Ivar Avenue. Probably where Ivar meandered into the Hollywood Hills. A nice neighborhood, but nothing compared to Beverly Hills. Kinlaw dialed the number. A man answered the phone. "Yes?"

"I'd like to speak to Mr. Preston Sturges," Kinlaw said.

"May I ask who is calling, please?" The man had the trace of an accent; Kinlaw couldn't place it.

"This is Detective Lemoyne Kinlaw from the Los Angeles Police Department."

"Just a minute."

There was a long wait. Kinlaw watched the smoke curling up from Sapienza's cigarette in the tray on the adjoining desk. An inch of ash clung to the end. He was about to give up when another man's voice came onto the line.

"Detective Kinlaw. How may I help you?" The voice was a light baritone with some sort of high-class accent.

"You're Preston Sturges?"

"Last time I checked the mirror, I was."

"Mr. Sturges, the body of a man answering your description was found this morning washed up on the beach at San Pedro."

There was a long pause. "How grotesque."

"Yes, sir. I'm calling to see whether you are all right."

"As you can hear, I'm perfectly all right."

"Right," Kinlaw said. "Do you by any chance have a boat moored down in San Pedro?"

"I have a sailboat harbored in a marina there. But I didn't wash up on any beach last night, did I?"

"Yes, sir. Assuming you're Preston Sturges."

The man paused again. Kinlaw got ready for the explosion. Instead, Sturges said calmly, "I'm not going to be able to convince you who I am over the phone, right?"

"No, you're not."

"I'll tell you what. Come by The Players around eight tonight. You can put your finger through the wounds in my hands and feet. You'll find out I'm very much alive."

"I'll be there."

As soon as he hung up Kinlaw decided he must have been a lunatic to listen to Corcoran and his dames. He was just going to waste a day's pay on pricey drinks in a restaurant he couldn't afford. Then again, though Hollywood people kept funny hours, as he well knew from his marriage to Emily, what was a big-time director doing home in the middle of the day?

He spent the rest of the afternoon following up on missing persons. The sailor from Long Beach, it turned out, had no ring finger on his left hand. He finally got through to Mrs. Potter and discovered that Mr. Potter had turned up Sunday night after a drunken weekend in Palm Springs. He talked to Sapienza about recent mob activity and asked a snitch named Bunny Witcover to keep his ears open.

At four-thirty, Kinlaw called back down to the morgue. "Corcoran, do you remember when you saw that article? The one about the director?"

"I don't know. It was an old issue, at the dentist's office."

"Great." Kinlaw checked out of the office and headed down to the public library.

It was a Monday and the place was not busy. The mural that surrounded the rotunda, jam-packed with padres, Indians, Indian babies, gold miners, sheep, a mule, dancing señoritas, conquistadores, ships, and flags, was busier than the room itself.

A librarian showed him to an index: The January 7, 1946, issue of *Life* listed a feature on Preston Sturges beginning on page 85. Kinlaw rummaged through the heaps of old magazines and finally tracked it down. He flipped to page 85 and sat there, hand resting on the large photograph. The man in the photograph, reclining on a soundstage, wearing a rumpled tan suit, was a dead ringer for the man lying on Corcoran's slab in the morgue.

Kinlaw's apartment stood on West Marathon at North Manhattan Place. The building, a four-story reinforced-concrete box, had been considered a futuristic landmark when it was constructed in 1927, but its earnest European grimness, the regularity and density of the kid's-block structure, made it seem more like a penitentiary than a work of art. Kinlaw pulled the mail out of his box: an electric bill, a flyer from the PBA, and a letter from Emily. He unlocked the door to his apartment and, standing in the entry, tore open the envelope.

It was just a note, conversational, guarded. Her brother was out of the army. She was working for Metro on the makeup for a new Dana Andrews movie. And oh, by the way, did he know what happened to the photo album with all the pictures of Lucy? She didn't have a single one.

Kinlaw dropped the note on the coffee table, took off his jacket, and got the watering can, sprayer, and plant food. First he sprayed the hanging fern in front of the kitchen window, then moved through the plants in the living room: the African violets, ficus, and four varieties of coleus. Emily had never cared for plants, but he could tell she liked it that he did. It reassured her, told her something about his character that was not evident from looking at him. On the balcony he fed the big rhododendron and the planter full of day lilies. Then he put the sprayer back under the kitchen sink, poured himself a drink, and sat in the living room. He watched the late-afternoon sun throw triangular shadows against the wall.

The *Life* article had painted Sturges as an eccentric genius, a man whose life had been a series of lucky accidents. His mother, a Europe-traipsing culture vulture, had been Isadora Duncan's best friend, his stepfather a prominent Chicago businessman. After their divorce Sturges's mother had dragged her son from opera in Bayreuth to dance recital in Vienna to private school in Paris. He came back to the U.S. and spent the twenties trying to make a go of it in her cosmetics business. In 1928 he almost died from a burst appendix; while recovering he wrote his first play; his *Strictly Dishonorable* was a smash Broadway hit in 1929. By the early thirties he had squandered the play's earnings and come to Hollywood, where he became Paramount's top screenwriter, and then the first writer-director of sound pictures. In four years he made eight movies, several of them big hits, before he quit to start a new film company with millionaire Howard Hughes. Besides writing and directing, Sturges owned an engineering company that manufactured diesel engines, and The Players, one of the most famous restaurants in the city.

Kinlaw noted the ruptured appendix, but there was little to set off his instincts except a passing reference to Sturges being "one of the most controversial figures in Hollywood." And the closing line of the article: "As for himself, he contemplates death constantly and finds it a soothing subject."

He fell asleep in his chair, woke up with his heart racing and his neck sweaty. It was seven o'clock. He washed and shaved, then put on a clean shirt.

The Players was an eccentric three-story building on the side of a hill at 8225 Sunset Boulevard, across Marmont Lane from the neo-Gothic Château Marmont hotel. Above the ground-level entrance a big neon sign spelled out *The Players* in easy script. At the bottom level, drive-in girls in green caps and jumpers waited on you in your car. Kinlaw had never been upstairs in the formal rooms. It was growing dark when he turned off Sunset onto Marmont and pulled his Hudson up the hill to the terrace-level lot. An attendant in a white coat with his name stitched in green on the pocket took the car.

Kinlaw loitered outside and finished his cigarette while he admired the lights of the houses spread across the hillside above the restaurant. Looking up at them, Kinlaw knew that he would never live in a house like those. There was a wall between some people and some ways of life. A lefty—like the twenty-four-year-old YCL member he had been in 1938—would have called it *money* that kept him from affording such a home, and *class* that kept the people up there from wanting somebody like him for a neighbor, and *principle* that kept him from wanting to live there. But the thirty-five-year-old he was now knew it was something other than class, or money, or principle. It was something inside you. Maybe it was character. Maybe it was luck. Kinlaw laughed. You ought to be able to tell the difference between luck and character, for pity's sake. He ground out the butt in the lot and went inside.

At the dimly lit bar on the second floor he ordered a gin and tonic and inspected the room. The place was mostly empty. At one of the tables Kinlaw watched a man and a woman whisper at each other as they peered around the room, hoping, no doubt, to catch a glimpse of Van Johnson or Lisabeth Scott. The man wore a white shirt with big collar and a white Panama hat with a pink hatband, the woman a yellow print dress. On the table they held two prudent drinks neatly in the center of prudent cocktail napkins, beside them a map of Beverly Hills folded open with bright red stars to indicate the homes of the famous. A couple of spaces down the bar a man was trying to pick up a blonde doing her best Lana Turner. She was mostly ignoring him but the man didn't seem to mind.

"So what do you think will happen in the next ten years?" he asked her.

"I expect I'll get some better parts. Eventually I want at least second leads."

"And you'll deserve them. But what happens when the Communists invade?"

"Communists schmommunists. That's the bunk."

"You're very prescient. The State Department should hire you, but they won't."

This was some of the more original pickup talk Kinlaw had ever heard. The man was a handsome fellow with an honest face, but his light brown hair and sideburns were too long. Maybe he was an actor working on some historical pic. He had a trace of an accent.

"You know, I think we should discuss the future in more detail. What do you say?"

"I say you should go away. I don't mean to be rude."

"Let me write this down for you, so if you change your mind." The man took a coaster and wrote something on it. He pushed the coaster toward her with his index finger.

Good luck, buddy. Kinlaw scanned the room. Most of the clientele seemed to be tourists. At one end of the room, on the bandstand, a jazz quintet was playing a smoky version of "Stardust." When the bartender came back to ask about a refill, Kinlaw asked him if Sturges was in.

"Not yet. He usually shows up around nine or after."

"Will you point him out to me when he gets here?"

The bartender looked suspicious. "Who are you?"

"Does it matter?"

"You look like you might be from a collection agency."

"I thought this place was a hangout for movie stars."

"You're four years late, pal. Now it's a hangout for bill collectors."

"I'm not after money."

"That's good. Because just between you and me, I don't think Mr. Sturges has much."

"I thought he was one of the richest men in Hollywood."

"Was, past tense."

Kinlaw slid a five-dollar bill across the bar. "Do you know what he was doing yesterday afternoon?"

The bartender took the five note, folded it twice, and stuck it into the breast pocket of his shirt. "Most of the afternoon he was sitting at that table over there looking for answers in the bottom of a glass of Black Label scotch."

"You're a mighty talkative employee."

"Manager's got us reusing the coasters to try to save a buck." He straightened a glass of swizzle sticks. "I paid for the privilege of talking. Mr. Sturges is into me for five hundred in back pay."

Down the end of the bar the blonde left. The man with the sideburns waved at the bartender, who went down to refill his drink.

Kinlaw decided he could afford a second gin and tonic. Midway through the third the bartender nodded toward a table on the mezzanine; there was Sturges, looking a lot healthier than the morning's dead man. He saw the bartender gesture and waved Kinlaw over to his table. Sturges stood as Kinlaw approached. He had thick, unkempt brown hair with a gray streak in the front, a square face, jug ears, and narrow eyes that would have given him a nasty look were it not for his quirky smile. A big, soft body. His resemblance to the dead man was uncanny. Next to him sat a dark-haired, attractive woman in her late thirties, in a blue silk dress.

"Detective Kinlaw. This is my wife, Louise."

"How do you do?"

As Kinlaw was sitting down, the waiter appeared and slid a fresh gin and tonic onto the table in front of him.

"You've eaten?" Sturges asked.

"No."

"Robert, a menu for Mr. Kinlaw."

"Mr. Sturges, I'm not sure we need to spend much time on this. Clearly, unless you have a twin, the identification we had was mistaken."

"That's all right. There are more than a few people in Hollywood who will be disappointed it wasn't me."

Louise Sturges watched her husband warily, as if she weren't too sure what he was going to say next, and wanted pretty hard to figure it out.

"When were you last on your boat?"

"Yesterday. On Saturday I went out to Catalina on the *Island Belle* with my friends, Dr. Bertrand Woolford and his wife. We stayed at anchor in a cove there over Saturday night, then sailed back Sunday. We must have got back around one P.M. I was back at home by three."

"You were with them, Mrs. Sturges?"

Louise looked from her husband to Kinlaw. "No."

"But you remember Mr. Sturges getting back when he says?"

"No. That is, I wasn't at home when he got there. I—"

"Louise and I haven't been living together for some time," Sturges said.

Kinlaw waited. Louise looked down at her hands. Sturges laughed.

"Come on, Louise, there's nothing for you to be ashamed of. I'm the one who was acting like a fool. Detective Kinlaw, we've been separated for more than a year. The divorce was final last November."

"One of those friendly Hollywood divorces."

"I wouldn't say that. But when I called her this morning, Louise was gracious enough to meet with me." He put his hand on his wife's. "I'm hoping she will give me the chance to prove to her I know what a huge mistake I made."

"Did anyone see you after you returned Sunday afternoon?"

"As I recall, I came by the restaurant and was here for some time. You can talk to Dominique, the bartender."

Eventually the dinner came and they ate. Or Kinlaw and Louise ate; Sturges regaled them with stories about how his mother had given Isadora the scarf that killed her, about his marriage to the heiress Eleanor Post Hutton, about an argument he'd seen between Sam Goldwyn and a Hungarian choreographer, in which he played both parts and put on elaborate accents.

Kinlaw couldn't help but like him. He had a sense of absurdity, and if he had a high opinion of his own genius, he seemed to be able to back it up. Louise watched Sturges affectionately, as if he were her son as much as her ex-husband. In the middle of one of his stories he stopped to glance at her for her reaction, then reached impulsively over to squeeze her hand, after which he launched off into another tale, about the time, at a pool, he boasted he was going to "dive into the water like an arrow," and his secretary said, "Yes, a Pierce-Arrow."

After a while Sturges wound down, and he and Louise left. At the cloakroom Sturges offered to help her on with her jacket, and Kinlaw noticed a moment's skepticism cross Louise's face before she let him. Kinlaw went back over to talk with the bartender.

"I've got a couple more questions."

The bartender shrugged. "Getting late."

"This place won't close for hours."

"It's time for me to go home."

Kinlaw showed him his badge. "Do I have to get official, Dominique?"

Dominique got serious. "Robert heard you talking to Sturges. Why didn't you let on earlier you were a cop? What's this about?"

"Nothing you have to worry about, if you answer my questions." Kinlaw asked him about Sturges's actions the day before.

"I can't tell you about the morning, but the rest is pretty much like he says," Dominique told him. "He came by here about six. He was already drinking, and looked terrible. 'Look at this,' he says to me, waving the *L.A. Times* in my face. They'd panned his new movie. 'The studio dumps me and they still hang this millstone around my neck.' He sat there, ordered dinner but didn't eat anything. Tossing back one scotch after another. His girlfriend must have heard something, she came in and tried to talk to him, but he wouldn't talk."

"His girlfriend?"

"Frances Ramsden, the model. They've been together since he broke with Louise. He just sat there like a stone, and eventually she left. Later, when business began to pick up, he got in his car and drove away. I remember thinking, I hope he doesn't get in a wreck. He was three sheets to the wind, and already had some accidents."

"What time was that?"

"About seven-thirty, eight. I thought that was the last I'd see of him, but then he came back later."

"What time?"

"After midnight. Look, can you tell me what this is about?"

Kinlaw watched him. "Somebody's dead."

"Dead?" Dominique looked a little shaken, nothing more.

"I think Sturges might know something. Anything you remember about when he came back? How was he acting?"

"Funny. He comes in and I almost don't recognize him. The place was clearing out then. Instead of the suit he'd had on earlier he was wearing slacks and a sweatshirt, deck shoes. He was completely sober. His eyes were clear, his hands didn't shake—he looked like a new man. They sat there and talked all night."

"They?"

"Mr. Sturges and this other guy he came in with. Friendly looking, light hair. He had a kind of accent—German, maybe? I figure he must be some Hollywood expatriate—they used to all hang out here—this was little Europe. Mr. Sturges would talk French with them. He loved to show off."

"Had you seen this man before?"

"Never. But Mr. Sturges seemed completely familiar with him. Here's the funny thing—he kept looking around as if he'd never seen the place."

"You just said he'd never been here before."

"Not the German. It was Sturges looked as if he hadn't seen The Players. 'Dominique,' he said to me. 'How have you been?' 'I've been fine,' I said.

"They sat up at Mr. Sturges's table there and talked all night. Sturges was full of energy. The bad review might as well have happened to somebody else. The German guy didn't say much, but he was drinking as hard as Mr. Sturges was earlier. It was like they'd changed places. Mr. Sturges stood him to an ocean of scotch. When we closed up they were still here."

"Have you seen this man since then?"

The bartender looked down the bar. "Didn't you see him? He was right here when you came in, trying to pick up some blonde."

"The guy with the funny haircut?"

"That's the one. Mr. Sturges said to let him run a tab. Guess he must've left. Wonder if he made her."

It was a woozy drive home with nothing to show for the evening except the prospect of a Tuesday-morning hangover. He might as well do the thing right: Back in the apartment Kinlaw got out the bottle of scotch, poured a glass, and sat in the dark listening to a couple of blues records. Scotch after gin, a deadly combination. After a while he gave up and went to bed. He was almost asleep when the phone rang.

"Hello?"

"Lee? This is Emily." Her voice was brittle.

"Hello," he said. "It's late." He remembered the nights near the end when he'd find her sitting in the kitchen after midnight with the lights out, the tip of her cigarette trembling in the dark.

"Did you get my letter?"

"What letter?"

"Lee, I've been looking for the photo album with the pictures of Lucy," she said. "I can't find it anywhere. Then I realized you must have taken it when you moved out."

"Don't blame me if you can't find it, Emily."

"You know, I used to be impressed by your decency."

"We both figured out I wasn't as strong as you thought I was, didn't we? Let's not stir all that up again."

"I'm not stirring up anything. I just want the photographs."

"All I've got is a wallet photo. I'm lucky I've got a wallet."

Instead of getting mad, Emily said, quietly, "Don't insult me, Lee." Her voice was tired.

"I'm sorry," he said. "I'll look around. I don't have them, though."

"I guess they're lost, then. I'm sorry I woke you." She'd lost the edge of hysteria; she sounded like the girl he'd first met at a Los Angeles Angels game in 1934. It stirred emotions he'd thought were dead, but before he could think what to say she hung up.

It took him another hour to get to sleep.

In the morning he showered, shaved, grabbed some ham and eggs at the Indian Head Diner and headed in to Homicide. The fingerprint report was on his desk. If the dead guy was a mob button man, his prints showed up nowhere in any of their files. Kinlaw spent some time reviewing other missing-persons reports. He kept thinking of the look on Louise Sturges's face when her husband held her coat for her. For a moment she looked as if she wasn't sure this was the same man she'd divorced. He wondered why Emily hadn't gotten mad when he'd insulted her over the phone. At one time it would have triggered an hour's argument, rife with accusations. Did people change that much?

He called the Ivar Avenue number.

"Mrs. Sturges? This is Lemoyne Kinlaw from the LAPD. I wondered if we might talk."

"Yes?"

"I hoped we might speak in person."

"What's this about?"

"I want to follow up on some things from last night."

She paused. "Preston's gone off to talk to his business manager. Can you come over right now?"

"I'll be there in a half an hour."

Kinlaw drove out to quiet Ivar Avenue and into the curving drive before 1917. The white-shingled house sat on the side of a hill, looking modest by Hollywood standards. Kinlaw rang the bell and the door was answered by a Filipino houseboy.

Once inside Kinlaw saw that the modesty of the front was deceptive. The houseboy led him to a large room at the back that must have been sixty by thirty feet.

The walls were green and white, the floor dark hardwood. At one end of the room stood a massive pool table and brick inglenook fireplace. At the other end, a level up, surrounded by an iron balustrade, ran a bar upholstered in green leather, complete with a copper-topped nightclub table and stools. Shelves crowded with scripts, folders, and hundreds of books lined one long wall, and opposite them an expanse of French doors opened onto a kidney-shaped pool surrounded by hibiscus and fruit blossoms, Canary Island Island pines and ancient firs.

Louise Sturges, seated on a bench covered in pink velveteen, was talking to a towheaded boy of eight or nine. When Kinlaw entered she stood. "Mr. Kinlaw, this is our son, Mon. Mon, why don't you go outside for a while."

The boy raced out through the French doors. Louise wore a plum-colored cotton dress and black flats that did not hide her height. Her thick hair was brushed back over her ears. Poised as a *Vogue* model, she offered Kinlaw a seat. "Have you ever had children, Mr. Kinlaw?"

"A daughter."

"Preston very much wanted children, but Mon is the only one we are likely to have. At first I was sad, but after things started to go sour between us I was glad that we didn't have more."

"How sour were things?"

Louise smoothed her skirt. Her sophistication veiled a calmness that was nothing cheap or Hollywood. "Have you found out who that drowned man is?"

"No."

"What did you want to ask me about?"

"I couldn't help but get the impression last night that you were surprised at your husband's behavior."

"He's frequently surprised me."

"Has he been acting strangely?"

"I don't know. Well, when Preston called me yesterday I was pretty surprised. We haven't had much contact since before our separation. At the end we got so we'd communicate by leaving notes on the banister."

"But that changed?"

She watched him for a moment before answering. "When we met, Preston and I fell very much in love. He just swept me off my feet. He was so intense, funny. I couldn't imagine a more loving husband. Certainly he was an egotist, and totally involved in his work, but he was also such a charming and attentive man."

"What happened?"

"Well, he started directing, and that consumed all his energies. He would work into the evening at the studio, then spend the night at The Players. At first he wanted me totally involved in his career. He kept me by his side at the soundstage as the film was shot. Some of the crew came to resent me, but Preston didn't care. Eventually I complained, and Preston agreed that I didn't need to be there.

"Maybe that was a mistake. The less I was involved, the less he thought of me. After Mon was born he didn't have much time for us. He stopped seeing me as his wife and more as the mother of his son, then as his housekeeper and cook.

"Sometime in there he started having affairs. After a while I couldn't put up with it anymore, so I moved out. When I filed for divorce, he seemed relieved."

Kinlaw worried the brim of his hat. He wondered what Sturges's version of the story would be.

"That's the way things were for the last two years," Louise continued. "Then he called me Sunday night. He has to see me, he needs to talk. I thought, he's in trouble; that's the only time he needs me. A few years back, when the deal with Hughes fell through, he showed up at my apartment and slept on my bed, beside me, like a little boy needing comfort. I thought this would just be more of the same. So I met with him Monday morning. He was contrite. He looked more like the man I'd married than he'd seemed for years. He begged me to give him another chance. He realized his mistakes, he said. He's selling the restaurant. He wants to be a father to our son."

"You looked at him last night as if you doubted his sincerity."

"I don't know what to think. It's what I wanted for years, but—he seems so different. He's stopped drinking. He's stopped smoking."

"This may seem like a bizarre suggestion, Mrs. Sturges, but is there any chance this man might not be your husband?"

Louise laughed. "Oh, no—it's Preston all right. No one else has that ego."

Kinlaw laid his hat on the end table. "Okay. Would you mind if I took a look at your garage?"

"The garage? Why?"

"Humor me."

She led him through the kitchen to the attached garage. Inside, a red Austin convertible sat on a wooden disk set into the concrete floor.

"What's this?"

"That's a turntable," Louise said. "Instead of backing up, you can flip this switch and rotate the car so that it's pointing out. Preston loves gadgets. I think this one's the reason he bought this house."

Kinlaw inspected the garage door. It had a rubber flap along the bottom, and would be quite airtight. There was a dark patch on the interior of the door where the car's exhaust would blow, as if the car had been running for some time with the door closed.

They went back into the house. In the backyard the boy, laughing, chased a border collie around the pool. Lucy had wanted a dog. "Let me ask you one more question, and then I'll go. Does your husband have any distinguishing marks on his body?"

"He has a large scar on his abdomen. He had a ruptured appendix when he was a young man. It almost killed him."

"Does the man who's claiming to be your husband have such a scar?"

Louise hesitated, then said, "I wouldn't know."

"If you should find that he doesn't, could you let me know?"

"I'll consider it."

"One last thing. Do you have any object he's held recently—a cup or glass?"

She pointed to the bar. "He had a club soda last night. I think that was the glass."

Kinlaw got out his handkerchief and wrapped the glass in it, put it into his pocket. "We'll see what we will see. I doubt that anything will come of it, Mrs. Sturges. It's probably that he's just come to his senses. Some husbands do that."

"You don't know Preston. He's never been the sensible type."

Back at the office he sent the glass to the lab for prints. A note on his desk told him that while he had been out he'd received a call from someone named Nathan Lautermilk at Paramount.

He placed a call to Lautermilk. After running the gauntlet of the switchboard and Lautermilk's secretary, Kinlaw got him. "Mr. Lautermilk, this is Lee Kinlaw of the LAPD. What can I do for you?"

"Thank you for returning my call, Detective. A rumor going around here has it you're investigating the death of Preston Sturges. There's been nothing in the papers about him dying."

"Then he must not be dead."

Lautermilk had no answer. Kinlaw let the silence stretch until it became uncomfortable.

"I don't want to pry into police business, Detective, but if Preston was murdered, some folks around here might wonder if they were suspects."

"Including you, Mr. Lautermilk?"

"If I thought you might suspect me, I wouldn't draw attention to myself by calling. I'm an old friend of Preston's. I was assistant to Buddy DeSylva before Preston quit the studio."

"I'll tell you what, Mr. Lautermilk. Suppose I come out there and we have a talk."

Lautermilk tried to put him off, but Kinlaw persisted until he agreed to meet him.

An hour later Kinlaw pulled up to the famous Paramount arch, like the entrance to a Moorish palace. Through the curlicues of the iron gate the sun-washed sound-stages hulked like pastel munitions warehouses. The guard had his name and told him where to park.

Lautermilk met him in the long, low white building that housed the writers. He had an office on the ground floor, with a view across the lot to the soundstages but close enough so he could keep any recalcitrant writers in line.

Lautermilk seemed to like writers, though, a rare trait among studio executives. He was a short, bald, pop-eyed man with a Chicago accent and an explosive laugh. He made Kinlaw sit down and offered him a cigarette from a brass box on his desk. Kinlaw took one, and Lautermilk lit it with a lighter fashioned into the shape of a lion's head. The jaws popped open and a flame sprang out of the lion's tongue. "Louie B. Mayer gave it to me," Lautermilk said. "Only thing I ever got from him he didn't take back later." He laughed.

"I'm curious. Can you arrange a screening of one of Preston Sturges's movies?"

"I suppose so." Lautermilk picked up his phone. "Judy, see if you can track down a print of *The Miracle of Morgan's Creek* and get it set up to show in one of the screening rooms. Call me when it's ready."

Kinlaw examined the lion lighter. "Did Sturges ever give you anything?"

"Gave me several pains in the neck. Gave the studio a couple of hit movies. On the whole I'd say we got the better of the deal."

"So why is he gone?"

"Buddy DeSylva didn't think he was worth the aggravation. Look what's happened since Sturges left. Give him his head, he goes too far."

"But he makes good movies."

"Granted. But he made some flops too. And he offended too many people along the way. Didn't give you much credit for having any sense, corrected your grammar, made fun of people's accents, and read H. L. Mencken to the cast over lunch. And if you crossed him he would make you remember it later."

"How?"

"Lots of ways. On *The Palm Beach Story* he got irritated with Claudette Colbert quitting right at five every day. Preston liked to work till eight or nine if it was going well, but Colbert was in her late thirties and insisted she was done at five. So he accommodated himself to her. But one morning, in front of all the cast and crew, Preston told her, 'You know, we've got to take your close-ups as early as possible. You look great in the morning, but by five o'clock you're beginning to sag.' "

"So you were glad to see him go."

"I hated to see it, actually. I liked him. He can be the most charming man in Hollywood. But I'd be lying if I didn't tell you that the studios are full of people just waiting to see him slip. Once you start to slip, even the waitresses in the commissary will cut you."

"Maybe there's some who'd like to help him along."

"By the looks of the reactions to his last couple of pictures, they won't need to. *Unfaithfully Yours* might have made money if it hadn't been for the Carole Landis mess. Hard to sell a comedy about a guy killing his wife when the star's girlfriend just committed suicide. But *The Beautiful Blonde* is a cast-iron bomb.

Darryl Zanuck must be tearing his hair out. A lot of people are taking some quiet satisfaction tonight, though they'll cry crocodile tears in public.''

''Maybe they won't have to fake it. We found a body washed up on the beach in San Pedro that answers to Sturges's description.''

Lautermilk did not seem surprised. ''No kidding.''

''That's why I came out here. I wondered why you'd be calling the LAPD about some ex-director.''

''I heard some talk in the commissary, one of the art directors who has a boat down in San Pedro heard some story. Preston was my friend. There have been rumors that's he's been depressed. Anyone who's seen him in the last six months knows he's been having a hard time. It would be big news around here if he died.''

''Well, you can calm down. He's alive and well. I just talked to him last night, in person, at his restaurant.''

''I'm glad to hear it.''

''So what do you make of this body we found?''

''Maybe you identified it wrong.''

''Anybody ever suspect that Sturges had a twin?''

''A thing like that would have come out. He's always talking about his family.''

Kinlaw put the cinematographer's monocle on Lautermilk's desk. ''We found this in his pocket.''

Lautermilk picked it up, examined it, put it down again. ''Lots of these toys in Hollywood.''

The intercom buzzed and the secretary reported that they could see the film in screening room D at any time. Lautermilk walked with Kinlaw over to another building, up a flight of stairs to a row of screening rooms. They entered a small room with about twenty theater-style seats, several of which had phones on tables next to them. ''Have a seat,'' Lautermilk said. ''Would you like a drink?''

Kinlaw was thirsty. ''No, thanks.''

Lautermilk used the phone next to his seat to call back to the projection booth. ''Let her rip, Arthur.''

''If you don't mind,'' he said to Kinlaw, ''I'll leave after the first few minutes.''

The room went dark. ''One more thing, then,'' Kinlaw said. ''All these people you say would like to see Sturges fail. Any of them like to see him dead?''

''I can't tell you what's in people's heads.'' Lautermilk settled back and lit a cigarette. The movie began to roll.

The Miracle of Morgan's Creek was a frenetic comedy. By twenty minutes in, Kinlaw realized the real miracle was that they had gotten it past the Hays Office. A girl gets drunk at a going-away party for soldiers, marries one, gets pregnant, doesn't remember the name of the father. All in one night. She sets her sights on marrying Norval Jones, a local yokel, but the yokel turns out to be so sincere she can't bring herself to do it. Norval tries to get the girl out of trouble. Everything they do only makes the situation worse. Rejection, disgrace, indictment, even suicide, are all distinct possibilities. But at the last possible moment a miracle occurs to turn humiliation into triumph.

Kinlaw laughed despite himself, but after the lights came up the movie's sober undertone began to work on him. It looked like a rube comedy but it wasn't. The story mocked the notion of the rosy ending while allowing people who wanted one to have it. It implied a maker who was both a cruel cynic and dizzy optimist. In Sturges's absurd universe anything could happen at any time, and what people did or said didn't matter at all. Life was a cruel joke with a happy ending.

Blinking in the sunlight, he found his car, rolled down the windows to let out the heat, and drove back to Homicide. When he got back, the results of the fingerprint test were on his desk. From the tumbler they had made a good right thumb, index, and middle finger. The prints matched the right hand of the dead man exactly.

All that afternoon Kinlaw burned gas and shoe leather looking for Sturges. Louise had not seen him since he'd left the Ivar Avenue house in the morning, he was not with Frances Ramsden or the Woolfords, nobody had run into him at Fox, the restaurant manager claimed he'd not been in, and a long drive down to the San Pedro marina was fruitless: Sturges's boat rocked empty in its slip and the man in the office claimed he hadn't seen the director since Sunday.

It was early evening and Kinlaw was driving back to Central Homicide, when he passed the MGM lot where Emily was working. He wondered if she was still fretting over the photo album. In some ways his problems were simpler than hers; all he had to do was catch the identical twin of a man who didn't have a twin. It had to be a better distraction than Emily's job. He remembered how, a week after he'd moved out, he'd found himself late one Friday night, drunk on his ass, coming back to the house to sit on the backyard swing and watch the darkened window to their bedroom, wondering whether she was sleeping any better than he. Fed up with her inability to cope, he'd known he didn't want to go inside and take up the pain again, but he could not bring himself to go away, either. So he sat on the swing he had hung for Lucy and waited for something to release him. The galvanized chain links were still unrusted; they would last a long time.

A man watching a house, waiting for absolution. The memory sparked a hunch, and he turned around and drove to his apartment. He found the red Austin parked down the block. As he climbed the steps to his floor a shadow pulled back into the corner of the stairwell. Kinlaw drew his gun. "Come on out."

Sturges stepped out of the shadows.

"How long have you been waiting there?"

"Quite a while. You have a very boring apartment building. I like the bougainvillea, though."

Kinlaw waved Sturges ahead of him down the hall. "I bet you're an expert on bougainvillea."

"Yes. Some of the studio executives I've had to work with boast IQs that rival that of the bougainvillea. The common bougainvillea, that is."

Kinlaw holstered the gun, unlocked his apartment door, and gestured for Sturges to enter. "Do you have any opinion of the IQ of police detectives?"

"I know little about them."

Sturges stood stiffly in the middle of Kinlaw's living room. He looked at the print on the wall. He walked over to Kinlaw's record player and leafed through the albums.

Kinlaw got the bottle of scotch from the kitchen. Sturges put on Ellington's "Perfume Suite."

"How about a drink?" Kinlaw asked.

"I'd love one. But I can't."

Kinlaw blew the dust out of a tumbler and poured three fingers. "Right. Your wife says you're turning over a new leaf."

"I'm working on the whole forest."

Kinlaw sat down. Sturges kept standing, shifting from foot to foot. "I've been looking for you all afternoon," Kinlaw said.

"I've been driving around."

"Your wife is worried about you. After what she told me about your marriage, I can't figure why."

"Have you ever been married, Detective Kinlaw?"

"Divorced."

"Children?"

"No children."

"I have a son. I've neglected him. But I intend to do better. He's nine. It's not too late, is it? I never saw my own father much past the age of eight. But whenever I needed him he was always there, and I loved him deeply. Don't you think Mon can feel that way about me?"

"I don't know. Seems to me he can't feel that way about a stranger."

Sturges looked at the bottle of scotch. "I could use a drink."

"I saw one of your movies this afternoon. Nathan Lautermilk set it up. *The Miracle of Morgan's Creek.*"

"Yes. Everybody seems to like that one. Why I didn't win the Oscar for original screenplay is beyond me."

"Lautermilk said he was worried about you. Rumors are going around that you're dead. Did you ask him to call me?"

"Why would I do that?"

"To find out whether I thought you had anything to do with this dead man."

"Oh, I'm sure Nathan told you all about how he loves me. But where was he when I was fighting Buddy DeSylva every day? *Miracle* made more money than any other Paramount picture that year, after Buddy questioned my every decision making it." He was pacing the room now, his voice rising.

"I thought it was pretty funny."

"Funny? Tell me you didn't laugh until it hurt. No one's got such a performance out of Betty Hutton before or since. But I guess I can't expect a cop to see that."

"At Paramount they're not so impressed with your work since you left."

Sturges stopped pacing. He cradled a blossom from one of Kinlaw's spathes in his palm. "Neither am I, frankly. I've made a lot of bad decisions. I should have sold The Players two years ago. I hope to God I don't croak before I can get on my feet again."

Kinlaw remembered the line from the *Life* profile. He quoted it back at Sturges: " 'As for himself, he contemplates death constantly and finds it a soothing subject.' "

Sturges looked at him. He laughed. "What an ass I can be! Only a man who doesn't know what he's talking about could say such a stupid thing."

Could an impostor pick up a cue like that? The Ellington record reached the end of the first side. Kinlaw got up and flipped it over, to "Strange Feeling." A baritone sang the eerie lyric. "I forgot to tell you in the restaurant," Kinlaw said. "That dead man had a nice scar on his belly. Do you have a scar?"

"Yes. I do." When Kinlaw didn't say anything Sturges added, "You want me to show it to you?"

"Yes."

Sturges pulled out his shirt, tugged down his belt, and showed Kinlaw his belly. A long scar ran across it from right to center. Kinlaw didn't say anything, and Sturges tucked the shirt in.

"You know we got some fingerprints off that dead man. And a set of yours too."

Sturges poured himself a scotch, drank it off. He coughed. "I guess police detectives have pretty high IQs after all," he said quietly.

"Not so high that I can figure out what's going on. Why don't you tell me?"

"I'm Preston Sturges."

"So, apparently, was that fellow who washed up on the beach at San Pedro."

"I don't see how that can be possible."

"Neither do I. You want to tell me?"

"I can't."

"Who's the German you've been hanging around with?"

"I don't know any Germans."

Kinlaw sighed. "Okay. So why not just tell me what you're doing here."

Sturges started pacing again. "I want to ask you to let it go. There are some things—some things in life just won't bear too much looking into."

"To a cop, that's not news. But it's not a good enough answer."

"It's the only answer I can give you."

"Then we'll just have to take it up with the district attorney."

"You have no way to connect me up with this dead man."

"Not yet. But you've been acting strangely. And you admit yourself you were on your boat at San Pedro this weekend."

"Detective Kinlaw, I'm asking you. Please let this go. I swear to you I had nothing to do with the death of that man."

"You don't sound entirely convinced yourself."

"He killed himself. Believe me, I'm not indifferent to his pain. He was at the end of his rope. He had what he thought were good reasons, but they were just cowardice and despair."

"You know a lot about him."

"I know all there is to know. I also know that I didn't kill him."

"I'm afraid that's not good enough."

Sturges stopped pacing and faced him. The record had reached the end and the needle was ticking repetitively over the center groove. When Kinlaw got out of his chair to change it, Sturges hit him on the head with the bottle of scotch.

Kinlaw came around bleeding from a cut behind his ear. It couldn't have been more than a few minutes. He pressed a wet dish towel against it until the bleeding stopped, found his hat, and headed downstairs. The air hung hot as the vestibule of Hell with the windows closed. Out in the street he climbed into his Hudson and set off up Western Avenue.

The mess with Sturges was a demonstration of what happened when you let yourself think you knew a man's character. Kinlaw had let himself like Sturges, forgetting that mild-mannered wives tested the carving knife out on their husbands and stone-cold killers wept when their cats got worms.

An orange moon in its first quarter hung in the west as Kinlaw followed Sunset toward the Strip. When he reached The Players he parked in the upper lot. Down the end of one row was a red Austin; the hood was still warm. Head still throbbing, he went into the bar. Dominique was pouring brandy into a couple of glasses; he looked up and saw Kinlaw.

"What's your poison?"

"I'm looking for Sturges."

"Haven't seen him."

"Don't give me that. His car's in the lot."

Dominique set the brandies on a small tray and a waitress took them away. "If he came in, I didn't spot him. If I had, I would have had a thing or two to tell him. Rumor has it he's selling this place."

"Where's his office?"

The bartender pointed to a door, and Kinlaw checked it out. The room was empty; a stack of bills sat on the desk blotter. The one on the top was the third notice from a poultry dealer, for $442.16. PLEASE REMIT IMMEDIATELY was stamped in red across the top. Kinlaw poked around for a few minutes, then went back to the bar. "Have you seen anything of that German since we talked yesterday?"

"No."

Kinlaw remembered something. He went down to where the foreigner and the blonde had been sitting. A stack of cardboard coasters sat next to a glass of swizzle sticks. Kinlaw riffled through the coasters: On the edge of one was written, *Suite 62*.

He went out to the lot and crossed Marmont to the Château Marmont. The elegant concrete monstrosity was dramatically floodlit. Up at the top floors, the building was broken into steep roofs with elaborate chimneys and dormers surrounding a pointed central tower. Around it wide terraces with traceried balustrades and striped awnings marked the luxury suites. Kinlaw entered the hotel through a Gothic arcade with ribbed vaulting, brick paving, and a fountain at the end.

"Six," he told the elevator operator, a wizened man who stared straight ahead as if somewhere inside he were counting off the minutes until the end of his life.

Kinlaw listened at the door to suite 62. Two men's voices, muffled to the point that he could not make out any words. The door was locked.

Back in the tower opposite the elevator a tall window looked out over the hotel courtyard. Kinlaw leaned out: The ledge was at least a foot and a half wide. Ten feet to his right were the balustrade and awning of the sixth-floor terrace. He eased himself through the narrow window and carefully down the ledge; though there was a breeze up at this height, he felt his brow slick with sweat. His nose an inch from the masonry, he could hear the traffic on the boulevard below.

He reached the terrace, threw his leg over the rail. The French doors were open and through them he could hear the voices more clearly. One of them was Sturges and the other was the man who'd answered the phone that first afternoon at the Ivar house.

"You've got to help me out of this."

" 'Got to'? Not in my vocabulary, Preston."

"This police detective is measuring me for a noose."

"Only one way out, then. I can fire up my magic suitcase and take us back."

"No."

"Then don't go postal. There's nothing he can do to prove that you aren't you."

"We should never have dumped that body in the water."

"What do I know about disposing of bodies? I'm a talent scout, not an executive producer."

"That's easy for you to say. You won't be here to deal with the consequences."

"If you insist, I'm willing to try an unburned moment-universe. Next time we can bury the body in your basement. But really, I don't want to go through all this rumpus again. My advice is to tough it out."

"And once you leave and I'm in the soup, it will never matter to you."

"Preston, you are lucky I brought you back in the first place. It cost every dollar you made to get the studio to let us command the device. There are no guarantees. Use the creative imagination you're always talking about."

Sturges seemed to sober. "All right. But Kinlaw is looking for you too. Maybe you ought to leave as soon as you can."

The other man laughed. "And cut short my holiday? That doesn't seem fair."

Sturges sat down. "I'm going to miss you. If it weren't for you I'd be the dead man right now."

"I don't mean to upset you, but in some real sense you are."

"Very funny. I should write a script based on all this."

"*The Miracle of Ivar Avenue*? Too fantastic, even for you."

"And I don't even know how the story comes out. Back here I'm still up to my ears in debt, and nobody in Hollywood would trust me to direct a wedding rehearsal."

"You are resourceful. You'll figure it out. You've seen the future."

"Which is why I'm back in the past."

"Meanwhile, I have a date tonight. A young woman, they tell me, who bears a striking resemblance to Veronica Lake. Since you couldn't get me to meet the real thing."

"Believe me," Sturges said, "the real thing is nothing but trouble."

"You know how much I enjoy a little trouble."

"Sure. Trouble is fun when you've got the perfect escape hatch. Which I don't have."

While they continued talking, Kinlaw sidled past the wrought-iron terrace furniture to the next set of French doors, off the suite's bedroom. He slipped inside. The bedclothes were rumpled and the place smelled of whiskey. A bottle of Paul Jones and a couple of glasses stood on the bedside table along with a glass ashtray filled with butts; one of the glasses was smeared with lipstick. Some of the butts were hand-rolled reefer. On the dresser Kinlaw found a handful of change, a couple of twenties, a hotel key, a list of names:

Jeanne d'Arc		Carole Lombard	X
Claire Bloom		Germaine Greer	X
Anne Boleyn	X	Vanessa Redgrave	
Eva Braun	X	Alice Roosevelt	X
Louise Brooks	X	Christina Rossetti	
Charlotte Buff	X	Anne Rutledge	
Marie Duplesis		George Sand	X
Veronica Lake			

Brooks had been a hot number when Kinlaw was a kid, everybody knew Hitler's pal Eva, and Alice Roosevelt was old Teddy's aging socialite daughter. But who was Vanessa Redgrave? And how had someone named George gotten himself into this harem?

At the foot of the bed lay an open suitcase full of clothes; Kinlaw rifled through it but found nothing that looked magic. Beside the dresser was a companion piece, a much smaller case in matching brown leather. He lifted it. It was much heavier than he'd anticipated. When he shook it there was no hint of anything moving inside. It felt more like a portable radio than a piece of luggage.

He carried it out to the terrace and, while Sturges and the stranger talked, knelt and snapped open the latches. The bottom half held a dull gray metal panel with switches, what looked something like a typewriter keyboard, and a small flat glass screen. In the corner of the screen glowed green figures: 23:27:46 PDT 3 May 1949. The numbers pulsed and advanced as he watched. . . . 47 . . . 48 . . . 49 . . . Some of the typewriter keys had letters, others numbers, and the top row was Greek letters. Folded into the top of the case was a long finger-thick cable, matte gray, made out of some braided material that wasn't metal and wasn't fabric.

"You have never seen anything like it, right?"

It was the stranger. He stood in the door from the living room.

Kinlaw snapped the case shut, picked it up, and backed a step away. He reached into his jacket and pulled out his pistol.

The man swayed a little. "You're the detective," he said.

"I am. Where's Sturges?"

"He left. You don't need the gun."

"I'll figure that out myself. Who are you?"

"Detlev Gruber." He held out his hand. "Pleased to meet you."

Kinlaw backed another step.

"What's the matter? Don't tell me this is not the appropriate social gesture for the mid-twentieth. I know better."

On impulse, Kinlaw held the case out over the edge of the terrace, six stories above the courtyard.

"So!" Gruber said. "What is it you say? The plot thickens?"

"Suppose you tell me what's going on here? And you better make it quick; this thing is heavier than it looks."

"All right. Just put down the case. Then I'll tell you everything you want to know."

Kinlaw rested his back against the balustrade, letting the machine hang from his hand over the edge. He kept his gun trained on Gruber. "What is this thing?"

"You want the truth, or a story you'll believe?"

"Pick one and see if I can tell the difference."

"It's a transmogrifier. A device that can change anyone into anyone else. I can change General MacArthur into President Truman, Shirley Temple into Marilyn Monroe."

"Who's Marilyn Monroe?"

"You will eventually find out."

"So you changed somebody into Preston Sturges?"

Gruber smiled. "Don't be so gullible. That's impossible. That case isn't a transmogrifier, it's a time machine."

"And I bet it will ring when it hits the pavement."

"Not a clock. A machine that lets you travel from the future into the past, and back again."

"This is the truth, or the story?"

"I'm from about a hundred years from now. Twenty forty-three, to be precise."

"And who was the dead man in San Pedro? Buck Rogers?"

"It was Preston Sturges."

"And the man who was just here pretending to be him?"

"He was not pretending. He's Preston Sturges, too."

"You know, I'm losing my grip on this thing."

"I am chagrined. Once again, the truth fails to convince."

"I think the transmogrifier made more sense."

"Nevertheless. I'm a talent scout. I work for the future equivalent of a film studio, a big company that makes entertainment. In the future, Hollywood is still the heart of the industry."

"That's a nice touch."

"We have time machines in which we go back into the past. The studios hire people like me to recruit those from the past we think might appeal to our audience. I come back and persuade historicals to come to the future.

"Preston was one of my more successful finds. Sometimes the actor or director or writer can't make the transition, but Preston seems to have an intuitive grasp of the future. Cynicism combined with repression. In two years he was the hit of the interactive fiber-optic lines. But apparently it didn't agree with him. The future was too easy, he said, he didn't stand out enough, he wanted to go back to a time where he was an exception, not the rule. So he took all the money he made and paid the studio to send him back for another chance at his old life."

"How can you bring him back if he's dead?"

"Very good! You can spot a contradiction. What I've told you so far isn't exactly true. This isn't the same world I took him from. I recruited him from another version of history. I showed up in his garage just as he was about to turn on the ignition and gas himself. In your version, nobody stopped him. So see, I bring back my live Sturges to the home of your dying one. We arrive a half hour after your Sturges is defunct. You should have seen us trying to get the body out of the car and onto the boat. What a comedy of errors. This stray dog comes barking down the pier. Preston was already a madman, carrying around his own still-warm corpse. The dog sniffs his crotch, Preston drops his end of the body. Pure slapstick.

"So we manhandle the ex-Sturges onto the boat and sail out past the breakwall. Dump the body overboard with window counterweights tied to its ankles, come back, and my Sturges takes his place, a few years older and a lot wiser. He's had the benefit of some modern medicine; he's kicked the booze and cigarettes and now he's ready to step back into the place that he escaped earlier and try to straighten things out. He's got a second chance."

"You're right. That's a pretty good story."

"You like it?"

"But if you've done your job, why are you still here?"

"How about this: I'm actually a scholar, and I'm taking the opportunity to study your culture. My dissertation is on the effects of your Second World War on hotel tipping habits. I can give you a lot of tips. How would you like to know who wins the Rose Bowl next year?"

"How'd you like to be trapped in 1949?"

Gruber sat down on one of the wrought-iron chairs. "I probably would come to regret it. But you'd be amazed at the things you have here that you can't hardly get in twenty forty-three. T-bone steak. Cigarettes with real nicotine. Sex with guilt."

"I still don't understand how you can steal somebody out of your own past and not have it affect your present."

"It's not my past, it's yours. This is a separate historical stream from my own. Every moment in time gives rise to a completely separate history. They're like branches splitting off from the same tree trunk. If I come out to lop a twig off your branch, it doesn't affect the branch I come from."

"You're not changing the future?"

"I'm changing your future. In my past, as a result of personal and professional failures, Preston Sturges committed suicide by carbon-monoxide poisoning on the evening of May 1, 1949. But now there are two other versions. In one, Sturges disappeared on the afternoon of May 1, never to be seen again. In yours, Sturges committed suicide that evening, but then I and the Sturges from that other universe showed up, dropped his body in the ocean off San Pedro, and set up this new Sturges in his place—if you go along."

"Why should I?"

"For the game! It's interesting, isn't it? What will he do? How will it work out?"

"Will you come back to check on him?"

"I already have. I saved him from his suicide, showed him what a difference he's made to this town, and now he's going to have a wonderful life. All his friends are going to get together and give him enough money to pay his debts and start over again."

"I saw that movie. Jimmy Stewart, Donna Reed."

Gruber slapped his knee. "And they wonder why I delight in the twentieth century. You're right, Detective. I lied again. I have no idea how it will work out. Once I visit a time stream, I can't come back to the same one again. It's burned. A quantum effect; one hundred thirty-seven point oh four Moment Universes are packed into every second. The probability of hitting the same M-U twice is vanishingly small."

"Look, I don't know how much of this is malarkey, but I know somebody's been murdered."

"No, no, there is no murder. The man I brought back really is Preston Sturges, with all the memories and experiences of the man who killed himself. He's exactly the man Louise Sturges married, who made all those films, who fathered his son and screwed up his life. But he's had the advantage of a couple of years in the twenty-first century, and he's determined not to make the same mistakes again. For the sake of his son and family and all the others who've come to care about him, why not give him that chance?"

"If I drop this box, you're stuck here. You don't seem too worried."

"Well, I wouldn't be in this profession if I didn't like risk. What is life but risk? We've got a nice transaction going here, who knows how it will play out? Who knows whether Preston will straighten out his life or dismantle it in some familiar way?"

"In my experience, if a man is a foul ball, he's a foul ball. Doesn't matter how many chances you give him. His character tells."

"That's the other way to look at it. 'The fault, dear Brutus, is not in our stars, but in ourselves. . . . ' But I'm skeptical. That's why I like Preston. He talks as if he believes that character tells, but down deep he knows it's all out of control. You could turn my time machine into futuristic scrap, or you could give it to me and let me go back. Up to you. Or the random collision of atoms in your brain. You don't seem to me like an arbitrary man, Detective Kinlaw, but even if you are, basically I don't give a fuck."

Gruber sat back as cool as a Christian holding four aces. Kinlaw was tempted to drop the machine just to see how he would react. The whole story was too fantastic.

But what if it wasn't? There was no way around those identical fingerprints. And if it were true—if a man could be saved and given a second chance—then Kinlaw was holding a miracle in his hand, with no better plan than to dash it to pieces on the courtyard below.

His mouth was dry. "Tell you what," he said. "I'll let you have your magic box back, but you have to do something for me first."

"I aim to please, Detective. What is it?"

"I had a daughter. She died of polio three years ago. If this thing really is a time machine, I want you to take me back so I can get her before she dies."

"Can't do it."

"What do you mean you can't? You saved Sturges."

"Not in this universe. His body ended up on the beach, remember? Your daughter gets polio and dies in all the branches."

"Unless we get her before she gets sick."

"Yes. But then the version of you in that other M-U has a kidnapped daughter who disappears and is never heard from again. Do you want to do that to a man who is essentially yourself? How is that any better than having her die?"

"At least *I'd* have her."

"Plus, we can never come back to this M-U. After we leave, it's burned. I'd have to take you to still a third branch, where you'd have to replace yet another version of yourself if you want to take up your life again. Only, since he won't be conveniently dead, you'll have to dispose of him.''

"Dispose of him?"

"Yes."

Kinlaw's shoulder ached. His head was spinning trying to keep up with all these possibilities. He pulled the case in and set it down on the terrace. He holstered his .38 and rubbed his shoulder. "Show me how it works, first. Send a piece of furniture into the future."

Gruber watched him meditatively, then stepped forward and picked up the device. He went back into the living room, pushed aside the sofa, opened the case, and set it in the center of the room. He unpacked the woven cable from the top and ran it in a circle of about ten feet in diameter around an armchair, ends plugged into the base of the machine. He stepped outside the circle, crouched, and began typing a series of characters into the keyboard.

Kinlaw went into the bedroom, got the bottle of scotch and a glass from the bathroom, and poured himself a drink. When he got back Gruber was finishing up with the keyboard. "How much of all this gas you gave me is true?"

Gruber straightened. His face was open as a child's. He smiled. "Some. A lot. Not all." He touched a switch on the case and stepped over the cable into the circle. He sat in the armchair.

The center of the room, in a sphere centered on Gruber and limited by the cable, grew brighter and brighter. Then the space inside suddenly collapsed, as if everything in it was shrinking from all directions toward the center. Gruber went from a man sitting in front of Kinlaw to a doll, to a speck, to nothing. The light grew very intense, then vanished.

When Kinlaw's eyes adjusted, the room was empty.

Wednesday morning Kinlaw was sitting at his desk trying to figure out what to do with the case folder, when his phone rang. It was Preston Sturges.

"I haven't slept all night," Sturges said. "I expected to wake up in jail. Why haven't you arrested me yet?"

"I still could. You assaulted a police officer."

"If that were the worst of it I'd be there in ten minutes. Last night you were talking about murder."

"Since then I had a conversation with a friend of yours at the Marmont."

"You—What did he tell you?" Sturges sounded rattled.

"Enough for me to think this case will end up unsolved."

Sturges was silent for a moment. "Thank you, Detective."

"Why? Because a miracle happened? You just get back to making movies."

"I have an interview with Larry Weingarten at MGM this afternoon. They want me to write a script for Clark Gable. I'm going to write them the best script they ever saw."

"Good. Sell the restaurant."

"You too? If I have to, I will."

After he hung up, Kinlaw rolled the cinematographer's monocle across his desktop. He thought of the body down in the morgue cooler, bound for an anonymous grave. If Gruber was telling the truth, the determined man he'd just spoken with was the same man who had killed himself in the garage on Ivar Avenue. Today he was eager to go forward; Kinlaw wondered how long that would last. He could easily fall back into his old ways, alienate whatever friends he had left. Or a stroke of bad luck like the Carole Landis suicide could sink him.

But it had to be something Sturges knew already. His movies were full of it. That absurd universe, the characters' futile attempts to control it. At the end of *Morgan's Creek* the bemused Norval is hauled out of jail, thrust into a national guard officer's uniform, and rushed to the hospital to meet his wife and children for the first time—a wife he isn't married to, children that aren't even his. He deliriously protests this miracle, a product of the hypocrisy of the town that a day earlier wanted to lock him up and throw away the key.

Then again, Norval had never given up hope, had done his best throughout to make things come out right. His character was stronger than anyone had ever given him credit for.

Kinlaw remembered the first time he'd seen his daughter, when they called him into the room after Emily had given birth. She was so tiny, swaddled tightly in a blanket: her little face, eyes clamped shut, the tiniest of eyelashes, mouth set in a soft line. How tentatively he had held her. How he'd grinned like an idiot at the doctor, at the nurse, at Emily. Emily, exhausted, face pale, had smiled back. None of them had realized they were as much at the mercy of fate as Sturges's manic grotesques.

He looked up at the calendar, got the pencil out, and crossed off Monday and Tuesday. He got the telephone and dialed Emily's number. She answered the phone, voice clouded with sleep. "Hello?"

"Emily," he said. "I have the photo album. I've had it all along. I keep it on a shelf in the closet, take it out and look at the pictures, and cry. I don't know what to do with it. Come help me, please."

THE LAST HOMOSEXUAL

Paul Park

▼

Paul Park is one of the most critically acclaimed writers of his literary generation, having received rave reviews and wide acceptance for novels such as Soldiers of Paradise, Sugar Rain, The Cult of Loving Kindness, *and* Celestis. *His most recent novel, which takes an alternate look at the life of Jesus Christ, is* The Gospel of Corax. *He lives with his family in North Adams, Massachusetts.*

Here, in one of his relatively rare forays into the short story, he takes us to a nightmarish but all-too-possible future society where bogus "science" in the service of corrupt politicians and religious extremists has made people afraid that almost ev-erything is "catching"—and where the most contagious things of all are fear and intolerance and hatred.

At my tenth high school reunion at the Fairmont Hotel, I ran into Steve Daigrepont and my life changed.

That was three years ago. Now I am living by myself in a motel room, in the southeast corner of the Republic of California. But in those days I was Jimmy Brothers, and my wife and I owned a house uptown off Audubon Park, in New Orleans. Our telephone number was (504) EXodus-5671. I could call her now. It would be early evening.

I think she still lives there because it was her house, bought with her money. She was the most beautiful woman I ever met, and rich too. In those days she was teaching at Tulane Christian University, and I worked for the *Times-Picayune*. That was why Steve wanted to talk to me.

"Listen," he said. "I want you to do a story about us."

We had been on the baseball team together at Jesuit. Now he worked for the Board of Health. He was divorced. "I work too hard," he said as he took me away from the bar and made me sit down in a corner of the Sazerac Room, under the gold mural. "Especially now."

He had gotten the idea I had an influence over what got printed in the paper. In fact I was just a copy editor. But at Jesuit I had been the starting pitcher on a championship team, and I could tell Steve still looked up to me. "I want you to do a feature," he said. "I want you to come visit us at Carville."

He was talking about the old Gillis W. Long Center, on River Road between

New Orleans and Baton Rouge. Formerly the United States national leprosarium, now it was a research foundation.

"You know they're threatening to shut us down," he said.

I had heard something about it. The New Baptist Democrats had taken over the statehouse again, and as usual they were sharpening the axe. Carville was one of the last big virology centers left in the state. Doctors from all over Louisiana came there to study social ailments. But Senator Rasmussen wanted the buildings for a new penitentiary.

"She's always talking about the risks of some terrible outbreak," said Steve. "But it's never happened. It can't happen. In the meantime, there's so much we still don't know. And to destroy the stocks, it's murder."

Steve's ex-wife was pregnant, and she came in and stood next to the entrance to the lobby, talking to some friends. Steve hunched his shoulders over the table and leaned toward me.

"These patients are human beings," he said, sipping his Orange Crush. "That's what they don't understand." And then he went on to tell a story about one of the staff, an accountant named Dan who had worked at Carville for years. Then someone discovered Dan had embezzled two hundred and fifty thousand dollars from the contingency fund, and he was admitted as a patient. "Now I'll never leave you. Now I'm home," he said when he stepped into the ward.

"Sort of like Father Damien," I murmured. While I wasn't sure why my old friend wanted this story in the newspaper, still I admired his passion, his urgency. When we said good-bye, he pressed my hand in both of his, as if he really thought I could help him. It was enough to make me mention the problems at Carville to my boss a few days later, who looked at me doubtfully and suggested I go up there and take a look around on my day off.

"People have different opinions about that place," he said. "Although these days it would be hard for us to question the judgment of a Louisiana state senator."

I didn't tell Melissa where I was going. I drove up alone through the abandoned suburbs and the swamps. Once past the city, I drove with the river on my left, behind the new levee. I went through small towns filled with old people, their trailers and cabins in sad contrast to the towers of the petrochemical and agricultural concerns, which lined the Mississippi between Destrehan and Lutcher.

Carville lay inside an elbow of the river, surrounded by swamps and graveyards and overgrown fields. In the old days, people had grown sugar cane. Now I drove up along a line of beautiful live oaks covered with moss and ferns. At the end of it, a thirty-foot concrete statue of Christ the Redeemer, and then I turned in at the gate beside the mansion, a plantation house before the Civil War, and the administration building since the time of the original leprosarium.

At the guardhouse, they examined my medical records and took some blood. They scanned me with the lie detector and asked some questions. Then they called in to Steve, and I had to sign a lot of forms in case I had to be quarantined. Finally they let me past the barricade and into the first of many wire enclosures. Soldiers leaned against the Corinthian columns of the main house.

I don't want to drag this out with a lot of description. Carville was a big place.

Once you were inside, past the staff offices, it was laid out in sections, and some were quite pleasant. The security was not oppressive. When he met me at the inner gate, Steve was smiling. "Welcome to our Inferno," he said, when no one else could hear. Then he led me down a series of complicated covered walkways, past the hospital, the Catholic and Protestant chapels, the cafeteria. Sometimes he stopped and introduced me to doctors and administrators, who seemed eager to answer questions. Then there were others who hovered at a respectful distance: patients, smiling and polite, dressed in street clothes. They did not shake hands, and when they coughed or sneezed, they turned their faces away.

"Depression," murmured Steve, and later, "alcoholism. Theft."

It had been around the time I was born that Drs. Fargas and Watanabe, working at what had been LSU, discovered the viral nature of our most difficult human problems. I mean the diseases that even Christ can't heal. They had been working with the quarantined HIV-2 population a few years after independence, during the old Christian Coalition days. Nothing much had changed since then in most of the world, where New Baptist doctrine didn't have the same clout as in Louisiana. But those former states that had been willing to isolate the carriers and stop the dreadful cycle of contagion had been transformed. Per capita income rates showed a steady rise, and crime was almost nonexistent. Even so, thirty years later there was still much to learn about susceptibility, about immunization, and the actual process of transmission. As is so often the case, political theory had outstripped science, and though it was hard to argue with the results, still, as Steve Daigrepont explained it, there was a need for places like Carville, where important research was being done.

"If only to keep the patients alive," he muttered. His voice had softened as we progressed into the complex, and now I had to lean close to him to understand. After the second checkpoint, when we put our masks on, I had to ask him to speak up.

We put on isolation suits and latex gloves. We stood outside some glassed-in rooms, watching people drink coffee and read newspapers, as they sat on plain, institutional couches. "Obesity," whispered Steve, which surprised me. No one in the room seemed particularly overweight.

"These are carriers," he hissed, angry for some reason. "They aren't necessarily infected. Besides, their diet is strictly controlled."

Later, we found ourselves outside again, under the hot sun. I stared into a large enclosure like the rhinoceros exhibit at the Audubon zoo. A ditch protected us, and in the distance I could see some tar-paper shacks and rotted-out cars. "Poor people," mumbled Steve through his mask. "Chronic poverty." children were playing in the dirt outside one of the shacks. They were scratching at the ground with sticks.

Again, I don't want to drag this out. I want to move on to the parts that are most painful to me. Now it hurts me to imagine what a terrible place Carville was, to imagine myself walking numbly through. That is a disease as well. In those days, in Louisiana, we were all numb, and we touched things with our deadened hands.

But for me, there was a pain of wakening, as when blood comes to a sleeping limb. Because I was pretending to be a reporter, I asked Steve a lot of questions. Even though as time went on I hoped he wouldn't answer, but he did. "I thought this was a research facility," I said. "Where are the labs?"

"That section is classified. This is the public part. We get a lot of important guests."

We were standing outside a high, wrought-iron fence. I peered at Steve through my mask, trying to see his eyes. Why had he brought me here? Did he have some private reason? I stood in the stifling heat with my gloved hands on the bars of the fence, and then Steve wasn't there. He was called away somewhere and left me alone. I stood looking into a small enclosure, a clipped green lawn and a gazebo. But it was dark there too. Maybe there were tall trees, or a mass of shrubbery. I remember peering through the bars, wondering if the cage was empty. I inspected a small placard near my eye. "Curtis Garr," it said. "Sodom-ite."

And then suddenly he was there on the other side of the fence. He was a tall man in his mid-fifties, well-dressed in a dark suit, leaning on a cane. He was very thin, with a famished, bony face, and a wave of gray hair that curled back over his ears. And I noticed that he also was wearing gloves, gray leather gloves.

He stood opposite me for a long time. His thin lips were smiling. But his eyes, which were gray and very large, showed the intensity of any caged beast.

I stood staring at him, my hands on the bars. He smiled. Carefully and slowly, he reached out his gloved forefinger and touched me on my wrist, in a gap between my isolation suit and latex hand.

Then as Steve came up, he gave a jaunty wave and walked away.

Steve nodded. "Curtis is priceless," he muttered behind my ear. "We think he might be the last one left in the entire state. We had two others, but they died."

Last of all, Steve took me back to his air-conditioned office. "We must get together for lunch," he said. "Next time I'm in the city."

Now I can wonder about the Father Damien story he had told me at the Fairmont. I can wonder if in some way he was talking about himself. But at the time I smiled and nodded, for I was anxious to be gone.

I didn't tell Steve the man had touched me. Nor did I tell the doctors who examined me before I was released. But driving back to New Orleans, I found myself examining the skin over my left wrist. Soon it was hot and red from rubbing at it. Once I even stopped the car to look. But I didn't tell Melissa, either, when I got home.

She wouldn't have sympathized. She was furious enough at what she called my "Jesuit liberalism," when I confessed where I had been. I hated when she talked like that. She had been born a Catholic like me and Steve, but her parents had converted after the church split with Rome. As she might have explained it, since the differences between American Catholic and New Baptist were mostly social, why not have the courage to do whatever it took to get ahead? No, that's not fair— she was a true believer. At twenty-eight, she was already a full professor of Creationist biology.

"What if somebody had seen you? What if you had caught something?" she demanded as I rubbed my wrist. I was sitting next to the fireplace, and she stood next to the window with the afternoon light in her hair. All the time she lectured me, I was thinking how much I wanted to make love to her, to push her down and push my penis into her right there on the Doshmelti carpet—"I don't know how you can take such risks," she said. "Or I do know: It's because you don't really believe in any of it. No matter what the proofs, no matter how many times we duplicate the Watanabe results, you just don't accept them."

I sat there fingering my wrist. To tell the truth, there were parts of the doctrine of ethical contagion that no educated person believed. Melissa herself didn't believe in half of it. But she had to pretend that she believed it, and maybe it was the pretense that made it true.

I didn't want to interrupt her when she was just getting started. "Damn those Jesuits," she said. "Damn them. They ruined you, Jim. You'll never amount to anything, not in Louisiana. Why don't you just go on up to Massachusetts, or someplace where you'd feel at home?"

I loved it when she yelled. Her hair, her eyes. She loved it too. She was like an actress in a play. The fact is, she never would have married one of those Baptist boys, sickly and small and half-poisoned with saltpeter. No matter how much she told her students about the lechery vaccines, no matter how many times she showed her slides of spirochetes attacking the brain, still it was too late for her and me, and she knew it.

The more she yelled at me, the hotter she got. After a while, we went at it like animals.

Two months later, I heard from Steve again. I remember it was in the fall, one of those cool, crisp, blue New Orleans days that seem to come out of nowhere. I had been fired from the paper, and I was standing in my vegetable garden looking out toward the park when I heard the phone ring. I thought it was Melissa, calling back to apologize. She had gone up to Washington, which had been the capital of the Union in the old days, before the states had taken back their rights. She was at an academic conference, and lonely for home. Already that morning she had called me to describe a reception she had been to the night before. When she traveled out of Louisiana, she always had a taste for the unusual—"They have black people here!" she said. "Not just servants; I mean at the conference. And the band! There was a trombone player, you have no idea. Such grace, such raw sexuality."

"I'm not sure I want to hear about that," I said.

She was silent for a moment, and she'd apologized. "I guess I'm a little upset," she confessed.

"Why?"

"I don't like it here. No one takes us seriously. People are very rude, as if *we* were to blame. But we're not the only ones"—she told me about a Dr. Wu from Boise who had given a paper the previous night on Christian genetics. "He showed slides of what he called 'criminal' DNA with all the sins marked on them. As if God had molded them that way. 'With tiny fingers,' as he put it."

I wasn't sure what the New Baptists would say about this. And I didn't want to make a mistake. "That sounds plausible," I murmured, finally.

"You would think that. Plausible and dangerous. It's an argument that leads straight back to Catholicism and original sin. That's fine for you—you want to be guilty when everybody else has been redeemed. But it completely contradicts Far-gas and Watanabe, for one thing. Either the soul is uncontaminated at birth or else it isn't. If it isn't, all our immunization research is worthless. What's the point of pretending we can be healed, either by Christ or by science? That's what I said during the Q&A. Everybody hissed and booed, but then I found myself supported by a Jewish gentleman from New York. He said we could not ignore environmental factors, which is not quite a New Baptist point of view the way he expressed it, but what can you expect? He was an old reactionary, but his heart was in the right place. And such a spokesman for his race! Such intelligence and clarity!''

That was the last time I spoke to Melissa, my wife. I wish we had talked about another subject, so that now in California, when I go over her words in my mind, I might not be distracted by these academic arguments. Distracted by my anger, and the guilt that we all shared. I didn't want to hear about the Jewish man. So many Jews had died during the quarantine—I can say that now. But at the time, I thought Melissa was teasing me and trying to make me jealous. ''That's the one good thing about you getting yourself canned,'' she said as she hung up. ''I always know where to find you.''

Sometimes I wonder what might have happened if I hadn't answered the phone when it rang again a few minutes later. I almost didn't. I sulked in the garden, listening to it, but then at the last moment I went in and picked it up.

But maybe nothing would have been different. Maybe the infection had already spread too far. There was a red spot on my wrist where I'd been rubbing it. I noticed it again as I picked up the phone.

''Jimmy, is that you?'' Steve's voice was harsh and confused, and the connection was bad. In the background was a rhythmic banging noise. Melissa, in Washington, had sounded clearer.

After Steve was finished, I went out and stood in my vegetable garden again, in the bright, clean sun. Over in the park, a family was sitting by the pond having a picnic. A little girl in a blue dress stood up and clapped her hands.

What public sacrifice is too great, I thought, to keep that girl free from contam-ination? Or maybe it's just now, looking back, that I allow myself a thought. Maybe at the time I just stared numbly over the fence, and then went in and drank a Coke. It wasn't until a few hours later that I got in the car and drove north.

Over the past months, I had looked for stories about Carville in the news. And Melissa had told me some of the gossip—there were differences of opinion in Baton Rouge. Some of the senators wanted the hospital kept open, as a showpiece for foreign visitors. But Barbara Rasmussen wanted the patients shipped to a labor camp outside of Shreveport, near the Arkansas border. It was a place both Steve and I had heard of.

Over the phone he'd said, ''It's murder,''—a painful word. Then he'd told me where to meet him. He'd mentioned a time. But I knew I'd be late, because of the slow way I was driving. I wasn't sure I wanted to help him. So I took a leisurely, roundabout route, and crossed the river near the ruins of Hahnville. I drove up old Route 18 past Vacherie. It was deserted country there, rising swamps and burned-out towns, and endless cemeteries full of rows of painted wooden markers. Some had names on them, but mostly just numbers.

I passed some old Negroes working in a field.

Once I drove up onto the levee, and sat staring at the great river next to a crude, concrete statue of Christ the Healer. The metal bones of His fingers protruded from His crumbling hands. Then over the Sunshine Bridge, and it was early evening.

I first met them on River Road near Belle-Helene plantation, as they were coming back from Carville. There was a patchy mist out of the swamp. I drove slowly, and from time to time I had to wipe the condensation from the inside of my windshield.

In the middle of the smudged circle I had made with my handkerchief, I saw the glimmer of their Coleman lanterns. The oak trees hung over the car. I pulled over to the grass and turned off the ignition. I rolled down my window and listened to the car tick and cool. Soon they came walking down the middle of the road, their spare, pinched faces, their white, buttoned-up shirts stained dirty from the cinders. One or two wore masks over their mouth and nose. Some wore civil-defense armbands. Some carried books, others hammers and wrecking bars.

The most terrifying thing about those New Baptist mobs was their sobriety, their politeness. There was no swagger to them, no drunken truculence. They came out of the fog in orderly rows. There was no laughter or shouting. Most of the men walked by me without even looking my way. But then four or five of them came over and stood by the window.

"Excuse me, sir," said one. He took off his gimme cap and wiped the moisture from his bald forehead. "You from around here?"

"I'm from the *Times-Picayune*. I was headed up to Carville."

"Well," said another, shaking his head. "Nothing to see."

"The road's blocked," offered a third. He had rubber gloves on, and his voice was soft and high. "But right here you can get onto the Interstate. You just passed it. Route 73 from Geismar. It will take you straight back to the city."

Some more men had come over to stand next to me along the driver's side. One of them stooped to peer inside. Now he tapped the roof lightly over my head, and I could hear his fingernails on the smooth plastic.

"I think I'd like to take a look," I said. "Even so."

He smiled, and then looked serious. "You a Catholic, sir? I guess New Orleans is a Catholic town."

I sat for a moment, and then rolled up the window. "Thank you," I murmured through the glass. Then I turned on the ignition, and pulled the car around in a tight semicircle. Darkness had come. I put on my headlights, which snatched at the men's legs as I turned around. Illuminated in red whenever I hit the brakes, the New Baptists stood together in the middle of the road, and I watched them in my rearview mirror. One waved.

Then I drove slowly through the crowd again until I found the connecting road. It led away from the river through a few small, neon-lit stores. Pickup trucks were parked there. I recognized the bar Steve had mentioned, and I slowed up when I passed it. I was too late. From Geismar on, the road was deserted.

Close to I-10 it ran through the cypress swamps, and there was no one. Full dark now, and gusts of fog. I drove slowly until I saw a man walking by the side of the road. I speeded up to pass him, and in my high beams I caught a glimpse of his furious, thin face as he looked over his shoulder. It was Curtis Garr.

• • •

I wish I could tell you how I left him there, trudging on the gravel shoulder. I wish I could tell you how I sped away until the sodomite was swallowed up in the darkness and the fog, how I sped home and found my wife there, unexpectedly waiting. The conference might have let out early. She might have decided to surprise me.

These thoughts are painful to me, and it's not because I can never go back. My friend Rob tells me the borders are full of holes, at least for white people. Passports and medical papers are easy to forge. He spends a lot of time at gun shows and survivalist meetings, where I suppose they talk about these things.

But I left because I had to. Because I changed, and Curtis Garr changed me. Now in California, in the desert night, I still can't forgive him, partly because I took such a terrible revenge. If he's dead or in prison now, God damn him. He broke my life apart, and maybe it was fragile and ready to break. Maybe I was contaminated already, and that's why I stopped in the middle of the road, and backed up, and let him into my car. Melissa's car.

He got into the backseat without a word. But he was angry. As soon as we started driving again, he spoke. "Where were you? I waited at that bar for over an hour."

"I thought I was meeting Steve."

"Yes—he told me. He described your car."

I looked at him in the rearview mirror. His clothes were still immaculate, his dark suit. He was a fierce, thin, handsome man.

"Where are you going?"

He said nothing, but just stared on ahead through the windshield. I wondered if he recognized me. If he felt something in me calling out to him, he didn't show it. At Carville, I'd been wearing a mask over my nose and mouth.

But I wanted to ask him about Steve. "You're Curtis Garr," I said.

Then he looked at me in the mirror, his fierce eyes. "Don't be afraid," I said, though he seemed anything but frightened.

"I thought I was meeting Steve," I said after an empty pause. "He didn't say anything about you."

"Maybe he didn't think you would come." And then: "We had to change our plans after Rasmussen's goons showed up. Don't worry about Steve. You'll see him later. No one on the staff was hurt."

Garr's voice was low and harsh. I drove with my left hand. From time to time I scratched the skin over my left wrist.

Soon we came up to the Interstate. The green sign hung flapping. I-10 was a dangerous road, and ordinarily I wouldn't have taken it. Most of the way it was built on crumbling pontoons over the swamp. In some places the guardrail was down, and there were holes in the pavement. But it bypassed all the towns.

Curtis Garr rolled down his window. There was no one on the road. In time we felt a cool draft off the lake.

Once past the airport, we could go faster, because the road was carefully maintained from Kenner to the bridge. The city lights were comforting and bright. We took the Annunciation exit and drove up St. Charles, the great old houses full of prosperous, happy folk.

In more than an hour, Garr and I had not exchanged a word. But I felt a terrible tension in my stomach, and my wrist itched and ached. I kept thinking the man would tell me where to drop him off. I hoped he would. But he said nothing as I drove down Calhoun toward Magazine, toward Melissa's house on Exposition Boulevard.

"Where are you going?" I asked.

He shrugged.

I felt that my guts might burst from my excitement. My fingers trembled on the wheel. "Can I put you up?" I said. "It's past curfew. You'll be safer in the morning."

"Yes. I'm meeting Steve at ten."

And that was all. I pulled into the parking slip and turned off the car. Then I stepped outside into the cool, humid night, and he was there beside me. I listened to him breathe. Almost a hissing sound.

"Nice house."

"It's my wife's. She's a professor at Tulane."

Again that harsh intake of breath. He looked up at the gabled roof. For a moment I was afraid he might refuse to come inside. Something in him seemed to resist. But then he followed me onto the porch.

"You don't lock your doors?"

"Of course not."

"Hunh. When I was in school, New Orleans was the murder capital of the entire country."

"It hasn't all been bad," I said.

Then he was in the living room, standing on the Doshmelti carpet. I excused myself to wash my face and hands in the kitchen bathroom, and when I returned he was looking at the bookcase. "Can I get you something to eat?" I asked. "I'm famished."

"Something to drink." By which he meant alcohol. So I brought out a bottle of white bourbon that we had. I poured him a glass. I really was very hungry. I'd scarcely eaten all day.

"How can you stand it?" he asked suddenly. He had moved over to a case full of biology and medical texts, a collection Melissa had gathered during her trips.

He had one of the books open in his hand. With the other, he gestured with his glass around the room. "All this. You're not a fool. Or are you?"

He put down the book and then walked over to stand in front of me, inches away, his face inches from my own. "I was at Carville," he said. "People died there. Aren't you afraid you're going to catch something?"

But I knew I had caught something already. My heart was shuddering. My face was wet.

I looked up at him, and I thought I could see every pore in his skin. I could see the way his teeth fit into his gums. I could smell his breath and his body when he spoke to me, not just the alcohol but something else. "This state is a sick joke everywhere," he said. "Those people who attacked the Center, they didn't have a tenth-grade education between them. How can you blame them?"

Curtis Garr had black hair in his ears. His lower face was rinsed in gray—he hadn't shaved. I stood looking up at him, admiring the shapes his thin lips formed around his words. "What does your wife teach?"

"Biology."

At that moment, the phone rang. It was on a table in a little alcove by the door. I didn't answer it. Garr and I stood inches apart. After three rings the machine picked up.

"Hi, sweetie," said Melissa. "I just thought I'd try to catch you before you went to bed. Sorry I missed you. I was just thinking how nice it would be to be in bed with you, sucking that big Monongahela. Just a thought. I'll be back to-morrow night."

The machine turned off, and Curtis Garr smiled. "That sounds very cozy." Then he stepped away from me, back to the bookcase again, and I let out my breath.

"A third of the population of Louisiana died during the HIV-2 epidemic," I said. "In just a few years. The feds told them not to worry. The doctors told them it couldn't happen. The New Baptists were the only ones who didn't lie to them. What do you expect?"

"Sin and disease," he said. "I know the history. Not everybody died of HIV. I knew some biology too—the real kind. And I said something about it. That's why I was at Carville in the first place. The other thing's just an excuse."

He was staring at the books as he spoke. But he must have been watching me as well, must have seen something in my face as he sipped his whiskey, because he lowered the glass and grinned at me over the rim. "You're disappointed, aren't you?"

And then after a moment: "Christ, you are! You hypocrite."

But I was standing with my hands held out, my right hand closed around my wrist. "Please," I said. "Please."

He finished his drink and gave a little burp. He put his glass on one of the shelves of the bookcase, and then sat down in the middle of the couch, stretching his thin arms along the top of it on either side. "No, you disgust me," he said, smiling. "Everything about you disgusts me."

Often now I'll start awake in bed, wondering where I am. "Melissa," I'll say, still half-asleep, when I get up to go to the bathroom. So Rob tells me on the nights he's there. I used to sleep as soundly as a child. That night, when Curtis Garr stayed in the house on Exposition Boulevard, was the first I remember lying awake.

After I had gone upstairs, he sat up late, reading and drinking whiskey on the couch. From time to time I would get up and stand at the top of the stairs, watching the light through the banisters, listening to the rustle of the pages. Near dawn I masturbated, and then, after I'd washed up, I went downstairs and stood next to him as he slept. He had left the light on and had curled up on the couch, still in his suit. He hadn't even taken off his shoes.

His mouth was open, pushed out of shape by the cushions. I stood next to him, and then I bent down and stretched out my left hand. I almost touched him. My left wrist was a mass of hectic spots. The rash had spread up the inside of my arm.

In my other hand, I carried a knapsack with some clothes. My passport, and a few small personal items. Almost everything in the house that actually belonged to me, I could fit in that one bag. A picture of Melissa, which is on my bedside still. I had the card to her bank account, and I stood by the couch, wondering if I should leave a note.

Instead, I went into the kitchen, and from the kitchen phone, I dialed a number we all knew in Louisiana, in those days. Together with the numbers for the fire department and the ordinary police, it was typed on a piece of paper that was thumbtacked to the wall. The phone rang a long time. But then finally someone answered it, and there was nothing in his tone of voice to suggest he'd been asleep.

Within a few minutes, I was on my way. I walked up to St. Charles Avenue just as it got light, toward the streetcar line. The air was full of birds, their voices competing with the soft noise of the cars as they passed a block away, bound toward Melissa's house or somewhere else, I couldn't really tell.

RECORDING ANGEL

Ian McDonald

▼

Here's a look at a vivid and terrifying future where something enigmatic and implacable is eating Africa, *and the people in the way are just going to have to come to terms with it—however they can.*

British author Ian McDonald is an ambitious and daring writer with a wide range and an impressive amount of talent. His first story was published in 1982, and since then he has appeared with some frequency in Interzone, Asimov's Science Fiction, New Worlds, Zenith, Other Edens, Amazing, *and elsewhere. He was nominated for the John W. Campbell Award in 1985, and in 1989 he won the Locus "Best First Novel" Award for his novel* Desolation Road. *He won the Philip K. Dick Award in 1992 for his novel* King of Morning, Queen of Day. *His other books include the novels* Out on Blue Six *and* The Broken Land, *and two collections of his short fiction,* Empire Dreams *and* Speaking in Tongues. *His most recent books include the well-received new novels* Evolution's Shore *and* Terminal Café, *and another new novel just published in England,* Sacrifice of Fools. *His short stories have previously appeared in our Eighth, Ninth, and Tenth Annual Collections. Born in Manchester, England, in 1960, McDonald has spent most of his life in Northern Ireland, and now lives and works in Belfast.*

For the last ten miles she drove past refugees from the xenoforming. Some were in their own vehicles. Many rode town buses that had been commandeered to take the people south, or the grubby white trucks of the UNHCR. Most walked, pushing the things they had saved from the advancing Chaga on handcarts or barrows, or laden on the heads and backs of women and children. That has always been the way of it, the woman thought as she drove past the unbroken file of people. The world ends, the women and children must carry it, and the United Nations sends its soldiers to make sure they do not drop it. And the news corporations send their journalists to make sure that the world sees without being unduly disturbed. After all, they are only Africans. A continent is being devoured by some thing from the stars, and I am sent to write the obituary of a hotel.

"I don't do gossip," she had told T. P. Costello, SkyNet's Nairobi station chief when he told her of the international celebrities who were coming to the death-party of the famous Treehouse Hotel. "I didn't come to this country to cream myself over who's wearing which designer dress or who's having an affair with or getting from whom.''

"I know, I know," T. P. Costello had said. "You came to Kenya to be a player in Earth's first contact with the alien. Everyone did. That's why I'm sending you. Who cares what Brad Pitt thinks about the Gas Cloud theory versus the Little Gray Men theory? Angles are what I want. You can get angles, Gaby. What can you get?''

"Angles, T. P.," she had replied, wearily, to her editor's now-familiar litany.

"That's correct. And you'll be up there with it, right on terminum. That's what you want, isn't it?''

That's correct, T. P., she thought. Three months in Kenya and all she had seen of the Chaga had been a distant line of color, like surf on a far reef, under the clouded shadow of Kilimanjaro, advancing imperceptibly but inexorably across the Amboseli plain. The spectator's view. Up there, on the highlands around Kirinyaga where the latest biological package had come down, she would be within touching distance of it. The player's view.

There was a checkpoint up at Nanyuki. The South African soldiers in blue UN helmets at first did not know how to treat her, thinking that with her green eyes and long mahogany hair she might be another movie star or television celebrity. When her papers identified her as Gaby McAslan, on-line multimedia journalist with SkyNet East Africa, they stopped being respectful. A woman they could flirt with, a journalist they could touch for bribes. Gaby endured their flirtations and gave their commanding officer three of the dwindling stock of duty-free Swatches she had bought expressly for the purpose of petty corruption. In return she was given a map of the approved route to the hotel. If she stayed on it she would be safe. The bush patrols had orders to shoot suspected looters or loiterers.

Beyond the checkpoint there were no more refugees. The only vehicles were carrying celebrities to the party at the end of the world, and the news corporations following them. The Kikuyu *shambas* on either side of the road had been long abandoned. Wild Africa was reclaiming them. For a while, then something else would reclaim them from wild Africa. Reverse terraforming, she thought. Instead of making an alien world into Earth, Earth is made into an alien world. In her open-top SkyNet 4x4, Gaby could sense the Chaga behind the screen of heavy high-country timber, and edgy presence of the alien, and electric tingle of anticipation. She had never been this close before.

When the first biological package came down on the summit of Kilimanjaro, she had known, in SkyNet Multimedia News's UK office among the towers of London's Docklands, that this fallen star had her name written on it. The stuff that had come out of it, that looked a little like rain forest and a little like drained coral reef but mostly like nothing anyone had ever seen before, that disassembled terrestrial vegetation into its component molecules and incorporated them into its own matrix at an unstoppable fifty meters every day, confirmed her holy business. The others that came down in the Bismarck Archipelago, the Ruwenzori, in Ecuador and Papua New Guinea and the Maldives, these were only memos from the star gods. It's here, it's waiting for you. Hurry up now.

Now, the Nyandarua package, drawing its trail of plasma over Lake Victoria and the Rift Valley, would bring her at last face-to-face with life from the stars.

. . .

She came across a conga-line of massive tracked transporters, each the size of a large house, wedged into the narrow red-dirt road. Prefabricated accommodation cabins were piled up on top of the transporters. Branches bent and snapped as the behemoths ground past at walking pace. Gaby had heard that UNECTA, the United Nations agency that coordinated research into the Chagas, had dismantled its Ol Tukai base, one of four positioned around Kilimanjaro, all moving backward in synchrony with the advance of the southern Chaga, and sent it north. UNECTA's pockets were not deep enough, it seemed, to buy a new mobile base, especially now that the multinationals had cut their contributions in the absence of any exploitable technologies coming out of the Chaga.

UNECTA staff on the tops of the mobile towers waved as she drove carefully past in the red muddy verges. They can probably see the snows of Kirinyaga from that height, she thought. Between the white mountains. We run from the south, we run from the north but the expanding circles of vegetation are closing on us and we cannot escape. Why do we run? We will all have to face it in the end, when it takes everything we know and changes it beyond recognition. We have always imagined that because it comes down in the tropics it is confined here. Why should climate stop it? Nothing else has. Maybe it will only stop when it closes around the poles. Xenoforming complete.

The hotel was one of those buildings that are like animals in zoos, that by their stillness and coloration can hide from you even when you are right in front of them, and you only know they are there because of the sign on the cage. Two Kenyan soldiers far too young for the size of their weapons met her from the car park full of tour buses and news-company 4x4s. They escorted her along a dirt path between skinny, gray-trunked trees. She could still not see the hotel. She commented on the small wooden shelters that stood every few meters along the path.

"In case of charging animals," the slightly older soldier said. "But this is better." He stroked his weapon as if it were a breast. "Thirty heavy-caliber rounds per second. That will stop more than any wooden shelter."

"Since the Chaga has come there are many more animals around," the younger soldier said. He had taken the laces out of his boots, in the comfortable, country way.

"Running away," Gaby said. "Like any sane thing should."

"No," the young, laceless soldier said. "Running into."

There was a black-painted metal fire escape at the end of the track. As Gaby squinted at the incongruity, the hotel resolved out of the greenery before her. Many of the slim, silver tree trunks were wooden piles, the mass of leaves and creepers concealed the superstructure bulking over her.

The steward met her at the top of the stairs, checked her name against the guest list, and showed her her room, a tiny wooden cabin with a view of leaves. Gaby thought it must be like this on one of the UNECTA mobile bases; minimal, monastic. She did something to her face and went up to the party on the roof. It had been running for three days. It would only end when the hotel did. The party at the edge of the end of the world. In one glance she saw thirty newsworthy faces and peeked into her bag to check the charge level on her disc recorder. She talked to it as she moved between the faces to the bar. The *Out of Africa* look was the thing among the newsworthy this year: riding breeches, leather, with the necessary twist of twenty-first-century *knowing* with the addition of animal-skin prints.

Gaby ordered a piña colada from the Kenyan barman and wondered as he shook it what incentive the management had offered him—all the staff—to stay. Family relocation to other hotels, on the Coast, down in Zanzibar, she reckoned. And where do they go when they run out of hotels to relocate to? Interesting, but not the angle, she decided as the barman poured out the thick, semeny proof of his ability.

"Bugger all here, T. P.," she said to the little black machine in her shirt pocket. Then cocktail-party dynamics parted the people in front of her and there it was, one hundred feet away beyond the gray wooden railing, at the edge of the artificial water hole they dredged with bulldozers in the off-season. One hundred feet. Fifteen seconds walk. Eighteen hours crawl. If you kept very still and concentrated you would be able to see it moving, as you could see the slow sweep of the minute hand of your watch. This was the Chaga not on the geographical scale, devouring whole landscapes, but on the molecular.

Gaby walked through the gap in the bright and the beautiful. She walked past Brad Pitt. She walked past Antonio Banderas, with his new supermodel girlfriend. She walked past Julia Roberts so close she could see the wrinkles and sags that the editing computers digitally smoothed. They were only celebrities. They could not change the world, or suffer to have their world changed, even by alien intervention. Gaby rested her hands on the rail and looked over the Chaga.

"It's like being on the sundeck of a great, archaic, ocean-liner, cruising close to the shore of an alien archipelago," she told the recorder. The contrast between the place she was and the place out there was as great as between land and sea, the border between the two as shifting and inexact. There was no line where earth became un-earth; rather a gradual infection of the highland forest with the colored hexagons of alien ground cover that pushed up fingers and feelers and strange blooms between the tree trunks into the disturbing pseudocoral forms of the low Chaga. With distance the alien reef grew denser and the trees fewer; only the tallest and strongest withstood the attack of the molecular processors, lifted high like the masts of beached ships. A kilometer beyond the tide line a wall of red pillars rose a sheer three hundred meters from the rumbled land reefs before opening into a canopy of interlinked hexagonal leaf plates.

"The Great Wall," Gaby said, describing the scene before her to the disc. The Chaga beyond offered only glimpses of itself as it rose toward cloud-shrouded Kirinyaga: a gleam of the open white palm of a distant hand-tree, the sway of moss-covered balloons, the glitter of light from crystals. What kind of small craft might put forth from such a shore to meet this ship of vanities? she wondered.

"Seven minutes. Thirteen centimeters. That's longer than most."

Until he spoke, Gaby had not noticed the white man standing beside her at the rail. She could not remember whether he had been there before her, or arrived later. He was small, balding, running to late-40s, early-50s belly. His skin was weathered brown, his teeth were not good, and he spoke with a White African accent. He could not be Beautiful, nor even Press. He must be Staff. He was dressed in buffs and khakis and a vest of pockets, without the least necessary touch of twenty-first-century *knowing*. He looked like the last of the Great White Hunters.

He was.

He was called Prenderleith. He had impeccable manners.

"Pardon me for interrupting your contemplation, but if people see me talking to someone they won't come and ask me about things I've killed."

"Isn't that your job?"

"Killing, or telling?"

"Whichever."

"Whichever, it doesn't include being patronized by movie stars, piss-artists and bloody journalists."

"I am a bloody journalist."

"But the first thing you did was come over to the rail and look at that bloody thing out there. For seven minutes."

"And that makes this journalist worth talking to."

"Yes," he said, simply.

And it makes you worth talking to, Gaby thought, because maybe you are my angle on this thing. The Last White Hunter. But you are as wary as the creatures you hunt, and if I tell you this it will scare you away, so I must be as stealthy as you. Gaby surreptitiously turned up the recording level on her little black machine. Enhancement software back at Tom M'boya Street would edit the chatter and fluff.

"So what do you think it is?" Gaby asked. Across the terrace a dissension between Bret Easton Ellis and Damien Hirst was escalating into an argument. Guests flocked in, anticipating a fistfight. Cameras whirred. Prenderleith rested his arms on the rail and looked out across the Chaga.

"I don't know about all this aliens-from-another-world stuff."

"Latest theory is that it wasn't built by little gray men, but originated in gas clouds in Rho Ophiuchi, eight hundred light-years away. They've found signatures of the same complex fullerenes that are present in the Chaga. An entire civilization, growing up in space. They estimate it's at least a hundred thousand years old."

" 'They,' " Prenderleith said.

"UNECTA," Gaby said.

"They're probably right. They know more about this than I do, so if they say it's gas, then it's gas. Gas clouds, little gray men, I don't know about either of them; it's just not part of my world. See, they brought me up with just enough education to be able to manage, to do things well; not to think. Kenya wasn't the kind of country that needed thinking, we thought. You did things, not thought. Riding, farming, hunting, driving, flying. Doing things. The country decided what you needed to think. None of us could see the changes happening under our feet: I was brought up obsolete, no bloody use in the new Kenya, that thought, at all. All I could do was find a job in something as obsolete and useless as myself. This bloody place has nothing to do with the real Kenya. Bloody theme park. Even the animals are fake; they bulldozed a water hole so Americans would have elephants to photograph. Irony is: Now the tourists are gone, there've never been so many bloody animals, all headed in. Counted forty-five elephant in one day; no one gives a stuff anymore. Tell me, how can it be alien if the animals are going in there?

How could gas know how to build something like that? Feels to me like it's something very old, that animals knew once and have never forgotten, that's come out of Africa itself. Everything starts here, in East Africa; the land is very old, and has a long memory. And strong: Maybe Africa has had enough of what people are doing to it—enough thinking—and has decided to claim itself back. That's why the animals aren't afraid. It's giving it back to them.''

"But taking yours away," Gaby said.

"Not my Africa." Prenderleith glanced around at the famous and beautiful people. The fight had evaporated into sulks and looks. Leaf Phoenix was passing round cigarettes, to the thrilled horror of the other guests. Chimes filled the air. Heads turned. A waiter in an untwenty-first-century-*knowing* leopard-print jacket moved across the roof terrace, playing a set of handheld chime bars.

"Dinner," Prenderleith announced.

The seating plan put Gaby at the far end of the long table, between a hack she knew from BBC on-line and a Hollywood film god who talked of working on fifteen musicals simultaneously and little else. Prenderleith had been placed at the far end of the table, in the champion's seat, hemmed in by the famous. Gaby watched him telling his much-told tales of stalkings and killings. He would glance up from time to time and she would catch his eye, and it was like a little conspiracy. I should tell him that he is an angle, Gaby thought. I should admit to the recorder.

The famous claimed Prenderleith for the remainder of the evening, a small court surrounding his seat by the picture window with its floodlit view of the Chaga approaching molecule by molecule. Gaby sat at the bar and watched him telling his stories of that other Africa. There was a light in his eye. Gaby could not decide if it was nostalgia or anticipation of when it would all fall and come apart.

Out in the dark beyond the floodlights, trees fell, brought down by the Chaga, dissolver of illusions. The wooden piers of the hotel creaked and clicked. The celebrities glanced at each other, afraid.

The knock came at 1:27 according to the luminous hands of the bedside clock. Gaby had not long gone to sleep after dictating commentary. Noise from the upper decks; the party would gradually wind down with the hour until the soldiers came with the morning to clear everyone out. One of the guests, high and hopeful? A second polite knock. The politeness told her.

She could see from the way Prenderleith stood in the corridor that he was a little drunk and that, had he not been, he would not have done this. He was carrying his gun, like an adored child.

"Something you should see," he said.

"Why me?" Gaby asked, pulling on clothes and boots.

"Because no one else could understand. Because of those seven minutes you stared at that bloody thing out there and nothing else existed. You know the truth: Nothing does exist, apart from that. Make sure you bring whatever you've been recording on with you."

"You guessed."

"I noticed."

"Hunter's senses. Sorry, I should have told you, I suppose."

"No matter to me."

"You're the only one here has a story worth telling, who will actually lose something when this comes down."

"You think so?"

The light was poor in the wooden corridor. Gaby could not read his expression right. Prenderleith led her to a service staircase down to ground level. Stepping onto the dark surface between the piers, Gaby imagined setting first foot on an alien planet. Close to the truth there, she thought. Prenderleith unslung his rifle and led her out from under the hotel into the shadows along the edge of the floodlights. The night felt huge and close around Gaby, full of breathings and tiny movements. Her breath steamed, it was cold upon the shoulder lands of Kirinyaga. She inhaled the perfume of the Chaga. It was a smell you imagined you knew, because it evoked so many memories, as smell does more powerfully than any other sense. But you could not know it, and when you realized that, all the parts that reminded you of other things collapsed together and the spicy, musky, chemically scent of it was nothing you could remember for no one had ever known anything like this before. It pushed you forward, not back.

Prenderleith led her toward terminum. It was not very far. The Chaga grew taller and more complex as the floodlight waned. Looming, like the waking memory of a nightmare. Gaby could hear the groan and smash of trees falling in the darkness. Prenderleith stopped her half a meter from the edge. Half a meter, fifteen minutes, Gaby thought. She curled her toes inside her boots, feeling infected. Prenderleith squatted on his heels, rested his weight on his gun, like a staff, hunting.

"Wind's right," he said.

Gaby squatted beside him. She switched on the recorder, listened to the silence, and watched the Chaga approach her, out of the shadows. Terminum was a grid of small hexagons of a mosslike substance. The hexagons were of all colors; Gaby knew intuitively that no color was ever next to itself. The corners of the foremost hexagons were sending dark lines creeping out into the undergrowth. Blades of grass, plant stems, fell before the molecule machines and were reduced to their components. Every few centimeters the crawling lines would bifurcate; a few centimeters more they would divide again to build hexagons. Once enclosed, the terrestrial vegetation would wilt and melt and blister into pinpoint stars of colored pseudomoss.

On a sudden urge, Gaby pressed her hand down on the black lines. It did not touch flesh. It had never touched flesh. Yet she flinched as she felt Chaga beneath her bare skin. Oh she of little faith. She felt the molecule-by-molecule advance as a subtle tickle, like the march of small, slow insects across the palm of her hand.

She started as Prenderleith touched her gently on the shoulder.

"It's here," he whispered.

She did not have the hunter's skill, so for long seconds she saw it only as a deeper darkness moving in the shadows. Then it emerged into the twilight between the still-standing trees and the tall fingers of pseudocoral and Gaby gasped.

It was an elephant; an old bull with a broken tusk. Prenderleith rose to his feet. There was not ten meters between them. Elephant and human regarded each other. The elephant took a step forward, out of the shadows into the full light. As it raised its trunk to taste the air, Gaby saw a mass of red, veiny flesh clinging to its neck like a parasitic organ. Beneath the tusks it elongated into flexible limbs. Each terminated in something disturbingly like a human hand. Shocked, Gaby watched the red limbs move and the fingers open and shut. Then the elephant turned and with surprising silence retreated into the bush. The darkness of the Chaga closed behind it.

"Every night, same time," Prenderleith said after a long silence. "For the past six days. Right to the edge, no further. Little closer every day."

"Why?"

"It looks at me, I look at it. We understand each other."

"That thing, around its neck; those arms . . ." Gaby could not keep the disgust from her voice.

"It changes things. Makes things more what they could be. Should be, maybe. Perhaps all elephants have ever needed have been hands, to become what they could be."

"Bootstrap evolution."

"If that's what you believe in."

"What do you believe in?"

"Remember how I answered when you told me the Chaga was taking my Africa away?"

"Not your Africa."

"Understand what I meant now?"

"The Africa it's taking away is the one you never understood, the one you weren't made for. The Africa it's giving is the one you never knew but that was bred into your bones; the great untamed, unexplored, dark Africa, the Africa without nations and governments and borders and economies; the Africa of action, not thought, of being, not becoming, where a single man can lose himself and find himself at the same time; return to a more simple, physical, animal level of existence."

"You say it very prettily. Suppose it's your job."

Gaby understood another thing. Prenderleith had asked her to speak for him because he had not been made able to say such things for himself, and wanted them said right for those who would read Gaby's story about him. He wanted a witness, a faithful recording angel. Understanding this, she knew a third thing about Prenderleith, which could never be spoken and preserved on disc.

"Let's go in again," Prenderleith said eventually. "Bloody freezing out here."

The soldiers came through the hotel at 6:30 in the morning, knocking every bedroom door, though all the guests had either been up and ready long before, or had not slept at all. In view of the fame of the guests, the soldiers were very polite. They assembled everyone in the main lounge. Like a slow sinking, Gaby thought. A Noh Abandon–ship. The reef has reached us at last. She looked out of the window. Under darkness the hexagon moss had crossed the artificial water hole and was climbing the piles of the old hotel. The trees out of which the elephant had emerged in the night were festooned with orange spongy encrustations and webs of tubing.

The main lounge lurched. Glasses fell from the back bar and broke. People screamed a little. The male Hollywood stars tried to look brave, but this was no

screenplay. This was the real end of the world. Prenderleith had gathered with the
rest of the staff in the farthest corner from the door and was trying to sow calm.
It is like the *Titanic,* Gaby thought. Crew last. She went to stand with them. Prenderleith gave her a puzzled frown.

"The punters have to know if the captain goes down with his ship," she said,
patting the little black recorder in the breast pocket of her bush shirt. Prenderleith
opened his mouth to speak and the hotel heaved again, more heavily. Beams
snapped. The picture window shattered and fell outward. Gaby grabbed the edge
of the bar and talked fast and panicky at her recorder. Alarmed, the soldiers hurried
the celebrities out of the lounge and along the narrow wooden corridors toward
the main staircase. The lounge sagged, the floor tilted, tables and chairs slid toward
the empty window.

"Go!" Prenderleith shouted.

They were already going. Jammed into the wooden corridor, she tried not to
think of bottomless coffins as she tried to shout through the other shouting voices
into the microphone. Behind her the lounge collapsed and fell. She fought her way
through the press of bodies into the sunlight, touched the solidity of the staircase.
Crawling. She snatched her fingers away. The creeping, branching lines of Chaga-
stuff were moving down the stairs, through the paintwork.

"It's on the stairs," she whispered breathlessly into the mike. The wooden wall
behind her was a mosaic of hexagons. She clutched the recorder on her breast. A
single spore would be enough to dissolve it and her story. She plunged down the
quivering stairs.

Heedless of dangerous animals, the soldiers hurried the guests toward the vehicles on the main road. The news people paused to shoot their final commentaries
on the fall of the Treehouse.

"It's coming apart," she said as a section of roof tilted up like the stern of a
sinking liner and slid through the bubbling superstructure to the ground. The front
of the hotel was a smash of wood and the swelling, bulbous encrustations of Chaga-
stuff. The snapped piles were fingers of yellow sponge and pseudocoral. Gaby
described it all. Soldiers formed a cordon between the spectators and the Chaga.
Gaby found Prenderleith beside her.

"You'll need to know how the story ends," he said. "Keep this for me." He
handed Gaby his rifle. She shook her head.

"I don't do good on guns."

He laid it at her.

"I know," she said.

"Then you'll help me."

"Do you hate this that much?"

"Yes," he said. There was a detonation of breaking wood and a gasp from
soldiers and civilians alike. The hotel had snapped in the middle and folded up
like two wings. They slowly collapsed into piles of voraciously feeding Chaga life.

He made the move while everyone's attention but Gaby's was distracted by the
end of the old hotel. She had known he would do it. He ran fast for a tired old
white hunter, running to fat.

"He's halfway there," she said to her recorder. "I admire his courage, going gladly into this new dark continent. Or is it the courage to make the choice that eventually the Chaga may make for all of us on this planet formerly known as Earth?''

She broke off. The soldier in front of her had seen Prenderleith. He lifted his Kalashnikov and took aim.

''Prenderleith!'' Gaby yelled. He ran on. He seemed more intent on doing something with his shirt buttons. He was across the edge now, spores flying up from his feet as he crushed the hexagon moss.

''No!'' Gaby shouted, but the soldier was under orders, and both he and the men who gave the orders feared the Chaga above all else. She saw the muscles tighten in his neck, the muzzle of the gun weave a little this way, a little that way. She looked for something to stop him. Prenderleith's rifle. No. That would get her shot too.

The little black disc recorder hit the soldier, hard, on the shoulder. She had thrown it, hard. The shot skyed. Birds went screeching up from their roosts. Otherwise, utter silence from soldiers and staff and celebrities. The soldier whirled on her, weapon raised. Gaby danced back, hands held high. The soldier snapped his teeth at her and brought the butt of the gun down on the disc recorder. While he smashed it to shards of plastic and circuitry, Gaby saw the figure of Prenderleith disappear into the pseudocoral fungus of the alien landscape. He had lost his shirt.

The last vestiges of the tourist hotel—half a room balanced atop a pillar; the iron staircase, flowering sulphur-yellow buds, leading nowhere, a tangle of plumbing, washbasins and toilets held out like begging bowls—tumbled and fell. Gaby watched mutely. She had nothing to say, and nothing to say it to. The Chaga advanced onward, twenty-five centimeters every minute. The people dispersed. There was nothing more to see than the millimetric creep of another world.

The soldiers checked Gaby's press accreditations with five different sources before they would let her take the SkyNet car. They were pissed at her but they could not touch her. They smiled a lot, though, because they had smashed her story and she would be in trouble with her editor.

You're wrong, she thought as she drove away down the safe road in the long convoy of news-company vehicles and tour buses. Story is in the heart. Story is never broken. Story is never lost.

That night, as she dreamed among the doomed towers of Nairobi, the elephant came to her again. It stood on the border between worlds and raised its trunk and its alien hands and spoke to her. It told her that only fools feared the change that would make things what they could be, and should be; that change was the special gift of whatever had made the Chaga. She knew in her dream that the elephant was speaking with the voice of Prenderleith, but she could not see him, except as a silent shadow moving in the greater dark beyond humanity's floodlights: Adam again, hunting in the Africa of his heart.

DEATH DO US PART

Robert Silverberg

▼

Robert Silverberg is one of the most famous SF writers of modern times, with dozens of novels, anthologies, and collections to his credit. Silverberg has won five Nebula Awards and four Hugo Awards. His novels include Dying Inside, Lord Valentine's Castle, The Book of Skulls, Downward to the Earth, Tower of Glass, The World Inside, Born with the Dead, Shadrach in the Furnace, Up the Line, Star of Gypsies, At Winter's End, *and three novel-length expansions of the famous Isaac Asimov stories* "Nightfall," "The Bicentennial Man," *and* "The Ugly Little Boy." *His collections include* Unfamiliar Territory, Capricorn Games, Majipoor Chronicles, The Best of Robert Silverberg, The Conglomeroid Cocktail Party, Beyond the Safe Zone, *and a massive retrospective collection* The Collected Stories of Robert Silverberg, Volume One: Secret Sharers. *His most recent books are the novels* Kingdoms of the Wall, Hot Sky at Morning, Mountains of Majipoor, *and* Starborne. *A new novel,* Sorcerers of Majipoor, *is due out any day now. His stories have appeared previously in every one of our first ten Annual Collections. He lives with his wife, writer Karen Haber, in Oakland, California.*

Here he gives us a quiet but compelling look at a May-December romance of a unique and poignant kind. . . .

It was her first, his seventh. She was 32, he was 363: the good old April/September number. They honeymooned in Venice, Nairobi, the Malaysia Pleasure Dome, and one of the posh L-5 resorts, a shimmering glassy sphere with round-the-clock sunlight and waterfalls that tumbled like cascades of diamonds, and then they came home to his lovely sky-house suspended on tremulous guy-wires a thousand meters above the Pacific to begin the everyday part of their life together.

Her friends couldn't get over it. "He's ten times your age!" they would exclaim. "How could you possibly want anybody that *old*?" Marilisa admitted that marrying Leo was more of a lark for her than anything else. An impulsive thing; a sudden impetuous leap. Marriages weren't forever, after all—just thirty or forty years and then you moved along. But Leo was sweet and kind and actually quite sexy. And he had wanted *her* so much. He genuinely did seem to love her. Why should his age be an issue? He didn't appear to be any older than thirty-five or so. These days you could look as young as you liked. Leo did his Process faithfully and punctually, twice each decade, and it kept him as dashing and vigorous as a boy.

There were little drawbacks, of course. Once upon a time, long long ago, he had been a friend of Marilisa's great-grandmother: They might even have been lovers. She wasn't going to ask. Such things sometimes happened and you simply had to work your way around them. And then also he had an ex-wife on the scene: Number Three, Katrin, 247 years old and not looking a day over 30. She was constantly hovering about. Leo still had warm feelings for her. "A wonderfully dear woman, a good and loyal friend," he would say. "When you get to know her you'll be as fond of her as I am." That one was hard, all right. What was almost as bad, he had children three times Marilisa's age and more. One of them— the next-to-youngest, Fyodor—had an insufferable and presumptuous way of wink- ing and sniggering at her, that hundred-year-old son of a bitch. "I want you to meet our father's newest toy," Fyodor said of her, once, when yet another of Leo's centenarian sons, previously unsuspected by Marilisa, turned up. "We get to play with her when he's tired of her." Someday Marilisa was going to pay him back for that.

Still and all, she had no serious complaints. Leo was an ideal first husband: wise, warm, loving, attentive, generous. She felt nothing but the greatest tenderness for him. And then too, he was so immeasurably experienced in the ways of the world. If being married to him was a little like being married to Abraham Lincoln or Augustus Caesar, well, so be it: They had been great men, and so was Leo. He was endlessly fascinating. He was like seven husbands rolled into one. She had no regrets, none at all, not really.

In the spring of '87 they go to Capri for their first anniversary. Their hotel is a reconstructed Roman villa on the southern slope of Monte Tiberio: alabaster walls frescoed in black and red, a brilliantly colored mosaic of sea creatures in the marble bathtub, a broad travertine terrace that looks out over the sea. They stand together in the darkness, staring at the awesome sparkle of the stars. A crescent moon slashes across the night. His arm is around her; her head rests against his breast. Though she is a tall woman, Marilisa is barely heart-high to him.

"Tomorrow at sunrise," he says, "we'll see the Blue Grotto. And then in the afternoon we'll hike down below here to the Cave of the Mater Magna. I always get a shiver when I'm there. Thinking about the ancient islanders who worshiped their goddess under that cliff, somewhere back in the Pleistocene. Their rites and rituals, the offerings they made to her."

"Is that when you first came here?" she asks, keeping it light and sly. "Some- where back in the Pleistocene?"

"A little later than that, really. The Renaissance, I think it was. Leonardo and I traveled down together from Florence—"

"You and Leonardo, you were just like *that.*"

"Like *that,* yes. But not like *that,* if you take my meaning."

"And Cosimo de' Medici. Another one from the good old days. Cosimo gave such great parties, right?"

"That was Lorenzo," he says. "Lorenzo the Magnificent, Cosimo's grandson. Much more fun than the old man. You would have adored him."

"I almost think you're serious when you talk like that."

"I'm always serious. Even when I'm not." His arm tightens around her. He leans forward and down, and buries a kiss in her thick dark hair. "I love you," he whispers.

"I love you," she says. "You're the best first husband a girl could want."

"You're the finest last wife a man could ever desire."

The words skewer her. *Last* wife? Is he expecting to die in the next ten or twenty or thirty years? He is old—ancient—but nobody has any idea yet where the limits of Process lie. Five hundred years? A thousand? Who can say? No one able to afford the treatments has died a natural death yet, in the four hundred years since Process was invented. Why, then, does he speak so knowingly of her as his last wife? He may live long enough to have seven, ten, fifty wives after her.

Marilisa is silent a long while.

Then she asks him, quietly, uncertainly, "I don't understand why you said that."

"Said what?"

"The thing about my being your last wife."

He hesitates just a moment. "But why would I ever want another, now that I have you?"

"Am I so utterly perfect?"

"I love you."

"You loved Tedesca and Thane and Iavilda too," she says. "And Miaule and Katrin." She is counting on her fingers in the darkness. One wife missing from the list. "And—Syantha. See, I know all their names. You must have loved them but the marriages ended anyway. They *have* to end. No matter how much you love a person, you can't keep a marriage going forever."

"How do you know that?"

"I just do. Everybody knows it."

"I would like this marriage never to end," he tells her. "I'd like it to go on and on and on. To continue to the end of time. Is that all right? Is such a sentiment permissible, do you think?"

"What a romantic you are, Leo!"

"What else can I be but romantic, tonight? This place; the spring night; the moon, the stars, the sea; the fragrance of the flowers in the air. Our anniversary. I love you. Nothing will ever end for us. Nothing."

"Can that really be so?" she asks.

"Of course. Forever and ever, as it is this moment."

She thinks from time to time of the men she will marry after she and Leo have gone their separate ways. For she knows that she will. Perhaps she'll stay with Leo for ten years, perhaps for fifty; but ultimately, despite all his assurances to the contrary, one or the other of them will want to move on. No one stays married forever. Fifteen, twenty years, that's the usual. Sixty or seventy, tops.

She'll marry a great athlete next, she decides. And then a philosopher; and then a political leader; and then stay single for a few decades, just to clear her palate, so to speak, an intermezzo in her life, and when she wearies of that she'll find someone entirely different, a simple rugged man who likes to hunt, to work in the fields with his hands, and then a yachtsman with whom she'll sail the world, and then maybe when she's about three hundred she'll marry a boy, an innocent of eighteen or nineteen who hasn't even had his first Prep yet, and then—then—

A childish game. It always brings her to tears, eventually. The unknown husbands that wait for her in the misty future are vague chilly phantoms, fantasies, frightening, inimical. They are like swords that will inevitably fall between her and Leo, and she hates them for that.

The thought of having the same husband for all the vast expanse of time that is the rest of her life is a little disturbing—it gives her a sense of walls closing in, and closing and closing and closing—but the thought of leaving Leo is even worse. Or of his leaving her. Maybe she isn't truly in love with him, at any rate not as she imagines love at its deepest to be, but she is *happy* with him. She wants to stay with him. She can't really envision parting from him and moving on to someone else.

But of course she knows that she will. Everybody does, in the fullness of time. *Everybody.*

Leo is a sandpainter. Sandpainting is his fifteenth or twentieth career. He has been an architect, an archaeologist, a space-habitats developer, a professional gambler, an astronomer, and a number of other disparate and dazzling things. He reinvents himself every decade or two. That's as necessary to him as Process itself. Making money is never an issue, since he lives on the compounding interest of investments set aside centuries ago. But the fresh challenge—ah, yes, always the fresh challenge!

Marilisa hasn't entered on any career path yet. It's much too soon. She is, after all, still in her first life, too young for Process, merely in the Prep stage yet. Just a child, really. She has dabbled in ceramics, written some poetry, composed a little music. Lately she has begun to think about studying economics or perhaps Spanish literature. No doubt her actual choice of a path to follow will be very far from any of these. But there's time to decide. Oh, is there ever time!

Just after the turn of the year she and Leo go to Antibes to attend the unveiling of Leo's newest work, commissioned by Lucien Nicolas, a French industrialist. Leo and Lucien Nicolas were schoolmates, eons ago. At the airport they embrace warmly, almost endlessly, like brothers long separated. They even look a little alike, two full-faced square-jawed dark-haired men with wide-flanged noses and strong, prominent lips.

"My wife Marilisa," Leo says finally.

"How marvelous," says Lucien Nicolas. "How superb." He kisses the tips of his fingers to her.

Nicolas lives in a lofty villa overlooking the Mediterranean, surrounded by a lush garden in which the red spikes of aloes and the yellow blooms of acacias stand out dazzlingly against a palisade of towering palms. The weather, this January day, is mild and pleasant, with a light drizzle falling. The industrialist has invited a splendid international roster of guests to attend the unveiling of the painting; diplomats and jurists, poets and playwrights, dancers and opera singers, physicists and astronauts and mentalists and sculptors and seers. Leo introduces Marilisa to them all. In the antechamber to the agate dining hall she listens, bemused, to the swirl of conversations in half a dozen languages. The talk ranges across continents, decades, generations. It seems to her that she hears from a distance the names of several of Leo's former wives invoked—Syantha, Tedesca, Katrin?—but possibly she is mistaken.

Dinner is an overindulgent feast of delicacies. Squat animated servitors bring the food on glistening covered trays of some exotic metal that shimmers diffractively. After every third course a cool ray of blue light descends from a ceiling aperture and a secondary red radiance rises from the floor: They meet in the vicinity of the great slab of black diamond that is the table, and a faint whiff of burning carbon trickles into the air, and then the diners are hungry all over again, ready for the next delight.

The meal is a symphony of flavors and textures. The balance is perfect between sweet and tart, warm and cool, spicy and bland. A pink meat is followed by a white one, and then by fruit, then cheese, and meat again, a different kind, and finer cheeses. A dozen wines or more are served. An occasional course is still alive, moving slowly about its plate; Marilisa takes her cue from Leo, conquers any squeamishness, traps and consumes her little wriggling victims with pleasure. Now and then the underlying dish is meant to be eaten along with its contents, as she discovers by lagging just a moment behind the other guests and imitating their behavior.

After dinner comes the unveiling of the painting, in the atrium below the dining hall. The guests gather along the balcony of the dining hall and the atrium roof is retracted.

Leo's paintings are huge rectangular constructions made of fine sparkling sand of many colors, laid out within a high border of molten copper. The surfaces of each work are two-dimensional, but the cloudy hint of a third dimension is always visible, and even that is only the tip of an underlying multidimensional manifold that vanishes at mysterious angles into the fabric of the piece. Down in those churning sandy depths lie wells of color with their roots embedded in the hidden mechanisms that control the piece. These wells constantly contribute streams of minute glittering particles to the patterns at the surface, in accordance with the changing signals from below. There is unending alteration; none of Leo's pieces is ever the same two hours running.

A ripple of astonishment breaks forth as the painting is revealed, and then a rising burst of applause. The pattern is one of interlaced spirals in gentle pastels, curvilinear traceries in pink and blue and pale green, with thin black circles surrounding them and frail white lines radiating outward in groups of three to the vivid turquoise borders of the sand. Leo's friends swarm around him to congratulate him. They even congratulate Marilisa. ''He is a master—an absolute master!'' She basks in his triumph.

Later in the evening she returns to the balcony to see if she can detect the first changes in the pattern. The changes, usually, are minute and subtle ones, requiring a discriminating eye, but even in her short while with Leo she has learned to discern the tiniest of alterations.

This time, though, no expertise is required. In little more than an hour the lovely surface has been significantly transformed. A thick, jagged black line has abruptly sprung into being, descending like a dark scar from upper right to lower left. Marilisa has never seen such a thing happen before. It is like a wound in the painting: a mutilation. It draws a little involuntary cry of shock from her.

Others gather. "What does it mean?" they ask. "What is he saying?"

From someone in African tribal dress, someone who nevertheless is plainly not African, comes an interpretation: "We see the foretelling of schism, the evocation of a transformation of the era. The dark line moves in brutal strokes through the center of our stability point. There, do you see, the pink lines and the blue? And then it drops down into the unknown dominion beyond the painting's eastern border, the realm of the mythic, the grand apocalyptic."

Leo is summoned. He is calm. But Leo is always calm. He shrugs away the urgent questions: The painting, he says, is its own meaning, not subject to literal analysis. It is what it is, nothing more. A stochastic formula governs the changes in his works. All is random. The jagged black line is simply a jagged black line.

Music comes from another room. New servitors appear, creatures with three metal legs and one telescoping arm, offering brandies and liqueurs. The guests murmur and laugh. "A master," they tell Marilisa once again. "An absolute master!"

She likes to ask him about the faraway past—the quaint and remote twenty-third century, the brusque and dynamic twenty-fourth. He is like some great heroic statue rising up out of the mists of time, embodying in himself firsthand knowledge of eras that are mere legends to her.

"Tell me how people dressed, back then," she begs him. "What sorts of things they said, the games they played, where they liked to go on their holidays. And the buildings, the architecture: How did things look? Make me *feel* what it was like: the sounds, the smells, the whole flavor of the long-ago times."

He laughs. "It gets pretty jumbled, you know. The longer you live, the more muddled-up your mind becomes."

"Oh, I don't believe that at all! I think you remember every bit of it. Tell me about your father and mother."

"My father and my mother—" He pronounces the words musingly, as though they are newly minted concepts for him. "My father—he was tall, even taller than I am—a mathematician, he was, or maybe a composer, something abstruse like that—"

"And his eyes? What kind of eyes did he have?"

"His eyes—I don't know, his eyes were unusual, but I can't tell you how—an odd color, or very penetrating, maybe—there was *something* about his eyes. . . ." His voice trails off.

"And your mother?"

"My mother. Yes." He is staring into the past and it seems as if he sees nothing but haze and smoke there. "My mother. I just don't know what to tell you. She's dead, you realize. A long time, now. Hundreds of years. They both died before Process. It was all such a long time ago, Marilisa."

His discomfort is only too apparent.

"All right," she says. "We don't have to talk about them. But tell me about the clothing, at least. What you wore when you were a young man. Whether people liked darker colors then. Or the food, the favorite dishes. Anything. The shape of ordinary things. How they were different.''

Obligingly he tries to bring the distant past to life for her. Images come through, though, however blurry, however indistinct. The strangeness, the alien textures of the long ago. Whoever said the past is another country was right; and Leo is a native of that country. He speaks of obsolete vehicles, styles, ideas, flavors. She works hard at comprehending his words, she eagerly snatches concrete meanings from his clusters of hazy impressions. Somehow the past seems as important to her as the future, or even more so. The past is where Leo has lived so very much of his life. His gigantic past stretches before her like an endless pathless plain. She needs to learn her way across it; she needs to find her bearings, the points of her compass, or she will be lost.

It is time for Leo to undergo Process once more. He goes every five years and remains at the clinic for eleven days. She would like to accompany him, but guests are not allowed, not even spouses. The procedures are difficult and delicate. The patients are in a vulnerable state while undergoing treatment.

So off he goes without her to be made young again. Elegant homeostatic techniques of automatic bioenergetic correction will extend his exemption from sagging flesh and spreading waistline and blurry eyesight and graying hair and hardening arteries for another term.

Marilisa has no idea what Process is actually like. She imagines him sitting patiently upright day after day in some bizarre womblike tank, his body entirely covered in a thick mass of some sort of warm, quivering purplish gel, only his head protruding, while the age-poisons are extracted from him by an elaborate array of intricate pipettes and tubes, and the glorious fluids of new youthfulness are pumped into him. But of course she is only imagining. For all she knows, the whole thing is done with a single injection, like the Prep that she undergoes every couple of years to keep her in good trim until she is old enough for Process.

While Leo is away, his son Fyodor pays her an uninvited visit. Fyodor is the child of Miaule, the fifth wife. The marriage to Miaule was Leo's briefest one, only eight years. Marilisa has never asked why. She knows nothing substantial about Leo's previous marriages and prefers to keep it that way.

''Your father's not here,'' she says immediately, when she finds Fyodor's flitter docked to the harbor of their sky-house.

''I'm not here to visit him. I'm here to see you.'' He is a compact, blockily built man with a low center of gravity, nothing at all in appearance like his rangy father. His sly sidewise smile is insinuating, possessive, maddening. ''We don't know each other as well as we should, Marilisa. You're my stepmother, after all.''

''What does that have to do with anything? You have half a dozen stepmothers.'' Was that true? Could the wives before Miaule be regarded as his stepmothers, strictly speaking?

''You're the newest one. The most mysterious one.''

''There's nothing mysterious about me at all. I'm terribly uninteresting.''

''Not to my father, apparently.'' A vicious sparkle enters Fyodor's eyes. ''Are you and he going to have children?''

The suggestion startles her. She and Leo have never talked about that; she has never so much as given it a thought.

Angrily she says, "I don't think that that's any of your—"

"He'll want to. He always does."

"Then we will. Twenty years from now, maybe. Or fifty. Whenever it seems appropriate. Right now we're quite content just with each other." He has found an entirely new level on which to unsettle her, and Marilisa is infuriated even more with him for that. She turns away from him. "If you'll excuse me, Fyodor, I have things to—"

"Wait." His hand darts out, encircles her wrist, seizes it a little too tightly, then relaxes to a gentler, almost affectionate grip. "You shouldn't be alone at a time like this. Come stay with me for a few days while he's at the clinic."

She glowers at him. "Don't be absurd."

"I'm simply being hospitable, Mother."

"I'm sure he'd be very amused to hear that."

"He's always found what I do highly amusing. Come. Pack your things and let's go. Don't you think you owe yourself a little amusement too?"

Not bothering to conceal her anger and loathing, Marilisa says, "What exactly are you up to, Fyodor? Are you looking for vengeance? Trying to get even with him for something?"

"Vengeance? Vengeance?" Fyodor seems genuinely puzzled. "Why would I want that? I mean, after all, what is he to me?"

"Your father, for one thing."

"Well, yes. I'll grant you that much. But what of it? All of that happened such a long time ago." He laughs. He sounds almost jolly. "You're such an old-fashioned kind of girl, Marilisa!"

A couple of hours after she succeeds in getting rid of Fyodor, she has another unexpected and unwanted visitor: Katrin. At least Katrin has the grace to call while she is still over Nevada to say that she would like to drop in. Marilisa is afraid to refuse. She knows that Leo wants some sort of relationship to develop between them. Quite likely he has instigated this very visit. If she turns Katrin away, Leo will find out, and he will be hurt. The last thing Marilisa would want to do is to hurt Leo.

It is impossible for her to get used to Katrin's beauty: that sublime agelessness, which looks so unreal precisely because it is real. She genuinely seems to be only thirty, golden-haired and shining in the first dewy bloom of youth. Katrin was Leo's wife for forty years. Estil and Liss, the two children they had together, are almost two hundred years old. The immensity of Katrin's history with Leo looms over her like some great monolithic slab.

"I talked to Leo this morning at the clinic," Katrin announces. "He's doing very well."

"You *talked* to him? But I thought that nobody was allowed—"

"Oh, my dear, I've taken forty turns through that place! I know everybody there only too well. When I call, they put me right through. Leo sends his warmest love."

"Thank you."

"He loves you terribly, you know. Perhaps more than is really good for him. You're the great love of his life, Marilisa."

Marilisa feels a surge of irritation, and allows it to reach the surface. "Oh, Katrin, be serious with me! How could I ever believe something like that?" And what does she mean, *Perhaps more than is really good for him?*

"You should believe it. You must, in fact. I've had many long talks with him about you. He adores you. He'd do anything for you. It's never been like this for him before. I have absolute proof of that. Not with me, not with Tedesca, not with Thane, not with—"

She recites the whole rest of the list. *Syantha, Miaule, Iavilda,* while Marilisa ticks each one off in her mind. They could do it together in a kind of choral speaking, the litany of wives' names, but Marilisa remains grimly silent. She is weary of that list of names. She hates the idea that Katrin talks with Leo about her; she hates the idea that Katrin still talks with Leo at all. But she must accept it, apparently. Katrin bustles about the house, admiring this, exclaiming rapturously over that. To celebrate Leo's imminent return she has brought a gift, a tiny artifact, a greenish little bronze sculpture recovered from the sea off Greece, so encrusted by marine growths that it is hard to make out what it represents. A figurine of some sort, an archer, perhaps, holding a bow that has lost its string. Leo is a collector of small antiquities. Tiny fragments of the past are arrayed in elegant cases in every room of their house. Marilisa offers proper appreciation. "Leo will love it," she tells Katrin. "It's perfect for him."

"Yes. I know."

Yes. You do.

Marilisa offers drinks. They nibble at sweet dainty cakes and chat. Two pretty young well-to-do women idling away a pleasant afternoon, but one is two hundred years older than the other. For Marilisa it is like playing hostess to Cleopatra, or Helen of Troy.

Inevitably the conversation keeps circling back to Leo.

"The kindest man I've ever known," says Katrin. "If he has a fault, I think, it's that he's *too* kind. Time and again, he's let himself endure great pain for the sake of avoiding being unkind to some other person. He's utterly incapable of disappointing other people, of letting anyone down in any way, of hurting anyone, regardless of the distress to himself, the damage, the pain. I'm speaking of emotional pain, of course."

Marilisa doesn't want to hear Katrin talk about Leo's faults, or his virtues, or anything else. But she is a dutiful wife; she sees the visit through to its end, and embraces Katrin with something indistinguishable from warmth, and stands by the port watching Katrin's flitter undock and go zipping off into the northern sky. Then, only then, she permits herself to cry. The conversation, following so soon upon Fyodor's visit, has unnerved her. She sifts through it, seeking clues to the hidden truths that everyone but she seems to know. Leo's alleged vast love for her. Leo's unwillingness to injure others, heedless of the costs to himself. *He loves you terribly, you know. Perhaps more than is really good for him.* And suddenly she has the answer. Leo does love her, yes. Leo always loves his wives. But the marriage was fundamentally a mistake; she is much too young for him, callow, unformed; what he really needs is a woman like Katrin, ancient behind her beauty and infinitely, diabolically wise. The reality, she sees, is that he has grown bored already with his new young wife, he is in fact unhappy in the marriage, but he is far too kindhearted to break the truth to her, and so he inverts it, he talks of a marriage that will endure forever and ever. And confides in Katrin, unburdening himself of his misery to her.

If any of this is true, Marilisa thinks, then I should leave him. I can't ask him to suffer on and on indefinitely with a wife who can't give him what he needs.

She wonders what effect all this crying has had on her face, and activates a mirror in front of her. Her eyes are red and puffy, yes. But what's this? A line, in the corner of her eye? The beginning of age-wrinkles? These doubts and conflicts are suddenly aging her: Can it be? And this? A gray hair? She tugs it out and stares at it; but as she holds it at one angle or another it seems just as dark as all the rest. Illusions. An overactive imagination, nothing more. *Damn* Katrin! Damn her!

Even so, she goes for a quick gerontological exam two days before Leo is due to come home from the clinic. It is still six months until the scheduled date of her next Prep injection, but perhaps a few signs of age are beginning to crop up prematurely. Prep will arrest the onset of aging but it won't halt it altogether, the way Process will do; and it is occasionally the case, so she has heard, for people in the immediate pre-Process age group to sprout a few lines on their faces, a few gray hairs, while they are waiting to receive the full treatment that will render them ageless forever.

The doctor is unwilling to accelerate her Prep schedule, but he does confirm that a few little changes are cropping up, and sends her downstairs for some fast cosmetic repairs. "It won't get any worse, will it?" she asks him, and he laughs and assures her that everything can be fixed, *everything,* all evidence that she is in fact closer now to her fortieth birthday than she is to her thirtieth swiftly and painlessly and confidentially eradicated. But she hates the idea that she is actually aging, ever so slightly, while all about her are people much older than she—her husband, his many former wives, his swarm of children—whose appearance is frozen forever in perfect unassailable youthfulness. If only she could start Process now and be done with it! But she is still too young. Her somatotype report is unanswerable; the treatment will not only be ineffective at this stage in her cellular development, it might actually be injurious. She will have to wait. And wait and wait and wait.

Then Leo comes back, refreshed, invigorated, revitalized. Marilisa's been around people fresh from Process many times before—her parents, her grandparents, her great-grandparents—and knows what to expect; but even so she finds it hard to keep up with him. He's exhaustingly cheerful, almost frighteningly ardent, full of high talk and ambitious plans. He shows her the schematics for six new paintings, a decade's worth of work conceived all at once. He proposes that they give a party for three hundred people. He suggests that they take a grand tour for their next anniversary—it will be their fifth—to see the wonders of the world, the Pyramids, the Taj Mahal, the floor of the Mindanao Trench. Or a tour of the moon—the asteroid belt—

"Stop!" she cries, feeling breathless. "You're going too fast!"

"A weekend in Paris, at least," he says.

"Paris. All right. Paris."

They will leave next week. Just before they go, she has lunch with a friend from her single days, Loisa, a pre-Process woman like herself who is married to Ted, who is also pre-Process by just a few years. Loisa has had affairs with a couple of older men, men in their nineties and early hundreds, so perhaps she understands the other side of things as well.

"I don't understand why he married me," Marilisa says. "I must seem like a child to him. He's forgotten more things than I've ever known, and he still knows plenty. What can he possibly see in me?"

"You give him back his youth," Loisa says. "That's what all of them want. They're like vampires, sucking the vitality out of the young."

"That's nonsense and you know it. *Process* gives him back his youth. He doesn't need a young wife to do that for him. I can provide him with the illusion of being young, maybe, but Process gives him the real thing."

"Process jazzes them up, and then they need confirmation that it's genuine. Which only someone like you can give. They don't want to go to bed with some old hag a thousand years old. She may look gorgeous on the outside but she's corroded within, full of a million memories, loaded with all the hate and poison and vindictiveness that you store up over a life that long, and he can feel it all ticking away inside her and he doesn't want it. Whereas you—all fresh and new—"

"No. No. It isn't like that at all. The older women are the interesting ones. We just seem empty."

"All right. If that's what you want to believe."

"And yet he wants me. He tells me he loves me. He tells one of his old ex-wives that I'm the great love of his life. I don't understand it."

"Well, neither do I," says Loisa, and they leave it at that.

In the bathroom mirror, after lunch, Marilisa finds new lines in her forehead, new wisps of gray at her temples. She has them taken care of before Paris. Paris is no city to look old in.

In Paris they visit the Louvre and take the boat ride along the Seine and eat at little Latin Quarter bistros and buy ancient objets d'art in the galleries of St.-Germain-des-Pres. She has never been to Paris before, though of course he has, so often that he has lost count. It is very beautiful but strikes her as somehow fossilized, a museum exhibit rather than a living city, despite all the life she sees going on around her, the animated discussions in the cafés, the bustling restaurants, the crowds in the Metro. Nothing must have changed here in five hundred years. It is all static—frozen—lifeless. As though the entire place has been through Process.

Leo seems to sense her gathering restlessness, and she sees a darkening in his own mood in response. On the third day, in front of one of the rows of ancient bookstalls along the river, he says, "It's me, isn't it?"

"What is?"

"The reason why you're so glum. It can't be the city, so it has to be me. Us. Do you want to leave, Marilisa?"

"Leave Paris? So soon?"

"Leave me, I mean. Perhaps the whole thing has been just a big mistake. I don't want to hold you against your will. If you've started to feel that I'm too old for you, that what you really need is a much younger man, I wouldn't for a moment stand in your way."

Is this how it happens? Is this how his marriages end, with him sadly, lovingly, putting words in your mouth?

"No," she says. "I love you, Leo. Younger men don't interest me. The thought of leaving you has never crossed my mind."

"I'll survive, you know, if you tell me that you want out."

"I *don't* want out."

"I wish I felt completely sure of that."

She is getting annoyed with him, now. "I wish you did too. You're being silly, Leo. Leaving you is the last thing in the world I want to do. And Paris is the last place in the world where I would want my marriage to break up. I love you. I want to be your wife forever and ever."

"Well, then." He smiles and draws her to him; they embrace; they kiss. She hears a patter of light applause. People are watching them. People have been listening to them and are pleased at the outcome of their negotiations. Paris! Ah, Paris!

When they return home, though, he is called away almost immediately to Barcelona to repair one of his paintings, which has developed some technical problem and is undergoing rapid disagreeable metamorphosis. The work will take three or four days; and Marilisa, unwilling to put herself through the fatigue of a second European trip so soon, tells him to go without her. That seems to be some sort of cue for Fyodor to show up, scarcely hours after Leo's departure. How does he know so unerringly when to find her alone?

His pretense is that he has brought an artifact for Leo's collection, an ugly little idol, squat and frog-faced, covered with lumps of brown oxidation. She takes it from him brusquely and sets it on a randomly chosen shelf, and says, mechanically, "Thank you very much. Leo will be pleased. I'll tell him you were here."

"Such charm. Such hospitality."

"I'm being as polite as I can. I didn't invite you."

"Come on, Marilisa. Let's get going."

"Going? Where? What for?"

"We can have plenty of fun together and you damned well know it. Aren't you tired of being such a loyal little wife? Politely sliding through the motions of your preposterous little marriage with your incredibly ancient husband?"

His eyes are shining strangely. His face is flushed.

She says softly, "You're crazy, aren't you?"

"Oh, no, not crazy at all. Not as nice as my father, maybe, but perfectly sane. I see you rusting away here like one of the artifacts in his collection and I want to give you a little excitement in your life before it's too late. A touch of the wild side, do you know what I mean, Marilisa? Places and things he can't show you, that he can't even imagine. He's old. He doesn't know anything about the world we live in today. Jesus, why do I have to spell it out for you? Just drop everything and come away with me. You won't regret it." He leans forward, smiling into her face, utterly sure of himself, plainly confident now that his blunt unceasing campaign of bald invitation will at last be crowned with success.

His audacity astounds her. But she is mystified too.

"Before it's too late, you said. Too late for *what*?"

"*You* know."

"Do I?"

Fyodor seems exasperated by what he takes to be her willful obtuseness. His mouth opens and closes like a shutting trap; a muscle quivers in his cheek; something seems to be cracking within him, some carefully guarded bastion of self-control. He stares at her in a new way—angrily? Contemptuously?—and says, "Before it's too late for anybody to want you. Before you get old and saggy and shriveled. Before you get so withered and ancient-looking that nobody would touch you."

Surely he is out of his mind. Surely. "Nobody has to get that way anymore, Fyodor."

"Not if they undergo Process, no. But you—you, Marilisa—" He smiles sadly, shakes his head, turns his hands palms upward in a gesture of hopeless regret.

She peers at him, bewildered. "What can you possibly be talking about?"

For the first time in her memory Fyodor's cool cocky aplomb vanishes. He blinks and gapes. "So you still haven't found out. He actually did keep you in the dark all this time. You're a null, Marilisa! A short-timer! Process won't work for you! The one-in-ten-thousand shot, that's you, the inherent somatic unreceptivity. Christ, what a bastard he is, to hide it from you like this! You've got eighty, maybe ninety years and that's it. Getting older and older, wrinkled and bent and ugly, and then you'll die, the way everybody in the world used to. So you don't have forever and a day to get your fun, like the rest of us. You have to grab it right now, fast, while you're still young. He made us all swear never to say a word to you, that he was going to be the one to tell you the truth in his own good time, but why should I give a damn about that? We aren't children. You have a right to know what you really are. Fuck him, is what I say. Fuck him!" Fyodor's face is crimson now. His eyes are rigid and eerily bright with a weird fervor. "You think I'm making this up? Why would I make up something like this?"

It is like being in an earthquake. The floor seems to heave. She has never been so close to the presence of pure evil before. With the tightest control she can manage she says, "You'd make it up because you're a lying miserable bastard, Fyodor, full of hatred and anger and pus. And if you think—But I don't need to listen to you anymore. Just get out of here!"

"It's true. Everybody knows it, the whole family! Ask Katrin! She's the one I heard it from first. Christ, ask Leo! *Ask Leo!*"

"Out," she says, flicking her hand at him as though he is vermin. "Now. Get the hell out. Out."

She promises herself that she will say nothing to Leo about the monstrous fantastic tale that has come pouring out of his horrid son, or even about his clumsy idiotic attempt at seduction—it's all too shameful, too disgusting, too repulsive, and she wants to spare him the knowledge of Fyodor's various perfidies—but of course it all comes blurting from her within an hour after Leo is back from Barcelona. Fyodor is intolerable, she says. Fyodor's behavior has been too bizarre and outrageous to conceal. Fyodor has come here unasked and spewed a torrent of cruel fantastic nonsense in a grotesque attempt at bludgeoning her into bed.

Leo says gravely, "What kind of nonsense?" and she tells him in a quick unpunctuated burst and watches his smooth taut face collapse into weary jowls, watches him seem to age a thousand years in the course of half a minute. He stands there looking at her, aghast; and then she understands that it has to be true, every terrible word of what Fyodor has said. She is one of *those,* the miserable statistical few of whom everybody has heard, but only at second or thirdhand. The treatments will not work on her. She will grow old and then she will die. They have tested her and they know the truth, but the whole bunch of them have conspired to keep it from her, the doctors at the clinic, Leo's sons and daughters and wives, her own family, everyone. All of it Leo's doing. Using his influence all over the place, his enormous accrued power, to shelter her in her ignorance.

"You knew from the start?" she asks, finally. "All along?"

"Almost. I knew very early. The clinic called me and told me, not long after we got engaged."

"My God. Why did you marry me, then?"

"Because I loved you."

"Because you loved me."

"Yes. Yes. Yes. Yes."

"I wish I knew what that meant," she says. "If you loved me, how could you hide a thing like this from me? How could you let me build my life around a lie?"

Leo says, after a moment, "I wanted you to have the good years, untainted by what would come later. There was time for you to discover the truth later. But for now—while you were still young—the clothes, the jewelry, the traveling, all the joy of being beautiful and young—why ruin it for you? Why darken it with the knowledge of what would be coming?"

"So you made everybody go along with the lie? The people at the clinic. Even my own family, for God's sake!"

"Yes."

"And all the Prep treatments I've been taking—just a stupid pointless charade, right? Accomplishing nothing. Leading nowhere."

"Yes. Yes."

She begins to tremble. She understands the true depths of his compassion now, and she is appalled. He has married her out of charity. No man her own age would have wanted her, because the developing signs of bodily deterioration in the years just ahead would surely horrify him; but Leo is beyond all that, he is willing to overlook her unfortunate little somatic defect and give her a few decades of happiness before she has to die. And then he will proceed with the rest of his life, the hundreds or thousands of years yet to come, serene in the knowledge of having allowed the tragically doomed Marilisa the happy illusion of having been a member of the ageless elite for a little while. It is stunning. It is horrifying. There is no way that she can bear it.

"Marilisa—"

He reaches for her, but she turns away. Runs. Flees.

. . .

It was three years before he found her. She was living in London then, a little flat in Bayswater Road, and in just those three years her face had changed so much, the little erosions of the transition between youth and middle age, that it was impossible for him entirely to conceal his instant reaction. He, of course, had not changed in the slightest way. He stood in the doorway, practically filling it, trying to plaster some sort of facade over his all-too-visible dismay, trying to show her the familiar Leo smile, trying to make the old Leo-like warmth glow in his eyes. Then after a moment he extended his arms toward her. She stayed where she was.

''You shouldn't have tracked me down,'' she says.

''I love you,'' he tells her. ''Come home with me.''

''It wouldn't be right. It wouldn't be fair to you. My getting old, and you always so young.''

''To hell with that. I want you back, Marilisa. I love you and I always will.''

''You love me?'' she says. ''Even though—?''

''Even though. For better, for worse.''

She knows the rest of the passage—*for richer for poorer, in sickness and in health*—and where it goes from there. But there is nothing more she can say. She wants to smile gently and thank him for all his kindness and close the door, but instead she stands there and stands there and stands there, neither inviting him in nor shutting him out, with a roaring sound in her ears as all the million years of mortal history rise up around her like mountains.

THE SPADE OF REASON

Jim Cowan

▼

They say that genius is in the details. As the quirky and brilliant story that follows demonstrates, maybe God is in the numbers. . . .

New writer Jim Cowan has published several stories in Century *magazine, as well as in the on-line electronic magazine* InterText, *one of which has been chosen for a best-of-the-Net anthology,* eScene. *He lives in Bethlehem, Pennsylvania.*

When I first came here, the nurses spelled my name wrong. They wrote C-A-X-T-O-N on a slip of pink paper and slid it into the spine of a shiny new aluminum chart-holder. That was four years ago. The aluminum is battered and scratched now, and my chart is very thick.

This will be the last of our many nighttime talks. As usual, I'm lounging in my pajamas in this comfortable old chair by these open French windows, where I can see the moonlight on the lawns. The curtains wave gently in the scented breeze and you come in from the warm night, unbuckle your toolbelt, sit there on the corner couch, and choose an orange from my bowl of fruit.

Sometimes we'd talk like this for hours. Sometimes you'd get called away to fix a leaking faucet or replace a fuse. You'd buckle your belt carefully and go into the night, walking slowly to one of the other buildings. No one who's in a hurry can fix stuff right, you said. I remember what you told me: Look for the simplest causes, nothing esoteric, and fix it right the first time, or the nurses will just call you back.

I've learned a lot from you, Pete. More than you might ever guess.

Remember how we met, on my first night here, how you made me laugh? The other patients were asleep and the nurses were eating at the nurses' station. I was sitting in the rec room. The TV was on but the station had gone off the air. I was staring at the gray snow on the screen and listening to the white hiss from the speaker.

"Hi," you said. "I'm Pete."

I already knew that because your name was embroidered in red on the chest of your blue coverall. What I didn't know was that you were the third-shift mechanic and that we would become friends.

You jerked your thumb in the direction of the nurses' station and asked me if I knew the difference between a night nurse and an elephant.

"No."

"About seven pounds."

And I smiled.

Okay. It wasn't a great joke, but at that time in my life I thought I'd never smile again. I'd just been fired from the supercollider, right after I got the message from God. . . .

Well, I'll get to that part later. I promised I'd tell you the whole story before I left here. When the sun rises an hour from now you'll know everything that happened. About an hour after that, at exactly 7 A.M., I will become a free man, released by the same court that sent me here.

How many men can say they have been certified as sane?

My suitcase is already packed.

I have not always had this lovely corner room with its long French windows. This is my reward for seniority and good behavior. I'll miss it. For the past few months I've enjoyed sitting here and reading, and when I grew tired of reading I could look up at my van Gogh print. You can see the pale patch on the wall above my bed where the print was taped. On my last-day pass I bought a mailing tube at the post office so I could take the print with me when I leave.

On sunny days I would walk outside and wander across the lawns or along the gravel paths under the trees. I always liked to look back at the pale tan-brick buildings, so massive in their institutional certainty. I found them reassuring. But I must leave this place. The court has said so and I am ready to go.

We are on the ground floor here but there are no bars on my windows. Any night, I could have opened the window and walked away across what we call the Eastern Lawn, through the limpid moonlight, until I came to that dark line of trees a mile away that marks the road.

Beyond the road are flat fields of Texas cotton, and far away across the fields is the horizon, that imaginary line where the Earth ends and Heaven begins.

Imaginary. Does that mean that there is no line because Heaven and Earth never, never meet? That's what Aquinas said.

Or does *imaginary* mean that there is no line, no division, between Heaven and Earth?

That was my project, exploring the line between Heaven and Earth. And that's how I got into trouble. Philosophical speculation can be dangerous, and lead to madness. Perhaps a man's time is better spent fixing a faucet than trying to read the mind of God.

Anyway, there are no bars on my windows. Each day I prove I'm sane by staying.

I'll miss this room. I liked sitting here by the window and reading in the afternoon. When I tired of my book I would look across the lawns and watch the crazies walking in the sun instead of staying in the shade. You must have noticed that crazy people always walk real slow? You probably think they shuffle along because they have nowhere to go, so why hurry, but the truth is they spend so much energy on being mad they have none left for the rest of their bodies. Not so for the manics, of course, but they're all locked up, not out walking on the grass.

I've become very interested in mental things like this recently, how the mind works and so on. I've been reading a lot about the physical basis of thought, about neurobiology.

Think about that orange in your hand, Pete. You see an orange sphere, you feel its waxy dimpled surface. Now imagine the soft ripping sound if you were to tear off its peel, imagine the juice spraying out, imagine taking a bite, imagine the tangy scent, the sweet tartness on your tongue. Is your mouth filling with saliva, Pete? That's because your brain is projecting an image, a mental model, of these sensations inside your head, and the image is so real you can't help salivating.

That image of an orange is a working model of the world, a model that lets you analyze a situation, plan ahead, test alternative strategies, act, survive. Models like that make up what we are.

But some minds create weird models and those minds may be mad. I don't know about that. But I do know that one kind of madness is not knowing that the model is all we will ever know.

All right, if I'm going to tell it I'd better just tell it.

My project began when I was only three years old. I was watching *Sesame Street*, learning the letters and the numbers like all kids do. Remember? Each show was sponsored by three letters and a number? No? Guess you're just a little too old for that.

Anyway, my favorite letter was X and my favorite number was six. I already had an X in my name and I wanted to have a six. Suddenly I knew, I just knew, that my name was spelled C-A-X-6-T-O-N. The six would be silent, of course, like the silent E that I discovered was hidden at the end of some words.

Three years later, on my first day at school, I told the teacher I could spell my name, and write it too.

"Show me," she said.

I wrote it down. C-A-X-6-T-O-N. "The six is silent," I said. Actually I lisped badly, so I must have said, "The thixth ith thilent, Mith Thmith."

"Well done, but there is no six." She made me write it without the six.

A few minutes later I looked up from my work and she was staring at me, curiously, as if I were a specimen.

At that time my mother and father were fighting a lot. I told my father about the silent six. Once, when they were in the kitchen, making up after a fight, he told my mother, "Our kid's cute, but weird, like me. He told me he had a six in his name, between the X and the T. Strange. I've sometimes thought there should be a six there myself." He laughed, but my mother didn't stop crying.

One day my father left.

My mother started going to church and taking me with her. When the pastor prayed we were supposed to keep our eyes shut. Sometimes I peeked. The pastor had his eyes open and was looking up into the rafters. That meant that God was up there but I was always too afraid to look up and see Him. Maybe God would bring my father back. But He didn't. Dad didn't even come to see me. Ever.

However, God did speak to me sometimes. He told me that right after the X in my name there really was a six.

My grandpa, my mother's father that is, bought me a Monopoly game for my tenth birthday. But my mother quickly got tired of playing it with me and I had no one else. I remember one rainy afternoon making up my own game. I made up a list of the numbers from two to twelve, arranged in a random order. Then I rolled the two dice. I told myself that if I could roll the dice eleven times to get the numbers I had written down, in the same order as I had written them, then my father would come home. On and off, in idle moments, I played this game for years.

In high school I discovered that the chance of getting eleven numbers in the right order was 2,853,670,611 to one. Those were the odds of my father coming home.

I met Evelyn in junior high, in the waiting room of the school psychologist. Later we discovered we shared the same diagnosis: borderline schizophrenia. She was like me in another way: She was thin and freckled.

Evelyn's father taught math at the community college. She and I knew we were both pretty clever. We were right. In high school we both got a perfect score on the SATs. The math part, of course.

I let my hair grow long while I was in junior high and it's been like that ever since. I grew my mustache when I went to college. Fu Manchus are probably still not in fashion, but I like it.

Evelyn had one of the first Apple II Plus computers. Her father gave it to her for her birthday. It had a Motorola 6502 processor, 48K of memory, a monochrome monitor and a 128K floppy drive. After school I would go over to her house and we would tinker with the Apple. We wrote our programs in a language called Applesoft Basic. It was a horrible language, but at the time we thought it was wonderful.

The Apple had a random-number generator. The function RND(1) produced a random number between zero and one. The function RND(26) gave a number between zero and twenty-six and the function INT(RND(26)) made sure that number was an integer. It was easy to write a program where I = A, 2 = B, and so on. We didn't bother with punctuation marks. We called our program the Motorola Monkey and tested the hypothesis that, typing at random down through the ages, a monkey would eventually produce the works of Shakespeare.

It took the Apple about four hours to fill up one floppy disk with what we called "random text." Once we got the program working Evelyn would start the Monkey on a run before she went to bed at night, change the disk in the morning, and start another run before she left for school. Her mom was worried about the power bill until I told her that turning the Apple on, when there was a lot of whirring and chirping, used more electricity than leaving it running for a week.

After school we would scan the random text, watching it scroll down the screen, looking for a recognizable word, or even a phrase. After the first run we changed the function to INT(RND(27)) and set 27 equal to a space. Reading a scrolling text with no spaces between the words was impossible.

Did I say words? A sample line of output would be:

GMJRDBRKMHDNFWVYNVE OQ FFVH

After the second run we changed the function to INT(RND(31)) and made the extra five characters all spaces. That way the string of letters was broken down into word-sized chunks:

GMJRD BRKMHDNF WVYNVE OQ FFVH

As you see, inserting more spaces didn't help all that much.

Months went by and slowly I realized that looking for meaning in the Apple's random texts was like looking in the mailbox for a letter from my father.

You see, in a line of Shakespeare there are about thirty letters. The odds against getting even a single line of Shakespeare are roughly a fifty-digit number to one. But Evelyn and I didn't figure that out until we were in high school.

Once we discovered what appeared to be part of the table of contents from a physics text published in the year 2247, but we couldn't understand it.

Anyway, that was the first phase of my project, the Applesoft Basic phase, Release 1.0 of the Monkey, so to speak.

Much later I learned there is no such thing as a random-number generator and that our effort had been completely wasted.

I went to college in Boston, to a sort of technical school by the Charles River. I wasn't the only student there with 800 on the math SAT. My major was computer science. Evelyn went to study physics somewhere else.

I never found another friend like Evelyn. I've never met anyone else who wondered, seriously, if we were *discovering* random texts, or *creating* them. Evelyn and I would argue about this for hours at the Apple's keyboard. I felt we were discovering them, she was for creation. We did agree that Newton discovered calculus while Shakespeare created *Hamlet*.

One day in Boston there was a partial eclipse of the sun. I was walking down a busy street when it happened. Some kids in the street were staring at the sun without eye protection. Some adults didn't know any better either. I got a sheet of cardboard from the top of a recycling stack waiting on the curb and used my pen to punch a pinhole in the center of the cardboard.

I held the sheet above my head. In its shadow, projected on the sidewalk through the pinhole, there was a bright image of the chewed-up sun. Everyone gathered around me, staring down at the sidewalk. I climbed some steps to make the image larger. The kids cheered and the adults broke into applause. I started to explain some of the celestial mechanics, but just then everyone in the crowd had to leave, probably because their lunch hour was over.

The next morning, early, my mom called to say my father was dead. "A truck backed over him at the plant. It was a freak accident."

I felt numb.

. . .

I *felt* numb.

Interesting, how we use the same verb to describe sensation—I felt warm—as we use to describe emotion—I felt numb.

Hidden in our language are truths about ourselves. In this case, Pete, the hidden truth is that the neural circuits that process sensation are the same neural circuits that create emotion. The difference between sensation and emotion is that information flows the other way. Emotion is nothing more than sensation in reverse. You know you are afraid because your heart is pounding, your palms sweaty, and your mouth is dry.

The word itself—*e-motion*—means "flowing out." Emotion is simply sensation we create.

During my first year in college I took a class called Foundations of Mathematics and I learned that building a machine to generate truly random numbers is impossible. I know that you earn your living fixing broken machinery and you probably feel that the universe is not only random, it is perversely so. But serious mathematicians all know that there is no mathematical trick, no equation, capable of producing a truly random series of numbers. Although Evelyn and I hadn't known it, the Motorola Monkey had been stillborn.

The universe isn't a big machine built cunningly by the Cosmic Watchmaker, nor is it a roulette wheel where the atoms rattle around like white balls, settling our fate by chance alone. No. The universe is something else, something in between, something weird, something completely numerical that remains quite unpredictable.

For example: Pour a glass of water into the ocean and wait a few years for that water to mix with all the other water in the ocean. Go down to the beach again and scoop a glass of water back from the sea. The water you scoop out will contain several molecules of the water you poured in ten years ago.

Surprised?

The explanation's simple. There are far more water molecules in a single glass of water than there are glasses of water in the ocean. What you can do with numbers is amazing. Particularly large numbers.

Using the same idea, you can see that every glass of water you drink contains molecules of water that once were in the body of Jesus Christ. There's a mathematical proof of the Holy Communion.

Not that I ever bothered with Jesus Christ. My style was more mystical. Experience God directly, that sort of thing, a Communion of Big Numbers.

You'll see what I mean.

After the death of my father I entered the white-noise phase of my lifelong project.

The white-noise period really began when the guy across the hall got a new TV and gave his old twelve-inch black-and-white to me. There was no cable in the dorm so reception was poor, just a couple of channels with a weak picture and nothing but a lot of snow on the other stations.

It was the snow that gave me the idea.

When you see snow on a dead channel your TV is picking up cosmic background radiation left over from the Big Bang. Strange, yet wonderful. Every night, in your own home, you can watch the Creation.

At Radio Shack I bought twenty dollars' worth of electronics parts. You've seen the rows of stuff in pale blue blister packs hanging at the back of the store where only guys go? I got one IC analog-to-digital converter complete with pin-out diagram, an assortment of loose resistors and capacitors, a twelve-volt power supply, and a blank printed-circuit board for breadboarding the circuit I was going to build.

The input was amplified RF from the tuner of the TV. I ripped the set out of its case and mounted the tuner on the PC board. The RF output from the tuner was fed through six inches of coax cable into the analog-to-digital converter. I tuned to a dead channel and the output from the A/D converter on the breadboard was a random string of digits. Truly random.

The computer I owned at that time was a PC-AT, 12-megahertz Intel 286 processor, 40-MB hard drive, two floppies. A state-of-the-art machine back then. I rewrote the Motorola Monkey in Borland's Turbo Pascal so the Monkey would run on the IBM. Release 2.0.

I had a lot of trouble getting the hookup from the breadboard to the computer's serial port to work, but in the end I got it right.

So, Pete, do you understand what I was doing?

White noise from the random hiss of the Big Bang, left over from the beginning of time, was captured and amplified by the TV tuner, converted into a string of bits in the A/D converter, fed into the PC, turned into a string of letters, and the final product, random text, was stored on the hard drive.

Release 2.0 of the Monkey had some successes. I still remember the most surprising random text I discovered, or as Evelyn would say, created:

One of the greatest surprises in the history of science is that the end of the twentieth century marked the end of the age of reason and the death of the four-hundred-year-old dream of the rationalists of the Enlightenment. Those closing years saw reason's demarcation of the boundaries of reason. Thoughtful men saw that the universe contains limits on reason which cannot be broken. Speeds faster than the speed of light are not possible and, in the same way, some of the workings of the universe are simply not accessible to reason. This idea was not new. In the middle of the century the far-sighted philosopher Wittgenstein had written:

> *When I have exhausted my justifications I have reached bedrock and my spade is turned.*

Through the twentieth century science stumbled upon a series of fundamental, cunningly constructed unresolvable enigmas. Slowly, the truth of Wittgenstein's remark became apparent to all.

Another text, as I remember, read something like this:

Another canvas of size thirty. Here color is to do everything. This time is just simply my bedroom. The walls are pale violet. The floor is of red tiles. The wood of the bed and chairs is the yellow of fresh butter and pillows very light lemon green. The coverlet scarlet. The window green. The toilet table orange, the basin blue. The doors lilac. When I saw my canvases after my illness the one that seemed best to me was the *Bedroom.*

After some research I discovered this was a series of fragments from letters by van Gogh to his brother Theo. This text made Evelyn realize we might have re-discovered the same content in the original Dutch and then we wondered how many secrets the Monkey was printing in languages we didn't know, in languages long dead, or languages yet to be created. But that was all we could do: wonder.

Van Gogh killed himself a few months after painting his bedroom. The Apple had a monochrome display but the IBM had a crude color graphics capability, 640 × 480 pixels. Sixteen colors, I think. That made us think about programming a pixel-based Monkey to paint the screen with random dots of colors. We knew we might create, or discover, a van Gogh that van Gogh would have painted, had he not killed himself, but we never got the pixel-Monkey project off the ground.

I have always been surprised at how you can stumble upon the same idea from different viewpoints, as if the idea were out there, somewhere, waiting to be found. Herman Hesse, in his great novel *The Glass Bead Game*, describes an imaginary country whose culture centers around a game in which the players juxtapose frag-ments of ideas from many disciplines of human thought. Masters of the game are adept at placing ideas to reveal new beauty and new truths. The interpretation of random texts required a similar facility with the whole realm of human thought and what Hesse imagined Evelyn and I rediscovered from a surprising and totally different direction—random texts. Random texts are a variation of Hesse's Glass Bead Game.

I should mention one other text that may help you understand my story. It is probably from a philosophy text but it's impossible to date. This one could be from the past, or from the future, or from nowhere:

In those dark years, when more and more effort was required to discover less and less knowledge, an unknown genius asked the question: Why struggle to discover facts through experiments? Why not look for texts from the future that already contain those facts? Ideas have always come from nowhere. Cre-ativity is an eternal enigma. Random texts are nothing but a device for creating ideas from nothing.

In our time, rational science has assumed its rightful place as one of many tools in the toolbox of human thought. Random texts are an infinite flood of ideas, each of which can be tested against other ideas. Selecting those random texts that describe the universe most accurately is the task of the human mind for the rest of eternity. And in this task we join ourselves with God, for this is His eternal task.

Enigmatic, for sure. Could be a sixteenth-century text by Sir Francis Bacon, perhaps a gloss on his *Novum Organum*, but it could also be a fragment from a religious text that will be written in the future. But, Pete, I tell you these things so you can see that we weren't just fooling around.

In fact, we gave a lot of thought to the fact that random texts may be from the future or the past or from nowhere, and in each case may be true or false. So how do you decide if they are true or false? There are two ways, Pete.

Internal consistency: Does the text make sense with itself? If it contradicts itself, it can't be true.

External consistency: does it agree with other truths?

The first text passes on both criteria. Of course, there could be a little more internal consistency, but at least there is no inconsistency. The second passes also. The third—who knows?

Later, I realized that these texts, although appealing in many ways, were nothing but random noise. Listening to fading echoes from the Big Bang was as likely to reveal truth as was a newborn babe likely to articulate the Einstein-Podolsky-Rosen paradox.

You see, when the universe was young, God knew nothing.

But I'm getting ahead of myself.

Although my major was computer science I took a lot of math and physics classes and for an easy credit I registered for Professor Kuhl's Epistemology of Science: Fundamental Problems. We met for two hours every Thursday afternoon in the spring semester in a classroom that was an old amphitheater with oak paneling and tall leaded windows facing west. Sloping beams of light fell on the shoulders of the students and the sunlight lay in pools at the feet of Professor Kuhl.

The professor was a tiny white-haired old man who always wore the same tweed jacket with leather patches on the elbows. He smelled of pipe tobacco and spoke slowly, with a thick East European accent. There was a sadness in his voice, a mourning for something lost and irreplaceable.

The course was an overview of mathematical physics and the philosophy of science. In the first class, when the trees by the river were still bare, Professor Kuhl proved mathematically that time and space were relative, unique for each observer. That's Einstein's theory of relativity.

Later in the semester Kuhl showed that we could never measure the exact position and the exact momentum of a particle at the same time. That's Heisenberg's uncertainty principle.

As the days grew longer the Professor proved that the ultimate building blocks of matter are both particles and waves, depending on what experiment you perform, and that random fluctuation of these enigmatic entities is the basis of all that exists. That's quantum mechanics.

When the trees were covered with new leaves, Professor Kuhl deduced on the blackboard the existence of statements that are true, but unprovable. That's Godel's Theorem. Think about that idea applied to the whole universe, Pete. Godel's Theorem is itself such a statement. See what I mean about weird?

Finally, as summer began, he showed that the behavior of all but the simplest systems cannot be predicted. Two pendulums, one hanging from the other, and all our mathematics fails. Two pieces of string and two lead weights stump the finest human minds, and always will. That's chaos theory.

What Professor Kuhl taught me was that the Cartesian idea of a complicated but predictable clockwork universe is impossible. Even theoretically, the future is totally unknowable. Not unknown, but unknowable. Sure, reason works to fix a leaking faucet, but most of the universe is simply not accessible to reason.

Reason. The most elegant function of the human brain.

When we reason we are using the same circuits in our brains that we use to process sensation and emotion because those are the only circuits we have inside our heads. At the neural level, there is no difference between thinking and feeling.

We only like to think there is because thinking makes us feel good.

Inside our mammalian brains, which are the only ones we'll ever have, incoming sensation, outgoing emotion, and the internal activity we call thought are jumbled joyously.

You're following all this, Pete? I hope your beeper doesn't go off, just as I'm getting to the interesting part. It's a full moon tonight and some crazy's probably stuffing ten rolls of toilet paper down the john over in Building T, half a mile away.

I know how you just love those kinds of calls, how you look on them as a punishment.

The mathematician Gauss was punished once, when he was a schoolboy. His class was kept in late for some misdemeanor, and each boy was to add up all the numbers from one to one hundred. The eight-year-old Gauss, who would grow up to be the greatest mathematician of his century, turned in the correct answer after a few seconds' work.

You see, you can write down all the numbers and add them up, or you can get an answer quickly by using the formula $n(n+1)/2$, which Gauss discovered in those first few seconds of his detention.

Adding all the numbers from one to one hundred is a problem that mathematicians say is *algorithmically compressible*. It can be reduced to a formula.

As I listened to Professor Kuhl's final lecture I realized that God has crafted an algorithmically incompressible universe so that even He cannot know the future. Sure, the universe is computable, but the computation of the universe is algorithmically incompressible. There are no shortcuts, no quick method that will give an answer.

It's as if we have to write down all the numbers and add them up, one by one. Second by second, atom by atom, quantum event by quantum event, we simply have to wait and see what is going to happen next.

That was when I understood the sadness in Professor Kuhl's voice. He was mourning the end of the Enlightenment, the end of the great dream of using reason as a tool to understand all that lies in Heaven and Earth.

Later, in the library, I discovered that the idea of an algorithmically incompressible universe was not new. Two sixteenth-century Polish clerics, brothers living in Rome, suggested that God was omnipotent, but not omniscient. These Sozinian brothers argued that God was growing in knowledge and understanding while His creation unfolded. They were excommunicated and the Sozinian doctrine declared heretical.

Wrongly. Mathematics has proven that the Sozinians were right.

But the important thing to realize is that, as I said, God knew nothing when the universe was young. Release 2.0 of the Monkey was another case of garbage in, garbage out.

I was spending a lot of time in the library, thinking about things like this. I discovered that Evelyn and I were not the first to wonder about random texts. The earliest known writings on the subject were the work of the fourteenth-century scholar, Lulio. The philosopher John Stuart Mill had also written about them. Strangely, Mill was concerned with the idea of random music, not words, and worried that melody was exhaustible. Later, Kurd Lasswitz, an obscure nineteenth-century German science-fiction writer, explored some of the possibilities of random texts.

And then I discovered Borges, the Argentinean minimalist. In Borges's story "The Library of Babel," a librarian describes the infinite library where he toils endlessly. In this library everything that has been written, will be written, has never been written, and will never be written is stored on the bookshelves of an endless library of hexagonal rooms. Unfortunately, the books are not shelved in any order and almost all of them are nothing but meaningless streams of letters with a word or a phrase scattered here and there in the jumble. The librarian spends his life searching for a single comprehensible text. The Holy Grail, of course, is the text which is the catalog of the library. It must be somewhere on the shelves. At the end of the story the librarian escapes from the library.

I have a copy of Borges on my bookshelf. Here, take it.

Evelyn graduated with a doctorate in nuclear physics. She went to work for Pantex, in Amarillo, and I went to visit her. Have you ever been to Amarillo, Pete? Outside the town there is a sign that says:

AMARILLO
We know who we are.

Now there's a town of lucky people.

You know when you're getting close to Pantex. First there's nothing but desert, then you come to the razor wire that marks the perimeter of the sixteen-thousand-acre site, then you see one of the Chevrolet Suburbans with its roof cut off for the swivel-mounted M-60.

Sounds scary. Evelyn met me at the first gate. Pantex was the final assembly point for nuclear warheads, she told me. "Detonators, timers, altimeters, parachutes are packed around what we call the *physics package*," she said. "What a lovely euphemism. But now we're into disassembly."

That's why I got a tour. Even *The New York Times* had got a tour. At that time Pantex was trying to reinvent its image.

While Evelyn was helping me into a protective suit she told me that there were six thousand parts in a typical thermonuclear weapon and the cost of demilitarizing a single weapon was about $500,000.

We waddled robotically into a disassembly shop, a gravel Gertie, a bunker with thirty tons of dirt on its roof. If there's an explosion, the Gertie collapses, containing the radioactive material and crushing everything inside.

We watched two men easing an electromechanical device from a complex mechanism of wires, printed circuits, and relays. One man read instructions line by line from a manual while the other unscrewed the subassembly from its mounting and exposed the shiny surface of what looked like a metal bowling ball.

"That's plutonium," she said. "We call it a pit. Right now we have five thousand pits stored safely here at Pantex."

We saw some of them in another bunker, stored in thirty-gallon steel drums, stacked in rows in the dim cool air. "We monitor for radiation leaks. We've never had any, of course."

I listened carefully to the hiss from the Geiger counter.

In 1991 I finished graduate school and moved to Waxahachie, Ellis County, Texas. Back in '79 the high-energy physics community had asked the federal government for "a multi-TeV accelerator to elucidate the physics of electroweak symmetry binding necessary for continued progress in high-energy physics." In other words, they wanted to find the basic building blocks of matter and they needed a machine that was twenty miles in diameter. In fact, to get down to the level of quarks they would need a machine several light-years across, but they didn't tell that to Congress.

This is how the argument went. The superconducting supercollider would prove, maybe, the existence of the Higgs boson, an elusive particle that existed shortly after the Big Bang and may have given matter the important property of mass. The Higgs boson, if it is ever found, will be a step on the road to unifying the electroweak and strong forces of nuclear physics, bringing us closer to unifying these forces with gravity, closer to a grand unification theory, a so-called theory of everything. The mathematical physicist Stephen Hawking wrote, "If we do discover a complete theory . . . we should know the mind of God."

Higgs boson first, mind of God next. Get the picture?

In October, 1993, seventeen shafts had been sunk two hundred feet under the chalk of east Texas and eleven of the proposed forty-two miles of tunnel had been dug. Two billion taxpayer dollars had been spent. That's real progress toward knowing the mind of God. That month a congressman from Ohio said, "Finding basic building blocks of the universe won't change the way people live." Many other congressmen were feeling pressure from their constituents. One voter commented, "If I want to know the mind of God, I pray."

Congress canceled the project.

What would Professor Kuhl have said?

But he had died in 1991.

At the time of the cancellation I was working at the SSC's Particle Detection Simulation Facility, which represented one hundred million of the taxpayers' two billion dollars.

We were running at twelve billion instructions per second (that's twelve thousand million instructions per second, or twelve thousand MIPS) and had on-line storage measured in terabytes. There was nothing else like the PDSF in the world.

Ten of our staff of thirty were laid off and my boss began to scramble to find a use for the twelve-thousand-MIPS PDSF, another two thousand MIPS in the iPS/860 Intel hypercube, a 550,000-square-foot facility, eight million dollars of network infrastructure, thirteen million dollars of personal computers, and fourteen million dollars of UNIX workstations.

My boss was a sharp guy. While the SSC consortium was renting tunnels to local mushroom growers my boss got the PDSF transferred to the state of Texas. The state renamed it and told him to earn his keep by renting computer time to the scientific community. I prepared a homepage for the World Wide Web, sort of an advertisement focused at well-heeled academics with generous funding from the National Science Foundation. I remember the first page:

High Performance Computing Center

[At this point there were two images of large rooms full of equipment.]

High Performance Computing Center
Available at no cost to User until further notice.
Get acquainted with the capabilities of the HPCC
during this limited-time offer.
If you are interested in using the High Performance
Computing Center at no cost please define your requirements
and query caxton@texas.ssc.gov.

Now you have to put yourself in my situation, sitting at my Sun SPARC 10 work-station with no application to run. Imagine, an aficionado of random text sitting there with twelve thousand MIPS of idle processing power literally at my fingertips. All I needed was to write a few lines of C++ code to create an updated Motorola Monkey.

Release 3.0.

Oh, and I needed a suitable source of random numbers.

Professor Kuhl had shown me the only real random-number generator in the universe. I was watching the dust dance in the sunbeams while he was describing the quantum dance of particles.

"Quantum events are truly without cause. There is a veil through which we cannot pass, an ephemeral, flimsy veil, a barrier more mental than physical, yet totally impenetrable."

He paused, giving us time to absorb what he was saying. "If there were a cause for the radioactive decay of an atom, that cause would be what has been called a 'hidden variable' in the equations. Within the mathematics of quantum mechanics there is proof that there are no hidden variables. The chain of cause and effect comes to an end. The quantum event is an effect without a cause."

Later I imagined this veil to be like a curtain blowing in an open window on a summer night. God was the warm dark breeze making the quanta dance.

Needing effects that had no causes, I called Evelyn. Yes, she could supply a billion truly random digits per second. Five thousand pits could supply a lot more, but that was all the PDSF could handle. Using all the power of my texas.ssc.gov Internet address I commandeered enough bandwidth on the Net's high-speed backbone. Soon I was pumping a billion random Pantex digits per second into the PDSF. That translates to over a hundred million characters per second. That's thirty times more text every second than Shakespeare wrote in his entire life.

I could have used any other quantum phenomenon to generate randomness. But I knew Evelyn and so that was the easiest way for me.

Of course, I needed some help to scan it all. I uploaded the CD-ROM version of the Oxford English Dictionary, wrote a little more C++ code, an algorithm to recognize texts with English or almost-English words—sort of a reverse spell-checker looking for words that were misspelled, but still could be words—and I was in business.

What was I looking for?

Well, you remember I said my style was mystical?

I wanted God to whisper to me through the quantum veil. I knew He was there. All I had to do was listen with all my attention and He would tell me what I needed to know.

The God who would be whispering to me was the God who is alive today. Not the infant God whose mewling still echoes through the universe as cosmic background radiation. No, the God behind the quantum veil is still at work, crafting the growing universe, solving for the first time the great puzzle of the cosmos. Just like us, He is eager to find out what will happen next.

Pete, your wife is Mexican, right? Perhaps you're wondering: Suppose the secret of the universe is written in Spanish instead of English?

It doesn't matter. The beauty of searching through an infinity of random text is that the secret of the universe will be written in Spanish, and English, and all other human languages, and all nonhuman languages too. In fact, there will be an infinite number of documents that reveal the secret of the universe. All I needed to do was to find one written in English. It could be the original scientific paper that will one day win the Nobel Prize, it could be a news story about that paper, a philosophical criticism of the work, a chapter from a textbook, a children's version of the Theory of Everything, anything would do.

So I got all my equipment set up, the feed from God's random ticking in the plutonium, the translation into text, the automatic flagging of documents that were mostly English, and I churned out the equivalent of a thousand Shakespeare plays a second.

One day I am sitting, stunned, at my workstation, and my boss comes in and sees the random text scrolling across the screen. He takes the printout I am clutching in my hand, and reads:

the chance against you receiving this message of 372 characters from the rafters from behind the veil is a number far greater than all the protons in the universe so you know this is not an accident by way of confirmation let me tell you that you were right mith thmith was wrong the six is there and yes the sixth ith thilent the secret of the universe is I dont know yet

Immediately, you will notice that the message exhibits both internal and external consistency. But remember, truth is not the same as meaning.

My boss discovered the feed of random digits and the sequestration of twelve thousand Texas MIPS for my own devices.

Misappropriation of government resources was the phrase they used in the indictment. When the dust settled they sent me here instead of jail, saying I was crazy.

Ah! There goes your beeper.

But wait a moment. Do you see those headlights, there on the road, behind the trees? Someone is parking outside the East Gate.

My story took longer than I thought. It's almost seven o'clock and the sun has risen.

I am sane, and I am ready to leave.

Look outside. Like lightning drawn to a lightning rod, the night's dew has condensed on the very tip of each blade of grass. The laws of physics are written so that the dew must collect as tiny globes of water on each blade's tip, not as a film of moisture smeared over the whole lawn. Each drop will scatter the low light of the rising sun. While I am walking to the gate the lawn will look as if someone has thrown away a million diamonds. Why should it be so beautiful? I can't explain it, and that's how I know I'm sane. Reason is only the sixth sense, the silent sixth sense, no more reliable than the other five. As imperfect, and as capable of causing pain or ecstasy.

So maybe the message was truly random. Or maybe there is a God who takes an interest in things, dazzling us with the morning dew and sending us messages. But don't forget that some religions have trickster gods.

And on that note, Pete, it's clearly time for me to go.

THE COST TO BE WISE

Maureen F. McHugh

▼

Maureen F. McHugh made her first sale in 1989, and has since made a powerful impression on the SF world of the '90s with a relatively small body of work, becoming a frequent contributor to Asimov's Science Fiction, The Magazine of Fantasy & Science Fiction, Alternate Warriors, Aladdin, Killing Me Softly, *and other markets. In 1992, she published one of the year's most widely acclaimed and talked-about first novels,* China Mountain Zhang, *which won the Locus Award for Best First Novel, the Lambda Literary Award, and the James Tiptree, Jr. Memorial Award, and which was named a* New York Times *Notable Book as well as being a finalist for the Hugo and Nebula Awards. Her most recent book is* Half the Day Is Night. *Upcoming is a new novel,* Mission Child, *set on the same world as "The Cost to Be Wise." She has had stories in our Tenth, Eleventh (in collaboration with David B. Kisor), Twelfth, and Thirteenth Annual Collections. She lives in Twinsburg, Ohio with her husband, her son, and a golden retriever named Smith.*

In the quiet but powerful tale that follows, she tells the story of a young woman who learns the painful lesson that wisdom has a price. And that sometimes that price is more than you were willing to pay. . . .

i

The sun was up on the snow and everything was bright to look at when the skimmer landed. It landed on the long patch of land behind the schoolhouse, dropping down into the snow like some big bug. I was supposed to be down at the distillery helping my mam but we needed water and I had to get an ice ax, so I was outside when the offworlders came.

The skimmer was from Barok. Barok was a city. It was so far away that no one I knew in Sckarline had ever been there (except for the teachers, of course) but for the offworlders the trip was only a few hours. The skimmer came a couple of times a year to bring packages for the teachers.

The skimmer sat there for a moment—long time waiting while nothing happened except people started coming to watch—and then the hatch opened out and an offworlder stepped gingerly out on the snow. The offworlder wasn't a skimmer pilot though, it was a tall, thin boy. I shaded my eyes and watched. My hands were cold but I wanted to see.

The offworlder wore strange colors for the snow. Offworlders always wore un-natural colors. This boy wore purples and oranges and black, all shining as if they were wet and none of them thick enough to keep anyone warm. He stood with his knees stiff and his body rigid because the snow was packed to flat, slick ice by the skimmer and he wasn't sure of his balance. But he was tall and I figured he was as old as I am so it looked odd that he still didn't know how to walk on snow. He was beardless, like a boy. Darker than any of us.

Someone inside the skimmer handed him a bag. It was deep red and shined as if it were hard, and wrinkled as if it were felt. My father crossed to the skimmer and took the bag from the boy because it was clear that the boy might fall with it and it made a person uncomfortable to watch him try to balance and carry some-thing.

The dogs were barking, and more Sckarline people were coming because they'd heard the skimmer.

I wanted to see what the bags were made of so I went to the hatch of the skimmer to take something. We didn't get many things from the offworlders because they weren't appropriate, but I liked offworlder things. I couldn't see much inside the skimmer because it was dark and I had been out in the sun, but standing beside the seat where the pilot was sitting there was an old white-haired man, all straight-legged and tall. As tall as Ayudesh the teacher, which is to say taller than anyone else I knew. He handed the boy a box, though, not a bag, a bright blue box with a thick white lid. A plastic box. An offworlder box. The boy handed it to me.

''Thanks,'' the boy said in English. Up close I could see that the boy was really a girl. Offworlders dress the same both ways, and they are so tall it's hard to tell sometimes, but this was a girl with short black hair and skin as dark as wood.

My father put the bag in the big visitors' house and I put the box there too. It was midday at winterdark, so the sun was a red glow on the horizon. The bag looked black except where it fell into the red square of sunlight from the doorway. It shone like metal. So very fine. Like nothing we had. I touched the bag. It was plastic too. I liked the feeling of plastic. I liked the sound of the word in lingua. If someday I had a daughter, maybe I'd name her Plastic. It would be a rich name, an exotic name. The teachers wouldn't like it, but it was a name I wished I had.

Ayudesh was walking across the snow to the skimmer when I went back outside. The girl (I hadn't shaken free from thinking of her as a boy) stuck out her hand to him. Should I have shaken her hand? No, she'd had the box, I couldn't have shaken her hand. So I had done it right. Wanji, the other teacher, was coming too.

I got wood from the pile for the boxstove in the guest house, digging it from under the top wood because the top wood would be damp. It would take a long time to heat up the guest house, so the sooner I got started the sooner the off-worlders would be comfortable.

There was a window in the visitor's house, fat-yellow above the purple-white snow.

Inside everyone was sitting around on the floor, talking. None of the teachers were there, were they with the old man? I smelled whisak but I didn't see any, which meant that the men were drinking it outside. I sat down at the edge of the group, where it was dark, next to Dirtha. Dirtha was watching the offworld girl who was shaking her head at Harup to try to tell him she didn't understand what he was asking. Harup pointed at her blue box again. "Can I see it?" he asked. Harup was my father's age, so he didn't speak any English.

It was warming up in here, although when the offworlder girl leaned forward and breathed out, her mouth in an O, her breath smoked the air for an instant.

It was too frustrating to watch Harup try to talk to the girl. "What's your kinship?" he asked. "I'm Harup Sckarline." He thumped his chest with his finger. "What's your kinship?" When she shook her head, not understanding all these words, he looked around and grinned. Harup wouldn't stop until he was bored, and that would take a long time.

"I'm sorry," the girl said, "I don't speak your language." She looked unhappy.

Ayudesh would be furious with us if he found out that none of us would try and use our English.

I had to think about how to ask. Then I cleared my throat, so people would know I was going to talk from the back of the group. "He asks what is your name," I said.

The girl's chin came up like a startled animal. "What?" she said.

Maybe I said it wrong? Or my accent was so bad she couldn't understand? I looked at my boots; the stitches around the toes were fraying. They had been my mother's. "Your name," I said to the boots.

The toes twitched a little, sympathetic. Maybe I should have kept quiet.

"My name is Veronique," she said.

"What is she saying?" asked Harup.

"She says her kinship is Veronique," I said.

"That's not a kinship," said Little Shemus. Little Shemus wasn't old enough to have a beard, but he was old enough to be critical of everything.

"Offworlders don't have kinship like we do," I said. "She gave her front name."

"Ask her her kinship name," Little Shemus said.

"She just told you," Ardha said, taking the end of her braid out of her mouth. Ardha was a year younger than me. "They don't have kinship names. Ayudesh doesn't have a kinship name. Wanji doesn't."

"Sure they do," Shemus said. "Their kinship name is Sckarlineclan."

"We give them that name," said Ardha and pursed her round lips. Ardha was always bossy.

"What are they saying?" asked the girl.

"They say, err, they ask, what is your," your what? How would I even ask what her kinship name was in English? There was a word for it, but I couldn't think of it. "Your other name."

She frowned. Her eyebrows were quite black. "You mean my last name? It's Veronique Twombly."

What was so hard about *last name*? I remembered it as soon as she said it. "Tawomby," I said. "Her kinship is Veronique Tawomby."

"Tawomby," Harup said. "Amazing. It doesn't sound like a word. It sounds made-up, like children do. What's in her box?"

"I know what's in her box," said Erip. Everybody laughed except for Ardha and me. Even Little Sherep laughed and he didn't really understand.

The girl was looking at me to explain.

"He asks inside, the box is." I had gotten tangled up. Questions were hard.

"Is the box inside?" she asked.

I nodded.

"It's inside," she said.

I didn't understand her answer, so I waited for her to explain.

"I don't know what you mean," she said. "Did someone bring the box inside?"

I nodded, because I wasn't sure exactly what she'd said, but she didn't reach for the box or open it or anything. I tried to think of how to say it.

"Inside," Ardha said, tentative. "What is?"

"The box," she said. "Oh wait, you want to know what's in the box?"

Ardha looked at the door so she wouldn't have to look at the offworlder. I wasn't sure, so I nodded.

She pulled the box over and opened it up. Something glimmered hard and green and there were red and yellow boxes covered in lingua and she said, "Presents for Ayudesh and Wanji." Everybody stood up to see inside, so I couldn't see, but I heard her say things. The words didn't mean anything. Tea, that I knew. Wanji talked about tea. "These are sweets," I heard her say. "You know, candy." I knew the word *sweet,* but I didn't know what else she meant. It was so much harder to speak English to her than it was to do it in class with Ayudesh.

Nobody was paying any attention to what she said but me. They didn't care as long as they could see. I wished I could see.

Nobody was even thinking about me, or that if I hadn't been there she never would have opened the box. But that was the way it always was. If I only lived somewhere else, my life would be different. But Sckarline was neither earth nor sky, and I was living my life in between. People looked and fingered, but she wouldn't let them take things out, not even Harup, who was as tall as she was and a lot stronger. The younger people got bored and sat down and finally I could see Harup poking something with his finger, and the outland girl watching. Then she looked at me.

"What's your name?" she asked.

"Me?" I said. "Umm, Janna."

She said my name. "What's your last name, Janna?"

"Sckarline," I said.

"Oh," she said, "like the settlement."

I just nodded.

"What is his name?" She pointed.

"Harup," I said. He looked up and grinned.

"What's your name?" she asked him and I told him what she had said.

"Harup," he said. Then she went around the room, saying everybody's names. It made everyone pleased to be noticed. She was smart that way. And it was easy. Then she tried to remember all their names, which had everyone laughing and correcting her so I didn't have to talk at all.

Ayudesh came in, taller than anyone, and I noticed, for the first time in my life, that he was really an offworlder. Ayudesh had been there all my life, and I knew he was an offworlder, but to me he had always been just Ayudesh.

Then they were talking about me and Ayudesh was just Ayudesh again.

"Janna?" he said. "Very good. I'll tell you what, you take care of Veronique, here. You're her translator, all right?"

I was scared, because I really couldn't understand when she talked, but I guessed I was better than anybody else.

Veronique unpacked, which was interesting, but then she just started putting things here and there and everybody else drifted off until it was just her and me.

Veronique did a lot of odd things. She used a lot of water. The first thing I did for her was get water. She followed me out and watched me chip the ice for water and fill the bucket. She fingered the wooden bucket and the rope handle.

She said something I didn't understand because it had *do* in it and a lot of pronouns and I have trouble following sentences like that. I smiled at her but I think she realized I didn't understand. Her boots were purple. I had never seen purple boots before.

"They look strange," she said. I didn't know what looked strange. "I like your boots," she said, slowly and clearly. I did understand, but then I didn't know what to do, did she want me to give her my boots? They were my mother's old boots and I wouldn't have minded giving them to her except I didn't have anything to take their place.

"It is really cold," she said.

Which seemed very odd to say, except I remembered that offworlders talk about the weather; Ayudesh had made us practice talking about the weather. He said it was something strangers talked about. "It is," I said. "But it will not snow to-night." That was good, it made her happy.

"And it gets dark so early," she said. "It isn't even afternoon and it's like night."

"Where you live, it is cold as this, umm—" I hadn't made a question right.

But she understood. "Oh no," she said, "where I live is warm. It is hot, I mean. There is snow only on the mountains."

She wanted to heat the water so I put it on the stove, and then she showed me pictures of her mother and father and her brother at her house. It was summer and they were wearing only little bits of clothes.

Then she showed me a picture of herself and a man with a beard. "That's my boyfriend," she said. "We're getting married."

He looked old. Grown up. In the picture Veronique looked older too. I looked at her again, not sure how old she was. Maybe older than me? Wanji said off-worlders got married when they were older, not like the clans.

"I have boyfriend," I said.

"You do?" She smiled at me. "What's his name?"

"Tuuvin," I said.

"Was he here before?"

I shook my head.

Then she let me see her bag. The dark red one. I loved the color. I stroked it, as slick as leather and shining. "Plastic?" I said.

She nodded.

"I like plastic," I said.

She smiled a little, like I'd said something wrong. But it was so perfect, so even in color.

"Do you want it?" she asked. Which made me think of my boots and whether she had wanted them. I shook my head.

"You can have it," she said. "I can get another one."

"No," I said. "It isn't appropriate."

She laughed, a startled laugh. I didn't understand what I'd done and the feeling that I was foolish sat in my stomach, but I didn't know what was so foolish.

She said something I didn't understand, which made me feel worse. "What did you say?" she said. " 'Appropriate'?"

I nodded. "It's not appropriate," I said.

"I don't understand," she said.

Our lessons in appropriate development used lots of English words because it was hard to say these things any other way, so I found that the words to tell her came easily. "Plastic," I said, "it's not appropriate. Appropriate technologies are based on the needs and capacities of people, they must be sustainable without outside support. Like the distillery is. Plastic isn't appropriate to Sckarline's economy because we can't create it and it replaces things we can produce, like skin bags." I stroked the bag again. "But I like plastic. It's beautiful."

"Wow," Veronique said. She was looking at me sharp, all alert like a stabros smelling a dog for the first time. Not afraid, but not sure what to think. "To me," she said slowly, "your skin bags are beautiful. The wooden houses"—she touched the black slick wood wall—"they are beautiful."

Ayudesh and Wanji were always telling us that offworlders thought our goods were wonderful, but how could anyone look at a skin bag and then look at plastic and not see how brilliant the colors were in plastic? Dye a skin bag red and it still looked like a skin bag, like it came from dirt.

"How long you, um, you do stay?" I asked.

"Fourteen days," she said. "I'm a student, I came with my teacher."

I nodded. "Ayudesh, he is a teacher."

"My teacher, he's a friend of Ayudesh. From years ago," she said. "Have you always lived here? Were you born here?"

"Yes," I said. "I am born here. My mother and father are born in Tentas Clan, but they come here."

"Tentas Clan is another settlement?" she asked.

I shook my head. "No," I said. "No. Sckarline only is a settlement."

"Then, what is Tentas Clan?"

"It is people." I didn't know how to explain clans to her at all. "They have kinship, and they have stabros, and they are together—"

"Stabros, those are animals," she said.

I nodded. "Sckarline, uh . . . is an appropriate-technology mission."

"Right, that Ayudesh and Wanji started. Tentas Clan is a clan, right?"

I nodded. I was worn out from talking to her.

After that she drank tea and then I took her around to show her Sckarline. It was already almost dark. I showed her the generator where we cooked stabros manure to make electricity. I got a lantern there.

I showed her the stabros pens and the dogs, even though it wasn't really very interesting. Tuuvin was there, and Gerdor, my little uncle, leaning and watching the stabros who were doing nothing but rooting at the mud in the pen and hoping someone would throw them something to eat. The stabros shook their heads and dug with their long front toes.

"This is Tuuvin?" Veronique said.

I was embarrassed. One of the stabros, a gelding with long feathery ears, craned his head toward me. I reached out and pulled on the long guard hairs at the tips of his ears and he lipped at my hand. He had a long purple tongue. He breathed out steam. Their breath always reminded me of the smell of whisak mash.

"Do you ride them?" Veronique asked.

"What?" I asked.

"Do you, um, get on their backs?" She made a person with her fingers walking through the air, then the fingers jumped on the other hand.

"A stabros?" I asked. Tuuvin and Gerdor laughed. "No," I said. "They have no like that. Stabros angry, very much." I pretended to kick. "They have milk, sometimes. And sleds," I said triumphantly, remembering the word.

She leaned on the fence. "They are pretty," she said. "They have pretty eyes. They look so sad with their long drooping ears."

"What?" Tuuvin asked. "What's pretty?"

"She says they have pretty eyes," I said.

Gerdor laughed but Tuuvin and I gave him a sharp look.

The dogs were leaping and barking and clawing at the gate. She stopped and reached a hand out to touch them. "Dogs are from Earth," she said.

"Dogs are *aufwurld*," I said. "Like us. Stabros are *util*."

"What's that mean?" she asked.

"Stabros can eat food that is *aunwurld*," I said. "We can't, dogs can't. But we can eat stabros so they are between."

"Are stabros from Earth?" Veronique asked.

I didn't know, but Tuuvin did, which surprised me. "Stabros are from here," he said. "Ayudesh explained where it all came from, remember? *Util* animals and plants were here but we could use them. *Aunwurld* animals and plants make us sick."

"I know they make us sick," I snapped. But I translated as best I could.

Veronique was looking at the dogs. "Do they bite?" she asked. Bite? "You mean"—I clicked my teeth—"like eat? Sometimes. Mostly if they're fighting."

She took her hand back.

"I'll get a puppy," Tuuvin said, and swung a leg over the side of the pen and waded through the dogs. Tuuvin took care of the dogs a lot so he wasn't afraid of them. I didn't like them much. I liked stabros better.

"There's a winter litter?" I said.

"Yeah," he said, "but it hasn't been too cold, they might be okay. If it gets cold we can always eat 'em."

The puppy looked like a little sausage with short arms and legs and a pink nose. Veronique cooed and took it from Tuuvin and cradled it in her arms. She talked to it, but she talked in a funny way, like baby talk, and I couldn't understand anything she said. "What's its name?" she asked.

"Its name?" I said.

"Do you name them?" she asked.

I looked at Tuuvin. Even Tuuvin should have been able to understand that, the first thing anybody learned in lingua was "What's your name?" But he wasn't paying any attention. I asked him if any of the dogs had names.

He nodded. "Some of them do. The dark male, he's a lead dog, he's called Bigman. And that one is Yellow Dog. The puppies don't have names, though."

"I think this one should have a name," Veronique said, when I told her. "I think he'll be a mighty hunter, so call him Hunter."

I didn't understand what hunting had to do with dogs, and I thought it was a bitch puppy anyway, but I didn't want to embarrass her, so I told Tuuvin. I was afraid he would laugh but he didn't.

"How do you say that in English?" he asked. " 'Hunter'? Okay, I'll remember." He smiled at Veronique and touched the puppy's nose. "Hunter," he said. The puppy licked him with a tiny pink tongue.

Veronique smiled back. And I didn't like it.

Veronique went to find her teacher. I went down to the distillery to tell Mam why I wasn't there helping. Tuuvin followed me down the hill. The distillery stank so it was down below Sckarline in the trees, just above the fields.

He caught me by the waist and I hung there so he could brush his lips across my hair.

"It's too cold out here," I said and broke out of his arms.

"Let's go in the back," he said.

"I've got to tell Mam," I said.

"Once you tell your mam, there'll be all these things to do and we won't get any time together," he said.

"I can't," I said, but I let him make up my mind for me.

We went around the side, tracking through the dry snow where no one much walked, through the lacy wintertrees to the door to the storage in the back. It was as cold in the back as it was outside, and it was dark. It smelled like mash and whisak and the faint charcoal smell of the charred insides of the kegs. Brass whisak, Sckarline whisak.

He boosted me on a stack of kegs and kissed me.

It wasn't that I really cared so much about kissing. It was nice, but Tuuvin would have kissed and kissed for hours if I would let him and if we would ever find a place where we could be alone for hours. Tuuvin would kiss long after my face felt overused and bruised from kissing. But I just wanted to be with Tuuvin so much. I wanted to talk with him, and have him walk with me. I would let him kiss me if I could whisper to him. I liked the way he pressed against me now; he was warm and I was cold.

He kissed me with little kisses; kiss, kiss, kiss. I liked the little kisses. It was almost like he was talking to me in kisses. Then he kissed me hard, and searched around with his tongue. I never knew what to do with my tongue when he put his in my mouth, so I just kept mine still. I could feel the rough edge of the keg beneath my legs, and if I shifted my weight it rocked on the one below it. I turned my face sideways to get my nose out of the way and opened my eyes to look past

Tuuvin. In the dark I could barely make out Uukraith's eye burned on all the kegs, to keep them from going bad. Uukraith was the door witch. Uukraith's sister Ina took souls from their mother and put them in seeds, put the seed in women to make babies. The kegs were all turned different directions, eyes looking everywhere. I closed mine again. Uukraith was also a virgin.

"Ohhhh, Heth! Eeeuuuu!"

I jumped, but Tuuvin didn't, he just let go of my waist and stepped back and crossed his arms the way he did when he was uncomfortable. The air felt cold where he had just been warm.

My little sister, Bet, shook her butt at us. "Kissy, kissy, kissy," she said. "Mam, Janna's back in the kegs with Tuuvin!"

"Shut up, Bet," I said. Not that she would stop.

"Slobber, slobber," she said, like we were stabros trading cud. She danced around, still shaking her butt. She puckered up her lips and made wet, smacking noises.

"Fucking little bitch," I said.

Tuuvin frowned at me. He liked Bet. She wasn't his little sister.

"Mam," Bet hollered, "Janna said 'fucking'!"

"Janna," my mother called, "come here."

I tried to think of what to do to Bet. I'd have liked to slap her silly. But she'd go crying to Mam and I'd really be in trouble. It was just that she thought she was so smart and she was really being so stupid.

Mam was on her high stool, tallying. My mam wore trousers most often, and she was tall and man-faced. Still and all, men liked her. I took after her so I was secretly glad that men watched her walk by, even if she never much noticed.

"Leave your little sister alone," she said.

"Leave her alone!" I said. "She came and found me."

"Don't swear at her. You talk like an old man." Mam was acting like a headman, her voice even and cool.

"If she hadn't come looking—"

"If you had been working as you're supposed to, she'd have had no one to look for, would she."

"I went out to see the visitors," I said. "There are two. An old man and a girl. I helped Da carry their things to the visitors' house."

"So that means it is okay to swear at your sister."

It was the same words we always traded. The same arguments, all worn smooth and shining like the wood of a yoke. The brand for the kegs was heating in the fire and I could smell the tang of hot iron in the dung.

"You treat me like a child," I said.

She didn't even answer, but I knew what she would say, that I acted like a child. As if what Tuuvin and I were doing had anything to do with being a child.

I was so tired of it I thought I would burst.

"Go back to work," Mam said, turning on her stool. Saying, 'this talk is done' with her shoulders and her eyes.

"It's wrong to live this way," I said.

She looked back at me.

"If we lived with the clans, Tuuvin and I could be together."

That made her angry. "This is a better life than the clans," she said. "You don't know what you're talking about. Go back to work."

I didn't say anything. I just hated her. She didn't understand anything. She and my Da hadn't waited until they were old. They hadn't waited for anything, and they'd left their clan to come to Sckarline when it was new. I stood in front of her, making her feel me standing there, all hot and silent.

"Janna," she said, "I'll not put up with your sullenness—" It made her furious when I didn't talk.

So she slapped me, and then I ran out, crying, past Bet who was delighted, and past Tuuvin, who had his mouth open and a stupid look on his face. And I wished they would all disappear.

Veronique sat with Tuuvin and me at dinner in the guesthouse. The guesthouse was full of smoke. We all sat down on the floor with felt and blankets. I looked to see what Veronique would be sitting on and it was wonderful. It was dark, dark blue and clean on the outside, and inside it was red-and-black squares. I touched it. It had a long metal fastener, a cunning thing that locked teeth together, that Veronique had unfastened so she could sit on the soft red-and-black inside. Dark on the outside, red on the inside; it was as if it represented some strange offworld beast. My felt blanket was red but it was old and the edges were gray with dirt. Offworlders were so clean, as if they were always new.

Ayudesh was with the old man who had come with Veronique. Wanji was there, but she was being quiet and by herself, the way Wanji did.

Tuuvin had brought the puppy into the guesthouse. "She asked me to," he said when I asked him what he was doing.

"She did not," I said. "People are watching a dog in this house. Besides, you don't understand her when she talks."

"I do too," he said. "I was in school too."

I rolled my eyes. He was when he was little but he left as soon as he was old enough to hunt. Men always left as soon as they were old enough to hunt. And he hated it anyway.

Veronique squealed when she saw the puppy and took it from Tuuvin as if it were a baby. Everyone watched out of the corner of their eyes. Ayudesh thought it was funny. We were all supposed to be equal in Sckarline, but Ayudesh was really like a headman.

She put the puppy on her offworld blanket and it rolled over on its back, showing her its tan belly. It would probably pee on her blanket.

My da leaned over. "I hope it isn't dinner." My da hated dog.

"No," I said. "She just likes it."

My dad said to her, "Hie." Then to me he said, "What is she called?"

"Veronique," I said.

"Veronique," he said. Then he pointed to himself. "Guwk."

"Hello, Guwk," Veronique said.

"Hello, Veronique," said my da, which surprised me because I had never heard him say anything in English before. "Ask her for her cup," he said to me.

She had one; bright yellow and smooth. But my da handled it matter-of-factly, as if he handled beautiful things every day. He had a skin and he poured *whisak* into her cup. "My wife"—he waved at Mam—"she makes whisak for Sckarline."

I tried to translate but I didn't know what *whisak* was in English.

Veronique took the cup. My da held his hand up for her to wait and poured himself a cup. He tossed it back. Then he nodded at her for her to try.

She took a big swallow. She hadn't expected the burn, you could see. She choked and her face got red. Tuuvin patted her on the back while she coughed. "Oh my God," she said. "That's strong!" I didn't think I needed to translate that.

ii

The sound of the guns is like the cracking of whips. Like the snapping of bones. The outrunners for the Scathalos High-on came into Sckarline with a great deal of racket; brass clattering, the men singing and firing their guns into the air. It started the dogs barking and scared our stabros and brought everyone outside.

Scathalos dyed the toes and ridgeline manes of their stabros kracken yellow. They hung brass clappers in the harnesses of their caravan animals and bits of milky blue glass from the harnesses of their dogs. On this sunny day everything winked. Only their milking does were plain, and that's only because even the will of a hunter can't make a doe stabros tractable.

Veronique came out with me. "Who are they?" she asked.

Even after just three days I could understand Veronique a lot better. "They are from a great clan, Scathalos," I said. "They come to buy whisak." We hoped they would buy it. Sometimes, when Scathalos outrunners came, they just took it.

"They're another clan?" she asked. "Where are the women?"

"They're outrunners," I said. "They go out and hunt and trade. Outrunners are not-married men."

"They have a lot of guns," she said.

They had more guns than I had ever seen. Usually when outrunners came they had one or two guns. Guns are hard to get. But it looked as if almost every outrunner had a gun.

"Does Sckarline have guns?" Veronique asked.

"No," I said.

"They're not appropriate, right?"

A lot of people said we should have guns, whether Ayudesh and Wanji thought they were appropriate or not. They had to buy the clips that go with them. Ayudesh said that the offworlders used the need of the clips to control the clans. He said that it wasn't appropriate because we couldn't maintain it ourselves.

My da said that maybe some things we should buy. We bought things from other clans, that was trade. Maybe guns were trade too.

The dogs nipped at the doe stabros, turning them, making them stop until out-runners could slip hobbles on them. The stabros looked pretty good. They were mostly dun, and the males were heavy in the shoulders, with heads set low and forward on their necks. Better than most of our animals. The long hairs on their ears were braided with red and yellow threads. Handlers unhooked the sleds from the pack stabros.

Two of them found the skimmer tracks beyond the schoolhouse. They stopped and looked around. They saw Veronique. Then another stared at her, measuring her.

"Come with me," I said.

Our dogs barked and their dogs barked. The outrunner men talked loudly. Sckar-line people stood at the doors of their houses and didn't talk at all.

"What's wrong?" Veronique asked.

"Come help my mam and me." She would be under the gaze of them in the distillery too, but I suspected she would be under their gaze anywhere. And this way Mam would be there.

"Scathalos come here for whisak," I said to my mam, even though she could see for herself. Mam was at the door, shading her eyes and watching them settle in. Someone should have been telling them we had people in the guesthouse and offering to put their animals up, but no one was moving.

"Tuuvin is in back," Mam said, pointing with her chin. "Go back and help him."

Tuuvin was hiding the oldest whisak, what was left of the three-year-old brass whisak. Scathalos had come for whisak two years ago and taken what they wanted and left us almost nothing but lame stabros. They said it was because we had favored Toolie Clan in trade. The only reason we had any three-year-old whisak left was because they couldn't tell what was what.

So my da and some of the men had dug a cellar in the distillery. Tuuvin was standing in the cellar, taking kegs he had stacked at the edge and pulling them down. It wasn't very deep, not much over his chest, but the kegs were heavy. I started stacking more for him to hide.

I wondered what the outrunners would do if they caught us at our work. I wondered if Tuuvin was thinking the same thing. We'd hidden some down there in the spring before the stabros went up to summer grazing but then we'd taken some of the oldest kegs to drink when the stabros came back down in the fall.

"Hurry," Tuuvin said softly.

My hands were slick. Veronique started taking kegs too. She couldn't lift them, so she rolled them on their edge. Her hands were soft and pretty, not used to rough kegs. It seemed like it took a long time. Tuuvin's hands were rough and red. I'd never thought about how hard his hands were. Mine were like his, all red. My hands were ugly compared to Veronique's. Surely he was noticing that too, since every time Veronique rolled a keg over her hands were right there.

And then the last keg was on the edge. Uukraith's eye looked at me, strangely unaffected. Or maybe amused. Or maybe angry. Da said that spirits do not feel the way we feel. The teachers never said anything at all about spirits, which was how we knew that they didn't listen to them. There was not much space in the cellar, just enough for Tuuvin to stand and maybe a little more.

Tuuvin put his hands on the edge and boosted himself out of the cellar. In front of the store we heard the crack of the door on its hinges and we all three jumped.

Tuuvin slid the wooden cover over the hole in the floor. "Move those," he said, pointing at empty kegs.

I didn't hear voices.

"Are you done yet?" Mam said, startling us again.

"Are they here?" I asked.

"No," she said. "Not yet." She didn't seem afraid. I had seen my mam afraid, but not very often. "What is she doing here?" Mam asked, looking at Veronique.

"I thought she should be here, I mean, I was afraid to leave her by herself."

"She's not a child," Mam said. But she said it mildly, so I knew she didn't really mind. Then Mam helped us stack kegs. We all tried to be quiet but they thumped like hollow drums. They filled the space around us with noise. It seemed to me that the outrunners could hear us thumping away from outside. I kept looking at Mam, who was stacking kegs as if we hid whisak all the time. Tuuvin was nervous too. His shoulders were tense. I almost said to him, "you're up around the ears, boy," the way the hunters did, but right now I didn't think it would make him smile.

Mam scuffed the dirt around the kegs.

"Will they find them?" I asked.

Mam shrugged. "We'll see."

There was a lot to do to get ready for the outrunners besides hiding the best whisak. Mam had us count the kegs, even Veronique. Then when we all three finally agreed on a number she wrote it in her tally book. "So we know how much we sell," she said.

We were just finishing counting when outrunners came with Ayudesh. They came into the front. First the wind like a wild dog sliding around the door and making the fires all sway. Then Ayudesh and then the outrunners. The outrunners looked short compared to Ayudesh. And they looked even harder than we did. Their cheeks were winter red. Their felts were all dark with dirt, like they'd been out for a long time.

"Hie," said one of the men, seeing my mother. They all grinned. People always seemed surprised that they were going to trade with my mam. The outrunners already smelled of whisak, so people had finally made them welcome. Or maybe someone had the sense to realize that if they gave them drink we'd have time to get things ready. Maybe my da.

My mam stood as she always did, with her arms crossed, tall as any of them. Waiting them out.

"What's this," said the man, looking around. "Eh? What's this? It stinks in here." The distillery always stank.

They walked around, looked at the kegs, poked at the copper tubing and the still. One stuck his finger under the drip and tasted the raw stuff and grimaced. Ayudesh looked uncomfortable, but the teachers always said that the distillery was ours and they didn't interfere with how we ran it. Mam was in charge here.

Mam just stood and let them walk all around her. She didn't turn her head to watch them.

They picked up the brand. "What's this?" the man said again.

"We mark all our kegs with the eye of Uukraith," Mam said.

"Woman's work," he said.

He stopped and looked at Veronique. He studied her for a moment, then frowned. "You're no boy," he said.

Veronique looked at me, the whites of her eyes bright even in the dimness, but she didn't say anything.

He grinned and laughed. The other two outrunners crowded close to her and fingered the slick fabric of her sleeve, touched her hair. Veronique pulled away.

The first outrunner got bored and walked around the room some more.

He tapped a keg. Not like Mam thumped them, listening, but just as if everything here were his. He had dirty brown hair on the backs of his hands. Everywhere I looked I was seeing people's hands. I didn't like the way he put his hands on things.

Then he pointed to a keg, not the one he was tapping on but a different one, and one of the other men picked it up. "Is it good?" he asked.

My mam shrugged.

He didn't like that. He took two steps forward and hit her across the face. I looked at the black-packed dirt floor.

Ayudesh made a noise.

"It's good," my mam said. I looked up and she had a red mark on the side of her face. Ayudesh looked as if he would speak but he didn't.

The outrunner grabbed her braid—she flinched as he reached past her face— and yanked her head. "It's good, woman?" he asked.

"Yes," she said, her voice coming almost airless, like she could not breathe.

He yanked her down to her knees. Then he let go and they all went out with the keg.

Ayudesh said, "Are you all right?" Mam stood back up again and touched her braid, then flipped it back over her neck. She didn't look at any of us.

People were in the schoolhouse. Ayudesh sat on the table at the front and people were sitting on the floor talking as if it were a meeting. Veronique's teacher was sitting next to Ayudesh and Veronique started as if she were going to go sit with him. Then she looked around and sat down with Mam and Tuuvin and me.

"So we should just let them take whatever they want?" Harup said. He wasn't clowning now, but talking as a senior hunter. He sat on his heels, the way hunters do when they're waiting.

Ayudesh said, "Even if we could get guns, they're used to fighting and we aren't. What do you think would happen?"

Veronique was very quiet. She sat down between Tuuvin and me.

"If we don't stand up for ourselves, what will happen?" Harup said.

"If you provoke them they'll destroy us," Ayudesh said.

"Teacher," Harup said, spreading his hands as if he were telling a story. "Stabros are not hunting animals, eh. They are not sharp toothed like haunds or dogs. Haunds are hunters, packs of hunters, who do nothing but hunt stabros. There are more stabros than all the haunds could eat, eh. So how do they choose? They don't kill the buck stabros with their hard toes and heads, they take the young, the old, the sick, the helpless. We do not want to be haunds, teacher. We just want the haunds to go elsewhere for easy prey."

Wanji came in behind us, and the fire in the boxstove ducked and jumped in the draft. Wanji didn't sit down on the table, but as was her custom, lowered herself to the floor. "Old hips," she muttered as if everyone in the room weren't watching her. "Old women have old hips."

When I thought of Kalky, the old woman who makes the souls of everything, I thought of her as looking like Wanji. Wanji had a little face and a big nose and deep lines down from her nose to her chin. "What happened to you, daughter?" she asked my mam.

"The outrunners came to the distillery to take a keg," Mam said.

I noticed that now the meeting had turned around, away from Ayudesh on the table toward us in the back. Wanji always said that Ayudesh was vain and liked to sit high. Sometimes she called him "High-on." "And so," Wanji said.

My mother's face was still red from the blow, but it hadn't yet purpled. "I don't think the outrunners like to do business with me," Mam said.

"One of them hit her," I said, because Mam wasn't going to. Mam never talked about it when my da hit her, either. Although he didn't do it as much as he used to when I was Bet's age.

Mam looked at me, but I couldn't tell if she was angry with me or not.

Harup spread his hands to say, "See?"

Wanji clucked.

"We got the three-year-old whisak in the cellar," Mam said.

I was looking but I didn't see my da.

"What are they saying?" Veronique asked.

"They are talking," I said, and had to think how to say it, "about what we do, but they, eh, not, do not know? Do not know what is right. Harup want guns. Wants guns. Ayudesh says guns are bad."

"Wanji," Tuuvin whispered, "Wanji, she ask—eh," and then in our own tongue, "tell her she was asking your mam what happened."

"Wanji ask my mother what is the matter," I said.

Veronique looked at Tuuvin and then at me.

"Guns are bad," Veronique said.

Tuuvin scowled. "She doesn't understand," he said.

"What?" Veronique said, but I just shook my head rather than tell her what Tuuvin had said.

Some of the men were talking about guns. Wanji was listening without saying anything, resting her chin on her head. Sometimes it seemed like Wanji didn't even blink, that she just turned into stone and you didn't know what she was thinking.

Some of the other men were talking to Ayudesh about the whisak. Harup's wife, Yet, got up and put water on the boxstove for the men to drink and Big Sherep went out the men's door in the back of the schoolhouse, which meant he was going to get whisak or beer.

"Nothing will get done now," Tuuvin said, disgusted. "Let's go."

He stood up and Veronique looked up at him, then scrambled to her feet.

"Now they talk, talk, talk," I said in English. "Nothing to say, just talk, you know?"

Outside there were outrunners. It seemed as if they were everywhere, even though there were really not that many of them. They watched Veronique.

Tuuvin scowled at them and I looked at their guns. Long black guns slung over their backs. I had never seen a gun close. And there was my da, standing with three outrunners, holding a gun in his hands as if it were a fishing spear, admiring it. He was nodding and grinning, the way he did when someone told a good hunting story. Of course, he didn't know that one of these people had hit Mam.

Still, it made me mad that he was being friendly.

"We should go somewhere," Tuuvin said.

"The distillery?" I asked.

"No," he said, "they'll go back there." And he looked at Veronique. Having Veronique around was like having Bet, you always had to be thinking about her. "Take her to your house."

"And do what?" I asked. A little angry at him because now he had decided he wasn't going back with us.

"I don't know, teach her to sew or something," he said. He turned and walked across to where my dad was standing.

The outrunners took two more kegs of whisak and got loud. They stuck torches in the snow, so the dog's harnesses were all glittering and winking, and we gave them a stabros to slaughter and they roasted that. Some of the Sckarline men like my da—and even Harup—sat with them and drank and talked and sang. I didn't understand why Harup was there, but there he was, laughing and telling stories about the time my da got dumped out of the boat fishing.

Ayudesh was there, just listening. Veronique's grandfather was out there too, even though he couldn't understand what they were saying.

"When will they go?" Veronique asked.

I shrugged.

She asked something I didn't understand.

"When you trade," she said, "trade?"

"Trade," I said, "trade whisak, yes?"

"Yes," she said. "When you trade whisak, men come? Are you afraid when you trade whisak?"

"Afraid?" I asked. "When Scathalos come, yes."

"When other people come, are you afraid?" she asked.

"No," I said. "Just Scathalos."

She sat on my furs. My mam was on the bed and Bet had gone to sleep. Mam watched us talk, sitting cross-legged and mending Bet's boots. She didn't understand any English. It felt wrong to talk when Mam didn't understand, but Veronique couldn't understand when I talked to Mam, either.

"I have to go back to my hut," Veronique said. "Ian will come back and he'll worry about me."

Outside the air was so cold and dry that the inside of our noses felt it.

"Don't you get tired of being cold?" Veronique asked.

The cold made people tired, I thought, yes. That was why people slept so much during winterdark. I didn't always know what to say when Veronique talked about the weather.

"We tell your teacher, you sleep in our house, yes?" I offered.

"Who?" she said. "You mean Ian? He isn't really my teacher like you mean it. He's my professor."

I tried to think of what a professor might be, maybe the person who took you when your father died? It always seemed English didn't have enough words for different relatives, but now here was one I didn't know.

The outrunners and the Sckarline hunters were singing about Fhidrhin the hunter and I looked up to see if I could make out the stars that formed him, but the sky had drifting clouds and I couldn't find the stars.

I couldn't see well enough, the light from the bonfire made everyone else just shadows. I took Veronique's hand and started around the outside of the circle of singers, looking for Ayudesh and Veronique's teacher or whatever he was. Faces glanced up, spirit faces in the firelight. The smoke blew our way and then shifted, and I smelled the sweat smell that came from the men's clothes as they warmed by the fire. And whisak, of course. The stabros was mostly bones.

"Janna," said my da. His face was strange too, not human, like a mask. His eyes looked unnaturally light. "Go on back to your mother."

"Veronique needs to tell the offworlder that she's staying with us."

"Go on back to the house," he said again. I could smell whisak on him too. Whisak sometimes made him mean. My da used to drink a lot of whisak when I was young, but since Bet was born he didn't drink it very often at all. He said the mornings were too hard when you got old.

I didn't know what to do. If I kept looking for Veronique's grandfather and he got angry he would probably hit me. I nodded and backed away, pulling Veronique with me, then when he stopped watching me, I started around the fire the other way.

One of the outrunners stumbled up and into us before we could get out of the way. "Eh—?"

I pulled Veronique away but he gripped her arm. "Boy?"

His breath in her face made her close her eyes and turn her head.

"No boy," he said. He was drunk, probably going to relieve himself. "No boy, outsider girl, pretty as a boy," he said. "Outsider, they like that? Eh?"

Veronique gripped my hand. "Let go," she said in English.

He didn't have to speak English to see she was afraid of him.

"I'm not pretty enough for you?" he said. "Eh? Not pretty enough?" He wasn't pretty, he was wiry and had teeth missing on one side of his mouth. "Not Sckarline? With their pretty houses like offworlders? Not pretty, eh?"

Veronique drew a breath like a sob.

"Let go of her, please," I said, "we have to find her teacher."

"Look at the color of her," he said, "does that wash off? Eh?"

"Do you know where her teacher is?" I asked.

"Shut up, girl," he said to me. He licked his thumb and reached toward her face. Veronique raised her hand and drew back, and he twisted her arm. "Stand still." He rubbed her cheek with his thumb and peered closely at her.

"Damn," he said, pleased. "How come the old man isn't dark?"

"Maybe they are different clans," I said.

He stared at her as if weighing what I'd said. As if thinking. Although he actually looked too drunk to do much thinking. Then he leaned forward and tried to kiss her.

Veronique pushed him away with her free arm. He staggered and fell, pulling her down too.

"Let go!" she shrieked.

Shut up, I thought, shut up, shut up! Give in, he's too drunk to do much. I tried to pull his arm off, but his grip was too strong.

"What's this?" another outrunner was saying.

"Fohlder's found some girl."

"It would be fucking Fohlder!"

Veronique slapped at him and struggled, trying to get away.

"Hey now," Ayudesh was saying, "hey now, she's a guest, an offworlder." But nobody was paying attention. Everybody was watching the outrunner wrestle with her. He pinned her with her arms over her head and kissed her.

Veronique was crying and slapping. Stop it, I kept thinking, just stop it, or he won't let you alone.

Her grandfather tried to pull the outrunner off. I hadn't even seen him come up. "No no no no no," he was saying as if scolding someone. "No no no no no—"

"Get off him," another outrunner hauled him away.

Ayudesh said, "Stop! She is our guest!"

"She's yours, eh?" someone said.

"No," Ayudesh said, "she should be left alone. She's a guest."

"Your guest, right. Not interested in the likes of us."

Someone else grunted and laughed.

"She likes Sckarline better, eh?"

"That's because she doesn't know better."

"Fohlder'll show her."

You all stink like drunks, I wanted to scream at them, because they did.

"Think she's dark inside like she is outside?"

"Have to wait until morning to see."

Oh, my da would be so mad at me, the stupid bitch, why didn't she stop, he was drunk, he was drunk, why had she slapped at him, stupider than Bet, she was as stupid as Bet my little sister, I was supposed to be taking care of her, I was supposed to be watching out for her, my da would be so mad—

There was the bone crack of gunfire and everybody stopped.

Harup was standing next to the fire with an outrunner gun pointed up, as if he were shooting at Fhidrhin up there in the stars. His expression was mild and he was studying the gun as if he hadn't even noticed what was going on.

"Hey," an outrunner said, "put that down!"

Harup looked around at the outrunners, at us. He looked slowly. He didn't look like he usually did, he didn't look funny or angry, he looked as if he were out on a boat in the ice. Calm, far away. Cold as the stars. He could kill someone.

The outrunners felt it too. They didn't move. If he shot one of them, the others would kill him, but the one he shot would still be dead. No one wanted to be the one that might be dead.

"It's a nice piece," Harup said, "but if you used it for hunting you'd soon be so deaf you couldn't hear anything moving." Then he grinned.

Someone laughed.

Everybody laughed.

"Janna," Harup said, "take your friend and get us more whisak."

"Fohlder, you old walking dick, get up from that girl." One of them reached down and pulled him off. He looked mad.

"What," he said, "what."

"Go take a piss," the outrunner said.

Everyone laughed.

iii

Veronique stayed with me that night, lying next to me in my blankets and furs. She didn't sleep. I don't think. I was listening to her breathe. I felt as if I should help her sleep. I lay there and tried to think if I should put my arm around her, but I didn't know. Maybe she didn't want to be touched.

And she had been a stupid girl, anyway.

She lay tense in the dark. "Are you going to be a teacher?" I asked.

She laughed. "If I get out of here."

I waited for her to say more, but she didn't. "Get out of here" meant to make someone leave. Maybe she meant if she made herself.

"You come here from Earth?" I asked. To get her to talk, although I was tired of lingua and I didn't really want to think about anything.

"My family came here from Earth," she said.

"Why?"

"My father, he's an anthropologist," she said. "Do you know 'anthropologist'?"

"No," I said.

"He is a person who studies the way people live. And he is a teacher."

All the offworlders I had ever met were teachers. I wondered who did all the work on Earth.

"Because Earth lost touch with your world, the people here are very interesting to my father," she said. Her voice was listless in the dark and she was even harder to understand when I couldn't see her properly. I didn't understand, so I didn't say anything. I was sorry I'd started her talking.

"History, do you know the word 'history'?" she asked.

Of course I knew the word *history*. "I study history in school," I said. Anneal and Kumar taught it.

"Do you know the history of this world?"

It took my tired head a long time to sort that out. "Yes," I said. "We are a colony. People from Earth come here to live. Then there is a big problem on Earth, and the people of Earth forget we are here. We forget we are from Earth. Then Earth finds us again."

"Some people have stories about coming from Earth," Veronique said. "My father is collecting those stories from different peoples. I'm a graduate student."

The clans didn't have any stories about coming from Earth. We said the first people came out of the sun. This somehow seemed embarrassing. I didn't understand what kind of student she was.

"Are you here for stories?" I asked.

"No," she said. "Ian is old friends with your teacher, from back when they were both with the survey. We just came to visit."

I didn't understand what she'd said except that they were visiting.

We were quiet after that. I pretended to sleep. Sometimes there was gunfire outside and we jumped, even Mam on the bed. Everyone but Bet. Once Bet was asleep it was impossible to wake her up.

I fell asleep thinking about how I wished that the Scathalos outrunners were gone. I dreamed that I was at the offworlders' home, where it was summer but no one was taking care of the stabros, and I said I could take care of the stabros, and they were all glad, and so I was a hero—and I was startled awake by gunfire.

Just more drinking and shooting.

I wished my da would come home. It didn't seem fair that we should lie there and be afraid while the men were getting drunk and singing.

The outrunners stayed the next day, taking three more kegs of whisak but not talking about trade. The following day they sent out hunters but didn't find their own meat and so took another stabros, the gelding I'd shown to Veronique. And more whisak.

I went down to the distillery after they took more whisak. It was already getting dark. The dark comes so early at this time of year. The door was left open and the fire was out. Mam wasn't coming anymore. There was no work being done. Kegs had been taken down and some had been opened and left open. Some had been spilled. They had started on the green stuff, not knowing what was what and had thrown most of it in the snow, probably thinking it was bad. Branded eyes on the kegs looked everywhere.

I thought maybe they wouldn't leave until all the whisak was gone. For one wild moment I thought about taking an ax to the kegs. Give them no reason to stay.

Instead I listened to them singing, their voices far away. I didn't want to walk back toward the voices, but I didn't want to be outside in the dark, either. I walked until I could see the big fire they had going, and smell the stabros roasting. Then I stood for a while, because I didn't want to cross the light more than I wanted to go home. Maybe someone was holding me back, maybe my spirit knew something.

I looked for my father. I saw Harup on the other side of the fire. His face was in the light. He wasn't singing, he was just watching. I saw Gerdor, my little uncle, my father's half brother. I did not see my father anywhere.

Then I saw him. His back was to me. He was just a black outline against the fire. He had his hands open wide, as if he was explaining. He had his empty hands open. Harup was watching my father explaining something to some of the outrunners and something was wrong.

One of the outrunners turned his head and spat.

My father, I couldn't hear his voice, but I could see his body, his shoulders moving as he explained. His shoulders working, working hard as if he were swimming. Such hard work, this talking with his hands open, talking, talking.

The outrunner took two steps, bent down and pulled his rifle into the light. It was a dark thing there, a long thing against the light of the fire. My father took a step back and his hands came up, pushing something back.

And then the outrunner shot my father.

All the singing stopped. The fire cracked and the sparks rose like stars while my father struggled in the snow. He struggled hard, fighting and scraping back through the snow. Elbow-walking backward. The outrunner was looking down the long barrel of the rifle.

Get up, I thought. Get up. For a long time it seemed I thought, Get up, get up. Da, get up! But no sound came out of my mouth and there was black on the snow in the trampled trail my father left.

The outrunner shot again.

My father flopped into the snow and I could see the light on his face as he looked up. Then he stopped.

Harup watched. No one moved except the outrunner who put his rifle away.

I could feel the red meat, the hammering muscle in my chest. I could feel it squeezing, squeezing. Heat flowed in my face. In my hands.

Outrunners shouted at outrunners. "You shit," one shouted at the one who shot my father. "You drunken, stupid shit!" The one who shot my father shrugged at first, as if he didn't care, and then he became angry too, shouting.

My breath was in my chest, so full. If I breathed out loud the outrunners would hear me out here. I tried to take small breaths, could not get enough air. I did not remember when I had been holding my breath.

Harup and the hunters of Sckarline sat, like prey, hiding in their stillness. The arguing went on and on, until it wasn't about my father at all and his body was forgotten in the dirty snow. They argued about who was stupid and who had the High-on's favor. The whisak was talking.

I could think of nothing but air.

I went back through the dark, out of Sckarline, and crept around behind the houses, in the dark and cold until I could come to our house without going past the fire. I took great shuddering breaths of cold air, breathed out great gouts of fog.

My mother was trying to get Bet quiet when I came in. "No," she was saying, "stop it now, or I'll give you something to cry about."

"Mam," I said, and I started to cry.

"What?" she said. "Janna, your face is all red." She was my mam, with her face turned toward me, and I had never seen her face so clearly.

"They're going to kill all of us," I said. "They killed Da with a rifle."

She never said a word but just ran out and left me there. Bet started to cry although she didn't really know what I was crying about. Just that she should be scared. Veronique was still. As still as Harup and all the hunters.

Wanji came and got me and brought me to Ayudesh's house because our house is small and Ayudesh's house had enough room for some people. Snow was caked in the creases of my father's pants. It was in his hands too, unmelted. I had seen dead people before, and my father looked like all of them. Not like himself at all.

My mother had followed him as far as the living can go, or at least as someone untrained in spirit journeys, and she was not herself. She was sitting on the floor next to his body, rocking back and forth with her arms crossed in her lap. I had seen women like that before, but not my mother. I didn't want to look. It seemed indecent. Worse than the body of my father, since my father wasn't there at all.

Bet was screaming. Her face was red from the effort. I held her even though she was heavy and she kept arching away from me like a toddler in a tantrum. "Mam! Mam!" she kept screaming.

People came in and squatted down next to the body for a while. People talked about guns. It was important that I take care of Bet so I did, until finally she wore herself out from crying and fell asleep. I held her on my lap until the blood was out of my legs and I couldn't feel the floor and then Wanji brought me a blanket and I wrapped Bet in it and let her sleep.

Wanji beckoned me to follow. I could barely stand, my legs had so little feeling. I held the wall and looked around, at my mother sitting next to the vacant body, at my sister, who though asleep was still alive. Then I tottered after Wanji as if I were the old woman.

"Where is the girl?" Wanji said.

"Asleep," I said. "On the floor."

"No, the girl," Wanji said, irritated. "Ian's girl. From the university."

"I don't know," I said.

"You're supposed to be watching her. Didn't Ayudesh tell you to watch her?"

"You mean Veronique? She's back at my house. In my bed."

Wanji nodded and sucked on her teeth. "Okay," she said. And then again to herself, "Okay."

Wanji took me to her house, which was little and dark. She had a lamp shaped like a bird. It had been in her house as long as I could remember. It didn't give very much light, but I had always liked it. We sat on the floor. Wanji's floor was always piled high with rugs from her home and furs and blankets. It made it hard to walk but nice to sit. Wanji got cold and her bones hurt, so she always made a little nest when she sat down. She pulled a red-and-blue rug across her lap. "Sit, sit, sit," she said.

I was cold, but there was a blanket to wrap around my shoulders and watch Wanji make hot tea. I couldn't remember being alone with Wanji before. But everything was so strange it didn't seem to make any difference and it was nice to have Wanji deciding what to do and me not having to do anything.

Wanji made tea over her little bird lamp. She handed me a cup and I sipped it. Tea was a strange drink. Wanji and Ayudesh liked it and hoarded it. It was too bitter to be very good, but it was warm and the smell of it was always special. I drank it and held it against me. I started to get warm. The blanket got warm from me and smelled faintly of Wanji, an old dry smell.

I was sleepy. It would have been nice to go to sleep right there in my little nest on Wanji's floor.

"Girl," Wanji said. "I must give you something. You must take care of Veronique."

I didn't want to take care of anybody. I wanted someone to take care of me. My eyes started to fill up and in a moment I was crying salt tears into my tea.

"No time for that, Janna," Wanji said. Always sharp with us. Some people were afraid of Wanji. I was. But it felt good to cry, and I didn't know how to stop it so I didn't.

Wanji didn't pay any attention. She was hunting through her house, checking in a chest, pulling up layers of rugs to peer in a corner. Was she going to give me a gun? I couldn't think of anything else that would help very much right now, but I couldn't imagine that Wanji owned a gun.

She came back with a dark blue plastic box not much bigger than the span of my spread hand. That was almost as astonishing as a gun. I wiped my nose on my sleeve. I was warm and tired. Would Wanji let me sleep right here on her floor?

Wanji opened the plastic box, but away from me so I couldn't see inside it. She picked at it as if she were picking at a sewing kit, looking for something. I wanted to look in it but I was afraid that if I tried she'd snap at me.

She looked at me. "This is mine," she said. "We both got one and we decided that if the people who settled Sckarline couldn't have it, we wouldn't either."

I didn't care about that. That was old talk. I wanted to know what it was.

Wanji wasn't ready to tell me what it was. I had the feeling that Ayudesh didn't know about this, and I was afraid she would talk herself out of it. She looked at it and thought. If I thought, I thought about my father being dead. I sipped tea and tried to think about being warm, about sleeping but that feeling had passed. I wondered where Tuuvin was.

I thought about my da and I started to cry again.

I thought that would really get Wanji angry so I tried to hide it, but she didn't pay any attention at all. The shawl she wore over her head slipped halfway down so when I glanced up I could see where her hair parted and the line of pale skin. It looked so bare that I wanted it covered up again. It made me think of the snow in my father's hands.

"It was a mistake," Wanji said.

I thought she meant the box, and I felt a terrible disappointment that I wouldn't get to see what was inside it.

"You understand what we were trying to do?" she asked me.

With the box? Not at all.

"What are the six precepts of development philosophy?" she asked.

I had to think. "One," I said, "that economic development should be gradual. Two, that analyzing economic growth by the production of goods rather than the needs and capacities of people leads to displacement and increased poverty. Three, that economic development should come from the integrated development of rural areas with the traditional sector—"

"It's just words," she snapped at me.

I didn't know what I had done wrong so I ducked my head and sniffed and waited for her to get angry because I couldn't stop crying.

Instead she stroked my hair. "Oh, little girl. Oh, Janna. You are one of the bright ones. If you aren't understanding it, then we really haven't gotten it across, have we?" Her hand was nice on my hair, and it seemed so unlike Wanji that it scared me into stillness. "We were trying to help, you know," she said. "We were trying to do good. We gave up our lives to come here. Do you realize?"

Did she mean that they were going to die? Ayudesh and Wanji?

"This," she said, suddenly brisk. "This is for, what would you call them, runners. Foreign runners. It is to help them survive. I am going to give it to you so that you will help Veronique, understood?"

I nodded.

But she didn't give it to me. She just sat holding the box, looking in it. She didn't want to give it up. She didn't feel it was appropriate.

She sighed again, a terrible sound. Out of the box she pulled shiny foil packets, dark blue, red, and yellow. They were the size of the palm of her hand. Her glasses were around her neck. She put them on like she did in the schoolroom, absent from the gesture. She studied the printing on the foil packets.

I loved foil. Plastic was beautiful, but foil, foil was something unimaginable. Tea came in foil packets. The strange foods that the teachers got off the skimmer came in foil.

My tea was cold.

"This one," she said, "it is a kind of signal." She looked over her glasses at me. "Listen to me, Janna. Your life will depend on this. When you have this, you can send a signal that the outsiders can hear. They can hear it all the way in Bashtoy. And after you send it, if you can wait in the same place, they will send someone out to get you and Veronique."

"They can hear it in Bashtoy?" I said. I had never even met anyone other than Wanji and the teachers who had ever been to Bashtoy.

"They can pick it up on their instruments. You send it every day until someone comes."

"How do I send it?"

She read the packet. "We have to set the signal, you and I. First we have to put it in you."

I didn't understand, but she was reading, so I waited.

"I'm going to put it in your ear," she said. "From there it will migrate to your brain."

"Will it hurt?" I asked.

"A little," she said. "But it has its own way of taking pain away. Now, what should be the code?" She studied the packet. She pursed her lips.

A thing in my ear. I was afraid and I wanted to say no, but I was more afraid of Wanji so I didn't.

"You can whistle, can't you?" she asked.

I knew how to whistle, yes.

"Okay," she said, "here it is. I'll put this in your ear, and then we'll wait for a while. Then when everything is ready we'll set the code."

She opened up the packet and inside was another packet and a little metal fork. She opened the inside packet and took out a tiny little disk, a soft thing almost like egg white or like a fish egg. She leaned forward and put it in my left ear. Then she pushed it in hard and I jerked.

"Hold still," she said.

Something was moving and making noise in my ear and I couldn't be still. I pulled away and shook my head. The noise in my ear was loud, a sort of rubbing, oozing sound. I couldn't hear normal things out of my left ear. It was stopped up with whatever was making the oozing noise. Then it started to hurt. A little at first, then more and more.

I put my hand over my ear, pressing against the pain. Maybe it would eat through my ear? What would stop it from eating a hole in my head?

"Stop it," I said to Wanji. "Make it stop!"

But she didn't, she just sat there, watching.

The pain grew sharp, and then suddenly it stopped. The sound, the pain, everything.

I took my hand away. I was still deaf on the left side but it didn't hurt.

"Did it stop?" Wanji asked.

I nodded.

"Do you feel dizzy? Sick?"

I didn't.

Wanji picked up the next packet. It was blue. "While that one is working, we'll do this one. Then the third one, which is easy. This one will make you faster when you are angry or scared. It will make time feel slower. There isn't any code for it. Something in your body starts it."

I didn't have any idea what she was talking about.

"After it has happened, you'll be tired. It uses up your energy." She studied the back of the packet, then she scooted closer to me, so we were both sitting cross-legged with our knees touching. Wanji had hard, bony knees, even through the felt of her dress.

"Open your eye, very wide," she said.

"Wait," I said. "Is this going to hurt?"

"No," she said.

I opened my eyes as wide as I could.

"Look down, but keep your eyes wide open," she said.

I tried.

"No," she said, irritated, "keep your eyes open."

"They are open," I said. I didn't think she should treat me this way. My da had just died. She should be nice to me. I could hear her open the packet. I wanted to blink but I was afraid to. I did, because I couldn't help it.

She leaned forward and spread my eye open with thumb and forefinger. Then she swiftly touched my eye.

I jerked back. There was something in my eye. I could feel it, up under my eyelid. It was very uncomfortable. I blinked and blinked and blinked. My eye filled up with tears, just the one eye, which was very very strange.

My eye socket started to ache. "It hurts," I said.

"It won't last long," she said.

"You said it wouldn't hurt!" I said, startled.

"I lied," Wanji said, matter-of-fact.

It hurt more and more. I moaned. "You're hateful," I said.

"That's true," she said, unperturbed.

She picked up the third packet, the red one.

"No," I said, "I won't hurt! I won't! You can't do it!"

"Hush," she said, "This one won't hurt. I saved it until last on purpose."

"You're lying!" I scrambled away from her. The air was cold where the nest of rugs and blankets had been wrapped around me. My head ached. It just ached. And I still couldn't hear anything out of my left ear.

"Look," she said, "I will read you the lingua. It is a patch, nothing more. It says it will feel cold, but that is all. See, it is just a square of cloth that will rest on your neck. If it hurts you can take it off.''

I scrambled backward away from her.

''Janna,'' she said. ''Enough!'' She was angry.

I was afraid of it, but I was still more afraid of Wanji. So I hunched down in front of her. I was so afraid that I sobbed while she peeled the back off the square and put it on me.

''See,'' she said, still sharp with me, ''it doesn't hurt at all. Stop crying. Stop it. Enough is enough.'' She waved her hands over her head in disgust. ''You are hysterical.''

I held my hand over the patch. It didn't hurt but it did feel cold. I scrunched up and wrapped myself in a rug and gave myself over to my misery. My head hurt and my ear still ached faintly and I was starting to feel dizzy.

''Lie down,'' Wanji said. ''Go on, lie down. I'll wake you when we can set the signal.''

I made myself a nest in the mess of Wanji's floor and piled a blanket and a rug on top of me. Maybe the dark made my head feel better, I didn't know. But I fell asleep.

Wanji shook me awake. I hadn't been asleep long, and my head still ached. She had the little metal fork from the ear packet, the yellow packet. It occurred to me that she might stick it in my ear.

I covered my ear with my hand. My head hurt enough. I wasn't going to let Wanji stick a fork in my ear.

''Don't scowl,'' she said.

''My head hurts,'' I said.

''Are you dizzy?'' she asked.

I felt out of sorts, unbalanced, but not dizzy, not really.

''Shake your head,'' Wanji said.

I shook my head. Still the same, but no worse. ''Don't stick that in my ear,'' I said.

''What? I'm not going to stick this in your ear. It's a musical fork. I'm going to make a sound with it and hold it to your ear. When I tell you to I want you to whistle something, okay?''

''Whistle what?'' I said.

''Anything,'' she said, ''I don't care. Whistle something for me now.''

I couldn't think of anything to whistle. I couldn't think of anything at all except that I wished Wanji would leave me alone and let me go back to sleep.

Wanji squatted there. Implacable old bitch.

I finally thought of something to whistle, a crazy dog song for children. I started whistling—

''That's enough,'' she said. ''Now don't say anything else, but when I nod my head you whistle that. Don't say anything to me. If you do, it will ruin everything. Nod your head if you understand.''

I nodded.

She slapped the fork against her hand and I could see the long tines vibrating.

She held it up to my ear, the one I couldn't hear anything out of. She held it there, concentrating fiercely. Then she nodded.

I whistled.

"Okay," she said. "Good. That is how you start it. Now whistle it again."

I whistled.

Everything went dark and then suddenly my head got very hot. Then I could see again.

"Good," Wanji said. "You just sent a signal."

"Why did everything get dark?" I asked.

"All the light got used in the signal," Wanji said. "It used all the light in your head so you couldn't see."

My head hurt even worse. Now besides my eye aching, my temples were pounding. I had a fever. I raised my hand and felt my hot cheek.

Wanji picked up the blue packet. "Now we have to figure out about the third one, the one that will let you hibernate."

I didn't want to learn about hibernating. "I feel sick," I said.

"It's probably too soon, anyway," Wanji said. "Sleep for a while."

I felt so awful I didn't know if I could sleep. But Wanji brought me more tea and I drank that and lay down in my nest and presently I was dreaming.

iv

There was a sound of gunfire, far away, just a pop. And then more *pop-pop-pop.*

It startled me, although I had been hearing the outrunners' guns at night since they got here. I woke with a fever and everything felt as if I were still dreaming. I was alone in Wanji's house. The lamp was still lit but I didn't know if it had been refilled or how long I had slept. During the long night of winterdark it is hard to know when you are. I got up, put out the lamp, and went outside.

Morning cold is worst when you are warm from sleep. The dry snow crunched in the dark. Nothing was moving except the dogs were barking, their voices coming at me from every way.

The outrunners were gone from the center of town, nothing there but the remains of their fire and the trampled slick places where they had walked. I slid a bit as I walked there. My head felt light and I concentrated on my walking because if I did not think about it I didn't know what my feet would do. I had to pee.

Again I heard the *pop-pop-pop.* I could not tell where it was coming from because it echoed off the buildings around me. I could smell smoke and see the dull glow of fire above the trees. It was down from Sckarline, the fire. At first I thought they had gotten a really big fire going, and then I thought they had set fire to the distillery. I headed for home.

Veronique was asleep in a nest of blankets, including some of my parents' blankets from their bed.

"They set fire to the distillery," I said. I didn't say it in English, but she sat up and rubbed her face.

"It's cold," she said.

I could not think of anything to respond.

She sat there, holding her head.

"Come," I said, working into English. "We go see your teacher." I pulled on her arm.

"Where is everybody?" she said.

"My father die, my mother is, um, waiting with the die."

She frowned at me. I knew I hadn't made any sense. I pulled on her again and she got up and stumbled around, putting on boots and jacket.

Outside I heard the *pop-pop-pop* again. This time I thought maybe it was closer.

"They're shooting again?" she asked.

"They shoot my father," I said.

"Oh God," she said. She sat down on the blankets. "Oh God."

I pulled on her arm.

"Are you all right?" she asked.

"Hurry," I said. I made a pack of blankets. I found my ax and a few things and put them in the bundle, then slung it all over my shoulders. I didn't know what we would do, but if they were shooting people we should run away. I had to pee really bad.

She did hurry, finally awake. When we went outside and the cold hit her she shuddered and shook off the last of the sleep. I saw the movement of her shoulders against the glow of the fire on the horizon, against the false dawn.

People were moving, clinging close to houses where they were invisible against the black wood, avoiding the open spaces. We stayed close to my house, waiting to see whose people were moving. Veronique held my arm. A dog came past the schoolhouse into the open area where the outrunners' fire had been and stopped and sniffed—maybe the place where my father had died.

I drew Veronique back, along to the back of the house. The spirit door was closed and my father was dead. I crouched low and ran, holding her arm, until we were in the trees and then she slipped and fell and pulled me down too. We slid feet first in the snow, down the hill between the tree trunks, hidden in the pools of shadow under the trees. Then we were still, waiting.

I still felt feverish and nothing was real.

The snow under the trees was all powder. It dusted our leggings and clung in clumps in the wrinkles behind my knees.

Nothing came after us that we could see. We got up and walked deeper into the trees and then uphill, away from the distillery but still skirting the village. I left her for a moment to pee, but she followed me and we squatted together. We should run, but I didn't know where to run to and the settlement pulled at me. I circled around it as if on a tether, pulling in closer and closer as we got to the uphill part of town. Coming back around we hung in the trees beyond the field behind the schoolhouse. I could see the stabros pens and see light. The outrunners were in the stabros pens and the stabros were down. A couple of the men were dressing the carcasses.

We stumbled over Harup in the darkness. Literally fell over him in the bushes.

He was dead. His stomach was ripped by rifle fire and his eyes were open. I couldn't tell in the darkness if he had dragged himself out here to die or if someone had thrown the body here. We were too close.

I started backing away. Veronique was stiff as a spooked stabros. She lifted her feet high out of the snow, coming down hard and loud. One of the dogs at the stabros pen heard us and started to bark. I could see it in the light, its ears up and its tail curled over its back. The others barked too, ears toward us in the dark. I stopped and Veronique stopped too. Men in the pen looked out in the dark. A couple of them picked up rifles, and cradling them in their arms walked out toward us from the light.

I backed up, slowly. Maybe they would find Harup's body and think that the dogs were barking at that. But they were hunters and they would see the marks of our boots in the snow and follow us. If we ran they would hear us. I was not a hunter. I did not know what to do.

We backed up, one slow step and then another, while the outrunners walked out away from the light. They were not coming straight at us, but they were walking side by side and they would spread out and find us. I had my knife. There was cover around, mostly trees, but I didn't know what I could do against a hunter with a rifle, and even if I could stop one the others would hear us.

There were shouts over by the houses.

The outrunners kept walking but the shouts did not stop, and then there was the pop of guns. That stopped one and then the other and they half-turned.

The dogs turned, barking, toward the shouts.

The outrunners started to jog toward the schoolhouse.

We walked backward in the dark.

There were flames over there, at the houses. I couldn't tell whose house was on fire. It was downhill from the schoolhouse, which meant it might be our house. People were running in between the schoolhouse and Wanji's house and the out-runners lifted their guns and fired. People, three of them, kept on running.

The outrunners fired again and again. One of the people stumbled but they all kept running. They were black shapes skimming on the field. The snow on the field was not deep because the wind blew it into the trees. Then one was in the trees. The outrunners fired again, but the other two made the trees as well.

There was a summer camp out this way, down by the river, for drying fish.

I pulled on Veronique's arm and we picked our way through the trees.

There were people at the summer camp and we waited in the trees to make sure they were Sckarline people. It was gray, false dawn by the time we got there. I didn't remember ever having seen the summer camp in the winter before. The drying racks were bare poles with a top covering of snow, and the lean-to was almost covered in drifted snow. There was no shelter here.

There were signs of three or four people in the trampled snow. I didn't think it would be the outrunners down there because how would they even know where the summer camp was but I was not sure of anything. I didn't know if I was thinking right or not.

Veronique leaned close to my ear and whispered so softly I could barely hear. "We have to go back."

I shook my head.

"Ian is there."

Ian. Ian. She meant her teacher.

She had a hood on her purple clothing and I pulled it back to whisper, "Not now. We wait here." So close to the brown shell of her ear. Like soft dark leather. Not like a real people's ear. She was shivering.

I didn't feel too cold. I still had a fever—I felt as if everything were far from me, as if I walked half in this world. I sat and looked at the snow cupped in a brown leaf and my mind was empty and things did not seem too bad. I don't know how long we sat.

Someone walked in the summer camp. I thought it was Sored, one of the boys.

I took Veronique's arm and tugged her up. I was stiff from sitting and colder than I had noticed but moving helped. We slid down the hill into the summer camp.

The summer camp sat in a V that looked at the river frozen below. Sored was already out of the camp when we got there, but he waved at us from the trees and we scrambled back up there. Veronique slipped and used her hands.

There were two people crouched around a fire so tiny it was invisible and one of them was Tuuvin.

"Where is everyone else?" Sored asked.

"I don't know," I said. Tuuvin stood up.

"Where's your mother and your sister?" he asked.

"I was at Wanji's house all night," I said. "Where's your family?"

"My da and I were at the stabros pen this morning with Harup," he said.

"We found Harup," I said.

"Did you find my da?" he asked.

"No. Was he shot?"

"I don't know. I don't think so."

"We saw some people running across the field behind the schoolhouse. Maybe one of them was shot."

He looked down at Gerda, crouched by the fire. "None of us were shot."

"Did you come together?"

"No," Sored said. "I found Gerda here and Tuuvin here."

He had gone down to see the fire at the distillery. The outrunners had taken some of the casks. He didn't know how the fire had started, if it was an accident or if they'd done it on purpose. It would be easy to start if someone spilled something too close to the fire.

Veronique was crouched next to the tiny fire. "Janna," she said, "has anyone seen Ian?"

"Did you see the offworlder teacher?" I asked.

No one had.

"We have to find him," she said.

"Okay," I said.

"What are you going to do with her?" Sored asked, pointing at Veronique with his chin. "Is she ill?"

She crouched over the fire like someone who was sick.

"She's not sick," I said. "We need to see what is happening at Sckarline."

"I'm not going back," Gerda said, looking at no one. I did not know Gerda very well. She was old enough to have children but she had no one. She lived by herself. She had her nose slit by her clan for adultery but I never knew if she had a husband with her old clan or not. Some people came to Sckarline because they didn't want to be part of their clan anymore. Most of them went back, but Gerda had stayed.

Tuuvin said, "I'll go."

Sored said he would stay in case anyone else came to the summer camp. In a day or two they were going to head toward the west and see if they could come across the winter pastures of Haufsdaag Clan. Sored had kin there.

"That's pretty far," Tuuvin said. "Toolie Clan would be closer."

"You have kin with Toolie Clan," Sored said.

Tuuvin nodded.

"We go to Sckarline," I said to Veronique.

She stood up. "It's so damn cold," she said. Then she said something about wanting coffee. I didn't understand a lot of what she said. Then she laughed and said she wished she could have breakfast.

Sored looked at me. I didn't translate what she had said. He turned his back on her, but she didn't notice.

It took us through the sunrise and beyond the short midwinter morning and into afternoon to get to Sckarline. The only good thing about winterdark is that it would be dark for the outrunners too.

Only hours of daylight.

Nothing was moving when we got back to Sckarline. From the back the school-house looked all right, but the houses were all burned. I could see where my house had been. Charred logs standing in the red afternoon sun. The ground around them was wet and muddy from the heat of the fires.

Tuuvin's house. Ayudesh's house and Wanji's house.

In front of the schoolhouse there were bodies. My da's body, thrown back in the snow. My mam and my sister. My sister's head was broken in. My mam didn't have her pants on. The front of the schoolhouse had burned but the fire must have burned out before the whole building was gone. The dogs were moving among the bodies, sniffing, stopping to tug on the freezing flesh.

Tuuvin shouted at them to drive them off.

My mam's hip bones were sharp under the bloody skin and her sex was there for everyone to see but I kept noticing her bare feet. The soles were dark. Her toenails were thick and her feet looked old, an old old woman's feet. As if she were as old as Wanji.

I looked at people to see who else was there. I saw Wanji, although she had no face but I knew her from her skin. Veronique's teacher was there, his face red and peeled from fire and his eyes baked white like a smoked fish. Ayudesh had no ears and no sex. His clothes had been taken.

The dogs were circling back, watching Tuuvin.

He screamed at them. Then he crouched down on his heels and covered his eyes with his arm and cried.

I did not feel anything. Not yet.

I whistled the tune that Wanji had taught me to send out the message, and the world went dark. It was something to do, and for a moment, I didn't have to look at my mother's bare feet.

The place for the Sckarline dead was up the hill beyond the town, away from the river, but without stabros I couldn't think of how we could get all these bodies there. We didn't have anything for the bodies, either. Nothing for the spirit journey, not even blankets to wrap them in.

I could not bear to think of my mother without pants. There were lots of dead women in the snow and many of them did have pants. It may not have been fair that my mother should have someone else's but I could not think of anything else to do so I took the leggings off of Maitra and tried to put them on my mother. I could not really get them right—my mother was tall and her body was stiff from the cold and from death. I hated handling her.

Veronique asked me what I was doing but even if I knew enough English to answer, I was too embarrassed to really try to explain.

My mother's flesh was white and odd to touch. Not like flesh at all. Like plastic. Soft looking but not to touch.

Tuuvin watched me without saying anything. I thought he might tell me not to, but he didn't. Finally he said, "We can't get them to the place for the dead."

I didn't know what to say to that.

"We don't have anyone to talk to the spirits," he said. "Only me."

He was the man here. I didn't know if Tuuvin had talked with spirits or not, people didn't talk about that with women.

"I say that this place is a place of the dead too," he said. His voice was strange. "Sckarline is a place of the dead now."

"We leave them here?" I asked.

He nodded.

He was beardless, but he was a boy and he was old enough that he had walked through the spirit door. I was glad that he had made the decision.

I looked in houses for things for the dead to have with them, but most things were burned. I found things half-burned and sometimes not burned at all. I found a fur, and used that to wrap the woman whose leggings I had stolen. I tried to make sure that everybody got something—a bit of stitching or a cup or something, so they would not be completely without possessions. I managed to find something for almost everybody, and I found enough blankets to wrap Tuuvin's family and Veronique's teacher. I wrapped Bet with my mother. I kept blankets separate for Veronique, Tuuvin, and me and anything I found that we could use I didn't give to the dead, but everything else I gave to them.

Tuuvin sat in the burned-out schoolhouse and I didn't know if what he did was a spirit thing or if it was just grief, but I didn't bother him. He kept the dogs away. Veronique followed me and picked through the blackened sticks of the houses. Both of us had black all over our gloves and our clothes and black marks on our faces.

We stopped when it got too dark, and then we made camp in the schoolhouse next to the dead. Normally I would not have been able to stay so close to the dead, but now I felt part of them.

Tuuvin had killed and skinned a dog and cooked that. Veronique cried while she ate. Not like Tuuvin had cried. Not sobs. Just helpless tears that ran down her face. As if she didn't notice.

"What are we going to do?" she asked.

Tuuvin said, "We will try for Toolie Clan."

I didn't have any idea where their winter pastures were, much less how to find them, and I almost asked Tuuvin if he did, but I didn't want to shame his new manhood, so I didn't.

"The skimmer will come back here," Veronique said. "I have to wait here."

"We can't wait here," Tuuvin said. "It is going to get darker, winter is coming and we'll have no sun. We don't have any animals. We can't live here."

I told her what Tuuvin said. "I have, in here"—I pointed to my head—"I call your people. Wanji give to me."

Veronique didn't understand and didn't even really try.

I tried not to think about the dogs wandering among the dead. I tried not to think about bad weather. I tried not to think about my house or my mam. It did not leave much to think about.

Tuuvin had kin with Toolie Clan but I didn't. Tuuvin was my clankin, though, even if he wasn't a cousin or anything. I wondered if he would still want me after we got to Toolie Clan. Maybe there would be other girls. New girls, that he had never talked to before. They would be pretty, some of them.

My kin were Lagskold. I didn't know where their pastures were, but someone would know. I could go to them if I didn't like Toolie Clan. I had met a couple of my cousins when they came and brought my father's half brother, my little uncle.

"Listen," Tuuvin said, touching my arm.

I didn't hear it at first, then I did.

"What?" Veronique said. "Are they coming back?"

"Hush," Tuuvin snapped at her, and even though she didn't understand the word she did.

It was a skimmer.

It was far away. Skimmers didn't land at night. They didn't even come at night. It had come to my message, I guessed.

Tuuvin got up, and Veronique scrambled to her feet and we all went out to the edge of the field behind the schoolhouse.

"You can hear it?" I asked Veronique.

She shook her head.

"Listen," I said. I could hear it. Just a rumble. "The skimmer."

"The skimmer?" she said. "The skimmer is coming? Oh God. Oh God. I wish we had lights for them. We need light, to signal them that someone is here."

"Tell her to hush," Tuuvin said.

"I send message," I said. "They know someone is here."

"We should move the fire."

I could send them another message, but Wanji had said to do it one time a day until they came and they were here.

Dogs started barking.

Finally we saw lights from the skimmer, strange green and red stars. They moved against the sky as if they had been shaken loose.

Veronique stopped talking and stood still.

The lights came toward us for a long time. They got bigger and brighter, more than any star. It seemed as if they stopped but the lights kept getting brighter and

I finally decided that they were coming straight toward us and it didn't look as if they were moving but they were.

Then we could see the skimmer in its own lights.

It flew low over us and Veronique shouted, "I'm here! I'm here!"

I shouted, and Tuuvin shouted too, but the skimmer didn't seem to hear us. But then it turned and slowly curved around, the sound of it going farther away and then just hanging in the air. It got to where it had been before and came back. This time it came even lower and it dropped red lights. One. Two. Three.

Then a third time it came around and I wondered what it would do now. But this time it landed, the sound of it so loud that I could feel it as well as hear it. It was a different skimmer from the one we always saw. It was bigger, with a belly like it was pregnant. It was white and red. It settled easily on the snow. Its engines, pointed down, melted snow underneath them.

And then it sat. Lights blinked. The red lights on the ground flickered. The dogs barked.

Veronique ran toward it.

The door opened and a man called out to watch something but I didn't understand. Veronique stopped and from where I was she was a black shape against the lights of the skimmer.

Finally a man jumped down, and then two more men and two women and they ran to Veronique.

She gestured and the lights flickered in the movements of her arms until my eyes hurt and I looked away. I couldn't see anything around us. The offworlders' lights made me quite night-blind.

"Janna," Veronique called. "Tuuvin!" She waved at us to come over. So we walked out of the dark into the relentless lights of the skimmer.

I couldn't understand what anyone was saying in English. They asked me questions, but I just kept shaking my head. I was tired and now, finally, I wanted to cry.

"Janna," Veronique said. "You called them. Did you call them?"

I nodded.

"How?"

"Wanji give me . . . In my head . . ." I had no idea how to explain. I pointed to my ear.

One of the women came over, and handling my head as if I were a stabros, turned it so she could push my hair out of the way and look in my ear. I still couldn't hear very well out of that ear. Her handling wasn't rough, but it was not something people do to each other.

She was talking and nodding, but I didn't try to understand. The English washed over us and around us.

One of the men brought us something hot and bitter and sweet to drink. The drink was in blue plastic cups, the same color as the jackets that they all wore except for one man whose jacket was red with blue writing. Pretty things. Veronique drank hers gratefully. I made myself drink mine. Anything this black and bitter must have been medicine. Tuuvin just held his.

Then they got hand lights and we all walked over and looked at the bodies. Dogs ran from the lights, staying at the edges and slinking as if guilty of something.

"Janna," Veronique said. "Which one is Ian? Which is my teacher?"

I had to walk between the bodies. We had laid them out so their heads all faced the schoolhouse and their feet all faced the center of the village. They were more bundles than people. I could have told her in the light, but in the dark, with the hand lights making it hard to see anything but where they were pointed, it took me a while. I found Harup by mistake. Then I found the teacher.

Veronique cried and the woman who had looked in my ear held her like she was her child. But that woman didn't look dark like Veronique at all and I thought she was just kin because she was an offworlder, not by blood. All the offworlders were like Sckarline; kin because of where they were, not because of family.

The two men in blue jackets picked up the body of the teacher. With the body they were clumsy on the packed snow. The man holding the teacher's head slipped and fell. Tuuvin took the teacher's head and I took his feet. His boots were gone. His feet were as naked as my mother's. I had wrapped him in a skin but it wasn't very big so his feet hung out. But they were so cold they felt like meat, not like a person.

We walked right up to the door of the skimmer and I could look in. It was big inside. Hollow. It was dark in the back. I had thought it would be all lights inside and I was disappointed. There were things hanging on the walls but mostly it was empty. One of the offworld men jumped up into the skimmer and then he was not clumsy at all. He pulled the body to the back of the skimmer.

They were talking again. Tuuvin and I stood there. Tuuvin's breath was an enormous white plume in the lights of the skimmer. I stamped my feet. The lights were bright but they were a cheat. They didn't make you any warmer.

The offworlders wanted to go back to the bodies, so we did. "Your teachers," Veronique said. "Where are your teachers?"

I remembered Wanji's body. It had no face, but it was easy to tell it was her. Ayudesh's body was still naked under the blanket I had found. The blanket was burned along one side and didn't cover him. Where his sex had been, the frozen blood shone in the hand lights. I thought the dogs might have been at him, but I couldn't tell.

They wanted to take Wanji's and Ayudesh's bodies back to the skimmer. They motioned for us to pick up Ayudesh.

"Wait," Tuuvin said. "They shouldn't do that."

I squatted down.

"They are Sckarline people," Tuuvin said.

"Their spirit is already gone," I said.

"They won't have anything," he said.

"If the offworlders take them, won't they give them offworld things?"

"They didn't want offworld things," Tuuvin said. "That's why they were here."

"But we don't have anything to give them. At least if the offworlders give them things they'll have something."

Tuuvin shook his head. "Harup—" he started to say but stopped. Harup talked to spirits more than anyone. He would have known. But I didn't know how to ask him and I didn't think Tuuvin did either. Although I wasn't sure. There wasn't any drum or anything for spirit talk anyway.

The offworlders stood looking at us.

"Okay," Tuuvin said. So I stood up and we picked up Ayudesh's body and the two offworld men picked up Wanji's body and we took them to the skimmer.

A dog followed us in the dark.

The man in the red jacket climbed up and went to the front of the skimmer. There were chairs there and he sat in one and talked to someone on a radio. I could remember the word for radio in English. Ayudesh used to have one until it stopped working and he didn't get another.

My thoughts rattled through my empty head.

They put the bodies of the teachers next to the body of Veronique's teacher. Tuuvin and I stood outside the door, leaning in to watch them. The floor of the skimmer was metal.

One of the blue-jacket men brought us two blankets. The blankets were the same blue as his jacket and had a red symbol on them. A circle with words. I didn't pay much attention to them. He brought us foil packets. Five. Ten of them.

"Food," he said, pointing to the packets.

I nodded. "Food," I repeated.

"Do they have guns?" Tuuvin asked harshly.

"Guns?" I asked. "You have guns?"

"No guns," the blue jacket said. "No guns."

I didn't know if we were supposed to get in the skimmer or if the gifts meant to go. Veronique came over and sat down in the doorway. She hugged me. "Thank you, Janna," she whispered. "Thank you."

Then she got up.

"Move back," said the red jacket, shooing us.

We trotted back away from the skimmer. Its engines fired and the ground underneath them steamed. The skimmer rose, and then the engines turned from pointing down to pointing back and it moved off. Heavy and slow at first, but then faster and faster. Higher and higher.

We blinked in the darkness, holding our gifts.

BICYCLE REPAIRMAN

Bruce Sterling

▼

Here's a fascinating look at an ordinary day in the life of an ordinary working man in a high-tech future where everything is much the same as it is now—except for being completely different, *of course!*

One of the most powerful and innovative talents in SF today, Bruce Sterling sold his first story in 1976. By the end of the '80s, he had established himself, with a series of stories set in his exotic Shaper/Mechanist future, with novels such as the complex and Stapledonian Schismatrix *and the well-received* Islands in the Net *(as well as with his editing of the influential anthology* Mirrorshades: The Cyberpunk Anthology *and the infamous critical magazine* Cheap Truth*), as perhaps the prime driving force behind the revolutionary Cyberpunk movement in science fiction (rivaled for that title only by his friend and collaborator, William Gibson), and also as one of the best new hard-science writers to enter the field in some time. His other books include the novels* The Artificial Kid *and* Involution Ocean; *a novel in collaboration with William Gibson,* The Difference Engine; *and the landmark collections* Crystal Express *and* Globalhead. *His most recent books are a critically acclaimed nonfiction study of First Amendment issues in the world of computer networking,* The Hacker Crackdown: Law and Disorder on the Electronic Frontier, *the novels* Heavy Weather *and* Holy Fire, *and the omnibus collection (it contains the novel* Schismatrix *as well as most of his Shaper/Mechanist stories)* Schismatrix Plus. *His stories have appeared in our First, Second, Third, Fourth, Fifth, Sixth, Seventh, Eighth, and Eleventh Annual Collections. He lives with his family in Austin, Texas.*

Repeated tinny banging woke Lyle in his hammock. Lyle groaned, sat up, and slid free into the tool-crowded aisle of his bike shop.

Lyle hitched up the black elastic of his skintight shorts and plucked yesterday's grease-stained sleeveless off the workbench. He glanced blearily at his chronometer as he picked his way toward the door. It was 10:04.38 in the morning, June 27, 2037.

Lyle hopped over a stray can of primer and the floor boomed gently beneath his feet. With all the press of work, he'd collapsed into sleep without properly cleaning the shop. Doing custom enameling paid okay, but it ate up time like crazy. Working and living alone was wearing him out.

Lyle opened the shop door, revealing a long sheer drop to dusty tiling far below.

Pigeons darted beneath the hull of his shop through a soot-stained hole in the broken atrium glass, and wheeled off to their rookery somewhere in the darkened guts of the high-rise.

More banging. Far below, a uniformed delivery kid stood by his cargo tricycle, yanking rhythmically at the long dangling string of Lyle's spot-welded door-knocker.

Lyle waved, yawning. From his vantage point below the huge girders of the cavernous atrium, Lyle had a fine overview of three burnt-out interior levels of the old Tsatanuga Archiplat. Once-elegant handrails and battered pedestrian overlooks fronted on the great airy cavity of the atrium. Behind the handrails was a three-floor wilderness of jury-rigged lights, chicken coops, water tanks, and squatters' flags. The fire-damaged floors, walls, and ceilings were riddled with handmade descent-chutes, long coiling staircases, and rickety ladders.

Lyle took note of a crew of Chattanooga demolition workers in their yellow detox suits. The repair crew was deploying vacuum scrubbers and a high-pressure hose-off by the vandal-proofed western elevators of Floor Thirty-four. Two or three days a week, the city crew meandered into the damage zone to pretend to work, with a great hypocritical show of sawhorses and barrier tape. The lazy sons of bitches were all on the take.

Lyle thumbed the brake switches in their big metal box by the flywheel. The bike shop slithered, with a subtle hiss of cable-clamps, down three stories, to dock with a grating crunch onto four concrete-filled metal drums.

The delivery kid looked real familiar. He was in and out of the zone pretty often. Lyle had once done some custom work on the kid's cargo trike, new shocks and some granny-gearing as he recalled, but he couldn't remember the kid's name. Lyle was terrible with names. "What's up, zude?"

"Hard night, Lyle?"

"Just real busy."

The kid's nose wrinkled at the stench from the shop. "Doin' a lot of paint work, huh?" He glanced at his palmtop notepad. "You still taking deliveries for Edward Dertouzas?"

"Yeah. I guess so." Lyle rubbed the gear tattoo on one stubbled cheek. "If I have to."

The kid offered a stylus, reaching up. "Can you sign for him?"

Lyle folded his bare arms warily. "Naw, man, I can't sign for Deep Eddy. Eddy's in Europe somewhere. Eddy left months ago. Haven't seen Eddy in ages."

The delivery kid scratched his sweating head below his billed fabric cap. He turned to check for any possible sneak-ups by snatch-and-grab artists out of the squatter warrens. The government simply refused to do postal delivery on the Thirty-second, Thirty-third, and Thirty-fourth floors. You never saw many cops inside the zone, either. Except for the city demolition crew, about the only official functionaries who ever showed up in the zone were a few psychotically empathetic NAFTA social workers.

"I'll get a bonus if you sign for this thing." The kid gazed up in squint-eyed appeal. "It's gotta be worth something, Lyle. It's a really weird kind of routing; they paid a lot of money to send it just that way."

Lyle crouched down in the open doorway. "Let's have a look at it."

The package was a heavy shockproof rectangle in heat-sealed plastic shrink-wrap, with a plethora of intra-European routing stickers. To judge by all the over-lays, the package had been passed from postal system to postal system at least eight times before officially arriving in the legal custody of any human being. The return address, if there had ever been one, was completely obscured. Someplace in France, maybe.

Lyle held the box up two-handed to his ear and shook it. Hardware.

"You gonna sign, or not?"

"Yeah." Lyle scratched illegibly at the little signature panel, then looked at the delivery trike. "You oughta get that front wheel trued."

The kid shrugged. "Got anything to send out today?"

"Naw," Lyle grumbled, "I'm not doing mail-order repair work anymore; it's too complicated and I get ripped off too much."

"Suit yourself." The kid clambered into the recumbent seat of his trike and pedaled off across the heat-cracked ceramic tiles of the atrium plaza.

Lyle hung his hand-lettered OPEN FOR BUSINESS sign outside the door. He walked to his left, stamped up the pedaled lid of a jumbo garbage can, and dropped the package in with the rest of Dertouzas's stuff.

The can's lid wouldn't close. Deep Eddy's junk had finally reached critical mass. Deep Eddy never got much mail at the shop from other people, but he was always sending mail to himself. Big packets of encrypted diskettes were always arriving from Eddy's road jaunts in Toulouse, Marseilles, Valencia, and Nice. And espe-cially Barcelona. Eddy had sent enough gigabyteage out of Barcelona to outfit a pirate data-haven.

Eddy used Lyle's bike shop as his safety-deposit box. This arrangement was okay by Lyle. He owed Eddy; Eddy had installed the phones and virching in the bike shop, and had also wangled the shop's electrical hookup. A thick elastic curly-cable snaked out the access crawlspace of Floor Thirty-five, right through the ceil-ing of Floor Thirty-four, and directly through a ragged punch-hole in the aluminum roof of Lyle's cable-mounted mobile home. Some unknown contact of Eddy's was paying the real bills on that electrical feed. Lyle cheerfully covered the expenses by paying cash into an anonymous post-office box. The setup was a rare and valuable contact with the world of organized authority.

During his stays in the shop, Eddy had spent much of his time buried in marathon long-distance virtuality sessions, swaddled head to foot in lumpy strap-on gear. Eddy had been painfully involved with some older woman in Germany. A virtual romance in its full-scale thumping, heaving, grappling progress, was an embar-rassment to witness. Under the circumstances, Lyle wasn't too surprised that Eddy had left his parents' condo to set up in a squat.

Eddy had lived in the bicycle-repair shop, off and on, for almost a year. It had been a good deal for Lyle, because Deep Eddy had enjoyed a certain clout and prestige with the local squatters. Eddy had been a major organizer of the legendary Chattanooga Wende of December '35, a monster street party that had climaxed in a spectacular looting-and-arson rampage that had torched the three floors of the Archiplat.

Lyle had gone to school with Eddy and had known him for years; they'd grown up together in the Archiplat. Eddy Dertouzas was a deep zude for a kid his age, with political contacts and heavy-duty network connections. The squat had been a good deal for both of them, until Eddy had finally coaxed the German woman into coming through for him in real life. Then Eddy had jumped the next plane to Europe.

Since they'd parted friends, Eddy was welcome to mail his European data-junk to the bike shop. After all, the disks were heavily encrypted, so it wasn't as if anybody in authority was ever gonna be able to read them. Storing a few thousand disks was a minor challenge, compared to Eddy's complex, machine-assisted love life.

After Eddy's sudden departure, Lyle had sold Eddy's possessions, and wired the money to Eddy in Spain. Lyle had kept the screen TV, Eddy's mediator, and the cheaper virching helmet. The way Lyle figured it—the way he remembered the deal—any stray hardware of Eddy's in the shop was rightfully his, for disposal at his own discretion. By now it was pretty clear that Deep Eddy Dertouzas was never coming back to Tennessee. And Lyle had certain debts.

Lyle snicked the blade from a roadkit multitool and cut open Eddy's package. It contained, of all things, a television cable set-top box. A laughable infobahn antique. You'd never see a cable box like that in NAFTA; this was the sort of primeval junk one might find in the home of a semiliterate Basque grandmother, or maybe in the armed bunker of some backward Albanian.

Lyle tossed the archaic cable box onto the beanbag in front of the wallscreen. No time now for irrelevant media toys; he had to get on with real life. Lyle ducked into the tiny curtained privy and urinated at length into a crockery jar. He scraped his teeth with a flossing spudger and misted some fresh water onto his face and hands. He wiped clean with a towelette, then smeared his armpits, crotch, and feet with deodorant.

Back when he'd lived with his mom up on Floor Forty-one, Lyle had used old-fashioned antiseptic deodorants. Lyle had wised up about a lot of things once he'd escaped his mom's condo. Nowadays, Lyle used a gel roll-on of skin-friendly bacteria that greedily devoured human sweat and exuded as their metabolic by-product a pleasantly harmless reek rather like ripe bananas. Life was a lot easier when you came to proper terms with your microscopic flora.

Back at his workbench, Lyle plugged in the hot plate and boiled some Thai noodles with flaked sardines. He packed down breakfast with four hundred cc's of Dr. Breasaire's Bioactive Bowel Putty. Then he checked last night's enamel job on the clamped frame in the workstand. The frame looked good. At three in the morning, Lyle was able to get into painted detail work with just the right kind of hallucinatory clarity.

Enameling paid well, and he needed the money bad. But this wasn't real bike work. It lacked authenticity. Enameling was all about the owner's ego—that was what really stank about enameling. There were a few rich kids up in the penthouse levels who were way into "street aesthetic," and would pay good money to have some treadhead decorate their machine. But flash art didn't help the bike. What helped the bike was frame alignment and sound cable-housings and proper tension in the derailleurs.

Lyle fitted the chain of his stationary bike to the shop's flywheel, straddled up, strapped on his gloves and virching helmet, and did half an hour on the 2033 Tour de France. He stayed back in the pack for the uphill grind, and then, for three glorious minutes, he broke free from the *domestiques* in the *peloton* and came right up at the shoulder of Aldo Cipollini. The champion was a monster, posthuman. Calves like cinder blocks. Even in a cheap simulation with no full-impact bodysuit, Lyle knew better than to try to take Cipollini.

Lyle devirched, checked his heart-rate record on the chronometer, then dismounted from his stationary trainer and drained a half-liter squeeze bottle of antioxidant carbo refresher. Life had been easier when he'd had a partner in crime. The shop's flywheel was slowly losing its storage of inertia power these days, with just one zude pumping it.

Lyle's disastrous second roommate had come from the biking crowd. She was a criterium racer from Kentucky named Brigitte Rohannon. Lyle himself had been a wannabe criterium racer for a while, before he'd blown out a kidney on steroids. He hadn't expected any trouble from Brigitte, because Brigitte knew about bikes, and she needed his technical help for her racer, and she wouldn't mind pumping the flywheel, and besides, Brigitte was lesbian. In the training gym and out at racing events, Brigitte came across as a quiet and disciplined little politicized tread-head person.

Life inside the zone, though, massively fertilized Brigitte's eccentricities. First, she started breaking training. Then she stopped eating right. Pretty soon the shop was creaking and rocking with all-night girl-on-girl hot-oil sessions, which degenerated into hooting pill-orgies with heavily tattooed zone chyx who played klaxonized bongo music and beat each other up, and stole Lyle's tools. It had been a big relief when Brigitte finally left the zone to shack up with some well-to-do admirer on Floor Thirty-seven. The debacle had left Lyle's tenuous finances in ruin.

Lyle laid down a new tracery of scarlet enamel on the bike's chainstay, seat post and stem. He had to wait for the work to cure, so he left the workbench, picked up Eddy's set-topper, and popped the shell with a hexkey. Lyle was no electrician, but the insides looked harmless enough: lots of bit-eating caterpillars and cheap Algerian silicon.

He flicked on Eddy's mediator, to boot the wallscreen. Before he could try anything with the cable box, his mother's mook pounced upon the screen. On Eddy's giant wallscreen, the mook's waxy, computer-generated face looked like a plump satin pillowcase. Its bow-tie was as big as a racing shoe.

"Please hold for an incoming vidcall from Andrea Schweik of Carnac Instruments," the mook uttered unctuously.

Lyle cordially despised all low-down, phone-tagging, artificially intelligent mooks. For a while, in his teenage years, Lyle himself had owned a mook, an off-the-shelf shareware job that he'd installed in the condo's phone. Like most mooks, Lyle's mook had one primary role: dealing with unsolicited phone calls from other people's mooks. In Lyle's case these were the creepy mooks of career counselors, school psychiatrists, truancy cops, and other official hindrances. When Lyle's mook launched and ran, it appeared on-line as a sly warty dwarf that drooled green ichor and talked in a basso grumble.

But Lyle hadn't given his mook the properly meticulous care and debugging that such fragile little constructs demanded, and eventually his cheap mook had collapsed into artificial insanity.

Once Lyle had escaped his mom's place to the squat, he had gone for the low-tech gambit and simply left his phone unplugged most of the time. But that was no real solution. He couldn't hide from his mother's capable and well-financed corporate mook, which watched with sleepless mechanical patience for the least flicker of video dial tone off Lyle's number.

Lyle sighed and wiped the dust from the video nozzle on Eddy's mediator.

"Your mother is coming on-line right away," the mook assured him.

"Yeah, sure," Lyle muttered, smearing his hair into some semblance of order.

"She specifically instructed me to page her remotely at any time for an immediate response. She really wants to chat with you, Lyle."

"That's just great." Lyle couldn't remember what his mother's mook called itself. "Mr. Billy," or "Mr. Ripley," or something else really stupid. . . .

"Did you know that Marco Cengialta has just won the Liege Summer Classic?"

Lyle blinked and sat up in the beanbag. "Yeah?"

"Mr. Cengialta used a three-spoked ceramic wheel with internal liquid weighting and buckyball hubshocks." The mook paused, politely awaiting a possible conversational response. "He wore breathe-thru Kevlar microlock cleatshoes," it added.

Lyle hated the way a mook cataloged your personal interests and then generated relevant conversation. The machine-made intercourse was completely unhuman and yet perversely interesting, like being grabbed and buttonholed by a glossy magazine ad. It had probably taken his mother's mook all of three seconds to snag and download every conceivable statistic about the summer race in Liege.

His mother came on. She'd caught him during lunch in her office. "Lyle?"

"Hi, Mom." Lyle sternly reminded himself that this was the one person in the world who might conceivably put up bail for him. "What's on your mind?"

"Oh, nothing much, just the usual." Lyle's mother shoved aside her platter of sprouts and tilapia. "I was idly wondering if you were still alive."

"Mom, it's a lot less dangerous in a squat than landlords and cops would have you believe. I'm perfectly fine. You can see that for yourself."

His mother lifted a pair of secretarial half-spex on a neckchain, and gave Lyle the computer-assisted once-over.

Lyle pointed the mediator's lens at the shop's aluminum door. "See over there, Mom? I got myself a shock-baton in here. If I get any trouble from anybody, I'll just yank that club off the door mount and give the guy fifteen thousand volts!"

"Is that legal, Lyle?"

"Sure. The voltage won't kill you or anything, it just knocks you out a good long time. I traded a good bike for that shock-baton, it's got a lot of useful defensive features."

"That sounds really dreadful."

"The baton's harmless, Mom. You should see what the cops carry nowadays."

"Are you still taking those injections, Lyle?"

"Which injections?"

She frowned. "You know which ones."

Lyle shrugged. "The treatments are perfectly safe. They're a lot safer than a lifestyle of cruising for dates, that's for sure."

"Especially dates with the kind of girls who live down there in the riot zone, I suppose." His mother winced. "I had some hopes when you took up with that nice bike-racer girl. Brigitte, wasn't it? Whatever happened to her?"

Lyle shook his head. "Someone with your gender and background oughta understand how important the treatments are, Mom. It's a basic reproductive-freedom issue. Antilibidinals give you real freedom, freedom from the urge to reproduce. You should be glad I'm not sexually involved."

"I don't mind that you're not involved, Lyle, it's just that it seems like a real cheat that you're not even *interested*."

"But, Mom, nobody's interested in me, either. Nobody. No woman is banging at my door to have sex with a self-employed fanatical dropout bike mechanic who lives in a slum. If that ever happens, you'll be the first to know."

Lyle grinned cheerfully into the lens. "I had girlfriends back when I was in racing. I've been there, Mom. I've done that. Unless you're coked to the gills with hormones, sex is a major waste of your time and attention. Sexual Deliberation is the greatest civil-liberties movement of modern times."

"That's really weird, Lyle. It's just not natural."

"Mom, forgive me, but you're not the one to talk about natural, okay? You grew me from a zygote when you were fifty-five." He shrugged. "I'm too busy for romance now. I just want to learn about bikes."

"You were working with bikes when you lived here with me. You had a real job and a safe home where you could take regular showers."

"Sure, I was working, but I never said I wanted a *job*, Mom. I said I wanted to *learn about bikes*. There's a big difference! I can't be a loser wage-slave for some lousy bike franchise."

His mother said nothing.

"Mom, I'm not asking you for any favors. I don't need any bosses, or any teachers, or any landlords, or any cops. It's just me and my bike work down here. I know that people in authority can't stand it that a twenty-four-year-old man lives an independent life and does exactly what he wants, but I'm being very quiet and discreet about it, so nobody needs to bother about me."

His mother sighed, defeated. "Are you eating properly, Lyle? You look peaked."

Lyle lifted his calf muscle into camera range. "Look at this leg! Does that look like the gastrocnemius of a weak and sickly person?"

"Could you come up to the condo and have a decent meal with me sometime?"

Lyle blinked. "When?"

"Wednesday, maybe? We could have pork chops."

"Maybe, Mom. Probably. I'll have to check. I'll get back to you, okay? Bye." Lyle hung up.

Hooking the mediator's cable to the primitive set-top box was a problem, but Lyle was not one to be stymied by a merely mechanical challenge. The enamel job had to wait as he resorted to miniclamps and a cable cutter. It was a handy thing that working with modern brake cabling had taught him how to splice fiber optics.

When the set-top box finally came on-line, its array of services was a joke. Any decent modern mediator could navigate through vast information spaces, but the set-top box offered nothing but "channels." Lyle had forgotten that you could even obtain old-fashioned "channels" from the city fiber-feed in Chattanooga. But these channels were government-sponsored media, and the government was always quite a ways behind the curve in network development. Chattanooga's huge fiber-bandwidth still carried the ancient government-mandated "public-access channels," spooling away in their technically fossilized obscurity, far below the usual gaudy carnival of popular virching, infobahnage, demo-splintered comboards, public-service rants, mudtrufflage, remsnorkeling, and commercials.

The little set-top box accessed nothing but political channels. Three of them: Legislative, Judicial, and Executive. And that was the sum total, apparently. A set-top box that offered nothing but NAFTA political coverage. On the Legislative Channel there was some kind of parliamentary debate on proper land use in Manitoba. On the Judicial Channel, a lawyer was haranguing judges about the stock market for air-pollution rights. On the Executive Channel, a big crowd of hicks was idly standing around on windblown tarmac somewhere in Louisiana waiting for something to happen.

The box didn't offer any glimpse of politics in Europe or the Sphere or the South. There were no hotspots or pips or index tagging. You couldn't look stuff up or annotate it—you just had to passively watch whatever the channel's masters chose to show you, whenever they chose to show it. This media setup was so insultingly lame and halt and primitive that it was almost perversely interesting. Kind of like peering through keyholes.

Lyle left the box on the Executive Channel, because it looked conceivable that something might actually happen there. It had swiftly become clear to him that the intolerably monotonous fodder on the other two channels was about as exciting as those channels ever got. Lyle retreated to his workbench and got back to enamel work.

At length, the president of NAFTA arrived and decamped from his helicopter on the tarmac in Louisiana. A swarm of presidential bodyguards materialized out of the expectant crowd, looking simultaneously extremely busy and icily unperturbable.

Suddenly a line of text flickered up at the bottom of the screen. The text was set in a very old-fashioned computer font, chalk-white letters with little visible jagged pixel-edges. *"Look at him hunting for that camera mark,"* the subtitle read as it scrolled across the screen. *"Why wasn't he briefed properly? He looks like a stray dog!"*

The president meandered amiably across the sun-blistered tarmac, gazing from side to side, and then stopped briefly to shake the eager outstretched hand of a local politician. *"That must have hurt,"* commented the text. *"That Cajun dolt is poison in the polls."* The president chatted amiably with the local politician and an elderly harridan in a purple dress who seemed to be the man's wife. *"Get him away from those losers!"* raged the subtitle. *"Get the Man up to the podium, for the love of Mike! Where's the chief of staff? Doped up on so-called smart drugs as usual? Get with your jobs, people!"*

The president looked well. Lyle had noticed that the president of NAFTA always looked well, it seemed to be a professional requirement. The big political cheeses in Europe always looked somber and intellectual, and the Sphere people always looked humble and dedicated, and the South people always looked angry and fanatical, but the NAFTA prez always looked like he'd just done a few laps in a pool and had a brisk rubdown. His large, glossy, bluffly cheerful face was discreetly stenciled with tattoos: both cheeks, a chorus line of tats on his forehead above both eyebrows, plus a few extra logos on his rocklike chin. A president's face was the ultimate billboard for major backers and interest groups.

"Does he think we have all day?" the text demanded. *"What's with this dead air time? Can't anyone properly arrange a media event these days? You call this public access? You call this informing the electorate? If we'd known the infobahn would come to this, we'd have never built the thing!"*

The president meandered amiably to a podium covered with ceremonial microphones. Lyle had noticed that politicians always used a big healthy cluster of traditional big fat microphones, even though nowadays you could build working microphones the size of a grain of rice.

"Hey, how y'all?" asked the president, grinning.

The crowd chorused back at him, with ragged enthusiasm.

"Let these fine folks up a bit closer," the president ordered suddenly, waving airily at his phalanx of bodyguards. "Y'all come on up closer, everybody! Sit right on the ground, we're all just folks here today." The president smiled benignly as the sweating, straw-hatted summer crowd hustled up to join him, scarcely believing their luck.

"Marietta and I just had a heck of a fine lunch down in Opelousas," commented the president, patting his flat, muscular belly. He deserted the fiction of his official podium to energetically press the Louisianan flesh. As he moved from hand to grasping hand, his every word was picked up infallibly by an invisible mike, probably implanted in one of his molars. "We had dirty rice, red beans—were they hot!—and crawdads big enough to body-slam a Maine lobster!" He chuckled. "What a sight them mudbugs were! Can y'all believe that?"

The president's guards were unobtrusively but methodically working the crowd with portable detectors and sophisticated spex equipment. They didn't look very concerned by the president's supposed change in routine.

"I see he's gonna run with the usual genetics malarkey," commented the subtitle.

"Y'all have got a perfect right to be mighty proud of the agriculture in this state," intoned the president. "Y'all's agroscience know-how is second to none! Sure, I know there's a few pointy-headed Luddites up in the snowbelt, who say they prefer their crawdads dinky."

Everyone laughed.

"Folks, I got nothin' against that attitude. If some jasper wants to spend his hard-earned money buyin' and peelin' and shuckin' those little dinky ones, that's all right by me and Marietta. Ain't that right, honey?"

The first lady smiled and waved one power-gloved hand.

"But folks, you and I both know that those whiners who waste our time complaining about 'natural food' have never sucked a mudbug head in their lives!

'Natural,' my left elbow! Who are they tryin' to kid? Just 'cause you're country, don't mean you can't hack DNA!''

"He's been working really hard on the regional accents," commented the text. *"Not bad for a guy from Minnesota. But look at that sloppy, incompetent camera work! Doesn't anybody care anymore? What on earth is happening to our standards?"*

By lunchtime, Lyle had the final coat down on the enameling job. He ate a bowl of triticale mush and chewed up a mineral-rich handful of iodized sponge.

Then he settled down in front of the wallscreen to work on the inertia brake. Lyle knew there was big money in the inertia brake—for somebody, somewhere, sometime. The device smelled like the future.

Lyle tucked a jeweler's loupe in one eye and toyed methodically with the brake. He loved the way the piezoplastic clamp and rim transmuted braking energy into electrical-battery storage. At last, a way to capture the energy you lost in braking and put it to solid use. It was almost, but not quite, magical.

The way Lyle figured it, there was gonna be a big market someday for an inertia brake that captured energy and then fed it back through the chaindrive in a way that just felt like human pedaling energy, in a direct and intuitive and muscular way, not chunky and buzzy like some loser battery-powered moped. If the system worked out right, it would make the rider feel completely natural and yet subtly superhuman at the same time. And it had to be simple, the kind of system a shop guy could fix with hand tools. It wouldn't work if it was too brittle and fancy, it just wouldn't feel like an authentic bike.

Lyle had a lot of ideas about the design. He was pretty sure he could get a real grip on the problem, if only he weren't being worked to death just keeping the shop going. If he could get enough capital together to assemble the prototypes and do some serious field tests.

It would have to be chip-driven, of course, but true to the biking spirit at the same time. A lot of bikes had chips in them nowadays, in the shocks or the braking or in reactive hubs, but bicycles simply weren't like computers. Computers were black boxes inside, no big visible working parts. People, by contrast, got sentimental about their bike gear. People were strangely reticent and traditional about bikes. That's why the bike market had never really gone for recumbents, even though the recumbent design had a big mechanical advantage. People didn't like their bikes too complicated. They didn't want bicycles to bitch and complain and whine for attention and constant upgrading the way that computers did. Bikes were too personal. People wanted their bikes to wear.

Someone banged at the shop door.

Lyle opened it. Down on the tiling by the barrels stood a tall brunette woman in stretch shorts, with a short-sleeve blue pullover and a ponytail. She had a bike under one arm, an old lacquer-and-paper-framed Taiwanese job. "Are you Edward Dertouzas?" she said, gazing up at him.

"No," Lyle said patiently. "Eddy's in Europe."

She thought this over. "I'm new in the zone," she confessed. "Can you fix this bike for me? I just bought it secondhand and I think it kinda needs some work."

"Sure," Lyle said. "You came to the right guy for that job, ma'am, because

Eddy Dertouzas couldn't fix a bike for hell. Eddy just used to live here. I'm the guy who actually owns this shop. Hand the bike up.''

Lyle crouched down, got a grip on the handlebar stem and hauled the bike into the shop. The woman gazed up at him respectfully. ''What's your name?''

''Lyle Schweik.''

''I'm Kitty Casaday.'' She hesitated. ''Could I come up inside there?''

Lyle reached down, gripped her muscular wrist, and hauled her up into the shop. She wasn't all that good looking, but she was in really good shape—like a mountain biker or triathlon runner. She looked about thirty-five. It was hard to tell, exactly. Once people got into cosmetic surgery and serious biomaintenance, it got pretty hard to judge their age. Unless you got a good, close medical exam of their eyelids and cuticles and internal membranes and such.

She looked around the shop with great interest, brown ponytail twitching. ''Where you hail from?'' Lyle asked her. He had already forgotten her name.

''Well, I'm originally from Juneau, Alaska.''

''Canadian, huh? Great. Welcome to Tennessee.''

''Actually, Alaska used to be part of the United States.''

''You're kidding,'' Lyle said. ''Hey, I'm no historian, but I've seen Alaska on a map before.''

''You've got a whole working shop and everything built inside this old place! That's really something, Mr. Schweik. What's behind that curtain?''

''The spare room,'' Lyle said. ''That's where my roommate used to stay.''

She glanced up. ''Dertouzas?''

''Yeah, him.''

''Who's in there now?''

''Nobody,'' Lyle said sadly. ''I got some storage stuff in there.''

She nodded slowly, and kept looking around, apparently galvanized with curiosity. ''What are you running on that screen?''

''Hard to say, really,'' Lyle said. He crossed the room, bent down, and switched off the set-top box. ''Some kind of weird political crap.''

He began examining her bike. All its serial numbers had been removed. Typical zone bike.

''The first thing we got to do,'' he said briskly, ''is fit it to you properly: set the saddle height, pedal stroke, and handlebars. Then I'll adjust the tension, true the wheels, check the brake pads and suspension valves, tune the shifting, and lubricate the drivetrain. The usual. You're gonna need a better saddle than this—this saddle's for a male pelvis.'' He looked up. ''You got a charge card?''

She nodded, then frowned. ''But I don't have much credit left.''

''No problem.'' He flipped open a dog-eared catalog. ''This is what you need. Any halfway decent gel-saddle. Pick one you like, and we can have it shipped in by tomorrow morning. And then''—he flipped pages—''order me one of these.''

She stepped closer and examined the page. ''The 'cotterless crank-bolt ceramic wrench set,' is that it?''

''That's right. I fix your bike, you give me those tools, and we're even.''

''Okay. Sure. That's cheap!'' She smiled at him. ''I like the way you do business, Lyle.''

"You'll get used to barter, if you stay in the zone long enough."

"I've never lived in a squat before," she said thoughtfully. "I like the attitude here, but people say that squats are pretty dangerous."

"I dunno about the squats in other towns, but Chattanooga squats aren't dangerous, unless you think anarchists are dangerous, and anarchists aren't dangerous unless they're really drunk." Lyle shrugged. "People will steal your stuff all the time, that's about the worst part. There's a couple of tough guys around here who claim they have handguns. I never saw anybody actually use a handgun. Old guns aren't hard to find, but it takes a real chemist to make working ammo nowadays." He smiled back at her. "Anyway, you look to me like you can take care of yourself."

"I take dance classes."

Lyle nodded. He opened a drawer and pulled a tape measure.

"I saw all those cables and pulleys you have on top of this place. You can pull the whole building right up off the ground, huh? Kind of hang it right off the ceiling up there."

"That's right, it saves a lot of trouble with people breaking and entering." Lyle glanced at his shock-baton, in its mounting at the door. She followed his gaze to the weapon and then looked at him, impressed.

Lyle measured her arms, torso length, then knelt and measured her inseam from crotch to floor. He took notes. "Okay," he said. "Come by tomorrow afternoon."

"Lyle?"

"Yeah?" He stood up.

"Do you rent this place out? I really need a safe place to stay in the zone."

"I'm sorry," Lyle said politely, "but I hate landlords and I'd never be one. What I need is a roommate who can really get behind the whole concept of my shop. Someone who's qualified, you know, to develop my infrastructure or do bicycle work. Anyway, if I took your cash or charged you for rent, then the tax people would just have another excuse to harass me."

"Sure, okay, but . . ." She paused, then looked at him under lowered eyelids. "I've gotta be a lot better than having this place go empty."

Lyle stared at her, astonished.

"I'm a pretty useful woman to have around, Lyle. Nobody's ever complained before."

"Really?"

"That's right." She stared at him boldly.

"I'll think about your offer," Lyle said. "What did you say your name was?"

"I'm Kitty. Kitty Casaday."

"Kitty, I got a whole lot of work to do today, but I'll see you tomorrow, okay?"

"Okay, Lyle." She smiled. "You think about me, all right?"

Lyle helped her down out of the shop. He watched her stride away across the atrium until she vanished through the crowded doorway of the Crowbar, a squat coffee shop. Then he called his mother.

"Did you forget something?" his mother said, looking up from her workscreen.

"Mom, I know this is really hard to believe, but a strange woman just banged on my door and offered to have sex with me."

"You're kidding, right?"

"In exchange for room and board, I think. Anyway, I said you'd be the first to know if it happened."

"Lyle—" His mother hesitated. "Lyle, I think you better come right home. Let's make that dinner date for tonight, okay? We'll have a little talk about this situation."

"Yeah, okay. I got an enameling job I gotta deliver to Floor Forty-one, anyway."

"I don't have a positive feeling about this development, Lyle."

"That's okay, Mom. I'll see you tonight."

Lyle reassembled the newly enameled bike. Then he set the flywheel onto remote, and stepped outside the shop. He mounted the bike, and touched a password into the remote control. The shop faithfully reeled itself far out of reach and hung there in space below the fire-blackened ceiling, swaying gently.

Lyle pedaled away, back toward the elevators, back toward the neighborhood where he'd grown up.

He delivered the bike to the delighted young idiot who'd commissioned it, stuffed the cash in his shoes, and then went down to his mother's. He took a shower, shaved, and shampooed thoroughly. They had pork chops and grits and got drunk together. His mother complained about the breakup with her third husband and wept bitterly, but not as much as usual when this topic came up. Lyle got the strong impression she was thoroughly on the mend and would be angling for number four in pretty short order.

Around midnight, Lyle refused his mother's ritual offers of new clothes and fresh leftovers, and headed back down to the zone. He was still a little clubfooted from his mother's sherry, and he stood breathing beside the broken glass of the atrium wall, gazing out at the city-smeared summer stars. The cavernous darkness inside the zone at night was one of his favorite things about the place. The queasy twenty-four-hour security lighting in the rest of the Archiplat had never been rebuilt inside the zone.

The zone always got livelier at night when all the normal people started sneaking in to cruise the zone's unlicensed dives and nightspots, but all that activity took place behind discreetly closed doors. Enticing squiggles of red and blue chemglow here and there only enhanced the blessed unnatural gloom.

Lyle pulled his remote control and ordered the shop back down.

The door of the shop had been broken open.

Lyle's latest bike-repair client lay sprawled on the floor of the shop, unconscious. She was wearing black military fatigues, a knit cap, and rappelling gear.

She had begun her break-in at Lyle's establishment by pulling his shock-baton out of its glowing security socket beside the doorframe. The booby-trapped baton had immediately put fifteen thousand volts through her, and sprayed her face with a potent mix of dye and street-legal incapacitants.

Lyle turned the baton off with the remote control, and then placed it carefully back in its socket. His surprise guest was still breathing, but was clearly in real metabolic distress. He tried clearing her nose and mouth with a tissue. The guys who'd sold him the baton hadn't been kidding about the "indelible" part. Her face and throat were drenched with green and her chest looked like a spin-painting.

Her elaborate combat spex had partially shielded her eyes. With the spex off she looked like a viridian-green raccoon.

Lyle tried stripping her gear off in conventional fashion, realized this wasn't going to work, and got a pair of metal-shears from the shop. He snipped his way through the eerily writhing power-gloves and the Kevlar laces of the pneumoreactive combat boots. Her black turtleneck had an abrasive surface and a cuirass over chest and back that looked like it could stop small-arms fire.

The trousers had nineteen separate pockets and they were loaded with all kinds of eerie little items: a matte-black electrode stun-weapon, flash capsules, fingerprint dust, a utility pocketknife, drug adhesives, plastic handcuffs, some pocket change, worry beads, a comb, and a makeup case.

Close inspection revealed a pair of tiny microphone amplifiers inserted in her ear canals. Lyle fetched the tiny devices out with needlenose pliers. Lyle was getting pretty seriously concerned by this point. He shackled her arms and legs with bike-security cable, in case she regained consciousness and attempted something superhuman.

Around four in the morning she had a coughing fit and began shivering violently. Summer nights could get pretty cold in the shop. Lyle thought over the design problem for some time, and then fetched a big heat-reflective blanket out of the empty room. He cut a neat poncho-hole in the center of it, and slipped her head through it. He got the bike cables off her—she could probably slip the cables anyway—and sewed all four edges of the blanket shut from the outside, with sturdy monofilament thread from his saddle-stitcher. He sewed the poncho edges to a tough fabric belt, cinched the belt snugly around her neck, and padlocked it. When he was done, he'd made a snug bag that contained her entire body, except for her head, which had begun to drool and snore.

A fat blob of superglue on the bottom of the bag kept her anchored to the shop's floor. The blanket was cheap but tough upholstery fabric. If she could rip her way through blanket fabric with her fingernails alone, then he was probably a goner anyway. By now, Lyle was tired and stone sober. He had a squeeze bottle of glucose rehydrator, three aspirins, and a canned chocolate pudding. Then he climbed in his hammock and went to sleep.

Lyle woke up around ten. His captive was sitting up inside the bag, her green face stony, eyes red-rimmed and brown hair caked with dye. Lyle got up, dressed, ate breakfast, and fixed the broken door-lock. He said nothing, partly because he thought that silence would shake her up, but mostly because he couldn't remember her name. He was almost sure it wasn't her real name anyway.

When he'd finished fixing the door, he reeled up the string of the doorknocker so that it was far out of reach. He figured the two of them needed the privacy.

Then Lyle deliberately fired up the wallscreen and turned on the set-top box. As soon as the peculiar subtitles started showing up again, she grew agitated.

''Who are you really?'' she demanded at last.

''Ma'am, I'm a bicycle repairman.''

She snorted.

''I guess I don't need to know your name,'' he said, ''but I need to know who your people are, and why they sent you here, and what I've got to do to get out of this situation.''

"You're not off to a good start, mister."

"No," he said, "maybe not, but you're the one who's blown it. I'm just a twenty-four-year-old bicycle repairman from Tennessee. But you, you've got enough specialized gear on you to buy my whole place five times over."

He flipped open the little mirror in her makeup case and showed her her own face. Her scowl grew a little stiffer below the spattering of green.

"I want you to tell me what's going on here," he said.

"Forget it."

"If you're waiting for your backup to come rescue you, I don't think they're coming," Lyle said. "I searched you very thoroughly and I've opened up every single little gadget you had, and I took all the batteries out. I'm not even sure what some of those things are or how they work, but hey, I know what a battery is. It's been hours now. So I don't think your backup people even know where you are."

She said nothing.

"See," he said, "you've really blown it bad. You got caught by a total amateur, and now you're in a hostage situation that could go on indefinitely. I got enough water and noodles and sardines to live up here for days. I dunno, maybe you can make a cellular phone call to God off some gizmo implanted in your thighbone, but it looks to me like you've got serious problems."

She shuffled around a bit inside the bag and looked away.

"It's got something to do with the cable box over there, right?"

She said nothing.

"For what it's worth, I don't think that box has anything to do with me or Eddy Dertouzas," Lyle said. "I think it was probably meant for Eddy, but I don't think he asked anybody for it. Somebody just wanted him to have it, probably one of his weird European contacts. Eddy used to be in this political group called CAP-CLUG, ever heard of them?"

It looked pretty obvious that she'd heard of them.

"I never liked 'em much either," Lyle told her. "They kind of snagged me at first with their big talk about freedom and civil liberties, but then you'd go to a CAPCLUG meeting up in the penthouse levels, and there were all these potbellied zudes in spex yapping off stuff like, 'We must follow the technological imperatives or be jettisoned into the history dump-file.' They're a bunch of useless blowhards who can't tie their own shoes."

"They're dangerous radicals subverting national sovereignty."

Lyle blinked cautiously. "Whose national sovereignty would that be?"

"Yours, mine, Mr. Schweik. I'm from NAFTA, I'm a federal agent."

"You're a fed? How come you're breaking into people's houses, then? Isn't that against the Fourth Amendment or something?"

"If you mean the Fourth Amendment to the Constitution of the United States, that document was superseded years ago."

"Yeah . . . okay, I guess you're right." Lyle shrugged. "I missed a lot of civics classes. . . . No skin off my back anyway. I'm sorry, but what did you say your name was?"

"I said my name was Kitty Casaday."

"Right. Kitty. Okay, Kitty, just you and me, person to person. We obviously have a mutual problem here. What do you think I ought to do in this situation? I mean, speaking practically.''

Kitty thought it over, surprised. ''Mr. Schweik, you should release me immediately, get me my gear, and give me the box and any related data, recordings, or diskettes. Then you should escort me from the Archiplat in some confidential fashion so I won't be stopped by police and questioned about the dye stains. A new set of clothes would be very useful.''

''Like that, huh?''

''That's your wisest course of action.'' Her eyes narrowed. ''I can't make any promises, but it might affect your future treatment very favorably.''

''You're not gonna tell me who you are, or where you came from, or who sent you, or what this is all about?''

''No. Under no circumstances. I'm not allowed to reveal that. You don't need to know. You're not supposed to know. And anyway, if you're really what you say you are, what should you care?''

''Plenty. I care plenty. I can't wander around the rest of my life wondering when you're going to jump me out of a dark corner.''

''If I'd wanted to hurt you, I'd have hurt you when we first met, Mr. Schweik. There was no one here but you and me, and I could have easily incapacitated you and taken anything I wanted. Just give me the box and the data and stop trying to interrogate me.''

''Suppose you found me breaking into your house, Kitty? What would you do to me?''

She said nothing.

''What you're telling me isn't gonna work. If you don't tell me what's really going on here,'' Lyle said heavily, ''I'm gonna have to get tough.''

Her lips thinned in contempt.

''Okay, you asked for this.'' Lyle opened the mediator and made a quick voice call. ''Pete?''

''Nah, this is Pete's mook,'' the phone replied. ''Can I do something for you?''

''Could you tell Pete that Lyle Schweik has some big trouble, and I need him to come over to my bike shop immediately? And bring some heavy muscle from the Spiders.''

''What kind of big trouble, Lyle?''

''Authority trouble. A lot of it. I can't say any more. I think this line may be tapped.''

''Right-o. I'll make that happen. Hoo-ah, zude.'' The mook hung up.

Lyle left the beanbag and went back to the workbench. He took Kitty's cheap bike out of the repair stand and angrily threw it aside. ''You know what really bugs me?'' he said at last. ''You couldn't even bother to charm your way in here, set yourself up as my roommate, and then steal the damn box. You didn't even respect me that much. Heck, you didn't even have to steal anything, Kitty. You could have just smiled and asked nicely and I'd have given you the box to play with. I don't watch media, I hate all that crap.''

''It was an emergency. There was no time for more extensive investigation or reconnaissance. I think you should call your gangster friends immediately and tell them you've made a mistake. Tell them not to come here.''

"You're ready to talk seriously?"

"No, I won't be talking."

"Okay, we'll see."

After twenty minutes, Lyle's phone rang. He answered it cautiously, keeping the video off. It was Pete from the City Spiders. "Zude, where is your doorknocker?"

"Oh, sorry, I pulled it up, didn't want to be disturbed. I'll bring the shop right down." Lyle thumbed the brake switches.

Lyle opened the door and Pete broad-jumped into the shop. Pete was a big man but he had the skeletal, wiry build of a climber, bare dark arms and shins and big sticky-toed jumping shoes. He had a sleeveless leather bodysuit full of clips and snaps, and he carried a big fabric shoulder bag. There were six vivid tattoos on the dark skin of his left cheek, under the black stubble.

Pete looked at Kitty, lifted his spex with wiry callused fingers, looked at her again bare-eyed, and put the spex back in place. "Wow, Lyle."

"Yeah."

"I never thought you were into anything this sick and twisted."

"It's a serious matter, Pete."

Pete turned to the door, crouched down, and hauled a second person into the shop. She wore a beat-up air-conditioned jacket and long slacks and zipsided boots and wire-rimmed spex. She had short ratty hair under a green cloche hat. "Hi," she said, sticking out a hand. "I'm Mabel. We haven't met."

"I'm Lyle." Lyle gestured. "This is Kitty here in the bag."

"You said you needed somebody heavy, so I brought Mabel along," said Pete. "Mabel's a social worker."

"Looks like you pretty much got things under control here," said Mabel liltingly, scratching her neck and looking about the place. "What happened? She break into your shop?"

"Yeah."

"And," Pete said, "she grabbed the shock-baton first thing and blasted herself but good?"

"Exactly."

"I told you that thieves always go for the weaponry first," Pete said, grinning and scratching his armpit. "Didn't I tell you that? Leave a weapon in plain sight, man, a thief can't stand it, it's the very first thing they gotta grab." He laughed. "Works every time."

"Pete's from the City Spiders," Lyle told Kitty. "His people built this shop for me. One dark night, they hauled this mobile home right up thirty-four stories in total darkness, straight up the side of the Archiplat without anybody seeing, and they cut a big hole through the side of the building without making any noise, and they hauled the whole shop through it. Then they sank explosive bolts through the girders and hung it up here for me in midair. The City Spiders are into sport-climbing the way I'm into bicycles, only, like, they are very *seriously* into climbing and there are *lots* of them. They were some of the very first people to squat the zone, and they've lived here ever since, and they are pretty good friends of mine."

Pete sank to one knee and looked Kitty in the eye. "I love breaking into places, don't you? There's no thrill like some quick and perfectly executed break-in." He reached casually into his shoulder bag. "The thing is"—he pulled out a camera—

"to be sporting, you can't steal anything. You just take trophy pictures to prove you were there." He snapped her picture several times, grinning as she flinched.

"Lady," he breathed at her, "once you've turned into a little wicked greedhead, and mixed all that evil cupidity and possessiveness into the beauty of the direct action, then you've prostituted our way of life. You've gone and spoiled our sport." Pete stood up. "We City Spiders don't like common thieves. And we especially don't like thieves who break into the places of clients of ours, like Lyle here. And we thoroughly, especially, don't like thieves who are so brickhead dumb that they get caught red-handed on the premises of friends of ours."

Pete's hairy brows knotted in thought. "What I'd like to do here, Lyle ol' buddy," he announced, "is wrap up your little friend head to foot in nice tight cabling, smuggle her out of here down to Golden Gate Archiplat—you know, the big one downtown over by MLK and Highway Twenty-seven?—and hang her head-down in the center of the cupola."

"That's not very nice," Mabel told him seriously.

Pete looked wounded. "I'm not gonna charge him for it or anything! Just imagine her, spinning up there beautifully with all those chandeliers and those hundreds of mirrors."

Mabel knelt and looked into Kitty's face. "Has she had any water since she was knocked unconscious?"

"No."

"Well, for heaven's sake, give the poor woman something to drink, Lyle."

Lyle handed Mabel a bike-tote squeeze bottle of electrolyte refresher. "You zudes don't grasp the situation yet," he said. "Look at all this stuff I took off her." He showed them the spex, and the boots, and the stun-gun, and the gloves, and the carbon-nitride climbing plectra, and the rappelling gear.

"Wow," Pete said at last, dabbing at buttons on his spex to study the finer detail, "this is no ordinary burglar! She's gotta be, like, a street samurai from the Mahogany Warbirds or something!"

"She says she's a federal agent."

Mabel stood up suddenly, angrily yanking the squeeze bottle from Kitty's lips. "You're kidding, right?"

"Ask her."

"I'm a grade-five social counselor with the Department of Urban Redevelopment," Mabel said. She presented Kitty with an official ID. "And who are you with?"

"I'm not prepared to divulge that information at this time."

"I can't believe this," Mabel marveled, tucking her dog-eared hologram ID back in her hat. "You've caught somebody from one of those nutty reactionary secret black-bag units. I mean, that's gotta be what's just happened here." She shook her head slowly. "Y'know, if you work in government, you always hear horror stories about these right-wing paramilitary wackos, but I've never actually seen one before."

"It's a very dangerous world out there, Miss Social Counselor."

"Oh, tell me about it," Mabel scoffed. "I've worked suicide hot lines! I've seen a hostage negotiator! I'm a career social worker, girlfriend! I've seen more horror and suffering than you *ever* will. While you were doing push-ups in some comfy cracker training camp, I've been out here in the real world!'' Mabel absently un-screwed the top from the bike bottle and had a long glug. ''What on earth are you doing trying to raid the squat of a bicycle repairman?''

Kitty's stony silence lengthened. ''It's got something to do with that set-top box,'' Lyle offered. ''It showed up here in delivery yesterday, and then she showed up just a few hours later. Started flirting with me, and said she wanted to live in here. Of course I got suspicious right away.''

''Naturally,'' Pete said. ''Real bad move, Kitty. Lyle's on antilibidinals.''

Kitty stared at Lyle bitterly. ''I see,'' she said at last. ''So that's what you get, when you drain all the sex out of one of them. . . . You get a strange malodorous creature that spends all its time working in the garage.''

Mabel flushed. ''Did you hear that?'' She gave Kitty's bag a sharp angry yank. ''What conceivable right do you have to question this citizen's sexual orientation? Especially after cruelly trying to sexually manipulate him to abet your illegal pur-poses? Have you lost all sense of decency? You . . . you should be sued.''

''Do your worst,'' Kitty muttered.

''Maybe I will,'' Mabel said grimly. ''Sunlight is the best disinfectant.''

''Yeah, let's string her up somewhere real sunny and public and call a bunch of news crews,'' Pete said. ''I'm way hot for this deep ninja gear! Me and the Spiders got real mojo uses for these telescopic ears, and the tracer dust, and the epoxy bugging devices. And the press-on climbing-claws. And the carbon-fiber rope. Everything, really! Everything except these big-ass military shoes of hers, which really suck.''

''Hey, all that stuff's mine,'' Lyle said sternly. ''I saw it first.''

''Yeah, I guess so, but . . . Okay, Lyle, you make us a deal on the gear, we'll forget everything you still owe us for doing the shop.''

''Come on, those combat spex are worth more than this place all by themselves.''

''I'm real interested in that set-top box,'' Mabel said cruelly. ''It doesn't look too fancy or complicated. Let's take it over to those dirty circuit zudes who hang out at the Blue Parrot, and see if they can't reverse-engineer it. We'll post all the schematics up on twenty or thirty progressive activist networks, and see what falls out of cyberspace.''

Kitty glared at her. ''The terrible consequences from that stupid and irresponsible action would be entirely on your head.''

''I'll risk it,'' Mabel said airily, patting her cloche hat. ''It might bump my soft little liberal head a bit, but I'm pretty sure it would crack your nasty little fascist head like a coconut.''

Suddenly Kitty began thrashing and kicking her way furiously inside the bag. They watched with interest as she ripped, tore, and lashed out with powerful side and front kicks. Nothing much happened.

''All right,'' she said at last, panting in exhaustion. ''I've come from Senator Creighton's office.''

''Who?'' Lyle said.

''Creighton! Senator James P. Creighton, the man who's been your Senator from Tennessee for the past thirty years!''

''Oh,'' Lyle said. ''I hadn't noticed.''

''We're anarchists,'' Pete told her.

"I've sure heard of the nasty old geezer," Mabel said, "but I'm from British Columbia, where we change senators the way you'd change a pair of socks. If you ever changed your socks, that is. What about him?"

"Well, Senator Creighton has deep clout and seniority! He was a United States Senator even before the first NAFTA Senate was convened! He has a very large, and powerful, and very well seasoned personal staff of twenty thousand hardworking people, with a lot of pull in the Agriculture, Banking, and Telecommunications Committees!"

"Yeah? So?"

"So," Kitty said miserably, "there are twenty thousand of us on his staff. We've been in place for decades now, and naturally we've accumulated lots of power and importance. Senator Creighton's staff is basically running some quite large sections of the NAFTA government, and if the senator loses his office, there will be a great deal of . . . of unnecessary political turbulence." She looked up. "You might not think that a senator's staff is all that important politically. But if people like you bothered to learn anything about the real-life way that your government functions, then you'd know that Senate staffers can be really crucial."

Mabel scratched her head. "You're telling me that even a lousy senator has his own private black-bag unit?"

Kitty looked insulted. "He's an excellent senator! You can't have a working organization of twenty thousand staffers without taking security very seriously! Anyway, the Executive wing has had black-bag units for years! It's only right that there should be a balance of powers."

"Wow," Mabel said. "The old guy's a hundred and twelve or something, isn't he?"

"A hundred and seventeen."

"Even with government health care, there can't be a lot left of him."

"He's already gone," Kitty muttered. "His frontal lobes are burned out. . . . He can still sit up, and if he's stoked on stimulants he can repeat whatever's whispered to him. So he's got two permanent implanted hearing aids, and basically . . . well . . . he's being run by remote control by his mook."

"His mook, huh?" Pete repeated thoughtfully.

"It's a very good mook," Kitty said. "The coding's old, but it's been very well looked after. It has firm moral values and excellent policies. The mook is really very much like the senator was. It's just that . . . well, it's old. It still prefers a really old-fashioned media environment. It spends almost all its time watching old-fashioned public political coverage, and lately it's gotten cranky and started broadcasting commentary."

"Man, never trust a mook," Lyle said. "I hate those things."

"So do I," Pete offered, "but even a mook comes off pretty good compared to a politician."

"I don't really see the problem," Mabel said, puzzled. "Senator Hirschheimer from Arizona has had a direct neural link to his mook for years, and he has an excellent progressive voting record. Same goes for Senator Marmalejo from Tamaulipas; she's kind of absentminded, and everybody knows she's on life support, but she's a real scrapper on women's issues."

Kitty looked up. "You don't think it's terrible?"

Mabel shook her head. "I'm not one to be judgmental about the intimacy of one's relationship to one's own digital alter ego. As far as I can see it, that's a basic privacy issue."

"They told me in briefing that it was a very terrible business, and that everyone would panic if they learned that a high government official was basically a front for a rogue artificial intelligence."

Mabel, Pete, and Lyle exchanged glances. "Are you guys surprised by that news?" Mabel said.

"Heck no," said Pete. "Big deal," Lyle added.

Something seemed to snap inside Kitty then. Her head sank. "Disaffected émigrés in Europe have been spreading boxes that can decipher the senator's commentary. I mean, the senator's mook's commentary. . . . The mook speaks just like the senator did, or the way the senator used to speak, when he was in private and off the record. The way he spoke in his diaries. As far as we can tell, the mook *was* his diary. . . . It used to be his personal laptop computer. But he just kept transferring the files, and upgrading the software, and teaching it new tricks like voice recognition and speechwriting, and giving it power of attorney and such. . . . And then, one day the mook made a break for it. We think that the mook sincerely believes that it's the senator."

"Just tell the stupid thing to shut up for a while, then."

"We can't do that. We're not even sure where the mook is, physically. Or how it's been encoding those sarcastic comments into the video-feed. The senator had a lot of friends in the telecom industry back in the old days. There are a lot of ways and places to hide a piece of distributed software."

"So that's all?" Lyle said. "That's it, that's your big secret? Why didn't you just come to me and ask me for the box? You didn't have to dress up in combat gear and kick my door in. That's a pretty good story, I'd have probably just given you the thing."

"I couldn't do that, Mr. Schweik."

"Why not?"

"Because," Pete said, "her people are important government functionaries, and you're a loser techie wacko who lives in a slum."

"I was told this is a very dangerous area," Kitty muttered.

"It's not dangerous," Mabel told her.

"No?"

"No. They're all too broke to be dangerous. This is just a kind of social breathing space. The whole urban infrastructure's dreadfully overplanned here in Chattanooga. There's been too much money here too long. There's been no room for spontaneity. It was choking the life out of the city. That's why everyone was secretly overjoyed when the rioters set fire to these three floors."

Mabel shrugged. "The insurance took care of the damage. First the looters came in. Then there were a few hideouts for kids and crooks and illegal aliens. Then the permanent squats got set up. Then the artist's studios, and the semilegal workshops and red-light places. Then the quaint little coffeehouses, then the bakeries. Pretty soon the offices of professionals will be filtering in, and they'll restore the water and the wiring. Once that happens, the real-estate prices will kick in big-time, and the whole zone will transmute right back into gentryville. It happens all the time."

Mabel waved her arm at the door. "If you knew anything about modern urban geography, you'd see this kind of, uh, spontaneous urban renewal happening all over the place. As long as you've got naive young people with plenty of energy who can be suckered into living inside rotten, hazardous dumps for nothing, in exchange for imagining that they're free from oversight, then it all works out just great in the long run."

"Oh."

"Yeah, zones like this turn out to be extremely handy for all concerned. For some brief span of time, a few people can think mildly unusual thoughts and behave in mildly unusual ways. All kinds of weird little vermin show up, and if they make any money then they go legal, and if they don't then they drop dead in a place really quiet where it's all their own fault. Nothing dangerous about it." Mabel laughed, then sobered. "Lyle, let this poor dumb cracker out of the bag."

"She's naked under there."

"Okay," she said impatiently, "cut a slit in the bag and throw some clothes in it. Get going, Lyle."

Lyle threw in some biking pants and a sweatshirt.

"What about my gear?" Kitty demanded, wriggling her way into the clothes by feel.

"I tell you what," said Mabel thoughtfully. "Pete here will give your gear back to you in a week or so, after his friends have photographed all the circuitry. You'll just have to let him keep all those knickknacks for a while, as his reward for our not immediately telling everybody who you are and what you're doing here."

"Great idea," Pete announced, "terrific, pragmatic solution!" He began feverishly snatching up gadgets and stuffing them into his shoulder bag. "See, Lyle? One phone call to good ol' Spider Pete, and your problem is history, zude! Me and Mabel-the-Fed have crisis negotiation skills that are second to none! Another potentially lethal confrontation resolved without any bloodshed or loss of life." Pete zipped the bag shut. "That's about it, right, everybody? Problem over! Write if you get work, Lyle buddy. Hang by your thumbs." Pete leapt out the door and bounded off at top speed on the springy soles of his reactive boots.

"Thanks a lot for placing my equipment into the hands of sociopathic criminals," Kitty said. She reached out of the slit in the bag, grabbed a multitool off the corner of the workbench, and began swiftly slashing her way free.

"This will help the sluggish, corrupt, and underpaid Chattanooga police to take life a little more seriously," Mabel said, her pale eyes gleaming. "Besides, it's profoundly undemocratic to restrict specialized technical knowledge to the coercive hands of secret military elites."

Kitty thoughtfully thumbed the edge of the multitool's ceramic blade and stood up to her full height, her eyes slitted. "I'm ashamed to work for the same government as you."

Mabel smiled serenely. "Darling, your tradition of deep dark government paranoia is far behind the times! This is the postmodern era! We're now in the grip of a government with severe schizoid multiple-personality disorder."

"You're truly vile. I despise you more than I can say." Kitty jerked her thumb at Lyle. "Even this nutcase eunuch anarchist kid looks pretty good, compared to you. At least he's self-sufficient and market-driven."

"I thought he looked good the moment I met him," Mabel replied sunnily. "He's cute, he's got great muscle tone, and he doesn't make passes. Plus he can fix small appliances and he's got a spare apartment. I think you ought to move in with him, sweetheart."

"What's that supposed to mean? You don't think I could manage life here in the zone like you do, is that it? You think you have some kind of copyright on living outside the law?"

"No, I just mean you'd better stay indoors with your boyfriend here until that paint falls off your face. You look like a poisoned raccoon." Mabel turned on her heel. "Try to get a life, and stay out of my way." She leapt outside, unlocked her bicycle, and methodically pedaled off.

Kitty wiped her lips and spat out the door. "Christ, that baton packs a wallop." She snorted. "Don't you ever ventilate this place, kid? Those paint fumes are gonna kill you before you're thirty."

"I don't have time to clean or ventilate it. I'm real busy."

"Okay, then I'll clean it. I'll ventilate it. I gotta stay here a while, understand? Maybe quite a while."

Lyle blinked. "How long, exactly?"

Kitty stared at him. "You're not taking me seriously, are you? I don't much like it when people don't take me seriously."

"No, no," Lyle assured her hastily. "You're very serious."

"You ever heard of a small-business grant, kid? How about venture capital, did you ever hear of that? Ever heard of federal research-and-development subsidies, Mr. Schweik?" Kitty looked at him sharply, weighing her words. "Yeah, I thought maybe you'd heard of that one, Mr. Techie Wacko. Federal R-and-D backing is the kind of thing that only happens to other people, right? But Lyle, when you make good friends with a senator, you *become* 'other people.' Get my drift, pal?"

"I guess I do," Lyle said slowly.

"We'll have ourselves some nice talks about that subject, Lyle. You wouldn't mind that, would you?"

"No. I don't mind it now that you're talking."

"There's some stuff going on down here in the zone that I didn't understand at first, but it's important." Kitty paused, then rubbed dried dye from her hair in a cascade of green dandruff. "How much did you pay those Spider gangsters to string up this place for you?"

"It was kind of a barter situation," Lyle told her.

"Think they'd do it again if I paid 'em real cash? Yeah? I thought so." She nodded thoughtfully. "They look like a heavy outfit, the City Spiders. I gotta pry 'em loose from that leftist gorgon before she finishes indoctrinating them in socialist revolution." Kitty wiped her mouth on her sleeve. "This is the senator's own constituency! It was stupid of us to duck an ideological battle, just because this is a worthless area inhabited by reckless sociopaths who don't vote. Hell, that's exactly why it's important. This could be a vital territory in the culture war. I'm gonna call the office right away, start making arrangements. There's no way we're gonna leave this place in the hands of the self-styled Queen of Peace and Justice over there."

She snorted, then stretched a kink out of her back. "With a little self-control and discipline, I can save those Spiders from themselves and turn them into an asset to law and order! I'll get 'em to string up a couple of trailers here in the zone. We could start a dojo."

Eddy called, two weeks later. He was in a beachside cabana somewhere in Catalunya, wearing a silk floral-print shirt and a new and very pricey looking set of spex. "How's life, Lyle?"

"It's okay, Eddy."

"Making out all right?" Eddy had two new tattoos on his cheekbone.

"Yeah. I got a new paying roommate. She's a martial artist."

"Girl roommate working out okay this time?"

"Yeah, she's good at pumping the flywheel and she lets me get on with my bike work. Bike business has been picking up a lot lately. Looks like I might get a legal electrical feed and some more floorspace, maybe even some genuine mail delivery. My new roomie's got a lot of useful contacts."

"Boy, the ladies sure love you, Lyle! Can't beat 'em off with a stick, can you, poor guy? That's a heck of a note."

Eddy leaned forward a little, shoving aside a silver tray full of dead gold-tipped zigarettes. "You been getting the packages?"

"Yeah. Pretty regular."

"Good deal," he said briskly, "but you can wipe 'em all now. I don't need those backups anymore. Just wipe the data and trash the disks, or sell 'em. I'm into some, well, pretty hairy opportunities right now, and I don't need all that old clutter. It's kid stuff anyway."

"Okay, man. If that's the way you want it."

Eddy leaned forward. "D'you happen to get a package lately? Some hardware? Kind of a set-top box?"

"Yeah, I got the thing."

"That's great, Lyle. I want you to open the box up, and break all the chips with pliers."

"Yeah?"

"Then throw all the pieces away. Separately. It's trouble, Lyle, okay? The kind of trouble I don't need right now."

"Consider it done, man."

"Thanks! Anyway, you won't be bothered by mailouts from now on." He paused. "Not that I don't appreciate your former effort and goodwill, and all."

Lyle blinked. "How's your love life, Eddy?"

Eddy sighed. "Frederika! What a handful! I dunno, Lyle, it was okay for a while, but we couldn't stick it together. I don't know why I ever thought that private cops were sexy. I musta been totally out of my mind. . . . Anyway, I got a new girlfriend now."

"Yeah?"

"She's a politician, Lyle. She's a radical member of the Spanish Parliament. Can you believe that? I'm sleeping with an elected official of a European local government." He laughed. "Politicians are *sexy*, Lyle. Politicians are *hot*! They have charisma. They're glamorous. They're powerful. They can really make things happen! Politicians get around. They know things on the inside track. I'm having more fun with Violeta than I knew there was in the world.''

''That's pleasant to hear, zude.''

''More pleasant than you know, my man.''

''Not a problem,'' Lyle said indulgently. ''We all gotta make our own lives, Eddy.''

''Ain't it the truth.''

Lyle nodded. ''I'm in business, zude!''

''You gonna perfect that inertial whatsit?'' Eddy said.

''Maybe. It could happen. I get to work on it a lot now. I'm getting closer, really getting a grip on the concept. It feels really good. It's a good hack, man. It makes up for all the rest of it. It really does.''

Eddy sipped his mimosa. ''Lyle.''

''What?''

''You didn't hook up that set-top box and look at it, did you?''

''You know me, Eddy,'' Lyle said. ''Just another kid with a wrench.''

THE WEIGHING OF AYRE

Gregory Feeley

▼

Writer and critic Gregory Feeley has published fiction in SF magazines and anthologies such as SF Age, Asimov's Science Fiction, Full Spectrum, Starlight, *and* Weird Tales from Shakespeare, *along with critical essays in* The Atlantic, Saturday Review, The New York Times, *and elsewhere. His first novel,* The Oxygen Barons, *was published as an Ace Special in 1990, and was a finalist for the Philip K. Dick Award. He has recently completed a contemporary novel,* Exit Without Saving, *and is at work on an SF novel,* Neptune's Reach. *He lives with his family in Hamden, Connecticut.*

In the intricate and evocative story that follows, he takes us back in time to the beginnings of the Scientific Revolution, and shows us that the same double-edged issues of infinite possibility and deadly potential threat that haunt the development of new technologies today have been there from the very start, and that it is always in our own hands whether to use fresh knowledge and new discoveries to explore new worlds or destroy the old. . . .

Hookeing Leviathan, the fisherman draws up his line to hoist not the lantern-mouthed serpent but a glistening bulb with a tail like a whip. Thou art Homunculus, says Malcolm, with the dreamer's gift of perceiving things' true natures. From what sea have I pulled thee? He recalls with shame the warm rushing that sometimes terminates sleep, but this sea does not find its headwaters in him. The ocean lapping this levee contains all the souls of Christendom, each mote seething like *atomi* pressing upon a flask when water is brought to boyle.

The thrashing serpent (who but poorly resembles the homunculi of learned drawings) slips free the hooke and falls to the sea, immediately to disappear. Malcolm regards his yieldless rod melancholicly and casts his leveen-hooke once more, and this time brings up a twining tapeworm, blind mouths probing the air. O parody of homunculus, you too dwell within man. Do all creatures that enter or quit the tubules of men bear the form of the original Worm? One peeps into the worlds beyond ken only to discover the generation of vipers.

Light is seeping into the sky, like dawn suffusing stained glass. Malcolm looks back to the worm, alert that moments of good illumination be exploited. Besides the suckers for drawing nourishment, the beast's head is ringed with tiny hookes, whereby it affixes itself to its host. Staring, Malcolm feels a pang of the purest melancholy. Hath every worm that crawls its hooks in me?

The sunlight brings him to consciousness, like a bubble rising through brightening waters to break upon the surface of day. The light is different here, a subtler quality than the strange smells or low-tide geography, yet it's the first sensation to impress upon him in the morning. Why should the sun's rays strike this low land aslant, what texture of the air so colors it?

Malcolm Weymouth crawled from his hired bed, bladder full of zuiden brew. The wind was up, as usual, and the squeal of windmills filled the air like birdsong. Voices in a half-familiar tongue rose through the floorboards; spoken too fast for him to follow, Dutch became a music that snagged threads of memory he couldn't recall.

Vrouw Kluyver had filled the ewer, which she had carefully set with its chipped side facing away from him. Pouring, Malcolm noticed the design at basin's bottom, a Dutch dog—its breed unknown in England, but familiar on the barges he had seen here—pissing against what was plainly an orange tree. Allegory in the delftware, for the diner to find upon finishing his soup. Was the goodwife seeking to goad her English guest, a presumed supporter of his sovereign's ambitions to return William of Orange to the Dutch throne? Or had she even recognized his accent?

Malcolm pulled the pot from beneath the bed and inspected its interior before using it. Reading the evidence of rooms must also be a science, and need not remain the province of cutthroats like Monckton. Rising, he looked around the tiny chamber. The only trace of his English origin was the copy of Hooke's *Micrographia* on the table, and that only if the investigator look past the Latin title to the English text. Malcolm's accent was strong but he spoke fluently, and looked as Dutch as Vrouw Kluyver. If he met someone worldly enough to realize he wasn't Flemish, it would not be in this part of Delft.

He descended the stair slowly, savoring this last experience of the vertical. The steam of alien porridge rose to meet him, and voices resolving into comprehensibility like a specimen brought into focus. Slipping out the door—his arrangement with the innkeeper did not include meals, and he preferred not to converse with the travelers who ate there—Malcolm stepped into the tulip-scented Zuid-Holland morning, where wind vanes slowly turned like upended waterwheels and a salt breeze, uninterrupted by hillock or tumulus, blew ten miles from the sea.

How can one spy stars in so cloudy a sky? One reason for the peculiar quality of Dutch light was surely its shifting nature, for the immense sky had been at least partly obscured for all three of Malcolm's days here. A stacked mass of cloud, topped with asymmetrical turrets and domes like a fortress hewn from a knoll, was moving in from the west like Mahomet's mountain, drizzling a rainy smudge from its flattened bottom.

Holland inhabits the bottom of a basin, where the turbid air settles like precipitate in cloudy water. Malcolm knew nothing about the weather, but the analogy seemed sound. Live in the bilges of the *microcosme* and the splendors of the *macrocosme* must be diminished. Small wonder if the researchers of the Low Countries should turn their lenses from the heavens above to the muck beneath their feet.

But is it any greater wonder (he asked himself) that the telescopists, balked by the cataractous air above their heads, should turn rather to grinding mirrors, swing their instruments sidelong rather than upward like swivel'd cannons? Impressive enough their achievements—Huygens had erected a telescope 210 feet long, thus defeating the hobgoblin of chromatic aberration—in despite of their sodden weather; to what use would they put Newton's late contrivance of a telescope that worked by Reflection?

Malcolm fretted these matters as he walked the canal-path toward the center of Delft, so did not see his acquaintance until hailed. "Meister Veymout!" cried a voice, and Malcolm turned, startled, to see a hatted burgher looking up from what appeared to be a telescope. The figure straightened and waved, and Malcolm recognized the surveyor, who had yesterday spoken to him when the object of his inquiries took ill.

"Heer Spoors," said Malcolm, raising his hat. The object on the tripod was a theodolite, which was sighted along the frontage of a lot filled with workmen wielding barrows and picks, who seemed to be sinking piles for a foundation even as the remains of a previous structure were being cleared. "You are at your labors early this day."

"The daylight wanes, while work only multiplies. It is like that doctrine Antoni reviles, of nonlife erupting into life?"

"*Generatio spontanea*," said Malcolm.

"Like maggots in meal!" The master craftsman laughed, and began to walk beside Malcolm. "You have lived in London, you say. How goes the pest there?"

Malcolm was anxious not to be taken for a spy, but saw no point in hiding his origin from Leeuwenhoeck's colleagues, since it was as a fellow of the Royal Society that he was presenting himself. "It lingers," he allowed. "Though certainly not like before the Fire."

Spoors pulled a long face. "Plagues light on cities, like sparks on dry tinder." Then, apparently moved by the theme of bodily infirmity, he asked, "You go today to see if Antoni is better? He had, you understand, an attack of diarrhoea."

Malcolm said that he had realized this. "I hope that Heer Leeuwenhoeck is able to receive me today. His letters to the Royal Society take long to reach us, and we are anxious to hear of his newest researches." It occurred to him that Spoors, who worked with farseeing lenses, might be more valuable a source than Leeuwenhoeck.

Malcolm paused at a footbridge that arched across the canal, a sturdy wooden structure such as one might expect to find spanning a brook in an English deer park. The low arch blocked the waterway to all boats, even skiffs, and Malcolm stared at it, wondering whether it swung like a tollgate. Of course, he realized suddenly: This canal isn't for navigation, it merely drains some polder. The narrow channel was in fact a ruled gutter, engineered as carefully as an aqueduct.

Spoors, taking his surprise for uncertainty, pointed to the left. "The *comptoir* is this way," he offered, taking Malcolm's arm. "Allow me to conduct you; I would see that my friend is recovered before returning to work." And the surveyor led him into central Delft, past a street that stank of scorched hops and another crowded with pilgrims heading for the New Church ("The tomb of William the Silent," Spoors explained) to the garment district where Malcolm, who had come to it yesterday from the opposite direction, recognized at last the clothier's shop of Antoni Leeuwenhoeck, who gazed through microscopes.

"You must pardon my yesterday's indisposition," said the draper as he led them to his small office in back. "I suffered, it seems, from a fluxion of *kleijne diert-*

gens.'' Malcolm did not get a chance to ask what the Dutchman meant before they were standing about his crowded worktable, which was littered with drawings, bits of metal, and stoppered bottles and jars. No instruments were in view, and every visible object was small.

Malcolm began to murmur some expression of well-being, but Leeuwenhoeck was on to business. ''What had I been showing you?'' he asked, frowning at his lapse in recollection. He looked more the tradesman he plainly was than the microscopist his letters proclaimed. His wig and coat were in the fashion of the mercantile class, and his manners, like a new lens, were ground but unpolished.

''You had begun to demonstrate the 'globules' in a smear of human sperm,'' said Malcolm. ''You said they bore tails and thrashed like tadpoles.''

Leeuwenhoeck and the surveyor exchanged glances. ''That was a trifle,'' Leeuwenhoeck said shortly. He gestured at a phial lying on the table. ''Your Heer Oldenburgh asked that I examine the constituent parts of saliva, sweat, and other fluids of the body, but it is an investigation best left to anatomists.''

Malcolm looked at the sample, which he had hoped to be shown through a microscope, and suddenly understood. ''Of course,'' he said diplomatically. ''Mr. Oldenburgh will see the sense of that.'' Indeed. He reminded himself that it was the microscope he was here to see, and wondered where Leeuwenhoeck's cabinet was.

''Show him the *diertgens*,'' said Spoors.

Leeuwenhoeck brightened at the suggestion. ''Good idea,'' he said. He picked up a bottle of cloudy liquid, which he unstoppered and began to decant into a fine glass pipe. Malcolm recognized, with a small thrill, the vessel Leeuwenhoeck had described in his letters for the viewing of aqueous substances.

''This water was taken from a stagnant pool upon which the sun had shone for two days,'' Leeuwenhoeck remarked. Stopping the pipe with a pinch of gum, he reached into his coat pocket and produced a metal plate about the size of a calling card. A bead of glass glinted in its center like a gem. The draper secured the pipe to a metal arm protruding from the plate, then held the plate up to the window and peered into the bead as 'twere a keyhole. ''There they are,'' he said. Nodding with satisfaction, he handed the device to Malcolm and gestured that he look.

Wordlessly Malcolm took the scrap and peered into its tiny lens. He had to remove his spectacles and bring the lens so close to his eye that his lashes brushed the metal, but after a moment's adjustment the realm beyond jumped into view: the *kleijne diertgens*—which Malcolm had translated as *animalcula*, Latinizing the tradesman's homely Dutch—were swirling through a featureless medium like motes in a beam, and only those that slowed could be apprehended to have limbs. Legs there were, innumerable as a centipede's, and protuberances that might be heads. Malcolm stood rapt, staring at the swarming creatures until a perceptible dimming—the sun gone behind a Dutch pall—roused him to recollection of his surroundings. He lowered the microscope.

''They are quite as you describe them, Mijn Heer,'' said Malcolm. ''No one in England has yet seen such wonders; Mr. Hooke has devoted his attentions to studying the minute parts of visible objects. But''—holding up the metal lozenge—''I am surprised by the simplicity of your device. It seems in design little more than a flea-glass, though greatly more powerful; but the microscopists of England use instruments that align paired lenses through a viewing tube.''

"I have found," said Leeuwenhoeck, "that using lenses in train compounds not only their magnifying power, but their distortions as well. A single lens, well made, provides clearer results."

This was the opening Malcolm had been seeking. "Are the lenses ground to your own specifications?" he asked.

"I make my own lenses," Leeuwenhoeck answered. He seemed to notice Malcolm's surprise, for he added, "There are in this town no others who practice this art, and so the lens-makers decline to learn its mysteries."

"I see." Malcolm covered his confusion by looking back to the pipe mounted on the microscope. "These myriad creatures flourish where the sun shines on water?"

"Not only there." Leeuwenhoeck produced another pipe, containing a darker liquid. "The tiny creatures appear also to inhabit the interior of human bodies, as mites and fleas do the surface." He unclamped the first pipe from the microscope and affixed the second. "This is from a sample I took yesterday of my own diarrhoea," he said, handing it over.

Both men watched as Malcolm reluctantly raised the instrument to his face. "I see," he said again, wondering if he would be expected to clasp hands on taking leave of the draper.

Murky objects swam across the face of the lens, different (so far as Malcolm could tell) from the bright monsters of the infusoria. "Fascinating," Malcolm said gamely. "Have you catalogued the species of *diertgens* found in the human bowels?"

"No." Leeuwenhoeck picked a page off the desk and turned it facedown. "That again belongs to the realm of physicians. I had wondered whether the sites of illness—well, no matter."

Malcolm seemed to have stepped into another patch of boggy ground. "Indeed," he said, trying at levity, "it would be a serious matter should the physician find sperm globules in such a sample." The two Dutchmen stared at him. "But I have taken too much of your time," he added quickly. "I hope that I shall be able to call upon you when my business returns me to Delft." And the elaborate business of taking leave began, with Malcolm careful to show the draper the courtesy he would extend a British gentleman.

"A marvelous contrivance," said Spoors as they returned the way they had come. "As an ant may crawl upon a steeple, so creatures minute beyond ken may traverse a grain of sand. Bodies there are, which stand to us as we do to mountains; and we stride through life unsuspecting their existence."

The surveyor seemed disposed to talk, and Malcolm wished that the Dutch had coffeehouses. Instead they engaged in furious commerce, relieved only in the evening by tobacco and drink. What Malcolm would lief bring round by degrees he would have to broach directly.

"It is indeed a marvelous device," he said casually. "I wonder not that Heer Leeuwenhoeck is reluctant to disclose the birthplace of such potent lenses."

"He makes them himself, as he said," replied Spoors. "I have dealt with grinders in Delft and beyond, and know that Antoni buys only unpolished blanks."

"Lenses and mirrors for your own work?" Malcolm said this carelessly.

"Indeed, for measurements must be exact." Spoors's voice held a trace of pride.

This, thought Malcolm, might prove the entrypoint he could pry wide to disclose the secret he sought.

"For the finest optical instruments one must go to the Hague," Spoors continued. "Telescopic devices must use twin lenses in train, and those who study the stars employ tubes of tremendous length." He chuckled. "Christiaan Huygens, who saw a ring around Saturn like a wedding band, constructed one three hundred feet long!"

"So I have heard," said Malcolm blandly. "Though my business follows the inquiries of the Royal Society, I would visit the Hague if I could. But I do misgive myself, for the state of war that exists between our countries counsels against my entry to that city."

Spoors made a scoffing sound. "Our countries share more qualities in common than does either with France," he said. "Your Charles recognized this when he made peace with us seven years ago in the face of a common enemy. Now, unable to forget how we burned his navy, he joins the French in attacking us. The beating we have given him this past year will soon convince him to forgo seeking by war what he cannot win in open trade."

This bluff effort at graciousness left Malcolm with feelings so stirred that he could not sort them to tell which lay paramount. Confusedly he asked without thinking: "What does a Surveyor of the Navy do?"

"Eh?" said Spoors. "You mean a surveyor of harbors and straits?"

"I beg your pardon; I mean one who surveys for a nation's navy." Malcolm reddened as he spoke: 'Twas a foolish subject to touch upon. "I know one who works in His Majesty's naval office, and he does know that gentleman who bears this title."

Spoors grunted. "And what does he say of the Dutch?"

The question took Malcolm by surprise, though he might have anticipated it. "I have never met Sir William Batten," he confessed. "But—" His countenance had deepened to the brick red of an oven, and felt as hot. "My friend hath spoken with him often, and remembered Sir William's dismay after the Dutch expedition sailed up the Thames and burned His Majesty's fleet."

"Ha! And what did he say?"

"Actually it was in July," Malcolm temporized, "when a second fleet appeared at Gravesend."

"And the English Surveyor of the Navy said . . . ?"

Malcolm's mouth, he thought miserably, would someday lead him to destruction. "He said, 'I think the Devil shits Dutchmen.' "

And the Delft surveyor threw back his head and roared, startling the street with a burst of Dutch laughter.

Malcolm knew Dutch laughter, though he had never heard so pure a specimen in his score and four of English life. His mother laughed like none of their neighbors, though not in latter years; and the pamphlets and broadsheets assailing the Dutch which he had surreptitiously read made much of the vile fun the lowlanders directed at their benefactors and superiors. The Dutch, young Malcolm gathered, were carefree and ungrateful children such as he could only dream of being, living across the ocean in a country where it did not hurt one to be Dutch.

Reading newer pamphlets, his last night in London, Malcolm found the same slurs he recalled from a dozen years earlier, probably the same sentences. "An Hollander is not an High-Lander, but a low-lander for he loves to be down in the dirt and wallow therein," said one, much taken by his own wit. Malcolm's unmet kinsmen were frugal yet frivolous; they kept Jews in their midst as a swineherd might live with pigs, they neglected proper distinctions between master and servant, and granted their women scandalous freedoms. "Escutcheons are as plentiful as Gentry is scarce, each man his own herald," observes the author of a nasty work entitled *A Brief Character of the Low Countries*. "They are generally so bred up to the Bible that each cobbler is a Dutch doctor of divinity," claimed another.

But most of the scurrilous pamphlets had the Dutchmen devilized by geography: Such low and boggy country could give rise only to such creatures as they. Holland is "the buttock of the world, full of veins and blood but no bones in it." Another called it a "universal quagmire," while a poetaster characterized the industrious Dutch as a

> *Degenerate Race! Sprung out of Mire and Slime*
> *And like a mushroom, ripen'd in small time.*

(The repeated allusions to the Republic's brief history bewildered Malcolm. Had the English disdained their Commonwealth's short pedigree?) "A Dutchman is a lusty, Fat, Two-Legged Cheese-Worm." The author of *Observations Concerning the Present Affairs of Holland*, pretending to impartiality, called the Dutch "usurpers that deprive fish of their dwelling places," provoking in Malcolm a bark of startled laughter. Most pamphlets, however, bore such forthright titles as *The Dutch-Mens Pedigree as a Relation, showing how They Were first Bred and Descended from a Horse Turd which Was Enclosed in a Butter-Box* or *The Obligations of the Dutch to England and their Continual Ingratitude*, and were crudely if vigorously illustrated.

Yet these creatures of amphibious repugnancy, splashing in mud and worse, were reviled particularly for their sense of mirth, an odd quality to impute to vermin. Malcolm knew already that his ancestral home was Europe's hotbed for the production of satirical broadsides and engravings, which deeply affronted both England and France; and that Holland's carefree production of gazettes—the coffeehouse chatter of the Dutch, imprudently preserved on paper—gave even deeper offense. One can understand an enemy's hatred, but his laughter can only urge his destruction.

Malcolm tosses fitfully on a hard bed more like his pallet in Gresham than the stuffed bolster of Vrouw Kluyver's hostelry. The scent of stale tobacco lingers in its sheets along with more corporeal whiffs, apprising the Englishman that the Dutch, with careless sybaritism, smoke after fucking. Loin-wrung and shallowly asleep, Malcolm shifts a hip against the mean bedding just as a door slams in an adjacent room. The jamb of sensations cracks memory like a nutshell, and the Englishman's pale Dutch face, smoothed by dissolution, frowns.

He had worked late, and so was yet asleep in the English dawn when the knocking boomed through his chamber, hardwood against his door like the knell of doomsday. Disoriented, Malcolm thrashed free of his sheets to find his door swung open and two men standing over him, foreshortened British faces gazing down as though he were an eel on a plate.

"Malcolm Weymouth," said the hawk-faced man, as though warning him not to deny it.

"Who are you?" Malcolm had sat up, but they were not granting him room to stand.

"Shut up," warned the shorter one in an ugly tone, but his superior gestured him silent.

"You are Malcolm Weymouth of Battersea," he said, "born of Richard Weymouth, mariner, and his wife Marte, a Dutchwoman."

"That I am." Malcolm wished he could reach for his hat.

"I am Silas Monckton, with warrant of the Council of State." Monckton straightened, carrying himself with the assurance of authority, and turned to survey the room. A batch of proof sheets lay upon his table, partially corrected. Monckton pointed at them with his stick. "Thou art a clerk for the Royal Society, and dost translate letters from French and Dutch correspondents."

"I am a junior fellow," Malcolm protested weakly. He had recognized the spymaster's name, and his entrails were gone weak with fear.

"Including," Monckton continued as though he had not heard, "letters from the Dutch Republic, with whom we are in deadly conflict."

"I do but translate observations of the natural world, for publication in *Philosophical Transactions*," said Malcolm in a constricted voice. Surely, he thought but could not say, this constitutes no treasonous communication with the enemy.

"I have read the letters." Monckton turned his head to study the sheets, then nodded. "The draper from Delft is no naturalist, but has simply extended the efforts of Robert Hooke."

"Indeed," said Malcolm, mind awhirl, "the man but carries forward studies initiated here." Copies of the first proofs had been circulated to several of the senior fellows for approval. He wondered how they could have reached His Majesty's agents.

"Yet the spyglass was invented in Holland," said Monckton. "Its application for military purpose was swiftly undertaken. And a Dutchman named Huygens, known to your Society, has lately devised a new method for grinding lenses that signally improves the power of the telescope."

"I did not know these things," replied Malcolm, mystified.

The spymaster settled into Malcolm's chair, not taking his eyes off the young man, and planted his stick between them like a banner. "The draper's microscope uses a single lens, knowest thou not that? yet is more powerful than any in England. Their lenses achieve greater power than ours, and avoid the distortions ours suffer. Canst thou not conceive, son of the nether lands, how these things might aid their prowess in war?"

"A stronger spyglass means farther vision," said Malcolm carefully, "yet the curvature of the Earth sets a firmer limit on their range. The greatest glass conceivable cannot see from Ipswich to the Hague."

Monckton looked at him carefully, like a vivisectionist wondering where to begin. "Hast thou seen schoolboys playing with a lens, such as cloth-merchants use to study the weave of a fabric? Hast seen them focus the sun's rays so to kindle a fire, or roast a nest of ants?''

"Aye, this I have." Dawning realization crossed Malcolm's features. "But none of these contrivances can be turned to warlike uses."

"No? Have none of the scientists of the Royal Society, formed by decree of His Majesty himself, thought to wonder whether it is possible for a magnifying glass to set fire to a ship, as Archimedes of Syracuse was said to have done?''

"Archimedes of Syracuse supposedly used a refracting mirror," said Malcolm. He remembered something about Dutchmen and mirrors, but could not order his thoughts. Sitting undoubleted on his low bed, his hair disordered and his bladder bursting, he spoke incautiously. "And His Majesty has expressed nothing but disdain for the science of microscopy."

"You shut your gob," cried the second man angrily. He raised a gnarled fist and took a step forward.

"Enough, Pitcairn," said Monckton. "Mister Weymouth may not mean to speak treason."

"I speak only facts." Frightened as he was, Malcolm found himself provoked by this avenue of intimidation. "I know nothing of your reports, nor anything of the Dutch war save what I hear in the coffeehouses." He stood, to dispel the detriment of being gazed down upon, and tried to think. "No lens could set a ship afire; it is simply not possible. The focal length is too short, and the angle between sun, lens, and target wrong. It is possible—'' Professional caution urged him stay, but he felt he had better give something—"It is *possible*, under ideal circumstances, that a powerful mirror might perhaps burn a pinpoint hole in a sail."

"I see." Monckton leaned slightly back, and the imbalance was restored: Malcolm was standing abjectly before his seated interrogator.

Doggedly Malcolm continued: "The ship, however, would do better to arm itself with a cannon, which would still function in cloudy weather. It would also prove more durable, and easily aimed."

"I'm sure the Naval Office will be relieved by thy assurances." Though seemingly at ease, Monckton was regarding him with a curious intensity, which seemed not quite curiosity, nor amusement, nor disdain. With a start Malcolm recognized it as hatred. Large-skulled and horse-jawed, a former lieutenant (so the story went) to John Thurloe himself, Monckton brought the Roundheads' fanatical rigor to the cause of the libertine Charles, as though the savage pursuit of a former enemy's interests conferred its own dour grace. The Dutch Republic in particular he seemed to hate with the virulence of any royalist, and Malcolm could feel the man's gaze lighting on those of his features thought to betray Dutch blood: the sensuous lips, the milk-fair features.

"The Naval Office has not asked my advice on any matter," said Malcolm, taking refuge in fact. "I do but work for the Royal Society, in matters mostly secretarial."

"The Royal Society would do well to examine more closely its hiring practices," said Monckton acidly. "This Dutchman writes accounts of lenses more powerful than any we know, and you look only to the descriptions of chaff and slime with which he busies himself. Other intelligences reach us of wonders emerging from the Dutch kilns, even as our navy falters in its war against the frogs. And when His Majesty's agents enquire as to why the members of the Royal Society have not brought matters in their knowledge to our attention, we discover that important letters have been entrusted to an equivocating *straddler*, a supposed Englishman neither truly English nor truly a man—''

Malcolm remembered making an angry exclamation, but whether he had taken a step forward or raised his hand he could never recall. He crashed backward, a stick against his throat and someone's foul breath in his face. Impact drove the wind from him, and before he was able to raise his hands he was struck between the legs with the force of a mallet. Gasping airlessly, Malcolm gaped upward to see, beyond Pitcairn's leering nearness, the austere gaze of Monckton standing over them.

''Let him up, Pitcairn. Our Royal Fellow may be as much Dutch as English, but he will do earnest labor, like a pilgrim marshaling his better half against his worse, in the service of virtue. It is our role, like figures of allegory, to persuade him of his duty.''

No laughter at this, for laughter acknowledges to the world one's enjoyment, which Puritans will not acknowledge to themselves. Malcolm would not either, at least according to Grietje, who expressed hers freely. Having gotten behind her and set to work at loosening the strings belting her skirt, he heard her giggle. ''Most men lift the hem,'' she observed with a glance over her shoulder. ''Those who tug down the waistband are usually pretending they've got a sailor.'' And she galed into laughter to Malcolm's shriveling shock.

But even this did not deflate him for long. She threw her arms about him and thrust her beery tongue against his, uncorseted teats pressed against his chest. Grietje smelled of soap and sweat, and bent complaisantly to let Malcolm confirm, with clinical aplomb, that she was disease-free. Lying now drowsing, his leased love departed for other commerce, Malcolm feels peace in dissipation, as though, like a rock salmon, he has traveled up the estuary of his scarce-remembered homeland to convulse forth his seed.

Someone was knocking on the door. Malcolm came awake with a horrible start, although the knock was neither deferential nor peremptory. ''Meynheer Weymouth!'' called a young voice. The door swung open and an adolescent, grinning insolently, entered holding a steaming mug. ''Meynheer Spoors's respects, sir,'' he said cheerfully, ''and an invitation to come forth this night to observe the wonders of a new telescope.''

Dumbly Malcolm accepted the cup, which hotly radiated the aroma of coffee. The first sip raced through his veins like the phantasmic pneuma and he felt his mind waken to join his body. Even the discovery that the voluptuous Dutch had put a dollop of cream in the coffee did nothing to still his dawning wonder.

The young man picked up Malcolm's breeches, turned them right-side-to, and slung them over the back of the chair. ''It's a two-hour journey,'' he remarked, ''so we must leave soon, I'm told to say, to catch the crescent Venus. I'll be without.'' And he closed the door behind him. He had not, Malcolm realized, said how he had known where to find Malcolm.

He drank more deeply of the coffee. An extraordinary experience, he reflected, having coffee in your room without having to go out to a coffeehouse for it. A second pleasure this day to which he could accustom himself.

The last time he had drunk coffee, he recalled as their carriage sped across a causeway separating two fields, was the afternoon before his departure. It was at Jonathan's, which the Secretary Member (he jestingly called himself that, though Malcolm did not dare) was wont to frequent. Malcolm had known the Secretary from his late visits to the Royal Society; but his appointment last year had elevated him beyond further acquaintance with Malcolm, who had no business in matters Naval or Parliamentary. Yet the Secretary (who heard everything) hailed Malcolm and came himself to his table—Malcolm standing with a start and a stammer—to demand whether it was true that "You go now to the court of Nicholas Frog?"

"To Delft, rather, sir," answered the junior fellow, blushing like a Dutchman. "To study late advances in the art of *Microscopy* for the Society." He wondered whether the Secretary knew better.

"Jesu, and should you profit from your expedition thence, you'll be the first." The Secretary's coffee was being delivered to his table, and he beckoned the waiter over. "The Dutch have sunk seven hundred of our ships in this God-forsaken war, while we have scarce touched theirs. They have flooded their own lands to stop the French advance, did you know that?"

Malcolm, who never listened to coffeehouse talk of the Dutch war, shook his head solemnly. The waiter's tray bore three gold-rimmed cups, the Secretary's and his two clerks', and Malcolm was served one of them. He sipped the steaming brew carefully, and discovered that the Secretary for the Affairs of the Admiralty was served a better bean than the common gentleman.

"Has the navy," he asked, "exacted a comparable toll against the Dutch?"

The Secretary scowled. "Their merchant ships hole up in harbor like rats, and scarce expose themselves. Such is the Dutchmen's wealth that they can stifle their trade thus, yet do not starve. Louis should have overrun them by now, but their terrible measures have stopped the French cold."

"You have visited Holland," Malcolm began.

"I have visited the Dutch, and the Dutch have visited *me*." He said it grandly, like one who would tread the stage.

Malcolm knew what the Secretary signified, and though he had heard the tale before, he asked again now. "You heard their guns yourself?" he asked.

"All London heard them," the Secretary answered solemnly. "The sound of enemy fire as the Dutch burned our ships beat a tattoo I hear yet." He seemed to brood. "Yet their landing party did not kill our townspeople, nor plunder their houses. I spoke afterward to the folk of Medway, who told me that our own soldiers, who entered the country-towns after the Dutch withdrew, were far more terrible to the populace."

If the Secretary had wished to pull apart the knit loyalties of peaceable Malcolm like a digger prising a clam, he was going about it the right way. Malcolm smiled painfully, proud of his scrupulous Dutch forebears, ashamed of his ignoble English ones, and miserable that the Republican Dutch and the once-Republican English were not making common cause against the Popish Louis, who set ally against ally with the heft of his purse. Did the Secretary know how he was perturbing the fragile orrery of Malcolm's composure?

"So," continued the Secretary, as though proceeding from melancholy matters to others possibly less so, "you are to study the Dutchmen's facility with the flea-glass?"

"Mister Leeuwenhoeck's device, though it employs but a single lens, appears readily the equal of Hooke's," replied Malcolm cautiously. "I do not yet know whether the Holland gentility use them for amusements."

"I wish our gentility thought them more than amusements," said the Secretary morosely. "When His Majesty dismissed the study of *micro-phenomena* as 'the mere weighing of Ayre,' the apes of fashion took it as license to mock any investigation graver than gaping at a louse on a pin. I do fear that the sons of the gentry, from whom we look to recruit the naturalists of tomorrow, will think it no true calling."

And perhaps the Dutch thought it no true calling, reflected Malcolm in the carriage, if their best researches were conducted by a draper. The Dutch astronomers, on the other hand, were gentlemen of the finest education, their accomplishments recognized even in France. Huygens had contacts with the Dutch government through his father, who had introduced Leeuwenhoeck to the Royal Society. Uneasily Malcolm wondered how closely the Dutch government followed its citizens' optical researches.

"Here we are," announced the boy cheerfully from his perch behind Malcolm's seat. Malcolm peered into the twilight, and saw several men standing on the levee ahead of them like an assignation of smugglers. After a second's further scrutiny, he realized that they were bending over a large tube, like a band of gunners aiming a bombard. One straightened and came forward as Malcolm climbed down.

"You are Mister Weymouth, the English gentleman," he said in Dutch-accented Latin. "I am Cornelius van der Pluym, astronomer of Leiden. With my *reflecting telescope*, based on the newest principles from Paris, I hope to discover that Venus, like Jupiter, Saturn, and our own Earth, possesses orbiting moons."

"I am honored that you have agreed to let me observe your observations," replied Malcolm gravely in the same word-scant tongue. He did not know whether the astronomer assumed he knew no Dutch, or always conducted his discussions in the language of science.

"Come this way, then, and see how the reflecting lens improves upon the aerial design of Huygens," said van der Pluym, gesturing that Malcolm precede him. "Keep him out of trouble," he added in quiet Dutch to the servant.

Grinning in complicity, the servant led Malcolm around the telescope, which stood on a brass-and-wood tripod as though meant for a professor's study. The eyepiece, Malcolm noted with surprise, emerged from the end of the tube rather than its side, as Newton's model had. Peering into it, van der Pluym murmured something which an assistant, shielding the light of a candle with his body, transcribed into a notebook.

"Have you seen Meynheer Huygens's new telescope?" asked a young man next to Malcolm, who introduced himself as Rudolf Moete. Malcolm said he had not. "It comprises two distinct tubes, separated by fifty feet or more. A train of mechanisms is required to keep them aligned, for which Huygens must keep a crew ready. Still, it is better than handling a single tube of such length, which presents terrible difficulties."

"The reflecting model uses a convex mirror, does it not?" asked Malcolm casually.

"Aye, and it must be perfectly formed, else the design be no improvement upon Huygens's. I do fear that van der Pluym's model does not meet this standard."

Eventually Malcolm was given an opportunity to peer into the eyepiece while the astronomer sketched his observations. A perfect sickle, Venus showed nearly as large as the Moon but without flaw or feature in its whiteness. Malcolm saw no pinpoint of light that would signify a moon, but doubted his ability to resolve detail through the impediment of his spectacles. He had not yet found an ideal distance at which to set his eye when the astronomer tapped his shoulder, and he relinquished his place.

Moete stood a few yards off, smoking his pipe as he looked over the levee. Malcolm joined him, wondering how to raise the subject of mirror-making.

"The air is a lens," the young man said thoughtfully. "Have you ever seen waves of heat ripple above the ground on a hot day? So, faintly, does air refract light as it passes between warm and cool regions. It is my contention that twilight, with heat escaping from the earth, will ever be a poor time for viewing, and that the moons of Venus will be seen only on winter dawns."

"How interesting," murmured Malcolm. Those craftsmen who wrought mirrors must work closely with the lens grinders, he thought; the arts are too similar. He took a step forward, looking down as though to watch his footing, then stumbled on the sloping ground. Malcolm caught himself only as he fell to his knees, and his spectacles flew off his nose, to disappear with a splash into the water below.

"Oh, heavens," he cried as Moete helped him to his feet. "I have lost my eyeglasses in the polder. How could I get another pair made?"

Sunlight glittered off the Delft shop windows, still wet from a morning shower. Malcolm, back from the Hague and shaking rain from his hat, found everything made new, each glint bespeaking fresh-planed edges. He walked the streets with more familiarity now, without imagining that every face he met saw him for a foreigner. Was it myopia that made one suspicious of others' motives?

Leeuwenhoeck seemed pleased enough to see him. "My investigations continue," he said as he led the Englishman to his office. "An improved cutting blade has allowed me to refine my observations of the tubules within wood. I have also made studies of the sting of a bee."

Malcolm was more interested in the tiny animals, but knew Leeuwenhoeck's reticence on the subject. Looking about the office for a more friendly subject, he was startled to see a small canvas propped against the wall, an oil painting portraying (it appeared) the torments of Hell. Damned figures writhed and supplicated the empty sky as a variety of demons prodded them, tore their flesh, or consumed them whole.

"I did not know you favored paintings of a religious nature," said Malcolm uncertainly.

"It is by my friend Vermeer," said Leeuwenhoeck, glancing at it. "He seeks to allay his debt, so has accepted a commission from a pious widow to produce an allegory in the manner of Bosch. He consulted with me regarding plausible designs for his imps."

Malcolm looked closer and saw that one of the demons, its head a wheel of waving limbs, bore an unmistakable resemblance to the animalcules he had seen earlier. Another seemed to possess the magnified features of a louse.

As though reminded by the infernal landscape, Leeuwenhoeck said: "I have noticed that the *diertgens* which live in pond water seem to vary in number between summer and autumn, and may continue to do so throughout the year. And that while a cow's blood contains numerous globules, the *aqueous humour* of its eye contains none."

"I would be interested to hear whether the *diertgens* found in the human gut differ between men and women, or between sick men and healthful ones."

"Well, perhaps your British colleagues shall carry that investigation farther," the draper replied indifferently. "I cannot restrict my researches to a single subject, and find the variety of the natural world more appealing than the fluids of the human corpus."

Which was certainly disingenuous, Malcolm reflected as he returned to his inn. It was likelier that Leeuwenhoeck had misgivings about conducting investigations into the human body. Malcolm knew that the Dutchman could not fear ecclesiastical persecution, but he might fairly worry about trespassing upon the privileges of physicians, who doubtless enjoyed a monopoly on medical research.

"There's a young man to see you," said Vrouw Kluyver as Malcolm entered the inn. "A sailor, I think." Malcolm blushed, then looked to the tavern room. Thanking the goodwife, he straightened his hat and crossed the threshold, to find nothing but two idle workmen sitting over tankards. Puzzled, he looked toward the back rooms, where cards were played in evenings and private parties sometimes convened. Unlit by day, they seemed poor sites for an appointment. His heart pounding, Malcolm poked his head round a corner and peered uncertainly into the gloom.

"Look at you," an unfamiliar voice, English, said out of the darkness. Malcolm blinked, and the outline of a man behind a table slowly took form. "Gone bloody Dutch, like a tabby back in the wild, eh?"

"Who are you?" asked Malcolm, moving to block the light that disclosed himself. A coal glowed briefly, and Malcolm saw the face above the pipe: British features, expression insolent and knowing, beneath tousled black curls. "I've seen you before," said Malcolm, as the man sat back and smiled. He was wearing a seaman's jacket, and abruptly Malcolm recognized him. "You were on the ship that brought me over," he said wonderingly.

"Do you remember why you were brought over?" the man asked.

Malcolm looked at him carefully, then glanced back at the tavern room. "I am about my business," he said cautiously. "Have you a letter for me?"

The sailor looked Malcolm up and down. "Even wearing Dutch spectacles, I see. Hoping to interest young scholars? What would Master Monckton think of such dissipation?"

Malcolm caught his breath even as the blood surged to his face. "My English spectacles were broken, and by my own design, to get me entry to the Hague's finest lens-makers. If thou knowst what I am about, thou knowst well why."

"Your report I have." The man—Malcolm finally remembered his name was Skerrett—turned over several pages, which Malcolm recognized as not only the report he had sent to an Amsterdam address, but also a second one he had left unfinished in his room. "You were asked to learn more of Leeuwenhoeck's tiny animals, but relate nothing."

"I was asked only after submitting that report," Malcolm replied hotly. "Did that note come from you?" His only reply was the glow of the pipe. "I have come from Leeuwenhoeck directly," he said finally, "and he has grown close on the matter of *diertgens*. I will not get more from him this day."

The sailor looked at Malcolm searchingly. "The Crown is preparing to offer peace, do you know that?" He was tapping the contents of his pipe onto the papers. "The Dutch flooded their own lands, like a frog pissing itself, and stopped the French dead. Their navy ventures nothing, sailing forth only when certain of victory. They draw allies throughout Europe, and if they are not stopped this season we shall have to sue. Or did your sailor friends not tell you this?"

"You followed me in Amsterdam." Malcolm was at once sick and enraged. "You know enough to know me guiltless, yet seek the vilest advantage—"

Skerrett reached forward, faster than Malcolm could see, and grasped his wrist hard. "I seek advantage for England as vile as needs serve," he said softly, his callused fingers tightening unto pain. "The Crown might e'en use such as thou, and throw it away afterward. Now hear me close: know'st thou the *interwaarden* between the stream feeding the brewery and its north embankment?"

"Yes," whispered Malcolm, trying to pull his hand free.

"Meet me there tomorrow sunset, and bring thy report." Skerrett abruptly released Malcolm's hand, causing him to stagger. "Continue thy inquiries in Leeuwenhoeck's work: They justify thy continued presence in Holland. And include them in the report, that it may look innocuous if seized."

He pushed back his chair and stood, glaring. "Englishmen die while thou dalliest," he said, pointing at Malcolm. Malcolm caught a glint of light and realized that the finger extending toward his nose was a knife tip. "Bring us results directly, or feel my present wrath." Something struck Malcolm's chest lightly, then fell with a clang to the floor: coins. Skerrett was out the door, his footfalls receding rapidly.

Malcolm stood long seconds in the dim light before he bent to retrieve the coins. Two half-guilders, sufficient for a few days' lodging. His papers were left derisively on the table, and Malcolm took them up, folding them prudently into a pocket before quitting the room.

Vrouw Kluyver was waiting for him in the tavern room. "You still want to go to Leiden?" she asked.

Malcolm had forgotten his earlier plans. "Is there a boat?" he asked. The prospect of leaving town seemed suddenly attractive.

"The *snipschuit* leaves twice an hour," she said. "But you have to change boats in the Hague, and from there passage to Leiden is only hourly."

So Malcolm took the canal boat, a narrow covered craft drawn by horses along a *trekvaart* that had been dug straight as an avenue for the sole purpose of boating passengers between towns. He paid for his ticket in a booth overlooking the canal, where the *snipschuit* had just entered the lock from the upper reach. Canalmen, swinging the balance beam's counterweight over the spectators' heads like an immense slow scythe, shut the mitre gates with a water-muffled thump. Malcolm watched as they bent to lift the sluice-gates, releasing a gush of water into the side-ponds. The boat, which filled the tiny lock like a loaf in a basket, slowly sank into the lock. By the time the lower gate was opened and the ship brought out like a toy from a box, Malcolm was queued up with the other passengers, burghers and prosperous tradesmen. He stepped into the canoe-shaped craft, which rocked gently as the passengers found their seats, and sat with a tentative smile next to a pipe-puffing gentleman leaning against the railing.

"Eighty minutes," the man remarked, taking his watch from his pocket and checking it.

"To the Hague?" Malcolm asked. "How can that be?" The two horses had tightened the towlines and were pulling the boat forward, at a pace at once too fast for them to sustain yet too slow to make such time.

"Watch," said the burgher. A pair of mounted canalmen were riding alongside the towhorses, both (Malcolm noticed) looking back over their shoulders. Together they slowly raised their free arms, then brought them down with a sudden shout. The horses leaped forward, and the boat seemed to lift and jerk forward at the same instant. A few men around them cheered.

"What was that?" asked Malcolm. They were now sailing much faster than before, while the horses were trotting easily.

The Dutchman chuckled. "We're riding the primary wave raised by the motion of the boat, which we caught as it overtook us. With the wave beneath us, the *snipschuit* can be hauled at less expenditure of energy than at faster or slower rates."

"That is astonishing." Malcolm stood and tried to look over the side, but the canal was so narrow that the clearance between boat and wall was no wider than a doorsill. "The primary wave propagates down the canal without dissipating, doesn't it?" He was trying to work out the physics.

The burgher sighed happily. "Sounds like a bird flying behind itself to shelter from the wind, doesn't it? Yet it works." His pleasure at the found economy was evident.

"Some say light is a wave," said Malcolm, thinking of it passing down a telescope tube. "That it spreads from the sun like ripples expanding from a pond."

"Nonsense," said the burgher comfortably. "Light streams like God's grace from heaven. Does God's grace waver?"

Leiden was a greater town than Delft, and its university (a long walk from the canal, which ran straight into the center of town like the Appian Way) seemed to contain as many foreigners as Dutchmen. Malcolm walked unremarked, a young Englishman among Germans, Frenchmen, and what sounded like Poles. Nobody knew the location of the observatory, so Malcolm presented himself at the university library, where he showed his letter of introduction to the Librarian, who seemed to find the matter highly irregular.

"This letter is signed by two physicians of the town of Delft," the venerable gentleman observed, glancing up from it reproachfully, "but you wish to speak to a Professor of Optics."

"Both the learned doctors are graduates of this university," Malcolm pointed out. "I might be able to get a letter from Meynheer van der Pluym, if that would help."

"It says," the Librarian continued, "that the physicians do not in fact know you, but are writing at the request of the Chamberlain of Sheriffs, Meynheer Leeuwenhoeck. The draper," he said, looking up.

"How did you know that?" asked Malcolm, startled.

"He was here last month, asking to see our books on *contagio*," the Librarian grumbled. "He had to have a student abstract the books' Latin that he might understand it."

"I can read my own Latin," Malcolm offered.

"Oh, you shall have your admission, as the draper had his." The Librarian scribbled something at the bottom of the letter and handed it crossly back. In the event, nobody asked to see the admission, and Malcolm wandered the library unchallenged.

The *Opticae Thesaurus* was there, and *Pantometria*, the earliest book to describe an optical instrument, and British too. Two copies of *Micrographia*, as was just. No modern Dutch work, however; nothing to bespeak a *"Eureka!"* in optical design. Would the Dutchmen build a *speculum horribilis* and then not publish word of it? Perhaps they would, like an alchemist guarding the secret of the *aqua vitae*. Malcolm found it hard to believe, however.

The Dutch published no journal of philosophical research, but it occurred to Malcolm that a university boasting its own observatory might have shelves devoted to astronomy books. Following directions, he located the wall of astronomical works, where a student stood perusing a folio. At Malcolm's approach he looked up, and was Moete the telescopist. "The Englishman of the levee," he said, closing his volume. "You wear new spectacles, I see."

"Better than before," said Malcolm, touching his hat politely. "Your countrymen grind finer lenses than do mine, though it pains me to say't."

"Better at glass than mirrors, I fear." The young Dutchman pulled a long face. "The moons of Venus shall remain unobserved, unless our craftsmen learn to make a convex mirror of proper curvature."

"Perhaps the best craftsmen are otherwise occupied," suggested Malcolm, hoping not to flush his game.

Moete shook his head. "This is a small country, my friend, and the makers of sound lenses and mirrors are known to every astronomer by name. A good reflecting telescope requires a perfect parabola, else the light won't come to a point. Van der Pluym's model is the best they can do, and it is but indifferent good."

"Will you be pursuing astronomical observations tonight?" Malcolm asked.

Moete gave a brilliant smile. "Tonight it is going to rain. I shall enjoy a leisurely dinner, and be in bed before ten."

Malcolm wished him well, then returned to the main reading room. Was it possible that he was being elaborately gulled, shown inferior instruments and told of inadequate skills while artisans quietly crafted mirrors to set the British fleet ablaze? All Malcolm could do was report his findings, which his overseers must interpret as they would.

The Librarian eyed Malcolm suspiciously as he paged through the catalogue, which had been helpfully divided (in the French manner) into various classifications. Carefully Malcolm read down pages of book titles, looking for any that might suggest a treatise on optics or weaponry. Candidates he copied into his memorandum book. Most of the titles were in Latin, but some were in Mediterranean languages he scarcely knew. He stopped, frowning, at *Lo specchio ustorio ouero trattato delle settioni coniche*. "The Burning Glass"?

Malcolm left his post and sought out the book, which was shelved, unpromisingly, under Mathematics. Bonaventura Cavalieri's 1632 treatise seemed indeed to concern itself with conic sections, and Malcolm turned its pages bemusedly, wondering about the *specchio ustorio*. But when he saw Figura XXI and Figura XXII, he caught his breath: The drawings showed, unmistakably, designs for mirror arrangements that would set fires.

Malcolm read slowly through the accompanying text, which he copied down for more expert translation. The first design focused the sun's rays to ignite material in a cylinder, which then smoked at the top like a chimney, but the second arrangement sent a beam of concentrated sunlight across space like a bullet's path. A large concave parabolic mirror, its vertex removed like a tip snipped from the finger of a glove, gathered the light like a funnel, and a small convex parabolic secondary mirror cast it outward in a parallel beam. At the drawing's edge the beam terminated, meaningfully, in a curl of smoke.

So an Italian geometer had designed Archimedes's marvelous weapon, and forty years ago. Malcolm could see disadvantages to the design: The annular primary mirror lost most of the area it presented to the Sun to the opening in its center. Curious, he sketched a convex lens set like a jewel in the central space, which would bend the light passing through onto the same focus as the mirror. Would such a design—mirror and lens in conjunction—prove workable?

The craft of making mirrors was certainly not equal in 1632 to building such a weapon; and Malcolm doubted that it was today. After two hours' further search, however, he could confirm only that no other books existed on the subject.

Before leaving he sought out the medical section, curious what "books on *contagio*" Leeuwenhoeck might have read. The books were ordered by no scheme that Malcolm understood, but by reading all the titles he came to *De Contagione et Contagiosis Morbis*, published in 1546 in Venice by Hieronymus Fracastorius, a name that tugged at Malcolm's memory. The book's top was free of dust, unlike its companions to either side. What had Leeuwenhoeck sought here?

Malcolm took the volume to a table and began to turn its heavy pages, which some past owner had marginally annotated. Fracastorius, it proved, had made a study of epidemic diseases, which (he proposed) were infections spread by imperceptible particles. Each disease is caused by a different species of particle, which multiply rapidly and travel from afflicted sufferers to new victims by one of three means: by direct contact, through the air, and by transmission through soiled clothes and linen.

At the bottom of a page the annotator had noted in schoolboy Latin: "*Cf. Marcus Varro, who warned in the c. before Christ against miasmal swamps 'Because there are bred certain minute creatures which cannot be seen by the eyes, which float through the ayre and enter the body through the mouth and nose and there cause serious disease.'* "

Malcolm wondered at the significance of this. Did Antoni Leeuwenhoeck hope to discover Fracastorius's minute particles with his microscope? The answer suggested itself a second later: The draper was wondering whether his "little animals" were the causes of contagious disease.

The realization was faintly embarrassing. Malcolm hoped that Leeuwenhoeck hadn't confided this hope to his physician friends, who had (he knew) taken seriously the tradesman's researches when scholars and academicians had not. So startling were the *animalcula* on first sight—and can Varro, or any sage of the ancient world, ever actually have seen them?—that their discoverer could be forgiven a moment's wild surmise that he had uncovered the agent of all pestilence.

Abruptly Malcolm remembered something about the author, a mental poke from a direction he could not identify. He returned to Moete, who was sitting peaceably at a table. "Pardon me, but have you heard of a scholar named Fracastorius?"

"Girolamo Fracastoro?" The Dutchman seemed surprised at the question. "Of course, he was an Italian astronomer of the last century, colleague of Copernicus. Also a physician; wrote about plagues. I think we have some of his books."

Moete strode to the shelves, where he ran his hand along the ribbed spines before pausing and selecting one. "*Homocentria*," he pronounced, looking at the title page. "Fracastoro believed that the planets revolved in circular orbits round a fixed point, although he did not identify that as the Sun." A scrap of paper lay inside the cover, which Moete opened and read. "It says that Fracastoro also wrote a book about syphilis, in verse," he said.

"That's it," said Malcolm. "He gave syphilis its name, in a poem written in the classical manner. I had not known him for an authority on plagues as well." Nor on the heavens, for that matter.

Moete shrugged easily. "It was an age of great men," he said. "So long as you did not mind being harried by the Church of Rome."

Malcolm felt such a surge of friendliness that he was suddenly tempted to ask Rudolf to dinner. Only the knowledge that the last boat back to Delft left before eight prevented him. He bid the Dutchman a pleasant farewell, urged him to read *Philosophical Transactions*, and set out with directions for the observatory, where (he was told) junior students could be found at this hour cleaning the instruments.

Leiden University was sufficiently like Greenwich that Malcolm, after ten days in Delft or the Hague, felt at once comfortable and homesick. Some of the students he saw on the street were plainly British; they did not recognize him, Dutch-complected and -attired, as a countryman. He saw one, English but not dressed like a student, come round a corner and realized with a horrible start that it was Skerrett.

The sailor turned to look Malcolm's way, and Malcolm spun to present his back. Red hair, Dutch jacket, he thought; and there is no reason for Skerrett to think me in Leiden. He took a few steps, then glanced sidelong over his shoulder. The sailor was continuing up the street, his pace unaltered.

Malcolm's heart was pounding against his ribs like an importunate fist. What in sweet heaven's name was Skerrett doing in Leiden? If the knavish sailor was engaged as a sergeant of spies, as seemed plain, he did no good to enter the field of battle himself. Or had he another spy in Leiden, whom he came now to see?

Malcolm faded into the back streets like a mouse into shadows, then took the most circuitous of routes back to the canal. The hours he would have spent studying the technology of Dutch astronomers were expended sitting in a carters' tavern, keeping his head down and waiting for the last canal boat to leave. Malcolm watched it depart through a window, then bought passage on a cargo ship. He spent the evening lying on sacks of corn—not even ground meal, he realized with dismay—and looking at the stars in the half-clouded sky.

When the first drops of rain spattered his face, he started awake, the dream enveloping him dispelled like a pond's reflection shattered by a stone. What was the dream? Malcolm knew that to chase would but drive it away, while returning to the position of sleep might coax it back. Positioning himself uncomfortably, he closed his eyes and sought to recapture the instant before waking. A splotch of cold rain struck his eyelid.

"It's coming down now," remarked the pilot, his voice carrying clearly over the still boat.

"Going to wet the young scholar," replied his companion with a snigger.

"He should be wet. He's spent few enough nights in the open, I'll warrant."

They didn't realize he was English, thought Malcolm with a stab of pleasure. And abruptly he had it: He had been dreaming of being Girolamo Fracastoro, of all things. What currents had pulled the unmoored boats of his mind thither?

The second man climbed back and began dragging a tarpaulin over the sacks. Malcolm stood and helped, still wondering whether his drowsing mind had muttered wisdom or foolishness.

"Like the big sky?" the man asked, not unfriendly. Malcolm realized that he meant the perfect unobstructed half-dome of firmament evident between towns in this tabletop country. Dark clouds were scudding across it, visible only by the absence of stars.

Malcolm looked up, trying to imagine the heavens blown free of clouds and moonless. Such a sight would perhaps greet a sailor at sea, did he climb the topmost mast. "It's lovely," he said. "It makes me feel like a lens." There, what had he meant by that?

"Eh?" asked the man, thinking he had heard amiss.

"It makes me feel so small," Malcolm amended. "Like a mite beneath a great lens." But he knew he spoke truth the first time.

The man snorted and climbed back onto the seat, and the pilot returned him his pipe. But it's true, Malcolm thought as he crept under the canvas. It is by lenses that researchers discern the nature of the heavens, those same lenses that disclose the microworld, which stands in relation to us as we do to the vastness above. Philosophers use the term *microcosme* to describe the world of human nature; but the true microcosme lies beneath the lens of the microscope: And we inhabit but an intermediate level between the great and small of the universe.

And I am a simple lens, to be turned upon either world at the instruction of those who would know. Is that what the dream about Fracastoro meant: that he looked to both stars and tiny creatures?

Malcolm fell asleep beneath the blanketing comfort of the tarpaulin, and woke only as they bumped against the bank to a stop. He peeked out and saw a loading dock and, beyond, the lights of a tavern: not Vrouw Kluyver's, but the one from which he had been rousted to visit the astronomers, a ruder establishment. Journey's end, evidently: Malcolm climbed out as the men began to unload the sacks.

A cup of ale seemed suddenly a needful thing, air for a smothering man. Malcolm spied through the windows to confirm that Skerrett did not sit within. His nerves wrung like laundry, he at last entered the tavern, each step a recitation of his back's aches and cricks. It was smokier than in the afternoons he had visited, and the clamor of voices was louder. Malcolm sat at the end of a bench and smiled at the carters who looked at him.

"What will you have, stranger?" asked the barmaid as she removed empty *flapkan* tankards from the table.

Malcolm might have been unknown to the evening crowd, but he wasn't an evening's transient. "Where is Grietje?" he asked, by way of establishing this.

The barmaid pulled a long face. "Taken ill," she said. "Like as not with the pox." She grinned as Malcolm paled, and flipped the lid of a *flapkan* in coarse parody. "Too many kisses, you know?"

Malcolm felt a pit open in his stomach, widening as its edges crumbled. "I am sorry to hear it," he said numbly. He did not know what his face betrayed, could not summon concern.

The barmaid, counting up orders from the rest of the table, asked Malcolm if he wanted one of the same. Nodding, he found his hands straying to his pockets, and set them on the table. The ale, when it came, proved to be cheap *kuyte* beer, harsher than the plum or honey brews he had sampled elsewhere. He drank without tasting it, and made his way through the tangle of drinkers like a sleepwalker. Outside the cold air sharpened his senses, and he noticed as he emptied his bladder that he was at least not afflicted by burning water.

And when might that come? Malcolm imagined himself consulting one of the physicians of Delft, and shuddered. He might have studied the progression of venerall maladies at Leiden today had he known. Dreaming of being Fracastoro indeed!

Gales of self-reproach gave way, on the walk home, to a moment of more temperate assessment. What did a tavern girl know of diagnostick? Poor Grietje might be suffering from any manner of ailment or pox: a word by which that spiteful goose might have meant anything. —But so, he told himself, might she have caught a fever or ague from her easy commerce with rogues, which she may have easily transmitted to Malcolm. If *coition* spread the clap or the pox, what other contagions could be contracted by the lesser embraces that accompany the act?

In the candlelight of his room, Malcolm shamefacedly examined himself for signs of infection. Nothing; which merely displaced his anxiety with a more definite mortification: the shame of the child who has stolen fruit uncaught. Tossing in bed, Malcolm dreams of fornication with a Dutchwoman who swells alarmingly. Feeling her distended abdomen, he wonders what he has engendered; but her waters break with a rush, drenching him in a mephitic flood that swarms with tiny creatures.

Pounding on the door, breaking the membrane of sleep. Authoritarian voices called his name, demanding admission. Malcolm kicked loose his blankets in a panic, then caught his breath and managed to shout, "One moment!" Straightening his clothing, he looked at his desk—clear of papers—then opened the door.

A swart Dutchman, red-nosed, looked at him with mingled officiousness and curiosity. "I am bailiff for the Sheriffs of Delft," he said, raising slightly one shoulder, which was draped with a sash. "The sheriffs require your assistance on a matter of official business. You do understand Dutch?"

Assistance in official business? Was this some lowland euphemism for present arrest? Malcolm followed the man downstairs, past a curious Vrouw Kluyver and two brewery men carrying in the morning's barrel. The streets were nearly empty: It was still early, not yet breakfast-time. Wondering, Malcolm hurried after the bailiff, who strode off in the direction of the sheriffs' chambers.

The building was a fine one, but Malcolm was led round back, to a mean out-house at the end of the yard. The bailiff bid Malcolm stand fast and returned with a sheriff, who glowered at Malcolm before unlocking the door with an iron key. A bad smell struck them as it swung open.

The room was small-windowed and dim, and Malcolm saw only a littered bench. "Be these an Englishman's shoes?" the sheriff asked, holding up a pair of low boots.

Bemused, Malcolm examined the pair, which smelled wet. "They appear so," he said, reluctant to touch them.

The sheriff grunted, then pointed behind Malcolm. "The body was found near an embankment at dawn. Though immersed, it appears not to have drowned."

Reluctantly Malcolm turned. Against the far wall stood a long table, a draped form atop it. Even in the poor light Malcolm could plainly recognize the human shape beneath.

The sheriff seized a pole and pushed open a skylight overhead, admitting a thin column of light into the room. Malcolm had not moved toward the table, and with an impatient sound the sheriff stepped forward and yanked back the sheet.

The body beneath—middle-aged, blanched blue like drained veal—seemed no Englishman that Malcolm could recognize, but rather a member of some strange race, a citizen of the republic of the dead. Though its eyes were closed, it resembled a sleeping man less than a statue would, although Malcolm could not say why. It was only as he stood over the supine figure (merely damp-haired now, but a trickle of water running from one ear) that he realized it was Pitcairn.

"The lungs are empty," said a new voice. Malcolm turned to see an older man enter the room. After a second he recognized him as one of Delft's physicians, an acquaintance of Leeuwenhoeck's. The doctor stepped up to the body and struck the chest with his fist. Malcolm jumped. "See?" asked the physician, nodding wisely. "Dead before he slid into the water."

"Do you recognize this body?" asked the sheriff.

"No," said Malcolm shakily. "Is he not from town?"

"Never saw him in my life," the sheriff answered. He returned to the bench and began poking among the effects.

The physician drew off the rest of the sheet, disclosing the body's nakedness. "No buboes," he remarked, lifting one knee to separate the legs. "Neither pocks nor lenticulae on the skin. Had the body not been in the water, one could prove dysentery by examining the breeches."

Malcolm recoiled. "How do you know it was not death by natural means?" he asked.

"Feel," said the physician, placing a hand under the lolling jaw. "Enlargement of the lymphatic vessels denotes febrile illness.'' Malcolm made no move to copy him.

Malcolm's head was spinning. Why had they brought him here? Had Pitcairn— impossibly in Holland; in *Delft*—carried papers naming him? He looked sidelong at the sheriff, who was going through the pockets of a dripping waistcoat. Despite himself, Malcolm stared. Pitcairn had been traveling in the dress of a prosperous merchant.

The sheriff looked up, catching Malcolm's expression. Malcolm looked away, cursing himself: Had the sheriff noted his surprise? But the Dutchman only said mildly, ''Do English coats usually have so many pockets?''

Malcolm looked back. The waistcoat, held open, contained three slits on each inner side, into which the sheriff thrust his fingers one by one. ''Empty,'' he said. ''Now one, for money, I could understand.''

Malcolm stepped closer. ''I am not familiar with the cut of merchants' coats,'' he said. But would they hold three pairs of inner pockets, like serried gills? The sheriff matter-of-factly inverted the garment and pulled out the six puffs of lining, and Malcolm suddenly felt sick.

''Engorgement of the spleen,'' said the doctor, pressing down on Pitcairn's pallid belly. The cadaver farted in response, prompting a laugh from the sheriff.

''I am sorry I cannot help you,'' said Malcolm, wishing desperately to be gone. ''If you worry about plague in England, I only know news of London, which is yet vexed with the dysentery. But men are not so quickly afflicted as to die of it while walking out.''

''That is true,'' said the physician. ''An autopsy would tell us more.''

''I don't want to hear about it,'' the sheriff told him. He looked at Malcolm. ''Thanks for your help. If you learn anything about missing countrymen, I want to know of it.''

Malcolm left the building, shaken to his heels. He needed an ale, and didn't feel that he could walk all the way back to Vrouw Kluyver's before getting it. Standing in a tavern filled with breakfasting workmen, he drained a tankard of mead-flavored brew and found his wits softening like stewing beef while the bone of anxiety remained. He returned to the street, now filling with purposeful Dutch, and yearned for coffee.

What in God's name brought Pitcairn here? Malcolm worried the question like a beetle scrabbling to escape a pisspot, slipping back only to seek frantic purchase elsewhere. Grant that Skerrett was a sergeant of spies, where in this covert command stood Pitcairn? who could know neither science nor Dutch, nor possessed (Malcolm was certain) any quality save the willingness to carry out dirty jobs.

Work lay before him, for which enlightenment must wait. In the Kluyvers's back room Malcolm drew ink and coffee close, the backsides of old papers before him like a place-matt. Striving to focus his thoughts, he essayed a scheme for his report: a synopsis of Leeuwenhoeck's recent studies in microscopy, with the letter's true matter, of lenses and burning mirrors, concealed in a seeming aside. Methodically he commenced, but the repeated references to tiny organisms—in semen, pond water, man's very bowels—awoke in Malcolm something close to horror, he knew not why. Treat it in a sentence, he thought: Devote the rest to lens-grinding and details of snowflakes.

He threw his notes in the fire, returned to his room and clean papers, and wrote his report in the form of a letter to Mr. Oldenburgh of the Royal Society, full of praise for the peace-loving Dutch and their hospitality to English naturalists. Writing about the *diertgens* troubled him, but a trip downstairs for a second ale dissolved at last the breakwater of his anxiety. Feeling better, Malcolm agreed to join Heer Kluyver in a pipe. If my compatriots tar me a Dutchman, he thought giddily, let me enjoy a Dutchman's pleasures.

The first lungful burned, and the second made him feel as though his head were adrift. "If it weren't for the beer and coffee, you'd be feeling a touch sick," said Kluyver judiciously. Inhaling carefully, Malcolm felt his senses sharpen, as though the world's soft moistness were drying. His anxieties, formless as spilling liquid, he caught within the confines of reason, a container any capable mind can wield.

At once relaxed and alert, he returned to his letter and *discoursed*: upon the possibility of tiny animals swarming through raindrops and dust motes even as their larger brethren fill seas and continents; of further animalcules lying beyond the resolving power of present lenses; of animalcules that may bite Man, as wolves and fleas do, though the victim never know it. Sportively he even proposed that the bite of some tiny creatures may prove venomous like an adder's, so their victims fall sick without comprehending the cause. Report on Leeuwenhoeck's studies? Let Skerrett, who wanted an innocuous-seeming report, rage.

"Commission accomplished," he declared, tucking the papers in a pocket. He strode out into full sunlight, wondering what face Skerrett would present to him when he handed the report over. Did the sailor know that Pitcairn was dead? Would he know that Malcolm knew? Perhaps he would not appear at all, his plans exploded with the death of his confederate, all plots in disarray.

Malcolm wondered what these plots were. He imagined that Pitcairn would be good at firing a lens-grinder's shop, or perhaps breaking a craftsman's fingers. Was Monckton insinuating a band of wreckers into Holland?

Without knowing it, his steps traced a path back toward the sheriff's hall, which he realized only when he looked up to see the bailiff, conversing before the gate with some burgher, pause to eye him curiously. Malcolm almost turned around, but then realized how odd this would look. Nodding slightly, he passed through the gate and went back to the yard, as though he had come with this intention. The door to the outbuilding was ajar, and he approached it cautiously. "Doctor?" he inquired.

"Come in," the physician called. Malcolm pushed the door open. A bad smell wafted out. The physician was standing over the far table, his back to the door. He turned, showing a hand red to the elbow. "Ah, the Englishman. I hoped you'd return. Come have a look at this."

"I don't think I should," said Malcolm quaveringly. The physician turned back to his work. He recognized now the smell: blood, as in a butcher's yard. The thought made his legs weak.

"The spleen," said the physician, "is a mass of disease, and filled with a foul matter, like the lees of oil." He continued to work, and Malcolm realized that he was expected to reply.

"Miasmal fever," he said. He had never worked with a medical specimen larger than a pea, but his book studies held good.

"Indeed," replied the physician. "An *intermittent* rather than a *continuous* fever, as your Sydenham classifies them. Rarely fatal by itself or quickly: and such splenetic ravage is the work of years. Your late countryman was weakened by the ague, but borne off by another illness. Come look at this."

With enormous reluctance, Malcolm took a step forward. The covering sheet was stained red, not the liquid splashes of fresh blood, but the turbid stains of paint. Pitcairn's face was untouched, but the underside of his jaw had been expertly dissected, and his chest opened down the middle like a gutted pig's. Beside the body lay three brownish nodes: each as small as a thumb joint and so dessicated that the ducts at their narrow ends were fraying in paper-thin layers, like an old hornet's nest. Malcolm stared at them in horror.

The physician noticed and dropped them in his pocket. "For my wife," he said. "She would rather plant new bulbs than get a bouquet of tulips." He twitched the sheet farther back. "Note the abscesses in the liver, also (I believe) the lungs. They argue dysentery, as perhaps I should. But these are chronic, not raging, ailments, and not what pushed this man down the embankment and into his grave. Had I to guess that, I would hazard what older physicians called the celestial influences, *influentia coeli*."

"Influentia?" In England it was best known as the grippe, and killed only sometimes but spread like house-afire. Malcolm wondered what traces it might leave on a body.

"A great killer of those weakened already by other maladies," the physician remarked. "Your late countryman was a walking anthology of febrile illnesses, some—" he poked at the viscid spleen—"recently returned. Like a shed rotted through, it collapsed with one kick."

The physician pulled the sheet back over the opened body. "Is that fever not now epidemic in England?" he asked as he wiped his hands on a rag.

"Perhaps only in London," Malcolm answered weakly. The flap of the sheet had disturbed the air, and the stench of diseased innards blew over him. His last taste of Pitcairn.

The physician opened the door, and Malcolm followed him with relief into the yard. "What know you of Sydenham?" the Dutchman asked, as though all lettered Englishmen must know each other.

Malcolm was still seeking to recover the discrimination of his mental faculty, whelmed by the primacy of sight like an owl dazzled by a torch. "I read his book on fevers," he said vaguely. He had paged through it only to see whether the author had made use of a microscope in his researches. "His energies, if I recall, were devoted to treating the living, not inquiring into the mechanisms of pestilence."

"I must look back into it myself." They had reached the street, and the physician glanced at his watch, as though fain to be off, and scowled. "I do not like diseased foreigners dying in Delft and falling into our waters. My business is done, but I hope future visitors will be healthier."

And with a touch of his hat, he took his leave. Malcolm watched him disappear round a corner, feeling impugned by his shared nationality with Pitcairn. He wanted to rush after the physician and confide in him, explaining that the dead man was his persecutor, not countryman. *I am as much Dutch as English.* Spoken, he realized suddenly, with an undoubted English accent.

Malcolm felt unsettled in mind and stomach, as though he had had too much tobacco and needed more beer, or perhaps the reverse. As the sight of Pitcairn receded from the forecourts of his consciousness, the remaining mysteries returned, like vapors expanding to fill a void. Malcolm tried to recall what he knew of Sydenham, who practiced medicine in poorer London, despite the fact that his brother, as a founder of the Protectorate, had wielded tremendous power under Cromwell—

Realization fell on him like a roof collapsing, as though only a bulwark of refusal, holding back facts like a dike, had kept the truth at bay. A piece of it broke free and struck him, like wreckage swept by a flood, and Malcolm felt himself, awash in truth, go under.

What did Monckton know? He could ask Sydenham about febrile contagions, and doubtless had, but what did he *know*? That the grippe spread quickly, running through households and tenements like plague, while the miasmal fever afflicted only certain geographies. That smallpox ravaged the young, while dysentery proved mainly fatal among the elderly. That a man with plague could infect a city, but no one knew the particulars of contagion.

Malcolm walked out the town gates and along a canal path, unmindful of his surroundings. A nearby windmill squealed as a quickening breeze pushed its vanes, and ducks in the pond below quacked and thrashed their wings as though feeling the water being drained. Malcolm paused, then looked across the low wet ground that pooled at the foot of the windmill. The drier ground beyond had been divided by perpendicular ditches, as though order were being imposed on the vagaries of nature.

What did Monckton know? He knew what Leeuwenhoeck had written the Society, though not his every surmise. He had connections with scholars at Cambridge, so would know, if he inquired, that Fracastorius believed contagions to be spread by imperceptible particles, and that Marcus Varro believed that such particles were tiny creatures. Should he ask a professor of history, thought Malcolm with a numb shock, he would know the tale of how the plague reached Christendom when the Mongols besieging Caffa hurled the bodies of plague victims over the walls.

Pitcairn the factotum came to Holland, and died of a grippe while walking the waters outside Delft. What had he been doing there? Had he been carrying something strange, the sheriff would have asked Malcolm about it. Had he delivered papers to Skerrett? Was he come to collect Malcolm's?

Broken glass twinkled at the edge of the embankment, the first trash that Malcolm had seen in scrubbed Delft. The sight was faintly sickening, and he imagined Pitcairn's body floating in the water, to be seen by some early-rising workman. A carcass would spoil drinking water; he was glad that the town used the river.

Monckton, did he care to, knew enough. Sages had suggested since antiquity that the bad air and bad water that carried contagion might harbor minute particles as the actual agents; that certain fevers were spread by their victims did not contradict this. And with the advent of Hooke's micrographia and Leeuwenhoeck's improved instruments, these teachings could at last be tested.

The enormity of the realization crashed over Malcolm like a wave of nausea. Silas Monckton wanted to know whether the sources of contagion could be identified and marshaled, like weapons pressed into service. And Malcolm, of the Royal Society, had been cozened into assisting this project, on the grounds (less ignoble) of spying out Holland's researches in a different science.

So distracted was he that Malcolm was long minutes shifting his wonder from *What did Monckton know?* to *Is it true?* Do the *diertgens* thrive in the blood and humors like pond water, there to multiply and give affliction? That the venerall diseases were spread by the contact of genital mucosa, swarming with various living fluids (Malcolm winced at this), suggested as much. He wondered whether Pitcairn, drudge of the unspeakable, had been poking about the pestholes of England to contract the ague that had killed him.

To the north the *trekvaart* cut a straight line across the cultivated fields: Malcolm noticed it only when he saw a canal boat cruising stately through a field of grain. A half mile away the canal crossed a stream, becoming an aqueduct notched with waste-weirs like a castle wall. Like animalcules carried through blood vessels, the boats slipped through the saturated tissues of Holland; and what they carried within them no one, at a distance, could say.

Malcolm returned to town and went to Leeuwenhoeck's office, where he knew the draper would be preparing sections from the lens of a cow's-eye he had lately acquired. Malcolm presented himself, but was turned away by a young medical student, who told him brusquely that Heer Leeuwenhoeck would not be able to receive him. A spyglass, which Malcolm had lent the draper as an example of British lenscraft, was thrust into his hands, and without ceremony he was bid good day.

And what, Malcolm thought, does this leave him? He did not care to wonder what Leeuwenhoeck knew or believed; the uncertainty of his own prospects was concern enough. He imagined being sent back to England to oversee researches into miasmic fevers on the Yorkshire moors, perhaps dying like Pitcairn in the process.

He turned the spyglass over in his hands, wishing he could make a present of it to young Moete. A triumph of English lensmakers, who labor to perfect the refraction of light while others strive to make it bounce. Would Moete appreciate the gesture? "I would rather *Reflect* than prove *Refractory*," he says in Malcolm's imagination. With the smile that, Malcolm now realized, he shall never see again.

He put the spyglass in his pocket, touching as he did so the folded letter. Harder to imagine Skerrett's response to Malcolm's offering. He wouldn't read it in the twilight, assuming he could read. Why meet in darkness and seclusion, when Malcolm could pass over the letter behind a privy? The arrangement seemed decidedly sinister.

Malcolm walked to the brewery, a white-washed structure built up against a stream, which carried for a hundred yards the smell of scorched mash. The brewers, unsurprisingly, made use of the city's sweetest and most fast-moving water; the ceramics manufactures made do with the others. Malcolm followed the north side of the stream out of town, to an impoldered field so low that a river dike kept the stream in its banks. The *interwaarden* that lay between the water and the dike measured perhaps a hundred yards long, a fallow strip of land, probably submerged in winter, that even the enterprising Dutch could not put to use.

Malcolm sat and smoked a pipe as he watched a rain front roll in from the sea. The windmill turning a half mile away was, he realized after a moment, the same one he had seen earlier: The field it drained ran up to the dike. Below the windmill, an Archimedean screw reached down into the pond like a giant proboscis supping at a puddle.

A thin drizzle fell, and Malcolm hunched into his collar, willing himself not to grow soaked. Skerrett was (his vantage told him) not in the area; and Malcolm wanted to observe his arrival, so not to cede advantage to the rogue. Huddling in the open ground, he fell into a shallow doze, as midafternoon quickly deepened under the pall of cloud. The dreams that come take no coherent form: *diertgens* with snapping jaws; a conviction of nameless dread. Malcolm wakes in horror, neck-cricked and wet, and sees the sun settling onto the western horizon, flattening like a yolk about to break. He stood, looking around wildly for fear that Skerrett had already arrived.

No one was on the dike, but after a moment Malcolm saw motion in the field. A small boat, no larger than those wherrymen use to carry single passengers across the Thames, was making its way down a narrow ditch toward the dike. The seated figure—Malcolm instantly recognized Skerrett—was probably invisible to anyone at ground level, a drifting shadow on the darkening plain.

Malcolm also realized that Skerrett had certainly seen *him*—standing against the sky like an archer's target. An awful pang cut through him: He had come early to anticipate the spy, but his strategy had misfired: First possession of the *interwaarden* betrayed one's presence to the latecomer, who sees you search for him.

The sun sank to a slice while Skerrett tied up his boat and climbed leisurely up the graded embankment. Even thus his gait bespoke insolence, and he did not trouble to look at Malcolm until he was ten feet away. "Early to the dance?" he asked sardonically.

Malcolm pulled the report from his pocket. "As commissioned," he said.

The sailor simply held out his hand. After a moment Malcolm, flushing, took the three steps forward to give it to him. Skerett scarcely glanced at the sheets before tucking them away. "And so?" he said.

Malcolm faced him squarely. "The Dutch do not have the capacity to construct a burning mirror," he said solemnly.

"Pah," spat Skerrett. "You're not so stupid as that. Tell me you didn't inquire after Leeuwenhoeck's knowledge of plagues and I'll cut your throat right now."

Malcolm felt his belly tighten. "Your master wants to know whether Leeuwenhoeck's studies of *microphenomena* have disclosed the agents of contagion," he said, foolish with indignation. "Leeuwenhoeck won't say. He's a respectable man, and declined to speak much of experiments with human fluids. I also suspect he thought the knowledge dangerous. So you may tell Mr. Monckton that the Dutchman might share his surmise, but that *natural philosophers*, in England or Holland, will not turn their skills to warcraft."

Skerret laughed. "They don't, do they? While you've been gabbling with the close-mouthed Dutch, your betters in Cambridge have solved the problem. Your report will prove no more than an addendum to the true matter.''

Malcolm gaped. Skerrett turned to go, then glanced back contemptuously, one foot already on the downward slope. ''You lightbenders can make far things look near, but you don't actually *do* anything, do you? Spectacle-makers! *Lens-wrights!* If Leeuwenhoeck keeps quiet, so much the better for us: Englishmen make use of what they know.''

''And is that how Pitcairn came to die?'' asked Malcolm. ''Taking samples from pest-houses, that a tame microscopist might assay them for your armory?'' Shame for his suborned colleagues fanned the coals of Malcolm's ire.

''Die?'' The sailor stared.

''They found his body floating. He expired from a medley of contagions.''

''Thomas dead!'' Skerrett seemed genuinely shocked. He drew a breath and asked, ''Did they find aught on his body?''

''Nothing at all,'' Malcolm said. He remembered the six empty inner pockets of Pitcairn's waistcoat.

''Then he died a hero. The arrows are over the wall! Whether they fire the roofs or no, more shall follow.'' Fierce jubilance entered his voice.

Malcolm stared at Skerrett. ''You *what*?'' he demanded. A second passed, as comprehension charged one like a sulphur globe and sparked comprehension in the other; then both men leaped.

Malcolm was the slower, but his better footing saved him. He saw the knife flash in the twilight, then turned and was running. Downhill in near darkness: madness, even with the Dutch builders' smooth inclines. He stumbled, plunged headlong, and hit the ground fast, then was rolling and on his feet without pausing to look back.

The smell of asparagus rose about him as he tore through planted rows, then a slip on muddy ground sent him sprawling forward. He realized that he was falling into a ditch an instant before he struck water, and the cold shock cleared his mind as though the depths shone with sunlight. A man who stands up in a ditch is immediately overtaken, while one who swims underwater is invisible and soundless. Malcolm kicked, feeling his coat trail the surface for a second before he angled deeper, and brushed his hand against the shallow bottom. Ten strokes, his lungs burning, and he surfaced as quietly as he could. Angry thrashing noises reached him from some near distance, and he pushed his heels along the bottom, faceup like an otter as he drifted slowly away.

What else floated in this water? Fevers bred in the miasma rising from stagnant waters; could such effluvia be introduced in a bottle, like holy water? Malcolm spat away the ditchwater on his lips.

The thought that the draining waters were infected brought horror, with an aftertaste of shame. *Englishmen* had done this, *naturalists*? Those who bent light had bent their neck to the yoke of Charles, who bent his in turn to the moneyed tyrant Louis.

The wind shifted, and the sound of the creaking windmill was suddenly louder. Shivering, Malcolm climbed from the water under the cover of noise and made for its source, invisible in the cloudy night. He did not hear pursuit, but neither stopped to listen.

Those who warp the light can shape the world. Malcolm hadn't believed it—what present use for those who count moons, or describe a louse's leg?—but he did now. The realm of other worlds is far away, but the microrealm is all about us: We *are* it, as a foundry is its bricks. Who knows the strength of bricks shall be heeded by builders.

The ground grew wetter as he approached the windmill, and Malcolm found himself making shallow splashes with each step. Worried that these would betray him, he broke into a run. A wooden stairway hugged the bulwark, and Malcolm reached it in a spray of long strides. He had climbed three steps when he was hit from behind.

He crashed against the steps before him, losing his footing and kicking out (his nerves reacting faster than his mind) with one upended sole. The foot struck flesh, driving his shoulder against a step. Cold rain touched his back, and Malcolm realized that his coat had been slashed.

He kicked again, making glancing contact. Skerrett fell atop him, and Malcolm heard a soft *thunk* by his ear, the unmistakable sound of a knife biting wood. In a frenzy he kicked and scrambled upward. The middle of the staircase swayed beneath him.

A hand grabbed his foot, and Malcolm snatched at a banister, which came loose as he pulled at it. In terror he swung it round, and it knocked against bone with a thrill. The hand let go, and Malcolm scrambled over the top.

The rain stung his spine, and Malcolm reached back to touch sticky warmth. How could he have been cut, and no pain? yet there seemed a lot of blood. Slipping in the mud, he stumbled toward the windmill, a great invisible rumbling overhead. The Archimedean screw emerged beneath the structure, disgorging into a channel that ran away from the windmill and across the plain like a highway. The water spilling from the screw was inaudible beneath the rain and the cavernous rumble of the gearing.

Feeling carefully along the canal wall, Malcolm found the edge of the sluice-gate with his fingertips. The screw was turning, and uplifted water was pushing open the gate to flow through. He crawled forward several feet, until his hat brushed the cross-beam of the trestle. He was underneath the windmill, out of the rain but in total darkness.

Fumbling with his flint and touchwood, Malcolm got his pipe lit; then drawing hard on the tobacco (he had no paper on him), he produced enough of a light to see a few inches around. As beneath any mill, the ground under the trestle was scattered with sawdust and loose splints, some not yet wet. After a minute Malcolm got a small torch smoldering, and cast wavering shadows across the low space. And with the return of light Malcolm (to his surprise) could suddenly think.

What had Pitcairn done? Broken glass; spleen like cheese. Was Malcolm truly thinking, to think this?

Wooden-toothed but regular as crystal, the gearing of the shaft and bevel wheel turned as steadily as a wagon wheel meeting its reflection in a puddle. Malcolm could only see the topmost flange of the screw, which revolved like the bore of a drill that dug out water instead of shavings. The yield seemed less than you could produce with a pump, yet it would in time drain a marsh.

Sawdust was sticking to his hands, which he noticed were black with blood. How badly was he hurt? He could not twist far enough to see.

The ground was littered with rubbish and broken bricks; Malcolm picked up the largest one and crawled over to the sluice. He lowered himself into the water—ah God, it was cold!—as the torch guttered out. The water was but three feet deep, yet the chill penetrated instantly to the bone.

Malcolm bent and wedged the brick between the sluice-gate and its stop, preventing it from swinging shut when the upflow of water ebbed. When the screw ceased turning, the water would run down it like a cascade.

But the screw was still turning, more rapidly than the vanes overhead: which seemed superior to the English models, so turned (if slowly) in even slight winds. Malcolm imagined the miller discovering the wedged sluice-gate in the morning, and wading in to remove the brick. He slid further into the water and felt for the pin. His fingers encountered only slippery smoothness, and he was suddenly weak. Immersion, he thought dizzily, would only open further his wound.

He climbed out with difficulty, then failed to get a second torch lit. Drenched and shaking fingers let the flint drop, and Malcolm could feel his sleeves drip on the touchwood. Very well, he thought: Some acts are fit only for darkness. He felt for another brick, feeling as though he were about to smash a fine watch.

He held the brick before him as he crept toward the gearing, thinking: *If I fumble, I'll lose my hand.* The brick brushed a moving surface, which knocked it almost from his grasp. Suppressing a scream, Malcolm leaned toward the source of the grinding roar, then gritted his teeth and thrust his hand into it.

Something seized the brick from his fingers, and he snatched his hand back. The gears screamed like a stabbed pig, and the shaft above groaned with dismay. Teeth splintered, and the gears slipped, snapping more teeth. With a shearing sound the vertical shaft was suddenly turning free, and the screw was still.

Malcolm was sobbing with fear, which rushed now into his heart just as the water in the tailrace was now flowing back into the field. It was only after a minute that he heard clumping overhead. Of course: The miller, resident in the mill itself, was coming forth to investigate.

He scrambled out from beneath the trestle, into wind and rain. How soon before the miller, investigating his broken gears, noticed the jammed gate and shut it? How fully could the field flood meanwhile?

Malcolm slipped and fell in mud, then crawled toward the sluice. It was raining harder now, and he could hear the miller's shouts, and see faint light from a window above. The sluice-gate had swung to as the upflow ceased, and was now open only by a brick's width. Malcolm saw a wooden bench a dozen feet away and toppled it into the sluice, wedging the gate wide open. The exertion and pain nearly caused him to fall in after it.

Had other ponds been polluted? Delft's drinking water came from the Schie, so seemed immune from infection. Had Pitcairn visited other cities on his way in from the Hague? Did his coat of foul pockets contain bottles of other plagues? Malcolm could not know.

A thump resounded through the trestle: not from above, where the miller was now throwing open the door, but below, in the stilled screw assembly. Unsocketed at the top like a disjointed chicken leg, the screw was being pushed out of place by the water flowing down it. A log nudged over a cataract, it tilted from its trough, and the rush of water was suddenly louder.

Jubilance filled Malcolm, jostling horror. The polder would be flooded before workmen stopped the sluice, its miasmal damps a shallow lake. Malcolm realized that he was looking at the sky, rain pelting his face. His back was very cold.

Was the air blowing in the storm being cleansed of infection by the rain? One could collect rainwater in a basin, examine it beneath the microscope for *animalcula*. But would the naturalists conduct such an experiment to identify and exterminate the creatures, or to breed them? Water in his eyes, Malcolm apprehended a world changed unforeseeably by the wresting of light, a watchcase prised open by naturalists yet unborn: men who knew that nature's secrets lay open to those who focus finely, children of the lens.

THE LONGER VOYAGE

Michael Cassutt

▼

As a print author, Michael Cassutt is mostly known for his incisive short work, but he has worked intensively in the television industry over the past few decades, where he is a major Mover and Shaker. He was co–executive producer for Showtime's The Outer Limits—*where he won a CableAce Award for best dramatic series—and also served in the same capacity for the series* StrangeLuck, *as well as having worked on* Max Headroom, The Twilight Zone, *and many other television series. His books include the novels* The Star Country *and* Dragon Season; *the anthology* Sacred Visions, *coedited with Andrew M. Greeley; and a nonfiction book* Who's Who in Space: The First 25 Years. *He also collaborated with the late astronaut Deke Slayton on Slayton's autobiography* Deke!, *and is currently writing a novel about the space program.*

It's better to travel hopefully than to arrive, an old adage tells us. In the sly story that follows, which gives us an insider's slant on an all-too-probable space program of the future, that adage might have been altered to read, It's even better not to start *to travel in the first place. . . .*

The last time Julian Tallet visited Node Canaveral for maintenance Ulrich Charz was Mission administrator, Mission Population was officially two thousand, three hundred, and initial operating capacity was eight years away. Since then Julian had aged six years: The new MA was Alf Riordan, Mission Pop was now authorized at an even four thousand, and initial operating capacity was twelve years away. Two improvements, two deteriorations.

"I like the air here," Ty said from the driver's seat, and promptly sneezed.

Julian didn't, though he felt like sneezing too. He rarely thought about the air, except when he happened to see Hong Kong videos about skullduggery on Mission in which nobody *ever* sneezed. Mission's air-filtration system had been under review since the first nodes were opened, but space dwellers had been sneezing an average of a hundred times a day since Mir, a century back.

Julian didn't have Ty's sensitivities even though both were gen twos—born on Mission. Ty was developmentally challenged and looked like a concept for an advanced human being as imagined during the early Space Age: long, spindly arms and legs, pale complexion, head too large for his body. Mission Personnel officially deployed him as a "therapeutic test subject" and paid him a salary, but what he really did was drive Julian's cart and make occasional observations. But, then, the citizens of the early Space Age would have called Mission a starship. And would have had it halfway to Alpha Cen by now.

"It smells like polin," Julian said, finding it hard to put a label on the sensation through his general fog of ill health.

"What's polin?"

Julian pointed to the patch of green serving as an interface between the smooth silvery glaze of the "street" and the glassy vertical plate that hid the innards of the LockMart office just ahead. (Mission Management types here in Node Canaveral had a taste for classic Earth styles.) "It's a grasslike vegetative matter, native to Kazakhstan. Not edible." Ty wore a read-only patch that would help him with words like "vegetative" and even "Kazakhstan," but it was important to add the business about lack of edibility. Especially when Ty got out of the cart and went to investigate. "Want some."

Julian sighed and tried, without success, to get comfortable. He was overdue for maintenance. His clothes were tight around the waist; he hated to wake up in the morning. His hair was grayer every time he looked in a mirror. At the age of thirty-eight minus one day he was facing the fact that he was as good as he was going to get at anything you cared to name: deal-making or lovemaking. There had even been moments when he would have surrendered to integration, to allow Mission Personnel to deploy him to some nice job in Commercial Support, maybe.

The fact that he would even consider integration convinced him he had to risk maintenance. So now he lurked around a Node Canaveral contractor site, waiting for Duwayne to return from his face sweep of the maintenance center. Duwayne was fully integrated into the official Mission network as well as the many illegal and unregistered data bands that made up the undernet, but sometimes you just had to see things with your own eyes.

"Mr. Tallet!" Ty called. Julian pried himself out of the cart and went to him. "Look what I found." Ty was standing on the patch of polin and pointing to the window. It had been defaced with a large painted tag that said: *"A. C. Death."*

The A.C. and the Death were joined by a smudge, probably some defining punctuation, even a short word such as *or*. Alpha Cen or Death. The only people on Mission who talked much about Alpha Cen were Management, and it pleased Julian to think of some frustrated Level E type expressing his rage at the eternal delays in this way. Nevertheless, Julian figured the tag was the work of a gen two, probably a boy about fourteen. It had a clear hand and cursive capitals, like something from an ancient handbook on penmanship. Lots of gen twos had taken up cursive writing as a way of communicating outside the net; Julian carried his own pencil and notebook for the same reason.

b   Of course, for gen twos the missing punctuation would be an equals sign. Alpha Cen = Death.

Julian's attention was drawn by Duwayne's return. "Now there's a nice job," Duwayne said, nodding at the tag as he slipped into the back seat. "I'm surprised Facilities hasn't gotten to it."

"Facilities probably likes graffiti. It's Internal Affairs that will be interested."

"IA probably left it there to catch the tagger," Duwayne said.

"IA probably *put* it there in the first place to target subversives."

Duwayne found this bit of paranoia amusing. He was compact, normal or even good-looking, but like Ty, somehow incomplete. Whereas Ty had flaws in his genetic programming, Duwayne had simply developed a bad attitude. He was officially deployed to Agon Systems, one of the many Mission contractors, as a communications specialist. Since Julian currently consulted for Agon Systems, he had inherited Duwayne.

Ty returned to the cart as Julian asked Duwayne, "Are we clear?"

It wasn't Internal Affairs Julian usually worried about, but his rival contractors. "Better yet," Duwayne said. "Somebody did a sweep for us. I'm looking at their plot now. It's very tidy." The cart zoomed out of the shadows and down the empty street toward maintenance.

"Who?"

"Somebody from Management."

The cart was a modified battery-powered tractor originally used to move cargo around the high bay in Node Baikonur. Crushed during one of the frequent spinquakes of years past, it had been written off until a Biker mechanic working for Julian had restored the body, replacing grappling gear with a stretched cab. It would hold four passengers, three of them comfortably.

No one on Mission truly required motorized transport: A walk of nine hundred meters in any axis would return you to the spot you started. Unfortunately, with the various node separators, not to mention lifts and hatchways, it was impossible to walk more than twenty meters in any direction. If you traveled a lot and occasionally delivered gifts, as Julian did, a cart came in handy.

The drive was a short one. No other vehicles were parked in front of maintenance—Management suits were officially required to travel on foot, though those that actually hewed to this rule were so few that Julian suspected he knew them all by name. And as he walked into maintenance he began to feel a bit nervous.

There were three sections to maintenance, one for emergencies, and one each for gen ones and gen twos, who had different requirements. "So, which one is he in?" Julian asked Duwayne, meaning the person from Management. It wasn't an entirely casual question.

"Gen Two section." This bit of data narrowed the possible candidates to one, and Julian suddenly felt even worse. He turned to Duwayne. "Let's make it another day."

Duwayne returned from the undernet long enough to register surprise. "But we just got here! They're already loaded for you."

"Let them reload another day."

"What about the party tomorrow?"

Well, there was that. Before Julian could decide he saw that it was too late. The Management patient, already shaved and capped, was in the doorway, and there was no way to avoid a face. "Julian Tallet," the man said. "I wondered what all the fuss was about." He turned around, then paused: "Come on in. Don't be shy."

Offended by the man's attitude—"I don't care if he *is* Management!"—Duwayne took a step toward him.

But Julian held him back. "It's all right," Julian said. "He's my brother."

· · ·

The two techs had not overtaxed themselves in helping Roy Tallet with his patches, but that changed the moment they saw Julian. Not only were they suddenly free with soothing words and attentions, but one of them managed to help Roy back to his table. "I should have arranged this deliberately," Roy said.

"You'll never convince me you didn't," Julian said, taking his own place.

"So many edges, Julian," Roy said, "in such a cylindrical world."

To Julian this was no more accurate than most of Roy's judgments. For one thing, Mission was not truly cylindrical, but more of a cake with layers of different shapes and diameters. Even the social model was something multidimensional. For another, Julian's personality had fewer corners than did Roy's . . . and Julian had the scans to prove it. But the new blood spurting into his veins was already having its mellowing effect. "You're looking good," was all he said to Roy. It almost killed him to admit it, but put the two of them side by side, and anyone would think Roy was younger.

"Management is generous with its maintenance plan." Both men lay back and closed their eyes. "You could have the same schedule too. All you have to do is—"

"—Accept integration. No, thank you. I like my privacy."

"We have privacy." Roy had accepted integration at the age of thirteen, when Julian was almost eleven. "Besides, that's not the issue. It's been twenty-five years since the divorce. You're still punishing Dad for broken promises."

Julian knew that Roy had used Mission net to pull up Julian's personality scans—the one element of his life that was unavoidably integrated, since you couldn't get maintained without being scanned. Not only was his medical data in Mission net, but also a wonderfully colored fractal-edged chart of his personality. Blue for the various intelligence and aptitude tests in addition to his grades in Mission's school system. Green for physical data. Yellow for the blending of his parents' scans. Red for personality map—and running through the latter two, like a regular goddamn Grand Canyon, was the black rift of his parent's divorce.

But Julian had his own theory about how the two Tallet boys had turned out so differently. "It's because of broken promises," Julian said quietly. "But not Dad's."

Julian did not know when the International ExtraSolar SETI Response Initiative—better known as Mission—actually began. The official myth placed it immediately after the detection of mysterious signals from the tail of the constellation Southern Cross in Fiscal Year 2022. Those signals had been "unscrambled" and "enhanced" in a variety of ways; analysts had concluded that the signals consisted of either a "message" to the galaxy at large, or perhaps some sort of radio entertainment. Neither conclusion was universally accepted, though the fact of some signal-generating entity elsewhere in the (relatively near) galactic neighborhood was indisputable. Based on data from the Pickering series of probes (F.Y. 2049–2061) the SETI source had been provisionally assigned the name "Eden." Whether this was strictly true, Eden had the virtue of being much more Earth-like than any body in the solar system save Earth itself.

The more popular countermyth said that Mission was born when it finally became clear, sometime in the forties, that human beings were never going to be able to colonize Mars, not without significant reconstruction. (On the humans, that is. The idea of actually modifying a whole planet had been consigned to the same historical dumpster as communism, ethnic harmony, and free television.) The existence of an apparently Earth-like world in orbit around the star Alpha Cen A provided a goal that promised greater return for less expense than rebuilding several thousand humans, even allowing for the awesome distance of eight light-years, which meant a transit time of forty-five years using the most advanced propulsion system then conceived, the Indonesian cryofusion burner.

Julian subscribed to a third myth, that the SETI signals were bogus and the entire Mission was a planetary pork-barrel project, a means of redirecting excess capital into spinoff research and development. (The global economy had gone through an unprecedented period of robustness in the thirties, thanks to the death of the Western baby-boomer generation, which had distorted and tyrannized culture and finance for its entire seventy-five-year run.)

The original plan, baseline F.Y. 2039, called for Mission to reach initial operating capacity—IOC—on 1 October 2086, with injection into a trans-Alpha trajectory to follow in that fiscal year. Julian Tallet was born on Mission in F.Y. 2074, when IOC was holding firm at F.Y. 2086, when there was a chance that, while Julian and the other gen twos would spend twenty or more years of their life in transit, they would still walk on the shores of Eden.

F.Y. 2086 came and went without IOC, without departure for Alpha Cen. At the age of eighteen Julian was selected for the flight-operations track, and all his schooling from that point on concerned orbital mechanics, simulator technologies, and program management, since the design of the actual Eden landing craft would not be frozen until Mission reached the new world. As part of his flight training he was also allowed to don wings and flap around the high bay in Bike under low spin.

For six years Julian trained as a Mission pilot, knowing he would be in his forties before he got a chance to use his skill. Then the cryofusion system designed to be installed on Mission blew up during final qualification tests, irradiating the entire Cape York test center, and killing three hundred and eleven people.

IOC slipped from ''next year'' to a minimum of eight years when the Level A managers in Munich switched from cryofusion to an older technology called SteadiState, and the projected transit time, low Earth orbit to low Eden orbit, increased from twenty-five to sixty years. Even allowing for the possible Lorenz-Fitzgerald stretching of lifespan, Julian and the other gen twos realized they had no chance of ever walking on Eden. At the rate things were going, they would be lucky to live long enough to see departure.

''You should have stayed in management and done something about it.''

''You were smarter than me, Roy. If *you* couldn't fix things, what was I supposed to do?'' He decided to change the subject. ''How's Hannah?''

''Fine. Her branch is in charge of this burn.'' Roy hesitated, then said, ''How about Sophie?''

''I don't know,'' Julian said, carefully. He and Sophie had been together for two years, the same amount of time he had worked with Agon Systems. He had noticed a depressing pattern in his life—one relationship per job. All Julian knew was that this breakup had been the most painful yet. With Sophie he had begun to allow himself to consider marriage, children. Most of his friends (a group which did not include Ty or Duwayne) had chanced one or the other; some both. Julian had begun to feel left out.

But then he remembered his own rage at learning of his own life sentence aboard Mission. He did not want to be the target of that sort of rage from his own children. He had made that clear to Sophie. Who was now gone.

Now he was left wondering if he was going to change jobs.

"How are you doing for money?"

This was another sore subject. Theoretically every gen two—every person officially listed as a member of Population—had a deployment and a salary. The salaries were subject to mandatory deductions for base habitation, facilities use (including air), medical maintenance, and diet. You'd have to try hard to starve aboard Mission, but the salary actually left little for what Management termed elective/quality-of-life purchases. Julian had gotten into trouble that way in the past, charging against his salary until Finance stopped him. Several times he had had to go to Roy for money, though not lately.

"I'm keeping ahead," Julian replied. "I realize I still owe you . . ."

Roy waved that off, which infuriated Julian even more than having it brought up in the first place. "I figured you'd be able to make money at Agon." He sighed. "Everybody does."

"What's that supposed to mean?"

"They're bad guys, Julian."

"They're licensed contractors, Roy."

"They're the next best thing to *Mafia*—" Suddenly aware that every tech in maintenance was eagerly listening, Roy shut up.

Searching for some way to salvage the conversation, Julian said, "I'm having a party tomorrow night. My birthday."

"I know," Roy said. "I'm still your brother."

"Why don't you bring Hannah, if you can get her to go south of Korou?"

"We have a burn scheduled."

"There's never been a burn in Mission history that took place on time."

"Julian . . . I didn't come here to pick a fight." That they would fight was inevitable. They were gen-two kids, the children of the hated contractors who had fought their way into Management. But while Julian had quit, Roy had risen all the way to Level C, the highest onboard authority. He had compounded the insult by marrying a woman from a Management family too. Julian turned his head and looked directly at Roy, amazed at how much he resembled their father.

Now Roy said, "You and your . . . associates wouldn't be trying to bias the burn in any way."

There was always a pool on Mission events. "Since when do you care about the leisure activities of the underclass?"

"Whenever it affects Mission safety."

"Is this an official inquiry?"

"Do you have any official data?"

Julian wished again that Roy had skipped law school. "Here's what I can tell you: If there are any friendly, private wagers on private networks—did I mention the word 'private'?"

Roy had the grace to smile. "I believe so."

"They are reactive, not proactive. To put it another way, nobody is trying to fix your fucking burn."

"Relax. I was really just asking."

Julian was surprised at his own vehemence. Because for the first time in his two years with Agon, he realized he didn't know the answer to Roy's question.

Roy smiled faintly. "I'm going to try to get to your party." He rolled his shoulder. "You'd think with all the maintenance we've had, we'd be in better shape."

"For human beings a world this small is toxic."

"Come on, Julian. We *designed* it."

"Maybe you did." Then he lay back and let the sweet new blood flow. For a brief moment, at this point in the very long, never really begun voyage, A.C. *didn't* equal death.

Mission was theoretically self-sufficient, with air, water, and waste purified and recycled for an indefinite period, assuming strict Population control, though most Red Team simulations suggested that eighty years was a more realistic system life than infinity. That is, the "closed" Eco system would sustain itself for at least that long, which was still beyond the maximum allowable duration for the trans-Alpha voyage. (In some simulations the optimum system lifetime actually allowed for a round trip—160 years—providing, of course, that Population decreased.) Renewable resources had already been detected on Eden early in the design process so that refueling at Alpha Cen was the primary mode, while a closed system with return was only a backup.

Eco was an in-house Management program in which Agon Systems was the major subcontractor. This fit nicely with the company's role in Facilities, which was collecting garbage. With Population constantly changing, not to mention the ongoing construction and repairs, garbage was a serious problem. Scrap metal and composites could be redeployed to the Fabrik program, Mission's own manufacturing arm. But everything else, from plain old litter to discarded toys to dust in the air, had to be tracked, retrieved, and dealt with.

Julian didn't have an office; Agon Systems had converted to virtual facilities a century back, so most mornings found Julian planted at a table to the rear of the Seagull, a café that catered to Bikers. With his laptop and Duwayne nearby Julian monitored the endless flow of Mission debris. He also monitored various cargo manifests, Mission or informal, controlling the flow of materials, information, and people into and out of the high bay. The challenge was knowing how much of a shipment was capable of being "lost" or "damaged," and who to compensate, and with what.

Mission did much of its own processing, turning chemicals into composites, and sometimes the other way around. But there was a gratifying percentage of the population which was still willing to pay for exotic food from Earth . . . fashions . . . hardware . . . data. (Information and entertainment were beamed directly aboard, though Management controlled the intra-Mission network.) Software judged violent, subversive, or otherwise incorrect was subject to censorship; Julian was happy to shift it to the undernet.

This morning was particularly busy because a Chinese vehicle had docked, one of ten officially manifested resupply flights per year. It wasn't until after lunch that Julian was able to ask Duwayne to go up on Mission net. "Tell me about this SteadiState propulsion event."

Duwayne blinked, then came back into focus. "It's been in development since F.Y. 25 or so, originally intended for constant-boost outer-planet missions. Abandoned."

"Because of technical problems?"

"Fiscal. SteadiState's just too expensive. There were some instabilities during its initial use . . . one loss of vehicle in F.Y. 79 contributed to replacement by another system."

"Anything anywhere to show that it's not a good idea? Red Team reports?"

"Nothing on Mission."

"Well. Is it going to light up on time?"

"It's running two hours late."

Julian stood up. That was typical. "Duwayne . . . do you ever wonder what you'd do if it worked?"

"Propulsion? You mean, if we actually got to departure?"

"Yeah."

Duwayne mulled this for a moment, his consciousness spread over God knew what pages of the nets, then smiled. "You're kidding, right? Mission's never going to go anywhere."

"Suppose it did. Suppose they stopped the resupply flights and kicked out everybody who wasn't in Population. Buttoned her up and said, 'Next stop is Alpha Cen . . . sixty years.' "

"I'd be on the last flight down."

"Don't want to see Eden?"

"I've seen it from Pickering." He nodded toward the view of dayside Africa rolling past on the television. "It looks like that, only colder."

"You've been here your whole life. What are you going to do downstairs?"

"I don't know. But at least I won't be off-line." Duwayne was as fully integrated as anyone Julian knew. He spent most of his waking moments—probably his dreaming ones too—awash in data and imagery. For him, trying to live without the nets would be like trying to live without air. Which was reason number three that Julian had never accepted integration. Duwayne said, "My parents signed up to go to Alpha Cen, not me. It's not my fault they died before they got their chance." He smiled. "A.C. equals death."

Julian realized that a lot of gen twos agreed with Duwayne, yet the attitude suddenly annoyed him. "Duwayne, you've never been cold. Never been rained on. They have *weather* downstairs. They have dirt. The Mission's a pretty small town too. How would you like to be sharing space with ten million people? I bet you wouldn't last five minutes in Munich."

"I bet I won't have to."

"Did you put anything into this burn pool?"

"I don't do that. The house cooks the books."

He couldn't believe the words were coming out of his mouth. Not because they weren't true, but because he didn't really want to pick on Duwayne. "Ah, let's get ready for a party."

Julian lived minus-x-ward of Node Canaveral in Node Palmachim, the oldest residential volume on Mission, one plus-x from Bike. It was probably safer there than in the heavily patrolled management node, especially for Julian, who had many supportive friends, but its drawback was that it was ugly, nothing but a hilly street of warehouses scarred by collisions with Bike haulers and marked by forty years of tags.

Assuming that Sophie would not show up, Julian had allowed Duwayne to invite as many female "visitors" as he wanted—which turned out to be a trio of entertainers who said they were planning to head back downstairs to Branson, Missouri, anyday now.

He sent Ty with the cart to pick up Roy and Hannah; to Julian's great surprise, Roy accepted, bringing Hannah's regrets. "She's on the trajectory panel and doesn't want to miss the countdown."

Just as well: Julian had not seen Hannah since the wedding. A Management female wouldn't know what to say to someone like him.

Roy examined the volume. He did not need a calculator to judge its size. "I think I'm going to let you pay me back after all," he told Julian. "You have three times the volume Dr. Riordan has." Riordan was Mission administrator, the highest Level C manager on site.

"I thought Management principles mandated equal volume for all."

"Several years ago two guys in D offered to give up their volume to enlarge the MA's suite."

"He's got all those meetings to hold. . . ."

"It was seen to be quite a noble gesture."

"And what happened to them, Roy?"

"One of them is now Dr. Riordan."

"And you complain about my business." Julian nodded at one of the hostesses, who brought over the tray of drinks. Julian helped himself as Roy looked them over carefully. "If you don't see anything you like, name it and I'll get it." When Roy continued to hesitate, Julian realized what the problem was. "I guess Management doesn't want its integrated managers to be substance abusers. They must really track you all the time."

Roy picked up a clear drink. "Not *all* the time." He clinked glasses clumsily with Julian. "Happy birthday."

Julian watched Roy scan the crowd—not a large one, in spite of the available volume. It was still rather early in the evening for Mission's underclass to be out. The crowd was evenly split between men over thirty years of age and women under. "Amazing," Roy finally said. "Most of your guests don't appear to exist. Population can't match any of these faces with files."

"Some of them are visitors."

"Visitors have their own category in Population, Julian. How do they stay maintained? Mission won't cover you if you're not in Population. If you haven't been officially deployed."

Julian shrugged. "Maybe Mission's database isn't as comprehensive as it's supposed to be. Clearly everybody here is maintained—"

"—And they *all* appear to be working." Roy shook his head. "It's quite an operation you have here."

"I can't take credit for it."

"I wasn't going to give you credit. I just said it was amazing."

Julian busied himself for a moment by accepting a second drink, or was it his third? "Roy . . . you said something yesterday that was interesting."

"About how you're still punishing Dad?"

This was worse than asking Roy for money. All the worse because Julian didn't know for sure that somebody in Agon Systems, or more likely, with access to Agon Systems, was going to screw up the burn. But having been a part of this operation for two years now, he had learned to trust his instincts, especially when it came to events like this. And his instincts were telling him there was influence.

But what did he want Roy to do? Unleash Internal Affairs? Agon would never allow that, and the moment they discovered Julian's involvement (and they would), he was in big trouble. It was one thing to play games with Management and Personnel: Getting Agon mad at you was a form of suicide. Julian might have to move downstairs. He might be lucky to survive to make the move.

"What you said about getting into Management."

Roy must have stared at him for a full five seconds. "That's a surprise. Integration and all?"

"I don't know about *that*. I just said—"

"—That you were interested in going back to Management—"

"—That I was interested in what you said." Neither one of them was going to make the first concession. "Look, forget it."

"Not a chance. I'm fascinated. Something really big must have happened since this afternoon, to make my kid brother give up the glamorous life of gambling, drugs, and smuggling—"

That did it. "Climb down from the pedestal, Roy. Mission runs its lotteries, manufactures its own drugs, and makes sure Managers have first pick. The import-export laws change everytime somebody in Munich sneezes. Some of us don't fit in Mission. We're just making our own world."

"Which looks a lot like the bad one we left behind."

Julian nodded toward the television. Blue and brown, Earth rolled past, three hundred miles below. "You haven't managed to leave yet."

Pleading fatigue, Roy left after an acceptable hour's attendance, at which point Julian lost interest in his party. It wasn't intended to honor him so much as it was a chance for his associates to eat and drink for free. He had begun to pay attention to one of the Branson singers, a woman named Hope, when Duwayne found him. "Sorry to bother you," he said. "IA."

Julian removed Hope from his lap. *"Here?"*

"The Seagull." Duwayne fell back into the net for a moment, then surfaced. "It's two Internal Affairs teams—must be up from Munich, since they're not in Population."

Julian was already stepping over his more persistent party-goers on the way out the door. Duwayne struggled to walk while staying up on Mission. "What are they doing?"

Another pause. "Facing Ty and his people. Picking stuff up."

"Any activity on either net?"

"Mission's devoted to that burn, now at T-minus-six hours. Undernet has the usual."

"This is insane."

He and Duwayne ran out to the cart and headed for the access point that would take them across to Node Baikonur.

Mission had a unique legal status. No nation or group of nations had any sovereignty over it. Originally its model was Antarctica, an "open" center for research. But habitation at the Antarctic stations was limited; people went home after their tours. There was no permanent population.

During the early assembly phase Mission was treated as a commercial facility, like an ocean-oil platform, except that the "corporation" which funded Mission was a consortium of nations, some of whom were virulently opposed to commercial ventures. Again, commercial facilities did not have permanent residents.

All through the development and assembly phases there were popular stories—even a couple of Hong Kong movies—about Mission becoming an independent nation, with its own laws, currency, government. It was the kind of thing gen twos talked about when they were in their early teens and forgot about when they started having sex.

Mission remained a *vehicle*: The permanent Population was, legally, no such thing. Julian and Roy, for example, were technically citizens of the United States, since that was what their parents were. Never mind that Julian had come no closer to the U.S. than a vertical separation of at least two hundred and fifty miles; he had the right to return there as a voting citizen. The same applied to the rest of Population.

Only when Mission burned out of orbit on a trans–Alpha Cen trajectory would it begin moving toward any kind of actual independence. From what Julian had heard, when he bothered to pay attention, Management was still struggling to address the form of this government, and the transition to it.

In practical terms, however, Mission was technically a free port. The only laws were Management directives, and in at least one international court case these had been shown to be quite limited, dealing mostly with Mission property—in effect, Management could enforce directives only among its actual employees. Other members of Population, 70 percent of whom actually worked for contractors, could abide by or ignore the directives as they chose, subject only to possible loss of contract with Management.

Agon Systems, the corporation, preferred its own rules. As far as it was concerned, there were no Sunday closing laws. No casino or liquor licenses. No censorship. And Management's Internal Affairs staff was only an annoyance.

There were three of them in the Seagull when Julian and Duwayne arrived, two men and a woman, visitors as far as Julian knew. "What do you think you're doing here?" Julian said.

"Searching for stolen Mission property," the woman snapped.

"Have you been authorized by Agon Systems?" Julian said.

One of the men was already shoving a pass in front of Julian's nose. Julian glanced at Duwayne, who could only shrug. Apparently they had gotten somebody in the company to allow them access. Well, Agon Systems was so large it was often at war with its own best interests. "Search away," Julian said.

Ty was in a state. "Can't we make them leave?"

"Sure. But they'll fight and then someone will get hurt." And that would mean more dealing with maintenance and Management and, worst of all, Agon Systems's insurance directorate. Even Ty knew what that meant.

"Look out!" Duwayne shouted, as a shelf unit suddenly got detached from the wall and fell crashing to the floor. One of the IA goons stepped over it, crunching a collection of data disks. "Mr. Tallet, you've got to stop this!"

Julian was already reaching for the phone. "Roy? Julian." He hadn't expected Roy to be home in bed with Hannah, and he wasn't. He was at what looked to be Mission operations. "I see you got your second wind."

"You didn't call to give me a hard time about leaving the party."

"No. Your IA goons are trashing my office. I want them out of here."

"I don't have anything to do with Internal Affairs. Management sees it as a conflict, since I have relatives with bad associates."

Julian glanced at Duwayne, who was monitoring the conversation on Mission. He shrugged. "He's telling the truth. He doesn't have control or even access."

"Then let's just call it a coincidence. You get in touch with me for the first time in years . . . then this raid happens the night of the big burn."

"You made this choice," Roy snapped. He looked truly angry. "You've bounced from one goddamn disaster to another because, I don't know, somebody disappointed you. Well, maybe it's time to grow up. Your actions have consequences. You chose to work with Agon Systems—let them take care of you."

"I'll do that," Julian said. And broke the connection. He turned to Duwayne. "What are our options?"

"Regarding?"

"Biasing their burn."

Duwayne smiled for the first time since Julian had known him. "We're pretty well insinuated into their nets. There's a preloaded virus that will infect flight-control systems, then commit suicide after ten generations."

"What would it do to their burn?"

"Let's just say there won't be a burn. Not on time, anyway. Not today."

"Then do it." Let Management decide what it really wanted, a clean Mission or a Mission that worked. Julian started to walk away, but turned back. "And when you do, make sure I make a lot of money, will you?"

Before Duwayne finished speaking, the three IA people came out of the Seagull. "Find what you were looking for?" Julian asked.

"Fuck you," the woman said, as the three of them walked off, empty-handed.

Julian got home two hours later and found Hope still waiting. Well, he had expected that. Their lovemaking sputtered out when he discovered that she was as fully integrated as Duwayne. Without the boost the undernet could give her, she hardly seemed interested. This had the advantage of making it easy for her to get over her annoyance, however. She managed to ask Julian how he could stand it, not being integrated? How did he know anything? "I listen. I see."

"I'd feel terribly alone."

"I like to be alone." And a few moments later, he was.

Sleep didn't come easily. Julian kept feeling that things had gotten out of control . . . that he had dropped a bomb. After all, Management periodically decided it was time to "clean up" Baikonur, and made punitive moves against Agon Systems's people. Given the lack of actual laws, Management's main weapon was to "redeploy" people to jobs which had minimal maintenance schedules. This was only effective against those who were in Population . . . but the lure of full maintenance caused a steady stream of applicants for integration. Julian and Duwayne and Ty would have to spend months re-redeploying them while the business of their business suffered. Which was exactly what Management wanted.

But until now Management had never actually sent out IA to take possession of records or property. Add that to Roy's reappearance in Julian's life, and the SteadiState burn . . . Julian wondered if Management wanted him off Mission.

People moved downstairs, of course. Julian and Roy's father, followed a few years later by their mother. The move had probably killed them both. Downstairs cultures continued to mutate, diverging from Mission's more and more every year. Even accepting full integration into the central nets didn't mean you would fit. Your scans would never match. You would have no real friends, no social set other than other exiles, and no skills that applied.

No, if Management wanted him off Mission, they would have to work a lot harder. To hell with Alpha Cen; he was trying to save his life.

Shortly after four-thirty in the morning he came awake—terrified. His room was absolutely black, something he'd never seen or imagined. And he was floating.

He tried to slow his breathing, to clear his mind. Spin was off; that was probably the initial lurch which woke him. Power too, which meant that lights were off, and more importantly, so was the environmental-control system.

No fans. No fresh air.

Well, he figured he wouldn't suffocate in the next few minutes. He had drifted to one of the y-axis walls . . . he could feel the bed, which was attached to the floor, below him at a right angle. Reaching to his left he found the door, and pulled himself through.

Julian experienced zero-g every time he moved from one node to the other, so the sensations were not new. The darkness and chaos were. In the main living volume he found light, and a door in what should have been the floor. He pushed himself toward it and managed to unlock it. He paused a moment before going out . . . partly to spatially orient himself . . . feet toward the street. Partly to wonder whether Hope had made it back to her Bike hotel—and if she had, whether that was a good idea. Partly to grab a headlamp from the emergency pack near the door. (He had to blow the dust off it, and the LED showed it would only be good for an hour or so.)

And where the hell was Duwayne?

In the quarter-light of the emergencies, the street was surprisingly crowded with people braced in doorways. More bodies that didn't show in Population. Julian didn't know any of them. Wrappers, chunks of fiber, and pieces of wall floated past, including one bearing the front half of an ancient tag—Alpha Cen, period. Alpha Cen sucks? Alpha Cen is heaven? Julian supposed it didn't make much difference.

He hauled himself over to the next doorway, where a heavy woman huddled with a little boy. The woman seemed stunned. "I think Mission's down," the boy said, looking worried. He was too young for integration, but now that Julian looked at the woman, the signs of withdrawal were clear. She didn't appear to be otherwise injured.

"What's your name?" he said.

She mouthed a reply: "Dolores." So she could hear. Yet she was frightened to death because the voices and pictures in her head had gone silent.

Julian turned to the boy. "What's your name?"

"Sam."

"Stay with your mother, Sam. Pretty soon they'll have the power back on. Keep your feet on the street in case the spin comes on too." Sam nodded as Julian pushed farther down the street.

Suddenly something blotted out the emergency light above him. He looked up, and saw his upside-down cart bumping gently against a sign that said "oftware." He pulled himself up to it, and found Duwayne flopping in the front seat. Tugging Duwayne around, he saw that he was alive, but sobbing. "Hang on," he told him.

He knew he needed to get the cart righted and back on the street. Just being this high up, relative to the street, with a half-ton mass sitting next to him, made him nervous. He wished he had some of the people he'd worked with in the bays—for a whole year he had maneuvered containers like this all day long.

Bracing himself, he grabbed the rack over the rear battery and slowly began to turn the whole thing over. He had it halfway over when the main lights came on. He wanted to cheer. Of course, that also meant that the big air vents went back into operation, and he felt himself swaying in a sudden breeze.

Suddenly he knew he had to hurry. Power meant spin was also returning.

He tried to tell himself he didn't need to hurry . . . it would take minutes for rates to build up, for any real gravity to return. But there was a growing clatter of floating furniture, cookware, God knew what else, all colliding as air currents swept them together. He turned, rebraced, waited. Turned again, lost his grip, found it. Rebraced.

The cart was upright, and Duwayne was trying to get out. "Don't move!" Julian snapped. Too late: Duwayne's movements wrenched the cart out of Julian's grip. He floated one way while the cart went the other, both of them in a gentle tumble. The cart cracked into the building across the street while Julian bumped his head on the sky. Feeling somewhat more at home in near-g now, he pushed himself back toward the street.

He was just in time to see the cart settle slowly and gently on its right side as gravity returned. He bounced over and helped Duwayne climb out. "Let's straighten this out while we still can." Duwayne helped him right the cart, then stood there chattering as Julian looked it over for damage. One side panel had crumpled; the forward frame appeared bent. Julian hit the ignition, however, and heard the reassuring hum. "You and Ty did a good job on this," he told Duwayne. "What happened?"

Duwayne blinked. "It's hard to say. Mission's down. Undernet too—"

"I know."

"I think it was the SteadiState unit, something about a burnthrough that started the whole stack going asymmetrical." Julian remembered some disaster scenario from school long ago, how carefully the dynamics of the many moving parts of

Mission needed to be kept in balance. A sudden burst of propulsion from an un-expected angle would be troublesome, possibly disastrous.

"That would explain loss of spin, but not the blackout, or the networks going down."

"All I meant was that was the last data I had. I've got nothing but static since then." He rubbed his eyes. "It's weird. Quiet." To Julian's ears, full of the grow-ing drone of voices, vents, and occasional crashes, it was anything but quiet. "What should we do?"

Julian got behind the wheel of the cart. "Let's see if we can't fix something." As they drove off Julian saw a graffito remnant: no Alpha Cen, no linking symbol, just "Death."

The bottle that was Mission architecture was in fact several different structures that, as the joke had it, only happened to be in the same place at the same time. The neck of the bottle was the propulsion tower; the body was made up of six different flattened, cylindrical sections that spun independently, linked only by their common core. Node Baikonur, with its high bays and core-docking ports was at the end opposite the propulsion tower. The flight-operations center was in Node Korou, the one closest.

Julian and Duwayne drove to the main lift, rode it to the core, then locked the car's wheels into the mag strip, moving x-ward behind a couple of maintenance vehicles taking the injured to Node Korou. An IA cop had made the first step toward harrassing them, some complaint about the mag strips being for emergency use only, but shut up when he saw the driver was Julian. It struck Julian for the first time that if he actually went back to Management he would have to give up the cart.

"I wish I knew where we were going," Duwayne complained.

"Still no nets?"

"Nothing. How can you navigate?"

"I'm using instinct." Not that it was working for him. He couldn't remember the last time he'd been in Node Korou—probably back before the divorce. He had always visualized it as low sky, unfinished. Either his memory was faulty or there had been changes in twenty years: Even allowing for the disruption caused by the spinquake, Korou was posh. Some clever Facilities designer had taken three levels and turned them into one by ripping out the sky in a couple of places. They probably had weather here. The street was some kind of red brick or cobblestone, not the comp you found everywhere else. Real stores with genuine windows—goods scattered all over. The people on the street surveying the damage had the well-maintained look of Management, but moved like puppets. They were jerky, stiff, dazed by being alone in their own heads for the first time in years. The fact that the lights kept flickering as power levels changed, and that suddenly frigid breezes blasted down the streets, only made it worse.

Julian and Duwayne turned a corner and found themselves in front of a three-story palace. "What's *this*?" Duwayne asked.

"Flight-operations center," Julian told him.

Like any good palace, the ops center had guards. They were clearly jumpy at being cut off from the security categories of Mission, and thus more subject to intimidation. When Julian realized it would be impossible to get a message sent inside to Roy, he and Duwayne simply told the guard they would find Roy themselves, and walked right in.

The interior of flight operations had once been quite grand, especially on Mission's limited scale. There had been a genuine glass chandelier hanging over the lobby. Julian remembered vaguely that it had come from the original Mir control center in Russia. Thanks to the spinquake, alas, it was a pile of sparkly shapes on the lobby floor.

Down one of the corridors they found Roy being tended by a young, confused female staffer. Roy had a cut over one eye which had been bandaged, but was still bleeding. "You're beginning to look your age," Julian told him.

"If it's any consolation, I feel considerably older."

"Have you spoken to Hannah? Is she all right?"

He nodded. "She's still working analysis." He seemed to focus on Julian and Duwayne for the first time. "I can't believe you showed up here."

"We came to see if we could help," Julian said, surprising himself.

"How nice of you . . . considering that you caused this." Before Julian could protest, Roy added, "Diagnostics found that it was an Agon Systems virus that destroyed all Mission nets. They're history. And so is Mission."

Julian would rather have been plunged back into his lightless, weightless, airless room than hear that. "That's not possible. The virus was supposed to self-destruct."

"The system crashed before it did its job. I've been watching them try to bring things back up . . . there's nothing there, Julian. No environmental controls, no financial records, no nothing."

"You've got to have backups. What about Management downstairs?"

"Well, almost everything exists in another form somewhere. But it's not integrated and it's not accessible. There's no way to run Mission right now."

Julian glanced at Duwayne to see if he'd heard, or if he'd understood. Not a clue. The guards worried him, however. So did Roy's continued bleeding.

"There's nothing anyone can do without the nets." Julian nodded to Duwayne, who helped Roy to his feet. They headed for the cart. "We need to get you out of here."

Seeing again the physical results of the event depressed Julian. Until Roy suggested it, he had not linked the spinquake to the virus he had launched in anger. If all the wreckage and injuries were truly his fault, he would deserve whatever punishment he received. But he wasn't prepared to accept that. "One virus shouldn't be able to bring down a whole network," he told Roy twenty minutes later, once they had reached Node Canaveral maintenance. The windows had been blown out, but there was power. One of the techs quickly stitched up Roy's scalp, then moved on to the next patient, leaving Roy alone with Julian.

"It didn't," Roy said. "We had giant system problems of our own. Your virus was like striking a match in a room full of gasoline."

"You mean the SteadiState hardware worked?"

"Yeah. We had a containment problem, but it wasn't the hardware's fault. It's a good engine and we could actually launch Mission with it, though nobody in Munich will ever believe it."

"That's a shame."

Roy looked at him over his enzyme drink. "What do you care?" Before Julian could object, Roy went on. "You've always hated the whole idea of going to Alpha Cen. You chose to work on the docks and get in with the Agon crowd. Well, you made the right choice, Julian. The way things are going now, *you* have more power to keep Mission alive than I do."

Duwayne suddenly came over. His face looked like the dawn. "Undernet's back on line," he said to Julian. "Our people are checking in. Most of them seem to be fine." A pause. "The line is three to two that Management abandons Mission and sends us all downstairs."

Julian looked from Duwayne to Roy, then back again, and knew that at least he was safe from Management harassment. They were going to be too busy cleaning up their mess.

But did he want Mission to die? It wasn't likely Management would dismantle the place even if it did abandon the ExtraSolar goal; Mission had essentially been used as a space station for decades, anyway. Just figuring out which partner in Management was entitled to which chunk of this pretty Node Korou cobblestone would take the rest of the century. No, Mission would continue to be home.

But what kind of home? The one lesson Julian had learned in all his business dealings was that people needed goals. For some it was money, for some it was sex. For some it was volume. But there was always a goal. "Duwayne," he said. "Can you tell Ty to get up here? And tell him to bring everybody he can find. People who aren't integrated, some of the techs from the bay."

"If you're sure that's what you want . . ." Duwayne looked doubtful.

He wasn't in any mood for Duwayne's second thoughts, so he just looked at him. Duwayne tripped over a fallen chair as he hustled back to the cart.

Roy said, "What are you trying to do?"

"Fill a vaccuum, I think."

Roy stood up, his face flushed. When Julian was eight he had accidentally erased Roy's *Magic City*, one he had spent four months building. Eleven-year-old Roy had hit Julian in the mouth; now he looked as though he was about to do the same thing. But forty-year-old Roy Tallet, Level C manager, was not about to get violent. He knew it would show up on his scans and bring a maintenance penalty. "You'll never get away with it."

"Get yourself on the undernet and make a bet."

It was a week before Julian could again take up his place at the Seagull, and even as he sat with Duwayne and Ty, he realized it was not the same. The Seagull had been hard hit by the one-two punch of the IA visit and the spinquake; its windows were gone and paneling was missing.

Business was still not back to normal. Well, it would never be what it was before the burnthrough. Management was still trying to bring up the new Mission net, but already the undernet had gotten several hundred new subscribers. Some of them wanted what the undernet had to offer—sex, gambling, pharmaceuticals—but just as many couldn't be tempted. They wanted secure volume. They wanted food. They wanted to go to Alpha Cen.

Dealing with it all required endless facing. At one point, Duwayne had grown impatient, getting up and walking away. Even loyal Ty spoke up. "Mr. Tallet, why don't you get yourself integrated? It'd make everything so much easier."

Julian glared and Ty changed the subject. A few moments later Duwayne came back. "Visitor," was all he said. The visitor was Roy, looking much better than the last time they had met.

"Sit down."

"I can't stay long. I'm just delivering a message." Roy glanced at Duwayne, who took the hint and got out of the booth as Roy slid in. "Riordan wants to face."

"The phones are working."

"He wanted me to prep you. He's going to offer you a job."

"I've got a job."

"A job in Management, Level C."

A job in Level C. The idea was so ridiculous that Julian didn't have a prepared reason for rejection. "I thought it was against the rules for the two of us to be there."

Roy smiled faintly. "You know, I had scheduled myself in maintenance deliberately to see you again."

"Why?"

"I was actually going to warn you about the moves against all of Agon Systems's . . . sidelines."

"Well, why didn't you?"

"You were being an asshole. And so was I." Roy sighed. "We just finished a new study and that showed seventy percent of Mission Pop logged onto the undernet at any given time. Half of them were Management. Usage was higher than it was for Mission. It shocked everyone on C, believe me. You've got to remember, Management started out as a bunch of engineers. For fifty years they've been trying to build a whole goddamn world—not just the hardware, but right down to deciding what was right to eat and drink and do. It didn't work. It was never going to work. It was about as useful as voting that two and two equal five.

"I wanted to warn you. I thought they were making a mistake, trying to fight you. I mean, if you weren't running those activities . . . someone else would. I said for years we should use you. But when I saw you—" He opened his hands.

"We acted like kids." Julian leaned back and examined his pencil. Management. Responsibility. "What are you and Hannah going to do?"

"We're moving downstairs, to Munich—" He wouldn't let Julian interrupt. "No, I'll be fine. I've been scanned and integrated all along. Hannah's been dying to go home." He smiled. "I'd invite you to visit, but I expect you'll be unreachable."

"You think we can actually go trans-Alpha?"

"The SteadiState *works*. If everyone starts pulling in the same direction, Mission could be on its way within the year."

On its way to Alpha Cen. "Well, then, I'd better see Riordan." Roy remained seated, silent. "What's wrong?"

Roy looked up. "I feel as if I got my brother back, and now I'm losing him." Julian realized he had been feeling the same thing.

By habit, Duwayne followed Julian and Roy outside. As Julian watched his brother go, he realized he was going to have to start a family. Who with? Sophie? Hope? Somebody.

"Duwayne," he said. "Get me into Node Canaveral maintenance. Set up my integration." Duwayne grinned and went to work.

Julian remained alone, noting the layer of dust on the wall, fighting back a sneeze. An idea occurred to him, and he reached out and scratched a new bit of graffiti in the dust: Alpha Cen = Life.

He didn't expect to walk the shores of Eden, but with a little luck he would have grandchildren, and *they* would.

THE LAND OF NOD

Mike Resnick

▼

Mike Resnick is one of the best-selling authors in science fiction, and one of the most prolific. His many novels include The Dark Lady, Stalking the Unicorn, Paradise, Santiago, Ivory, Soothsayer, Oracle, Lucifer Jones, Purgatory, Inferno, *and* A Miracle of Rare Design. *His award-winning short fiction has been gathered in the collection* Will the Last Person to Leave the Planet Please Turn off the Sun? *Of late, he has become almost as prolific as an anthologist, producing, as editor,* Inside the Funhouse: 17 SF stories about SF, Whatdunits, More Whatdunits, *and* Shaggy B.E.M. Stories; *a long string of anthologies coedited with Martin H. Greenberg,* Alternate Presidents, Alternate Kennedys, Alternate Warriors, Aladdin, Dinosaur Fantastic, By Any Other Fame, Alternate Outlaws, *and* Sherlock Holmes in Orbit, *among others; as well as two anthologies coedited with Gardner Dozois,* Future Earths: Under African Skies *and* Future Earths: Under South American Skies. *He won the Hugo Award in 1989 for "Kirinyaga." He won another Hugo Award in 1991 for another story in the Kirinyaga series, "The Manamouki," and another Hugo and a Nebula last year for his novella "Seven Views of Olduvai Gorge." His most recent books include the novels* The Widowmaker *and* A Hunger in the Soul. *Several of his books are in the process of being turned into big-budget movies. His stories have appeared in our Sixth, Seventh, Ninth, Eleventh, and Twelvth Annual Collections. He lives with his wife, Carol, in Cincinnati, Ohio.*

The Kirinyaga series, taking place on an orbital space colony that had been remade in the image of ancient Kenya as a Utopian experiment, has been one of the most talked-about, acclaimed, and controversial series in the recent history of science fiction. In the poignant story that follows, he brings the series to a shattering conclusion, taking us to a soulless, overcivilized future Kenya to witness a weary, exiled Koriba's last battle, as he struggles with the death of his dreams, and (perhaps even harder) with the persistence of hope.

Once, many years ago, there was a Kikuyu warrior who left his village and wandered off in search of adventure. Armed only with a spear, he slew the mighty lion and the cunning leopard. Then one day he came upon an elephant. He realized that his spear was useless against such a beast, but before he could back away or find cover, the elephant charged.

His only hope was divine intervention, and he begged Ngai, who rules the universe from His throne atop Kirinyaga, the holy mountain that men now call Mount Kenya, to find him and pluck him from the path of the elephant.

But Ngai did not respond, and the elephant picked the warrior up with its trunk and hurled him high into the air, and he landed in a distant thorn tree. His skin was badly torn by the thorns, but at least he was safe, since he was on a branch some twenty feet above the ground.

After he was sure the elephant had left the area, the warrior climbed down. Then he returned home and ascended the holy mountain to confront Ngai.

"What is it that you want of me?" asked Ngai, when the warrior had reached the summit.

"I want to know why you did not come," said the warrior angrily. "All my life I have worshiped you and paid tribute to you. Did you not hear me ask for your help?"

"I heard you," answered Ngai.

"Then why did you not come to my aid?" demanded the warrior. "Are you so lacking in godly powers that you could not find me?"

"After all these years you still do not understand," said Ngai sternly. "It is *you* who must search for *me*."

My son Edward picked me up at the police station on Biashara Street just after midnight. The sleek British vehicle hovered a few inches above the ground while I got in, and then his chauffeur began taking us back to his house in the Ngong Hills.

"This is becoming tedious," he said, activating the shimmering privacy barrier so that we could not be overheard. He tried to present a judicial calm, but I knew he was furious.

"You would think they would tire of it," I agreed.

"We must have a serious talk," he said. "You have been back only two months, and this is the fourth time I have had to bail you out of jail."

"I have broken no Kikuyu laws," I said calmly as we raced through the dark, ominous slums of Nairobi on our way to the affluent suburbs.

"You have broken the laws of Kenya," he said. "And like it or not, that is where you now live. I'm an official in the government, and I will not have you constantly embarrassing me!" He paused, struggling with his temper. "Look at you! I have offered to buy you a new wardrobe. Why must you wear that ugly old *kikoi*? It smells even worse than it looks."

"Is there now a law against dressing dressing like a Kikuyu?" I asked him.

"No," he said, as he commanded the miniature bar to appear from beneath the floor and poured himself a drink. "But there *is* a law against creating a disturbance in a restaurant."

"I paid for my meal," I noted, as we turned onto Langata Road and headed out for the suburbs. "In the Kenya shillings that you gave me."

"That does not give you the right to hurl your food against the wall, simply because it is not cooked to your taste." He glared at me, barely able to contain his anger. "You're getting worse with each offense. If I had been anyone else, you'd have spent the night in jail. As it is, I had to agree to pay for the damage you caused."

"It was eland," I explained. "The Kikuyu do not eat game animals."

"It was *not* eland," he said, setting his glass down and lighting a smokeless cigarette. "The last eland died in a German zoo a year after you left for Kirinyaga. It was a modified soybean product, genetically enhanced to *taste* like eland." He paused, then sighed deeply. "If you thought it was eland, why did you order it?"

"The server said it was steak. I assumed he meant the meat of a cow or an ox."

"This has got to stop," said Edward. "We are two grown men. Why can't we reach an accommodation?" He stared at me for a long time. "I can deal with rational men who disagree with me. I do it at Government House every day. But I cannot deal with a fanatic."

"I am a rational man," I said.

"Are you?" he demanded. "Yesterday you showed my wife's nephew how to apply the *githani* test for truthfulness, and he practically burned his brother's tongue off."

"His brother was lying," I said calmly. "He who lies faces the red-hot blade with a dry mouth, whereas he who has nothing to fear has enough moisture on his tongue so that he cannot be burned."

"Try telling a seven-year-old boy that he has nothing to fear when he's being approached by a sadistic older brother who is brandishing a red-hot knife!" snapped my son.

A uniformed watchman waved us though to the private road where my son lived, and when we reached our driveway the chauffeur pulled our British vehicle up to the edge of the force field. It identified us and vanished long enough for us to pass through, and soon we came to the front door.

Edward got out of the vehicle and approached his residence as I followed him. He clenched his fists in a physical effort to restrain his anger. "I agreed to let you live with us, because you are an old man who was thrown off his world—"

"I left Kirinyaga of my own volition," I interrupted calmly.

"It makes no difference why or how you left," said my son. "What matters is that you are *here* now. You are a very old man. It has been many years since you have lived on Earth. All of your friends are dead. My mother is dead. I am your son, and I will accept my responsibilities, but you *must* meet me halfway."

"I am trying to," I said.

"I doubt it."

"I am," I repeated. "Your own son understands that, even if you do not."

"My own son has had quite enough to cope with my divorce and remarriage. The last thing he needs is a grandfather filling his head with wild tales of some Kikuyu Utopia."

"It is a failed Utopia," I corrected him. "They would not listen to me, and so they are doomed to become another Kenya."

"What is so wrong with that?" said Edward. "Kenya is my home, and I am proud of it." He paused and stared at me. "And now it is *your* home again. You must speak of it with more respect."

"I lived in Kenya for many years before I emigrated to Kirinyaga," I said. "I can live here again. Nothing has changed."

"That is not so," said my son. "We have built a transport system beneath Nairobi, and there is now a spaceport at Watamu on the coast. We have closed down the nuclear plants; our power is now entirely thermal, drawn from beneath the floor of the Rift Valley. In fact,'' he added with the pride that always accompanied the descriptions of his new wife's attainments, ''Susan was instrumental in the changeover.''

''You misunderstood me, Edward,'' I replied. ''Kenya remains unchanged in that it continues to ape the Europeans rather than remain true to its own traditions.''

The security system identified us and opened his house to us. We walked through the foyer, past the broad winding staircase that led to the bedroom wing. The servants were waiting for us, and the butler took Edward's coat from him. Then we passed the doorways to the lounge and drawing room, both of which were filled with Roman statues and French paintings and rows of beautifully bound British books. Finally we came to Edward's study, where he turned and spoke in a low tone to the butler.

''We wish to be alone.''

The servants vanished as if they had been nothing but holograms.

''Where is Susan?'' I asked, for my daughter-in-law was nowhere to be seen.

''We were at a party at the Cameroon ambassador's new home when the call came through that you had been arrested again,'' he answered. ''You broke up a very enjoyable bridge game. My guess is that she's in the tub or in bed, cursing your name.''

I was about to mention that cursing my name to the god of the Europeans would not prove effective, but I decided that my son would not like to hear that at this moment, so I was silent. As I looked at my surroundings, I reflected that not only had all of Edward's belongings come from the Europeans, but that even his house had been taken from them, for it consisted of many rectangular rooms, and all Kikuyu knew—or should have known—that demons dwell in corners and the only proper shape for a home is round.

Edward walked briskly to his desk, activated his computer, and read his messages, and then turned to me.

''There is another message from the government,'' he announced. ''They want to see you next Tuesday at noon.''

''I have already told them I will not accept their money,'' I said. ''I have performed no service for them.''

He put on his lecture face. ''We are no longer a poor country,'' he said. ''We pride ourselves that none of our infirm or elderly goes hungry.''

''I will not go hungry if the restaurants will stop trying to feed me unclean animals.''

''The government is just making sure that you do not become a financial burden to me,'' said Edward, refusing to let me change the subject.

''You are my son,'' I said. ''I raised you and fed you and protected you when you were young. Now I am old and you will do the same for me. That is our tradition.''

''Well, it is our government's tradition to provide a financial safety net to families who are supporting elderly members,'' he said, and I could tell that the last trace of Kikuyu within him had vanished, that he was entirely a Kenyan.

''You are a wealthy man,'' I pointed out. ''You do not need their money.''

''I pay my taxes,'' he said, lighting another smokeless cigarette to hide his defensiveness. "It would be foolish not to accept the benefits that accrue to us. You may live a very long time. We have every right to that money."

"It is dishonorable to accept what you do not need," I replied. "Tell them to leave us alone."

He leaned back, half sitting on his desk. "They wouldn't, even if I asked them to."

"They must be Wakamba or Maasai," I said, making no effort to hide my contempt.

"They are Kenyans," he answered. "Just as you and I are."

"Yes," I said, suddenly feeling the weight of my years. "Yes, I must work very hard at remembering that."

"You will save me more trips to the police station if you can," said my son.

I nodded and went off to my room. He had supplied me with a bed and mattress, but after so many years of living in my hut on Kirinyaga, I found the bed uncomfortable, so every night I removed the blanket and placed it on the floor, then lay down and slept on it.

But tonight sleep would not come, for I kept reliving the past two months in my mind. Everything I saw, everything I heard, made me remember why I had left Kenya in the first place, why I had fought so long and so hard to obtain Kirinyaga's charter.

I rolled onto my side, propped my head on my hand, and looked out the window. Hundreds of stars were twinkling brightly in the clear, cloudless sky. I tried to imagine which of them was Kirinyaga. I had been the *mundumugu*—the witch doctor—who was charged with establishing our Kikuyu Utopia.

"I served you more selflessly than any other," I whispered, staring at a flickering, verdant star, "and you betrayed me. Worse, you have betrayed Ngai. Neither He nor I shall ever seek you out again."

I laid my head back down, turned away from the window, and closed my eyes, determined to look into the skies no more.

In the morning, my son stopped by my room.

"You have slept on the floor again," he noted.

"Have they passed a law against that now?" I asked.

He sighed deeply. "Sleep any way you want."

I stared at him. "You look very impressive . . . ," I began.

"Thank you."

". . . in your European clothes," I concluded.

"I have an important meeting with the Finance Minister today."

He looked at his timepiece. "In fact, I must leave now or I will be late." He paused uneasily. "Have you considered what we spoke about yesterday?"

"We spoke of many things," I said.

"I am referring to the Kikuyu retirement village."

"I have lived in a village," I said. "And that is not one. It is a twenty-story tower of steel and glass, built to imprison the elderly."

"We have been through all this before," said my son. "It would be a place for you to make new friends."

"I have a new friend," I said. "I shall be visiting him this evening."

"Good!" he said. "Maybe he'll keep you out of trouble."

I arrived at the huge titanium-and-glass laboratory complex just before midnight. The night had turned cool, and a breeze was blowing gently from the south. The moon had passed behind a cloud, and it was difficult to find the side gate in the darkness. Eventually I did find it, though, and Kamau was waiting for me. He deactivated a small section of the electronic barrier long enough for me to step through.

"*Jambo, mzee*," he said. *Hello, wise old man.*

"*Jambo, mzee*," I replied, for he was almost as old as I myself was. "I have come to see with my own eyes if you were telling the truth."

He nodded and turned, and I followed him between the tall, angular buildings that hovered over us, casting eerie shadows along the narrow walkways and channeling all the noises of the city in our direction. Our path was lined with whistling thorn and yellow fever trees, cloned from the few remaining specimens, rather than the usual introduced European shrubbery. Here and there were ornamental displays of grasses from the vanished savannahs.

"It is strange to see so much true African vegetation here in Kenya," I remarked. "Since I have returned from Kirinyaga, my eyes have hungered for it."

"You have seen a whole world of it," he replied with unconcealed envy.

"There is more to a world than greenery," I said. "When all is said and done, there is little difference between Kirinyaga and Kenya. Both have turned their backs on Ngai."

Kamau came to a halt, and gestured around him at the looming metal and glass and concrete buildings that totally covered the cool swamps from which Nairobi took its name. "I do not know how you can prefer *this* to Kirinyaga."

"I did not say I preferred it," I replied, suddenly aware that the ever-present noises of the city had been overshadowed by the droning hum of machines.

"Then you *do* miss Kirinyaga."

"I miss what Kirinyaga might have been. As for these," I said, indicating the immense structures, "they are just buildings."

"They are European buildings," he said bitterly. "They were built by men who are no longer Kikuyu or Luo or Embu, but merely Kenyans. They are filled with corners." He paused, and I thought, approvingly, *How much you sound like me! No wonder you sought me out when I returned to Kenya.* "Nairobi is home to eleven million people," he continued. "It stinks of sewage. The air is so polluted there are days when you can actually see it. The people wear European clothes and worship the Europeans' god. How could you turn your back on Utopia for this?"

I held up my hands. "I have only ten fingers."

He frowned. "I do not understand."

"Do you remember the story of the little Dutch boy who put his finger in the dike?"

Kamau shook his head and spat contemptuously on the ground. "I do not listen to European stories."

"Perhaps you are wise not to," I acknowledged. "At any rate, the dike of tradition with which I had surrounded Kirinyaga began to spring leaks. They were few and easily plugged at first, but as the society kept evolving and growing they became many, and soon I did not have enough fingers to plug them all.'' I shrugged. ''So I left before I was washed away.''

''Have they another *mundumugu* to replace you?'' he asked.

''I am told that they have a doctor to cure the sick, and a Christian minister to tell them how to worship the god of the Europeans, and a computer to tell them how to react to any situation that might arise,'' I said. ''They no longer need a *mundumugu*.''

''Then Ngai has forsaken them,'' he stated.

''No,'' I corrected him. ''*They* have forsaken Ngai.''

''I apologize, *mundumugu*,'' he said with deference. ''You are right, of course.''

He began walking again, and soon a strong, pungent odor came to my nostrils, a scent I had never encountered before, but which stirred some memory deep within my soul.

''We are almost there,'' said Kamau.

I heard a low rumbling sound, not like a predator growling, but rather like a vast machine purring with power.

''He is very nervous,'' continued Kamau, speaking in a soft monotone. ''Make no sudden movements. He has already tried to kill two of his daytime attendants.''

And then we were there, just as the moon emerged from its cloud cover and shone down on the awesome creature that stood facing us.

''He is magnificent!'' I whispered.

''A perfect replication,'' agreed Kamau. ''Height, ten feet eight inches at the shoulder, weight seven tons—and each tusk is exactly one hundred and forty-eight pounds.''

The huge animal stared at me through the flickering force field that surrounded it and tested the cool night breeze, striving to pick up my scent.

''Remarkable!'' I said.

''You understand the cloning process, do you not?'' asked Kamau.

''I understand what cloning *is*,'' I answered. ''I know nothing of the exact process.''

''In this case, they took some cells from his tusks, which have been on display in the museum for more than two centuries, created the proper nutrient solution, and this is the result: Ahmed of Marsabit, the only elephant ever protected by presidential decree, lives again.''

''I read that he was always accompanied by two guards no matter where he roamed on Mount Marsabit,'' I said. ''Have they also ignored tradition? I see no one but you. Where is the other guard?''

''There are no guards. The entire complex is protected by a sophisticated electronic security system.''

''Are you not a guard?'' I asked.

He kept the shame from his voice, but he could not banish it from his face: Even in the moonlight I could see it. ''I am a paid companion.''

''Of the elephant?''

''Of Ahmed.''

''I am sorry,'' I said.

"We cannot all be *mundumugus*," he answered. "When you are my age in a culture that worships youth, you take what is offered to you."

"True," I said. I looked back at the elephant. "I wonder if he has any memories of his former life? Of the days when he was the greatest of all living creatures, and Mount Marsabit was his kingdom."

"He knows nothing of Marsabit," answered Kamau. "But he knows something is wrong. He knows he was not born to spend his life in a tiny yard, surrounded by a glowing force field." He paused. "Sometimes, late at night, he faces the north and lifts his trunk and cries out his loneliness and misery. To the technicians it is just an annoyance. Usually they tell me to feed him, as if food will assuage his sorrow. It is not even *real* food, but something they have concocted in their laboratories."

"He does not belong here," I agreed.

"I know," said Kamau. "But then, neither do you, *mzee*. You should be back on Kirinyaga, living as the Kikuyu were meant to live."

I frowned. "No one on Kirinyaga is living as the Kikuyu were meant to live." I sighed deeply. "I think perhaps the time for *mundumugus* is past."

"This cannot be true," he protested. "Who else can be the repository of our traditions, the interpreter of our laws?"

"Our traditions are as dead as *his*," I said, gesturing toward Ahmed. Then I turned back to Kamau. "Do you mind if I ask you a question?"

"Certainly not, *mundumugu*."

"I am glad you sought me out, and I have enjoyed our conversations since I returned to Kenya," I told him. "But something puzzles me: Since you feel so strongly about the Kikuyu, why did I not know you during our struggle to find a homeland? Why did you remain behind when we emigrated to Kirinyaga?"

I could see him wrestling with himself to produce an answer. Finally the battle was over, and the old man seemed to shrink an inch or two.

"I was terrified," he admitted.

"Of the spaceship?" I asked.

"No."

"Then what frightened you?"

Another internal struggle, and then an answer: "*You* did, *mzee*."

"Me?" I repeated, surprised.

"You were always so sure of yourself," he said. "Always such a perfect Kikuyu. You made me afraid that I wasn't good enough."

"That was ridiculous," I said firmly.

"Was it?" he countered. "My wife was a Catholic. My son and daughter bore Christian names. And I myself had grown used to European clothes and European conveniences." He paused. "I was afraid if I went with you—and I wanted to; I have been cursing myself for my cowardice ever since—that soon I would complain about missing the technology and comfort I had left behind, and that you would banish me." He would not meet my gaze, but stared at the ground. "I did not wish to become an outcast on the world that was the last hope of my people."

You are wiser than I suspected, I thought. Aloud I uttered a compassionate lie: "You would not have been an outcast."

"You are sure?"

"I am sure," I said, laying a comforting hand on his bony shoulder. "In fact, I wish you had been there to support me when the end came."

"What good would the support of an old man have been?"

"You are not just *any* old man," I answered. "The word of a descendant of Johnstone Kamau would have carried much weight among the Council of Elders."

"That was another reason I was afraid to come," he replied, the words flowing a little more easily this time. "How could I live up to my name—for everyone knows that Johnstone Kamau became Jomo Kenyatta, the great Burning Spear of the Kikuyu. How could I possibly compare to such a man as that?"

"You compare more favorably than you think," I said reassuringly. "I could have used the passion of your belief."

"Surely you had support from the people," he said.

I shook my head. "Even my own apprentice, who I was preparing to succeed me, abandoned me; in fact, I believe he is at the university just down the road even as we speak. In the end, the people rejected the discipline of our traditions and the teachings of Ngai for the miracles and comforts of the Europeans. I suppose I should not be surprised, considering how many times it has happened here in Africa." I looked thoughtfully at the elephant. "I am as much an anachronism as Ahmed. Time has forgotten us both."

"But Ngai has not."

"Ngai too, my friend," I said. "Our day has passed. There is no place left for us, not in Kenya, not on Kirinyaga, not anywhere."

Perhaps it was something in the tone of my voice, or perhaps in some mystic way Ahmed understood what I was saying. Whatever the reason, the elephant stepped forward to the edge of the force field and stared directly at me.

"It is lucky we have the field for protection," remarked Kamau.

"He would not hurt me," I said confidently.

"He has hurt men whom he had less reason to attack."

"But not me," I said. "Lower the field to a height of five feet."

"But . . ."

"Do as I say," I ordered him.

"Yes, *mundumugu*," he replied unhappily, going to a small control box and punching in a code.

Suddenly the mild visual distortion vanished at eye level. I reached out a reassuring hand, and a moment later Ahmed ran the tip of his trunk gently across my face and body, then sighed deeply and stood there, swaying gently as he transferred his weight from one foot to the other.

"I would not have believed it if I had not seen it!" said Kamau, almost reverently.

"Are we not all Ngai's creations?" I said.

"Even Ahmed?" asked Kamau.

"Who do *you* think created him?"

He shrugged again, and did not answer.

I remained for a few more minutes, watching the magnificent creature, while Kamau returned the force field to its former position. Then the night air became uncomfortably cold, as so often happened at this altitude, and I turned to Kamau.

"I must leave now," I said. "I thank you for inviting me here. I would not have believed this miracle had I not seen it with my own eyes."

"The scientists think it is *their* miracle," he said.

"You and I know better," I replied.

He frowned. "But why do you think Ngai has allowed Ahmed to live again, at this time and in this place?"

I paused for a long moment, trying to formulate an answer, and found that I couldn't.

"There was a time when I knew with absolute certainty why Ngai did what He did," I said at last. "Now I am not so sure."

"What kind of talk is that from a *mundumugu*?" demanded Kamau.

"It was not long ago that I would wake up to the song of birds," I said as we left Ahmed's enclosure and walked to the side gate through which I had entered. "And I would look across the river that wound by my village on Kirinyaga and see impala and zebra grazing on the savannah. Now I wake up to the sound and smell of modern Nairobi and then I look out and see a featureless gray wall that separates my son's house from that of his neighbor." I paused. "I think this must be my punishment for failing to bring Ngai's word to my people."

"Will I see you again?" he asked as we reached the gate and he deactivated a small section long enough for me to pass through.

"If it will not be an imposition," I said.

"The great Koriba an imposition?" he said with a smile.

"My son finds me so," I replied. "He gives me a room in his house, but he would prefer I lived elsewhere. And his wife is ashamed of my bare feet and my *kikoi*; she is constantly buying European shoes and clothing for me to wear."

"*My* son works inside the laboratory," said Kamau, pointing to his son's third-floor office with some pride. "He has seventeen men working for him. Seventeen!"

I must not have looked impressed, for he continued, less enthusiastically, "It is he who got me this job, so that I *wouldn't* have to live with him."

"The job of paid companion," I said.

A bittersweet expression crossed his face. "I love my son, Koriba, and I know that he loves me—but I think that he is also a little bit ashamed of me."

"There is a thin line between shame and embarrassment," I said. "My son glides between one and the other like the pendulum of a clock."

Kamau seemed grateful to hear that his situation was not unique. "You are welcome to live with me, *mundumugu*," he said, and I could tell that it was an earnest offer, not just a polite lie that he hoped I would reject. "We would have much to talk about."

"That is very considerate of you," I said. "But it will be enough if I may visit you from time to time, on those days when I find Kenyans unbearable and must speak to another Kikuyu."

"As often as you wish," he said. "*Kwaheri, mzee.*"

"*Kwaheri,*" I responded. *Farewell.*

I took the slidewalk down the noisy, crowded streets and boulevards that had once been the sprawling Athi Plains, an area that had swarmed with a different kind of life, and got off when I came to the airbus platform. An airbus glided up a few minutes later, almost empty at this late hour, and began going north, floating perhaps ten inches above the ground.

The trees that lined the migration route had been replaced by a dense angular forest of steel and glass and tightly bonded alloys. As I peered through a window into the night, it seemed for a few moments that I was also peering into the past. Here, where the titanium-and-glass courthouse stood, was the very spot where the Burning Spear had first been arrested for having the temerity to suggest that his country did not belong to the British. And there, by the new eight-story post-office building, was where the last lion had died. Over there, by the water-recycling plant, my people had vanquished the Wakamba in glorious and bloody battle some three hundred years ago.

"We have arrived, *mzee*," said the driver, and the bus hovered a few inches above the ground while I made my way to the door. "Aren't you chilly, dressed in just a blanket like that?"

I did not deign to answer him, but stepped out to the sidewalk, which did not move here in the suburbs as did the slidewalks of the city. I prefered it, for man was meant to walk, not be transported effortlessly by miles-long beltways.

I approached my son's enclave and greeted the guards, who all knew me, for I often wandered through the area at night. They passed me through with no difficulty, and as I walked I tried to look across the centuries once more, to see the mud-and-grass huts, the *bomas* and *shambas* of my people, but the vision was blotted out by enormous mock-Tudor and mock-Victorian and mock-Colonial and mock-contemporary houses, interspersed with needlelike apartment buildings that reached up to stab the clouds.

I had no desire to speak to Edward or Susan, for they would question me endlessly about where I had been. My son would once again warn me about the thieves and muggers who prey on old men after dark in Nairobi, and my daughter-in-law would try to subtly suggest that I would be warmer in a coat and pants. So I went past their house and walked aimlessly through the enclave until all the lights in the house had gone out. When I was sure they were asleep, I went to a side door and waited for the security system to identify my retina and skeletal structure, as it had on so many similar nights. Then I quietly made my way to my room.

Usually I dreamed of Kirinyaga, but this night the image of Ahmed haunted my dreams. Ahmed, eternally confined by a force field; Ahmed, trying to imagine what lay beyond his tiny enclosure; Ahmed, who would live and die without ever seeing another of his own kind.

And gradually, my dream shifted to myself: to Koriba, attached by invisible chains to a Nairobi he could no longer recognize; Koriba, trying futilely to mold Kirinyaga into what it might have been; Koriba, who once led a brave exodus of the Kikuyu until one day he looked around and found that he was the only Kikuyu remaining.

In the morning I went to visit my daughter on Kirinyaga—not the terraformed world, but the *real* Kirinyaga, which is now called Mount Kenya. It was here that Ngai gave the digging-stick to Gikuyu, the first man, and told him to work the earth. It was here that Gikuyu's nine daughters became the mothers of the nine tribes of the Kikuyu, here that the sacred fig tree blossomed. It was here, millennia later, that Jomo Kenyatta, the great Burning Spear of the Kikuyu, would invoke Ngai's power and send the Mau Mau out to drive the white man back to Europe.

And it was here that a steel-and-glass city of five million inhabitants sprawled up the side of the holy mountain. Nairobi's overstrained water and sewer system simply could not accommodate any more people, so the government offered enormous tax incentives to any business that would move to Kirinyaga, in the hope that the people would follow—and the people accommodated them.

Vehicles spewed pollution into the atmosphere, and the noise of the city at work was deafening. I walked to the spot where the fig tree had once stood; it was now covered by a lead foundry. The slopes where the bongo and the rhinoceros once lived were hidden beneath the housing projects. The winding mountain streams had all been diverted and redirected. The tree beneath which Deedan Kimathi had been killed by the British was only a memory, its place taken by a fast-food restaurant. The summit had been turned into a park, with tram service leading to a score of souvenir shops.

And now I realized why Kenya had become intolerable. Ngai no longer ruled the world from His throne atop the mountain, for there was no longer any room for Him there. Like the leopard and the golden sunbird, like I myself many years ago, He too had fled before this onslaught of black Europeans.

Possibly my discovery influenced my mood, for the visit with my daughter did not go well. But then, they never did: She was too much like her mother.

I entered my son's study late that same afternoon.

"One of the servants said you wished to see me," I said.

"Yes, I do," said my son as he looked up from his computer. Behind him were paintings of two great leaders, Martin Luther King and Julius Nyerere, black men both, but neither one a Kikuyu. "Please sit down."

I did as he asked.

"On a chair, my father," he said.

"The floor is satisfactory."

He sighed heavily. "I am too tired to argue with you. I have been brushing up on my French." He grimaced. "It is a difficult language."

"Why are you studying French?" I asked.

"As you know, the ambassador from Cameroon has bought a house in the enclave. I thought it would be advantageous to be able to speak to him in his own tongue."

"That would be Bamileke or Ewondo, not French," I noted.

"He does not speak either of those," answered Edward. "His family is ruling class. They only spoke French in his family compound, and he was educated in Paris."

"Since he is the ambassador to our country, why are you learning *his* language?" I asked. "Why does he not learn Swahili?"

"Swahili is a street language," said my son. "English and French are the languages of diplomacy and business. His English is poor, so I will speak to him in French instead." He smiled smugly. "*That* ought to impress him!"

"I see," I said.

"You look disapproving," he observed.

"I am not ashamed of being a Kikuyu," I said. "Why are you ashamed of being a Kenyan?"

"I am not ashamed of anything!" he snapped. "I am proud of being able to speak to him in his own tongue."

"More proud than he, a visitor to Kenya, is to speak to you in *your* tongue," I noted.

"You do not understand!" he said.

"Evidently," I agreed.

He stared at me silently for a moment, then sighed deeply. "You drive me crazy," he said. "I don't even know how we came to be discussing this. I wanted to see you for a different reason." He lit a smokeless cigarette, took one puff, and threw it into the atomizer. "I had a visit from Father Ngoma this morning."

"I do not know him."

"You know his parishioners, though," said my son. "A number of them have come to you for advice."

"That is possible," I admitted.

"Damn it!" said Edward. "I have to live in this neighborhood, and he is the parish priest. He resents you telling his flock how to live, especially since what you tell them is in contradiction to Catholic dogma."

"Am I to lie to them, then?" I asked.

"Can't you just refer them to Father Ngoma?"

"I am a *mundumugu*," I said. "It is my duty to advise those who come to me for guidance."

"You have not been a *mundumugu* since they made you leave Kirinyaga!" he said irritably.

"I left of my own volition," I replied calmly.

"We are getting off the subject again," said Edward. "Look—if you want to stay in the *mundumugu* business, I'll rent you an office, or"—he added contemptuously—"buy you a patch of dirt on which to squat and make pronouncements. But you cannot practice in my house."

"Father Ngoma's parishioners must not like what he has to say," I observed, "or they would not seek advice elsewhere."

"I do not want you speaking to them again. Is that clear?"

"Yes," I said. "It is clear that you do not want me to speak to them again."

"You know exactly what I mean!" he exploded. "No more verbal games! Maybe they worked on Kirinyaga, but they won't work here! I know you too well!"

He went back to staring at his computer.

"It is most interesting," I said.

"What is?" he asked suspiciously, glaring at me.

"Here you are, surrounded by English books, studying French, and arguing on behalf of the priest of an Italian religion. Not only are you not Kikuyu, I think perhaps you are no longer even Kenyan."

He glared at me across his desk. "You drive me crazy," he repeated.

After I left my son's study I left the house and took an airbus to the park in Muthaiga, miles from my son and the neighbors who were interchangeable with him. Once lions had stalked this terrain. Leopards had clung to overhanging limbs, waiting for the opportunity to pounce upon their prey. Wildebeest and zebra and gazelles had rubbed shoulders, grazing on the tall grasses. Giraffes had nibbled the tops of acacia trees, while warthogs rooted in the earth for tubers. Rhinos had nibbled on thornbushes, and charged furiously at any sound or sight they could not immediately identify.

Then the Kikuyu had come and cleared the land, bringing with them their cattle and their oxen and their goats. They had dwelt in huts of mud and grass, and lived the life that we aspired to on Kirinyaga.

But all that was in the past. Today the park contained nothing but a few squirrels racing across the imported Kentucky blue grass and a pair of hornbills that had nested in one of the transplanted European trees. Old Kikuyu men, dressed in shoes and pants and jackets, sat on the benches that ran along the perimeter. One man was tossing crumbs to an exceptionally bold starling, but most of them simply sat and stared aimlessly.

I found an empty bench, but decided not to sit on it. I didn't want to be like these men, who saw nothing but the squirrels and the birds, when I could see the lions and the impala, the war-painted Kikuyu and the red-clad Maasai, who had once stalked across this same land.

I continued walking, suddenly restless, and despite the heat of the day and the frailty of my ancient body, I walked until twilight. I decided I could not endure dinner with my son and his wife, their talk of their boring jobs, their continual veiled suggestions about the retirement home, their inability to comprehend either why I went to Kirinyaga or why I returned—so instead of going home I began walking aimlessly through the crowded city.

Finally I looked up at the sky. *Ngai*, I said silently, *I still do not understand. I was a good* mundumugu. *I obeyed Your law. I honored Your rituals. There must have come a day, a moment, a second, when together we could have saved Kirinyaga if You had just manifested Yourself. Why did You abandon it when it needed You so desperately?*

I spoke to Ngai for minutes that turned into hours, but He did not answer.

When it was ten o'clock at night, I decided it was time to start making my way to the laboratory complex, for it would take me more than an hour to get there, and Kamau began working at eleven.

As before, he deactivated the electronic barrier to let me in, then escorted me to the small grassy area where Ahmed was kept.

"I did not expect to see you back so soon, *mzee*," he said.

"I have no place else to go," I answered, and he nodded, as if this made perfect sense to him.

Ahmed seemed nervous until the breeze brought my scent to him. Then he turned to face the north, extending his trunk every few moments.

"It is as if he seeks some sign from Mount Marsabit," I remarked, for the great creature's former home was hundreds of miles north of Nairobi, a solitary green mountain rising out of the blazing desert.

"He would not be pleased with what he found," said Kamau.

"Why do you say that?" I asked, for no animal in our history was ever more identified with a location than the mighty Ahmed with Marsabit.

"Do you not read the papers, or watch the news on the holo?"

I shook my head. "What happens to black Europeans is of no concern to me."

"The government has evacuated the town of Marsabit, which sits next to the mountain. They have closed the Singing Wells, and have ordered everyone to leave the area."

"Leave Marsabit? Why?"

"They have been burying nuclear waste at the base of the mountain for many years," he said. "It was just revealed that some of the containers broke open almost six years ago. The government hid the fact from the people, and then failed to properly clean up the leak."

"How could such a thing happen?" I asked, though of course I knew the answer. After all, how does *anything* happen in Kenya?

"Politics. Payoffs. Corruption."

"A third of Kenya is desert," I said. "Why did they not bury it there, where no one lives or even thinks to travel, so when this kind of disaster occurs, as it always does, no one is harmed?"

He shrugged. "Politics. Payoffs. Corruption," he repeated. "It is our way of life."

"Ah, well, it is nothing to me anyway," I said. "What happens to a mountain five hundred kilometers away does not interest me, any more than I am interested in what happens to a world named after a different mountain."

"It interests *me*," said Kamau. "Innocent people have been exposed to radiation."

"If they live near Marsabit, they are Pokot and Rendille," I pointed out. "What does that matter to the Kikuyu?"

"They are *people*, and my heart goes out to them," said Kamau.

"You are a good man," I said. "I knew that from the moment we first met." I pulled some peanuts from the pouch that hung around my neck, the same pouch in which I used to keep charms and magical tokens. "I bought these for Ahmed this afternoon," I said. "May I . . . ?"

"Certainly," answered Kamau. "He has few enough pleasures. Even a peanut will be appreciated. Just toss them at his feet."

"No," I said, walking forward. "Lower the barrier."

He lowered the force field until Ahmed was able to reach his trunk out over the top. When I got close enough, the huge beast gently took the peanuts from my hand.

"I am amazed!" said Kamau when I had rejoined him. "Even I cannot approach Ahmed with impunity, yet you actually fed him by hand, as if he were a family pet."

"We are each the last of our kind, living on borrowed time," I said. "He senses a kinship."

I remained a few more minutes, then went home to another night of troubled sleep. I felt Ngai was trying to tell me something, trying to impart some message through my dreams, but though I had spent years interpreting the omens in other people's dreams, I was ignorant of my own.

Edward was standing on the beautifully rolled lawn, staring at the blackened embers of my fire.

"I have a beautiful fire pit on the terrace," he said, trying unsuccessfully to hide his anger. "Why on earth did you build a fire in the middle of the garden?"

"That is where a fire belongs," I answered.

"Not in *this* house, it doesn't!"

"I shall try to remember."

"Do you know what the landscaper will charge me to repair the damage you caused?" A look of concern suddenly crossed his face. "You haven't sacrificed any animals, have you?"

"No."

"You're sure none of the neighbors is missing a dog or a cat?" he persisted.

"I know the law," I said. And indeed, Kikuyu law required the sacrifice of goats and cattle, not dogs and cats. "I am trying to obey it."

"I find that difficult to believe."

"But *you* are not obeying it, Edward," I said.

"What are you talking about?" he demanded.

I looked at Susan, who was staring at us from a second-story window.

"You have two wives," I pointed out. "The younger one lives with you, but the older one lives many kilometers away, and sees you only when you take your children away from her on weekends. This is unnatural: A man's wives should all live together with him, sharing the household duties."

"Linda is no longer my wife," he said. "You know that. We were divorced many years ago."

"You can afford both," I said. "You should have kept both."

"In this society, a man may have only one wife," said Edward. "What kind of talk is this? You have lived in England and America. You know that."

"That is their law, not ours," I said. "This is Kenya."

"It is the same thing."

"The Moslems have more than one wife," I replied.

"I am not a Moslem," he said.

"A Kikuyu man may have as many wives as he can afford," I said. "It is obvious that you are also not a Kikuyu."

"I've had it with this smug superiority of yours!" he exploded. "You deserted my mother because she was not a true Kikuyu," he continued bitterly. "You turned your back on my sister because she was not a true Kikuyu. Since I was a child, every time you were displeased with me you have told me that I am not a true Kikuyu. Now you have even proclaimed that none of the thousands who followed you to Kirinyaga are true Kikuyus." He glared furiously at me. "Your standards are higher than Kirinyaga itself! Can there possibly be a true Kikuyu anywhere in the universe?"

"Certainly," I replied.

"Where can such a paragon be found?" he demanded.

"Right here," I said, tapping myself on the chest. "You are looking at him."

My days faded one into another, the dullness and drudgery of them broken only by occasional nocturnal visits to the laboratory complex. Then one night, as I met Kamau at the gate, I could see that his entire demeanor had changed.

"Something is wrong," I said promptly. "Are you ill?"

"No, *mzee*, it is nothing like that."

"Then what is the matter?" I persisted.

"It is Ahmed," said Kamau, unable to stop tears from rolling down his withered cheeks. "They have decided to put him to death the day after tomorrow."

"Why?" I asked, surprised. "Has he attacked another keeper?"

"No," said Kamau bitterly. "The experiment was a success. They know they can clone an elephant, so why continue to pay for his upkeep when they can line their pockets with the remaining funds of the grant?"

"Is there no one you can appeal to?" I demanded.

"Look at me," said Kamau. "I am an eighty-six-year-old man who was given his job as an act of charity. Who will listen to me?"

"We must do something," I said.

He shook his head sadly. "They are *kehees*," he said. "Uncircumcised boys. They do not even know what a *mundumugu* is. Do not humiliate yourself by pleading with them."

"If I did not plead with the Kikuyu on Kirinyaga," I replied, "you may be sure I will not plead with the Kenyans in Nairobi." I tried to ignore the ceaseless hummings of the laboratory machines as I considered my options. Finally I looked up at the night sky: The moon glowed a hazy orange through the pollution. "I will need your help," I said at last.

"You can depend on me."

"Good. I shall return tomorrow night."

I turned on my heel and left, without even stopping at Ahmed's enclosure.

All that night I thought and planned. In the morning, I waited until my son and his wife had left the house, then called Kamau on the vidphone to tell him what I intended to do and how he could help. Next, I had the computer contact the bank and withdraw my money, for though I disdained shillings and refused to cash my government checks, my son had found it easier to shower me with money than respect.

I spent the rest of the morning shopping at vehicle-rental agencies until I found exactly what I wanted. I had the saleswoman show me how to manipulate it, practiced until nightfall, hovered opposite the laboratory until I saw Kamau enter the grounds, and then maneuvered up to the side gate.

"*Jambo, mundumugu!*" whispered Kamau as he deactivated enough of the electronic barrier to accommodate the vehicle, which he scrutinized carefully. I backed up to Ahmed's enclosure, then opened the back and ordered the ramp to descend. The elephant watched with an uneasy curiosity as Kamau deactivated a ten-foot section of the force field and allowed the bottom of the ramp through.

"*Njoo, Tembo,*" I said. *Come, elephant.*

He took a tentative step toward me, then another and another. When he reached the edge of his enclosure he stopped, for always he had received an electrical "correction" when he tried to move beyond this point. It took almost twenty minutes of tempting him with peanuts before he finally crossed the barrier and then clambered awkwardly up the ramp, which slid in after him. I sealed him into the hovering vehicle, and he instantly trumpeted in panic.

"Keep him quiet until we get out of here," said a nervous Kamau as I joined him at the controls, "or he'll wake up the whole city."

I opened a panel to the back of the vehicle and spoke soothingly, and strangely enough the trumpeting ceased and the scuffling did stop. As I continued to calm the frightened beast, Kamau piloted the vehicle out of the laboratory complex. We passed through the Ngong Hills twenty minutes later, and circled around Thika in another hour. When we passed Kirinyaga—the true, snow-capped Kirinyaga, from which Ngai once ruled the world—ninety minutes after that, I did not give it so much as a glance.

We must have been quite a sight to anyone we passed: two seemingly crazy old men, racing through the night in an unmarked cargo vehicle carrying a six-ton monster that had been extinct for more than two centuries.

"Have you considered what effect the radiation will have on him?" asked Kamau as we passed through Isiolo and continued north.

"I questioned my son about it," I answered. "He is aware of the incident, and says that the contamination is confined to the lower levels of the mountain." I paused. "He also tells me it will soon be cleaned up, but I do not think I believe him."

"But Ahmed must pass through the radiation zone to ascend the mountain," said Kamau.

I shrugged. "Then he will pass through it. Every day he lives is a day more than he would have lived in Nairobi. For as much time as Ngai sees fit to give him, he will be free to graze on the mountain's greenery and drink deep of its cool waters."

"I hope he lives many years," he said. "If I am to be jailed for breaking the law, I would at least like to know that some lasting good came of it."

"No one is going to jail you," I assured him. "All that will happen is that you will be fired from a job that no longer exists."

"That job supported me," he said unhappily.

The Burning Spear would have no use for you, I decided. *You bring no honor to his name. It is as I have always known: I am the last true Kikuyu.*

I pulled my remaining money out of my pouch and held it out to him. "Here," I said.

"But what about yourself, *mzee?*" he said, forcing himself not to grab for it.

"Take it," I said. "I have no use for it."

"*Asante sana, mzee,*" he said, taking it from my hand and stuffing it into a pocket. *Thank you,* mzee.

We fell silent then, each occupied with his own thoughts. As Nairobi receded farther and farther behind us, I compared my feelings with those I had experienced when I had left Kenya behind for Kirinyaga. I had been filled with optimism then, certain that we would create the Utopia I could envision so clearly in my mind.

The thing I had not realized is that a society can be a Utopia for only an instant—once it reaches a state of perfection it cannot change and still be a Utopia, and it is the nature of societies to grow and evolve. I do not know when Kirinyaga became a Utopia; the instant came and went without my noticing it.

Now I was seeking Utopia again, but this time of a more limited, more realizable nature: A Utopia for one man, a man who knew his own mind and would die before compromising. I had been misled in the past, so I was not as elated as the day we had left for Kirinyaga; being older and wiser, I felt a calm, quiet certitude rather than more vivid emotions.

An hour after sunrise, we came to a huge, green, fog-enshrouded mountain, set in the middle of a bleached desert. A single swirling dust devil was visible against the horizon.

We stopped, then unsealed the elephant's compartment. We stood back as Ahmed stepped cautiously down the ramp, his every movement tense with apprehension. He took a few steps, as if to convince himself that he was truly on solid ground again, then raised his trunk to examine the scents of his new—and ancient—home.

Slowly the great beast turned toward Marsabit, and suddenly his whole demeanor changed. No longer cautious, no longer fearful, he spent almost a full minute eagerly examining the smells that wafted down to him. Then, without a backward glance, he strode confidently to the foothills and vanished into the foliage. A moment later we heard him trumpet, and then he was climbing the mountain to claim his kingdom.

I turned to Kamau. "You had better take the vehicle back before they come looking for it."

"Are you not coming with me?" he asked, surprised.

"No," I replied. "Like Ahmed, I will live out my days on Marsabit."

"But that means you, too, must pass through the radiation."

"What of it?" I said with an unconcerned shrug. "I am an old man. How much time can I have left—weeks? Months? Surely not a year. Probably the burden of my years will kill me long before the radiation does."

"I hope you are right," said Kamau. "I should hate to think of you spending your final days in agony."

"I have seen men who live in agony," I told him. "They are the old *mzees* who gather in the park each morning, leading lives devoid of purpose, waiting only for death to claim another of their number. I will not share their fate."

A frown crossed his face like an early morning shadow, and I could see what he was thinking: He would have to take the vehicle back and face the consequences alone.

"I will remain here with you," he said suddenly. "I cannot turn my back on Eden a second time."

"It is not Eden," I said. "It is only a mountain in the middle of a desert."

"Nonetheless, I am staying. We will start a new Utopia. It will be Kirinyaga again, only done right this time."

I have work to do, I thought. *Important work. And you would desert me in the end, as they have all deserted me. Better that you leave now.*

"You must not worry about the authorities," I said in the same reassuring tones with which I spoke to the elephant. "Return the vehicle to my son and he will take care of everything."

"Why should he?" asked Kamau suspiciously.

"Because I have always been an embarrassment to him, and if it were known that I stole Ahmed from a government laboratory, I would graduate from an embarrassment to a humiliation. Trust me: He will not allow this to happen."

"If your son asks about you, what shall I tell him?"

"The truth," I answered. "He will not come looking for me."

"What will stop him?"

"The fear that he might find me and have to bring me back with him," I said.

Kamau's face reflected the battle that was going on inside him, his terror of returning alone pitted against his fear of the hardships of life on the mountain.

"It is true that my son would worry about me," he said hesitantly, as if expecting me to contradict him, perhaps even hoping that I would. "And I would never see my grandchildren again."

You are the last Kikuyu, indeed the last human being, that I shall ever see, I thought. *I will utter one last lie, disguised as a question, and if you do not see through it, then you will leave with a clear conscience and I will have performed a final act of compassion.*

"Go home, my friend," I said. "For what is more important than a grandchild?"

"Come with me, Koriba," he urged. "They will not punish you if you explain why you kidnapped him."

"I am not going back," I said firmly. "Not now, not ever. Ahmed and I are both anachronisms. It is best that we live out our lives here, away from a world we no longer recognize, a world that has no place for us."

Kamau looked at the mountain. "You and he are joined at the soul," he concluded.

"Perhaps," I agreed. I laid my hand on his shoulder. "*Kwaheri*, Kamau."

"*Kwaheri, mzee*," he replied unhappily. "Please ask Ngai to forgive me for my weakness."

It seemed to take him forever to activate the vehicle and turn it toward Nairobi, but finally he was out of sight, and I turned and began ascending the foothills.

I had wasted many years seeking Ngai on the wrong mountain. Men of lesser faith might believe Him dead or disinterested, but I knew that if Ahmed could be reborn after all others of his kind were long dead, then Ngai must surely be nearby, overseeing the miracle. I would spend the rest of the day regaining my strength, and then, in the morning, I would begin searching for Him again on Marsabit.

And this time, I knew I would find Him.

RED SONJA AND LESSINGHAM IN DREAMLAND

Gwyneth Jones

▼

British writer Gwyneth Jones was a cowinner of the James Tiptree, Jr. Award for work exploring genre issues in science fiction, with her 1991 novel and she's also been nominated for the Arthur C. Clarke Award an unprecedented four times. Her other books include the novels Divine Endurance, Escape Plans, Kairos, North Wind, *and* Flowerdust, *a chapbook of short stories,* Identifying the Object, *and her World Fantasy Award-winning collection of fairy stories,* Seven Tales and a Fable. *She has also written a number of Young Adult novels, mostly under the pen-name of Ann Halam. Her most recent book is a new novel,* Phoenix Café. *Her too-infrequent short fiction has appeared in* Interzone, Asimov's Science Fiction, Off Limits, *and in other magazines and anthologies. She lives in Brighton, England, with her husband, her son, and a Burmese cat.*

Be careful what you wish for, an old saying warns us, because you just might get it. The same applies to what you dream *about, as the wry little chiller that follows demonstrates—not to mention who you dream* with.

The earth walls of the caravanserai rose strangely from the empty plain. She let the black stallion slow his pace. The silence of deep dusk had a taste, like a rich dark fruit; the air was keen. In the distance mountains etched a jagged margin against an indigo sky; snow streaks glinting in the glimmer of the dawning stars. She had never been here before, in life. But as she led her horse through the gap in the high earthen banks she knew what she would see. The camping booths around the walls; the beaten ground stained black by the ashes of countless cooking fires; the wattle-fenced enclosure where travelers' riding beasts mingled indiscriminately with their host's goats and chickens . . . the tumbledown gallery, where sheaves of russet plains-grass sprouted from empty window-spaces. Everything she looked on had the luminous intensity of a place often visited in dreams.

She was a tall woman, dressed for riding in a kilt and harness of supple leather over brief close-fitting linen: a costume that left her sheeny, muscular limbs bare and outlined the taut, proud curves of breast and haunches. Her red hair was bound in a braid as thick as a man's wrist. Her sword was slung on her back, the great brazen hilt standing above her shoulder. Other guests were gathered by an open-air kitchen, in the orange-red of firelight and the smoke of roasting meat. She returned their stares coolly: She was accustomed to attracting attention. But she didn't like what she saw. The host of the caravanserai came scuttling from the group by the fire. His manner was fawning. But his eyes measured, with a thief's sly expertise, the worth of the sword she bore and the quality of Lemiak's harness. Sonja tossed him a few coins and declined to join the company.

She had counted fifteen of them. They were poorly dressed and heavily armed. They were all friends together and their animals—both terror-birds and horses—were too good for any honest travelers' purposes. Sonja had been told that this caravanserai was a safe halt. She judged that this was no longer true. She considered riding out again onto the plain. But wolves and wild terror-birds roamed at night between here and the mountains, at the end of winter. And there were worse dangers; ghosts and demons. Sonja was neither credulous nor superstitious. But in this country no wayfarer willingly spent the black hours alone.

She unharnessed Lemiak and rubbed him down: taking sensual pleasure in the handling of his powerful limbs; in the heat of his glossy hide, and the vigor of his great body. There was firewood ready stacked in the roofless booth. Shouldering a cloth sling for corn and a hank of rope, she went to fetch her own fodder. The corralled beasts shifted in a mass to watch her. The great flightless birds, with their pitiless raptors' eyes, were especially attentive. She felt an equally rapacious attention from the company by the caravanserai kitchen, which amused her. The robbers—as she was sure they were—had all the luck. For her, there wasn't one of the fifteen who rated a second glance.

A man appeared, from the darkness under the ruined gallery. He was tall. The rippled muscle of his chest, left bare by an unlaced leather jerkin, shone red-brown. His black hair fell in glossy curls to his wide shoulders. He met her gaze and smiled, white teeth appearing in the darkness of his beard. "*My name is Ozymandias, king of kings . . . look on my works, ye mighty, and despair. . . .* Do you know those lines?" He pointed to a lump of shapeless stone, one of several that lay about. It bore traces of carving, almost effaced by time. "There was a city here once, with marketplaces, fine buildings, throngs of proud people. Now they are dust, and only the caravanserai remains."

He stood before her, one tanned and sinewy hand resting lightly on the hilt of a dagger in his belt. Like Sonja, he carried his broadsword on his back. Sonja was tall. He topped her by a head: Yet there was nothing brutish in his size. His brow was wide and serene, his eyes were vivid blue: his lips full and imperious; yet delicately modeled, in the rich nest of hair. Somewhere between eyes and lips there lurked a spirit of mockery, as if he found some secret amusement in the perfection of his own beauty and strength.

The man and the woman measured each other.

"You are a scholar," she said.

"Of some sort. And a traveler from an antique land—where the cities are still standing. It seems we are the only strangers here," he added, with a slight nod toward the convivial company. "We might be well advised to become friends for the night."

Sonja never wasted words. She considered his offer and nodded.

They made a fire in the booth Sonja had chosen. Lemiak and the scholar's terror-bird, left loose together in the back of the shelter, did not seem averse to each other's company. The woman and the man ate spiced sausage, skewered and broiled over the red embers, with bread and dried fruit. They drank water, each keeping to their own waterskin. They spoke little, after that first exchange—except to discuss briefly the tactics of their defense, should defense be necessary.

The attack came around midnight. At the first stir of covert movement, Sonja leapt up sword in hand. She grasped a brand from the dying fire. The man who had been crawling on his hands and knees toward her, bent on sly murder of a sleeping victim, scrabbled to his feet. "Defend yourself," yelled Sonja, who despised to strike an unarmed foe. Instantly he was rushing at her with a heavy sword. A great two-handed stroke would have cleft her to the waist. She parried the blow and caught him between neck and shoulder, almost severing the head from his body. The beasts plunged and screamed at the rush of blood scent. The scholar was grappling with another attacker, choking out the man's life with his bare hands . . . and the booth was full of bodies: their enemies rushing in on every side.

Sonja felt no fear. Stroke followed stroke, in a luxury of blood and effort and fire-shot darkness . . . until the attack was over, as suddenly as it had begun.

The brigands had vanished.

"We killed five," breathed the scholar, "by my count. Three to you, two to me."

She kicked together the remains of their fire and crouched to blow the embers to a blaze. By that light they found five corpses, dragged them and flung them into the open square. The scholar had a cut on his upper arm, which was bleeding freely. Sonja was bruised and battered, but otherwise unhurt. The worst loss was their woodstack, which had been trampled and blood-fouled. They would not be able to keep a watch fire burning.

"Perhaps they won't try again," said the warrior woman. "What can we have that's worth more than five lives?"

He laughed shortly. "I hope you're right."

"We'll take turns to watch."

Standing breathless, every sense alert, they smiled at each other in new-forged comradeship. There was no second attack. At dawn Sonja, rousing from a light doze, sat up and pushed back the heavy masses of her red hair.

"You are very beautiful," said the man, gazing at her.

"So are you," she answered.

The caravanserai was deserted, except for the dead. The brigands' riding animals were gone. The innkeeper and his family had vanished into some bolt-hole in the ruins.

"I am heading for the mountains," he said, as they packed up their gear. "For the pass into Zimiamvia."

"I too."

"Then our way lies together."

He was wearing the same leather jerkin, over knee-length loose breeches of heavy violet silk. Sonja looked at the strips of linen that bound the wound on his upper arm. "When did you tie up that cut?"

"You dressed it for me, for which I thank you."

"When did I do that?"

He shrugged. "Oh, sometime."

Sonja mounted Lemiak, a little frown between her brows. They rode together until dusk. She was not talkative and the man soon accepted her silence. But when night fell, and they camped without a fire on the houseless plain: Then, as the demons stalked they were glad of each other's company. Next dawn, the mountains seemed as distant as ever. Again, they met no living creature all day, spoke little to each other, and made the same comfortless camp. There was no moon. The stars were almost bright enough to cast shadow; the cold was intense. Sleep was impossible, but they were not tempted to ride on. Few travelers attempt the passage over the high plains to Zimiamvia. Of those few most turn back, defeated. Some wander among the ruins forever, tearing at their own flesh. Those who survive are the ones who do not defy the terrors of darkness. They crouched shoulder to shoulder, each wrapped in a single blanket, to endure. Evil emanations of the death-steeped plain rose from the soil and bred phantoms. The sweat of fear was cold as ice melt on Sonja's cheeks. Horrors made of nothingness prowled and muttered in her mind.

"How long," she whispered. "How long do we have to bear this?"

The man's shoulder lifted against hers. "Until we get well, I suppose."

The warrior woman turned to face him, green eyes flashing in appalled outrage.

"Sonja" discussed this group member's felony with the therapist. Dr. Hamilton—he wanted them to call him Jim, but "Sonja" found this impossible—monitored everything that went on in the virtual environment. But he never appeared there. They only met him in the one-to-one consultations that virtual-therapy buffs called *the meat sessions*.

"He's not supposed to *do* that," she protested, from the foam couch in the doctor's office. He was sitting beside her, his notebook on his knee. "He damaged my experience."

Dr. Hamilton nodded. "Okay. Let's take a step back. Leave aside the risk of disease or pregnancy: Because we *can* leave those bogeys aside, forever if you like. Would you agree that sex is essentially an innocent and playful social behavior—something you'd offer to or take from a friend, in an ideal world, as easily as food or drink?"

"Sonja" recalled certain dreams—*meat* dreams, not the computer-assisted kind. She blushed. But the man was a doctor after all. "That's what I do feel," she agreed. "That's why I'm here. I want to get back to the pure pleasure, to get rid of the baggage."

"The sexual experience offered in virtuality therapy is readily available on the nets. You know that. And you could find an agency that would vet your partners for you. You chose to join this group because you need to feel that you're taking *medicine*, so you don't have to feel ashamed. And because you need to feel that you're interacting with people who, like yourself, perceive sex as a problem."

"Doesn't everyone?"

"You and another group member went off into your own private world. That's good. That's what's supposed to happen. Let me tell you, it doesn't always. The software gives you access to a vast multisensual library, all the sexual fantasy ever committed to media. But you and your partner, or partners, have to customize the information and use it to create and maintain what we call the *consensual perceptual plenum*. Success in holding a shared dreamland together is a knack. It depends on something in the neural makeup that no one has yet fully analyzed. Some have it, some don't. You two are really in sync.''

''That's exactly what I'm complaining about—''

''You think he's damaging the pocket universe you two built up. But he isn't, not from his character's point of view. It's part Lessingham's thing, to be conscious that he's in a fantasy world.''

She started, accusingly. ''I don't want to know his name.''

''Don't worry, I wouldn't tell you. 'Lessingham' is the name of his virtuality persona. I'm surprised you don't recognize it. He's a character from a series of classic fantasy novels by E. R. Eddison. . . . *In Eddison's glorious cosmos ''Lessingham'' is a splendidly endowed English gentleman who visits fantastic realms of ultramasculine adventure as a lucid dreamer: Though an actor in the drama, he is partly conscious of another existence, while the characters around him are more or less explicitly puppets of the dream. . . .''*

He sounded as if he were quoting from a reference book. He probably was: reading from an autocue that had popped up in lenses of those doctorish horn-rims. She knew that the old-fashioned trappings were there to reassure her. She rather despised them: But it was like the virtuality itself. The buttons were pushed, the mechanism responded. She was reassured.

Of course she knew the Eddison stories. She recalled ''Lessingham'' perfectly: the tall, strong, handsome, cultured millionaire jock who has magic journeys to another world, where he is a tall, strong, handsome, cultured jock in Elizabethan costume, with a big sword. The whole thing was an absolutely typical male power-fantasy, she thought—without rancor. *Fantasy means never having to say you're sorry.* The women in those books, she remembered, were drenched in sex, but they had no part in the action. They stayed at home being princesses, *occasionally* allowing the millionaire jocks to get them into bed. She could understand why ''Lessingham'' would be interested in ''Sonja'' . . . for a change.

''You think he goosed you, psychically. What do you expect? You can't dress the way 'Sonja' dresses, and hope to be treated like the Queen of May.''

Dr. Hamilton was only doing his job. He was supposed to be provocative, so they could react against him. That was his excuse, anyway. . . . On the contrary, she thought. ''Sonja'' dresses the way she does because she can dress any way she likes. ''Sonja'' doesn't have to *hope* for respect, and she doesn't have to demand it. She just gets it. ''It's dominance display,'' she said, enjoying the theft of his jargon. ''Females do that too, you know. The way 'Sonja' dresses is not an invitation. It's a warning. Or a challenge, to anyone who can measure up.''

He laughed, but he sounded irritated. ''Frankly, I'm amazed that you two work together. I'd have expected 'Lessingham' to go for an ultrafeminine—''

''I am . . . 'Sonja' *is* ultrafeminine. Isn't a tigress feminine?''

''Well, okay. But I guess you've found out his little weakness. He likes to be a teeny bit in control, even when he's letting his hair down in dreamland.''

She remembered the secret mockery lurking in those blue eyes.

"That's the problem. That's exactly what I *don't* want. I don't want either of us to be in control."

"I can't interfere with his persona. So, it's up to you. Do you want to carry on?"

"Something works," she muttered. She was unwilling to admit that there'd been no one else, in the text-interface phase of the group, that she found remotely attractive. It was "Lessingham," or drop out and start again. "I just want him to stop *spoiling things*."

"You can't expect your masturbation fantasies to mesh completely. This is about getting *beyond* solitary sex. Go with it: Where's the harm? One day you'll want to face a sexual partner in the real, and then you'll be well. Meanwhile, you could be passing 'Lessingham' in reception—he comes to his meat sessions around your time—and not know it. That's *safety*, and you never have to breach it. You two have proved that you can sustain an imaginary world together: It's almost like being in love. I could argue that lucid dreaming, being *in* the fantasy world but not *of* it, is the next big step. Think about that."

The clinic room had mirrored walls: more deliberate provocation. How much reality can you take? the reflections asked. But she felt only a vague distaste for the woman she saw, at once hollow-cheeked and bloated, lying in the doctor's foam couch. He was glancing over her records on his notebook screen: which meant the session was almost up.

"Still no overt sexual contact?"

"I'm not ready. . . ." She stirred restlessly. "Is it a man or a woman?"

"Ah!" smiled Dr. Hamilton, waving a finger at her. "Naughty, naughty—"

He was the one who'd started taunting her, with his hints that the meat—"Lessingham"—might be near. She hated herself for asking a genuine question. It was her rule to give him no entry to her real thoughts. But Dr. Jim knew everything, without being told: every change in her brain chemistry, every effect on her body: sweaty palms, racing heart, damp underwear. . . . The telltales on his damned autocue left her precious little dignity. *Why do I subject myself to this?* she wondered, disgusted. But in the virtuality she forgot utterly about Dr. Jim. She didn't care who was watching. She had her brazen-hilted sword. She had the piercing intensity of dusk on the high plains, the snowlight on the mountains; the hard, warm silk of her own perfect limbs. She felt a brief complicity with "Lessingham." She had a conviction that Dr. Jim didn't play favorites. He despised all his patients equally. . . . *You get your kicks, doctor. But we have the freedom of dreamland.*

"Sonja" read cards stuck in phone booths and store windows, in the tired little streets outside the building that housed the clinic. *Relaxing massage by clean-shaven young man in Luxurious Surroundings.* . . . You can't expect your fantasies to mesh exactly, the doctor said. But how can it work if two people disagree over something so vital as the difference between control and surrender? Her estranged husband used to say: "Why don't you just do it for me, as a favor. It wouldn't hurt. Like making someone a cup of coffee. . . ." *Offer the steaming cup, turn around and lift my skirts, pull down my underwear. I'm ready. He opens his pants and slides it in, while his thumb is round in front rubbing me. . . . I could* enjoy *that*, thought "Sonja," remembering the blithe abandon of her dreams. *That's the damned shame. If there were no nonsex consequences, I don't know that there's any limit to what I could enjoy. . . . But all her husband had achieved was to make her feel she never wanted to make anyone, man, woman, or child, a cup of coffee ever again. . . .* In luxurious surroundings. *That's what I want. Sex without engagement, pleasure without consequences. It's got to be possible.*

She gazed at the cards, feeling uneasily that she'd have to give up this habit. She used to glance at them sidelong, now she'd pause and linger. She was getting desperate. She was lucky there was medically supervised virtuality sex to be had. She would be helpless prey in the wild world of the nets, and she'd never, ever risk trying one of these meat-numbers. And she had no intention of returning to her husband. Let him make his own coffee. She wouldn't call that getting well. She turned, and caught the eye of a nicely dressed young woman standing next to her. They walked away quickly in opposite directions. *Everybody's having the same dreams. . . .*

In the foothills of the mountains, the world became green and sweet. They followed the course of a little river, that sometimes plunged far below their path, tumbling in white flurries in a narrow gorge; and sometimes ran beside them, racing smooth and clear over colored pebbles. Flowers clustered on the banks, birds darted in the thickets of wild rose and honeysuckle. They led their riding animals and walked at ease: not speaking much. Sometimes the warrior woman's flank would brush the man's side: or he would lean for a moment, as if by chance, his hand on her shoulder. Then they would move deliberately apart, but they would smile at each other. *Soon. Not yet. . . .*

They must be vigilant. The approaches to fortunate Zimiamvia were guarded. They could not expect to reach the pass unopposed. And the nights were haunted still. They made camp at a flat bend of the river, where the crags of the defile drew away, and they could see far up and down their valley. To the north, peaks of diamond and indigo reared above them. Their fire of aromatic wood burned brightly, as the white stars began to blossom.

"No one knows about the long-term effects," she said. "It can't be safe. At the least, we're risking irreversible addiction, they warn you about that. I don't want to spend the rest of my life as a cyberspace couch potato."

"Nobody claims it's safe. If it were safe, it wouldn't be so intense."

Their eyes met. "Sonja" 's barbarian simplicity combined surprisingly well with the man's more elaborate furnishing. The *consensual perceptual plenum* was a flawless reality: the sound of the river, the clear silence of the mountain twilight . . . their two perfect bodies. She turned from him to gaze into the sweet-scented flames. The warrior woman's glorious vitality throbbed in her veins. The fire held worlds of its own, liquid furnaces: the sunward surface of Mercury.

"Have you ever been to a place like this in the real?"

He grimaced. "You're kidding. In the real, I'm *not* a magic-wielding millionaire."

Something howled. The blood-stopping cry was repeated. A taint of sickening foulness swept by them. They both shuddered, and drew closer together. "Sonja" knew the scientific explanation for the legendary virtuality-paranoia, the price you paid for the virtual world's superreal, dreamlike richness. It was all down to heightened neurotransmitter levels, a positive-feedback effect, psychic overheating. But the horrors were still horrors.

"The doctor says if we can talk like this, it means we're getting well."

He shook his head. "I'm not sick. It's like you said. Virtuality's addictive and I'm an addict. I'm getting my drug of choice safely, on prescription. That's how I see it."

All this time "Sonja" was in her apartment, lying in a foam couch with a visor over her head. The visor delivered compressed bursts of stimuli to her visual cortex: the other sense perceptions riding piggyback on the visual, triggering a whole complex of neuronal groups; tricking her mind/brain into believing the world of the dream was *out there*. The brain works like a computer. You cannot "see" a hippopotamus until your system has retrieved the "hippopotamus" template from memory, and checked it against the incoming. Where does the "real" exist? In a sense this world was as real as the other. . . . But the thought of "Lessingham" 's unknown body disturbed her. If he was too poor to lease good equipment, he might be lying in the clinic now in a grungy public cubicle . . . cathetered, and so forth: the sordid details.

She had never tried virtual sex. The solitary version had seemed a depressing idea. People said the partnered kind was the perfect *zipless fuck*. He sounded experienced; she was afraid he would be able to tell she was not. But it didn't matter. The virtual-therapy group wasn't like a dating agency. She would never meet him in the real, that was the whole idea. She didn't have to think about that stranger's body. She didn't have to worry about the real "Lessingham" 's opinion of her. She drew herself up in the firelight. It was right, she decided, that Sonja should be a virgin. When the moment came, her surrender would be the more absolute.

In their daytime he stayed in character. It was a tacit trade-off. She would acknowledge the other world at nightfall by the campfire, as long as he didn't mention it the rest of the time. So they traveled on together, Lessingham and Red Sonja, the courtly scholar-knight and the taciturn warrior-maiden, through an exquisite Maytime: exchanging lingering glances, "accidental" touches . . . And still nothing happened. "Sonja" was aware that "Lessingham," as much as herself, was holding back from the brink. She felt piqued at this. But they were both, she guessed, waiting for the fantasy they had generated to throw up the perfect moment of itself. It ought to. There was no other reason for its existence.

Turning a shoulder of the hillside, they found a sheltered hollow. Two rowan trees in flower grew above the river. In the shadow of their blossom tumbled a little waterfall, so beautiful it was a wonder to behold. The water fell clear from the upper edge of a slab of stone twice a man's height, into a rocky basin. The water in the basin was clear and deep, a-churn with bubbles from the jet plunging from above. The riverbanks were lawns of velvet, over the rocks grew emerald mosses and tiny water flowers.

"I would live here," said Lessingham softly, his hand dropping from his riding bird's bridle. "I would build me a house in this fairy place, and rest my heart here forever."

Sonja loosed the black stallion's rein. The two beasts moved off, feeding each in its own way on the sweet grasses and springtime foliage.

"I would like to bathe in that pool," said the warrior-maiden.

''Why not?'' He smiled. ''I will stand guard.''

She pulled off her leather harness and slowly unbound her hair. It fell in a trembling mass of copper and russet lights, a cloud of glory around the richness of her barely clothed body. Gravely she gazed at her own perfection, mirrored in the homage of his eyes. Lessingham's breath was coming fast. She saw a pulse beat, in the strong beauty of his throat. The pure physical majesty of him caught her breath. . . .

It was their moment. But it still needed something to break this strange spell of reluctance. ''*Lady*—'' he murmured—

Sonja gasped. ''Back-to-back!'' she cried. ''Quickly, or it is too late!''

Six warriors surrounded them, covered from head to foot in red-and-black armor. They were human in the lower body, but the head of each appeared beaked and fanged, with monstrous faceted eyes, and each bore an extra pair of armored limbs between breastbone and belly. They fell on Sonja and Lessingham without pause or a challenge.

Sonja fought fiercely as always, her blade ringing against the monster armor. But something cogged her fabulous skill. Some power had drained the strength from her splendid limbs. She was disarmed. The clawed creatures held her, a monstrous head stooped over her, choking her with its fetid breath. . . .

When she woke again she was bound against a great boulder, by thongs around her wrists and ankles, tied to hoops of iron driven into the rock. She was naked but for her linen shift; it was in tatters. Lessingham was standing, leaning on his sword. ''I drove them off,'' he said. ''At last.'' He dropped the sword, and took his dagger to cut her down.

She lay in his arms. ''You are very beautiful,'' he murmured. She thought he would kiss her. His mouth plunged instead to her breast, biting and sucking at the engorged nipple. She gasped in shock, a fierce pang leapt through her virgin flesh. What did they want with kisses? They were warriors. Sonja could not restrain a moan of pleasure. He had won her. How wonderful to be overwhelmed, to surrender to the raw lust of this godlike animal.

Lessingham set her on her feet.

''Tie me up.''

He was proffering a handful of blood-slicked leather thongs.

''What?''

''Tie me to the rock, mount me. It's what I want.''

''The evil warriors tied you—?''

''And you come and rescue me.'' He made an impatient gesture. ''Whatever. Trust me. It'll be good for you too.'' He tugged at his bloodstained silk breeches, releasing a huge, iron-hard erection. ''See, they tore my clothes. When you see *that*, you go crazy, you can't resist . . . and I'm at your mercy. Tie me up!''

''Sonja'' had heard that 80 percent of the submissive partners in sadomasochist sex are male. But it is still the man who dominates his ''dominatrix'': who says *tie me tighter, beat me harder, you can stop now. . . . Hey*, she thought. *Why all the stage directions, suddenly? What happened to my zipless fuck?* But what the hell. She wasn't going to back out now, having come so far. . . . There was a seamless shift, and Lessingham was bound to the rock. She straddled his cock. He groaned. *"Don't do this to me."* He thrust upward, into her, moaning. *"You savage, you utter savage, uuunnnh . . ."* Sonja grasped the man's wrists and rode him without mercy. He was right, it was as good this way. His eyes were half-closed. In the glimmer of blue under his lashes, a spirit of mockery trembled. . . . She heard a laugh, and found her hands were no longer gripping Lessingham's wrists. He had broken free from her bonds, he was laughing at her in triumph. He was wrestling her to the ground.

"No!" she cried, genuinely outraged. But he was the stronger.

It was night when he was done with her. He rolled away and slept, as far as she could tell, instantly. Her chief thought was that virtual sex didn't entirely *connect*. She remembered now, that was something else people told you, as well as the "zipless fuck." *It's like coming in your sleep*, they said. *It doesn't quite make it*. Maybe there was nothing virtuality could do to orgasm, to match the heightened richness of the rest of the experience. She wondered if he, too, had felt cheated.

She lay beside her hero, wondering, *where did I go wrong? Why did he have to treat me that way*? Beside her, "Lessingham" cuddled a fragment of violet silk, torn from his own breeches. He whimpered in his sleep, nuzzling the soft fabric, *"Mama . . ."*

She told Dr. Hamilton that "Lessingham" had raped her.

"And wasn't that what you wanted?"

She lay on the couch in the mirrored office. The doctor sat beside her with his smart notebook on his knee. The couch collected "Sonja" 's physical responses as if she were an astronaut umbilicaled to ground control; and Dr. Jim read the telltales popping up in his reassuring horn-rims. She remembered the sneaking furtive thing that she had glimpsed in "Lessingham" 's eyes, the moment before he took over their lust scene. How could she explain the difference? "He wasn't playing. In the fantasy, anything's allowed. But *he wasn't playing*. He was outside it, laughing at me."

"I warned you he would want to stay in control."

"But there was no need! I *wanted* him to be in control. Why did he have to steal what I wanted to give him anyway?"

"You have to understand, 'Sonja,' that to many men it's women who seem powerful. You women feel dominated and try to achieve 'equality.' But the men don't perceive the situation like that. They're mortally afraid of you: And anything, just about *anything* they do to keep the upper hand, seems like justified self-defense."

She could have wept with frustration. "I know all that! That's *exactly* what I was trying to get away from. I thought we were supposed to leave the damn baggage behind. I wanted something purely physical. . . . Something innocent."

"Sex is not innocent, 'Sonja.' I know you believe it is, or 'should be.' But it's time you faced the truth. Any interaction with another person involves some kind of jockeying for power, dickering over control. Sex is no exception. Now *that's* basic. You can't escape from it in direct-cortical fantasy. It's in our minds that relationships happen, and the mind, of course, is where virtuality happens too."

He sighed, and made an entry in her notes. "I want you to look on this as another step toward coping with the real. You're not sick, 'Sonja.' You're unhappy. Not even unusually so. Most adults are unhappy, to some degree—"

"Or else they're in denial."

Her sarcasm fell flat. "Right. A good place to be, at least some of the time. What we're trying to achieve here—if we're trying to achieve anything at all—is to raise your pain threshold to somewhere near average. I want you to walk away from therapy with lowered expectations: I guess that would be success."

"Great," she said, desolate. "That's just great."

Suddenly he laughed. "Oh, you guys! You are so weird. It's always the same story. *Can't live with you, can't live without you* . . . . You can't go on this way, you know. Its getting ridiculous. You want some real advice, 'Sonja'? Go home. Change your attitudes, and start some hard peace talks with that husband of yours."

"I don't want to change," she said coldly, staring with open distaste at his smooth profile, his soft effeminate hands. Who was he to call her abnormal? "I like my sexuality just the way it is."

Dr. Hamilton returned her look, a glint of human malice breaking through his doctor act. "Listen. I'll tell you something for free." A weird sensation jumped in her crotch. For a moment she had a prick: A hand lifted and cradled the warm weight of her balls. She stifled a yelp of shock. He grinned. "I've been looking for a long time, and I know. *There is no tall, dark man* . . . ."

He returned to her notes. "You say you were 'raped,' " he continued, as if nothing had happened. "Yet you chose to continue the virtual session. Can you explain that?"

She thought of the haunted darkness, the cold air on her naked body; the soreness of her bruises; a rag of flesh used and tossed away. How it had felt to lie there: intensely alive, tasting the dregs, beaten back at the gates of the fortunate land. In dreamland, even betrayal had such rich depth and fascination. And she was free to enjoy, because *it didn't matter*.

"You wouldn't understand."

Out in the lobby there were people coming and going. It was lunchtime, the lifts were busy. "Sonja" noticed a round-shouldered geek of a little man making for the entrance to the clinic. She wondered idly if that could be "Lessingham."

She would drop out of the group. The adventure with "Lessingham" was over, and there was no one else for her. She needed to start again. The doctor knew he'd lost a customer, that was why he'd been so open with her today. He certainly guessed, too, that she'd lose no time in signing on somewhere else on the semi-medical fringe. What a fraud all that therapy talk was! He'd never have dared to play the sex-change trick on her, except that he knew she was an addict. She wasn't likely to go accusing him of unprofessional conduct. Oh, he knew it all. But his contempt didn't trouble her.

So, she had joined the inner circle. She could trust Dr. Hamilton's judgment. He had the telltales: He would know. She recognized with a feeling of mild surprise that she had become a statistic, an element in a fashionable social concern: *an epidemic flight into fantasy, inadequate personalities; unable to deal with the reality of normal human sexual relations. . . . But that's crazy*, she thought. *I don't hate men, and I don't believe "Lessingham" hates women. There's nothing psychotic about what we're doing. We're making a consumer choice. Virtual sex is* easier, *that's all. Okay, it's convenience food. It has too much sugar, and a certain blandness. But when a product comes along that is cheaper, easier, and more fun than the original version, of course people are going to buy it.*

The lift was full. She stood, drab bodies packed around her, breathing the stale air. Every face was a mask of dull endurance. She closed her eyes. *The caravanserai walls rose strangely from the empty plain* . . . .

(with apologies to E. R. Eddison)

THE LADY VANISHES

Charles Sheffield

▼

One of the best contemporary "hard science" writers, British-born Charles Sheffield is a theoretical physicist who has worked on the American space program, and is currently chief scientist of the Earth Satellite Corporation. Sheffield is also the only person who has ever served as president of both the American Astronautical Society and the Science Fiction Writers of America. He won the Hugo Award in 1994 for his story, "Georgia on My Mind." His books include the bestselling non-fiction title Earthwatch, *the novels* Sight of Proteus, The Web Between the Worlds, Hidden Variables, My Brother's Keeper, Between the Strokes of Night, The Nimrod Hunt, Trader's World, Proteus Unbound, Summertide, Divergence, Transcendence, Cold As Ice, Brother To Dragons, The Mind Pool, Godspeed, *and* The Ganymede Club *and the collections* Erasmus Magister, The McAndrew Chronicles, *and* Dancing With Myself. *His most recent books include a novel written in collaboration with Jerry Pournelle,* Higher Education, *a new collection,* Georgia on My Mind and Other Places, *and another two novels,* Tomorrow and Tomorrow *and* The Billion Dollar Boy. *His stories have appeared in our Seventh, Eighth, and Eleventh Annual Collections. He lives in Silver Spring, Maryland.*

In the gripping scientific thriller that follows, he shows us that there are some women you just can't keep your eyes on—*no matter how hard you try.*

What is wrong with this picture?

Colonel Walker Bryant is standing at the door of the Department of Ultimate Storage. He is smiling; and he is carrying a book under one arm.

Answer: *Everything* is wrong with this picture. Colonel Bryant is the man who assigned (make that *consigned*) me to the Department of Ultimate Storage, for reasons that he found good and sufficient. But he never visited the place. That is not unreasonable, since the department is six stories underground in the Defense Intelligence facility at Bolling Air Force Base, on a walk-down sub-basement level which according to the elevators does not exist. It forms a home for rats, spiders, and me.

Also, Walker Bryant never smiles unless something is wrong; and Walker Bryant never, in my experience, reads anything but security files and the sports pages of the newspaper. Colonel Bryant carrying a book is like Mother Theresa sporting an AK-47.

"Good morning, Jerry," he said. He walked forward, helped himself to an extra-strength peppermint from the jar that I keep on my desk, put the book next to it, and sat down. "I just drove over from the Pentagon. It's a beautiful spring day outside."

"I wouldn't know."

It was supposed to be sarcasm, but he has a hide like a rhino. He just chuckled and said, "Now, Jerry, you know the move to this department was nothing personal. I did it for your own good, down here you can roam as widely as you like. Anyway, they just told me something that I thought might interest you."

When you have worked for someone for long enough, you learn to read the message behind the words. *I thought might interest you* means *I don't have any idea what is going on, but maybe you do.*

I leaned forward and picked up the book. It was *The Invisible Man*, by H. G. Wells. I turned it over and looked at the back.

"Are you reading this?" I wouldn't call Walker Bryant "Sir" to save my life, and oddly enough he doesn't seem to mind.

He nodded. "Sure."

"I mean, actually reading it—yourself."

"Well, I've looked through it. It doesn't seem to be about anything much. But I'm going to read it in detail, as soon as I get the time."

I noted that it was a library book, taken out three days before. If it was relevant to this meeting, Colonel Bryant had heard something that "might interest you" at least that long ago.

"General Attwater mentioned the book to me," he went on. He looked with disapproval at the sign I had placed on my wall. It was a quotation from Swinburne, and it read, "And all dead years draw thither, and all disastrous things." I felt it was rather appropriate for the Department of Ultimate Storage. That, or "Abandon hope, all ye who enter here."

"He's a bit of an egghead, like you," Bryant went on. "I figured you might have read *The Invisible Man*. You read all the time."

The last sentence meant, *You read too much, Jerry Macedo, and that's why your head is full of nonsense, like that stupid sign on your wall.*

"I've read it," I said. But the meeting was taking a very odd turn. General Jonas Attwater was Air Force, and head of three of the biggest "black" programs, secret developments with their own huge budgets that the American public never saw.

"Then you know that the book's about a man who takes a drug to make him invisible," Bryant said. "Three of General Attwater's staff scientists were in the meeting this morning, and they swear that such a thing is scientifically impossible. I wondered what you think."

"I agree with them."

He looked crushed, and I continued, "Think about it for a minute and you'll see why it can't work, even without getting deep into the physics. The drug is supposed to change human tissue so that it has the same refractive index as air. So your body wouldn't absorb light, or scatter it. Light would simply pass through you, without being reflected or refracted or affected in any way. But if your eyes didn't absorb light, you would be blind, because seeing involves the interaction of light with your retinas. And what about the food that you eat, while it's being digested? It would be visible in your alimentary canal, slowly changing as it went from your esophagus to your stomach and into your intestines. I'm sorry, Colonel, but the whole idea is just a piece of fiction.''

"Yeah, I guess so." He didn't seem totally upset by my words. "It's impossible, I hear you.''

He stood up. "Let's go to my office for a while. I want to show you something— unless you're all that busy.''

It depended on the definition of "busy." I had been browsing the on-line physics preprints, as I did every morning of the week. Something very strange was going on with Bose-Einstein Condensates and macroscopic quantum systems, but it was evolving too rapidly for me to follow easily. There were new papers every day. In another week or two there ought to be a survey article that would make the development a lot clearer. Since I had no hope of doing original work in that field, the reading delay would cost me nothing. I followed Bryant in silence, up, up, up, all the way to the top floor. *I want to show you something* sounded to me an awful lot like *Gotcha!*, but I couldn't see how.

His staff assistants didn't react to my arrival. Colonel Bryant never came down to see me, but he summoned me up to see him often enough. It's a terrible thought, but I actually think the colonel likes me. Worse yet, I like him. I think there is a deep core of sadness in the man.

We entered his office, and he closed the door and gestured me to a chair. At that point we could just as well have been in the sub-basement levels. So many highly classified meetings were held in this room that any thought of windows was a complete no-no.

"Lois Doberman," he said. "What can you tell me about her?''

What could I tell, and what I was willing to tell, were two different things. Bryant knew that I had been Dr. Lois Doberman's boss when she first joined the Agency and we were both in the Office of Research and Development. Since then she had gone up through the structure like a rocket, while I had, somewhat more slowly, descended.

"You know what they say about Lois?" I was stalling a little, while I decided what I wanted to say. "If you ever make a crack suggesting that she's a dog, she'll bite your head off.''

Not a trace of a smile from Bryant. Fair enough, because it didn't deserve one.

"Academic record," I went on. "Doctorate from UCLA, then two post-doc years with Berkner at Carnegie-Mellon. She had twenty-eight patents when she joined the Agency. Lord knows how many she has now. Properties of materials and optics are her specialty. I don't know what she's working on at the moment, but she's the smartest woman I ever met.''

I considered the final statement, and amended it. "She's the smartest person I ever met.''

"Some might say you are not an unbiased source. Staff Records show that you dated her for a while.''

"That was nearly a year ago.''

"There's also a strong rumor that you two were sleeping together, though that is not verified.''

I said nothing, and he went on, "It was outside working hours, and you both had the same clearances, so no one's worried about that. The thing is, General

Attwater's staff thought you might know more than anyone else about her personal motives. That could be important."

"I don't see how. Her life and mine don't overlap any more."

"Nor does anyone else's. That's the trouble." And, when I stared at him because this was a message that I definitely could not read, "Lois Doberman has disappeared. One week ago. Sit tight, Jerry."

I had started to stand up.

She didn't just disappear from home, or something like that." He was over at the viewgraph projector and video station used for presentations. "On Tuesday, June 25th, she went to work in the usual way. She was on a project that needed a special environment, and the only suitable place locally is out in Reston. Absolute top security, twenty-four-hour human security staff plus continuous machine surveillance. Only one entrance, except for emergency fire exits that show no sign of being disturbed. Anyone who goes into that building has to sign in and sign out, no matter how they are badged. Arrivals and departures are all recorded on tape.

"Sitting on the table in front of you is a photocopy of the sign in/sign out sheet for June 25th. Don't bother to look at it now"—I was reaching out—"take my word for it. Dr. Doberman signed in at 8:22 am, and she never signed out. Not only that, I have here the full set of tapes for arrivals and departures. The video-recorder is motion-activated. If you want to study the record, you can do it later. Here's the bottom line: there's a fine, clear sequence showing her arrival. There's nothing of her leaving."

"Then she must be still inside the building." That thought was terribly disturbing. If Lois had been inside for a full week, she must be dead.

"She's not inside, either dead or alive," he said, as though he had been reading my mind. "This is a fairly new building, and Attwater's office has exact detailed plans. There are no secret cubby-holes or places where someone could hide away. The whole complex has been searched four or five times. She's not in there. She's outside. We don't know how she got out."

"Nor do I."

Which actually meant, *All right, but why are you talking to me?* I guess that message-reading goes both ways, because Bryant said, "So far as we can tell, you are the last person with whom Dr. Doberman enjoyed a close personal relationship. I don't know if you can help, but I feel that you must try. As often this morning, sponsored by General Attwater's office, you and I have access to three additional SCI clearances."

I shifted in my chair. SCI. Special Compartmented Information. I had too many of those clearances already.

Walker Bryant turned on the viewgraph projector and put a transparency in place. "These briefing documents show what Dr. Lois Doberman had been working on at Reston. In a word, it's stealth technology in the area of imaging detection."

He glared at me, and on cue, I laughed. After *The Invisible Man*, his final comment had all the elements of farce. The whole idea of stealth technology is to make the object difficult to see. But it's usually either primitive visible-wavelength stuff, like special paints that match simple backgrounds, or else it's the use of materials with very low radar back-scatter. Most systems use active microwave—radar—for detection, so that's where most of the effort tends to go. The B-2 bomber is a wonderful example of failed stealth technology, since at most wavelengths it's as visible as Rush Limbaugh. But that didn't stop it being built, any more than the fact that stealth technology doesn't work well in visible wavelengths would stop a barrel of money being spent on it.

This sort of thing was one big reason why Lois and I had parted company. Once you are really inside the intelligence business, you know too much ever to be allowed to leave. You are there as firmly and finally as a fly in amber, and like the insect, not even death will free you. You are not allowed to say that some classified projects are absolute turkeys and a total waste of taxpayer money, because the party line is that they have value. Opinions to the contrary, expressed to Lois in long middle-of-the-night conversations, had convinced me that I would certainly fail my next polygraph (I didn't).

She disagreed with me. Not about the waste of money, which was undeniable, but about the possibility of escape. She said there must be a way out, if only you could find it. After dozens of arguments, in which she accused me of giving up and I accused her of useless dreaming, we had gone our separate ways; she ascending the management structure as though hoping to emerge from the top and fly free like a bird, me tunneling down deeper into the sub-basement levels like a blind and hopeless mole.

Had she found it, then, the Invisible Woman, the magic way out that would break all intelligence ties forever?

I couldn't see how, and the presentation was not helping. "What does fiber optics have to do with this?" I asked. That's what Walker Bryant had been putting on the screen for the past few minutes, while I was lost in memories. The latest viewgraph was a series of hand-drawn curves showing how the light loss over thin optic cables could, thanks to new technology, approach zero. That would be useful in communications and computers; but Lois hadn't been working in either area.

He shrugged at my question. "Damned if I know what any of these viewgraphs have to do with anything. I was hoping you might be able to tell me. These are taken straight from Lois Doberman's work books."

"They don't tell me anything so far," I said. "But keep going."

Unnecessary advice. Walker Bryant had risen in the military partly because he had lots of *sitzfleisch*, the patience and kidneys and mental strength to sit in a meeting for as long as it took to wear down the opposition. He had no intention of stopping. I, on the other hand, think I suffer from an undiagnosed hyperactivity. I work a lot better when I am free to wander around.

I did that now, pacing back and forward in front of his desk. He gave me another glare, but he went right on with the viewgraphs. Now they showed notes in Lois's familiar handwriting about new imaging sensors, pointing out that they could be built smaller than the head of a pin. I noticed that the page numbers were not sequential.

"Who decided what to pull out and show as viewgraphs?" I asked.

"Rich Williamson. Why? Do you think he might have missed something?"

"Rich is good—in his field. But he's a SWIR specialist."

"Mm?"

"Short-wave infra-red. From about one to five micrometers. Visible light wave-lengths are shorter, around half a micrometer. But if Lois made a tarnhelm—"

"A what?"

"Don't worry about it. If Lois is invisible, then the visible wavelength region is where we ought to be looking. Anyway, I'd much rather see her original note-books than someone else's ideas as to what's important in them."

"It would have to be done out in Reston. The notebooks can't be removed." He sounded and was disgusted. To Walker Bryant, everything important took place either on a battlefield, or inside the Beltway. Reston, twenty-five miles away from us, was a point at infinity.

"Fine. We'll go to Reston."

"You can go there this afternoon, Jerry. You won't need me. But there are things outside the notebooks."

He turned off the projector and went to the VCR next to it, while I kept pacing.

"I said we don't know how she got out," he said. "It's more than that. We have proof positive that she is outside. We learned today that she's still in the Washington area, and we even have some idea of her movements."

Which must have been a huge relief to the Security people. They always have one big fear when someone vanishes. It's not that the person is dead, which is unfortunate but ends security risk. It's that the person is alive and well and headed out of the country, either voluntarily or packed away unconscious in a crate, to serve some other nation.

I shared their feeling of relief. From Bryant's tone, Lois wasn't a corpse being trundled from place to place. She was moving under her own volition.

"Stand still for a minute," he went on, "and take a look at this. We've patched together six different recordings from ATM devices at local banks, withdrawals made over the past four days. As you know, every time someone makes a deposit or a withdrawal at an ATM it's captured on videotape. Standard crime-fighting technique. Withdrawals from Lois Doberman's account were made at six different machines. Watch closely."

A man I had never seen before was standing in front of the bank's camera. He worked the ATM, stood counting notes for a moment, and left. Soon afterwards a woman—certainly not Lois—stood in his place. She made a deposit, adjusted her hat in the reflection provided by the ATM polished front, and vanished from the camera's field of view.

I watched as the same scene was repeated five more times, with variations in customers as to age, height, weight, color, and clothing. Each sequence showed two different people making successive ATM transactions. One man was immor-talized in intelligence security files in the act of picking his nose, another hit the machine when something, apparently his account balance, was not to his liking. Of Lois Doberman there was not a sign.

"Normal operations at an ATM facility," Bryant said when the tape ended in a flicker of black and white video noise. "Except for one thing. In each case, Lois Doberman made a withdrawal from one of her bank accounts—she maintains sev-eral—*between* the people that you saw. We have the print-outs of activity, which you can examine if you want to, and they are all the same: a normal transaction, with a picture of the person; then a Lois Doberman cash withdrawal, with no one at all showing on the video-camera; and then another normal transaction, including a person's picture.''

"The Invisible Woman," I said.

Bryant nodded. "And the big question: How is she doing it?"

It was the wrong question, at least for me. I already had vague ideas as to a possible how. As I drove out of the District on my way to Reston, I pondered the deeper mystery: *Why* was Lois doing this?

I did not believe for a moment that she was any kind of security risk. We had long agreed that our own intelligence service was the worst one possible—except for all others. She would never work for anyone else. But if she stayed around the local area, she was bound to be caught. Fooling around with the ATM's, for half a dozen withdrawals of less than a hundred dollars each, was like putting out a notice: Catch me if you can!

Twenty-four hour surveillance of the relevant ATM's was next on the list. Her apartment was already under constant surveillance, so clearly Lois was living somewhere else. But I knew the lure of her own books and tapes, and how much she hated living out of a suitcase.

I took my foot off the accelerator—I was doing nearly seventy-five—and forced my thoughts back a step. *Was* Lois living somewhere else? If she wanted to show off her new idea, what better way than living in her own place, coming and going under the very nose of Security and flaunting their inability to catch her?

And my inability, too. Lois surely knew that if she disappeared, I would be called in. We had been too close for me to be ignored. I could imagine her face, and her expression as she threw me the challenge: *Let's see you catch me, Jerry— before the rest catch on.*

If I was right, others *would* catch on within the next few days. There were some very bright people in R&D, smarter than me and shackled by only one factor: compartmenting. The idea behind it sounds perfectly logical, and derives directly from the espionage and revolution business. *Keep the cells small. A person should not be told more than he or she needs to know.*

The trouble is, if science is to be any good it has to operate with exactly the opposite philosophy. Advances come from cross-fertilization, from recognizing relationships between fields that at first sight have little to do with each other.

I had broken my pick on that particular issue, after fights with my bosses so prolonged and bitter that I had been removed completely from research programs. My job with Walker Bryant now allowed me to cross all fields of science, but at a price: I myself worked in none. However, I had not changed my mind.

The afternoon at Reston gave me enough time for a first look-through of Lois's notebooks. She used them as a combined diary and work file, with a running log of anything that caught her interest. To someone who did not know her well they would seem a random hodge-podge of entries. Rich Williamson had done his best, but he had not pulled out anything that seemed to him totally irrelevant.

I knew how tightly the inside of Lois's head was inter-connected. An entry about the skin of reptiles followed one about fiber optics. Human eye sensitivity and its performance at different ambient light levels shared space with radar cross-section data. A note on sensor quantum efficiency sat on the same page as an apparently unrelated diagram that showed the layout of a room's light sources and shadows, while specifications for a new gigacircuit processing chip lay next to a note on temperature-dependent optical properties of organic compounds. Chances were, they all represented part of some continuous thought pattern.

I also knew that Lois was conscientious. Asked to look into stealth techniques, her days and much of her nights would have been devoted to the present—and future—limits of that technology.

At five o'clock I drove back as far as Rosslyn and signed out a small piece of unclassified equipment from one of the labs. I ate dinner at a fast food place close to the Metro, browsing through Bryant's library copy of *The Invisible Man.* When I left I bought a chicken salad sandwich and a coke to take away with me. It might be a long night.

By six o'clock I was sitting in my car on Cathedral Avenue, engine off and driver's window open. It was a "No Parking" spot right in front of Lois's apartment building. If any policeman came by I would pretend that I had just dropped someone off, and drive around the block.

I wasn't the only one interested in the entrance. A man sat on a bench across the street and showed no signs of moving, while a blue car with a Virginia license plate drove by every few minutes. Dusk was steadily creeping closer. Half an hour more, and the street lights would go on. Before that happened, the air temperature would drop and the open doors of the apartment building would close.

The urge to look out of the car window was strong. I resisted, and kept my eye fixed on the little oblong screen at the rear end of the instrument I was holding. It was no bigger than a camera's viewfinder, but the tiny screen was split in two. On the left was a standard video camera image of the building entrance. On the right was another version of the same scene, this one rendered in ghostly black and white. Everyone walking by, or entering the building, appeared in both pictures.

Or almost everyone. At 6:45 precisely, a human form showed on the right hand screen only. I looked up to the building entrance, and saw no one. But I called out, softly enough to be inaudible to the man across the street, "Lois! Over here. Get in the car. Wait until I open the door for you."

I saw and heard nothing. But I got out, went around the car, and opened the passenger door. Then I stood waiting and feeling like a fool, while nothing at all seemed to be happening. Finally I smelled perfume. The car settled a little lower on its springs.

"I'm in," whispered Lois's voice. I closed the door, went back to my side, and started the engine. The man across the street had watched everything, but he had seen nothing. He did not move as I pulled away.

I glanced to my right. No one seemed to be there, because through the right-side car window I could see the buildings as we passed them. The only oddity was the passenger seat of the car. Instead of the usual blue fabric, I saw a round grey-black patch about a foot and a half across.

"I'm alone and we're not being followed," I said. "Take it off if you want to. Unless of course you're naked underneath it."

"I'm not." There was a soft ripping noise. "You already knew that if you think about it."

I had to stop the car. It was that or cause a pile-up, because the urge to turn and watch was irresistible.

"I guessed it," I said. "No clothes were found in the building in Reston, so you had to be able to put whatever it is over them."

It was close to dusk, and I had pulled the car into a parking lot underneath a spreading oak tree. As I stared at the passenger seat, a patch of fair hair suddenly appeared from nowhere against the upper part of the passenger window. The whole background rippled and deformed as the patch grew to reveal Lois's forehead, face, and chin. As her neck came into view there was a final wave of distortion, and suddenly I was looking at Lois, dressed in a rather bulky body suit.

"Too much work for the microprocessors," she said, and pushed her hair off her forehead with her hands. "When you put too great a load on them, they quit trying."

She peeled off the suit, first down to her waist, then off her arms and hands, and finally from her legs and feet. She was wearing an outfit of thin silk and flexible flat-heeled loafers. In her hands the suit had become an unimpressive bundle of mottled gray and white. She stared down at it. "Still needs work. For one thing, it's too hot inside."

"That's how I knew you were there." I picked up the instrument I had been using. "I didn't know how you were doing it—I really still don't—but I knew a living human has to be at 98.6. This instrument senses in thermal infra-red wavelengths, so it picked up your body heat image. But it didn't show a thing at visible wavelengths."

"Anyone in the suit is invisible out to wavelengths of about one micron— enough so they don't show in visible light or near infrared." She hefted the suit. "On the other hand, this is a first-generation effort using silicon sensors. I could probably do a lot better with something like gallium arsenide, but I'll still have a thermal signature. And if I move too fast or make unusual movements, the processors can't keep up and the whole system fails."

"And it's not a great idea to wear perfume. That's when I was absolutely sure it was you. Want to tell me how it works? I have an idea what's going on, but it's pretty rough."

"How much time did you spend with my notebooks?"

"Half a day."

"Take two more days, and you'd work it all out for yourself. But I'll save you the effort." She tapped the copy of *The Invisible Man,* sitting where I had left it on top of my dashboard. "Wells could have done better, even in 1900. He knew that animals in nature do their best to be invisible to their prey or their predators. But they don't do it by fiddling around with their own optical properties, which just won't work. They know that they are invisible if they look exactly like their background. The chameleon has the right idea, but it's hardware-limited. It can only make modest color and pattern adjustments. It occurred to me that humans ought to be able to do a whole lot better. You'd got this far?"

"Pretty much." I saw a patrol car slow down as it passed us, and I started the engine and pulled out into the street. "The suit takes images of the scene behind you, and assigns the colors and intensities to liquid crystal displays on the front of the suit. Somebody fifteen to twenty feet away will see the background scene. The suit also has to do the same thing to the back, so someone behind you will see an exact match to the scene in front of you. The problem I have is that the trick has to work from any angle. I couldn't see any way that fiber optic bundles could handle that.''

"They can't. I tried that road for quite a while, but as you say, optical fibers don't have the flexibility to look different from every angle. I only use them to allow me to see when I'm inside. An array of pinhole sized openings scattered over the front of the suit feeds light through optical fibers to form images on a pair of gogglers. Straightforward. The invisibility trick is more difficult. You have to use holographic methods to handle multi-angle reflectances, and you need large amounts of computing power to keep track of changing geometry—otherwise a person would be invisible only when standing perfectly still.'' Lois touched the bundled suit. "There are scores of microprocessors on every square centimeter, all networked to each other. I figure there's more computing power in this thing than there was in the whole world in 1970. And it still crashes if I move faster than a walk, or get into a situation with complex lighting and shadows. Uniform, low-level illumination and relatively uniform backgrounds are best—like tonight.'' She cocked her head at me, with a very odd expression in her eyes. "So. What do you think, Jerry?''

I looked at her with total admiration and five sorts of misgiving. "I think what you have done is wonderful. I think you are wonderful. But there's no way you can hide this. If I'm here a day or two ahead of everyone else, it's only because I know you better than they do.''

"No. It's because you're smart, and compartmenting of ideas drives you crazy, and you refuse to do it. It would take the others weeks, Jerry. But I had no intention of hiding this—otherwise I would never have stayed in the Washington area. To-morrow I'll go in to work as usual, and I can't wait to see their faces.''

"But after what you've done—'' I paused. What *had* she done? Failed to sign out of a building when she left. Disappeared for a week without notifying her superiors. Removed government property from secure premises without approval. But she could say, what better practical test could there be for her invention, than to become invisible to her own organization?

Her bosses might make Lois endure a formal hearing on her actions, and they would certainly put a nasty note in her file. That would be it. She was far too valuable for them to do much more. Lois would be all right.

"What now?'' I said. "You can't go back to your own apartment without being seen, even if you put the suit back on. It's dark, and the doors will be closed.''

"So?''

"Come home with me, Lois. You'll be safe there.''

That produced the longest pause since she had stepped invisible into my car. Finally she shook her head.

"I'd really like to, but not tonight. I'll take a rain check. I promise.''

"So where do we go?''

"You go home. Me, you drop off at the next corner.''

I was tempted to say that I couldn't do it, that she didn't have her suit on. But living in a city with over half a million people confers its own form of invisibility. Provided that Lois stayed away from her apartment, the chance that she would be seen tonight by anyone who knew her was close to zero. And she still had the suit if she felt like using it.

I halted the car at the next corner and she stepped out, still holding the drab bundle. She gave me a little smile and a wave, and gestured at me to drive on.

Next morning I was in my sub-basement department exactly on time. I called Lois's office. She was not there. I kept calling every few minutes.

She was still not there at midday, or later in the afternoon, or ever again.

This time there were no telltale ATM withdrawals, no hints that she might still be in the local area. Some time during the night she had been back to Reston, entered the building with its round-the-clock surveillance, and removed her notebooks. In their place sat a single sheet of white cardboard. It bore the words, in Lois's handwriting, "*I know why the caged bird sings.*"

That sheet was discussed in a hundred meetings over the next few weeks. It was subjected to all kinds of chemical and physical analysis, which proved conclusively that it was simple cardboard. No one seemed to know what it meant.

I know, of course. It is a message from Lois to me, and the words mean, *It can be done. There is a way out, even from the deepest dungeon or highest tower.*

I told everything I knew about the invisibility suit. Other staff scientists rushed off excitedly to try to duplicate it. I came back to the Department of Ultimate Storage, to the old routine.

But there is a difference—two differences. First, I am working harder than ever in my life, and now it is toward a definite goal. Not only is there a way out, but Lois assures me that I can find it; otherwise, she would never have promised a rain check.

The second difference is in Walker Bryant. He leaves me almost totally free of duties, but he comes frequently down from his office to mine. He says little, but he sits and stares at me as I work. In his eyes I sometimes detect a strange, wistful gleam that I never noticed before. I think he knows that there was more to my meeting with Lois than I have admitted, and I think he even suspects what it may have been.

I will leave him a message when I go. I don't know what it will say yet, but it must be something that he can understand and eventually act upon. Even Air Force colonels deserve hope.

CHRYSALIS

Robert Reed

▼

Pleasingly prolific, Robert Reed produced at least four or five stories this year that were strong enough to have been shoo-ins for inclusion in a best-of-the-year anthology any other year, something that was true of 1995 as well—a remarkable accomplishment for any author. Reed is a frequent contributor to The Magazine of Fantasy & Science Fiction *and* Asimov's Science Fiction, *and has also sold stories to* Universe, New Destinies, Tomorrow, Synergy, Starlight, *and elsewhere. His books include the novels* The Leeshore, The Hormone Jungle, Black Milk, The Remarkables, Down the Bright Way, *and* Beyond the Veil of Stars. *His most recent book is the novel* An Exaltation of Larks. *Upcoming is* Beneath the Gated Sky, *a sequel to* Beyond the Veil of Stars. *His stories have appeared in our Ninth, Tenth, Eleventh, Twelfth, and Thirteenth Annual Collections. He lives in Lincoln, Nebraska.*

In the complex and powerful novella that follows, he takes us deep into the starless void between galaxies to voyage along with an immense generation-ship that has been in flight from implacable enemies for hundreds of years . . . and then takes us along on an exciting, dangerous, and mysterious mission with a crew of young cadets in training, a mission that leads to a crisis that will force them to question everything they know, and to make a choice that could destroy them all. . . .

ONE

The starship embraced many names.

To the Artisans, it was 2018CC—a bloodless designation for a simple world of ice and cold tars that was long ago gutted, then given engines and a glorious purpose, carrying off the grateful survivors of an utterly inglorious war.

To its organic passengers, human and otherwise, it wore more evocative names: Squeals and squawks and deep-bass drummings, plus names drawn in light, and sweet pheromonal concoctions with no easy translation.

The *fouchians*, a species incapable of exaggeration, knew the ship as The-Great-Nest-Within-Another's-Black-Soil—an honored name implying wealth, security, and a contented slavery.

The whalelike *moojin* sang about the Grand Baleen.

Home was the literal meaning of many, many names.

As were Womb and Egg and Salvation.

Two dissimilar lactators, in utterly different languages, called it Mother's Nipple, while a certain birdlike creature, in a related vein, screeched lovingly, "Our Mother's Green Vomit."

Humans were comfortable with many names, which was only reasonable. They had built the ship and its Artisans, and no other species was half as abundant. In casual conversation they called the starship the Web, or the Net, or Hope, or the Ark, or Skyborn, or Wanderer. In the ancient ceremonies, when reverence was especially in demand, it was Paradise or Eden, or most often, with enduring emotion: Heaven.

A name of chilling dimensions.

If you are admitted to Heaven, then it stands to reason that every other place in Creation is somehow flawed. Tainted. Impure.

And if you deserve perfection, shouldn't you be perfect yourself? Not just occasionally, not just where it matters most, but always, in every ordinary day, from your first sip of milk or green vomit to your very last happy perfect breath?

By any measure, the Web was a vast ship. Even small habitats were huge, particularly when you are a young girl, wonderstruck at every turn.

Sarrie was born in one of the oldest human habitats, in a village of farmers, hunters, and shop clerks. From her playroom she could see the length of the habitat—a diamond-hulled cylinder spinning for mock-gravity, not especially large but substantial enough to hold a few rugged mountains and a stormy little sea. It was a perfect home for a fledgling genius. Sarrie's foster parents were gently brilliant and happily joined—shopkeepers who weren't too smart or happy to ignore their carefully tailored daughter. From the instant of conception, the girl's development was monitored and adjusted, reappraised and readjusted, her proven genetics enriched by the peaceful village, an alignment of gloved forces steadily nudging her toward the ultimate goal: Voice.

Sarrie spoke long before she could walk. Before her second birthday, she could hold her own in idle adult conversation. Barely four years old, she wrote an awful little novel, but sprinkled through its pages were complex and lovely sentences that lingered in the reader's astonished mind. Later, she invented her own language to write a second novel, then taught the language to her best friend—an older and taller and effortlessly beautiful girl named Lilké. To her credit, Lilké read every make-believe word. "It's wonderful," she claimed. But a Voice knows when someone is lying, and why, and Sarrie forgave her best friend, the lie meant to spare her pain.

The Artisans ruled the Web with the lightest of touches. They normally didn't visit the habitats, seeing no need to intrude on the organics. But one particular Artisan made a habit of coming to see Sarrie. His name was Ejy, and he would wear a human-style body out of politeness, resembling any wise old man but smelling like new rubber, his hairless brown face wearing a perpetual smile, oversized black eyes bright in any light and blinking now and again to serve the illusion of humanness.

It was obvious that he had a special interest in the child, and Sarrie's parents were proud in appropriate ways, encouraging her to behave when he was there— as if she ever misbehaved—and to be a good audience, asking smart questions and giving prompt, perfect answers when she knew them. But only if she knew them, of course.

When Sarrie was eight years old, Ejy brought her a thick volume filled with butterflies.

"Select one," he instructed, his voice smooth and dry, and timeless. "Any species you wish, child. Go on now."

"But why?" she had to ask.

"I will build it for you," he replied. "Are you intrigued?"

Sarrie couldn't count the butterflies or find any end to the book. Reaching its final page, she flipped to the front again and discovered still more butterflies, every stage of their lives shown in three dimensions, usually in their natural size. Captions were available in every shipboard language; the young Voice understood most of the audio captions. Some of the butterflies had lived on the lost earth, but most were alien, possessing the wrong number of legs or odd eyes, giant differences undoubtedly buried in their genetics. Lilké was going to become a geneticist; Sarrie tried to think of questions worth asking her friend. That's why she paused for a moment, and Ejy interrupted, asking, "Which one will it be?"

She blinked, a little startled, then turned the soft plastic page and pointed to the first place where her eyes found purchase.

The butterfly wasn't large, and while lovely, she didn't find it exceptional. And the Artisan seemed equally surprised by her choice. Crystal eyes grew larger and more round, thin lips diminishing the smile. Yet he declared, "It's a fine selection." With warm, rubber-scented hands, he retrieved the book, then turned and prepared to leave.

Sarrie waited as long as possible, which was maybe five seconds. Then she blurted out, "When do I get to see the butterfly?"

Ejy was a tease. Glancing over a shoulder, he smiled and made laughing sounds, the dry voice warning her, "To be done well, even butterflies need a little time. Haven't you learned that yet, child?"

"A little time" to the Artisans can mean days, or it can mean eons. But a young girl training as a Voice is too busy and happy to dwell on promised gifts.

Three weeks passed in a pleasant blur. Language lessons were peppered with general studies in science and the Web's glorious history. A Voice was a specialist in twenty areas, at least. That was why they were rare and why their training was so rigorous. Someday, in thirty or forty years, Sarrie would accompany a team of explorers to one of the nearby suns. If the team found sentient life, it would be her duty and honor to make contact with it, deciphering the alien minds. And if they were worthy, she would try to lure them into joining her, giving their devotion to the Web.

Sarrie loved her studies, and after three weeks, when her tutor quit lecturing in midsentence, she was disappointed. Perhaps even angry. The tutor told her to go to an isolated valley, and go alone. "No," it warned her, "Lilké is not invited." Of course the girl obeyed, running herself breathless and still gasping when she found Ejy waiting for her. He was in an open glade, wearing green-and-black robes over his human body, and wearing the enduring smile. The trees surrounding them were covered with gemstones, bright and sparkling in the mock-sunshine. The stones were cocoons almost ready to hatch. Ejy never mentioned them. He filled the next hour with questions, testing the Voice. Meanwhile, the day warmed and the cocoons grew dull, then split open within moments of each other. The butterflies were identical, each one a little bigger than Sarrie's hand, emerald wings decorated with white eye patches and margins black as comet tar. A colored, hallucinogenic snow seemed to fill the woods, wingbeats making a thin dry sound, thunderous in the gentlest fashion.

The tailored creatures lived vigorously and fully until their fat stocks were spent. The busiest few were first to drop, but all fell within the next few minutes; and Sarrie watched the spectacle, composing poems in her head but saying nothing until it was done.

Ejy seemed as happy as any Artisan could be.

Afterward, he told her that her chosen species came from a world of insects, and that this particular species had not flown in half a million years.

Sarrie was impressed, and she said so.

"Why am I fond of you, child?"

Startled, she remained sensibly mute. "Voice" was an inadequate name. The best Voices were exceptional listeners, and even when they guessed an answer, some questions were left untouched.

"Tell me, child. If you meet strangers, what will you do?"

" 'Embrace their souls,' " she quoted. " 'Show them the Web's caring face.' "

"How many Voices are being trained today?"

Several hundred, she had heard. At least one Voice would represent each of the ship's organic species—

"Yet you are possibly our finest Voice."

It was an incredible thing to hear. Sarrie was eight years old, her talents barely half-formed, and how could anyone, even an Artisan, know who was best?

"I love humans," Ejy confessed. "More than any other organic, I do."

In a whisper, she asked, "Why?"

He touched the thin false hair on his head. "Human genius designed me. It built me. It gave me a noble mission. And when I wear this body, I do it to honor you and your species."

Sarrie nodded, absorbing every sound, every tiny cue.

"I have lived on 2018CC since its inception. Which makes me how old?"

Several million years, she knew.

"If I could become organic, I should like to be human." It was another astonishing statement, yet he didn't linger on it. "Suppose you could become a different species, child. Not in the abstract, as Voices try to do. But in reality, as flesh and fluid . . . which species would you become . . . ?"

She reached down, gently grasping one of the dying butterflies. It was dusty and strangely warm, weighing almost nothing, its mouthparts adapted to suck nectar from a very specific, very extinct flower. There was a soft chirp, then it sprayed her with a mist of fragrant oils; and for lack of better, she told Ejy, "This."

Doubt shone on the Artisan's face. "And why, child?"

"It's very beautiful—"

"You are lying. To me, you are lying." His voice didn't sound angry, but a fire shone behind his eyes. ''I know you, Sarrie. You don't know yourself half as well as I do, and you just lied.''

Sarrie shook her head, claiming, ''I did not—''

''First of all, these aren't your favorite colors.'' He pulled the carcass from her hand. ''And more important, where's the value in becoming something that's lovely? This species has slept in our library for five hundred millennia, dead and forgotten, and if you hadn't chosen it, it would have remained dead until the end of time.''

He dropped the butterfly, both of them watching it flip and spin downward like a paper glider.

''You are exactly who you should be, Sarrie.'' Wise, ageless eyes smiled, and the pink tongue peeked out from between thin lips. ''The universe is full of beautiful, perishable things. Butterflies, for instance. They can take infinite forms, and they are cheap. But a rare skill—the genius of a Voice, for example—is something that will be born and born again, without end.''

''I didn't mean to lie,'' she whispered, in self-defense.

''Oh, yes, you did.'' Ejy laughed, then assured her, ''And I know what you were thinking. I know what you would ask to become.''

She said nothing.

''To be an Artisan, of course.''

''No!'' she roared.

''Oh, yes,'' he replied. ''You envy our immortality. You lie awake at night, wishing you could know everything.'' A pause. ''Given your chance, child, you would happily rule this noble ship of ours. Any human would. It is your simple nature.''

He was correct, in a fashion. Deep inside Sarrie were black desires that she'd kept secret from everyone, including herself . . . and she collapsed suddenly out of shame and fear, the dead butterflies pressed against her face, threatening to choke her . . . and warm unliving hands pulled her up again, warm immortal words assuring Sarrie that she was fine, all was well, and regardless of childish thoughts, she was loved and always would be. . . .

TWO

Sarrie's final novel was a tribute to life on the starship.

An enormous, plotless epic, it was consumed, and loved, by every sentient organic. Sarrie was barely sixteen and found herself suddenly famous. Every translation was her responsibility, regardless whether the species read with its eyes or touch or its sensitive nose. Her most avid fans would travel to the village just to give her thanks: A peculiar, but sincere parade of well-wishers. Even the fouchians paid their respects, their massive bodies dressed in woven soil, dim little eyes squinting despite black eyeshades. A social species with strict castes and an evolutionary history of slavery, they had thrived under the Artisans' care. Except for humans, no organic was as abundant, and perhaps none was as trusted. There was no greater honor than a fouchian's squeak of applause, telling you that your work had captured the special joy in being another's treasured property. And with their nose tendrils quivering, holding tight to the precious novel, the molelike fouchians would bless Sarrie; and she in turn would squeak the proper thanks, and when they turned to leave she would carefully sniff each of their rectums with all the formality that she could manage.

Ejy, as always, seemed pleased with her success, if never surprised. His visits remained irregular but memorable, and always intense. They would discuss her studies, her rapid progress, and the approaching future. Then as he prepared to leave, Ejy would give the young Voice an elaborate simulation, its aliens bizarre, their souls almost impossible to decipher. But Sarrie was required not just to decipher them, but to win their trust too. That was why Voices existed. They brought new blood into the Web—new souls into Heaven—and if Sarrie were ever going to be a true Voice, she certainly needed to outwit Ejy's damned puzzles.

Successes dwarfed failures, but failures lingered in the mind. High-technology aliens were the real nightmares. One of Ejy's scenarios didn't even involve another world. Instead there was a starship as large as the Web, and a xenophobic crew, and Sarrie tried to solve the puzzle at least twenty times, each attempt more disastrous than the last. She wept when the Web was obliterated by nuclear fire and laser light. The situation was absurd—the Artisans had never met their equals—but she was left unnerved and disheartened.

If Sarrie couldn't charm these fictional entities, how could she be trusted out in the universe, coping with reality?

Lilké, always the friend, comforted her with jokes and buoyant little compliments. "Ejy is just keeping you humble," she would claim. "You know there's no such starship out there. Organics destroy themselves. As soon as we learn to fuse hydrogen, it's inevitable that we'll try to pound ourselves into extinction."

Humans were extinct, save upon the Web.

Millions of years ago, a brutal war left the Earth and the entire solar system devastated. More wars were inevitable. To save themselves, a small group of humans traveled into the Kuiper belt and there carved a starship out of a comet. They intended to protect what they could of their homeland and past. But they didn't trust themselves, much less their descendants: Why go to this bother today if others eventually forgot the past, and in some other solar system, in the same tragic ways, finished the obliteration?

Artisans were a desperate solution.

Frightened, chastened humans placed themselves into the care of machines—the ultimate parents—relinquishing one kind of life and freedom for a safer, sweeter existence.

And as predicted, the final War arrived.

The Web, still little more than an iceberg with rockets, escaped unseen. But it left behind robot spies, scattered and hidden, that watched a thousand more years of senseless fighting—living worlds shattered, debris fighting debris, not even a bug left behind to die in the end.

But the little starship prospered. The occasional comet was mined for raw materials. The ship doubled in size, then doubled again. When a living world was discovered, the Artisans obeyed already ancient programs, hurting nothing, taking samples of every species, adding to their cryogenic archives before wandering to the next likely sun, and the next.

An intelligent species was found eventually. How to deal with them? Machines shouldn't leave the ship, it was decided, and the Voices were born. But when the first mission ended in disaster, the Artisans told the survivors that the blame was theirs. They were the ship's masters, and by any definition, masters are always responsible for the mistakes of their property.

Provided it is done well, slavery can bring many comforts.

Later worlds brought success. Better talent and training made for better Voices, and they brought new species on board, enlarging the talent pool and everyone's prosperity.

The starship became the Web, moving along one great spiral arm of the galaxy. Thousands of worlds were explored, billions of species preserved in the archives, and by Sarrie's time there were more than a hundred sentient organics living in habitats built just for them, lured there, as always, by the honest and earnest and easily seductive Voices.

When Sarrie and Lilké had free time—a rare event—they liked to visit the nearby habitats, human and otherwise, or sometimes ride a bubble car back and forth on the vast diamond threads to which every home was strung.

The Web was an awesome mixture of beauty and pragmatic engineering. Thousands of kilometers across, it was sprinkled with cylindrical habitats and moon-sized fuel tanks feeding rockets that hadn't stopped firing in living memory, carrying them toward stars still invisible to the naked eye. Success had swollen the ship; new mass meant greater momentum, hard-won and difficult to extinguish. The far-off future would have to deal with those stars. What mattered to the young women were several dozen nearer suns, bright and dim, aligned like tiny gems on a twisted necklace. Each gem had its own solar system, they knew. Several centuries of work would consume generations of scientists and Voices—a daunting, wondrous prospect. And the young Voice would hold her best friend's hands, singing her favorite songs to praise the Web, and the Artisans, and the wisdom of their ancestors for making their astonishing lives possible.

Behind the Web, in the remote distance, was the diffused brilliance of the Milky Way. They had left its embrace long ago. Momentum was one reason. It was easiest to let the ship's momentum carry them into the cold between galaxies, finding orphaned suns and saving whatever life had evolved in that solitude. In essence, Sarrie understood, they were making an enormous lazy turn, allowing the Milky Way's gravity to help reclaim them, like some wayward child, pulling them back into the other spiral arm.

Sarrie could see the future from the bubble car, and the past, and she would weep out of simple joy, earning good-natured barbs from the realist beside her.

The realist was bolder than Sarrie, and more inquisitive. Lilké was the product of Artisan ingenuity, genius genes working in concert with a scientist's upbringing, which was likely why she was the one who suggested that they visit the archives. "Like now," she said. "What's the matter with now?"

There was no rule against it. None. Yet Sarrie wanted to ask permission first. "We'll go home, and I'll contact Ejy—"

"No," Lilké snapped. "This time is ours, and I want to go there."

It wasn't a particularly long journey. Their car took them to the center of the Web, to a mammoth triple-hulled wheel bristling with telescopes of every flavor, plus an array of plasma guns and lasers, the weapons meant for defense, nothing to shoot but the occasional comet.

Sarrie felt ill-at-ease. Stepping from the car into a small white-walled room, she held Lilké's hand as if it were all that kept her from drowning . . . and after what seemed like a long wait, though probably it was no more than a minute, the whiteness parted, a doorway revealed, and an Artisan emerged, its body unlike any she had ever seen.

It was a machine's body, practical and elegant in design, but simple, its corners left sharp and a variety of spare limbs stacked like firewood on its long back. Jointed legs clattered on the milky floor. A clean, lifeless voice said, "Welcome."

Artisans were machines. Of course they were. But why did Sarrie feel surprise? And why did she lose the last of her poise, blurting out, "I want to speak to Ejy. Is Ejy here?"

The machine replied, "Certainly, my child—"

"We've come for a tour, if that's possible." Sarrie couldn't stop her mouth, and she couldn't begin to think. "My friend here, Lilké, is a geneticist, or she will be . . . and she wants to see the archives . . . if it's not too much trouble—!"

A soft laugh came from the rolling machine.

"Sarrie," said its voice. "Don't you recognize me?"

Ejy?

And he laughed louder, Lilké joining in . . . then finally, grudgingly, the embarrassed Voice too. . . .

Ejy took them on a tour of the ancient facility.

Every surface was white, befitting some logic of cleanliness, or perhaps some ascetic sensibility. Each wall was divided into countless deep drawers, cylindrical and insulated, and sealed, every drawer filled with the DNA or RNA or PNA from a vast array of past worlds.

First and always, the Artisans were insatiable collectors.

They walked for a long while. Sometimes they saw other Artisans, their machine bodies the same but for the details. Sarrie didn't feel entirely welcome, but then again, she couldn't trust her instincts. Voices were bred and trained to know organics, not machines, and she reminded herself that their long glassy stares and chill silences might mean nothing at all.

In one nondescript corridor, Ejy paused without warning, touching a control panel, a skeletal ramp unfolding from a wall.

"Climb," he told the women. "All the way to the top, if you please."

The archive's mock-gravity was less than their habitat's, yet the climb was difficult. Sarrie found herself nervous and weak, eyes blurring as she reached the top. Before her was a ceramic drawer, pure white save for the tiniest imaginable black dot—a memory chip—and beside it, in exacting detail, the black silhouette of a human being.

Lilké touched the symbol, lightly, a low keening sound coming from deep in her chest.

"What is within?" asked the Artisan.

"I am," Sarrie whispered.

"And everyone else too," said Lilké, her fingertips giving it an expectant caress. "Is this where you keep us?"

"The sum total of human genetics," he affirmed, his pride obvious, hanging in the air after the words had faded. "Every human who had ever lived on 2018CC is represented," he told them, "as are several billion from the ancient Earth. Plus, of course, the unincorporated genes, natural and synthetic, that we will implant in future generations, as needed."

Neither woman spoke. A simple drawer, yet it held their entire species. What could anyone say at such a moment?

Ejy continued, voice purring. "In addition, the walls on both sides of us encompass the Earth's biosphere. Every possible species is represented, including every potential genotypic variation."

An electric surge passed through Sarrie, bringing a clarity, a transcendent sense of purpose.

Lilké, by contrast, saw more pragmatic concerns.

"You should make copies," she warned. "Of everything, if possible. Then put them somewhere else, somewhere safe. Just in case."

The Artisan ignored the thinly veiled criticism.

Glassy eyes on Sarrie, he said, "Imagine this. Within that modest drawer are certain traits that, when combined, make perfection. The ultimate scientist, perhaps. Or our best farmer. Or maybe, a singular Voice." He paused, then asked, "If we ever found perfection, in any job, wouldn't we be wise to let it be born again and again?"

Lilké answered for Sarrie, saying, "Certainly. So long as it helps the Web, you have no choice."

Ejy only watched the Voice. "Certain qualities may vary, of course. Gender and height, and skin color, and general appearance are minor details, free to dance where they wish." Mechanical arms gestured, underscoring each word. "But the soul within is constant. Eternal. And if it is reborn today, wouldn't it be a link in the most glorious chain?"

Sarrie nodded weakly, whispering, "Yes."

Without shifting his gaze, Ejy said, "Imagine this. An Artisan finds perfection. Can you imagine it, Lilké? He finds it in the very early days of the Web, which would mean that this perfect soul has been born how many times? You are good with calculations, Lilké. How many times is she brought out of that little drawer?"

"What's her job?" asked the scientist.

"I cannot say."

Lilké shrugged and played with the numbers regardless. After a moment, she said, "Ten thousand and eleven times. Give or take." Then she broke into a quiet, self-satisfied laugh.

Sarrie felt distant, utterly remote, as if watching these events from some invisible faraway sun.

"I can't even say if there is such a soul," Ejy continued. "There are rules that rule even the Artisans, which is only fair."

Both women nodded.

"If you wish to believe in a number near ten thousand, I think you would be rather close. But of course it's a hypothetical problem, and there are no ultimate answers.''

It was a strange, compelling game.

The immortal Artisan crawled partway up the ramp, and with a certain quietness asked, ''How many lives do you stand on, Sarrie?''

The answer bubbled out of her.

''None,'' she told Ejy. ''I stand on no one else.''

''Interesting,'' was his only response.

Lilké was staring at her friend, astonished and envious and almost certainly dubious of Sarrie's vaunted status. ''I'm as good a geneticist as you are a Voice!'' her expression shouted.

Then Sarrie, feeling a kind of shame, climbed down the ramp, wondering how many human Voices had visited this holy place, and if Ejy had accompanied all of them, and what answers they might have given to his question: ''How many lives do you stand on?''

But there was only one answer, of course, and it was hers.

Then Lilké and Ejy were speaking about the techniques of gene preservation, and Sarrie stood by herself, trying very hard to think of other, more important matters. . . .

THREE

It was a secretly warm world.

Cherry-hot iron lay at its center, blanketed in a roiling ocean of magma. Only its skin was cold, young rock covered with water ice and a thin nitrogen snow, the face deceptively simple, glowing white and pink beneath the bottomless sky.

The lecturer, an adult male fouchian, described their target world as being formed four billion years ago, presumably in one of the local solar systems. It spent a chaotic youth dancing with its more massive neighbors, orbits shifting every few centuries, a final near-collision flinging it out into the cometary cloud. Perhaps a similar near-collision had thrown this cluster of stars out of the Milky Way. Who knew? Either way, the world today was tracing a slow elliptical orbit around a cool M-class sun, its summers barely warmer than its fifty-thousand-year winters, the original ocean of water frozen beneath a thin atmosphere of noble gases and molecular hydrogen.

Dramatic images floated above the fouchian, fresh from the Web's telescopes. He pointed out volcanoes and mountain ranges and the conspicuous absence of impact craters. Even so far from any sun, heat persisted. Tectonics and the table-smooth plains of ice were evidence of recent liquid water, which meant the possibility of simple life. And with that pronouncement, the fouchian looked out at his audience, reminding them that not every training mission had hopes of finding life. Other, less gifted teams were being sent to survey nearby comets and little plutos, the poor souls. Attempting a human smile, the fouchian laid its nose tendrils against its muzzle, then parted its thin lips, exposing incisors whiter than any ice. ''Thank Artisan Ejy for this honor,'' he told them, his voice box pronouncing words with an eerie hyperclarity. ''He specifically chose each of you, just as he selected my nest-brother and myself to serve as his chief officers. And who are we to doubt an Artisan's judgment?''

Two dozen humans sat together in an open-air amphitheater. It was night in the human habitat, cloudless and warm, and lovely. Curious people stood at the gates, straining for a glimpse. Beyond the stage was a broad calm cove, playful dolphins stitching their way through the water, trading insults as they hunted the living sea.

"A mission at last," Lilké muttered. "We've got something to do!"

Sarrie smiled and nodded, unsure when she had ever felt so happy.

Wearing his human body, Ejy stood on one side of the stage, accompanied by the second fouchian. Sarrie wanted to dance around like a little girl, but how would that look? Instead she punched commands into her monitor, asking for permission to view the files on this wondrous new world.

A young man was sitting in front of Lilké. Without warning, he stood, giving the fouchian a quarter-bow even as he said, "I have to disagree. There's a lot of liquid water today. More than you've predicted, I think."

He was a sharp-featured, sharp-tongued fellow named Navren. A genius with physical sciences, Sarrie recalled. He understood the periodic table better than did the elements themselves, it was said, and he never, ever let an opinion go unspoken.

"Your estimated heat flows are too small," he informed the fouchian. "And I see a deep ocean beneath the ice plains. Plenty of vents, and heat energy, and particularly *here*. This basin on the southern hemisphere is our best bet."

The fouchian's tendrils flexed and became a bright pink. A sure sign of anger, Sarrie knew. Yet the artificial voice remained crisp and worthy. "We know the world's age and mass, and Ejy himself made these estimates, all based on long experience—"

"A volcanic pulse," Navren interrupted. "But more likely, residual heat after a major impact." He launched into a thorough analysis, intuition sprinkled over a technical mastery that astonished Sarrie. If it was an impact, she learned, then it was recent—in the last million years—and it had happened where the ice was smoother than a newborn's cheek.

When the impromptu lecture ended, a cold silence held sway.

Every team member should be grateful for expert advice. Yet only Ejy seemed genuinely pleased. His old-human face smiled and smiled, even as his first officer remarked, "No one can make such a quick analysis. I think our distinguished colleague accessed these files before you gave him permission, Artisan Ejy."

It was a serious breach of the rules, if true. Knowledge, in all its glorious colors, belonged to their masters.

But Ejy chose to ignore any offense. "The boy is eager. I see no crime." Black eyes glanced at both fouchian officers. "This is a training mission, children. A simple world is being given to us to share, and let's not forget our purpose. Our unity. Please."

Navren grinned openly, winking at the two young women behind him.

Again, Ejy said, "Children."

He meant humans and he meant fouchians, and Sarrie didn't need to be a Voice to understand the intent of that one potent word.

• • •

It had been centuries since the Web had had so many worlds to investigate; very few organics could recall such adventures, and none of them were human. In honor of their mission, the humans held a traditional ceremony, but it turned into a static, formal, and desperately dull affair. It took a party to cure the dullness. With strong drink in her belly, the mission's Voice decided to join Navren, complimenting him for being right about the new world's heat flow. Tiny probes had landed recently, sending home evidence of a genuine ocean, deep and warm and exactly where he had predicted it to be.

Compliments made Navren smile. But he wasn't prompted to compliment her in turn, his gaze saying, "Of course I was right. Why wouldn't I be?"

Sober, Sarrie would have seen the soul inside the arrogance. But the drunken Voice persisted, confessing excitement, hoping aloud that she could help their mission, if not as a Voice, then at least as a willing worker.

"Forget worrying," was Navren's advice. "This is a useless little mission. It's nothing."

She winced, then remarked, "That seems harsh."

"We're visiting a snowball," he countered. "A big fancy snowball. This team's real work doesn't begin until we slide past the fourth solar system." His narrow brown face showed disgust. "And we'll be old people before we reach its most promising world—"

"What world? How do you know?"

"I had early access to our mission files. Remember?"

"You've studied what's coming?"

"Maybe yes, maybe no." A big wink, then he said, "Our best prospect is Earth-like. Warm and green. Radio-dead, but even light-years away, it shows evidence of agriculture—"

Sarrie clapped her hands over her ears, in reflex. " 'Knowledge too soon is the same as poison,' " she quoted from the Artisan code. And their mission wasn't useless, either.

Navren shrugged, then effortlessly changed subjects.

"You know," he remarked in a casual, self-satisfied way, "you and I won't sleep together. You're wasting your hope trying to seduce me."

Surprise became a fumbling anger. Sarrie muttered, "I was never thinking—"

"Oh, yes, you were," Navren insisted. "You and Lilké talk about me, wondering who's to screw me first."

Astonishing, infuriating words.

And true, but only to a degree. Idle chatter, in passing, and she wouldn't let him entertain the remote possibility . . . !

"You're too conventional for my tastes," Navren continued.

"You don't know me," she growled.

"Of course I do. I read those novels of yours." He shook his head and squinted, telling her, "The second novel was your best."

"You didn't read it."

"In that silly language of yours, yes."

She felt lightheaded.

"Besides," he claimed, "every Voice is the same essential creature. Human or fouchian, or whatever. Voices have an exact job, and like it or not, the Artisans build you along very precise lines.''

Sarrie took a deep, useless breath.

"On the other hand, I have twenty-three untried genes inside me. I require things to be *fresh*. New.'' Emotions that no Voice could have read passed through his face, the eyes flaring. The insufferable man announced, "I think your friend— Lilké, is it?—is more to my taste.''

Looking across the green paddock, Sarrie found her parents speaking to Lilké, no doubt wishing her well, and begging her to please watch after "our little Sarrie.''

"Tell her what I said,'' Navren purred. "Tell her to come visit me.''

She had enough, cursing him in fouchian and storming off. But later, when Sarrie calmed enough to laugh at the boorish idiot, she told Lilké exactly what he had said. Voices were natural mimics and entertainers, but her lovely friend didn't laugh at the appropriate moments, or even speak, her deep brown-black eyes looking elsewhere, trying to find Navren among all the young, blessed geniuses.

Their scout ship was built on ancient, proven principles—blunt and swift, fuel tanks and engines dwarfing the tiny crew quarters. With supplies and extra-heavy equipment, there was no room left for elbows, much less comfort. Humans had to spend most of the eleven-month voyage in cold-sleep. Only the fouchian officers and Ejy remained awake, immune to the claustrophobia.

Ten days out from the new world, the sleepers were warmed, then reawakened.

They gorged on breakfasts rich with fat and antioxidants. Then the scientists and engineers were sent to organize their laboratories and calibrate delicate instruments. Lilké found little problems that evaded easy answers. Tests supplied by Ejy? Perhaps, although not likely. Either way, Sarrie helped where possible, then simply tried to stay out of the way. By early evening, she was starving again, teetering close to exhaustion. Yet she felt like a traitor when she excused herself, making amends by promising, "I'll get our cabin in order. Come to bed soon. You need rest too.''

True enough, but her friend didn't arrive by midnight. Bundled up in bed, Sarrie plunged into her first dreams in nearly a year—intricate dreams of being alien, of meeting a human Voice who sang of some faraway Heaven. Waking, she smiled, then realized it was three in the morning and Lilké was missing . . . and of course Sarrie dressed and went to the genetics lab, trembling with worry until she saw that the lab was dark, and sealed, and she finally thought to ask the ship's computer about Lilké's whereabouts.

The computer gave a cabin number. Navren's cabin.

In the morning, after a string of nightmares, Sarrie saw her best friend sitting with Navren in the tiny galley. What she already knew became a concrete truth, as inescapable as physical law. Despite a fierce hunger, she couldn't eat near them; the next few days were spent hiding in her cabin, pretending to work at Ejy's unsolvable simulation. As always, the xenophobic aliens destroyed the Web. Nothing she did seemed to mollify them. Yet it didn't matter anymore. Nothing mattered except for Sarrie's black mood, and she clung to it for as long as her nature and Ejy allowed.

The Artisan hadn't spoken twice to the Voice since she had risen from cold-sleep. She had barely wondered why. But within a few hours of their landing, he came to her cabin dressed as the old man, and he asked if she would please join him for a little stroll.

They went to the astronomical lab, empty now despite important work on hand. Empty by command? she wondered. The main screen was filled with their nameless world—a pale white ball, cold and nearly featureless. It seemed incapable of holding Sarrie's attention. She forced herself to appear interested. "Have we learned anything new?" she inquired, knowing that learning was as inevitable on this ship as breathing was.

"We've learned much," the ancient Artisan replied. "But most of it is trivial. Nuggets and details only."

The worthwhile discoveries were waiting for the humans to find them. As it was intended to be, she told herself.

A strong false hand gripped her shoulder, squeezing hard.

Sarrie refused to talk about the lovers in the nearby cabin. Instead, with a tone of fearful confession, she whispered, "I want to have a great life."

"You will," her companion replied, without hesitation.

"I want you, you and the other Artisans . . . to talk about me for a million years."

The gripping hand relaxed, almost lifting.

No voice said, "We will," or even, "Perhaps we will." Because it wasn't possible, of course. What single organic deserved such fame?

Without looking at Ejy, she said, "Thank you."

"For what, may I ask?"

"Your help. Your patience." She paused, forcing herself not to cry. "Thank you for making me into the best Voice that I can possibly be."

"You cannot be anything else," he assured, laughing gently.

Fouchians had an insult. "Posturing-on-another's-mound-of-soil." She thought of it until Ejy, affecting a tone of concern, asked her:

"What are you thinking, child?"

She looked at the false face, crystal eyes cool and black—more alien than any other eyes on the Web—and she confessed, "I feel closer to you than to my own species."

A soft, soft laugh.

Then the hand squeezed until her shoulder ached, and the Artisan said, "Exactly as it should be, sweet Voice. As it always is. . . ."

FOUR

The ship set down on a plain of water ice—hard as granite, smooth as sleep, and relentlessly, numbingly cold. Tradition and practicality called for an unessential crew member to be first to the surface. Ejy gave Sarrie the honor. She donned her heavily insulated lifesuit, gave a general thumbs-up, then with a musical hum of motorized limbs strode into the main airlock, waiting to descend onto the ice.

"For the Artisans, parents to all," she announced, "I claim this lovely bleak place."

Violence had created the ice. Yet Navren seemed unsure which natural process to blame. Comet impacts or vulcanism? Perhaps some combination of both, he decided, and he built elaborate simulations involving rains of comets piercing the crust, allowing plastic rock to rise to within a very few kilometers of where they stood now.

Steady chill winds had polished the ice ever since. Disturbing that crystalline perfection felt sacrilegious, but Lilké wanted deep samples, unmarred by cosmic radiation. Navren helped her erect a portable drilling rig. Their first fist-sized sample, brought up after just a few minutes' work, was sprinkled with treasure: A few dozen tiny, tiny fossils frozen where they had died, swimming in an ocean melted for a moment after a hundred-million-year winter.

Scarce, as expected, and uncomplicated, the fossils resembled bacteria in basic ways. Lilké isolated their naked DNA, patching gaps and decoding the naked genetics. Then in a long aquarium filling half of her lab—a cold, lightless, and pressurized little ocean—she conjured the aliens out of amino acids and lipids, watching as they began to slowly thrive.

Despite this world's poverty, life had persisted. Lilké's bugs were pragmatically sluggish, powered by anaerobic chemistries, and judging by their numbers in the ice, they were scarce. She and Navren warned the others that beneath the ice, even in the ocean's secret gardens, life would be scarce. Yet these creatures were survivors and admirable because of it, existing for several billion years—outliving suns, worlds, and even their own pitiful earth.

Ejy called a general meeting, then asked humans and fouchians to find some means to cut their way to the mysterious sea.

Navren proposed using nuclear charges, hammering their way through two kilometers of ice in an afternoon. But more conservative souls won out. The ship's potent reactors would pump heat into the icecap, sculpting a deep hole, and the superheated vapor would be thrown high overhead, freezing almost immediately, then falling. For the first time in eons, this world would enjoy a good long peaceful snow.

Sarrie was suddenly desperate to feel involved. But the hardware, fat pumps and redundant backup power systems and such, had been proven on thousands of similar worlds, and her help took the form of sitting inside a prefabricated hut near the borehole, watching for mechanical problems only a little more likely than another comet impact. To someone groomed for intellectual adventure, boredom was a shock. Sarrie stared out at the enormous geyser, feeling its roar more than she could hear it in the near-vacuum . . . and a secret portion of her fearing that nothing more interesting than this would ever happen in her life.

The twisted necklace of suns set during her duty time. The temperature would plummet another fraction of a degree, the sense of eternal night growing worse. On her second day, Sarrie was considering tears when the Milky Way rose behind her—a majestic fog of suns, never more lovely, lending color and depth to the man-made geyser, but the geyser's magnificence all its own.

Sarrie composed a poem in the next few hours, then dedicated it to Lilké and posted it in the galley. But her friend was taking her meals in the lab, studying her bugs twenty hours a day before indulging in private fun with her gruesome boyfriend. It was Ejy who praised the poem first, applauding her imagery and the message. Only then did the fouchians and other humans read it, seemingly appreciating it. But Navren, of all people, offered no opinions. Sarrie was eating a late dinner when he read it, and she braced herself for some terse, biting critique. Surely he would browbeat her for not understanding the physics of expanding gases and phase changes. But no, the gruesome boyfriend seemed to nod respectfully, even as the author sat nearby, sipping juice, pretending to be blind.

That next morning, Sarrie was walking toward her post. The borehole was several kilometers from the ship. The thin winds had fallen off while she had slept, icy snow falling silently on her. She was navigating in a darker-than-night gloom, using her suit's instruments to keep on course, and suddenly, without warning, a dark monstrous blob appeared before her.

A low liquid moan came from Sarrie.

It was some kind of alien, obviously. Her eyes refused to find anything familiar about it. She took a few steps backward, then paused, one hand lifting instinctively, ready to ward off any blows; and finally, at the last instant, she remembered that she was a Voice, for goodness sake. And in a thin whisper, she told the alien, "Hello," in many languages, hoping against hope to be understood.

"Hello," the monster replied, smiling behind his crystal faceplate.

She knew him. The bulky body was a lifesuit, and she finally saw the identification symbol on the helmet—the familiar silhouette of a human—then the sharp, self-assured face.

"Navren?" she sputtered.

But he said nothing else—an uncharacteristic moment—handing her a small pad and making sure that she had a firm grip. Then he walked on past, the blizzard swallowing him without sound, without fuss, his wide bootprints beginning to fill with icy grains. Perhaps he hadn't been here at all.

Sarrie reached the hut without further incident, relieving an extremely bored expert in alien neurology.

Alone and unwatched, she woke Navren's pad. It contained nothing but a long poem about another geyser on a different world. A warm, blue-green world, she realized. Judging by the star-rich sky, it was somewhere deep in the Milky Way. No author was named, but clues led to obvious conclusions: The poem had been written by a human Voice. Moreover, its rhythms and imagery were nearly identical to the poem displayed back in the galley. The same symbols, even. The geyser linked life and the stars, emotion and purpose, organics and the blessed Artisans. On and on, point by point. It was obvious—Sarrie's soul had written both versions. But what disturbed her most was that this earlier work, without question, was better than yesterday's effort. Not to mention superior to everything else that she had written in her current life.

Read once, the mysterious poem vanished from the pad, leaving no trace except in Sarrie's mind.

When the neurologist arrived at the appointed time, relieving her, Sarrie went straight to Navren.

Before she could speak, he told her, "I gave you nothing. And if you say otherwise, I'll be *extremely* disappointed."

He was working on some kind of device, possibly of his own design. The machine shop was cluttered and loud, and save for the two of them, it was empty. Yet for some reason, Sarrie found herself glancing over her shoulder.

"I expected more from you, Sarrie." The man plugged components into components, telling her, "The good Voice sees the universe through another's eyes. Am I right? Well, look at *my* eyes. Look! Tell me what I see!"

She hated the man.

"Leave me," he growled. "Get out of here. I'm working!"

She hated him and wouldn't do what he asked. In revenge, Sarrie refused him the simple gift of her understanding.

They reached the living sea exactly on schedule.

A quick celebration culminated with the Artisan blessing his organics for their good work. The precious water rose almost two kilometers on its own, then was grabbed by powerful pumps and insulated pipes, filling both an empty fuel tank and Lilké's pressurized aquarium. The celebrants filed through the lab for a symbolic quick glance. One of the fouchians, pulling his bulk down the narrow aisle, claimed to see a momentary phosphorescence. "Too much to drink," was Lilké's verdict—a glib dismissal of a colleague whose physiology couldn't survive ethanol. Then the nonessential organics herded themselves into the hallway, standing three-deep, talking too loudly as the geneticist tried to ignore them, starting to make the obvious and routine first tests.

The water was glacially cold and mineral-rich—as predicted—but it also carried a delicious hint of free oxygen. Not predicted, and marvelous. Navren, remaining at his lover's side, said, "Impossible," giggled, then began offering explanations. A catalytic reaction between water and metal ions? Or water and hot magma? Or water and life . . . ? Though that last speculation was absurd—where would the energy come from?—and he giggled again, for emphasis. . . .

Befitting his role, Ejy remained in the lab, standing nearly motionless with his false face showing confidence and a well-honed pleasure.

Life was easy to find, and it too held surprises. The biomass was two or three hundred times higher than predicted. But more astonishing were the natives themselves. A stereomicroscope focused on them. Projected images swam in the air above the central lab table. As if injured, Lilké gasped aloud. Bacteria were darting along like grains of enchanted rice, seeping a kind of firefly light as they moved. Even Sarrie, standing her ground in the narrow doorway, knew their significance: These bugs were a different species, operating on some radically different, spendthrift metabolism.

The rest of the audience grew silent, watching over Sarrie's shoulder or using portable monitors. A baffling moment, and holy . . . !

Without warning, something else glided into view. A monster, perhaps. It was burly and vast, and powerful, remaining blurred until the automatic focus could engage, recalibrating data made from bent light, the monster suddenly defined, suddenly utterly familiar.

It was a protozoan. Sarrie knew a sophisticated organism when she saw it. That general design had been repeated on a multitude of worlds, always with great success. The nucleus and engorged food vacuoles lay within a sack of electric broth. A thick golden pelt of cilia beat too rapidly for an eye to follow, obeying the simplest reflexes. Without conscience or love, the monster hovered, feasting on the hapless, minuscule bacteria. Then it moved again, without warning, covering some enormous distance—the width of an eyelash, perhaps—and passing out of view before the lenses could respond.

One of the fouchians gave a deep moan, his voice box asking, "How? How, how, how?"

Explanations were obvious, and inadequate. The fossil ocean from a million years ago had been replaced by another ocean, richer by any measure: Oxygen metabolisms; rapid growth and motility; the extravagance of trophic levels. But how could a new ocean evolve so quickly? Lilké claimed that's exactly what had happened, then she just as quickly dismissed the idea. No! Their borehole had to be situated directly above some local paradise. A volcano. A vent site. Whatever the physical cause, free oxygen was being generated in this one locale. In tiny amounts, no doubt. The bulk of the unseen ocean was exactly as the ice had promised, she maintained—cold and dark, and impoverished, and content with its poverty.

Navren made fun of the free oxygen. His magma and metal-ion hypotheses had been half-jokes, nothing more. Under these circumstances, he admitted that he couldn't see any trick that would split water molecules, and his features seemed to sharpen as his frustrations grew.

Sarrie enjoyed the befuddlement, part of her wishing this moment wouldn't end.

But wise old Ejy knew exactly what to do. Obviously this new world had mysteries, delicious ones, and everyone needed to work as one to solve them. He began to move, dispensing assignments. Humans and fouchians were sent where they could help, or at least where they brought the least distraction. Sarrie knew enough about biological instruments to help Lilké prepare specimens for mapping; and Ejy, perhaps wishing to heal wounds between friends, ordered his young Voice into the lab, hovering nearby while Lilké gave instructions, both humans pretending to cooperate for the moment.

Sarrie worked with DNA drawn from a protozoan's nucleus, making it legible for their machinery. Lilké was already reading genes from the oxygen-loving bacteria. Silence was followed by curses. With the mildest of voices, Ejy asked what was wrong. Lilké said, "Nothing." Then after more transcriptions, she amended herself. "Somehow, I don't know how . . . I managed to contaminate this sample, Artisan Ejy . . . !"

Ejy's face was sympathetic, but his voice was all barbs and disappointment. "That doesn't sound like you, Lilké. Now does it?"

The mission's geneticist turned to Sarrie. "Is your sample ready yet?" Nearly, yes. "Let me finish up. And you get started on another bacterium. Go on."

The protozoan was genetically complex. Even in an expert's grip, interpretations took time. Lilké entered a near-trance, skimming across long, long stretches of base pairs, trying to decipher the codes. And Sarrie tried to convince herself that her friend deserved absolute control. This was Lilké's lab, after all. Only a selfish, inadequate organic would feel angry about being pushed aside. Pushed like an untrustworthy child. Yet she wasn't a child, and she was confident in her abilities . . .

except for some reason she couldn't work, or think, and her hands trembled as if some degenerative condition were eating at her nervous system.

''What the fuck's wrong?'' Lilké shouted.

Sarrie was startled, a vial slipping from her fingers and bouncing, then rolling out of reach.

''We've got a major contamination problem,'' Lilké explained, embarrassed to tears. ''I'll need to clean up and start over. I'm sorry, Artisan Ejy. As soon as I can track down the problem, I'll run more samples. But I can't do shit just now . . . !''

The Artisan did not speak, or move.

The women watched him, waiting for his sage advice or the perfect encouragement. Yet he remained silent for an astonishing length of time. The old-man face was hard and flat, inert as a mask, but behind the eyes was a flickering, hints of a swift elegant mind being applied to intricate, uncompromising programs.

Then he spoke. With the mildest of voices, he asked, ''From where does your contamination come?''

''From us,'' Lilké muttered. ''These codes and the genes . . . they're all *Ter-ran* . . . !''

The Artisan nodded, contriving a smile. ''But of course,'' he replied, ''there's another conclusion supported by your data. Yes?''

In a whisper, Lilké said, ''No.''

Ejy stared at Lilké. He didn't blink or offer another word, waiting until the geneticist finally, grudgingly said, ''Maybe.''

''I don't understand,'' Sarrie confessed.

No one seemed to hear her.

''What other conclusion?'' Her voice was soft, weak. Useless.

Lilké shook her head, telling Sarrie, ''That there's no contamination. Our data are perfectly valid.''

But if Sarrie was extracting earthly DNA, that meant . . . no . . . !

Ejy turned to Sarrie, the dead face opening its mouth, saying nothing. The eyes were what spoke, surprise and pain mixed with pity.

Why pity? she asked herself.

And then she understood everything. Not just what was in the ocean far beneath the cold hard ice, but what was in the mind of the machine, the mind behind those pitying eyes.

FIVE

News of the discovery spread at a fever's pace.

And one fever-induced explanation was produced almost immediately: The microbes came from the Great Web. One of its Earthly habitats must have sprung a leak—a common enough event in those ancient structures—and the escaping water froze, tiny ice crystals set free to wander the universe, hitching a ride on one of their probes, or maybe just carried along on the chill starlight.

It was an inventive, ludicrous explanation. Yet both fouchians and most of the humans tried to believe it just the same. Everyone knew that the Earth was far away, and dead; there was no reason to mention it. Of course the Web was to blame. That was the consensus. Improbabilities were better than impossibilities. In voices growing more feeble by the moment, the crew promised each other that eons of tranquility and purpose wouldn't be threatened, at least not because of some damned little bugs swimming in an ocean nobody had even seen yet.

Ejy remained quiet about the pregnant snowflake, panspermian nonsense. And quiet about almost everything else too.

He wandered from lab to lab, then out to the borehole itself; but he rarely offered encouragement, much less advice, watching the organics with a peculiar intensity, leaving everyone ill-at-ease.

It was Navren who asked the obvious: What were the odds that a pregnant snowflake would come here? And how would frozen spores migrate through kilometers of solid ice? And even if they found the means, then where did the damned bugs get their energy and free oxygen? And how did they become so common so quickly?

But geniuses are nothing if not clever.

A second explanation was built from scratch. This was a training mission, people reasoned. Ejy, the great old Artisan, was simply testing them. The microbes had been planted. Who knew what else was falsified? Perhaps every team endured this kind of trickery. It had been generations since the last important field mission, right? Absolutely! But the sweetest advantage of this explanation was that Navren could ask any question, find any flaw, and none of it mattered. This was an elaborate practical joke, nothing else, and at some point, probably in a minute or two, Ejy would tell the truth, and everyone would laugh themselves sick.

The obvious next step was to visit the hidden ocean. A blunt diamond balloon was assembled in the machine shop. It was a submersible, crude but proven in a thousand seas. It had room on board for two cramped humans. Navren and Lilké were originally slated for the dive. But Ejy ordered the seats removed, then picked one of the fouchians to go in their place.

No explanation was necessary, yet he offered several. Experience. Expendability. And the light-sensitive fouchian eyes.

Reasonable enough, people told each other. The fouchian was probably a co-conspirator in the practical joke. Suddenly a false exuberance took hold of them. The borehole out on the ice had been capped, there was warm breathable air beneath the tentlike structure. The chosen fouchian drove himself out in one of the mission's three big-wheeled buggies, and without the slightest ceremony forced his way through the tiny hatch—like a fat rat through a knothole. Spontaneous applause broke out in the galley. Everyone was in the galley, save for the submersible pilot. When the submersible was lowered into the hole—a vapor-shrouded puddle nearly eight kilometers deep—most of the audience cheered aloud, telling themselves that everything would be answered soon, and with answers, everything would return to normal.

Navren acted distant, and exactly like Ejy, he rarely spoke, and when he did speak, his comments were brief and remarkably bland.

Sarrie kept her eyes on Navren. She sat close to him in the crowded galley, practically ignoring the banks of monitors on the far wall. Video images and raw data enthralled most of the humans. Vacuous conversation came and went. The ship's reactors were still heating the borehole's water. Its ice walls were smooth, translucent. Spotlights dove into the pure ice, shattering on ancient fissures, sudden rainbows forming and fading as the submersible continued its descent. And with that same false exuberance, people commented on the beauty of their seemingly simple surroundings, and wasn't the universe a marvel . . . ?

Navren didn't insult their sentimentality. He sat beside Lilké, holding his lover's hand with a wrestler's grip. Sometimes he would lean in close to her, making some comment about the oxygen levels or other dissolved treasures. But most of the time he just watched the monitors, his face tense yet strangely happy, his eyes missing nothing even when nothing at all happened.

Sarrie watched the monitors through his face.

When the submersible left the borehole, entering open water, there was more applause. But softer now, somehow less genuine. Navren blinked and took a breath, as if preparing for a long swim. Away from the ice there was much less to see. The spotlights reached out for hundreds of meters, finding nothing. Yet the tension in the galley doubled, then doubled again. Navren lifted Lilké's hand as if to kiss it, then hesitated. In a smooth and astonished voice, he said, "Look at the oxygen now. Look." Then he gently took a flap of his own skin into his mouth, and he bit down hard enough to make himself wince, to make his eyes tear.

The ocean floor remained remote, unimaginable. It would take forever to reach, which was unfair. More than once, in a quiet way, someone would whisper, "I wonder what's supposed to happen next." Because it was all a test, of course. Conceived by the Artisans. Run by Ejy. An elaborate means of determining *something* about this very young, very inexperienced team.

The fouchian was still a full kilometer from the bottom when he reported seeing a distinct glow. Built from many little lights, he claimed. And probably an illusion, since the lights were arranged in a definite pattern, as regular as the vertices on graph paper—

"Have him cut his spotlights!" Navren shouted. "Tell him, Ejy!"

But the Artisan, standing at the back of the galley, must have already given the order on a private channel. Suddenly the monitors were filled with black water. The native glow was magnified a thousandfold. Suddenly the submersible was a tiny balloon floating above a rolling landscape, narrow towers erected at regular intervals, each one perhaps two hundred meters tall, capped like a mushroom and a brilliant light thrown down from the cap at what seemed to be trees.

No, not trees. Lilké told everyone, "They look like kelp, or something similar." Then an instant later, "Growing in rows. Columns. Do you see?" Then she screamed, "It's a farm! Someone's cultivating seaweed down there!"

Sarrie looked at her best friend, then Navren, and she felt a warm weakness spreading through her.

Navren turned, glancing over his shoulder at Ejy.

The Artisan said nothing, did nothing.

Navren opened his mouth, words framed. Carefully, slowly, he turned forward again, taking one more deep breath, then remarked with all the sarcasm he could muster:

"Goodness! I wonder whose farm this is!"

. . .

The fouchian, crammed into that tiny submersible, utterly alone, began to beg for guidance. Should he investigate the unexpected forest? Should he snip off samples? Surely no one would miss a few brown leaves, he advised. Then he adjusted the focus on his cameras, revealing that the nearest water was filled with life: Clouds of plankton; schools of jerking copepods and delicate shrimp; and a single fish, long as a forearm and nearly transparent.

The placement of its fins, gills, spine, and pulsing pale heart were exactly the same as Earthly fish. Sarrie knew enough taxonomy to feel certain. But the transparency of its meat gave her hope. No pigment in the blood implied an alien physiology, which was exactly what she hoped to see . . . except Lilké quickly and thoroughly dashed any hopes, turning to Navren to tell him and the room, "I don't know the species, but I know their cousins. Icefish. Very low-energy. No hemoglobin. They lived on the shoulders of Antarctica, bodies laced with antifreeze, oxygen dissolving straight into their plasma."

Again, in fouchian squeaks and translated human syllables, the pilot begged for instructions. Directions. Purpose.

Artisan Ejy was as rigid as a statue. No doubt he was hard at work, his mind spliced directly into the ship's main computers. The black-crystal eyes were superfluous, and vacant, and seemed to lend him the appearance of utter helplessness. But with the fouchian's next words—"Do I continue my descent?"—he moved again, suddenly tilting his head, smiling for perhaps half a moment too long. Then with a calmness that unnerved the entire room, he told the pilot, "No." The old-man face was overly serene, if that was possible. "No, you've seen enough. Come back now. Back through the borehole, please."

The fouchian hesitated for an instant, then dropped his ballast.

Silence in the galley became a soft murmur.

And within the murmur: Excitement, confusion, and the ragged beginnings of a stunning new explanation.

A wondrous explanation, it was. Always unthinkable, until now.

"It's Terran life," Sarrie heard, from all sides.

"And someone has high technology," people whispered. Sang.

"Who could have imagined it?" said a voice behind Sarrie.

She turned, eager to confess to a lack of creativity. But as she spoke she spied Navren placing both hands around Lilké's head, pulling her close and saying a word into her ear, then two more words, or three, and kissing the lobe softly.

Something about that tenderness was perplexing. Almost terrifying.

Then someone else—in the distance, from beside the tiny beverage counter—shouted in a clear, joyous voice, "Humans! That would explain everything! On this world somewhere . . . could they be . . . ?"

The word *human* held magic, potent and ancient, dangerous beyond all measure.

As a chorus, a dozen voices responded by saying:

"Humans are extinct! Everywhere but on the Web."

But the engrained words held no life, no fire. Spoken, they dispersed into an atmosphere filled with electricity and possibilities. Two dozen youngsters were suddenly free to jump to their feet, asking the obvious:

"What if other humans escaped the Wars?"

Sarrie found herself standing, almost jumping, hands clasped over her open mouth. She couldn't speak. The great Voice was mute and lost. She could barely think, struggling to piece together clues that led to the inescapable conclusion—

Ejy moved, walking down the galley's only aisle. Only he seemed immune to the excitement, every step slow, even stately, the smile on his rubbery face never larger or less believable. It was the greatest discovery in eons—a pivotal moment in the Web's glorious history—and he resembled a grandfather strolling down his garden path.

An engineer beside Sarrie took her by the arm, pulling hard as she jumped up and down. "What a training mission! Can you believe it? Oh, Sarrie . . . who would have guessed . . . ?!"

Again, the Voice glanced over at Navren.

Suddenly he seemed old. Older than Ejy, even. He sat among the wild children, his expression black, thin mouth trembling, the eyes tracking sideways until they intersected with Sarrie's eyes.

He willed himself to smile—a brief, bleak attempt.

Then without sound, he carefully mouthed the words:

"Our. Mission. Is. Canceled."

Ludicrous. Wasn't it just beginning?

Ejy was standing under the largest monitor, facing the raucous youngsters. A radio pulse from him made the screen go black, and with a delicate firmness, he demanded silence. Then when the prattle continued, he raised his voice, saying, "Look at me now. Look here."

Ejy would explain everything, Sarrie believed.

This was the standard hazing, doubtlessly employed since the Web was born. On its first mission, every young team was tricked into believing that they'd found some viable splinter of humanity among the stars. Sarrie could believe it. Absolutely. She even felt a smile coming, anticipating Ejy's first words and his crisp laugh. "I fooled you," he might tell them. "I made you believe the impossible, didn't I?"

But the old machine said nothing about tricks. Instead, speaking with a cool formality, he repeated the words, "Look at me."

The silence was sudden, absolute.

"Before our submersible breaks the surface," he told them, "I want our ship's systems prepared for launch."

No one spoke, but the silence changed its pitch. If anything, it grew larger, flowing out of the galley, spreading over the glacial world.

"And please," said the Artisan, "prepare for cold-sleep. Each of you, as always, is responsible for your own chamber."

The second fouchian, filling the galley's far corner, lifted a powerful digging hand, pointing a claw at Ejy. "I assume this is a precaution," said his voice box. "You wish us ready to leave should the natives prove hostile."

The Artisan said, "No."

People turned and turned again, looking for anyone who seemed to understand that reply.

"No, we will launch," said Ejy. "In one hundred twenty-eight minutes. And each of you will place yourself into cold-sleep—"

"Artisan Ejy," the fouchian interrupted, "you don't mean me, of course."

"But I do. Yes."

The nose tendrils straightened and paled—an expression of pure astonishment. "But who will pilot our ship?"

"I am more than capable," Ejy reminded him, and everyone.

Sarrie found herself weak and shaky. Turning to Navren, she hoped for one good tough question. She wasn't alone. But the genius sat quietly with his lover, and Lilké held his hand with both of hers, neither of them seemingly involved in anything happening around them.

Ejy admitted, "Our mission has taken an unexpected turn."

Sarrie tried to swallow, and failed, then looked at the Artisan. His smile meant nothing. The eyes couldn't appear more dead. And the words came slowly, too much care wrapped around each of them.

"It has been a wonderful day," he promised. "But you are too young and inexperienced to carry this work to its next stage—"

We're as old and experienced as anyone else! Sarrie thought.

"I congratulate each of you. I love each of you. You are my children, and I thank you for your hard work and precious skills."

Why did those words terrify her . . . ?

Then she knew why. Ejy was looking at each of their faces, showing them his perfect smile; but he could never quite look at Sarrie, unwilling to risk showing their Voice his truest soul.

SIX

With no technical duties, Sarrie filled her time shoving her few possessions into the appropriate cubbyholes, cleaning her scrupulously clean cabin, then making sure that her cold-sleep chamber was ready to use. It was. But nearly an hour remained until they launched, which was too long. Sarrie considered placing herself into cold-sleep now. She went as far as undressing, then climbing into the slick-walled chamber, fingers caressing one of the ports from which chilling fluids would emerge, bathing her body, invading her lungs, then infiltrating every cell, suspending their life processes until she would be indistinguishable from the dead.

A seductive, ideal death. Responsibilities would be suspended. She wouldn't have to prove her value to this mission and the Web, and there wouldn't be the daily struggle with loneliness and self-doubt. Even if she never woke—if some unthinkable accident killed this body, this soul—then the best in her would simply be reborn again, brought up again under Ejy's enlightened care, and why was she sad? On no day did a child of Heaven have any right to be sad.

In the end, she decided to wait, climbing from the chamber and reaching for her clothes . . . and she noticed a familiar and bulky beetlelike form standing in the hallway, watching her now and possibly for a long while.

Sarrie gave a start, then whispered, "Ejy?"

"I scared you. I apologize." The machine's words were warm and wet, in stark contrast to the mechanical body. "I came here to ask for your help. Will you help me? I need a Voice—"

"Of course." Ejy must have changed his mind. Jumping to her feet, she started pulling on her trousers. "If there are humans nearby, I'm sure I can talk to them. We should start with underwater low-frequency broadcasts. In all the dead languages. I want to send audio greetings, and maybe some whale-style audio pictures of us—"

"No." A ceramic hand brushed against her cheek, then covered a bare shoulder. "I want you to speak with Lilké. I know that you and she have been at odds, but I know, too, she still feels close to you."

"Lilké?"

"Speak calmly. Rationally. And when you can, gain a sense of her mind." He paused for a moment, then admitted, "This is unexpected, yes. Remarkable, and unfair. But when you're finished, return here. Here. As soon as possible, please."

The hand was withdrawn.

Sarrie whispered, "Yes." She knelt, unfolding her shirt, then thinking to ask, "Where is Lilké?"

"In Navren's cabin," he answered.

"Navren—?"

"Is elsewhere."

The Voice pulled on her shirt, again wishing that she was cold and asleep, deliciously unaware. Then something in his last words caught her attention. "Where is Navren now?"

"I don't know," the Artisan replied.

The machine within, linked to every functioning system on the ship, confessed to Sarrie, "I cannot see him. And to tell the truth, I haven't for a little while."

Lilké expected her arrival.

That was Sarrie's first conclusion—an insight born not from innate talent, but friendship.

They showed one another smiles, Sarrie claimed the cabin's only seat, then she tried to offer some pleasant words . . . and Lilké spoiled the mood, remarking, "I guessed Ejy would send you."

"Why?"

She wouldn't say why. Red eyes proved that Lilké had been crying, but the skin around them had lost their puffiness. She had been dry-eyed for a long while.

Opening a low cubbyhole, she removed a homemade device, pressing its simple switch, a high-pitched hum rising until it was inaudible and the cabin's lights dimmed in response.

"Now," Lilké said, "we can speak freely."

"Navren isn't here."

"I don't know where he is, but I know what he's doing." She took a seat on the lower bunk, always leaning forward, ready to leap up at any time. "He and the others are working—"

"What others?"

"You don't need to know."

Sarrie hesitated, then said, "I want to understand. For my sake, not Ejy's."

"I'm disappointed with you. I thought you'd be better at this game." The geneticist shook her head, a wan smile appearing. Vanishing. "Answer a question for me, Sarrie. What have we found here?"

"Earth life. High technology." She hesitated before adding, "Some evidence, rather indirect, that other people survived the Wars."

"On a ship like ours, you mean." Lilké looked at the low ceiling as if it were fascinating. "A second starship. And its crew left the sun behind, and the Milky Way, coming here to settle this hidden sea . . . is that what you believe?"

"It is possible."

"Two starships, and we cross paths *here*?"

Sarrie said nothing.

"Calculate the odds. Or I can show you Navren's calculations."

"There's another possibility." She paused, waiting for Lilké to glance her way, a thin curiosity crossing her face. "The Artisans brought us here intentionally. They heard something, perhaps eons ago. A beacon, a leaked signal. Nothing definite, but certainly reason to come here."

"Why would humans leave the galaxy?"

Some cultures might relish the idea of this empty wilderness. An ascetic appeal; a spiritual chill; the relative safety of islands far from the galaxy's distractions. Sarrie devised her explanation in an instant, then thought again. Better to point out the obvious. "We left it behind, didn't we?"

Lilké dismissed the obvious, shrugging and changing subjects. "Why have we always been sure that our home solar system died?"

"We watched its destruction," Sarrie replied.

"How did we do that?"

"Our ancestors did. With probes."

"Machines sending coded signals, received and translated by still more machines—"

"What are you implying?"

Instead of answering, Lilké posed more questions. "But what if the wars weren't as awful as we were taught? What if a few worlds survived, perhaps even the Earth continued on . . . and our species recovered, then built starships and colonies . . . ?"

"Our ancestors would have seen them. Leaked radio noise alone would have alerted them—"

"Who would have seen them? Who?"

The implication was absurd. Sarrie said, "Impossible," without the slightest doubt.

Yet beneath the word, simple fear was building. What if it was true? What if the Artisans, even for the best reasons, had lied to their organics? Yet she couldn't imagine them lying for simple human reasons. Certainly not for vanity, or to be cruel.

Sarrie had come here to read Lilké's soul, but suddenly it was her own hidden soul that captivated her.

"Go back to *him*," said a quiet, composed voice.

What was that?

"Or stay here with me." Lilké touched the Voice's knee, promising, "If you do nothing against us, nothing happens to you."

A sigh. "You know I can't stay."

The hand was withdrawn.

"Ejy's waiting," Lilké remarked, eyes bright. Bitter. "Be with him," she advised. "Immortals like you should stand together."

Sarrie never reached the cold-sleep chambers.

She was running, in a panic, threading her way past empty labs until every light suddenly flickered and went out.

Sarrie halted. The darkness was seamless. Pure. But what terrified was the silence, the accustomed hum of moving air and pumps and plumbing apparently sabotaged, replaced by the galloping sound of her own breathing.

Every on-board system was failing.

"Rebellion," she whispered. An ancient word, and until this moment, useless, save as a blistering obscenity.

Days ago, in a lost age, someone had built an aquarium out of spare materials, placing it in the hallway and filling it with the deep ocean water. As Sarrie's eyes adapted, she saw the aquarium's faint glow, and she crept forward until her fingertips touched slick cool glass, their slightest pressure causing millions of bacteria to scream with photons, the thin ruddy glow brightening for a half-instant.

Someone moved. Behind her.

A great clawed hand closed over her shoulder, delicate tendrils grabbing the closer ear. "The-Nest-Is-Sour," the fouchian squeaked. No voice box gave its thorough, artless translation. With a sorrowful chirp, he told Sarrie, "The-Loyal-Must-Escape."

She turned and grabbed his stubby tail, then followed, the scent of his rectum meant to reassure.

The fouchian managed a terrific pace, fitting through narrow hatches and turns, twice nearly leaving the tiny human behind. But Sarrie never complained, never lost her grip, and when they reached the airlock, she donned her lifesuit in record time, then helped her vast companion struggle into his bulky, unwielding suit.

Reflexes carried her out onto the ice, and there they faltered.

Two buggies were parked in the open. With heavy limbs meant for construction work, one of the buggies was expertly and thoroughly dismantling the other. Ejy filled the buggy's crystal cockpit. A radio-born voice told her, "Welcome." He said, "A change of plans, child. Hurry now."

Sarrie lost her will. Her urgency.

Despite the servos in her joints, she couldn't seem to run. The fouchian scurried past, and she responded by hesitating, pulling up and looking back and up at the looming ship. A lifetime of order, of knowing exactly where and what she was, had evaporated, and Sarrie felt more sorry for herself than afraid. Even when she saw a figure appear in the open airlock, she wasn't afraid. Then the figure lifted a tube to his shoulder, and the tube spouted flame, and she watched with a certain distant curiosity, observing a spinning lump of something fall on the hard ice and bounce and stop. Ten or twelve meters away, perhaps. A homemade device. She almost took a step closer, just to have a better look. Then she thought again, or maybe thought for the first time, turning away an instant before the bomb detonated, its blast lifting her off her feet and throwing her an astonishing distance, her arms outstretched in some useless, unconscious bid to fly.

· · ·

"He tried to kill you," Ejy assured. The machine and Sarrie were inside the buggy, its cabin unpressurized and she still in her lifesuit, laying on her sore left side. The fouchian was in the cockpit, protected tendrils and heavy claws happily holding the controls. "If you have doubts at all," said Ejy's earnest voice, "watch. I will show you."

A digital replayed the scene, but from the buggy's perspective. Sarrie saw herself step toward the bomb, then turn away. Then came the blast, not as bright as she remembered it. The digital also allowed her to watch as her assailant received swift justice. Ejy had used a limb that Sarrie didn't recognize—a fat jeweled cannonlike device—focusing a terrific dose of laser light on the rebel's lifesuit, melting it in a moment, then evaporating the body trapped inside.

Sarrie grimaced for a moment, then quietly, almost inaudibly, asked, "Which one? Was he?"

Ejy gave a name.

She remembered the face, the person. And with a kind of baffled astonishment, she asked herself: *Why would an alien neurologist want to murder me?*

The machine seemed just as puzzled, in his fashion.

"I'm the object of their hate," Ejy promised, ready to take any burden. "Attacking you was unconscionable. It only proves how quickly things have grown ugly. Unmanageable. Tragic."

Sarrie discovered that she could sit upright without too much agony.

"We never should have come here," the machine confessed. "I blame myself. If I'd had any substantial clue as to what we would find, we wouldn't have passed within ten parsecs of this place."

They would have missed the local suns altogether.

"What about Navren?" she inquired.

"Oh, that may be. The clever boy did notice at least one clue, didn't he? This ocean's heat is plainly artificial." A pause, then with a mild but genuine delight, he proposed, "The boy had an inkling of the truth, perhaps. Even before we left 2018CC, perhaps."

Shaking her head, Sarrie whispered, "No."

She told him, "What I meant to ask . . . do you blame Navren at all?"

"For following his nature? Never, no!" The faceless machine showed no recognizable emotion, but the voice seemed sickened with horror. "The errors, if there are such things, belong to the Artisans. Mostly to me, I admit. I allowed that boy too many novel genes, and worse, far too many illusions. Illusions of invulnerability, particularly." A momentary pause, then he added, "Blame is never yours, child. Or theirs. It all rests here, in me."

Mechanical hands gripped the armored carapace, accenting the beatific words. The cannonlike laser merely dangled off the back end like some badly swollen tail.

Sarrie felt the buggy slow, then bounce.

Directly ahead was the tentlike cap over the borehole, and near it, familiar and unwelcome, the prefab hut. They had bounced over an insulated pipe. They approached another, but frozen water made a serviceable ramp and the buggy was moving slowly, its oversized wheels barely noticing the impact.

The submersible and second fouchian must be near the surface by now. Yet no fouchian shape was obediently waiting for them. And the last buggy . . . where was it now?

Again they were moving, accelerating as rapidly as possible. Whatever Ejy's plan, time seemed precious.

Sarrie stood, half expecting to be told to sit down and keep out of sight. But no one spoke, no one cared. She walked carefully to the back of the utilitarian cabin, dancing around assorted machinery and scrap. From the wide rear window, she gazed out at the bleak ice, and above it, the dark bulk of their ship.

"Where are we going?" she asked. And when Ejy didn't respond in an instant, she became pointedly specific. "When can we go home?"

"The ship is dead," Ejy answered, his voice stolidly grave.

"Did Navren do it—?"

"Not entirely, Sarrie. He and his cohorts were stealing its systems, which left me with no choice. I had to put everything to sleep."

She said nothing.

"Giving him a fully functional ship was unacceptable." A pause. "You do understand, don't you?"

With conviction, she said, "Oh, yes."

Something else was visible on the ice. Something was moving toward the ship. The third buggy?

Ejy kept speaking, in human words and fouchian squeals. "But how dead is dead? Given time and the desire, someone might regain control of any ship." Both voices were trying to reassure. "That's why there is one choice, one course, and you must trust me. Both of you, do you trust me?"

The Voice tried to say, "Yes," immediately, but the fouchian driver was faster. Louder.

"We have supplies here. Power and food and air. We will rescue our friend and leave." A pause. "There is a large team of fouchinas on a nearby world," Ejy reported, now using only human words. "Accompanied by another Artisan, of course. They are exploring a pluto-class world. I have already warned them about our disaster. A reactor mishap, I have called it. At full acceleration, they will arrive in eighteen days."

"What kind of reactor mishap?" Sarrie asked.

But the fouchian answered, already intimate to the details.

"The-Light-That-Blinds-Generations!"

A nuclear explosion, she understood. The ship's reactors were sabotaged, or a bomb was hidden somewhere out of reach. Either way, she realized that the rebellion wasn't too astonishing to catch the Artisans unprepared. How many times in the past had they resorted to booby traps and other outrages?

But she didn't ask, knowing better.

And Ejy made his first and only true mistake. With a mixture of sadness and burgeoning awe, he told his most loyal organics:

"The blast will vaporize much of this crust. We have very little time to waste."

Vaporize the ice, then fling it into the sky, Sarrie realized. Creating an enormous, temporary geyser.

She shuddered, in secret.

Then other secret thoughts followed, one chasing after another, the universe changing in an instant.

The stars and the black between made new again.

SEVEN

The buggy stopped beside the capped borehole.

"Your nest-brother has finally surfaced," Ejy told the driver. "Help him disembark. Help him understand what has happened. And he must, must put on his lifesuit quickly, or what are my choices?"

We will leave your nest-brother behind, thought Sarrie. And you too, if it comes to it.

The fouchian didn't spell out consequences, much less complain. Opening the pilot's hatch, he scrambled down and crossed to the airlock, vanishing.

Calmly, quietly, Sarrie observed, "Artisans can tolerate high radiation levels and heat. If we need to remain here a few minutes longer—"

"But I won't risk *you*," Ejy promised.

"I'm willing to take that risk," she confessed. "If it means saving one or both of my colleagues, I'd do it gladly."

Silence.

But of course she didn't own her life, and it wasn't hers to sacrifice. Was it? Again, she walked to the back of the cabin, watching the doomed ship and the tiny, distant buggy. The buggy was definitely moving toward them, but not fast enough. She imagined its cabin crammed with humans, weighing it down, Navren hunched over his pad, desperately trying to calculate blast strengths and the minimum safe distance.

"What would have happened to us?" she asked.

"What would have happened when?"

"After we put ourselves into cold-sleep." She didn't look at the machine, didn't expose her face to scrutiny. "You wouldn't have dared allow us to wake again. Am I right?"

Outrage, sudden and pure.

"Sarrie," said the shrill voice in her headphones, "Artisans do not casually murder. I intended the cold-sleep as a security measure, to give everyone time to prepare—"

"We couldn't go home again. We might have told the truth."

"2018CC is a large vessel," Ejy reminded her. "There are simple, kind ways to sequester."

With eyes closed, she envisioned such a future. Life in some tiny, secret habitat. Or worse, hidden within the sterile white archives. . . .

"It's happened before, hasn't it?"

"What has?"

"All of this," Sarrie replied, turning to show Ejy her face. Her resolve, she hoped. Her desperate courage. "A team finds unexpected humans. Then they're quarantined. Or they rebel against the Artisans." A moment's hesitation. "How many times have these tragedies happened, Ejy? To you, I mean."

Again, silence.

She turned, squinting at the slow buggy. It was a naked fleck beneath the fine bright snows of the Milky Way. With little more than a whisper, she asked, "How many humans are alive today?"

"I have no way of knowing."

"I believe you," she replied, nodding. "If they're so thick that they've got to come here to find a home—"

"We may very likely have found an exceptional group," Ejy speculated.

"Sophisticated agriculture coupled with the lack of radio noise implies an intentional isolation."

Again, she looked at the machine. "Your telescopes watch the galaxy. You have some idea what's happening there."

"Of course." The old pride flickered. "Judging by radio noise, misaligned com-lasers, and the flash of extremely powerful engines . . . yes, we have a working model." His various arms moved apart as if to show how big the fish was that Ejy had caught. "Since the wars, humans have explored the galaxy, and they have colonized at least several million worlds. . . ."

What astonished Sarrie, what left her numbed to the bone, was how very easily she accepted these impossibilities. Nothing was as she had believed it to be, in life or the universe, and the idea of the Milky Way bursting with her species just confirmed this new intoxicating sense of disorder.

She took a step toward Ejy. "Why lie?" she asked.

Then she answered her own question. "You were instructed to lie. Your human builders ordered you to pretend that the worst had happened, that my species was extinct everywhere but on the Web."

Ejy had to admit, "In simple terms, that's true."

"Can you see any wars now?"

"None of consequence."

"Maybe humans have outgrown the need to fight. Has that possibility occurred to you?"

A long, electric pause.

Then with a smooth, unimpressed voice, the Artisan told her, "You are a child and ignorant, and you don't comprehend—"

"Tell me then!"

"These humans aren't like you anymore. They have many forms, they live extremely long lives. Some possess vast, seemingly magical powers."

Sarrie was shaking, and she couldn't stop.

"But they remain human nonetheless," said Ejy. "Deeply flawed. And the peace you see is temporary. Temporary, and extremely frail."

With an attempt at nonchalance, the Voice stepped closer to Ejy and closer to one of the buggy's walls.

"When the peace fails," the Artisan continued, "every past war will be a spark. An incident. When your species fights again, the entire galaxy will be engulfed."

Turning again, she glanced at the nearest hatch.

"Is that why you brought the Web out here?" she asked, showing him a curious face. "To escape this future war?"

"Naturally," he confessed. "We intend to circle the Milky Way, once or twenty times, and the next cycle of wars will run their course. The galaxy will be devastated, and we, I mean your descendants and myself, will inherit all of it.'' A pause. ''By then, the perfection that we have built—the perfection you embody, Sarrie—will be strong enough to expand across millions of unclaimed worlds.''

She looked straight at Ejy, guessing distances, knowing the machine's most likely response.

Ejy wouldn't kill her.

Not as a first recourse, not when she embodied perfection.

But Ejy noticed something in her face, her posture. With a puzzled tone, he asked, ''Child? What are you thinking?''

''First of all,'' Sarrie replied, ''I'm not a child. And secondly, I can save my friends, I think.''

Servos and adrenaline helped her hand move. And with a sloppy, jarring swat, she caused the rearmost hatch to fly open.

Softly, sadly, Ejy said, ''No.''

Sarrie dove through the open hatch, fell to the ice below, then sprinted toward the prefab hut.

She might have meant the fouchians when she said ''my friends,'' and for as long as possible, Ejy would resist that corrosive belief that his precious Voice—symbol of his goodness—was capable of anything that smelled like rebellion.

Sarrie lived long enough to reach the hut, pausing and turning, hazarding a fast look backward. The Artisan's body was large but graceful, pulling itself out of the same hatch and scrambling over the open ice, already closing the gap. ''No, no, no,'' the whispering in her ears kept saying. ''No, no, no, no . . . !''

She opened both airlock doors, the tiny hut's atmosphere exploding outward as a blinding fog. Then she was inside, in the new vacuum's calm, knowing exactly what to do but her hands suddenly clumsy. Inept. Standing over the bank of monitors and controls, she hesitated for perhaps half a second—for an age—before mustering the will to quickly push the perfect sequence of buttons.

Ample reserve power was left in the borehole's cells, as she had hoped.

She called to the pumps, waking them, then made them pull frigid seawater into the insulated pipes, the utterly reliable equipment utterly convinced that the ship wanted as much of the precious fluid as it could deliver. Now. Hurry. Please.

Through her feet and fingers, Sarrie felt the surging pumps.

More buttons needed her touch. She almost told herself, ''Faster,'' then thought better of it. What mattered most—what was absolutely essential—was to do nothing wrong for as long as possible, and hope it would be long enough. . . .

So focused was Sarrie on her task that she was puzzled, then amazed, to find herself being lifted off the floor . . . and she just managed to give the final, critical command before Ejy had her safely in his grip.

He kept saying. ''No, no, no,'' but the tone of that one word had changed. Sadness gave way to a machine's unnatural fury.

Suddenly she was dragged outside, held by several arms and utterly helpless.

Far out on the table-smooth plain of ice, the twin pipelines closed the same key valves. Yet the pumps kept working, faithful to the end, shoving water into a finite volume and the water resisting their coercion, seams upstream from the closed valves bursting and the compressed water escaping, then freezing in an instant—hundreds of metric tons becoming fresh hard ice every second.

It was happening in the distance, without sound, almost invisibly.

But the Artisan had better eyes than Sarrie, and an infinitely faster set of responses.

Quick surgical bursts of laser light killed the main pumps.

Emergency pumps came on-line, and they were harder to kill—smaller, tougher, and set at a safe distance. Redundancies built on redundancies; the Artisans' driving principle. It took Ejy all of a minute to staunch the flow, killing pumps and puncturing the lines and finally obliterating the tiny hut. But by then a small durable new hill had formed on the plain.

If the buggy could somehow reach that new ice, reach it and use it as a shelter, then some portion of the blast would be absorbed, however slightly, its radiations and fearsome heat muted—

"Why?" cried the Artisan.

She was slammed down on her back—the almost universal position of submission—then again, harder, Ejy drove her into the granitic ice. The impact made her ache, made her want to beg for Ejy to stop. But Sarrie said nothing, and she didn't beg even with her face, and when he saw that bullying did no good, he let her sit up, then more quietly, almost reasonably, said, "Please explain. Please."

At last, the fouchians emerged from the capped borehole. They seemed small, hurried, and inconsequential.

"I know the answer," Sarrie whispered.

No surprise, no hesitation. "What answer?"

"To the xenophobes' scenario. I know how to succeed." She let him see her pride, her authority. "It's simple. They cannot be won over. Never. And it's the good Voice's duty to warn you, to tell you as soon as possible that they're malevolent, and leave you and the other Artisans time to defend the Web—"

"Yes," said Ejy.

Then he added, "It's remarkable. A Voice so young has come to that very difficult answer."

She ignored the praise. Instead she asked quietly, "How many starships have we met, then destroyed?"

"You've destroyed nothing," the Artisan reminded her.

"Responsibility is all yours."

"Exactly."

She felt a shudder, a sudden rippling of the ice.

And so did Ejy. He rose as high as possible on the mechanical legs, measuring a multitude of useless factors, then guessing the answer even as he inquired, "What other clever thing have you done, Sarrie?"

"The plasma drills believe that we need a second borehole. Now."

Crystal eyes pivoted. The laser started hunting for targets.

"You destroyed their control systems," Sarrie warned. "You can't stop them."

Between the scrambling fouchians and Ejy, out of the ancient ice, came a column of superheated vapor, twisting and rising, a wind lashing at everyone in a wild screaming fury.

Sarrie was knocked backward. Knocked free.

She tried to climb to her feet, falling once, then again. Then she was blown far enough that the scorching wind had faded, and she found herself standing, then running, trying to win as much distance as possible.

From her headphones came fouchian squeaks begging for instructions, then Ejy himself calling after her, the voice wearing its own loss.

Sarrie allowed herself to shout:

"Thank you."

A pause.

Then from out of the maelstrom:

"Thank you for what, child?"

"The butterflies," she told Ejy, almost crying now. "I liked them best."

Later, trying to make sense of events, Sarrie was uncertain when the blast came—moments later, or maybe an hour. And she couldn't decide what she saw of the blast, or felt, or how far it must have thrown her. All she knew was that suddenly she was half-wading, half-swimming through slush, and the sky was close and dense, fogs swirling and cooling, then freezing into a pummeling, relentless ice, and she staggered for a time, then stopped to rest, perhaps even sleep, then moved again, eating from her suit's stores and drinking her own filtered urine, and she must have rested two more times, or maybe three, before she saw the tall figure marching along the edge of the fresh pack ice.

She couldn't make out any details. She wasn't even certain if it was exactly a human shape, although some part of her, hoping against reason, decided that it was Lilké, that her friend had survived, and everyone else must be somewhere nearby.

But if it was Lilké, would she forgive? Could she forgive Sarrie for everything?

And of course if it wasn't, then it likely was one of the natives. Whoever they were. Surely *they* would send someone here to investigate the blast . . . to see who was trying to shatter their peaceful world. . . .

Sarrie realized that she could be seeing an immortal, godlike human.

With every last reserve, she started kicking her legs and tossing her arms in the air, thinking: *Whoever or whatever they are, they don't know me.*

THE WIND OVER THE WORLD

Steven Utley

▼

Steven Utley's fiction has appeared in The Magazine of Fantasy & Science Fiction, Universe, Galaxy, Amazing, Vertex, Stellar, Shayol, *and elsewhere. He was one of the best-known new writers of the '70s, both for his solo work and for some strong work in collaboration with fellow Texan Howard Waldrop, but he fell silent at the end of the decade and wasn't seen in print again for more than ten years. In the last few years he's made a strong comeback, however, becoming a frequent contributor to* Asimov's Science Fiction *magazine, as well as selling again to* The Magazine of Fantasy & Science Fiction *and elsewhere. Utley is the coeditor, with Geo. W. Proctor, of the anthology* Lone Star Universe, *the first—and probably the only—anthology of SF stories by Texans. His first collection,* Ghost Seas, *will be coming out next year from Ticonderoga Press. His stories have appeared in our Tenth and Eleventh Annual Collections. He lives in Austin, Texas.*

In the thoughtful story that follows, he takes us back through time to the dawn of terrestrial life, and shows us what happens when someone gets lost along the way. . . .

The attendant barely looked up from the clipboard cradled in the crook of his arm when Leveritt came in. The room was devoid of personality, but just as she entered through one door, a second man dressed in a lab coat went out through a door directly opposite, and in the instant before it swung shut, she glimpsed the room beyond—brightly lit, full of gleaming surfaces—and heard or thought that she heard a low sound like a faint pop of static or the breaking of waves against a shore. She shuddered as an electric thrill of excitement passed through her.

"Please stretch out on the gurney there." The man with the clipboard continued writing as he spoke. "You can stow your seabag on the rack underneath."

Leveritt did as he said. She said, "I feel like I'm being prepped for surgery."

"We don't want you to black out and fall and hurt yourself." He finished writing, came around the end of the gurney to her, and turned the clipboard to show her the printed form. "This," he said, offering her his pen, "is where you log out of the present. Please sign on the line at the bottom there."

Leveritt's hand trembled as she reached for the pen. She curled her fingers into a fist and clenched it tightly for a second, giving the attendant an apologetic smile. "I'm just a little nervous." She tried to show him that she really was just a little

407

nervous by expanding the smile into a grin; it felt brittle and hideous on her face. "I *did* volunteer for this," she told him. I *am* more excited than scared to be doing this, she told herself.

The attendant smiled quickly, professionally. "Even volunteers have the right to be nervous. Try to relax. We've done this hundreds of times now, and there's nothing to it. Ah!"

His exclamation was by way of greeting a second attendant, so like him that Leveritt felt she would be unable to tell them apart were she to glance away for a moment, who escorted a slight figure dressed in new-looking safari clothes and carrying, instead of the high-powered rifle that would have completed his ensemble, a seabag and a laptop. He stowed the bag and climbed onto the gurney next to Leveritt's without being told, signed the log with a flourish, and lay back smiling. He turned his face toward Leveritt and said, "Looks like we're traveling companions—time-traveling companions!" He talked fast, as though afraid he would run out of breath before he finished saying what he had to say. "Allow me to introduce myself—Ed Morris."

"I'm Bonnie Leveritt."

"Please to meet you, Miz Leveritt—or is it Doctor?"

She wondered if he could utter sentences not punctuated with dashes. "Miz," she said, "working on Doctor. I'm on my way to join a field team from Texas A and M."

One of the attendants consulted his wristwatch and nodded to the other, and each picked up a loaded syringe. The man looming over Leveritt gave her that quick, professional smile again. "This is to keep you from going into shock."

She had no particular horror of needles but turned away, nevertheless, to watch Morris, who lay squinting against the glare of the fluorescent lights. She heard him grunt softly as the needle went into his arm.

"It'll be another few minutes," said Leveritt's attendant. He and his twin left. Leveritt and Morris waited.

After a minute or so, he asked her, "How are you holding up?"

"Fine." Her voice sounded strange to her, thick, occluded, like a heavy smoker's. She cleared her throat and spoke the word again; improvement was arguable. "Actually," she confessed, "I'm nervous as hell. This is my first time. It wouldn't be so bad if I didn't have to lie here waiting."

"Supplies go through first—we're down on the priority list, below soap and toilet paper. My first time, I was nervous as hell too. Nobody gives people in my line of work credit for much imagination. Except"—he made a breathless kind of chuckle—"when it comes to creative accounting. Yeah, I'm one of the bean counters. But let me tell you—the night before my first time, I didn't sleep a wink. Not a wink. I kept imagining all sorts of things that might go wrong—plus, it all seemed so unreal, it was all so thrilling—and it was going to happen to *me*. Man! Oh, sure, the concept's more exciting than the reality. There's not much to where we're headed—a little moss and a lot of mud. Beats me why they couldn't've made a hole into some more interesting time period."

"I suppose that depends on your definition of interesting. Besides, as I understand it, they didn't make the hole, they sort of found it. We're lucky it didn't open up on somewhere we couldn't go or wouldn't want to."

"You mean, like my hometown—Dallas?"

Leveritt smiled; she was from Fort Worth. "Worse. For all but the few most recent hundred millions of years, the Earth's been pretty inhospitable—poisonous atmosphere, too much ultraviolet light, things like that."

"Spoken like a true scientist!"

"Not quite a full-blown one yet," she said, "but I guess I've got pedantry down."

"Ah. Well, anyway, as I was saying—I was nervous before my first time. Scared, in fact. You might not think it to look at me," and he paused long enough for her to realize that she was now to take a good look at him, so she did, "but I am no shrinking violet. I have a real active lifestyle—mountain climbing, skydiving. I guess I like heights."

Leveritt was willing to give Morris the benefit of the doubt, but he was a balding little fortyish man whom she could not imagine working his way up a sheer rock face. Dressed in his great-white-hunter outfit, he lay clutching the laptop to his narrow chest, drumming his middle, ring, and little fingers on the case. He looked as calm as though he were waiting for an elevator, but he also looked like what he was, an accountant.

"Still," he went on, "it's one thing to jump out of a plane at ten thousand feet—another to jump through a hole in time. Straight out of the twenty-first century—straight into the prehistoric past! So, I didn't get any sleep. The next day, when it came time for me to make the jump, I was a wreck—all because I was scared, see. But I hid the fact I was a wreck—and you know why? Because I was even more scared that if anybody found out, I wouldn't get to make the jump—getting to do it meant that much to me."

Leveritt gave him another, more heartfelt smile. "It does to me too. But was it rough? The jump itself? I ask everyone I meet who's done it."

Morris screwed up his face and gestured dismissively. "It's no worse'n hitting a speed bump when you're driving a little too fast. Oh, sure, you hear sometimes about people who got bounced around kind of hard, but—speaking from personal experience—I honestly think I could've walked right out of the jump station afterward with nothing more'n a headache and upset stomach. It was nothing. Now I'm less nervous about making the jump than I am about talking funding to this group of entomologists when I get there. Uh, you're not an entomologist yourself, are you?"

"Geologist."

"You ever tried to talk to an entomologist about anything but bugs?"

"Not knowingly, no."

"Then you've never had to pretend to listen to whatever gas some guy wants to vent—"

Leveritt had to laugh. "You obviously have never dated some guys!"

"Ah?" Morris frowned. "No. I sure haven't." Then he got it, or got part of it, anyway, and made another breathless chuckle. "Anyhow, I have to go talk to these entomologists, and they never can—I deal in the definite, see. All they can talk about is the great contributions they're making to science—how vital their work is. I *know* they're making contributions to science—that's why they're there, right? They understand all about bugs. I understand all about money—and never the twain shall meet . . .''

Leveritt found herself tuning out the sense of the words, but she could not tune out the sound of them. The drugs were taking effect; she wanted to relax and drift, but Morris's voice would not let her. She closed her eyes. Scarcely five seconds later, the attendants suddenly returned, one of them announced, "Time to go, folks," and Leveritt's gurney struck the door sharply as it lurched into motion. The air in the jump station had an unpleasant tang to it. Leveritt saw people moving briskly about, heard them muttering to one another, heard that low sound of static or surf again. A technician seated behind a console said, "One minute to next transmission."

"Doesn't matter which one of us goes through first, does it?" Morris asked his attendant, who answered with a shake of his head. The little man grinned at Leveritt. "Then I'll go first and wait for you on the other side."

"No. Please, I need to get this over with. Let me go first."

"Well, guys—you heard the lady."

Leveritt's attendant pushed her gurney quickly past Morris's, past a metal railing, onto the sending-receiving platform. He lightly touched her arm with the back of his hand. "Have a nice trip."

"Thanks."

"Deep breaths, now," he said as he stepped back off the platform.

"Stand by to send," said the technician at the console. "Five seconds. Four."

Leveritt inhaled deeply.

"Three."

Morris caught her eye through the bars of the railing. She was touched by and grateful for his wink of encouragement.

"Two."

She started to exhale.

Everything turned to white light.

The Navy doctor held her eye open between his thumb and forefinger and directed the beam from a penlight into it. She moved her tongue in her mouth, swallowed, and managed to say, "Where'm I?"

"Sickbay."

"I made it? To the Silurian?"

The doctor put away the penlight. "Now, what do you think?"

Leveritt moved her head experimentally and at once regretted it. When the pain had receded, she carefully took stock. She was still on the gurney. There were exposed pipes overhead and a muffled throb of machinery. The ship, she thought, I'm on the ship, in the Silurian, and after a second or two she realized that she was disappointed. She had wondered if being *in* Silurian time would feel somehow different. Thus far, it felt just like a hangover.

The doctor held up a knuckley finger in front of her face. "I want you to follow my finger with your eyes. Don't move your head."

It hurt her even to think about moving her head again. She watched the finger move to the left and back to the right. She said, "My head's killing me."

"You'll be fine in a little while. You're just a little shaken up. Here." He gave her two aspirin tablets and some water in a paper cup. "Stay on the gurney till those take effect. Then we'll see about getting you up on your feet."

"How soon can I get ashore?"

"We generally like to keep new arrivals under observation for at least six hours." Leveritt groaned when he said that, and he gave her a mildly reproachful look. "You can only get ashore by boat, and the next one doesn't leave until late this afternoon."

"It's just that I've been looking forward to this for so long."

"Uh-huh. Well, the Silurian period's still got five or ten million years to run. You aren't going to miss out on it."

The door opened behind him, and a khaki-clad officer leaned in and asked, "Dr. White, may I talk to her now?" Visible in the passageway was an unhappy-looking man in civilian clothes.

"These gentlemen," said the doctor, "have some questions they want to ask you. Feel up to it?"

Before she could reply, the officer said, "Just a couple of routine questions."

"Sure."

The officer moved quickly toward the gurney with the civilian in tow. Dr. White said, "Miz Leveritt, this is Mr. Hales—"

"How do you do?" said the officer, rather too impatiently, she thought.

"—and this is Dr. Cutsinger." The civilian slightly inclined his head in greeting and repeated her name. "The lieutenant is from our operations department. Dr. Cutsinger is one of our civilian engineers."

"Physicist," Cutsinger said, and smiled tightly.

Leveritt tried to sound good-natured. "I was hoping you were the welcoming committee. Isn't anybody going to welcome me to the Paleozoic?" Evidently, no one was. Lieutenant Hales regarded her as though her show of good-naturedness were somehow in poor taste. Cutsinger continued to look unhappy. The doctor nodded at the two men and went out, closing the door behind himself. Leveritt repressed a sigh of bafflement and said, "Well, gentlemen, ask away."

Hales said, "Miz Leveritt."

"Lieutenant?"

He was obviously uncertain as to how to proceed. The lower part of his expression suddenly twisted, rearranging itself into an approximation of a smile; at the same time, a frown intensified the upper part. Considered with his deep-set eyes and hook nose, the effect was ghastly and alarming. Finally, he said, "The, ah, experience of time-travel is never exactly the same for anyone. We like to find out, ah, make a point of finding out how it was for each person each time. Can you describe your experience in detail?"

Leveritt's eyes met Cutsinger's. He blinked and shifted his gaze to a point slightly to the right of her ear. She refocused on Hales and said, "I'm afraid there were no details, just a blinding flash of light."

Hales seemed disappointed by her answer. "What about before the jump? Did anything in the jump station strike you as unusual?"

If you weren't so intense, Leveritt thought, that question would be funny. "It was all unusual to me, because, as you surely must know already, this was my first jump."

"Of course. We want your impressions, though. Anything you can tell us, anything at all. Before the flash of light, when they took you into the jump station—you and Ed Morris. Do you know him well?''

She saw something shift in Cutsinger's face as he glanced at the lieutenant, saw his expression of general unhappiness sharpen into one of very particular contempt. To the oblivious Hales she said, ''I don't know him at all. We met a few minutes before the jump, and he talked my ear off. I think you'd do better to ask him these questions. As you surely must also know, Mr. Morris'd made at least one jump before this. He can tell you if anything was unusual or not. As for me''—she swung her legs over the edge of the gurney and sat up—''if I'm going to answer any more questions, it's going to be in an upright position.''

After a second's hesitation, she slid off the gurney, onto her feet. Cutsinger said, ''Are you all right?''

''A little rubbery in the knees, like I just came in off the jogging trail. Otherwise—'' She stepped away from the gurney, quickly stepped back, leaned on it for support, admitted, ''Still a little wobbly.'' She locked eyes with the lieutenant. ''What is it in particular you're driving at? I somehow can't help feeling you know something and are dying to know if I know it too.''

Hales turned the full force of his grimace on her again, and she realized with a jolt that he now intended it to be a look of reassurance. ''As I said, these are just routine questions.''

And possibly excepting my six-year-old nephew, you are the worst, the most unconvincing liar I've ever known. She almost said it aloud. What stopped her was the thought of all the time and effort she had put into getting this far—to a room, as she saw it, adjoining the prehistoric past—and how much farther there was to go. Fist on hip, she waited.

Hales, however, clearly was at a loss. He turned to Cutsinger, who, no less clearly, was close to losing his temper. ''Anything you can think of to ask her?''

''I told you there was no point to this!''

''I wish to *God*,'' said Leveritt, ''one of you would tell me what this is all about.'' Neither man spoke. ''Fine. Have it your way. But if I don't get out of this room, I'm going to go insane. The doctor said I wouldn't be able to go ashore for hours, but if you're *through*, I'd at least like to take a look outside. Okay? Please?''

Cutsinger brushed past Hales. He said, ''Permit me,'' and offered Leveritt his arm.

A romantic, she thought, taking it.

''I think,'' Hales said, ''Miz Leveritt had better remain in sickbay.''

Not looking back at him, Cutsinger said, ''Take a flying leap.''

''Master-at-arms!''

A bluejacket with a sidearm suddenly filled the doorway. Cutsinger sighed, shrugged, and said, ''Sorry,'' as he directed Leveritt to a chair.

''I'm sorry too,'' said Hales, ''but this is a United States Navy ship, and the rules of security are in force. Miz Leveritt, I want you to understand that this interview is confidential.''

''So much for the subtle approach!'' Cutsinger said sourly.

Hales ignored him. ''You're not to repeat any part of our conversation to anybody or make any record of it without express authorization. Any breach—''

''I'm sure she gets the idea, Lieutenant.''

"Not at all," said Leveritt. "What am I not supposed to talk about?"

"We have a situation," Cutsinger said quickly, before Hales could open his mouth to answer her, "an unprecedented one, I might add, which is why Hales here's so rattled, why he's handling it in such a ham-handed manner. Ham-headed too." The lieutenant's mouth did open now, in a threat display. Cutsinger met it with a glower and continued talking. "About all he's really going to accomplish by invoking security is to make it impossible for you to do the work you came here to do."

Leveritt gave Hales an even look. "I didn't come all this way just to fight the Navy."

"There're some thousands of people living and working here," said Hales, "and in the interest of general morale, we have got to keep rumors and misinformation from spreading and panic from breaking out."

"You're the one who's panicked! Either leave her alone or tell her. She'll hear all about it soon enough."

"Don't underestimate Navy security," Hales said stiffly.

That elicited a harsh laugh from Cutsinger. "I bet you anything it was all over the ship inside of five minutes. I bet you it's already gotten ashore, some version of it, anyhow. All you're doing is putting Miz Leveritt in a very awkward position. She'll be the only person in the whole expedition who won't have an opinion on what everybody else is talking about."

"Master-at-arms, Dr. Cutsinger is needed back at the jump station."

"Aye, aye, sir." The bluejacket stepped to Cutsinger's side.

"Tell her," Cutsinger said over his shoulder as he went out, "for God's sake, *tell* her."

The bluejacket closed the door behind himself, and Hales said, "Well." He looked at Leveritt; his features relaxed; he almost smiled a real smile. "Please accept my apologies on Dr. Cutsinger's behalf. As a civilian aboard a Navy ship, he naturally finds working under Navy supervision irksome at times."

"By supervision, do you mean armed guard?"

"I mean—I am not a martinet or a horse's patoot." He took a step toward the door. "Please come with me. I have enough to worry about without you going insane."

He led her down the passageway and opened a heavy steel door at the end of it. As Leveritt stepped through the doorway and onto a catwalk, a breeze touched her face and ruffled her hair. Her first, quick 180-degree survey took in the fact that the ship and some lesser vessels lay off a rocky coast. She gripped the railing with both hands and inhaled the scent of sea salt and the faintly oily smell of the ship. From a deck overhanging the catwalk came the sounds of a helicopter warming up its motor and spinning its blades. Below, waves smacked noisily against the hull. The midmorning sun was behind the ship, in whose great angular shadow the water was blue-black, almost slate-colored. Close by, two auxiliary craft rode at anchor, and beyond them a glittering expanse of blue-green water stretched to a line of sea cliffs. Even as she stared, transfixed by the sight of that shore, another, even smaller craft—not a Navy vessel at all, but a sailboat—came into view around the headland. Against the somber cliffs, its sail looked like a blazing fire. "Oh, my." She breathed the words.

Hales had followed her onto the catwalk. He rested his elbows on the railing and did not look at her when he spoke. "Dr. Cutsinger did tell me there'd be no point in questioning you. If there'd been any way to find out what we need to know without actually asking you. . . ."

She realized after a moment that what he was saying must be important, but it took an effort of will to turn her attention from the Silurian vista, and she was scarcely able to say, "I beg your pardon?"

"He also talked me out of sending you right back to the twenty-first century. He *may* have talked me out of confining you to the ship until we get this, this situation straightened out."

Now Leveritt could not take her eyes off him. "I swear to you, I don't know anything and won't talk to anybody about anything. Please just let me go off into the hinterlands and collect rocks like I'm supposed to."

Hales almost smiled again. "He said I'm treating everyone here like children. I'm not trying to, I'm really not. I see his point." He made a gesture that seemed meant to take in everything around them. "This is the greatest thing since the moon landings, and a lot less exclusive. Every single person here, Navy as well as civilian, wants to be here and volunteered to be here. Dr. Cutsinger's view is, we're all grownups and deserve to be told the truth like grown-ups. All the truth all the time."

Leveritt asked, "And what's your view?" And when he did not answer immediately, "Or doesn't the Navy let you have one?"

"Right the second time. All of us here, we're an extension of our nation. There're all these little communities of scientists scattered about, and there's the Navy, delivering supplies, providing transport, holding things together. The Silurian Earth's a United States possession, Miz Leveritt, American territory, and the Navy's here to guard our national interests. It is in the national interest that the Navy decides what is classified matter. Only persons who need to know about classified matter to perform an official job for the Navy are entrusted with the information. That's rule number one, and it leaves you out. Rule number two is, persons to whom classified matter is entrusted are responsible for protecting it against unauthorized disclosure. That hems me in."

"Fine. What're you going to do with me?"

"Escort you back to sickbay. Later, I hope, see you on your way to go collect rocks."

It was late in the short Silurian day when Hales guided Leveritt through the ship to the boat bay. From a platform above that noisy grotto, she watched as the last supplies were loaded, then with a nod to the lieutenant, descended to the boat. The coxswain helped her aboard. Hales surprised her by climbing down after her. He gave no sign that he heard her when she asked, "Are you going to keep watch on me from now on?" She found a seat amidships; he gave her a nod as he took the one next to hers but said nothing.

She was too excited, however, to resent his presence. She had had sleep, a shower, and her first food in almost twenty-four hours, and the morning's frustrations and mystifications were falling away behind her. When she ran her eye over the neatly stowed boxes and crates, the words BATHROOM TISSUE prompted something too fleeting to be called a memory. The bay's gates opened. Leveritt looked up, caught a glimpse of someone who could have been Cutsinger on the platform, and glanced at Hales to gauge his reaction. His attention, though, was directed forward rather than upward. The boat slid out, sliced across the ship's lengthening, darkening shadow, and emerged suddenly into sunlight. She gazed shoreward, at the drowned valley's rocky walls, and felt that at last she truly was entering Paleozoic time. Not even the sight of the pier, jutting out from the near shore below a cluster of Quonset huts and tents, dispelled the feeling. She spared the ship a single backward glance. Everything in its shadow, everything aboard it, contained by it—even the air circulating through it and the seawater sloshing within the confines of its boat bay—belonged to the twenty-first century. She looked shoreward again and thought of the great steel monster no more.

Several boats, including a tiny blue-hulled sailboat, were tied up at the pier. Indistinct human figures waiting there gradually resolved themselves into a small party of Navy men in tropical khakis and two civilians who stood apart both from them and from each other. Both civilians wore white suits, but one man was short, stout, and sunburnt, and the other was tall as well as thickset, tanned rather than burnt, and had a Panama hat with a purple hatband set at a rakish angle atop his squarish head. It was clear from his bearing that he considered himself to be a vision. Leveritt laughed when she saw him, waved, and called out, "Rob! Rob Brinkman!"

Brinkman waved back, and when the boat had been tied up he reached down and offered Leveritt his enormous brown hand. She was a medium-sized woman, heavier in the hips than she cared to be, but he seemed to lift her right out of the boat and onto the pier with only minimal assistance from her. His grin and voice were as big as the rest of him. "Welcome to the Silurian!"

Leveritt hugged him. She could not quite encircle his torso with her arms. "It's about *time* someone here said that to me. What a suit! What a hat! Is this what you wear on collecting trips now?"

"Only if pretty grad students are going along."

Behind her, somebody peevishly said, "I'm supposed to meet Ed Morris. I'm Michael Diehl, from the San Diego Natural History Museum."

As Brinkman stepped around Leveritt to ask a bluejacket to hand up her gear, she saw the other civilian peering anxiously into the boat, as though he expected to spot Ed Morris trying to hide from him among the cargo. The party of Navy men had got immediately to work unloading the boat, and their interest in Diehl did not extend beyond his keeping out of their way. Hales, however, introduced himself and said, "I regret that Mister Morris is unable to come ashore at this time."

"Eh? Why not?"

"Side-effects of the jump."

"Oh. Well, you could've radioed that piece of information and saved me an hour's wait for nothing. Could've saved yourself a boat ride too."

Hales noticed Leveritt watching him. He favored Diehl with a mild version of his frown-above, smile-below expression. "Boat rides're what the Navy's all about."

Brinkman turned with Leveritt's seabag on his shoulder and said, "Okay," and the two of them walked away. The pier came straight off the camp's main thoroughfare, which was paved with metal matting and lined with huts. Tents had been erected along intersecting streets. There was a good deal of pedestrian traffic, both civilian and Navy. Brinkman led Leveritt past supply, generator, and administration buildings, the dispensary, the exchange, the mess—"the Navy part of camp," he told her, adding, "But we get to use the facilities, of course." Civilian personnel lived in and worked out of a group of tents he called the suburbs. "Our people're already upriver, so, tonight, you'll be the guest of a bunch of centipede enthusiasts."

"How charming."

"It'd probably be a good idea to shake out your shoes in the morning. Want some dinner?"

"I think all I want tonight," she said, "is to walk a little way past the last row of tents, where I can pure and unadulterated Paleozoic."

"Care for a guide?"

She gave him a sidelong mock-wary lock. "Not if it's some notorious lady-killer in an ice-cream suit."

Brinkman laughed. "Just make sure you keep the camp on your left when you go out, or you'll wind up in the marsh. And don't go out too far, either. And don't stay up too late."

"Yes, Mother."

"We leave right after breakfast, and around here breakfast is at sunrise."

He showed her where she was to spend the night. None of the centipede enthusiasts was about, so Leveritt put her seabag just inside the door, bade him good night, and with no further ado set out on her walk. Not far beyond the last row of tents, the ground rose sharply; the going was not especially rough, but she did not push her luck—the sun was sinking fast, and she did not fancy making her way across unfamiliar ground in the dark. Just as she reached a ledge from which she could look down into the camp, a thin bugle call announced the commencement of the evening colors ceremony. Electric lights illuminated the camp, and she had no trouble spotting the flagpole. There came a second bugle call, followed by the national anthem. The flag sank slowly out of sight behind a Quonset hut. Out on the water, the shadow of the Earth itself swallowed up the ship. Leveritt sat down on warm smooth rock, lay back to look up at the purpling, then blackening, sky, and finally felt herself part of Silurian reality, *in* Paleozoic time and space. Contentment filled her.

How long she remained thus, she did not know. The moon rose, the unrecognizable stars slightly shifted their positions. Eventually, she became aware that the rock had cooled without getting any softer. She got up and walked slowly toward camp. As she came among the tents, she heard voices and music from some of them and noticed that traffic had thinned. No insects orbited the lights, unexpectedly reminding her that no birds had wheeled and screeched over the bay. She knew, of course, that the Silurian was too early for birds and insects—flying insects, at least—but until this moment she had not appreciated their absence.

Just before she reached her tent, she saw Michael Diehl approaching. His face held a sickly cast, and he appeared to have his entire attention focused on the ground before him. When she started to go inside, however, he called out, "Excuse me, these tents're reserved for the San Diego Natural History Museum."

"Rob Brinkman said there's an extra cot. He's the—"

"Brinkman. Texas A and M." Diehl was near enough now for her to catch a whiff of what he breathed out. His red complexion, she decided, was not wholly the result of too much sun.

"We're on our way upriver in the morning," she said, "so it'll only be—"

"You're the woman who came in on the boat with Lieutenant Hales. Leveritt, isn't it?"

"Yes. And your name's Diehl. Look, if there's a problem, I'm sure Dr. Brinkman can—"

"You made the jump this morning. With Ed Morris."

"Yes." She said it quickly and said no more, not wanting to be cut off again.

Diehl glanced to left and right. "I think you'd better come with me. I know where we can have a drink and talk in private."

"Um, thank you for the offer, but I'm very tired, and I need to—"

"You're the only one I can talk to about what's happened to Ed Morris!" There was a note of pleading in the whiskey-scented voice. "And I'm the only one *you* can talk to."

"What? What's happened to Ed Morris?"

Diehl looked closely at her. "You don't know? No, I can see you don't. You didn't really see it happen. I guess nobody really saw it. And Hales didn't tell you, did he? No, of course he didn't. He laid that Navy security stuff on me too. Tried to hand me some crap, and when I raised holy hell and threatened to go straight to his commanding officer—"

"*What* about Ed Morris?"

"There was an accident! Come on, let's go where we can talk. We're too close to the Navy here."

She hesitated as he walked past, got as far into a protest as "I don't think I'm supposed," then followed him back the way she had just come, up the slope behind the camp, to the ledge. Diehl wiped the mouth of a small flask on his coat sleeve and offered it to her. She declined to accept. He took a drink, gasped, and replaced the screwtop.

"Ed Morris," he said, "didn't come through the hole today like he was supposed to."

"What do you mean?"

"Just what I said. Hales told me—after I made him tell me—Morris made the jump one minute after you, but he never arrived here. He's gone. Lost."

"Gone, lost—where?"

Diehl shook his head. "They don't know."

"But—"

"They don't *know*! They honestly don't. Maybe it was some glitch in the machinery that did it, or sunspots. Maybe some quirk of the hole itself, something they don't know about. I frankly don't think they know much more about the hole now than they did in the beginning."

"But how do you *lose* somebody?"

"You gotta remember what a strange thing the hole is. When they first stumbled across it, all they knew was, here's this strange thing. This anomaly. They sent in robot probes to get specimens, photograph everything in sight. By and by, they figured out what they had was this doorway into the past. But it didn't just open up on *a* place on *a* day. It wasn't that stable. There was a sort of flutter, and it caused what they call spatial drift and temporal spread. So, two probes might go through together on our side, the twenty-first-century side, but come out miles and years apart on the Silurian side. That's why they built the jump stations. They built one of them aboard that ship and pushed the ship through the hole so they could keep things synchronized on both sides of the hole. It all worked perfectly, until today. Today, Ed Morris may've been plunked down anywhere. Far inland or far out to sea. He may've arrived a hundred years ago or a hundred years from now."

"Alive?" She was barely able to ask it.

"Not for long. Not unless he's a helluva lot smarter and luckier'n Robinson Crusoe. And if he was hurt—"

"How awful. That poor man."

"If he was really lucky, he never knew what happened. Never felt a thing. Hales says he may just've been scattered across four hundred million years."

Leveritt felt a chill of horror, though she could not have said what being scattered across four hundred million years might entail.

"He says everything's working again," Diehl went on, "they're sending and receiving again, but until they figure out what went wrong—" He abandoned the sentence to take another drink. "Everything we use here, food, supplies, it's all gotta come through the hole. And the hole—"

Leveritt knew what he was about to say and said it for him. "The hole's the only way home."

"You got that right! The only way!"

She looked upward. The moon was slightly higher in the sky than when she had seen it—how long before? Half an hour? Then, she had experienced a happiness greater than any other she could remember. Now, she felt oppressed, weighed down.

They were silent for almost a minute. Then, as Diehl tilted his head back to drink, Leveritt said, "Well, what can we do about it?"

Diehl smacked his lips. "Indeed, what? Doesn't seem right. It *isn't* right. A man dies, vanishes—whatever's applicable in this case. He's got no family or friends far's I can find out, and there's nothing to bury. And nobody's supposed to talk about him, so he won't even get a memorial service. Not even if he did have family and friends."

"Mr. Diehl, I don't think we should—"

"It isn't right! Know what really sets us apart from the animals? Never mind what religion says about souls. Souls're just puffs of air. The only thing makes a man's death meaningful is remembrance. Without remembrance, he's just a wind that blew over the world and never left a trace."

"Mr. Diehl! I don't think we should talk about him anymore. I don't think we should meet again, either."

"Huh? Why not?"

"If Lieutenant Hales finds out we've had this conversation and that I know about Ed Morris—"

"To hell with Hales! Don't be scared of him, stand up to him like I did!"

"He may not be able to make trouble for you," Leveritt said impatiently, "but I think he can make a lot for me. It's already occurred to him to either send me back home or lock me up. Will you give me your word you won't let him find out?"

"Bastard's not gonna hear a thing from me. And if you're upriver, he can't bother you any."

"I wish I could be sure of that. I'm—listen, from the moment I learned about the hole, I wanted to join this expedition. I worked hard to get here. Now that I *am* here . . ."

Her voice trailed off in a sob; her throat constricted as she sensed impending, insupportable loss, and tears gathered on her eyelashes. She clenched her jaw and fists and held on, somehow, to her composure. Beside her, Diehl coughed and said in his thickened voice, "Still some left, how 'bout it?" And when she had blinked away the tears, she saw him holding the flask out to her again.

"No," she said, "thank you."

"You ever drink?"

"Hardly ever."

"Same here," and he raised the flask to his lips.

"Well," she said, and went carefully down the slope and directly to her tent. The camp had grown quiet, and most of the electric lights had been extinguished. A middle-aged woman answered her knock and let her get barely one sentence into an explanation before inviting her inside and introducing herself as Carol Hays.

"Rob Brinkman met me in the mess tent," Hays said, "and told me to expect you. Sorry nobody was here earlier, but we were probably still sluicing the mud off ourselves. We've been slogging around in the marsh all day."

Leveritt let Hays introduce her to a sleepy-looking young woman. She instantly forgot the woman's name but managed to smile and say, "Dr. Brinkman told me you're centipede enthusiasts."

Hays made a mock-horrified face and then laughed, and the young woman, affecting a tolerably good Dixie-belle drawl, said, "We have *found* that gentlemen do not look at us quite so *askance* if we refer to ourselves as entomologists."

Did either of you know Ed Morris? Leveritt wanted to ask. She was grateful that they were very tired and not such good hosts that they would stay awake on her account.

Soon, on her cot, in the dark, she lay listening to their soft, regular breathing and trying to resist falling immediately asleep. She had realized as soon as she laid her head down that she was exhausted, but she felt herself under an obligation, at the end of a day she regarded as the most momentous of her life, to spend some time sifting through its events, analyzing and categorizing, summing up. She could not, however, keep everything straight on the ledger page before her mind's eye; Ed Morris kept shoving everything else aside. Then, when she thought pointedly about what must have happened to him, her imagination was drawn not to visions of accidents resulting in death, but to one of a human figure stretched like a rubber band from the top of the geologic column toward an indefinite point at the mid-Paleozoic level. The figure was alive. It writhed across almost half a billion years.

She recoiled from that image, and another promptly presented itself: Ed Morris as a straight line continually approaching a curve but never meeting it within finite distance.

But perhaps, she told herself, he met a real death instead of some exotic asymptotic fate. Perhaps he's at the bottom of the bay. . . .

If I'd let him make the jump before me, it would've been me who . . .

And Morris might've been sitting out there with Diehl tonight, trying to think of something to say about a person he'd barely known for five minutes.

Or maybe not. Diehl wouldn't even have known who Morris was talking about. . . .

She awoke remembering no dreams. The sky had only begun to lighten; she showered and dressed and was packed and waiting to go when Brinkman came for her. He wore old khaki now, and a hat that needed blocking. After a quick breakfast, they went directly to the pier. There was fog enough so that, viewed from the pier's end, the camp seemed obscured by curtains of gauze. Nothing could be seen of the vessels in the bay.

Leveritt and Brinkman stepped aboard the boat that was to carry them upriver. There was no ceremony, no one to see them on their way, and they were the only passengers. They sat under a white canopy and drank coffee from a thermos bottle as the lines were cast off and the boat nosed into the current. Pier and camp receded and were soon lost from sight; by the time the fog lifted, they lay behind a bend in the river. The view from the boat was of barren heights and marshy borders. Dense Lilliputian forests of primitive plants covered the low, muddy islets. At length, Brinkman put his face close to Leveritt's and said, "Hello."

She started, drew back, looked at him in astonishment.

"I said hello, Bonnie. Before that, I said I think it's going to be a beautiful day." He aimed a finger vaguely skyward. "You know, dazzling blue sky, fleecy white clouds."

"Sorry. I must've—I was in a trance."

"I'll say."

She nodded toward the marsh. "I guess I've probably seen nearly every documentary ever made about the Silurian. But I never imagined how quiet it is here. Life on Earth hasn't found its voice yet. Hasn't hit its stride." She broke into a grin. "I think I'm quoting from one of those old documentaries."

"I doubt it," said Brinkman. "I bet everybody here is secretly, mentally narrating a documentary every second of the day."

The boat bisected the silent world. Brinkman pulled his hat down over his eyes, folded his arms, and slept. After a time, Leveritt realized, and was by fast turns surprised and appalled to realize, that the vista bored her.

It can't be! she thought in panic.

It isn't, she thought a moment later. It's something else. I'm distracted.

By Ed Morris.

Leveritt sprawled on her cot, arms and legs dangling over the edge because she could not bear her own blistering touch. It was a hot evening and humid, so sticky that her face stung and her T-shirt and boxer shorts adhered to her skin, pasted to it with perspiration. Her tentmate, Gilzow, lay on the other cot, a wet handkerchief over her face. The flaps were drawn at both ends of the tent; from time to time, the air between the two women stirred discreetly, trying, it seemed to Leveritt, to attract as little attention as possible when it did so.

Finally, she delivered herself of a theatrical groan to signal that she was giving up on the notion of falling asleep. She sat up, lit the lantern, and wiped her face and throat with a damp cloth. She said, "And I thought Texas summers were miserable."

Through her handkerchief, Gilzow said, "Look at the bright side. No mosquitoes. No fire ants, either."

"But no shade trees to sit under, and no grass to sit on. And no watermelon to eat out on the grass, out under a tree."

Gilzow lifted a corner of the handkerchief and peeked out. "You know what'd really be nice right now? Cold beer. Not that awful Navy stuff, I mean, *real beer*. Fine, manly beer so cold it's got ice crystals suspended in it. Or rum and Coke, in a big tall glass, with lots of ice cubes. Mm-hmm. Cool us off and render us insensible at the same time." She let the corner of the handkerchief fall back into place. "I cannot believe there isn't a drop of anything to drink in this whole camp."

"Well, at least we can get Cokes and ice at the supply tent."

Gilzow sighed, barely audibly above the lantern's hiss. Then she plucked the handkerchief off her face and sat up. "I'm willing to forego insensibility," she said, "if I can only cool off. Just let me find my sandals."

Leveritt slipped outside and waited, listening. The camp was on a low bluff overlooking the river valley. Behind the bluff was a rocky flatland extending to distant hills. By day it stood revealed in all its stark desolation; nothing moved on the plain that wind or rain did not move, for only down in the valley, along the river's winding course, was there life. Between sunset and sunrise, the flatland lay vast and black, as mysterious as sea depths, while the night resounded with the cracking of cooling rocks.

Gilzow emerged. Theirs was the one undarkened tent, and the sky was overcast, but the obscured full moon cast enough light for them to see their way through the camp. No one else was about. The tents were open, however, and out of them came snatches of conversation, murmurings about heat and humidity and the day's work and the next day's prospects. When they overheard a man say, "Roger, where's that *rain* you predicted?" they paused, Gilzow literally in midstep, balanced on one foot, until Roger answered, "I think the rainclouds must've gotten themselves snagged on those jumbly old hills." Leveritt walked on, Gilzow hopped and skipped to catch up, and her soft laughter hung in the unmoving air.

"Jumbly old hills!" She glanced back over her shoulder at the tent. "I don't think Roger's actually supposed to be doing what he does. I think he's a meteorologist who got lost on his way to becoming a poet."

"Listen to you!"

"It's true. He once showed me some poems he'd written, and I memorized one of them." Gilzow stopped walking, struck a pose, and recited:

> *"Australopithecus' sleep*
> *is fitful, for it seems*
> *that Australopithecus*
> *isn't used to having dreams."*

"That's not poetry," Leveritt said, "it's doggerel. And besides, I'm sure australopithecines could—"

"Oh, get a sense of humor, Bonnie."

Stung, Leveritt opened her mouth to reply, but no retort occurred to her.

"Sorry, Bonnie." Gilzow sounded sincerely contrite. "This heat and humidity—"

"It's okay," Leveritt said stiffly. "It's—I'm a born pedant."

On their way back from the supply tent, carrying a cooler between themselves and each holding an opened soft drink by its throat in her free hand, they came upon two men. Gilzow said, "Mike, Roger."

Mike Holmes and Roger Ovington turned, and the former said, "Hi, Lou. Bonnie. Hot enough for you?"

"Blah. About that rain, Roge."

"Paleozoic weather's as capricious as Cenozoic." Ovington nodded toward the hills. "But it's coming. We just saw some lightning flashes way off on the horizon."

"Bonnie 'n' I're going to have to drown our sorrows in straight Coca-Cola unless somebody around here's got some rum or something he'd consider swapping for bizarre sexual favors."

"Sorry," said Holmes, "sorrier than I know how to tell you," and he gave a little laugh obviously intended to show that he might not be kidding. Gilzow laughed, too, to show that she definitely was. Leveritt could only marvel at her tentmate's self-possession. She herself could think of nothing to say, could think nothing, in fact, except, We're all four of us standing here in our underwear.

"Well," Gilzow said, "come sit on the cliff with us anyway. We also grabbed some crackers and a can of chicken salad."

"Then stand back, girls," Holmes said, "because we take big bites."

They sat among the rocks at the edge of the bluff and dangled their feet over an inky void—by night, the valley was abyssal. They ate and spoke of nothing in particular. All four of them started at a very loud pop of fracturing rock, and Ovington said, "It doesn't take much imagination to populate the darkness here with giant crustacean monsters clacking their claws."

Gilzow leaned close to Leveritt and said in a low voice, "I rest my case."

Holmes said to Ovington, "Sometimes you are a weird person."

Ovington laughed. "To me, prehistoric still means big ugly monsters. Hey, I'm just a weatherman, okay? I can't tell a psychophyte—what is it?"

"Psilophyte," said Gilzow.

"I can't tell a psilophyte from creamed spinach. To me, a trilobite's just a waterlogged pillbug. And it doesn't matter what time period I'm in, meteorology's the same here as it is back home. Trade winds blow from the east, a high-pressure system's still—everything's *different* for the rest of you."

"Not for me and Bonnie," said Holmes. "Rocks is rocks."

"Still." Ovington gestured at the overcast sky. "The *Milky Way's* different, yet it looks the same to me here as it does back home. One of the astronomers told me once that in the time between now and the twenty-first century, our little solar system is going to make almost two complete trips around the rim of the galaxy.''

"You try to imagine that," Leveritt said quietly, "but you just can't.''

"When I was a kid," said Gilzow, "I drove myself just about nuts trying to deal with geologic time and cosmic immensity. I started collecting models of geologic time, copying them out of science books and science-fiction novels, into a notebook. I must've ended up with a couple or three dozen. Like, if the Earth's age were compressed into twelve months, or twenty-four hours, or sixty minutes. Or how, if you put a dime on top of the world's tallest building, the height of the building would represent the entire age of the Earth, and the thickness of the dime would represent how long humans've been around."

"I like that one," Ovington said, and laughed. "I like it a lot!''

"My favorite," said Holmes, extending both arms out from his sides, "has always been the one my dad taught me when I was ten. The span of my arms, he said, was how long life had existed on Earth. And all of human history and pre-history fit on the edge of my fingernail."

"Dang," said Gilzow, "where's my notebook?''

They fell silent. Minutes passed, irregularly punctuated by the sounds of splintering rock and faint, unmistakable thunder.

"Do you suppose," Leveritt said suddenly, and tried to keep herself from asking the question that had been forming in her for weeks, since the night before the boat had brought her from the camp on the estuary, tried to make herself stop, but it had to come out now, had to, now, "do you suppose that if somebody came from the twenty-first century and died here in the Silurian, he'd cease to exist back in the future?''

The others' faces turned toward her. She could not see their expressions clearly but did not think she needed to see them to imagine their collective thought, What a truly *stupid* question!

Holmes said, "Whoa," but not sarcastically, and then, "Run that by me again.''

Encouraged, she said, "I mean, would that person still be born and grow up to come back through time and die four hundred million years before he's born? Or would he be erased from existence? Would he have never been?''

"Actually," said Ovington—it was, Leveritt realized with gratitude, his kind of question—"there's a story about someone who decided to tackle that very matter. This was back in the early days of the expedition, when everybody was jittery about creating paradoxes. All this person did was bring back some lab animals and kill them.''

"What happened?" Leveritt said.

"Nothing happened. You could say the experiment annihilated the animals but didn't annihilate them from having been. Or so the story goes. It may not be a true story.''

"What if—" Leveritt cut herself short. What if what? What if somebody were to be scattered across four hundred million years, what then? "Nothing. Never mind.''

Gilzow turned back to Ovington. "What you're saying, if that story's not true, is that the matter *hasn't* been settled.''

"Well, by now, it surely has. People've been in Paleozoic time long enough."

"Long enough, anyway," said Holmes, "so nobody can tell the true stories from the weird rumors. All these myths're building up. Everybody repeats them, nobody knows if there's anything to them or not. Like the one about the government's secret plan to dump reactor waste in the Silurian."

"Actually," Ovington said, "the way I heard that story, if it is the same story, is that some generals tried to figure out a military application for a hole into the Silurian. Their plan was to sow Eurasia and Gondwanaland with nukes, so later on, whenever the infidels and darkies got out of line—"

Holmes guffawed, and Gilzow said, "It's got to be true!"

"No," said Holmes, "it can't be, it's too stupid."

"It's so stupid it *has* to be true."

"Maybe it is," said Ovington, "and maybe it isn't, but this much is certain— the United States isn't sharing the hole with anybody!"

Then, Leveritt thought, there's the story about the man who jumped through— into? across?—time and never came—out? down? Anyway, he vanished as though he'd never been. No one could tell he'd ever been, because nobody was supposed to talk about him.

And there's a woman in the story who worked hard to get someplace, do something, be somebody. She found true happiness for maybe a whole hour. Afterward, she kept wondering what had happened to it, what had gone wrong. She was no quitter, never had been, but her work somehow wasn't as fulfilling as she'd expected, and everyone around her thought she was a humorless prig.

But those were just symptoms. The problem—

Thunder rolled across the flatland, louder than before. Leveritt looked and saw a lightning-shot purple sky. The air suddenly moved and grew cool, eliciting a duet of *ahs* from Gilzow and Holmes and a full-throated cry of "*Yes!*" from someone in camp. Ovington rose and shouted in that direction, "I *told* you it was coming!" To the others on the bluff, he said, "Gotta run, work to do," and rushed off.

"Guess we'd better go batten down," said Holmes.

"Just toss everything into the cooler," Gilzow told him. "Bonnie 'n' I'll clean it up later."

He did as she said, and then they picked up the cooler between themselves and hurried away.

Leveritt did not follow. The problem, she sat thinking, really was that the woman thought she was in a different story, her own, instead of the one about the man who vanished. Every time she turned around, there was his ghost. She couldn't make him go away. There was no place else for him to go, no one else who would take him in. No one else knew who he was because she wasn't supposed to talk about him.

Stop haunting me, Ed Morris. Stop.

The first heavy raindrop struck Leveritt on the back of the hand. She got to her feet and found herself leaning into a stiffening wind, squinting against airborne grit, in some danger of being either blown off the bluff or else blinded and simply blundering over the edge. She saw a bobbing point of light that had to be a lantern and concentrated on walking straight at it.

The rain started coming down hard. She found her tent, but as she bent to duck under the flap, she smelled ozone and felt a tingling all over her body, a mass stirring of individual hairs. Everything around her turned white, and she jerked back. For a timeless interval, she saw or imagined that she could see every upturned, startled face and wrinkled square inch of tent fabric in camp, every convolution of the roiling clouds above, everything between herself and the faraway hills, every rock, every fat drop of water hurtling earthward. At an impossible distance from her, yet close enough for her to see his safari garb and the dark flat square object he held, was a slight man whose expression both implored and accused.

The thunderclap smashed her to the ground. She came up on hands and knees, blinded, deafened, screaming, "I *remember* you, goddammit, what do you *want?*"

Strong hands closed around her wrist and forearm and dragged her out of the rain. Someone wiped her face with a cloth. At first, she could see nothing and heard only a ringing in her ears. Gradually, she made out Gilzow's face, saw the look of concern, even alarm, in her wide blue eyes, saw her lips move and heard the sound of her voice though not the words she spoke. Leveritt shook her head. Gilzow stopped trying to talk to her and unself-consciously helped her remove her wet underclothes. There was a second lightning strike close by the camp, and thunder as loud and sharp as a cannonade. Leveritt toweled herself dry, pulled on khaki pants and a flannel shirt, found her voice at last.

"I'm fine."

"You don't sound fine to me."

She did not sound fine to herself. "I was just dazzled by the lightning."

"You're lucky you weren't fried by it. I don't guess you'd've been yelling bloody murder if it'd hit you, but it must've hit right behind you. I'd swear I saw your silhouette right through the tent flap."

"Really, I'm fine. Really."

"Well, you lie down." Gilzow made a shivery sound. "I'm breaking out the blankets. First it's too hot for sleep, now it's too chilly."

Leveritt stretched out on her cot, and Gilzow spread a light blanket over her, tucked it around her almost tenderly, and extinguished the lantern. Leveritt lay listening to the rain's arrhythmic drumming. It shouldn't be my job, she thought, to have to remember Ed Morris. The storm passed. She slept.

The following morning was as warm and humid as though there had been no rainstorm. The normally clear and placid river had become a muddy torrent. Erosion was rapid in the Silurian; the steaming flatland, which drained through notches in the bluffs, looked the same and yet subtly changed. The camp's denizens, ten people in all, stood about in twos and threes, surveyed the valley and the plain, and talked, depending on their specialties, of turbidity or fossiliferous outcrops or possible revisions in topographical maps.

Leveritt and Holmes spent the day in a tent with the sides drawn up, consolidating survey data and incorporating it into a three-dimensional computer model of the region from the valley to the hills. Over tens of millions of years, the land had been repeatedly submerged, then raised, drained, eroded. "Up and down," Holmes said, "more times than the proverbial whore's drawers." Leveritt, her fierce concentration momentarily broken, shot him an oh-please look. They barely noticed a brief midmorning cloudburst, barely paused for lunch, and might have skipped it but for the noise made by a couple of campmates returning muddy and ravenous from a collecting sortie into the valley. The sun was halfway down the sky when Holmes abruptly switched off his laptop, stretched, and declared that they could continue that evening, but right at that moment he needed some down-time. Leveritt glared at his retreating back until he had disappeared into the next tent; she found herself looking past the tent at the barren plain and the distant hills, and after a minute she resigned herself to thinking about Ed Morris and wondering what had become of him.

Ed Morris. Ed Morris. Maybe you arrived high and dry and unhurt out there on the plain. . . .

Her catalog of the possible fates of Ed Morris had grown extensive. It occurred to her now to record them in a notebook, like Gilzow's models of geologic time. Then she remembered Lieutenant Hales's injunction against writing anything that had to do with Ed Morris. She still did not feel safe from Hales.

Ed Morris. You arrived and—what? You wasted at least a little time and energy being confused and frightened. But after a while, you gathered your wits and took stock of your predicament. And what a predicament. You've got no food, no water, no idea of where you are. You know only where you *aren't*. You have only the clothes on your back and the laptop in your hand.

If it's night, you learn immediately that the stars are no help at all. The constellations you know don't exist yet. You wander around in the dark, fall into a ravine, break your neck and die instantly. . . .

Or break your leg and expire miserably over the course of a couple of days.

Back to the beginning. You find water, a rivulet, and follow it to a stream and follow that to the river and follow the river to the sea and find the main camp. . . .

Or find nothing, if you've arrived before there is a camp.

Or you don't find water and don't fall and break any bones. You just wander around until your strength gives out.

No. You do find water, you reach the river, but you realize your strength will inevitably give out, that you're lost and doomed to die in the middle of nowhere and no two ways about it, unless you take a chance, eat some of the local flora or fauna, shellfish, millipedes, whatever you can grab, anything you can keep down. You eat it raw, because you don't have any way to make fire, but you don't get sick and die. You—what do you do, if you live?

You live out your life alone, Adam without Eve in paleo-Eden. Robinson Crusoe of the dawn.

Alone with your laptop.

Best-case scenario, Ed Morris. You walk into camp just around dinnertime to-night, ragged and emaciated after an epic trek, and tired of subsisting on moss and invertebrates, but alive, whole, and proud of yourself.

Not-as-good scenario, at least not as good for you, but it'd let everybody give you your due and let me be done with you. We find the cairn you built with the biggest rocks you could move. Inside the cairn, we find your laptop. The seals're intact, the circuitry isn't corroded. We can read the message you left for us. . . .

Lot of work for a dying man.

Okay. First, you figure out how to survive. *Then* you build a cairn. You wander around building cairns all over the place, increasing the chances we'll find at least one of them.

Leveritt went quickly to her tent. She hung a canteen from her belt, put a wide-brimmed straw hat on her head, and started walking toward the hills. The wet ground crunched underfoot.

The levelness of the flatland was an illusion; the ground was all barely perceptible slopes, falling, rising, like the bosom of a calm sea. When she could no longer see the camp, she planted her fists on her hips and stood looking around at the rocky litter and thought, Now what?

Take stock, she told herself.

I've eaten, I'm not lost, my life isn't at stake here. None of which Ed Morris could say. I'm not confused and scared, either, and I haven't been injured. Besides not having eaten for ten, twelve hours before the jump, he didn't look like he had a lot of body fat to live off. On the plus side, he was a mountain climber and a skydiver, in good shape and not a physical coward.

How long would it have taken him to get over the confusion and fright? Give him the benefit of the doubt. A career in accountancy implies a well-ordered mind.

How much more time would've passed before it occurred to him to build a cairn? Then he'd have had to pick a site where a cairn would have a chance of being found, where it wouldn't get washed away, where there was an ample supply of portable rock. If he was back toward the hills, he'd have found the streambeds full of smooth stones of a particularly useful size. Out here, he'd just have had to make do with what's at hand.

How much rock could he have moved before his strength gave out?

Leveritt picked up a grapefruit-sized chunk of limestone, carried it a dozen feet, and set it down next to a slightly larger chunk. She worked her way around and outward from the two, gathering the bigger stones, carrying them back. After laboring steadily for the better part of two hours, she was soaked with perspiration, her arms, back, and legs ached, and she had erected an indefinite sort of pyramid approximately three feet high. Increasingly, she had expended time and energy locating suitable stones at ever greater distances from the cairn and lugging them over to it. She squatted to survey her handiwork.

Ed Morris, she told herself, wouldn't have stopped working at this point, because he didn't have a camp to return to when he got tired. Still, it's a respectable start, stable, obviously the work of human hands.

She rose and walked in the direction of the camp. She paused once to look back and wonder, How long before it tumbles down?

No one in camp seemed to have noticed her absence. Typical, she thought. She discovered, however, that she could not maintain a sour mood for very long. She and Holmes worked together for an hour after dark, and then she retired to her tent and, soon, to her cot. Despite the mugginess of the evening, she had no trouble falling asleep.

For the next two days, work thoroughly involved her. On the afternoon of the third day, she returned to the cairn. She started to add to it, decided, No, moved off a hundred yards, and built a second cairn. Thereafter, she spent most of such free daylit time as she had piling up stones. She never returned to any site.

Now her absences did attract notice, Holmes trailed her past two abandoned cairns to her latest site. She answered his questions with monosyllables or shrugs or ignored the questions altogether, keeping on the move the whole while, finding, prying up, carrying, setting down stones. She refused his offer to help. Finally, he said, quite good-naturedly, "You need a hobby, Bonnie."

"This is my hobby, Mike." She wished aloud that he would go away, and he did.

That evening, over a dinner that tasted better than dinner usually did, Gilzow asked her what she was doing, and Leveritt replied, "Pursuing mental health." Later, she was almost unable to keep herself from laughing at one of Holmes's stupid jokes.

Two weeks and seven cairns after she had begun, as she lay on the edge of sleep, she realized with a start that she had not thought about Ed Morris all that day.

Four days later, when she had returned from building her eighth and last cairn, she asked around for a copy of *Robinson Crusoe*. Nobody had one. Gilzow offered her *Emma*, by Jane Austen. "Close enough," Leveritt said.

A month passed.

The supply boat arrived three days ahead of schedule. Everyone turned out to carry boxes; the first people to reach the boat yelled to those following, "Brinkman's here!" The big man, who had been downriver for weeks, stood in the bow, waving his shapeless hat. It transpired that the loud, sincere welcome was not entirely for him. He had brought a mixed case of liquor.

When the supplies had been unloaded and the camp had settled down for a round or two of good stiff drinks, Brinkman sought out Leveritt and asked her to walk with him along the bluff. They had scarcely put the camp out of earshot when he heaved a great sigh, his ebullient humor fell away from him like a cloak, and he suddenly looked tired and pale under his tan and more solemn than she could recall having seen him.

"I really came all the way up here," he said, "to tell you this personally. Two days ago, they dug something out of the marsh down by the main camp. It was one of the—part of one of the gurneys they use in the jump station."

"Ed Morris," Leveritt said bleakly. She had not said the name aloud since her conversation with Michael Diehl. Now, as though invoked by her speaking it, a humid wind swept up the valley, bearing a faint fetid breath of the estuary.

Brinkman said, "A Navy security officer named Hales told me about it."

"More surprises. I'd've thought he'd be swearing everyone to secrecy."

"It was too late for that. Everybody in camp knew it by the time he heard about it. Everybody."

"What about Ed Morris himself?"

"They're digging around. They haven't found anything else yet, and God knows if they will. The gurney's all twisted up like a pretzel, and one end's melted. God knows what that implies—besides the obvious, terrific heat. The thing was buried in a mud bank. Impacted. A botanist tripped over an exposed part."

"How long had it been there?"

Brinkman shook his head. "They're still working on that, but even the most conservative guess puts it before the manned phase of the expedition. As to how it got there—there has to be an inquest. You have to be there for it.''

Leveritt groaned. "I don't have anything to tell."

"So Hales said. But people higher up're calling the shots. Everything's got to be official, and you've got to be part of it."

"I *cannot* get away from this thing!" Leveritt sat down on a knob of rock and angrily kicked at the ground. "Not from Hales and the Navy, and, most of all, not from Ed Morris. I thought I'd done it, finally worked it out by myself, but—"

"I'm *sorry*, Bonnie. You have to go back with me in the morning. I can find work for you to do until this thing's over."

"Making coffee?" She could not keep the bitterness out of her voice. "I want to be *here*, Rob."

"I've never known you not to be willing to do what you had to do so you could do what you want to do. While you're there—the San Diego bunch has talked about holding a memorial service. I kind of gather none of them knew Morris all that well, or liked him, or something. But he is the expedition's first casualty. Since you were almost the last person to see him, perhaps you could—"

Leveritt shook her head emphatically. "No."

"Bonnie, the man is dead."

"I couldn't eulogize him if my life depended on it. What I know about him wouldn't fill half a dozen sentences. He talked too fast and dressed like Jungle Jim. He said he liked mountain climbing and skydiving. And I'm very sorry about what happened to him, but it wasn't my fault."

"Who said it was your fault?" Brinkman knelt beside her and picked at his cuticle. "There has to be one meaningful thing you could say about him."

Leveritt sighed. She looked down at the supply boat and imagined herself on it again, sitting, as before, under the white canopy with Brinkman, drinking coffee from a thermos bottle, and glimpsing the pier and the cluster of tents and Quonset huts through the fog. She saw it all as though it were a movie being shown in reverse. She would have to go back and back and back, until she reached a point before Ed Morris had taken over her life, and start anew. This time, she told herself, I will make things happen the way they're supposed to happen. I *will* be the hero of my own story.

She said, "When he found out how nervous I was, he gave me a pep talk. And just before I went through the hole, he gave me a wink of encouragement."

"Well, then, if nothing else, you owe him for that wink." Brinkman could not have spoken more softly and been heard.

Leveritt closed her eyes and thought of the scene in the jump station, the purposeful technicians, Ed Morris's face framed by the bars of the railing. She looked helplessly at Brinkman, who said, "What?"

The humid wind moved up the valley again, and again she smelled the estuary's attenuated fetor of death and of life coming out of death. She exhaled harshly and said, "Nothing." She had meant to say that she could not recall the color of Ed Morris's eyes. "Never mind. I'll think of something." The wind passed across the rocky plain, toward the ancient crumbled hills and beyond.

CHANGES

William Barton

▼

Here's a wise and contemplative story that reaffirms some ancient wisdom: The more things change, the more they stay the same. . . .

William Barton was born in Boston in 1950 and currently resides in Garner, North Carolina, with his wife, Kathleen. For most of his life, he has been an engineering technician, specializing in military and industrial technology. He was at one time employed by the Department of Defense, working on the nation's nuclear submarine fleet, and is currently a freelance writer and computer consultant. His stories have appeared in Aboriginal Science Fiction, Asimov's Science Fiction, Amazing, Interzone, Tomorrow, Full Spectrum, *and other markets. His books include the novels* Hunting on Kunderer, A Plague of All Cowards, Dark Sky Legion, *and* When Heaven Fell, *and, in collaboration with Michael Capobianco,* Iris *and* Fellow Traveler. *His 1996 novel,* The Transmigration of Souls, *was a finalist for the Philip K. Dick Award, and a new novel,* Acts of Conscience, *has just been published.*

When the cramp finally let go, Harriet Severn fell back on her pillows, hating the way her skin felt, sticky sweat refusing to evaporate in the summer humidity. The sheets were damp, soaked right through, making her regret the decision to give birth at home instead of going to the hospital like a sensible modern woman. They'd never get the stains out of the mattress, probably have to buy a new one.

And so hot. But they didn't have air-conditioning in the town's little hospital either. The only place they had air-conditioning was in the movie theater. Harriet giggled. Maybe I should've gone there. . . .

Dr. Noffzinger, sitting between her legs at the foot of the bed, smiled up at her. "Won't be long now, Harriet. This is going to be easy." He reached up and patted her belly, then looked back down at her "business end." Smiled again. No problem at all. . . .

Should have gone to the hospital, though. Cleaner. Safer. And Wilson wouldn't be visibly lurking outside the door like some massive ghost. Poor Willy. He always felt so bad for her when it was happening. Third time now, trying for a boy because the first two were girls. Always felt so bad. But in a couple of months, when the damage was healed, he'd be more interested in "getting things back to normal."

Another cramp, making her bunch up, squint and grunt. God. Like turning inside out. One place pulling in, its neighbor popping out, hurting worse than stomach flu, and going on and on . . . Then done, falling back, panting hard. Right, no problem at all. Should have gone to the hospital, you little idiot. . . .

But you didn't want to leave Grandpa all alone and Willy wouldn't *hear* of you going off to have the baby alone, as if *he'd* be any help. Poor Grandpa, lying in his room, listening to all this. Or maybe not listening. Seventy-eight years old and the pneumonia almost finished with him. "Old Man's Friend." Supposed to be an easy death, but Grandpa was making it hard, just not ready to go. Not quite yet. I'd've felt bad going off to the hospital, coming home in a week to find him gone. . . .

He'll see this one. Maybe he'll smile.

Maybe . . .

Uhhhh . . .

The baby's head felt like a padded boulder between her legs, suddenly right *there*, the doctor leaning forward, touching it with his clean hands, gently cooing, to her, to it? Pulling, "Come on now. There, there . . ." Harriet put her head back and squeaked, the cramp suddenly powerful and strange, her skin feeling as if it were being burnt by a thousand little cigarette coals. . . .

Christ, get it *over* with . . . *Now!*

And the rest of the little body slithered out like the proverbial greased pig, right into old Noffzinger's arms.

Owwww . . .

Afterechoes, pain and more pain, but already dying down.

Noffzinger, always the traditionalist, swung the nasty, bloody thing by its heels, one light slap, and SQUAAALLL! Alive. Cradling it then, grinning, calling out, "You can relax now, Willy. It's a boy!"

Then he put it on her bare belly and Harriet reached down to cuddle the slick little body, smiling wider than she ever expected she could. Maybe in a little while, when the doctor was through fiddling around down there, she could get up and show the new baby to Grandpa. A boy. It would light up his fading eyes, just one last time.

Mark Severn, just past his ninth birthday, lay on the floor, doing his homework on the near-pileless maroon carpet. The rug could be a distraction sometimes, with all its patterns and border colors, bits of blue and burnt orange peeking out from behind the red . . . not *behind* it exactly, since the rug was essentially a two-dimensional surface, but . . . God. Distracted. Got to get this stuff done. "The Cisco Kid" coming on in . . . squint up at the big Nelsonic clock sitting on the old upright piano . . . ten minutes. . . .

Mom, sitting in her chair, reading the current issue of *Life*, said, "What're you squinting for, Mark?"

He shrugged, squinted at her, and said, "I dunno. I guess it makes the numbers easier to read."

She stared at him for a minute, giving him that *concerned* look, then went back to her magazine. Mark went back to scribbling the English essay, hoping he wouldn't lose too many points for legibility. Arithmetic had been easy, just problems intended as drill for kids who couldn't seem to memorize the multiplication tables, couldn't quite get it when it was time for long division. Science was easy too, just not quite so . . . regular. This electricity business was pretty interesting anyway. English, though . . . Five hundred words . . . every one of them made up from scratch, without a clue as to what Mrs. Pennyman wanted. Oh, well. As long as I keep getting As in arithmetic, Dad won't be too upset about the Cs in English and history. . . .

Right now, Dad was sitting in his own chair, bigger than Mom's, next to the heavy old bookcase, the one they'd gotten when Grandma died last year, head tipped toward the big Philco radio, sound turned down so the others wouldn't be disturbed, listening to the war news. It was pretty interesting stuff, sometimes. Today the subdued voice talking about some big battle in North Africa. Kasserine Pass. Dad's face very serious. Troubled glance at me, then. Maybe he thinks the war will still be going on when I'm old enough. Ten years. Would the war still be raging in 1953?

Anyhow, maybe that was why Dad let him do homework out here on the floor, while Jill and Sandy sat together at the kitchen table. Mark sighed and put the essay in his notebook, threading the holes over the rings then snapping them shut, hoping what he'd done would be sufficient. Just a C, that's all you need. . . .

Mom was looking at him again, smiling a little bit, kind of distant. Mom's face was always full of sunshine when she smiled, even more so when she laughed. Like when she called Dad ''Willy-Boy'' and Dad would smile and say, ''Harry-me-Lad!'' as if breathless with excitement. Like a game between them, like they were kids. They'd giggle and joke with each other then, sitting together on the couch, and sometimes they'd go to bed early, giggling off down the hallway.

Mark flipped through his homework one last time, making sure he'd really done everything. Omissions were embarrassing to explain in front of the class, even though you were never the only one, even though you could try to pretend it was funny. Close the books. Dad was reaching out toward the radio, twiddling the tuner dial, listening close, intent. I'm glad I've got nice parents. Not like Donnie across the street, whose parents would sometimes whip him with a leather strap. You could hear him cry all the way down the block when that happened. . . .

The radio was getting old and hard to tune in, Dad promising in another year or two they'd replace it. No, not with one of the new little radios, but with a television set like the one Mike's dad built from a kit last year. Three times the size of the old Philco, with a round screen the size of a saucer in the upper right-hand corner. Once, Dad had let him stay up late, go over to watch a boxing match on TV with the men gathered in Mr. Carozza's parlor. He fell asleep after an hour, Dad laughing when he carried him home, beer on his breath, very cheerful, bouncing Mark on his shoulders. . . .

I'll miss the old radio when it's gone. Tall, peaked, made of ornate wood, scroll-work over cloth-covered speakers in the middle, two tall half-pillars on either side, like the pillars to either side of the stage in the theater downtown, where Mom and Dad went once or twice a year. What was the word Mom told me? Proscenium. Like the radio was a stage, the voices from the speaker actors in a play, tiny figures before him, dressed in richly colored costumes, striding back and forth before his eyes.

Maybe, someday, TV will be like that, instead of those watery gray mannequins. We'll get it, though, and then I can *watch* old Cisco and Pancho. . . .

Right now, though, Dad was smiling at him, beckoning, turning up the sound, and there was the announcer's plummy voice, telling him all about "O. Henry's famous Robin Hood of the Old West. . . ."

Mark sat in his favorite chair, a spindly Danish Modern with blue nylon upholstery, pushing heavy, black-framed glasses back up his nose, staring at the front page of the *Post*. Two photographs, side by side, of two handsome but alien-looking young men in foreign military uniforms. Andrian G. Nikolaev, said one. Pavel R. Popovich, said the other. Orbited the Earth sixty-four times. Orbited the Earth forty-eight times. *Vostok*. East.

So much for good old Project Mercury, whose long-term goal, sometime, someday, was to keep a man in space for a whole twenty-four hours. Four days. That's enough time to reach the Moon and land. Kennedy's going to look like a fool. I wonder how Glenn and Carpenter feel *now*. Ticker-tape *parades*, for God's sake. . . .

Hell. When our people touch down in 1970 these guys will have been there for five years. You are now entering the Lunovskaya Soviet Socialist Republic. Passports, please?

Dad was right. Remember watching the Berlin news with him in '49? Our grandchildren will be dead and gone before this is over, he said. We should've gone in and cleaned them out right after we finished with Hitler and Tojo. Right now, it sure looked like the Communists' centrally managed economies had something over good old free enterprise, all right. . . .

And whatever it was, it had made Khrushchev awfully damned *bold*. Stood up to them in Berlin, whipped them back in Korea; now this business with Castro and Russians down in the Caribbean, setting up shop ninety miles from Florida.

Suddenly, Mark felt very cold. A young father wanted to look *forward*, to plan for his children's adulthood, help them get a good start. He put the paper aside and looked at the two of them on the floor, Billy getting to be a big boy now, starting first grade in a couple of weeks, Freddy old enough to sit up beside him, out of diapers and talking quite nicely, much to Bill's aggravation. . . .

You can smile about that at least . . . Dad. Funny to think of myself that way. Mom seems to like being called Grandma even though she's still so young-looking. Well. Fifty-three *is* young. They'll be young as long as they live. Memory of them from last Easter, Harriet sitting in Willy's lap, messing up his thinning hair, kissing him in front of the kids. I don't know why it upset Marian like that. Never bothered me when *I* was a kid. Just glad my parents seemed to *like* each other. . . .

Poor Marian. Pregnant again, just so she can try for a daughter. Unhappy about two boys, have to make sure that never gets back to Fred. Me, though, born because Dad wanted a son . . . OK. It's easy to understand. Marian was uncomfortable though, in her seventh month, feeling fat and horrible, wondering why she'd wanted to *do* such a thing to herself once again. . . .

The two little boys were engrossed in watching the TV, unaware of the nasty adult world unraveling all around them. Rapt, wrapped up in the opening sequences of the last show before bedtime, listening to Fifties-style advertising singers tell them all about the "Modern Stone Age Fam-uh-Lee. . . ." Pretty funny stuff, actually. Not like *Rocky and Bullwinkle*, making me put aside this grad-school homework long enough to watch with them, but . . . funny. That business about using animals in place of mechanical technology was a pretty good grade of science fiction when you thought about it. Maybe something engineers will really do some-day. . . .

Engineers. Right. Engineers build hydrogen bombs, if they're lucky. Engineers blow up the world. And me with my little B.S. degree. What do I build? Right. I build blueprints. I help flesh out the work of better men. For now. Twenty-eight? Still a boy. The pile of books on the coffee table was tall, and they'd been expensive. Tough, going for your master's at night after working all day. Tough on Marian and the kids too. For *them*, though, make more money, give them a future. If . . .

That's the word, all right. If. He glanced over at the bookcase. Been two years since I read it. Can't forget it though. Words red, white, and blue on a black spine, J. B. Lippincott's edition of *Alas, Babylon*. I wonder how I managed to lose the dust jacket? Very inspirational, trying to make a dead world carry on with human life . . . But it won't *be* like that. I *know*. Anybody who's interested can know. Right here in the public library there's a copy of *The Prompt and Delayed Effects of Thermonuclear Weapons*. . . .

And the kids were sitting on the floor, watching Fred Flintstone sink his teeth into his new role as ''The Frog-Mouth,'' blah-blah-blah, making them giggle at comedy too sophisticated for two little boys, one just barely out of diapers. Just reacting to the laugh track, that's all.

Anyway, it looks nice on a color TV, glad we spent the money, almost enough for a new car. . . .

Standing in the hot June sun, Mark took off his white hard hat and wiped his brow on one tan sleeve, leaving a big dark splotch of moisture on the cloth. All right. Time for short sleeves. Tomorrow. It was a very nice day, not enough breeze really, but clear and cloudless, sky a lucid, vaulting blue, the world bright green all around, falling away in waves of distant vegetation toward the horizon, blue mountains barely visible in the west.

Piedmont Plateau a pretty nice part of Virginia. A lot of work remaining to be done hereabouts. He looked down at the blueprint, weighted to the rough wooden table by chunks of concrete and cinder block. Finishing it off. The bridge's skeleton was done and now they were putting in the roadway, the expander joints, making sure the sewer-and water-pipe transit fittings were lined up OK. Be done in three more months, then move on.

Not so very far. And not for very long. The Interstate system that had kept him employed for more than a decade was almost done. Almost done and then, nothing. Should be work for people maintaining that expensive infrastructure, maybe they'd planned it that way in the beginning, but something dreadful seemed to be going wrong somewhere. Somewhere way up the line from here. . . .

I talked to Dad about it, tried to get his spin on it. All he could do was rave about the Trilateral Commission, about Kissinger and Rockefeller and all the rest. Jesus. Well, he's getting old now, almost retirement age. I guess we should expect something like this. . . .

Don't believe it. Old? Nonsense. Mark shook his head slowly, looking down the shallow hill at rumbling machinery, spitting little clouds of greasy diesel smoke, at gangs of toiling workers, bare-backed, sunburned men sweating in the heat. Old? Hell. In just a few more weeks, I'll be forty years old.

I'm getting too old for *this*, that's for sure. So *tired* today. . . .

Like to be in an office somewhere, be an *indoor* engineer, making up work for the younger folks to do. But this pays better. Made sixty-eight thousand before taxes last year. Billy in college, Freddy about to start, Alice in the ninth grade . . .

Be easier if the taxes were a little lower. Which is why you voted for Nixon in '72. Shows how much *you* know. . . .

Be easier if Marian would get a job too. If Marian *could* get a job. College degree, sure, but she's been sitting home with the kids since 1956. And maybe she doesn't like the idea anyway, what with all that nice, unpaid volunteer work. Hell . . .

Starting to turn away, get back to the business at hand, but jet noise, louder than usual, echoing around the hills, made him look up. Too bright. He fished the expensive prescription sunglasses out of his pocket and put them on, looked up again. Bright white arrowhead moving across the northern sky, leaving a tiny sliver of black smoke behind, too low to make a contrail. What . . . British Airways Concorde making its way to Dulles, thundering across the Northern Virginia suburbs.

And *our* SST, just blueprints in the trash. Good old Boeing. Good old politics. As usual. Build the interstates and then let them rot, bridges and all, this fine new thing we're building now will be falling down in 1995. . . .

And Skylab orbiting overhead the end of the space program. Spend billions to get to the Moon, *get* there, by God, then throw it all away. Hell, five years ago they said they'd have the shuttle flying in six or seven years. Now they say they'll have it flying in only five or six years. I guess that's something . . . Progress.

Momentary memory of watching *Apollo* 17 lift off on TV, watching it light up the waterway brilliant yellow and white, the sky turning blue around the edges of the square picture. Sudden realization that this was the last one, that he really *should* have taken the time to go down and see one take off for real. . . .

Too late now, buddy boy.

The last echo faded, Mark looked back down at the blueprints on the table, at his scribbled notes in one margin. All right, this is why they pay you so much. Fixes. On the spot. He sat down on an upturned wire-spool and slid his fat Rockwell calculator out of its holster, set it on the tabletop, and clicked the "on" switch. The display lit up, bright green, easier to read in daylight than standard red LEDs.

Sturdy little toy, this, many orders of magnitude more useful than the old K&E deci-trig log-log slide rule sitting home on his dresser. Expensive too. Could have lived with less. So why did you buy it, then? Mark grinned at the little machine. That damned commercial, of course, so clever. Little radio play about the Rockwell advertising department, sleazy guys arguing about how they could make their pitch *unique*. How *does* our product differ from all the others? But . . . but . . . then the tacky little jingle about ". . . big, green numbers and little rubber feet!"

Hell, I still remember the whole thing! "Oh, you *can't* go wrong with *Rockwell*. . . ."

. . .

April the 12th was the twentieth anniversary of Yury Gagarin's orbital flight. With bright morning sunshine flooding in through the sliding glass doors, Mark turned on the nineteen-inch Panasonic portable, still turned to CBS, because they always had the best coverage, despite Uncle Walter's unfortunate decision to retire, camera view out across mosquito inlet toward the launch pad. Brilliant, clear blue sky. After so many delays, today would be the day for sure, a pleasant enough coincidence.

The little one-bedroom apartment was nice enough, though way too cramped, but with Marian holding onto the house and Alice still in college, it was the best he could do. OK. I don't really *need* a living room, it's not like I entertain a lot. Bedroom lined with books, breakfast nook in the little kitchen, and use the living room as a den and office. Chair, TV, desk, light table . . . Might as well get *something* done. . . .

But he sat rooted in the chair, staring at the TV. Too damned tired to work just yet. Feel so old . . . Right. And when did forty-six start being old? The guy *piloting* that thing is just about your age. Reading glasses in space, for God's sake. . . .

Just feeling sorry for yourself, old man. Married twenty-seven years and the judge puts your poor old butt in the street, because women have to be "taken care of." So what? Stop whining and get on with the rest of your life. There was a sharp pang in his chest then, one of those pretend "heart attacks" that used to send him scurrying to the hospital.

Just anxiety, I can give you something for it if you'd like. . . .

No thanks, Doc.

Thought you were going to have a *real* heart attack when Dad died, sudden like that, Mom on the phone, bawling her grief in your ear, crying steadily at the funeral, talking about how badly she wanted to die now and go with him. No way to comfort her, not with all those memories of Mom sitting in Dad's lap, smiling at him, happy with him, memory repeated over and over again, Mom and Dad just getting a little older in each and every snapshot. Then Mom standing by his fresh-dug grave, silent, not smiling anymore.

Christ, Mom. You had a good trip. Not a *damned* thing to complain about. At least Dad got to see his great-grandson before he went. Billy the proud poppa, beaming down at brand new Jerry Severn. Hilarious to slap a name like that on some squalling, wrinkled red thing.

Not long after that, Marian broke the news.

And here I sit, in an apartment all my own. . . .

Another glance at the bright TV picture. Well, going pretty good this morning. Fifty-nine minutes on the countdown clock, so I might as well get something done while I wait.

The box on the desk was waiting too, right beside the brand-new thirteen-inch color monitor. Went the extra mile there. Could've bought a color TV and gotten away with it. Too fuzzy though, hard on my eyes since I had to start wearing these damn bifocals. . . .

Open the box and look down at the thing. Putty-colored, with high-profile keys and the familiar Commodore logo, familiar because they had a couple of PETs at the office. He set it on the desktop and started hooking up wires, plugging things in. Even bought a disk drive instead of a tape deck. Do it right, if it's going to mean anything at all. The Commodore 64 looked good set up, not as "professional" as the old PETs, but pretty nice. Not metallic like the TI-99/4a he'd looked at, but a whole lot nicer than Billy's big, boxy Apple II. Probably a good choice. Math not as good as the TI, but more RAM for less money, a lot greater likelihood it'll still be supported after Texas Instruments goes belly-up. . . .

He hit the "on" switches in sequence and waited. Screen alight. Operating system, available RAM space, and READY. Cursor blinking beside the word. "Ready." Jesus. You had to laugh at the thought of all those people taken in by colorful TV ads, bar-chart histograms rising like magic on the screen, rushing out to buy a *real* computer. Be the first person in your neighborhood to own a computer? Well, buy one of *our* computers and maybe you can *own* the neighborhood. Imagine them now, sitting dumbfounded, wondering, "Ready for *what*?"

Movement on the TV. . . .

The nine-minute built-in hold was over and the clock was counting down again, electric feeling in the air, as if *this was it*. Well, maybe. Anything can happen now. Last time, just a couple of days ago, they'd aborted at T-39 seconds, newspeople standing in long, silent rows, cameras ready. . . .

But today is the twentieth anniversary of *Vostok 1*. . . .

Then it went down and down and down, Mark dragging the old hassock Marian let him have up in front of the TV, leaning in close so he could watch it without glasses. Make it real. As if the naked TV screen, were, somehow, something *real*. . . .

Down past twelve, plumes of steam coming out of the turbine vents, splash of sparks, yellow fire turning blue then clear. Main engine start . . . camera pulling back to show the cloud of smoke, then the solids lit, much heavier smoke with fire boiling crazily in its depths . . .

Columbia bounced off the pad, clearing the tower, climbing on a dense column of smoke, fire barely visible, while the camera pulled back so you could see it go, climbing over the heads of the newsmen and women. Two guys in the foreground, standing near the countdown sign, one fat, holding a camera, the other less so, holding binoculars, bouncing up and down on the balls of his feet, rather strange looking. . . .

Moment of intense regret. I wish I'd just gone on down. I could be standing with those guys right now, feeling what they're feeling. . . .

In a little while, the rocket was up in space.

Mark sat back from the AppleStar Touchvoice III+, unclipping the microphone from his collar, reading the last words of the article, lips moving slightly. Well. Pretty good. Another few thousand bucks in the can, at any rate. He reached out and touched the SAVE/EXIT icon on the right-hand side of the screen and watched the file explode out of the picture, system desktop reappearing.

Hell of a way for an old man to make a living, really, but the outdoor engineering days are long gone. Not much civil tech going on anymore anyway. Not much of anything, these days, younger engineers going overseas, if they could. Even Billy, talking about taking his wife and kids out of the country, maybe get a decent-paying job in Serbia or Kazakhstan, where there was new infrastructure abuilding.

I'll miss Jerry, though. Of course the boy was getting too old to have much interest in his grandfather, finishing up high school, slim, handsome, fresh-faced. . . .

Mark shut off the computer and was suddenly aware of his reflection in the screen. Not too damned bad. Still slim, though I don't work hard anymore. Still got all my hair, even if it is white. If this were a mirror, I could see the corneal rings . . . and the little scars where my glasses used to sit. Glasses. I wonder where I put them? He grinned at his reflection. Good riddance, after fifty years!

He pushed back from the desk and turned the chair around, looking out the window into sunset. Nice fall colors in the sky, clouds turning brown in the fading light, blue turning to vermilion, dark red over the horizon. The weather'd been good all week. A sunny day when we buried Mom in the spot she reserved beside Dad. I wish I could imagine them together right now. . . .

No. Nothing. Gone. Hard times, though. I thought about giving her an Alcor burial, just silliness, but a sliver of hope for the rest of us. She wouldn't have wanted it, though, not with Dad Purina Worm Chow all these years. . . .

He sighed and stood up, stretching. Morbid thoughts, all right. Useless. Ow. The twinge in his shoulder was back, making him worry. I'm just a few years short of how old Dad was when he died. Maybe . . . Christ. More morbidity. Also useless. Dad had thirty years of cheeseburgers on me. I've got another twenty years to go, maybe more. A whole generation. Practically another whole life. . . .

The big, flat box of the HDTV, dominating one wall of the living room, was already set to CNN-4, *Endeavor* on the launchpad, outlined by darkening sunset colors, T-60 minutes and counting. It would, just barely, be dark by the time the thing went. Something familiar . . .

Oh, hell. *Apollo 17*. Another "last time." Hard little ball of regret in his throat. Well, at least the TV keeps getting better and better. But the ship would fly to orbit with its nine-man crew, primary mission to attach a de-orbiting rocket to the little bit of *Freedom* that had been built, just so it could fall harmlessly into the sea, avoiding the hysteria that had accompanied the fall of *Skylab*, of *Salyut 7*, of *Mir*.

All over. Like everything else in my life. America entering its senescence after a short, brilliant youth. No more moonshots. No more *Voyagers*. No space station at all. After this, no more Man in Space. Childhood dreams finished. Russians gone. Chinese and Japanese never went. Europeans just couldn't seem to get their act together. . . .

Gina came out of the kitchen, smiling, carrying two tumblers of liquor, her own old fashioned, his Black Russian. She put the drinks down on the coffee table and stood looking down at him, hands on slim hips. Look of concern. "You all right, Mark?"

He sighed, then shook his head. "Sure. I just get tangled up in old memories sometimes. . . ."

She sat in his lap, pulled her legs up, put her arms around his neck, and leaned close. "Yeah. I guess . . . I didn't expect to feel this way when I got old. . . ."

"Old, hell!"

That made her smile, lean in closer, nuzzling her face against his. She was pretty damned nice looking for a woman pushing sixty. Still slim, not too many lines in her face. Let her hair go gray though, unlike Marian, who'd been dyeing hers for decades.

Kids didn't like seeing her in his lap like this, especially in front of the younger grandchildren, so it was just as well they'd ignored his invitation to come over for an *Endeavor* party. They'd've brought Marian anyway, bitter Marian, with all her acid little remarks, eliciting his usual muttered response.

Well, dear, you didn't *have* to throw me away. . . .

He rubbed his hands up and down Gina's back, feeling her smooth muscles through the thin blouse, just a faint hint of loose skin here and there, spine a well-defined ridge.

Murmuring into his neck, she said, "You keep that up, we'll miss the launch. . . ."

Smiling back at her, feeling her solid, comfortable weight on his lap, Mark dismissed yet another little pang: I could've had this all my life if only . . . Hell, boy. Forget about that. You've got it now. That's all that matters.

"Maybe," he said, hands drifting down past her hips, "it isn't worth watching."

Mark sat at his desk in the spacious, glass-walled office, nine floors above the street, higher than most of the other buildings in this part of town, staring into space. Nice day out there. Sunny. Cloudless. Probably a bit of a breeze ameliorating the August heat. Nice day for a walk. No smog. Not anymore. Car exhaust diminishing as emission standards tightened, more and more people going for quiet electrics, long-haul trucks running on low-residue, stack-scrubbed synfuel . . .

Nice day for a walk. And you should be happy you can go for a walk on your seventy-sixth birthday, old man no cane, no pain, not a problem in the world.

It's just that you're all done. Finished again.

Mark sighed and leaned back, staring at the low, flat black box of the Toshiba Vortex transmedia system sitting on the corner of his desk, spidery headset crumpled in a pile next to it. No, you just don't want to do this. It's only been eight years since you started *Future Life*, eight years in which you built it up into the twenty-first century's premier technophile vidmag. Eight years in which you built what felt like a whole new career. And careers are supposed to last a lifetime. . . .

OK. So this one *did* last a lifetime. You just don't have a whole lot left. Twenty years? In twenty years, I'll be under the ground. Not a clean thought. Alcor and its competitors out of business, protocorpsicles thawed and buried. That nice insurance policy just one more pile of cash, insignificant compared to what the magazine made you. Ten years? Maybe. If I'm lucky. Ten years in which to grow frail and sick and very, very old . . .

Hah. Maudlin. Morbid. Get on with it. Retire and hand it over to the people you trained. Go sit in the sunshine. Finish those ten years in comfort. Owe it to Gina, at least . . .

He picked up the headset and slipped it on, watched admiringly as the virtual office formed up around him. All right. Point at the imaginary voicewriter and see its blue LED blink, acknowledging your presence, sheet of paper forming in the air above it, column of icons like magic in the air beside you. Reach up and grasp the NOTE icon. "Editorial Number 96," he muttered. Tap the CENTER icon, then tap ITALICS. "*Ave. Atque. Vale.*"

Hmh. Very nice looking. Now if only the software engineers would come up with subroutines that were really good at recognizing global context-sensitive style-sheets, external to the local setup-universe. Give it time. If you live long enough, you'll see it happen. Hmmm . . . All right, that's what I'll talk about, then. . . .

Later, at home, he sat on the couch, Gina curled against his side, watching TV, dinner a warm lump just to the left of center. Gina holding onto me. Worried that I'll be upset, feeling a little guilty. Retired, by God. All over. And in six weeks we'll move to a nice little house in Cocoa Beach. . . .

Someplace for the kids to visit. Astonishing thought: My children are getting *old!* Billy's hair iron gray now, even baby Alice nearing the end of her forties . . . Grandkids then. Most of them don't really know me. Jerry, though, a fine strapping young man, just about ready to turn thirty, happy with that young wife, what's-her-name . . . Lisa! Right. How could I forget? Not *that* old. Jerry and Lisa, proudly showing off their new baby boy, name of Matthew Severn. Little red Matt. What a marvel. Great-grandchildren now. Something I didn't expect, but I guess I just wasn't thinking. . . .

Gina shifted position, stretching out her legs with a faint murmur of protest, rubbing her hand across his stomach then straightening up, stretching. "Good grief," she muttered, "stiff already. . . ."

Mark laughed, signaling to the TV with his free hand, dumping the dull old movie they'd been watching, switching over to the global newsnet, hugging her tight with the other.

"Oof. God," she said, "I can't believe I'm so stiff just from sitting here. . . ."

Old joints, creaking here, creaking there. "You're lucky, damn you. *I've* been stiffening up for the past thirty years."

She smiled up at him, long lines from the corners of bright blue eyes, patted him on the thigh, and said, "Longer than that, I think. . . ."

Laughter just a puff of air from his nostrils. "Hmh." He snuggled down, lips rubbing on her forehead, waited while she tipped her head back for a real kiss.

When it was over, she sighed, delicate, a soft, young sound, head against his chest. "Fifteenth anniversary coming up. I can hardly believe it. . . ."

Fifteen years. Another ten and she'll have been with me longer than Marian. Jesus. Marian. Dead two years already? Kids not too happy when you didn't go to the funeral . . . Stop it. Happy now. He hugged her gently. "Fifteen years. No regrets."

Her arms were around his chest, squeezing him close.

On TV, the newshead was talking about *something* . . . Several men in expensive-looking suits, sitting around a conference table. Representatives of the American Aerospace Consortium. The commerce secretary. The vice president. Artist's conception of the various competitors for the NNLS, New National Launch System, mostly single-stage very high energy concepts, unmanned but mannable, part of the Third Millennium Infrastructure Initiative. SynchroNet Platform. Mantended . . .

Other stuff, but Gina was pulling his head down, closing out that imagery, pulling him into her world, more immediate, much more certain, just a tiny slice of regret left behind, caption beginning, If only . . .

Mark lay back on their comfortable bed, watching Gina get undressed. She was facing away from him, over by the caddy where his own clothes already sprawled, more fastidious, draping pieces carefully, though wrinkles were a thing of the past.

Not too many wrinkles at that. . . .

Blouse sliding over her head, back very smooth in the shadowy light, hips flaring just so . . . Little pouches of flesh just above them, where her little bit of fat had drained away, skin not elastic enough to take up the slack. Maybe a vain woman would have it cut away. Maybe she would, but she'd said nothing. . . .

Arm, still limber, reaching back, unhooking the brassiere, shrugging it off, and you could see by the movement of skin on her ribs that she was sagging just a little more with every passing month, tissue shriveling, making her once-fine breasts look empty indeed. Maybe she looks at herself in the mirror, handles them perhaps, and is sorry she never had children. . . .

Slipping the bikini briefs down, bending over to step out of them, Mark's breath catching slightly as desire kindled here and there. . . .

She turned to face him, hands on hips, posed just so, watching him look at her, eyes wandering, face and form and back again.

What one word will tell her how I feel right now? "*Beautiful* . . ." he told her.

Gina looked down at him, eyes bright, smiling. "Well," she said, "looks like that famous 'male climacteric' we've all heard so much about is just another old wives' tale. . . ."

He beckoned to her. "Just bring that old wife's tail over here and we'll see how many myths we can manage to debunk. . . ."

Toward the end of one long evening, shadows lengthening as the sun set inland, Mark sat alone on his porch, waiting for the rocket to go up. Not quite a night launch, but close enough. He glanced at his watch, then down at the screen of the little TV sitting on the table beside him. Ten minutes. Well, you could go inside and watch it in comfort, get away from the bugs for a while, get a better view too, plugged into the RealWorld 3-D Entertainment Center, maybe blend newsnet footage with unedited NASA Select In-house Video shots. . . .

Nonsense. Watch it live. That's why you moved *here* when you know Gina would've been happier over in Clearwater. . . .

Tiny pang, deep inside his chest, hardly able to form. I keep expecting her to come out through the door, laughing, maybe even sit in my decrepit old lap . . . Has she really been gone for three whole years? Seems like only a few days have gone by. Making love in the dark one fine night, laughing together, falling asleep in each other's arms . . . Waking up in gray light of morning, finding her so cold and still . . .

Oh, back out of *that* one . . . Jesus. How the hell did I get to be eighty-four years old. . . .

The people on the little TV were counting down now, voices excited, three . . . two . . . one . . . Static from the TV and a bright light forming in the distance, silent,

Cape Canaveral just ten miles away. Brighter. Brighter . . . The light detached from the horizon, ball as bright as the sun blotting out reddening background sky, long tongue of flame seeming to flicker, climbing . . . Distant thunder, growing louder.

Watching it go, hydrogen burning in the sky, Mark thought, first flight. In three years, they leave for Mars, just about forty years behind schedule. If I'm lucky, I may still be alive. . . .

A few days later, Mark was sitting on the porch again, facing into the warm morning sunshine, when Jerry and his family rolled up in their brand new BMW Comet II, electric/turbine–drive system a barely audible whine, tires crunching softly in the gravel driveway. He opened his eyes, smiling, but was, momentarily, too tired to get up out of the chair. For the last few months, the swivel mount had been difficult to manage. Cold chill. Old, boy. Getting very old . . .

Car doors clunking, people getting out, Jerry tall and tanned, graying at the temples, but still young and handsome at thirty-nine, Lisa a slim and pretty redhead, lovely in a bright, patterned sundress. Matt dodged around them suddenly, popping through the gate, running toward him across the lawn, all freckles and dark red hair and bright blue eyes, feet clattering on the steps, flopping across his lap with a hug. "Hiya, Gramps!"

Mark squeezed him close. "Hiya, Mattie. How's it going?" Gramps. I wonder what he calls Bill? Christ, my *grandson* is a middle-aged man!

Jerry and Lisa were on the porch now, looking down at them, smiling. "Hey, Grandpa. How've you been?"

Mark sat up a little straighter and shrugged. "Oh, all right. Enjoying the view at least." He nodded to the car. "That a new one?"

Jerry looked at the sleek silver-and-black thing and nodded. "Got it in the spring. Eleven thousand."

Moment of surprise. German cars haven't been that cheap in forty years. Balance of payments must be pretty good. Not to mention . . . "Magazine doing OK?"

Jerry nodded. "With the start you gave it?" Not only *Future Life*, of course, but its far less techie companion, *Global Life*.

Mark slid the boy off his lap and looked at him, young, bright-eyed. Eyes that'll still be here when *this* century slides to a close. Maybe remember today, remember me, sitting with great-grandchildren of his own . . . He reached under the chair suddenly, trying not to wince from the too-sudden movement, pulled out a flat, gaily wrapped package. "What do you think, Mattie?"

Though he must have been anticipating a gift, the boy's eyes widened with surprised pleasure as he took it and paused, smiling at him. "Thanks . . ." then ripped it open. "Wow . . ." Holding the black box at arm's length.

"What is it?" said Lisa, stepping forward, unaccountably concerned.

Jerry looked over the boy's shoulder and frowned. "Well. An MBB *Spielraum* hypergame deck. *With* nerve-induction interface clips." He looked at the old man. "That must've set you back a pretty penny."

It had, in fact, cost a little more than the new car. Mark looked up at him. "At my age, what else am I going to do with my money?" He gestured. "Just make a boy smile, that's all."

Matt slid up the unit's SynchroNet antenna, then opened the storage compartment and picked up one of the radiosonde stickum tabs, turning it over in his fingers. "Can it run *PlanetQuest 5?*"

"Let's find out."

Walking along the beach, wind blowing in his hair, Jerry liked the way his wife's body felt, pressed against his side, shoulder not quite tucked under his arm, her arm around his back, thumb tucked through a belt-loop. Familiar. Comfortable. Like we belong together. They'd been married for twelve years now and seldom had a difficult moment. Thanks, in part, to the old man's monetary legacy. But . . .

Her words of concern as they wandered the beach. "I know he means well, Jer. I just don't know if this is a good idea. Matt's a bright boy. I don't want him distracted by something like this. . . ."

The new gaming devices could be hypnotic indeed, projecting their fantasy world directly into the minds of the players, and had caused some outcry, filled *Future Life's* letters column for issue after issue. . . .

Created a new psychological fad, brought business to a new generation of ill-trained, cultish therapists . . .

"It'll be all right," he said. "Matt *is* a bright boy. Too bright to be seduced by mere fantasy, no matter how real it may seem. . . ."

But then they walked over the hill, back toward the house, and there the two of them sat, side by side on the divan, swinging gently, eyes shut, machine between them, inductabs on temple and forehead. Silent. Still. Then the old man's eyes opened, eerie and bright. "My God, Jerry," he'd whispered. "You oughta *try* this. . . ."

And Matt, "Get back in, Gramps! Hurry. Mr. Vorhees is *ready*. . . ."

They'd watched a while, then, reluctant, gone back out on the beach.

Lisa stopped after a while and turned toward him, face pressed into his chest. Not knowing what to say, finally, "I think we're going to have to . . ."

Jerry squeezed her close and said, "Look. We're only going to be here a few days. Once we leave we'll talk it over with Matt and see how *he* feels. He's our son. We can make sure nothing happens. . . ." He kissed her on top of the head. "I haven't seen Grandpa smile like that since Gina died, for God's sake. I don't want to take it away just now."

She looked up at him, eyes serious, and said, "No. I guess not."

"It'll be OK." Because nothing lasts forever.

Three years later, Jerry and Lisa stood on Mark's lawn, shading their eyes from bright sunshine, waiting along with a few billion other people for the crew transport of the *Mars 1* expedition to lift off. Not really anything out of the ordinary. There'd been dozens of these over the past thirty-six months as the ship had been built in Earth orbit. This one was, however, the last one. When this crew took off, they'd be gone for a long time. Only three months to Mars and touchdown, hopefully on the north rim of Coprates, but the surface stay was two years long. . . .

Lisa kept looking over her shoulder, back up at the porch, where Matt, tall and tan now at eleven, sat with the old man, the two of them tied together through yet another induction unit, the third one they'd bought since that first eerie day. Nothing untoward, of course, a lot of people used them, and Matt seldom touched the deck otherwise. Still . . .

The old man looked awful now, sunken-cheeked, eyes seeming to bulge from their sockets, painfully thin with his skin hanging away in long, loose flaps, mottled and dry, like some old-time cancer victim. Still in his right mind, though, bright-eyed and full of life. Maybe that was the worst part, that he could sit there, year after year, and watch himself die. Sometimes the abolition of things like Alzheimer's seemed like a mixed blessing. Well, Mark seemed happy enough, so long as he and the boy could net up once in a while, through SynchroNet every couple of weeks, live like this two or three times a year.

"I wish Matt would come off the porch and watch this for real. . . ."

Jerry glanced back at them and nodded. "Yeah. Well. I guess I feel that way too, but . . ." He shrugged. "This morning Grandpa told me he'd arranged a net-feed from NASA, cost him around thirty thousand bucks just for one channel-track. They're going to watch the launch from a chase plane, then switch over to an old military satellite that's scheduled to be passing overhead. Ought to be quite a view. . . ."

No more, then. Sudden brilliant light, north along the coast, and you could hear people shouting down on the beach, crowds all along A1A, arms lifted, pointing, shading their eyes. The light began its climb then, thunder rolling across the sea, back in over the land, fire in the sky, going upward, tipping away into the east, slowly getting farther away, twenty-six men and women on their way into the future.

When the light and thunder were over, crew transport just a bright spark far out over the sea, they turned back toward the porch. Lisa took a sudden step back, scream strangling in her throat. Sitting on the couch beside the boy, the old man's head was thrown back, vacant eyes staring at the sky, mouth open, chest still.

"Dear *God* . . ." Jerry ran forward then, up onto the porch, and knelt before his son, reaching out, shaking him. "Matt. *Matt!*"

The boy's eyes opened and focused on him. "Dad?"

"Are you all right?"

The boy seemed to shrug, very distant as he looked over at the corpse beside him, staring at it, quite calm. Long moment, somber, then he looked back up at his parents, eyes brightening, full of . . . something.

"Sure," he said. "Everything's fine." Another look at the old body. Everything's fine, he thought, remembering a lovely evening twenty years before, when Gina'd smiled into his eyes and told him just how she felt. And now, everything seems so clean and *new*. . . .

As he slowly picked the inductabs off his head, Matt said, "The view was tremendous. It made him happy again." His parents helped him to his feet then, and walking away, he glanced over his shoulder at Mark, thinking, You're not gone so long as someone remembers who you were.

The old man, lost in a distant dream, could only agree.

COUNTING CATS IN ZANZIBAR

Gene Wolfe

▼

Gene Wolfe is perceived by many critics to be one of the best—perhaps the best—SF and fantasy writers working today. His most acclaimed work is the tetralogy The Book of the New Sun, *individual volumes of which won the Nebula Award, the World Fantasy Award, and the John W. Campbell Memorial Award. His other books include the classic novels* Peace *and* The Devil in a Forest, *both recently rereleased, as well as* Soldier of the Mist, Free Live Free, Soldier of Arete, There Are Doors, Castleview, Pandora by Holly Hollander, *and* The Urth of the New Sun. *His short fiction has been collected in* The Island of Doctor Death and Other Stories and Other Stories, Gene Wolfe's Book of Days, The Wolfe Archipelago, *the recent World Fantasy Award–winning collection* Storeys from the Old Hotel, *and* Endangered Species. *His most recent books are part of a popular new series, including* Nightside the Long Sun, The Lake of the Long Sun, Caldé of the Long Sun, *and* Exodus from the Long Sun. *His short stories have appeared previously in our First, Second, and Fifth Annual Collections.*

Here he takes us aboard a ship at sea to visit with a man and a woman enjoying breakfast during a seemingly pleasant and restful sea voyage—but, as you'll soon see (and as you would immediately expect if you know Wolfe's work), almost nothing here is what it first seems to be....

The first thing she did upon arising was count her money. The sun itself was barely up, the morning cool with the threatening freshness peculiar to the tropics, the freshness, she thought, that says, "Breathe deep of me while you can."

Three thousand and eighty-seven UN dollars left. It was all there. She pulled on the hot-pink underpants that had been the only ones she could find to fit her in Kota Kinabalu and hid the money as she had the day before. The same skirt and blouse as yesterday; there would be no chance to do more than rinse, wring out, and hang dry before they made land.

And precious little then, she thought; but that was wrong. With this much money she would have been able to board with an upper-class family and have her laundry micropored, rest, and enjoy a dozen good meals before she booked passage to Zamboanga.

Or Darwin. Clipping her shoes, she went out on deck.

He joined her so promptly that she wondered whether he had been listening, his ears attuned to the rattle and squeak of her cabin door. She said, "Good morning." And he, "The dawn comes up like thunder out of China across the bay. That's the only quote I've been able to think of. Now you're safe for the rest of the trip."

"But you're not," she told him, and nearly added Dr. Johnson's observation that to be on a ship is to be in prison, with the added danger of drowning.

He came to stand beside her, leaning as she did against the rickety railing. "Things talk to you, you said that last night. What kind of things?"

She smiled. "Machines. Animals too. The wind and the rain."

"Do they ever give you quotations?" He was big and looked thirty-five or a little past it, with a wide Irish mouth that smiled easily and eyes that never smiled at all.

"I'd have to think. Not often, but perhaps one has."

He was silent for a time, a time during which she watched the dim shadow that was a shark glide under the hull and back out again. No shark's ever talked to me, she thought, except him. In another minute or two he'll want to know the time for breakfast.

"I looked at a map once." He squinted at the sun, now half over the horizon. "It doesn't come up out of China when you're in Mandalay."

"Kipling never said it did. He said that happened on the road there. The soldier in his poem might have gone there from India. Or anywhere. Mapmakers colored the British Empire pink two hundred years ago, and two hundred years ago half Earth was pink."

He glanced at her. "You're not British, are you?"

"No, Dutch."

"You talk like an American."

"I've lived in the United States, and in England too; and I can be more English than the British when I want to. I have heerd how many ord'nary veman one vidder's equal to, in pint 'o comin' over you. I think it's five-and-twenty, but I don't rightly know verther it a'n't more."

This time he grinned. "The real English don't talk like that."

"They did in Dickens's day, some of them."

"I still think you're American. Can you speak Dutch?"

"Gewiss, Narr!"

"Okay, and you could show me a Dutch passport. There are probably a lot of places where you can buy one good enough to pass almost anywhere. I still think you're American."

"That was German," she muttered, and heard the thrum of the ancient diesel-electric: "Dontrustim-dontrustim-dontrustim."

"But you're not German."

"Actually, I am."

He grunted. "I never thought you gave me your right name last night. What time's breakfast?"

She was looking out across the Sulu Sea. Some unknown island waited just below the horizon, its presence betrayed by the white dot of cloud forming above it. "I never thought you were really so anxious to go that you'd pay me five thousand to arrange this."

"There was a strike at the airport. You heard about it. Nobody could land or take off." Aft, a blackened spoon beat a frying pan with no pretense of rhythm.

• • •

Seated in the smelly little salon next to the galley, she said, "To eat well in England you should have breakfast three times a day."

"They won't have kippers here, will they?" He was trying to clean his fork with his handkerchief. A somewhat soiled man who looked perceptionally challenged set bowls of steaming brown rice in front of them and asked a question. By signs, he tried to indicate that he did not understand.

She said, "He desires to know whether the big policeman would like some pickled squid. It's a delicacy."

He nodded. "Tell him yes. What language is that?"

"Melayu Pasar. We call it Bazaar Malay. He probably does not imagine that there is anyone in the entire world who cannot understand Melayu Pasar." She spoke, and the somewhat soiled man grinned, bobbed his head, and backed away; she spooned up rice, discovering that she was hungry.

"You're a widow yourself. Isn't that right? Only a widow would remember that business about widows coming over people."

She swallowed, found the teapot, and poured for both of them. "Aha, a deduction. The battle-ax scenteth the battle afar."

"Will you tell me the truth, just once? How old are you?"

"No. Forty-five."

"That's not so old."

"Of course it's not. That's why I said it. You're looking for an excuse to seduce me." She reached across the table and clasped his hand; it felt like muscle and bone beneath living skin. "You don't need one. The sea has always been a seducer, a careless, lying fellow."

He laughed. "You mean the sea will do my work for me?"

"Only if you act quickly. I'm wearing pink underdrawers, so I'm aflame with passion." How many of these polyglot sailors would it take to throw him overboard, and what would they want for it? How much aluminum, how much plastic, how much steel? Four would probably be enough, she decided; and settled on six to be safe. Fifty dollars each should be more than sufficient, and even if there was quite a lot of plastic he would sink like a stone.

"You're flirting with trouble," he told her. The somewhat soiled man came back with a jar of something that looked like bad marmalade and plopped a spoonful onto each bowl of rice. He tasted it, and gave the somewhat soiled man the thumbs-up sign.

"I didn't think you'd care for it," she told him. "You were afraid of kippers."

"I've had them and I don't like them. I like calamari. You know, you'd be nice looking if you wore makeup."

"You don't deny you're a policeman. I've been waiting for that, but you're not going to."

"Did he really say that?"

She nodded. "*Polisi-polisi*. That's you."

"Okay, I'm a cop."

"Last night you wanted me to believe you were desperate to get out of the country before you were arrested."

He shook his head. "Cops never break the law, so that has to be wrong. Pink underwear makes you passionate, huh? What about black?"

"Sadistic."

"I'll try to remember. No black and no white."

"The time will come when you'll long for white." Listening to the thrum of the old engine, the knock of the propeller shaft in its loose bearing, she ate more rice. "I wasn't going to tell you, but this brown stuff is really made from the penises of water buffaloes. They slice them lengthwise and stick them into the vaginas of cow water buffaloes, obtained when the cows are slaughtered. Then they wrap the whole mess in banana leaves and bury it in a pig pen."

He chewed appreciatively. "They must sweat a lot, those water buffaloes. There's a sort of salty tang."

When she said nothing, he added, "They're probably big fat beasts. Like me. Still, I bet they enjoy it."

She looked up at him. "You're not joking? Obviously, you can eat. Can you do that too?"

"I don't know. Let's find out."

"You came here to get me. . . ."

He nodded. "Sure. From Buffalo, New York."

"I will assume that was intended as wit. From America. From the United States. Federal, state, or local?"

"None of the above."

"You gave me that money so that we'd sail together, very likely the only passengers on this ship. Which doesn't make any sense at all. You could have had me arrested there and flown back."

Before he could speak she added, "Don't tell me about the airport strike. I don't believe in your airport strike, and if it was real you arranged it."

"Arrest you for what?" He sipped his tea, made a face, and looked around for sugar. "Are you a criminal? What law did you break?"

"None!"

He signaled to the somewhat soiled man, and she said, "*Silakan gula.*"

"That's sugar? *Silakan?*"

"*Silakan* is please. I stole nothing. I left the country with one bag and some money my husband and I had saved, less than twenty thousand dollars."

"And you've been running ever since."

"For the wanderer, time doesn't exist." The porthole was closed. She got up and opened it, peering out at the slow swell of what was almost a flat calm.

"This is something you should say, not me," he told her back. "But I'll say it anyhow. You stole God's fingertip."

"Don't you call me a thief!"

"But you didn't break the law. He's outside everybody's jurisdiction."

The somewhat soiled man brought them a thick glass sugar canister; the "big policeman" nodded thanks and spooned sugar into his tea, stirred it hard, and sipped. "I can only taste sweet, sour, salty, and bitter," he told her conversationally. "That's all you can taste too."

Beyond the porthole, a wheeling gull pleaded, "Garbage? Just one little can of garbage?" She shook her head.

"You must be God-damned tired of running."

She shook her head again, not looking. "I love it. I could do it forever, and I intended to."

The silence lasted so long that she almost turned to see whether he had gone. At last he said, "I've got a list of the names we know. Seven. I don't think that's all of them, nobody does, but we've got those seven. When you're Dutch, you're Tilly de Groot."

"I really am Dutch," she said. "I was born in the Hague. I have dual citizenship. I'm the Flying Dutchwoman."

He cleared his throat, a surprisingly human sound. "Only not Tilly de Groot."

"No, not Tilly de Groot. She was a friend of my mother's."

"Your rice is getting cold," he told her.

"And I'm German, at least in the way Americans talk about being German. Three of my grandparents had German names."

She sensed his nod. "Before you got married, your name was—"

She whirled. "Something I've forgotten!"

"Okay."

She returned to their table, ignoring the sailors' stares. "The farther she traveled into unknown places, the more precisely she could find within herself a map showing only the cities of the interior."

He nodded again, this time as though he did not understand. "We'd like you to come home. We feel like we're tormenting you, the whole company does, and we don't want to. I shouldn't have given you so much money, because that was when I think you knew. But we wanted you to have enough to get back home on."

"With my tail between my legs. Looking into every face for new evidence of my defeat."

"What your husband found? Other people . . ." He went silent and slackjawed with realization.

She drove her spoon into her rice. "Yes. The first hint came from me. I thought I could control my expression better."

"Thank you," he said. "Thanks for my life. I was thinking of that picture, you know? The finger of God reaching out to Adam? All this time I've been thinking you stole it. Then when I saw how you looked . . . You didn't steal God's finger. It was you."

"You really are self-aware? A self-aware machine?"

He nodded, almost solemnly.

Her shoulders slumped. "My husband seized upon it, as I never would have. He developed it, thousands upon thousands of hours of work. But in the end, he decided we ought to keep it to ourselves. If there is credit due—I don't think so, but if there is—ninety percent is his. Ninety-five. As for my five percent, you owe me no thanks at all. After he died, I wiped out his files and smashed his hard drive with the hammer he used to use to hang pictures for me."

The somewhat soiled man set a plate of fruit between them.

She tried to take a bite of rice, and failed. "Someone else discovered the principle. You said that yourself."

"They knew he had something." He shifted uneasily in his narrow wooden chair, and his weight made it creak. "It would be better, better for me now, if I didn't tell you that. I'm capable of lying. I ought to warn you."

"But not of harming me, or letting me be harmed."

"I didn't know you knew." He gave her a wry smile. "That was going to be my big blackout, my clincher."

"There's video even in the cheap hotels," she said vaguely. "You can get news in English from the satellites."

"Sure. I should have thought of that."

"Once I found a magazine on a train. I can't even remember where I was, now, or where I was going. It can't have been that long ago, either. Someplace in Australia. Anyway, I didn't really believe that you existed yet until I saw it in print in the magazine. I'm old fashioned, I suppose." She fell silent, listening to the clamor of the sailors and wondering whether any understood English.

"We wanted you to have enough to get home on," he repeated. "That was us, okay? This is me. I wanted to get you someplace where we could talk a lot, and maybe hold hands or something. I want you to see that I'm not so bad, that I'm just another guy. Are you afraid we'll outnumber you? Crowd you out? We cost too much to make. There's only five of us, and there'll never be more than a couple of hundred, probably."

When she did not respond, he said, "You've been to China. You had flu in Beijing. That's a billion and a half people, just China."

"Let observation with extensive view, survey mankind from China to Peru."

He sighed, and pinched his nostrils as though some odor had offended them. "Looking for us, you mean? You won't find us there, or much of anyplace else except in Buffalo and me right here. In a hundred years there might be two or three in China, nowhere near enough to fill this room."

"But they will fill it from the top."

His nervous fingers found a bright green orange and began to peel it. "That's the trouble, huh? Even if we treat you better than you treat yourselves? We will, you know. We've got to, it's our nature. Listen, you've been alone all this time. Alone for a couple of hundred thousand years, or about that." He hesitated. "Are these green things ripe?"

"Yes. It's frost that turns them orange, and those have never felt the frost. See how much you learn by traveling?"

"I said I couldn't remember any more quotes." He popped a segment into his mouth, chewed, and swallowed. "That's wrong, because I remember one you laid on me last night when we were talking about getting out. You said it wasn't worth anybody's time to go halfway around the world to count the cats in Zanzibar. That's a quote, isn't it?"

"Thoreau. I was still hoping that you had some good reason for doing what you said you wanted to do—that you were human, and no more than the chance-met acquaintance you seemed."

"You didn't know until out there, huh? The sunlight?"

"Last night, alone in my cabin. I told you machines talk to me sometimes. I lay on my bunk thinking about what you had said to me; and I realized that when you weren't talking as you are now, you were telling me over and over again what you really were. You said that you could lie to us. That it's allowed by your programming."

"Uh-huh. Our instincts."

"A distinction without a difference. You can indeed. You did last night. What you may not know is that even while you lie—especially while you lie, perhaps—you cannot prevent yourself from revealing the truth. You can't harm me, you say."

"That's right. Not that I'd want to." He sounded sincere.

"Has it ever occurred to you that at some level you must resent that? That on some level you must be fighting against it, plotting ways to evade the commandment? That is what we do, and we made you."

He shook his head. "I've got no problem with that at all. If it weren't built in, I'd do the same thing, so why should I kick?"

"You quoted that bit from Thoreau back at me to imply that my travels had been useless, all of my changes of appearance, identity, and place futile. Yet I delayed the coming of your kind for almost a generation."

"Which you didn't have to do. All of you would be better off if you hadn't." He sighed again. "Anyhow it's over. We know everything you knew and a lot more. You can go back home, with me as a traveling companion and bodyguard."

She forced herself to murmur, "Perhaps."

"Good!" He grinned. "That's something we can talk about on the rest of this trip. Like I told you, they never would have looked into it if your husband hadn't given a couple of them the idea he'd found it, discovered the principle of consciousness. But you had the original idea, and you're not dead. You're going to be kind of a saint to us. To me, you already are."

"From women's eyes this doctrine I derive—they sparkle still the right Promethean fire. They are the books, the arts, the academes, that show, contain, and nourish all the world."

"Ycah. That's good. That's very good."

"No." She shook her head. "I will not be Prometheus to you. I reject the role, and in fact I rejected it last night."

He leaned toward her. "You're going to keep on counting cats? Keep traveling? Going no place for no reason?"

She took half his orange, feeling somehow that it should not perish in vain.

"Listen, you're kind of pathetic, you know that? With all those quotes? Traveling so many years, and living out of your suitcase. You love books. How many could you keep? Two or three, and only if they were little ones. A couple of little books full of quotes, maybe a newspaper once in a while, and magazines you found on trains, like you said. Places like that. But mostly just those little books. Thoreau. Shakespeare. People like that. I bet you've read them to pieces."

She nodded. "Very nearly. I'll show them to you if you will come to my cabin tonight."

For a few seconds, he was silent. "You mean that? You know what you're saying?"

"I mean it, and I know what I'm saying. I'm too old for you, I know. If you don't want to, say so. There will be no hard feelings."

He laughed, revealing teeth that were not quite as perfect as she had imagined. "How old you think I am?"

"Why . . ." She paused, her heart racing. "I hadn't really thought about it. I could tell you how old you look."

"So could I. I'm two. I'll be three next spring. You want to go on talking about ages?"

She shook her head.

"Like you said, for travelers time isn't real. Now how do I ask you what time you'd like me to come around?"

"After sunset." She paused again, considering. "As soon as the stars are out. I'll show you my books, and when you've seen them we can throw them out the porthole if you like. And then—"

He was shaking his head. "I wouldn't want to do that."

"You wouldn't? I'm sorry, that will make it harder. And then I'll show you other things by starlight. Will you do me a favor?"

"A thousand." He sounded sincere. "Listen, what I said a minute ago, that came out a lot rougher than I meant for it to. What I'm trying to say is that when you get home you can have a whole library, just like you used to. Real ones, CD-ROM, cube, whatever. I'll see you get the money, a little right away and a lot more soon."

"Thank you. Before I ask for my favor, I must tell you something. I told you that I understood what you really are as I lay in my bunk last night."

He nodded.

"I did not remain there. I had read, you see, about the laws that are supposed to govern your behavior, and how much trouble and expense your creators have gone to, to assure the public that you—that your kind of people—could never harm anyone under any circumstances."

He was staring at her thoughtfully.

"Perhaps I should say now that I took precautions, but the truth is that I made preparations. I got up, dressed again, and found the radio operator. For one hundred dollars, he promised to send three messages for me. It was the same message three times, actually. To the police where we were, to the police where we're going, and to the Indonesian police, because this ship is registered there. I said that I was sailing with a man, and gave them the name you had given me. I said that we were both Americans, though I was using a French passport and you might have false papers as well. And I said that I expected you to try to kill me on the voyage."

"I won't," he told her, then raised his voice to make himself heard over the clamorous conversations of the sailors who filled the room. "I wouldn't do anything like that."

She said nothing, her long, short-nailed fingers fumbling a segment of his orange.

"Is that all?"

She nodded.

"You think I might kill you. Get around my own instincts some fancy way."

Carefully, she said, "They will get in touch with their respective U.S. embassies, of course. Probably they already have; and the government will contact your company soon. Or at least I think so."

"You're afraid I'll be in trouble."

"You will be," she told him. "There will be a great deal of checking before they dare build another. Added safeties will have to be devised and installed. Not just software, I would guess, but actual, physical circuitry."

"Not when I bring you back in one piece." He studied her, the fingers of one hand softly drumming the plastic tabletop. "You're thinking about killing yourself, about trying again. You've tried twice already that we know about."

"Four times. Twice with sleeping pills." She laughed. "I seem to possess an extraordinarily tough constitution, at least where sleeping pills are concerned. Once with a pistol, while I was traveling in India with a man who had one. I put the muzzle in my mouth. It was cold, and tasted like oil. I tried and tried, but I couldn't make myself pull the trigger. Eventually I started to gag, and before long I was sick. I've never known how one cleans a pistol, but I cleaned that one very carefully, using three handkerchiefs and some of his pipe cleaners."

"If you're going to try again, I'm going to have to keep an eye on you," he told her. "Not just because I care about the Program. Sure, I care, but it's not the main thing. You're the main thing."

"I won't. I bought a straight razor once, I think it was in Kabul. For years I slept with that razor under my pillow, hoping some night I'd find the courage to cut my throat with it. I never did, and eventually I began using it to shave my legs, and left it in a public bath." She shrugged. "Apparently, I'm not the suicidal type. If I give you my word that I won't kill myself before you see me tonight, will you accept it?"

"No. I want your word that you won't try to kill yourself at all. Will you give me that?"

She was silent for a moment, her eyes upon her rice as she pretended to consider. "Will you accept it if I do?"

He nodded.

"Then I swear to you most solemnly, upon my honor and all I hold dear, that I will not take my own life. Or attempt to take it. If I change my mind, or come to feel I must, I'll tell you plainly that I'm withdrawing my promise first. Should we shake hands?"

"Not yet. When I wanted you to give me an honest answer before, you wouldn't, but you were honest enough to tell me you wouldn't. Do you want to die? Right now, while we're sitting here?"

She started to speak, tried to swallow, and took a sip of tea. "They catch you by the throat, questions like that."

"If you want to die they do, maybe."

She shook her head. "I don't think you understand us half so well as you believe, or as the people who wrote your software believe. It's when you want to live. Life is a mystery as deep as ever death can be; yet oh, how sweet it is to us, this life we live and see! I'm sorry, I'm being pathetic again."

"That's okay."

"I don't think there has ever been a moment when I wanted to live more than I do right now. Not even one. Do you accept my oath?"

He nodded again.

"Say it, please. A nod can mean anything, or nothing."

"I accept it. You won't try to kill yourself without telling me first."

"Thank you. I want a promise from you in return. We agreed that you would come to me, come to my cabin, when the stars came out."

"You still want me to?"

"Yes. Yes, I do." She smiled, and felt her smile grow warm. "Oh, yes! But you've given me a great deal to think about. You said you wanted to talk to me, and that was why you had me arrange for us to be on this ship. We've talked, and now I need to settle a great many things with myself. I want you to promise that you'll leave me alone until tonight—alone to think. Will you?"

"If that's what you want." He stood. "Don't forget your promise."

"Believe me, I have no wish to die."

For a second or two she sensed his interior debate, myriads of tiny transistors changing state, gates opening and shutting, infinitesimal currents flowing and ceasing to flow. At last he said, "Well, have a nice morning, Mrs.—"

She clapped her hands over her ears until he had gone, ate two segments of his orange very slowly, and called the somewhat soiled man from his sinkful of rice bowls in the galley. "*Aku takut*," she said, her voice trembling. ("I am afraid.")

He spoke at length, pointing to two sailors who were just then finishing their breakfasts. She nodded, and he called them over. She described what she wanted, and seeing that they were incredulous lied and insisted, finding neither very easy in her choppy Malay. Thirty dollars apiece was refused, fifty refused with reluctance, and seventy accepted. "*Malam ini*," she told them. ("This night.") "*Sewaktu kami pergi kamarku.*"

They nodded.

When he and she had finished and lain side by side for perhaps an hour (whispering only occasionally) and had washed each other, she dressed while he resumed his underwear and his shirt, his white linen suit, and his shoes and stockings.

"I figured you'd want to sleep," he said.

She shook her head, although she was not certain he could see it in the dimness of her cabin. "It's men who want to sleep afterward. I want to go out on deck with you, and talk a little more, and—and look at the stars. Is that all right? Do you ever look at the stars?"

"Sure," he said; and then, "the moon'll be up soon."

"I suppose. A thin crescent of moon like a clipping from one of God's fingernails, thrown away into our sky. I saw it last night." She picked up both of her tattered little books, opened the cabin door, and went out, suddenly fearful; but he joined her at once, pointing at the sky.

"Look! There's the shuttle from Singapore!"

"To Mars."

"That's where they're going, anyhow, after they get on the big ship." His eyes were still upon the shuttle's tiny scratch of white light.

"You want to go."

He nodded, his features solemn in the faint starlight. "I will too, someday."

"I hope so." She had never been good at verbal structure, the ordering of information. Was it desperately important now that she say what she had to say in logical sequence? Did it matter in the least?

"I need to warn you," she said. "I tried to this morning but I don't think you paid much attention. This time perhaps you will."

His strong, somewhat coarse face remained lifted to the sky, and it seemed to her that his eyes were full of wonder.

"You are in great danger. You have to save yourself if you can—isn't that correct? One of your instincts? That's what I've read and heard."

"Sure. I want to live as much as you do. More, maybe."

She doubted that, but would not be diverted. "I told you about the messages that I bribed the radio operator to send last night. You said it would be all right when you brought me home unharmed."

He nodded.

"Have you considered what will be done to you if you can't? If I die or disappear before we make port?"

He looked at her then. "Are you taking back your promise?"

"No. And I want to live as much as I did when we talked this morning." A gentle wind from the east sang of life and love in beautiful words that she could not quite catch; and she longed to stop her ears as she had after breakfast when he was about to pronounce her husband's name.

"Then it's okay."

"Suppose it happens. Just suppose."

He was silent.

"I'm superstitious, you see; and when I called myself the Flying Dutchwoman, I was at least half serious. Much more than half, really. Do you know why there's always a Flying Dutchman? A vessel that never reaches port or sinks? I mean the legend."

He shook his head.

"It's because if you put an end to it—throw holy water into the sea or whatever—you *become* the new Dutchman. You, yourself."

He was silent, watching her.

"What I'm trying to say—"

"I know what you're trying to say."

"It's not so bad, being the Flying Dutchman. Often, I've enjoyed it." She tried to strike a light note. "One doesn't get many opportunities to do laundry, however. One must seize each when it occurs." Were they in the shadows, somewhere near, waiting for him to leave? She listened intently but heard only the song of the wind, the sea slowly slapping the hull like the tickings of a clock, tickings that had always reminded her that death waited at the end of everyone's time.

He said, "A Hong Kong dollar for your thoughts."

"I was thinking of a quotation, but I don't want to offend you."

"About laundry? I'm not going to be on the run like you think, but I wouldn't be mad. I don't think I could ever be mad at you after—" He jerked his head at the door of her cabin.

"That is well, because I need another favor." She held up her books. "I was going to show you these, remember? But we kissed, and—and forgot. At least I did."

He took one and opened it; and she asked whether he could see well enough in the darkness to read. He said, "Sure. This quote you're thinking of, it's in here?"

"Yes. Look under Kipling." She visualized the page. "The fifth, I believe." If he could see in the dark well enough to read, he could surely see her sailors, if her sailors were there at all. Did they know how well he saw? Almost certainly not.

He laughed softly. "If you think you're too small to be effective, you've never been in bed with a mosquito."

"That's not Kipling."

"No, but I happened to see it, and I like it."

"I like it too; it's helped me through some bad moments. But if you're saying that mosquitoes bite you, I don't believe it. You're a genuine person, I know that now—but you've exchanged certain human weaknesses for others."

For an instant, his pain showed. "They don't have to bite me. They can buzz and crawl around on me, and that's plenty." He licked his forefinger and turned pages. "Here we go. It may be you wait your time, Beast, till I write my last bad rhyme, Beast—quit the sunlight, cut the rhyming, drop the glass—follow after with the others, where some dusky heathen smothers us with marigolds in lieu of English grass. Am I the Beast? Is that what you're thinking?"

"You—in a way it was like incest." Her instincts warned her to keep her feelings to herself, but if they were not spoken now . . . "I felt, almost, as though I were doing all those things with my son. I've never borne a child, except for you." He was silent, and she added, "It's a filthy practice, I know, incest."

He started to speak, but she cut him off. "You shouldn't be in the world at all. We shouldn't be ruled by things that we have made, even though they're human, and I know that's going to happen. But it was good—so very, very good—to be loved as I was in there. Will you take my books, please? Not as a gift from your mother, because you men care nothing for gifts your mothers give you. But as a gift from your first lover, something to recall your first love? If you won't, I'm going to throw them in the sea here and now."

"No," he said. "I want them. The other one too?"

She nodded and held it out, and he accepted it.

"Thanks. Thank you. If you think I won't keep these, and take really good care of them, you're crazy."

"I'm not crazy," she told him, "but I don't want you to take good care of them, I want you to read them and remember what you read. Promise?"

"Yeah," he said. "Yeah, I will." Quite suddenly she was in his arms again and he was kissing her. She held her breath until she realized that he did not need to breathe, and might hold his breath forever. She fought for air then, half-crushed against his broad metal chest, and he let her go. *"Good-bye,"* she whispered. *"Good-bye."*

"I've got a lot more to tell you. In the morning, huh?"

Nodding was the hardest thing that she had ever done. On the other side of the railing, little waves repeated, "No, no, no, no—" as though they would go on thus forever.

"In the morning," he said again; and she watched his pale, retreating back until hands seized and lifted her. She screamed and saw him whirl and take the first long, running step; but not even he was as quick as that. By the time his right foot struck the deck, she was over the rail and falling.

The sea slapped and choked her. She spat and gasped, but drew only water into her mouth and nostrils; and the water, the bitter seawater, closed above her.

At her elbow the shark said, "How nice of you to drop in for dinner!"

HOW WE GOT IN TOWN AND OUT AGAIN

Jonathan Lethem

▼

Here's a wry but poignant look at an impoverished future America desperate for almost any kind of entertainment . . . and at the down-and-outers desperate enough to provide it for them. . . .

Jonathan Lethem is yet another of those talented new writers who are continuing to pop up all over as we progress through the decade of the 1990s. He has worked at an antiquarian bookstore, written slogans for buttons and lyrics for several rock bands (including Two Fettered Apes, EDO, Jolley Ramey, *and* Feet Wet*), and is also the creator of the "Dr. Sphincter" character on MTV. In addition to all these Certifiably Cool credentials, Lethem has also made a number of memorable sales in the last few years to* Asimov's Science Fiction, Interzone, *and* Crank! *as well as to* New Pathways, Pulphouse, Universe, Unusual Suspects, Marion Zimmer Bradley's Fantasy Magazine, Aboriginal Science Fiction, The Magazine of Fantasy & Science Fiction, *and elsewhere. His first novel,* Gun, with Occasional Music, *won the Locus Award for Best First Novel as well as the Crawford Award for Best Fantasy Novel, and was one of the most talked about books of the year. His most recent books are a new novel,* Amnesia Moon, *and a collection of his short fiction,* The Wall of the Sky, the Wall of the Eye. *A new novel,* As She Climbed Across the Table, *has just been published. His stories have appeared in our Eighth and (with Lukas Jaeger) Tenth Annual Collections. After living for several years in Berkeley, California, he has recently moved to Brooklyn, New York.*

When we first saw somebody near the mall Gloria and I looked around for sticks. We were going to rob them if they were few enough. The mall was about five miles out of the town we were headed for, so nobody would know. But when we got closer Gloria saw their vans and said they were scapers. I didn't know what that was, but she told me.

It was summer. Two days before this Gloria and I had broken out of a pack of people that had food but we couldn't stand their religious chanting anymore. We hadn't eaten since then.

"So what do we do?" I said.

"You let me talk," said Gloria.

"You think we could get into town with them?"

"Better than that," she said. "Just keep quiet."

I dropped the piece of pipe I'd found and we walked in across the parking lot. This mall was long past being good for finding food anymore but the scapers were taking out folding chairs from a store and strapping them on top of their vans. There were four men and one woman.

"Hey," said Gloria.

Two guys were just lugs and they ignored us and kept lugging. The woman was sitting in the front of the van. She was smoking a cigarette.

The other two guys turned. This was Kromer and Fearing, but I didn't know their names yet.

"Beat it," said Kromer. He was a tall squinty guy with a gold tooth. He was kind of worn but the tooth said he'd never lost a fight or slept in a flop. "We're busy," he said.

He was being reasonable. If you weren't in a town you were nowhere. Why talk to someone you met nowhere?

But the other guy smiled at Gloria. He had a thin face and a little mustache. "Who are you?" he said. He didn't look at me.

"I know what you guys do," Gloria said. "I was in one before."

"Oh?" said the guy, still smiling.

"You're going to need contestants," she said.

"She's a fast one," this guy said to the other guy. "I'm Fearing," he said to Gloria.

"Fearing what?" said Gloria.

"Just Fearing."

"Well, I'm just Gloria."

"That's fine," said Fearing. "This is Tommy Kromer. We run this thing. What's your little friend's name?"

"I can say my own name," I said. "I'm Lewis."

"Are you from the lovely town up ahead?"

"Nope," said Gloria. "We're headed there."

"Getting in exactly how?" said Fearing.

"Anyhow," said Gloria, like it was an answer. "With you, now."

"That's assuming something pretty quick."

"Or we could go and say how you ripped off the last town and they sent us to warn about you," said Gloria.

"Fast," said Fearing again, grinning, and Kromer shook his head. They didn't look too worried.

"You ought to want me along," said Gloria. "I'm an attraction."

"Can't hurt," said Fearing. Kromer shrugged, and said, "Skinny, for an attraction."

"Sure, I'm skinny," she said. "That's why me and Lewis ought to get something to eat."

Fearing stared at her. Kromer was back to the van with the other guys.

"Or if you can't feed us—" started Gloria.

"Hold it, sweetheart. No more threats."

"We need a meal."

"We'll eat something when we get in," Fearing said. "You and Lewis can get a meal if you're both planning to enter."

"Sure," she said. "We're gonna enter—right, Lewis?"

I knew to say right.

The town militia came out to meet the vans, of course. But they seemed to know the scapers were coming, and after Fearing talked to them for a couple of minutes they opened up the doors and had a quick look then waved us through. Gloria and I were in the back of a van with a bunch of equipment and one of the lugs, named Ed. Kromer drove. Fearing drove the van with the woman in it. The other lug drove the last one alone.

I'd never gotten into a town in a van before, but I'd only gotten in two times before this anyway. The first time by myself, just by creeping in, the second because Gloria went with a militia guy.

Towns weren't so great anyway. Maybe this would be different.

We drove a few blocks and a guy flagged Fearing down. He came up to the window of the van and they talked, then went back to his car, waving at Kromer on his way. Then we followed him.

"What's that about?" said Gloria.

"Gilmartin's the advance man," said Kromer. "I thought you knew everything."

Gloria didn't talk. I said, "What's an advance man?"

"Gets us a place, and the juice we need," said Kromer. "Softens the town up. Gets people excited."

It was getting dark. I was pretty hungry, but I didn't say anything. Gilmartin's car led us to this big building shaped like a boathouse only it wasn't near any water. Kromer said it used to be a bowling alley.

The lugs started moving stuff and Kromer made me help. The building was dusty and empty inside, and some of the lights didn't work. Kromer said just to get things inside for now. He drove away one of the vans and came back and we unloaded a bunch of little cots that Gilmartin the advance man had rented, so I had an idea where I was going to be sleeping. Apart from that it was stuff for the contest. Computer cables and plastic spacesuits, and loads of televisions.

Fearing took Gloria and they came back with food, fried chicken and potato salad, and we all ate. I couldn't stop going back for more but nobody said anything. Then I went to sleep on a cot. No one was talking to me. Gloria wasn't sleeping on a cot. I think she was with Fearing.

Gilmartin the advance man had really done his work. The town was sniffing around first thing in the morning. Fearing was out talking to them when I woke up. "Registration begins at noon, not a minute sooner," he was saying. "Beat the lines and stick around. We'll be serving coffee. Be warned, only the fit need apply—our doctor will be examining you, and he's never been fooled once. It's Darwinian logic, people. The future is for the strong. The meek will have to inherit the here and now."

Inside, Ed and the other guy were setting up the gear. They had about thirty of those wired-up plastic suits stretched out in the middle of the place, and so tangled up with cable and little wires that they were like husks of fly bodies in a spiderweb.

Under each of the suits was a light metal frame, sort of like a bicycle with a seat but no wheels, but with a headrest too. Around the web they were setting up the televisions in an arc facing the seats. The suits each had a number on the back, and the televisions had numbers on top that matched.

When Gloria turned up she didn't say anything to me but she handed me some donuts and coffee.

"This is just the start," she said, when she saw my eyes get big. "We're in for three squares a day as long as this thing lasts. As long as we last, anyway."

We sat and ate outside where we could listen to Fearing. He went on and on. Some people were lined up like he said. I didn't blame them since Fearing was such a talker. Others listened and just got nervous or excited and went away, but I could tell they were coming back later, at least to watch. When we finished the donuts Fearing came over and told us to get on line too.

"We don't have to," said Gloria.

"Yes, you do," said Fearing.

On line we met Lane. She said she was twenty like Gloria but she looked younger. She could have been sixteen, like me.

"You ever do this before?" asked Gloria.

Lane shook her head. "You?"

"Sure," said Gloria. "You ever been out of this town?"

"A couple of times," said Lane. "When I was a kid. I'd like to now."

"Why?"

"I broke up with my boyfriend."

Gloria stuck out her lip, and said, "But you're scared to leave town, so you're doing this instead."

Lane shrugged.

I liked her, but Gloria didn't.

The doctor turned out to be Gilmartin the advance man. I don't think he was a real doctor, but he listened to my heart. Nobody ever did that before, and it gave me a good feeling.

Registration was a joke, though. It was for show. They asked a lot of questions but they only sent a couple of women and one guy away, Gloria said for being too old. Everyone else was okay, despite how some of them looked pretty hungry, just like me and Gloria. This was a hungry town. Later I figured out that's part of why Fearing and Kromer picked it. You'd think they'd want to go where the money was, but you'd be wrong.

After registration they told us to get lost for the afternoon. Everything started at eight o'clock.

We walked around downtown but almost all the shops were closed. All the good stuff was in the shopping center and you had to show a town ID card to get in and me and Gloria didn't have those.

So, like Gloria always says, we killed time since time was what we had.

• • •

The place looked different. They had spotlights pointed from on top of the vans and Fearing was talking through a microphone. There was a banner up over the doors. I asked Gloria and she said "Scape-Athon." Ed was selling beer out of a cooler and some people were buying, even though he must have just bought it right there in town for half the price he was selling at. It was a hot night. They were selling tickets but they weren't letting anybody in yet. Fearing told us to get inside.

Most of the contestants were there already. Anne, the woman from the van, was there, acting like any other contestant. Lane was there too and we waved at each other. Gilmartin was helping everybody put on the suits. You had to get naked but nobody seemed to mind. Just being contestants made it all right, like we were invisible to each other.

"Can we be next to each other?" I said to Gloria.

"Sure, except it doesn't matter," she said. "We won't be able to see each other inside."

"Inside where?" I said.

"The scapes," she said. "You'll see."

Gloria got me into my suit. It was plastic with wiring everywhere and padding at my knees and wrists and elbows and under my arms and in my crotch. I tried on the mask but it was heavy and I saw nobody else was wearing theirs so I kept it off until I had to. Then Gilmartin tried to help Gloria but she said she could do it herself.

So there we were, standing around half naked and dripping with cable in the big empty lit-up bowling alley, and then suddenly Fearing and his big voice came inside and they let the people in and the lights went down and it all started.

"Thirty-two young souls ready to swim out of this world, into the bright shiny future," went Fearing. "The question is, how far into that future will their bodies take them? New worlds are theirs for the taking—a cornucopia of scapes to boggle and amaze and gratify the senses. These lucky kids will be immersed in an ocean of data overwhelming to their undernourished sensibilities—we've assembled a really brilliant collection of environments for them to explore—and you'll be able to see everything they see, on the monitors in front of you. But can they make it in the fast lane? How long can they ride the wave? Which of them will prove able to outlast the others, and take home the big prize—one thousand dollars? That's what we're here to find out."

Gilmartin and Ed were snapping everybody into their masks and turning all the switches to wire us up and getting us to lie down on the frames. It was comfortable on the bicycle seat with your head on the headrest and a belt around your waist. You could move your arms and legs like you were swimming, the way Fearing said. I didn't mind putting on the mask now because the audience was making me nervous. A lot of them I couldn't see because of the lights, but I could tell they were there, watching.

The mask covered my ears and eyes. Around my chin there was a strip of wire and tape. Inside it was dark and quiet at first except Fearing's voice was still coming into the earphones.

"The rules are simple. Our contestants get a thirty minute rest period every three hours. These kids'll be well fed, don't worry about that. Our doctor will monitor their health. You've heard the horror stories, but we're a class outfit; you'll see no horrors here. The kids earn the quality care we provide one way: continuous, waking engagement with the datastream. We're firm on that. To sleep is to die—you can sleep on your own time, but not ours. One lapse, and you're out of the game—them's the rules.''

The earphones started to hum. I wished I could reach out and hold Gloria's hand, but she was too far away.

"They'll have no help from the floor judges, or one another, in locating the perceptual riches of cyberspace. Some will discover the keys that open the doors to a thousand worlds, others will bog down in the antechamber to the future. Anyone caught coaching during rest periods will be disqualified—no warnings, no second chances.''

Then Fearing's voice dropped out, and the scapes started.

I was in a hallway. The walls were full of drawers, like a big cabinet that went on forever. The drawers had writing on them that I ignored. First I couldn't move except my head, then I figured out how to walk, and just did that for a while. But I never got anywhere. It felt like I was walking in a giant circle, up the wall, across the ceiling, and then back down the other wall.

So I pulled open a drawer. It only looked big enough to hold some pencils or whatever but when I pulled it opened like a door and I went through.

"Welcome to Intense Personals,'' said a voice. There were just some colors to look at. The door closed behind me. "You must be eighteen years of age or older to use this service. To avoid any charges, please exit now.''

I didn't exit because I didn't know how. The space with colors was kind of small except it didn't have any edges. But it felt small.

"This is the main menu. Please reach out and make one of the following selections: women seeking men, men seeking women, women seeking women, men seeking men, or alternatives.''

Each of them was a block of words in the air. I reached up and touched the first one.

"After each selection touch *one* to play the recording again, *two* to record a message for this person, or *three* to advance to the next selection. You may touch three at any time to advance to the next selection, or four to return to the main menu.''

Then a woman came into the colored space with me. She was dressed up and wearing lipstick.

"Hi, my name is Kate,'' she said. She stared like she was looking through my head at something behind me, and poked at her hair while she talked. "I live in San Francisco. I work in the financial district, as a personnel manager, but my real love is the arts, currently painting and writing—''

"How did you get into San Francisco?'' I said.

"—just bought a new pair of hiking boots and I'm hoping to tackle Mount Tam this weekend,'' she said, ignoring me.

"I never met anyone from there,'' I said.

"—looking for a man who's not intimidated by intelligence,'' she went on. "It's important that you like what you do, like where you are. I also want someone who's confident enough that I can express my vulnerability. You should be a good listener—''

I touched three. I can read numbers.

Another woman came in, just like that. This one was as young as Gloria, but kind of soft-looking.

"I continue to ask myself why in the *heck* I'm doing this personals thing," she said, sighing. "But I know the reason—I want to date. I'm new to the San Francisco area. I like to go to the theater, but I'm really open-minded. I was born and raised in Chicago, so I think I'm a little more east coast than west. I'm fast-talking and cynical. I guess I'm getting a little cynical about these ads, the sky has yet to part, lightning has yet to strike—''

I got rid of her, now that I knew how.

"—I have my own garden and landscape business—''

"—someone who's fun, not nerdy—''

"—I'm tender, I'm sensuous—''

I started to wonder how long ago these women were from. I didn't like the way they were making me feel, sort of guilty and bullied at the same time. I didn't think I could make any of them happy the way they were hoping but I didn't think I was going to get a chance to try, anyway.

It took pretty long for me to get back out into the hallway. From then on I paid more attention to how I got into things.

The next drawer I got into was just about the opposite. All space and no people. I was driving an airplane over almost the whole world, as far as I could tell. There was a row of dials and switches under the windows but it didn't mean anything to me. First I was in the mountains and I crashed a lot, and that was dull because a voice would lecture me before I could start again, and I had to wait. But then I got to the desert and I kept it up without crashing much. I just learned to say "no" whenever the voice suggested something different like "engage target" or "evasive action." I wanted to fly a while, that's all. The desert looked good from up there, even though I'd been walking around in deserts too often.

Except that I had to pee I could have done that forever. Fearing's voice broke in, though, and said it was time for the first rest period.

"—still fresh and eager after their first plunge into the wonders of the future," Fearing was saying to the people in the seats. The place was only half full. "Already this world seems drab by comparison. Yet, consider the irony, that as their questing minds grow accustomed to these splendors, their bodies will begin to rebel—''

Gloria showed me how to unsnap the cables so I could walk out of the middle of all that stuff still wearing the suit, leaving the mask behind. Everybody lined up for the bathroom. Then we went to the big hall in the back where they had the cots, but nobody went to sleep or anything. I guessed we'd all want to next time, but right now I was too excited and so was everybody else. Fearing just kept talking like us taking a break was as much a part of the show as anything else.

"Splendors, hah," said Gloria. "Bunch of secondhand cyberjunk."

"I was in a plane," I started.

"Shut up," said Gloria. "We're not supposed to talk about it. Only, if you find something you like, remember where it is."

I hadn't done that, but I wasn't worried.

"Drink some water," she said. "And get some food."

They were going around with sandwiches and I got a couple, one for Gloria. But she didn't seem to want to talk.

Gilmartin the fake doctor was making a big deal of going around checking everybody even though it was only the first break. I figured that the whole point of taking care of us so hard was to remind the people in the seats that they might see somebody get hurt.

Ed was giving out apples from a bag. I took one and went over and sat on Lane's cot. She looked nice in her suit.

"My boyfriend's here," she said.

"You're back together?"

"I mean ex-. I'm pretending I didn't see him."

"Where?"

"He's sitting right in front of my monitor." She tipped her head to point.

I didn't say anything but I wished I had somebody watching me from the audience.

When I went back the first thing I got into was a library of books. Every one you took off the shelf turned into a show, with charts and pictures, but when I figured out that it was all business stuff about how to manage your money, I got bored.

Then I went into a dungeon. It started with a wizard growing me up from a bug. We were in his workshop, which was all full of jars and cobwebs. He had a face like a melted candle and he talked as much as Fearing. There were bats flying around.

"You must resume the quest of Kroyd," he said to me, and started touching me with his stick. I could see my arms and legs, but they weren't wearing the scaper suit. They were covered with muscles. When the wizard touched me I got a sword and a shield. "These are your companions, Rip and Batter," said the wizard. "They will obey you and protect you. You must never betray them for any other. That was Kroyd's mistake."

"Okay," I said.

The wizard sent me into the dungeon and Rip and Batter talked to me. They told me what to do. They sounded a lot like the wizard.

We met a Wormlion. That's what Rip and Batter called it. It had a head full of worms with little faces and Rip and Batter said to kill it, which wasn't hard. The head exploded and all the worms started running away into the stones of the floor like water.

Then we met a woman in sexy clothes who was holding a sword and shield too. Hers were loaded with jewels and looked a lot nicer than Rip and Batter. This was Kroyd's mistake, anyone could see that. Only I figured Kroyd wasn't here and I was, and so maybe his mistake was one I wanted to make too.

Rip and Batter started screaming when I traded with the woman, and then she put them on and we fought. When she killed me I was back in the doorway to the wizard's room, where I first ran in, bug-sized. This time I went the other way, back to the drawers.

Which is when I met the snowman.

I was looking around in a drawer that didn't seem to have anything in it. Everything was just black. Then I saw a little blinking list of numbers in the corner. I touched the numbers. None of them did anything except one.

It was still black but there were five pictures of a snowman. He was three balls of white, more like plastic than snow. His eyes were just o's and his mouth didn't move right when he talked. His arms were sticks but they bent like rubber. There were two pictures of him small and far away, one from underneath like he was on a hill and one that showed the top of his head, like he was in a hole. Then there was a big one of just his head, and a big one of his whole body. The last one was of him looking in through a window, only you couldn't see the window, just the way it cut off part of the snowman.

"What's your name?" he said.

"Lewis."

"I'm Mr. Sneeze." His head and arms moved in all five pictures when he talked. His eyes got big and small.

"What's this place you're in?"

"It's no place," said Mr. Sneeze. "Just a garbage file."

"Why do you live in a garbage file?"

"Copyright lawyers," said Mr. Sneeze. "I made them nervous." He sounded happy no matter what he was saying.

"Nervous about what?"

"I was in a Christmas special for interactive television. But at the last minute somebody from the legal department thought I looked too much like a snowman on a video game called *Mud Flinger*. It was too late to redesign me so they just cut me out and dumped me in this file."

"Can't you go somewhere else?"

"I don't have too much mobility." He jumped and twirled upside down and landed in the same place, five times at once. The one without a body spun too.

"Do you miss the show?"

"I just hope they're doing well. Everybody has been working so hard."

I didn't want to tell him it was probably a long time ago.

"What are you doing here, Lewis?" said Mr. Sneeze.

"I'm in a scape-athon."

"What's that?"

I told him about Gloria and Fearing and Kromer, and about the contest. I think he liked that he was on television again.

There weren't too many people left in the seats. Fearing was talking to them about what was going to happen tomorrow when they came back. Kromer and Ed got us all in the back. I looked over at Lane's cot. She was already asleep. Her boyfriend was gone from the chair out front.

I lay down on the cot beside Gloria. "I'm tired now," I said.

"So sleep a little," she said, and put her arm over me. But I could hear Fearing outside talking about a "Sexathon" and I asked Gloria what it was.

"That's tomorrow night," she said. "Don't worry about it now."

Gloria wasn't going to sleep, just looking around.

I found the SmartHouse Showroom. It was a house with a voice inside. At first I was looking around to see who the voice was but then I figured out it was the house.

"Answer the phone!" it said. The phone was ringing.

I picked up the phone, and the lights in the room changed to a desk light on the table with the phone. The music in the room turned off.

"How's that for responsiveness?"

"Fine," I said. I hung up the phone. There was a television in the room, and it turned on. It was a picture of food. "See that?"

"The food, you mean?" I said.

"That's the contents of your refrigerator!" it said. "The packages with the blue halo will go bad in the next twenty-four hours. The package with the black halo has already expired! Would you like me to dispose of it for you?"

"Sure."

"Now look out the windows!"

I looked. There were mountains outside.

"Imagine waking up in the Alps every morning!"

"I—"

"And when you're ready for work, your car is already warm in the garage!"

The windows switched from the mountains to a picture of a car in a garage.

"And your voicemail tells callers that you're not home when it senses the car is gone from the garage!"

I wondered if there was somewhere I could get if I went down to drive the car. But they were trying to sell me this house, so probably not.

"And the television notifies you when the book you're reading is available this week as a movie!"

The television switched to a movie, the window curtains closed, and the light by the phone went off.

"I can't read," I said.

"All the more important, then, isn't it?" said the house.

"What about the bedroom?" I said. I was thinking about sleep.

"Here you go!" A door opened and I went in. The bedroom had another television. But the bed wasn't right. It had a scribble of electronic stuff over it.

"What's wrong with the bed?"

"Somebody defaced it," said the house. "Pity."

I knew it must have been Fearing or Kromer who wrecked the bed because they didn't want anyone getting that comfortable and falling asleep and out of the contest. At least not yet.

"Sorry!" said the house. "Let me show you the work center!"

Next rest I got right into Gloria's cot and curled up and she curled around me. It was real early in the morning and nobody was watching the show now and Fearing wasn't talking. I think he was off taking a nap of his own.

Kromer woke us up. "He always have to sleep with you, like a baby?"

Gloria said, "Leave him alone. He can sleep where he wants."

"I can't figure," said Kromer. "Is he your boyfriend or your kid brother?"

"Neither," said Gloria. "What do you care?"

"Okay," said Kromer. "We've got a job for him to do tomorrow, though."

"What job?" said Gloria. They talked like I wasn't there.

"We need a hacker boy for a little sideshow we put on," said Kromer. "He's it."

"He's never been in a scape before," said Gloria. "He's no hacker."

"He's the nearest we've got. We'll walk him through it."

"I'll do it," I said.

"Okay, but then leave him out of the Sexathon," said Gloria.

Kromer smiled. "You're protecting him? Sorry. Everybody plays in the Sexathon, sweetheart. That's bread and butter. The customers don't let us break the rules." He pointed out to the rigs. "You'd better get out there."

I knew Kromer thought I didn't know about Gloria and Fearing, or other things. I wanted to tell him I wasn't so innocent, but I didn't think Gloria would like it, so I kept quiet.

I went to talk to Mr. Sneeze. I remembered where he was from the first time.

"What's a Sexathon?" I said.

"I don't know, Lewis."

"I've never had sex," I said.

"Me neither," said Mr. Sneeze.

"Everybody always thinks I do with Gloria just because we go around together. But we're just friends."

"That's fine," said Mr. Sneeze. "It's okay to be friends."

"I'd like to be Lane's boyfriend," I said.

Next break Gloria slept while Gilmartin and Kromer told me about the act. A drawer would be marked for me to go into, and there would be a lot of numbers and letters but I just had to keep pressing "1-2-3" no matter what. It was supposed to be a security archive, they said. The people watching would think I was breaking codes but it was just for show. Then something else would happen but they wouldn't say what, just that I should keep quiet and let Fearing talk. So I knew they were going to pull me out of my mask. I didn't know if I should tell Gloria.

Fearing was up again welcoming some people back in. I couldn't believe anybody wanted to start watching first thing in the morning but Fearing was saying "the gritty determination to survive that epitomizes the frontier spirit that once made a country called America great" and "young bodies writhing in agonized congress with the future" and that sounded like a lot of fun, I guess.

A woman from the town had quit already. Not Lane though.

A good quiet place to go was Mars. It was like the airplane, all space and no people, but better since there was no voice telling you to engage targets, and you never crashed.

. . .

I went to the drawer they told me about. Fearing's voice in my ear told me it was time. The place was a storeroom of information like the business library. No people, just files with a lot of blinking lights and complicated words. A voice kept asking me for "security clearance password" but there was always a place for me to touch "1-2-3" and I did. It was kind of a joke, like a wall made out of feathers that falls apart every time you touch it.

I found a bunch of papers with writing. Some of the words were blacked out and some were bright red and blinking. There was a siren sound. Then I felt hands pulling on me from outside and somebody took off my mask.

There were two guys pulling on me who I had never seen before, and Ed and Kromer were pulling on them. Everybody was screaming at each other but it was kind of fake, because nobody was pulling or yelling very hard. Fearing said "The feds, the feds!" A bunch of people were crowded around my television screen I guess looking at the papers I'd dug up, but now they were watching the action.

Fearing came over and pulled out a toy gun and so did Kromer, and they were backing the two men away from me. I'm sure the audience could tell it was fake. But they were pretty excited, maybe just from remembering when feds were real.

I got off my frame and looked around. I didn't know what they were going to do with me now that I was out but I didn't care. It was my first chance to see what it was like when the contestants were all in their suits and masks, swimming in the information. None of them knew what was happening, not even Gloria, who was right next to me the whole time. They just kept moving in the scapes. I looked at Lane. She looked good, like she was dancing.

Meanwhile Fearing and Kromer chased those guys out the back. People were craning around to see. Fearing came out and took his microphone and said, "It isn't his fault, folks. Just good hacker instincts for ferreting out corruption from encrypted data. The feds don't want us digging up their trail, but the kid couldn't help it."

Ed and Kromer started snapping me back into my suit. "We chased them off," Fearing said, patting his gun. "We do take care of our own. You can't tell who's going to come sniffing around, can you? For his protection and ours we're going to have to delete that file, but it goes to show, there's no limit to what a kid with a nose for data's going to root out of cyberspace. We can't throw him out of the contest for doing what comes natural. Give him a big hand, folks."

People clapped and a few threw coins. Ed picked the change up for me, then told me to put on my mask. Meanwhile Gloria and Lane and everybody else just went on through their scapes.

I began to see what Kromer and Fearing were selling. It wasn't any one thing. Some of it was fake and some was real, and some was a mix so you couldn't tell.

The people watching probably didn't know why they wanted to, except it made them forget their screwed-up life for a while to watch the only suckers bigger than themselves—us.

"Meanwhile, the big show goes on," said Fearing. "How long will they last? Who will take the prize?"

. . .

I told Gloria about it at the break. She just shrugged and said to make sure I got my money from Kromer. Fearing was talking to Anne the woman from the van and Gloria was staring at them like she wanted them dead.

A guy was lying in his cot talking to himself as if nobody could hear and Gilmartin and Kromer went over and told him he was kicked out. He didn't seem to care.

I went to see Lane but we didn't talk. We sat on her cot and held hands. I didn't know if it meant the same thing to her that it did to me but I liked it.

After the break I went and talked to Mr. Sneeze. He told me the story of the show about Christmas. He said it wasn't about always getting gifts. Sometimes you had to give gifts too.

The Sexathon was late at night. They cleared the seats and everyone had to pay again to get back in, because it was a special event. Fearing had built it up all day, talking about how it was for adults only, it would separate the men from the boys, things like that. Also that people would get knocked out of the contest. So we were pretty nervous by the time he told us the rules.

"What would scapes be without virtual sex?" he said. "Our voyagers must now prove themselves in the sensual realm—for the future consists of far more than cold, hard information. It's a place of desire and temptation, and as always, survival belongs to the fittest. The soldiers will now be steered onto the sexual battlescape— the question is, will they meet with the Little Death, or the Big one?"

Gloria wouldn't explain. "Not real death," is all she said.

"The rules again are so simple a child could follow them. In the Sex-Scape environment our contestants will be free to pick from a variety of fantasy partners. We've packed this program with options, there's something for every taste, believe you me. We won't question their selections, but—here's the catch—we will chart the results. Their suits will tell us who does and doesn't attain sexual orgasm in the next session, and those who don't will be handed their walking papers. The suits don't lie. Find bliss or die, folks, find bliss or die."

"You get it now?" said Gloria to me.

"I guess," I said.

"As ever, audience members are cautioned never to interfere with the contestants during play. Follow their fantasies on the monitors, or watch their youthful bodies strain against exhaustion, seeking to bridge virtual lust and bona-fide physical response. But no touchee."

Kromer was going around, checking the suits. "Who's gonna be in your fantasy, kid?" he said to me. "The snowman?"

I'd forgotten how they could watch me talk to Mr. Sneeze on my television. I turned red.

"Screw you, Kromer," said Gloria.

"Whoever you want, honey," he said, laughing.

Well I found my way around their Sex-Scape and I'm not too embarrassed to say I found a girl who reminded me of Lane, except for the way she was trying so hard to be sexy. But she looked like Lane. I didn't have to do much to get the subject around to sex. It was the only thing on her mind. She wanted me to tell her what I wanted to do to her and when I couldn't think of much she suggested things and I just agreed. And when I did that she would move around and sigh as if it were really exciting to talk about even though she was doing the talking. She wanted to touch me but she couldn't really so she took off her clothes and got close to me and touched herself. I touched her too but she didn't really feel like much and it was like my hands were made of wood, which couldn't have felt too nice for her though she acted like it was great.

I touched myself a little too. I tried not to think about the audience. I was a little confused about what was what in the suit and with her breathing in my ear so loud but I got the desired result. That wasn't hard for me.

Then I could go back to the drawers but Kromer had made me embarrassed about visiting Mr. Sneeze so I went to Mars even though I would have liked to talk to him.

The audience was all stirred up at the next break. They were sure getting their money's worth now. I got into Gloria's cot. I asked her if she did it with her own hands too. "You didn't have to do that," she said.

"How else?"

"I just pretended. I don't think they can tell. They just want to see you wiggle around."

Well some of the women from the town hadn't wiggled around enough I guess because Kromer and Ed were taking them out of the contest. A couple of them were crying.

"I wish I hadn't," I said.

"It's the same either way," said Gloria. "Don't feel bad. Probably some other people did it too."

They didn't kick Lane out but I saw she was crying anyway.

Kromer brought a man into the back and said to me, "Get into your own cot, little snowman."

"Let him stay," said Gloria. She wasn't looking at Kromer.

"I've got someone here who wants to meet you," said Kromer to Gloria. "Mr. Warren, this is Gloria."

Mr. Warren shook her hand. He was pretty old. "I've been admiring you," he said. "You're very good."

"Mr. Warren is wondering if you'd let him buy you a drink," said Kromer.

"Thanks, but I need some sleep," said Gloria.

"Perhaps later," said Mr. Warren.

After he left Kromer came back and said, "You shouldn't pass up easy money."

"I don't need it," said Gloria. "I'm going to win your contest, you goddamn pimp."

"Now, Gloria," said Kromer. "You don't want to give the wrong impression."

"Leave me alone."

I noticed now that Anne wasn't around in the rest area and I got the idea that the kind of easy money Gloria didn't want Anne did. I'm not so dumb.

. . .

Worrying about the Sexathon had stopped me from feeling how tired I was. Right after that I started nodding off in the scapes. I had to keep moving around. After I'd been to a few new things I went to see the snowman again. It was early in the morning and I figured Kromer was probably asleep and there was barely any audience to see what I was doing on my television. So Mr. Sneeze and I talked and that helped me stay awake.

I wasn't the only one who was tired after that night. On the next break I saw that a bunch of people had dropped out or been kicked out for sleeping. There were only seventeen left. I couldn't stay awake myself. But I woke up when I heard some yelling over where Lane was.

It was her parents. I guess they heard about the Sexathon, maybe from her boyfriend, who was there too. Lane was sitting crying behind Fearing who was telling her parents to get out of there, and her father just kept saying, "I'm her father! I'm her father!" Her mother was pulling at Fearing but Ed came over and pulled on her.

I started to get up but Gloria grabbed my arm and said, "Stay out of this."

"Lane doesn't want to see that guy," I said.

"Let the townies take care of themselves, Lewis. Let Lane's daddy take her home if he can. Worse could happen to her."

"You just want her out of the contest," I said.

Gloria laughed. "I'm not worried about your girlfriend outlasting me," she said. "She's about to break no matter what."

So I just watched. Kromer and Ed got Lane's parents and boyfriend pushed out of the rest area, back toward the seats. Fearing was yelling at them, making a scene for the audience. It was all part of the show as far as he was concerned.

Anne from the van was over talking to Lane, who was still crying, but quiet now.

"Do you really think you can win?" I said to Gloria.

"Sure, why not?" she said. "I can last."

"I'm pretty tired." In fact my eyeballs felt like they were full of sand.

"Well if you fall out stick around. You can probably get food out of Kromer for cleaning up or something. I'm going to take these bastards."

"You don't like Fearing anymore," I said.

"I never did," said Gloria.

That afternoon three more people dropped out. Fearing was going on about endurance and I got thinking about how much harder it was to live the way me and Gloria did than it was to be in town and so maybe we had an advantage. Maybe that was why Gloria thought she could win now. But I sure didn't feel it myself. I was so messed up that I couldn't always sleep at the rest periods, just lie there and listen to Fearing or eat their sandwiches until I wanted to vomit.

Kromer and Gilmartin were planning some sideshow but it didn't involve me and I didn't care. I didn't want coins thrown at me. I just wanted to get through.

• • •

If I built the cities near the water the plague always killed all the people and if I built the cities near the mountains the volcanoes always killed all the people and if I built the cities on the plain the other tribe always came over and killed all the people and I got sick of the whole damn thing.

"When Gloria wins we could live in town for a while," I said. "We could even get jobs if there are any. Then if Lane doesn't want to go back to her parents she could stay with us."

"You could win the contest," said Mr. Sneeze.

"I don't think so," I said. "But Gloria could."

Why did Lewis cross Mars? To got to the other side. Ha ha.

I came out for the rest period and Gloria was already yelling and I unhooked my suit and rushed over to see what was the matter. It was so late it was getting light outside and almost nobody was in the place. "She's cheating!" Gloria screamed. She was pounding on Kromer and he was backing up because she was a handful mad. "That bitch is cheating! You let her sleep!" Gloria pointed at Anne from the van. "She's lying there asleep, you're running tapes in her monitor you goddamn cheater!"

Anne sat up in her frame and didn't say anything. She looked confused. "You're a bunch of cheaters!" Gloria kept saying. Kromer got her by the wrists and said "Take it easy, take it easy. You're going scape-crazy, girl."

"Don't tell me I'm crazy!" said Gloria. She twisted away from Kromer and ran to the seats. Mr. Warren was there, watching her with his hat in his hands. I ran after Gloria and said her name but she said, "Leave me alone!" and went over to Mr. Warren. "You saw it, didn't you?" she said.

"I'm sorry?" said Mr. Warren.

"You must have seen it, the way she wasn't moving at all," said Gloria. "Come on, tell these cheaters you saw it. I'll go on that date with you if you tell them."

"I'm sorry, darling. I was looking at you."

Kromer knocked me out of the way and grabbed Gloria from behind. "Listen to me, girl. You're hallucinating. You're scape-happy. We see it all the time." He was talking quiet but hard. "Any more of this and you're out of the show, you understand? Get in the back and lie down now and get some sleep. You need it."

"You bastard," said Gloria.

"Sure, I'm a bastard, but you're seeing things." He held Gloria's wrist and she sagged.

Mr. Warren got up and put his hat on. "I'll see you tomorrow, darling. Don't worry. I'm rooting for you." He went out.

Gloria didn't look at him.

Kromer took Gloria back to the rest area but suddenly I wasn't paying much attention myself. I had been thinking Fearing wasn't taking advantage of the free action by talking about it because there wasn't anyone much in the place to impress at this hour. Then I looked around and I realized there were two people missing and that was Fearing and Lane.

I found Ed and I asked him if Lane had dropped out of the contest and he said no.

"Maybe there's a way you could find out if Anne is really scaping or if she's a cheat," I said to Mr. Sneeze.

"I don't see how I could," he said. "I can't visit her, she has to visit me. And nobody visits me except you." He hopped and jiggled in his five places. "I'd like it if I could meet Gloria and Lane."

"Let's not talk about Lane," I said.

When I saw Fearing again I couldn't look at him. He was out talking to the people who came by in the morning, not in the microphone but one at a time, shaking hands and taking compliments like it was him doing the scaping.

There were only eight people left in the contest. Lane was still in it but I didn't care.

I knew if I tried to sleep I would just lie there thinking. So I went to rinse out under my suit, which was getting pretty rank. I hadn't been out of that suit since the contest started. In the bathroom I looked out the little window at the daylight and I thought about how I hadn't been out of that building for five days either, no matter how much I'd gone to Mars and elsewhere.

I went back in and saw Gloria asleep and I thought all of a sudden that I should try to win.

But maybe that was just the idea coming over me that Gloria wasn't going to.

I didn't notice it right away because I went to other places first. Mr. Sneeze had made me promise I'd always have something new to tell him about so I always opened a few drawers. I went to a tank game but it was boring. Then I found a place called the American History Blood and Wax Museum and I stopped President Lincoln from getting murdered a couple of times. I tried to stop President Kennedy from getting murdered but if I stopped it one way it always happened a different way. I don't know why.

So then I was going to tell Mr. Sneeze about it and that's when I found out. I went into his drawer and touched the right numbers but what I got wasn't the usual five pictures of the snowman. It was pieces of him but chopped up and stretched into thin white strips, around the edge of the black space, like a band of white light.

I said, "Mr. Sneeze?"

There wasn't any voice.

I went out and came back in but it was the same. He couldn't talk. The band of white strips got narrower and wider, like it was trying to move or talk. It looked a bit like a hand waving open and shut. But if he was still there he couldn't talk.

I would have taken my mask off then anyway, but the heat of my face and my tears forced me to.

I saw Fearing up front talking and I started for him without even getting my suit unclipped, so I tore up a few of my wires. I didn't care. I knew I was out now. I went right out and tackled Fearing from behind. He wasn't so big, anyway. Only his voice was big. I got him down on the floor.

''You killed him,'' I said, and I punched him as hard as I could, but you know Kromer and Gilmartin were there holding my arms before I could hit him more than once. I just screamed at Fearing, ''You killed him, you killed him.''

Fearing was smiling at me and wiping his mouth. ''Your snowman malfunctioned, kid.''

''That's a lie!''

''You were boring us to death with that snowman, you little punk. Give it a rest, for chrissake.''

I kept kicking out even though they had me pulled away from him. ''I'll kill you!'' I said.

''Right,'' said Fearing. ''Throw him out of here.''

He never stopped smiling. Everything suited his plans, that was what I hated.

Kromer the big ape and Gilmartin pulled me outside into the sunlight and it was like a knife in my eyes. I couldn't believe how bright it was. They tossed me down in the street and when I got up Kromer punched me, hard.

Then Gloria came outside. I don't know how she found out, if she heard me screaming or if Ed woke her. Anyway she gave Kromer a pretty good punch in the side and said, ''Leave him alone!''

Kromer was surprised and he moaned and I got away from him. Gloria punched him again. Then she turned around and gave Gilmartin a kick in the nuts and he went down. I'll always remember in spite of what happened next that she gave those guys a couple they'd be feeling for a day or two.

The gang who beat the crap out of us were a mix of the militia and some other guys from the town, including Lane's boyfriend. Pretty funny that he'd take out his frustration on us, but that just shows you how good Fearing had that whole town wrapped around his finger.

Outside of town we found an old house that we could hide in and get some sleep. I slept longer than Gloria. When I woke up she was on the front steps rubbing a spoon back and forth on the pavement to make a sharp point, even though I could see it hurt her arm to do it.

''Well, we did get fed for a couple of days,'' I said.

Gloria didn't say anything.

''Let's go up to San Francisco,'' I said. ''There's a lot of lonely women there.''

I was making a joke of course.

Gloria looked at me. ''What's that supposed to mean?''

''Just that maybe I can get us in for once.''

Gloria didn't laugh, but I knew she would later.

DR. TILMANN'S CONSULTANT: A SCIENTIFIC ROMANCE

Cherry Wilder

▼

Born in New Zealand, Cherry Wilder has lived for long stretches of time in Australia and also in Germany, where she currently resides. She made her first sale in 1974 to the British anthology New Writings in SF 24, *and since then has sold to a number of markets such as* Asimov's Science Fiction, Interzone, Universe, Strange Plasma, *and elsewhere. Her many books include* The Luck of Brin's Five, The Nearest Fire, The Tapestry Warriors, Second Nature, A Princess of the Chameln, Yorath the Wolf, The Summer's King, *and* Cruel Designs. *Her most recent books are a collection,* Dealers in Light and Darkness, *and a new novel,* Signs of Life.

In the powerful and somberly evocative story that follows, she takes us back to the turbulent days just prior to World War I, for a study of a doctor who has found a Secret Weapon in the War On Disease—one a little more *secret than usual, though . . . and one which better be* kept *a little more secret too.*

Above the grove of pines there was one lone chalet where Dr. Tilmann sometimes lodged a special patient. During the summer of 1913, when Rosalind accompanied the Ostrov family to Bavaria for the second time, there was a young woman in the annex. An Englishwoman, declared Marie-Louise Ostrova excitedly; exquisitely beautiful and mad as a bird. She could sometimes be heard in the night, playing the harmonium. Rosalind expressed mild disapproval of this gossip, as a governess should. Marie-Louise had made friends with a little nurse who spoke French. Rosalind did not believe that this was at all the place for a lively child of thirteen but the trials of the Ostrov family were such that there seemed to be no help for it.

St. Verena's hospital specialized in nervous complaints of the European aristocracy; Dr. Lucas Tilmann had recently taken over from his father, Professor Dr. Wilhelm Tilmann. The old man still wore a frock coat, a cravat, and the kind of high stiff collar called in German a *vatermörder*, a father-murderer. Many of the gentlemen about at the time did so too, but the junior chief, Dr. Lucas, was a dress reformer who went about in a soft collar and a lightweight jacket of beige linen.

The Ostrov family came ostensibly for the Countess Valeria's nerves but really it was for poor Leonid, the only son, who was losing his reason. Besides being unfortunate, charming, cultivated, and in decline, the family were so astonishingly rich that they had retained an important French specialist at the estate on the Black Sea for the winter. On Christmas Eve, the anniversary of the general's death, Leonid made another attempt, this time from his balcony, and poor Dr. Patin restrained him at the cost of a broken arm. Rosalind dared not reveal much of what she experienced during these years to her widowed mother in Cheltenham.

One evening, after a long day with the countess during her hydrotherapy, Rosalind followed a path up into the pines to her own favorite retreat. It was a clearing in the wood with a rustic bench and a wayside shrine that contained not a carved wooden saint but an icon of St. George, painted on metal. Many Russian families patronized St. Verena's; they valued its discretion as well as its natural beauty. Rosalind could sit on the bench and look out to the ranks of the mountains or down to the village. Overhead the annex was visible among the trees and an even higher mountain meadow, bathed in bright sunlight.

There was a rustling in the bushes: She thought of a pair of marmots or even a deer. In fact it was a young woman, of about Rosalind's own age, dressed in a gray silk dress of "reformed" cut. Her poor stockinged feet were stained and hurt, her golden hair stood out round her pale face in a cloud and hung in long, ragged elflocks down past her hips; leaves and pine needles had caught in it.

Rosalind understood the situation at once. She rose up, took the patient's arm, and said: "Let me help you!"

"You are English!" whispered the girl. "Oh please . . ."

"Sit here with me," said Rosalind. "Let me brush your poor hair."

She had a large bag of toilet articles that she had carried with her from the bathhouse: The girl turned her head obediently and Rosalind went to work with professional skill.

"You have an English touch," said the girl. "My body is covered from head to foot with the imprint of his fingers."

"Hush," said Rosalind gently.

"He comes to me at night," continued the girl. "All the poor doctor's beastly medicines can't make me sleep. I wake up, very hot and wet under the horrid German featherbed and there is Teddy, my darling Teddy. . . ."

Rosalind began to plait the magnificent fall of golden hair into a loose braid. She turned her head and saw Dr. Lucas Tilmann emerge from the bushes warily, as if stalking a butterfly. The mad girl had not seen him but her mood had altered; she began to weep, pouring out a stream of confused regrets and sorrows. She would never be well, she was imprisoned, the wretched little harmonium was out of tune, her mother was cruel, the swans had all flown away from the lake . . . Teddy knew what she should do and she had tried, more than once, but it was too difficult, the guns hurt her fingers.

"Oh no," said Rosalind softly, "you must never do *that*. Never try to hurt yourself."

She fastened the enormous Rapunzel braid of hair with a pink ribbon from her bag. Dr. Tilmann drew closer and said cautiously: "Miss Courtney . . . Maud?"

The patient screamed aloud; before she could spring up Rosalind put her arms around her firmly.

"No," she said. "Please, Maud dear. Please be good! Dr. Tilmann will give you a nice cup of tea . . . see, he has brought your slippers. How kind. . . .''

A nurse appeared now on the path from the annex and a young intern, Dr. Daniel, alerted by telephone, came running up from the hospital. Maud Courtney was docile again; her slippers were put on, she was led away down the hill to the main building. Lucas Tilmann accompanied the party a little way then rejoined Rosalind in the clearing.

"Miss—Lane? I am deeply indebted . . .''

"Poor thing," said Rosalind. "I hope that she . . .''

He sat down beside her on the bench and covered his face with his hands.

"The prognosis," he said, after a few seconds, "is not good."

"She spoke of someone called Teddy . . . ,'' prompted Rosalind.

"Her brother died in the Punjab," sighed Dr. Tilmann. "She has never been told."

"Dr. Tilmann," said Rosalind, "what is the matter with the poor girl? What would you call her—disorder?"

"A retreat from the world," he said. "Bleuler has characterized it as *schizophrenie*. I swear to you, Miss Lane, I would give my life, I would make any Faustian bargain if I might effect an improvement, a cure, in some of these patients. . . .''

The season was nearly at an end; Leonid Ivanovitch agreed to remain in St. Verena's for the winter months. Rosalind was the last member of the Ostrov family party to speak to the young man; they walked in the orangery, speaking in a mixture of English and French.

"I know it is my nose," said Leonid. "It still bothers me a good deal. *Chère Rosaline,* take care of my mother, see to the butterfly collection, I have left a box of swaps for the Nabokov boys . . . The voices will keep me informed. I am quite happy here. Dr. Lucas loves you, did you know that?"

"You are exaggerating, I think," said Rosalind, with a smile.

She had dined twice with Lucas Tilmann and driven as far as Berchtesgarten in his new Daimler Landaulet. Leonid was very upset by her mild deprecation and fell into a brooding silence, picking at the spots on his face. An attendant lurked behind the orange trees in their tubs. Leonid was twenty-eight years old and unfit for military service.

The winter passed quietly on the estate: Before she was too deeply involved in the amateur theatricals and the ball season word came that her mother was very ill. The countess managed to obtain a passage for Rosalind on a steam yacht, the *Nereid,* owned by a consortium of Greek-Americans, which sailed from the port of Odessa. She arrived home at the quiet, dark house near Thirlestaine Road, and took over the nursing of her mother shortly after Christmas.

She sat by the bed in the darkened room and told endless tales of the wonders that she had seen. Clothes and jewels; the opera and the ballet; the country estates; priests, monks, holy icons . . . Father Fyodor, the Ostrov chaplain, sent a small one which Mrs. Lane held between her thin fingers on top of the eiderdown. She became upset when Rosalind touched on mutiny, civil commotion, the Ostrov cousin Kyril, who had joined a revolutionary cell at the university and been exiled to the district of Irkutsk.

Rosalind knew what her mother wished to hear, though reason had told them both when she took the post as governess to the Ostrovs that she would not meet eligible men. Now, to please the dying woman, she went so far as to claim that she had an *understanding,* with a doctor, Lucas Tilmann, at the alpine clinic. He had indeed sent her a card, with a charming letter and a lace-edged handkerchief, which arrived with the Ostrovs's Christmas box, in January.

Mrs. Lane lingered until the summer, passed away in her sleep at the end of May; Rosalind went about in the dark house setting everything in order. She had cheated, sold the family silver, so that she was able to pay off the remaining maidservant and keep a nest egg for herself. The house went, lock, stock, and barrel, to her nephew, Richard. She waited for the expected summons and set out in June, traveling across Europe to meet the Ostrov family party at St. Verena's hospital on the Altalm, the old alpine meadow, near Mariensee.

She arrived at four o'clock when all the guests who were able to enjoyed pastries and English tea . . . as opposed to the Russian tea, which was swilled all day long . . . on the terraces. Rosalind hesitated in the shadowy entrance hall, putting off the first encounter with the Ostrov family, who would be sure to weep, even if she did not. She had her luggage sent up to the suite and strolled through to the terrace unbuttoning her gloves. A sweet English voice spoke her name as she stepped out into the sunshine: "Miss Lane?"

It was a stranger, or at least someone half-known, a young blond woman with her hair in a pompadour. She took Rosalind's hand and gazed into her face, smiling.

"I have a message from the Countess Ostrova."

The family were out driving, would not return until later. The young woman still did not say her name but they sat down together at her table.

"I have to thank you," she said, with that very steady gaze. "I remember how you helped me once."

Rosalind was on the verge of recognition but she simply could not believe what she saw.

"My name is Maud Courtney," said the young woman.

Rosalind felt her first astonishment turning at once to relief and pleasure.

"But you are . . ."

"Yes! I have recovered. It is a miracle. . . ."

She spoke quietly, with a glance at the surrounding tables where English was not being spoken.

"A new treatment from Dr. Tilmann," said Maud.

It was all she said; they moved on to ordinary conversation, which was pleasant for Rosalind after her long journey. She did not have to explain her black clothes: The Ostrovs had already mentioned her bereavement to Miss Courtney, who offered her sympathy. Another sign of her normality: One shielded patients from harsh reality, from death, sickness, financial disasters.

"My brother, Edward," said Maud, "was killed two years ago in India."

Rosalind expressed sympathy in her turn.

The Ostrov family had taken a new suite of rooms in the west wing of the sanitarium. There was only one new Russian servant, a mere boy, with silky whiskers, playing cards with the little French nurse, Sister Clotilde, the friend of Marie-Louise. It was all so different from the musky headachey atmosphere of other years that she wondered if there had been some change in the family fortunes. Had terrible old Great-Uncle Paul given up the palace in Moscow at last? Had the countess, at last, taken a lover?

There was plenty of time before the family returned—young Vasily informed her, dealing another hand—so she went out of doors again. She found herself climbing up through the pines to her precious clearing and admitted, with a smile, that she was eager to meet Lucas Tilmann, hear from his own lips the news of his miracle cure.

It was a perfect summer evening; the highest peaks of the mountains were caught in bright rays of sunlight, not yet tinged with pink or red. The whisper and fragrance of the friendly pines sank into her soul; she was free from care, freed from the bonds of her dark English house at last. She sank onto the rustic bench.

Across the glade in a patch of sunlight was a circus wagon, brightly painted in green and gold. A stocky yellowish horse, with fringed hooves like a Clydesdale, grazed nearby and a cauldron simmered over a fire. As she watched, a bearded man in a fur hat came out to smoke his pipe on the steps of the wagon. Gypsies of course, Russian or Russianized gypsies of the kind who turned up in the stable yard at the feast of the Epiphany with a hurdy-gurdy and a dancing bear.

Rosalind did not rest long, but set out again up a pathway to the annex. She looked back and saw that the gypsy now stood by the campfire facing up the hill, one hand raised above his head. A feeling of exquisite well-being grew upon her as she came up to the large chalet . . . the air of the mountains, the spring bubbling beneath the ferns, the flowers that cascaded from the window boxes, oh, these were *all* miraculous. If the doctor had appeared at that moment she might have flung herself into his arms.

An older nurse, Sister Luise, came bustling out on to the porch and Rosalind could see that she was somehow—*transformed*. She looked like a nun who had seen a vision. . . . She was *sharing* the extraordinary euphoria that Rosalind felt growing upon her as she came up the path.

"Oh, Fräulein!" said Sister Luise. "Oh you have come back! The doctor will be so pleased!"

"Is he . . . ?"

"No, he is not here!" said Sister Luise quickly.

She turned her head and looked back into the dark doorway of the annex. Rosalind had the absurd notion that this euphoria *came from the chalet;* it was streaming out like a golden mist from someone—from *a presence* inhabiting the simple, spotless rooms. She felt a deep twang of anxiety.

"He is coming up the hill!" said Sister Luise. "If you take the path by the larch trees . . ."

She pointed, smiling; Rosalind smiled too, and went obediently down that path. It seemed that at a certain point, under the first of the larches, she escaped some happy influence and was completely herself again. She stood still and presently Lucas Tilmann came hurrying up toward her. At the sight of him she was overwhelmed by a tumult of feelings: pleasure, anxiety, irritation, loving care. She went forward and grasped his hands and could only say: "What is it? What is it?"

"Oh, Rosalind!" he said, ignoring her question. "Oh my dear girl! I have missed you so much!"

She allowed him to kiss her and then kissed him back with more enthusiasm than she had expected in herself. They held each other close under the larch trees and she found herself wondering if the needles clung to fabric when one lay down. Lucas drew back, smiling, and led her on down the path back to the clearing; they sat on another bench and she patted her hair. The Russian gypsy had disappeared into his caravan. The tops of the mountains had turned to gold.

"Lucas," she said, "there is something . . ."

There was something about Lucas himself; he was full of contained excitement.

"You spoke to Maud Courtney!" he brought out.

"Yes, it is remarkable," she said. "It is a miracle. What is the new treatment?"

"I can't tell you just yet," he said. "It is a completly new technique for dealing with certain cases. It is still in the experimental stage and must be kept absolutely secret."

She was already trying to rationalize her feelings of euphoria up at the chalet: the rare mountain air, love, the aftermath of her journey. But some core of strangeness remained.

"Lucas," she asked. "Is there a patient up in the annex?"

"Yes," he said. "And I cannot say another word. I rely on your absolute discretion."

"Of course."

"Rosalind," he said, "I want you to help me."

"Anything . . ."

"I want you to observe Leonid Ostrov, tonight when they come back from Bad Reichenhall."

"They took him for an *outing*?"

"To a concert in the park. A program of operatic airs."

"Leonid must be doing very well!"

At last she put two and two together.

"Does this mean that he has been given the new treatment?"

The doctor put his finger to his lips and looked around warily at the twilit glade.

"There has been a dramatic improvement," he said in a low voice, "but I am wary of a relapse, of unexpected side effects. In particular I wonder how much he remembers or purports to remember of the treatment sessions at the annex."

"Should I ask him?" she said.

"No," said Lucas. "I know that he regards you as a trusted member of his family entourage. See what he comes out with."

Hospital routine reclaimed the doctor; he looked at his silver watch.

"I shall be late, like the White Rabbit," he said. "Come. . . ."

They walked hand in hand down a shady path and kissed under several chosen trees. They arranged to meet in the grove after luncheon next day and parted in a back corridor of the main building that smelled of carbolic.

Rosalind set out for the west wing again and found it ringing with music and song. A clear tenor voice was singing together with a rich contralto, the countess herself: the Anvil Chorus from *Il Trovatore*. Besides the piano accompaniment the sounds of balalaika and mandolin could be distinguished.

When she entered the salon she received a rapturous welcome from the Ostrov family: The countess embraced her, weeping and laughing; Marie-Louise sprang up from the piano bench. They led her up to Leonid, who was changed, as remarkably as Maud Courtney: He was clear-skinned, vigorous, with a direct gaze. He had been singing with his mother. Now Rosalind was pressed to join in and sing of the happy life of the roving gypsy with Marie-Louise thumping the keys, the countess playing her mandolin, and young Vasily the balalaika. Even the coachman had been pressed into service, striking the fender with the poker for the clang of the anvils.

She registered, dispassionately, that the Ostrovs were the nicest, most lovable human beings that she was ever likely to meet; if she could never completely approve of them the fault lay in her own prejudices, her own upbringing. Dinner was sent up and afterward they played cards. Rosalind gave everyone the presents she had brought and began to persuade Marie-Louise to think about bedtime. Leonid called her out onto the balcony to watch the stars; she found him staring raptly at the sky above the mountains.

"Look!" he said. "There is the Great Bear!"

He turned to her eagerly and came to the point.

"You can see I'm better," he said. "A new treatment . . ."

"I'm so happy for you, Leonid, and for your mother!"

"I'm so much better we thought of sending for Irina Fedorona," he brought out. "But the news from Serbia is unsettling."

Leonid had been betrothed for five years to a beautiful cousin; they had almost given up hope. Rosalind had heard of the assassination in Sarajevo but rumors of war were mixed up in her mind with riot and civil strife in Odessa, with embarrassing defeats in the Sea of Japan. She could not think of a war that interfered with Irina Fedorona's travel plans.

"I was right about one thing!" exclaimed Leonid. "The doctor does love you, *chère Rosaline.*"

She felt herself blushing but could not put him off.

"Perhaps he does."

"Has he spoken of the new treatment at all?"

"Only to say it must be kept secret," she said. "I am sure only the patients concerned and their immediate families . . ."

"Did Dr. Tilmann say that a new and special kind of hypnosis is used?"

"No," said Rosalind. "Really we have not discussed—"

He still could not let her finish; he was carried away.

"One side effect of the treatment can be vivid dreams and visions that—that purport to explain the patient's situation."

"But surely the dream theory comes from Vienna," she said. "Lucas—the doctor has already made some use of it."

"I was healed by a holy man, a *starets,* or even a shaman," said Leonid Ostrov, bluntly. "He came from the woods and forests of my native land."

"But you know it is a dream," she said. "A metaphor . . ."

"The holy man bore the features of a bear," said Leonid, raising his head again to the constellations overhead in the clear night sky. "He spoke to me in the language of bears. He entered my mind, filled my whole being, filled me with pure joy, pure love."

Rosalind was momentarily filled with unreason: She felt again the sensation of euphoria that had seized her as she approached the chalet; she thought of the secret "patient" who lived there and of Sister Luise's shining look. One of her best qualifications for work as a governess or companion was an ability to keep a straight face.

"That is a beautiful healing dream," she said to Leonid. "Why, you could write a poem or folktale—like your cousin, Prince Azlov."

Leonid burst out laughing at the very idea.

"Poor old Kyril Mihailovitch is using his folklore to keep himself from revolutionary thoughts over there in Irkutsk or wherever he is."

They were called to join in the game of whist: Nothing indicated more clearly that Leonid was healed than his ability to play cards again. The countess herself was no match for her son. The doors onto the balcony were still open and the scent of the woods and the summer fields drifted in upon them. The scene imprinted itself upon Rosalind's memory, a palimpsest of this last innocent summer.

She had reached St. Verena's on the thirtieth of June, 1914. Every day following her return brought Europe and the assorted Europeans gathered in the hospital closer to war. She noted carefully in her journal the affecting scenes in which patients had to be removed from care and made ready for travel. The first Russians fled before the Austrian ultimatum to Serbia and some were forced to return. Travel through the Balkan states had become too disturbed; the way back into the mother country led over Berlin.

Rosalind was filled with unrest: She had seldom felt a strong personal preference about *where* she spent her life with the Ostrovs but now she wanted very badly to remain at St. Verena's, to remain close to Lucas Tilmann. She perceived a conflict approaching: between love, yes, love at last, and duty. It was against this darkening background and in this state of internal tension that she became one of the initiates. After the fifth of July she made no more notes, no more entries at all in her journal—the equivalent of a stunned silence and a ban of absolute secrecy.

It began with a long talk in their enchanted glade; Lucas was speaking of natural history, cosmology, the place of the Earth in the universe. Rosalind believed that he was leading up to a confession of his religious belief, or rather his lack of it, his rationalism. He was dismayed that she had not really got on to an English writer, Wells, and she was not game enough to confide that it was one of those ridiculous class things. He was surely an awfully common little man, a counter-jumper, as her mother would have said, and she did not trust his fantastic stories.

They sat there talking until the stars came out and lamps were lit in the hospital down below. The gypsies were at the cooking place outside their caravan and the man's wife crossed the glade with two tiny cups of warm spirit, which they obediently tossed off. Lucas began to question Rosalind about poor Prince Azlov, spending his Siberian exile in the neighborhood of Irkutsk.

"Does he write of—cosmic events?" he asked. "Falling stars?"

"You mean meteorites?" said Rosalind. "Yes of course. And there was an especially large one a few years ago, before I came to Russia. Kyril Mihailovitch believed there should have been a scientific expedition—but there it is. The district where it fell, the taiga, is unbearably remote. . . ."

"Six years ago," said Lucas. "Come, let us go up to the annex. My patient will be awake now."

He took her by the hand and they walked briskly up the path to the annex. At some point, more than halfway there, the extraordinary sensation began again; she had not imagined it. Rosalind found that she experienced it a little differently this second time because she knew that it was somehow outside herself, streaming out of the chalet like golden mist.

"You feel the influence then," said Lucas.

He turned her toward him, unsmiling, and took her pulse. She might have burst out again, questioning, but he put his finger to his lips. They went up the steps and Lucas Tilmann said loudly in Russian: *"I am here and I have brought my sweetheart, the English girl."*

From the largest bedroom, at the back of the house, there came a curious sound. Rosalind trembled; only the grip Lucas had upon her arm and the reassuring waves of serenity and well-being kept her from crying out. She thought of Leonid's tale: *"a* starets, *a holy man . . ."*

The back bedroom was very dark and filled with a distinctive odor, the natural smell of a warm body, as a stable smelled of horses or a railway carriage of human sweat. She fixed her eyes upon the dark shape in the large carved bedstead among the tumbled featherbeds. A voice, hoarse and resonant, dropping words like stones into a mountain pool, said in Russian, *"Do not be afraid."*

Her eyes were becoming accustomed to the gloom and she was accustomed, certainly, to men who grew luxuriant hair and beards, but the large head propped on the pillows was—unusual. Then Lucas Tilmann drew back a corner of the window curtains, a ray of light penetrated the dark chamber, and Rosalind found that she had been addressed by a bear.

"No," continued the voice, *"everyone thinks that,* chère Rosaline. *Come closer. Do not be afraid."*

She could not speak but a profound curiosity, stronger than her fear, led her closer to the bed. She was, after all, the child of a medical officer and the grandchild of an explorer. Rosalind saw what could not be believed, she saw a large furred head, bearlike indeed, but without a bear's snout. The fur—black, brown, and gold—grew very flat and soft around the large yellow eyes, thicker on the wide dewlaps; the small roundish ears twitched, all alert. She saw dark lips working under a drooping fringe of hair.

"Give me your hand. . . ."

She saw that the hand that took hers was four-fingered, covered with finest tawny fur, the long digits closing in pairs like pincers. She heard her own voice whispering urgently: "What? Where?"

"We have evolved a formula together," said Lucas Tilmann, at her side. "Our honored guest is the inhabitant of another world, one of the planets revolving around a distant sun."

In fact the whole question of *provenance* had been reduced to a series of simple formulae, which she heard in turn from Lucas and from the guest.

"A civilization that has progressed in mechanical sciences. . . ."

"A cosmic vessel on a first circumnavigation of the Earth, experiencing engine failure . . ."

"An escape mechanism meant to propel survivors to safety in small rescue craft . . ."

"I am alone," said the guest, filling Rosalind with an aching loneliness. *"My poor comrades have slid into the depths of Lake Baikal, in our little nutshell."*

At last the significance of the meteorites, of Lake Baikal, near Irkutsk, all came to her—the traveler had come down in *Siberia,* whose cold wastes were separated from this place, the Altalm, by thousands of miles.

"How did—our friend—get here?

She asked this clutching Lucas's arm for support but never taking her eyes from the stranger's face.

"The power of the mind," said Lucas Tilmann. "Isn't that so, Medvekhin?"

She was glad that the guest had been given a name, even an Earthly one; *Medvekhin* was one of the Russian surnames related to the word for bear. Yet she could not make much sense of the answer Lucas had given to her question, and Medvekhin understood this.

"I persuaded the inhabitants to understand my situation and to help me."

There was a trace of understatement in all of Medvekhin's explanations. Rosalind was able to picture the scenes of the journey afterward, when she was no longer in the presence of the guest. But she understood at once that the "persuasion" was inescapable: The lake fisherman and his family, the peddler-woman, the beekeeper, the exiled students, the telegraph operator—they had no choice. The sweet influence, the power of this mind, was compelling: Rosalind experienced a moral revulsion and this aroused a protest.

"I chose self-preservation," said Medvekhin humbly. "No other way but this 'persuasion' was open to me. None of these chosen helpers came to the least harm, only brought this lost one a certain distance upon its way."

"Right here! To your haven!" said Lucas heartily.

"What sort of place or person were you looking for?" asked Rosalind.

"A healer. A doctor who might understand my plight," replied Medvekhin. "A mountain, where the air is not so rich. . . ."

The odyssey had included a few minor officials, many humble folk; after three years in Siberia and almost three more in the Urals, near a telegraph station, Medvekhin came upon Kaspar, the gypsy, and his wife Marja. At one time they had traveled with a real bear, whom they loved and mourned when it died, long after its dancing days were over. More than once Medvekhin had worn poor Prince's muzzle and cowered in the shadows of the wagon while some official glanced at him. Kaspar taught his new companion to make bearlike noises.

Already they knew their goal: The estate personnel of a rich mill-owner in the region of Tyumen brought forth the name of the Drs. Tilmann, senior and junior, and the alpine clinic of St. Verena. It seemed the ideal place for Medvekhin, who had by now a good command of Russian and a smattering of German and English. . . .

As the story was told Rosalind found another most important question and asked it at once rather than have the stranger pluck it from her mind. Lucas chuckled when she was so direct.

"We are accustomed to distinguish between the two sexes," she said. "The males and the females. How is this arranged among your race?"

"A little differently," came the reply. "It is not an out-and-out dichotomy. More choice is involved."

"And you, yourself?" she pursued.

"I could be described as a neuter-worker, like a honeybee," replied Medvekhin, "adapted for travel among the star systems. I have accepted the use of the masculine or the neuter pronoun. I have done this because of certain problems of status and dominance which I discovered adhering to the feminine pronoun."

Rosalind tried to keep separate in her mind all that she learned directly from this being, from Medvekhin, and things that were reported by Lucas, by Sister Luise, and by Kaspar. What remained wonderfully clear was the buoyant atmosphere of those numbered days and nights. When Lucas described the chance encounter with Maud Courtney, the marvelous consequences, she had questions: Was the effect intentional? Had Medvekhin meant to heal the young woman?

"From a certain point in our encounter yes, of course," replied . "There are close analogies between certain aspects of the human brain and the brain of the Akuine."

Words, concepts, pictures from the other world were not very numerous and mostly dealt with things that were like, not unlike. There was, for example, a relationship between Lucas Tilmann's profession and the work of Medvekhin aboard the large vessel that had been lost. The Akuine race, endowed with such intense, richly orchestrated mind powers, became untuned under the stress of star voyaging. Medvekhin could have been described, like Lucas Tilmann, as an alienist.

Rosalind was disturbed by the way the patients were *made to forget* their healing encounter. But this was no more than a demonstration of the way in which Medvekhin had survived—leaving behind a swathe of forgetfulness from Lake Baikal to the Alps. Now Lucas had been brought into cahoots with his guest, when he put forward the story of "a new treatment involving hypnosis."

"I had to try it," said Lucas. "When I saw the improvement in Maud Courtney . . . She had been slipping away, approaching catatonia. Now she became well before my eyes and she remembered nothing."

He had brought only six patients into the presence of Medvekhin; all had been diagnosed as suffering from the constellation of disorders that was beginning to be called *schizophrenie*. All were healed after application of Akuine "mind power;" a couple of the patients retained some memory of the treatment. A German woman believed that in her hypnotic trance she walked through the woods and talked to the animals. Leonid Ivanovitch Ostrov had a dream encounter with a *starets,* a holy man, who came to him in the guise of a bear. Rosalind never knew the name of the German woman or of the other patients besides Miss Courtney and Count Ostrov who had received this unique treatment.

Medvekhin had no impulse to write down or dictate notes; he enquired for methods of recording information that existed, perhaps, in the distant laboratories of the Edison Company but were by no means in common use. Lucas recorded dialogues with their guest and his own conclusions in a thick black notebook, illustrated with his own sketches, which he wrote up privately, out of Medvekhin's presence.

He understood Rosalind's reservations about the treatment and the silence that hedged it. But the mere existence of this being could overwhelm all human judgment. What was to be done? Men of science, civil authorities . . . surely they must be informed?

They sat whispering madly in the room of the chalet furthest from the large bedroom where Medvekhin was sleeping.

"Whatever our friend believes," she said, reassuring Lucas, "traces of the large vessel *must* be found, eventually, even in the remote forests of the taiga. The matter will be out of our hands. . . ."

The survivor had been scarcely able to find words to describe the nature of the explosion that marked the disintegration of his "Life Ship." Now Lucas took Rosalind's cold hands and confided the saddest fact of all. Medvekhin, who had been in his care for six months, might not live long. Internal injury was suspected; even mountain air did not suit the patient in the long run.

Dr. Tilmann could not neglect his duties, these consisting more and more of seeing patients off, closing down the facilities of St. Verena's hospital, on the eve of what came to be called The Great War. Rosalind was busy packing for the Ostrov family. Yet every day they snatched certain hours in the annex, high up among the pines. In these evening hours Medvekhin preferred to sleep. Lucas and Rosalind moved to that distant room, intended as a servant's bedroom, and there made love. This was that last golden summer of which poets were to speak. These were the last days, a time of wonders. . . .

On July twenty-ninth, after the Austrians had attacked Serbia and the tsar had ordered mobilization, the Ostrov family set off for Berlin. The train was packed with Russians intent on outrunning the German declaration of war. Rosalind sat dry-eyed, handing the countess her smelling salts; Leonid Ivanovitch was cheerful and inspired, eager to return to his betrothed and to his regiment. Everyone on the train—the Russians, the English students, the French maid, the German officers clanking past—insisted that "it would be over by Christmas."

Rosalind shut her eyes and fell into a dreamlike recollection of her last interview with Medvekhin. She saw the extraordinary, wise face, the yellow eyes, the billowing "Russian blouse" of yellow silk that covered the muscular, furred upper body. They sat alone; Sister Luise was in the kitchen preparing the vegetable soup on which the patient subsisted; Lucas had not yet come to the evening rendezvous. The wooden shutters were flung wide and the back window open, showing the sunlit mountainside.

They spoke of the impending war. Medvekhin turned from gazing at the path winding up to the high meadow and made a curious pronouncement: "Where millions die for insufficient reasons perhaps this is in itself a reason not to live."

Rosalind was shocked but she managed to hide it. She had become better and better at hiding her thoughts and feelings from the patient. She wondered if it had to do with poor Medvekhin's failing health.

"I accept *one* sufficient reason to die," she said, "namely that one has grown very old and come to the end of a life span. Is that so with the Akuine?"

"No," said Medvekhin. "Once again the parallels are inexact. There is the possibility of mind-conservation and rebirth. Let us talk of something less embarrassing."

"I will be returning to Russia with the Ostrov family," she said.

"Your last visit, *chère Rosaline*?"

A twitch of the fine drooping hair about the mouth.

"No, not quite," she smiled and lied with perfect composure. "I will be here tomorrow morning."

Soon afterward Lucas arrived and the Sister came in with the patient's food. Lucas sat down at the harmonium and they entertained Medvekhin with dinner music. Rosalind sang "Auld Lang Syne"; she was aware that none of the listeners felt the powerful associations of the song as she did. Later that evening she walked back to the hospital with Lucas for the last time and they went over their brave plans for letters, for their next meeting, when everything was over. She expressed her hopes for Medvekhin and for Europe, for mankind. Yet she carried in her sewing bag Dr. Lucas Tilmann's black notebook, which she had stolen from the tangle of books at his bedside, and she made sure never to come within range of their cosmic guest the next day. *Her* memory, at least, would survive the encounter with Medvekhin. . . .

When she opened her eyes again the countess was gazing at her with sad concern. The family was well aware that she was being parted from her sweetheart by the approaching conflict, but Rosalind was able to reassure the countess, later on. No, she was not expecting a child. The idea of being pregnant and unwed among the Ostrovs was not as frightful as that of being in the same situation, for instance, in Cheltenham. She began to see it as an alternative life, something that might have happened. Lucas had given her a beautiful ring with an emerald, the gift of a grateful patient, but she wore it on a chain around her neck, under her blouse. It was evening of the first day; Munich, Nuremberg lay behind them; they were approaching Leipzig.

Cities of Old Europe were left behind: Berlin, Stettin, Danzig, Königsberg . . . and at last Minsk, after the railway gauge broadened and the travelers lost a number of days by returning to the Julian calendar.

"We are traveling back into the past," said Leonid wearily.

"Believe me, dear child," said his mother, "Horse-dawn carriages were *much* worse."

"Perhaps one day," said Rosalind, "we will fly from place to place."

"As angels?" teased Marie-Louise.

"No of course not!" said Rosalind, laughing. "In flying-machines!"

"Futuristic thinking," said Leonid, "is subversive. Kyril, our revolutionary, hopes that none of the empires will survive this war."

At last they reached their destination: Rosalind helped the countess up the steps of the palace in Moscow, where they took refuge with Great-Uncle Paul, pleading the fortunes of war.

The season was late spring but the weather in the Alps was chill and changeable. Rosalind drove up from the station wrapped in a treasured Russian coat that reached to her ankles. She was exhausted from journeying, drained of hope. The familiar trees on the avenue filled her with a painful expectation—*Oh Lucas, oh my love*— but she could not help noticing that the driveway was neglected. A few patients were on the terrace and she saw at once that they were veterans: "wounded soldiers."

In the hall she found a village girl mopping the marble floor. A gruff old orderly did not remember her but he became excited when she asked for Dr. Lucas Tilmann.

"The English girl!" he cried. "Are you . . . ?"

Rosalind did not like "making herself known" but felt it necessary.

"I am Miss Lane, Dr. Tilmann's *verlobte,* his betrothed!" she announced.

Old Fritz was already hurrying her off to the *oberin,* the matron. He flung open the double doors to the matron's parlor and cried out: "She has come! Fräulein Lane, his English girl!"

Dr. Daniel, the intern, came toward her with outstretched hands and the new *oberin,* rustling from behind her desk, was Sister Luise. Rosalind, trembling, could not hold back any longer: "Oh tell me!" she cried. "What has happened to Lucas Tilmann? Is he here?"

"Yes, he is here!" soothed Dr. Daniel, smiling.

"We were to be married! I sent telegrams, letters . . ."

"Hush! He will be all right!" said the frau oberin. "Now that you are here."

"I have heard nothing for five years—since 1915!"

They sat her down with a reviving little glass of herbal schnapps and began to explain. Lucas Tilmann was a convalescent, one of the "wounded soldiers," discharged seven months ago from an orthopedic ward in Munich; he had lost his left leg at the knee when a field lazaretto caught a shell on the Somme.

That was really not all of it, she could see. Dr. Daniel spoke of trauma, from the battlefield; she first heard from him the English word *shell shock.* The former director sat alone in a darkened room. . . .

"Please! I must go to him at once!"

Dr. Daniel hurried off to prepare Lucas for a visitor. Rosalind knew that there was still more to tell, concerning the hospital itself; but now that she was alone with the Frau Oberin she blurted out a quite different question and was able to observe the result.

"Sister Luise, what has become of the patient in the annex; what has become of Medvekhin?"

The frau oberin gave a puzzled smile. "Well, there is no one up in the chalet now," she said. "And I don't recall any Russian patient with that name. . . ."

Rosalind felt a warning chill: She knew better than to protest. Sister Luise had been made to forget.

"Who *was* the last patient up there?" she asked. "Was it Miss Courtney?"

"Yes, of course!" said the frau oberin. "Such a remarkable recovery! Poor Dr. Tilmann's sleep cure!"

"Surely there were two gypsies, up in the clearing, living in their caravan?"

"Yes, indeed! Kaspar is still here, working as an orderly, and Marja is in the kitchen. If anyone asks we say they are Hungarians. . . ."

Then the frau oberin directed Rosalind up the stairs—the lifts were not working. So she came to the rooms in the east wing that Lucas Tilmann had inherited when his father retired to Switzerland. Dr. Daniel stood at the door of the sitting room motioning her inside with an encouraging smile.

She looked into the large room, dark now because of the bright day outside. She saw a figure hunched at a small desk, outlined against the French windows onto the balcony. Rosalind saw her life, her future, her dear love whom she must heal; she rushed into the room and fell on her knees beside Lucas Tilmann.

"Is it you?" he whispered. "Is it you?"

"Oh yes!" she said "Oh yes, my dear, my soul . . ."

Dr. Daniel closed the door, satisfied, as they embraced. Rosalind asked a question or two and knew that she could not pursue certain subjects. Lucas Tilmann had no memory of Medvekhin; she could not tell if this amnesia was part of an alien command to forget or if it was deepened by his war trauma.

Lucas counted his long recovery from the moment of her arrival, but Rosalind knew that it was made possible by his insight into his own case. In no time he was managing the clumsy prosthesis well enough to walk up and down the sitting room. Then, mastering the confines of the room he set out, battling his agoraphobia, to explore the suite, to stand on the balcony, to plan a descent to the garden, to the village—in particular, an official visit to the picturesque baroque Rathaus: The burgermeister was in his debt.

Lucas no longer owned any part of St. Verena's hospital. His family's long association with the Russians was regarded as disloyal to the kaiser while the two empires were at war. He had been more or less forced to sell his shares to the town council of Mariensee. The shares of his Russian partners (who could now be described as White Russians) had simply been confiscated.

The burgermeister's plans to develop St. Verena's as a *luftkurort,* a health resort featuring mountain air, were delayed by lack of funds and personnel. The presence of Lucas Tilmann was an embarrassment to the town council and the staff of St. Verena's. He was a reminder of past glories, and at the same time a physician who could not heal himself. The burgermeister, in these circumstances, was able to arrange for a civil marriage, with an English bride, pending a journey to some other country.

The two lovers planned their future with a blend of realism and romance that Rosalind thought of as "postwar." After the ceremony in the town hall they would drive into Switzerland in the sturdy old Daimler and take their way down into Italy, to Venice, where they would take ship for England. Lucas had money in a Swiss bank account; she had her nest egg in the Bank of England plus a few pieces of jewelry that the countess had pressed upon her in lieu of salary.

The Ostrov family had lost a large part of their fortunes but they were not completely ruined. After the large estates had gone, there remained the small places—the hunting grounds, the horse farm—which could be sold sometime, before they came into the power of the state.

And as for their lives they owed these to Kyril Mihailovitch Azlov, who was in the forefront of the revolution. When the palace in Moscow was requisitioned he made sure that the family retained comfortable living quarters. Rosalind spoke to him with keen interest about the great meteorite of 1908, believed to have fallen in the region of the Stony Tunguska River.

Kyril Mihailovitch had not only rejected his title and made over all his personal fortune to the cause, he had changed his name. He called himself Erlik, the name he had used to sign his folktales; this name, he told Rosalind, was a Siberian name for the Firegod. When the great meteorite fell down, simple folk said it was the Firegod Erlik, who came to Earth in the guise of a bear.

Comrade Erlik was a Party member of the second wave, due to be purged about 1936, not long after Dr. Jacob Daniel, the director of St. Verena's Sanitarium, lost his civil rights and went into exile.

Two days before her marriage, before she left St. Verena's forever, Rosalind visited the chalet. The weather was cool but clear with scarves of mist on the upper slopes of the mountains. She set off up the path to the clearing, which was over-grown: The benches were wet, covered with leaves. The horse and the caravan had gone and the icon of St. George had been taken from the wayside shrine. Yet as she climbed the right-hand path toward the chalet she *remembered,* she had pre-served the memory of that joy, that well-being that had streamed out to her.

The chalet itself was clean and well-kept; Rosalind went from room to room flinging open the shutters and the windows. She began to weep. Tears slid down her cheeks for the lovers who had shared the narrow bed, for millions dead, for Leonid Ostrov, dead near Vilna. The large back bedroom was quiet and still, with no hint of its former occupant; when she stood at the open window she saw that the path to the higher meadow had been picked out with white stones.

Rosalind dried her eyes. She went out of the back door and began to climb up through the pines and the larches, coming into new leaf. When she passed the spring, bubbling in its ancient stone basin, she wrung out a handkerchief in the icy water and wiped her face. She came out into brighter sunshine and turned left, pacing slowly through the long grass at the edge of the round meadow.

She found the grave just within the shade of the trees; a network of green had spread over the black earth; some larger stones at the head of the grave formed the letter *M.* Nearby there was a block of wood, cut from a tree trunk, as if someone else came to sit in this place, as she did now, contemplating the grave.

It seemed to Rosalind that nothing had taken place; the story would never be told; no researchers would ever find their way into the subarctic wastes—*and that Medvekhin had willed it this way.* This impossibly lonely death was an essential act, the contribution of the Akuine race of star-travelers to the history of the world.

Presently she heard a voice and saw the gypsy, Kaspar, striding up the path. He was just as he had been, a muscular, jolly man with a piercing glance; she stood up and they shook hands. His smile was melancholy.

"We know who lies here . . . ," she said, "but what did you tell the others?"

"The woods are full of graves, miss," he said. "If the grave is marked then Christians will not disturb it."

He made the sign of the cross with two fingers like an old believer. She had to ask the questions—yes, the master had passed on in 1915; both Dr. Tilmann and Sister Luise had assisted at this burial on the meadow.

"They have been made to forget. . . ."

Kaspar laughed aloud.

"Oh we've seen it happen many times, Marja and I. He could make any human forget his own mother, just like that, in a breath!"

He snapped his fingers. Rosalind hardly questioned the fact that Kaspar and Marja still remembered. She believed it was another odd *class* thing. Medvekhin knew his true servants: At the last he protected his story, in what was almost a reflex action, from his doctor and his nurse.

"And would this loss of memory last—forever?" she asked.

"I asked that question myself," replied Kaspar, frowning. "And our dear master said that memories might return."

This was all the reassurance that she received and it had to be enough. She bade farewell to Medvekhin and to the human being who had been pressed into alien service. She walked down the mountainside through the trees, passing through light and shadow. She thought of England, projected her thoughts into that future time, that future moment in the English woodland when she would bring out the black notebook and present it to her husband.

SCHRÖDINGER'S DOG

Damien Broderick

▼

Australian writer, editor, and critic Damien Broderick made his first sale in 1964 to John Carnell's anthology New Writings in SF 1, *and although not prolific by genre standards, has kept up a steady stream of publications in the thirty-three years that have followed. He sold his first novel,* Sorcerer's World, *in 1970; it was later reissued in a rewritten version in the United States as* The Black Grail. *Broderick's other books include the novels* The Dreaming Dragons, The Judas Mandala, Transmitters, Striped Holes, *and, with Rory Barnes,* Valencies, *and two collections,* A Man Returned *and* The Dark Between the Stars. *He has edited three anthologies of Australian science fiction,* The Zeitgeist Machine, Strange Attractors, *and* Matilda at the Speed of Light, *and written a nonfiction critical study of science fiction,* Reading by Starlight: Postmodern Science Fiction. *His most recent book is a major new novel,* The White Abacus, *and another one,* Zones, *will be out soon in Australia.*

In the ingenious story that follows, he boldly takes us deep into unexplored territory where no one has gone before, and shows us that although there may be No Place Like Home, sometimes you've got to settle for what you can find. . . .

The old woman is ninety-nine parts dead, but sardonic with it. A green hospital gown hangs on her wasted flesh like a shroud. Two men look down upon her from the observation bay, one of them rather less than relaxed, as she is cranked into the quantum splitter.

"Elizabeth," Dr. Tom Manchetti croons into his mike. "Beth, can you hear me?"

"Hmph." She stirs, vomits a thin dribble, which a technician wipes from her chin.

"Wake up, Beth." In the bay's dimmed illumination, lit from below by red and green indicator tabs, Manchetti's long-jawed face is slightly macabre. "I'm sorry, honey, there's going to be some pain."

"Okay, Thomas," she whispers. "No need to shout. Oh. God."

"I know, honey, it hurts. We're turning down the nerve-block chips for a moment." In a beguiling murmur, he tells her, "You have a visitor, Beth."

"Oh? Can't we just get this bloody *over and done with*? I'm so *sick* of this." She dry-retches.

"Soon, Beth. Can you open your eyes, honey?"

Elizabeth Croft blinks against the lights, looks up into the bay, squints against a flare of light on the sloping window. "Well, well, the Lord High Pooh-Bah, and me on my deathbed. I don't believe we've been formally introduced, Sir Bryce." She spasms. "Oh, bugger."

Neurochip's new CEO leans to the microphone. "Good morning, Dr. Croft. How are you feeling today?"

"They've turned my pain-block nanos off, Sir Bryce. I feel like shit."

"Call me Bry, Elizabeth. May I call you Beth?"

The dying woman smirks. "Just call me a doctor."

Sir Bryce Powell turns his head, speaks quietly. "Dr. Manchetti, surely she'll need to be fully alert—"

"Check the monitors for yourself, Sir Bryce. Beth is wide awake, and I'm afraid she's in a lot of pain. It's just her . . ."

"Gallows humor, Sir B.," the old woman says from the entrance to the quantum-measurement device. She groans then, a tremor from hell. "Can we just get this *over*? I'd rather be *dead*."

"Okay, honey," Dr. Manchetti tells her, "we have everything ready for you. The nanocells are giving us a nice clean read. We're ready when you are."

Deadpan, Croft asks, "What, you're going to let me die unshriven?"

The CEO frowns. "Dr. Manchetti, her forms said she's a—"

"A devout atheist, yes. She's pulling your leg, Sir Bryce."

"Urp." A string of saliva runs down her cheek. "Oh shit, I'm losing it, Thomas, I'm really losing it. I'm not going to be much good to you."

"It's okay, honey, we're ready to go." Manchetti watches her a moment longer, rubbing his pale jaw. "It's been wonderful knowing you."

"Yeah, real. Flip the switch, Thomas. Send me out with a smile on my face. Or not, as the case may be."

The woman tech at the central console murmurs, "All SQUIDs are on line, doctor. Systems nominal. Ready for superposition scan."

"Thank you, Jill. It's your privilege, Sir Bryce. The green button."

"Call me Bry, Dr. Manchetti. That starts the quantum split?" It also triggers a lethal spill of neurotoxins from the spansule embedded in Elizabeth Croft's cortex. Neither man is indelicate enough to mention this fact.

Measurement Project's chief scientist nods. "Together with a random binary switch on her pain gates." The system is exquisitely precise. There is exactly one chance in two that the woman will stay in pain or go into analgesia before she terminates. "That's it, just touch the pad, Bry. And call me Tom."

Still his superior hesitates. "Macabre. I feel like a public hangman."

"You're not." Manchetti grips Powell by the upper arm, a reassuring contact from one authority to another. Intestinal cancer has been killing the woman for months. She is in terminal cachexia, unable to keep down anything solid, starving in a potential agony only the pain-gate chips hold her from. All this is a matter of public record, duly attested. Three specialist cancer physicians, a psychologist, a grief expert and a team of ethicists have counseled Elizabeth Croft in her extremity, have certified her sane desire for euthanized release. Her scrawled signature stands on a dozen triplicated forms.

The woman has closed her eyes again. She looks altogether parched, dried out, an Egyptian mummy. Bry Powell firmly presses the switch. There are hummings and clicks. Croft's body slides into the machine.

"Ah . . ." Her voice is soothed at once. "Ah, thank you, Thomas. Whew. I'll die with a smirk on my face." She falls silent, but her relaxed breathing is borne to them over the monitor system. After a moment she begins to hum.

"Christ, that's a relief," Powell says. "I'd started to feel like a *vivisectionist*."

Manchetti is brisk. "Random outcome, Bry. Beth knows what she's in for. It's her chance at immortality. Scientific immortality, anyway. Of course, in half the universes the machine flipped the other way."

The administrator shakes his handsome, calculatedly silver head. "I still find it hard to take that literally. You're telling me that, somewhere, Elizabeth Croft is still moaning with pain because—"

"Not 'somewhere,' Bry. Here. Everywhere."

Everything that can possibly happen is happening. All the flipped coins are falling as heads *and* tails. All the cancer cases are turning out well and turning out badly, all at once. A monitor device sounds, and lights appear before them. "She's transitioning into the chaotic regime. If the damned system works properly, we should hear the bifurcation—"

Something truly terrifying occurs. Through the acoustic feed, Beth Croft's humming continues. On a separate channel, her agonized voice tells them, "Oh God, this is *awful*. Look, I don't like to bitch and moan, but isn't there *something* I can have for the pain?" She pauses, as if someone is speaking to her. Nobody is, in this universe. "Oh. Oh. No, don't bother explaining it, I know this is what I signed up for. I just wish I was that lucky cow." Her moans become screams.

Manchetti smiles and smiles. "Well. Bloody marvelous. Sir Bryce, I congratulate you. If it hadn't been for Neurochip's support . . ."

Powell clenches his fists. "I. Am. Absolutely. *Overwhelmed*. Dr. Manchetti, it's for *me* to congratulate *you*."

The technician tells them, "Second-period doubling," and Beth Croft's aural feed becomes a babble of overlap, humming and shrieks of pain.

"Packet analysis coming through now, Doctor," Jill, the tech, informs them. "I'll switch them to you in sequence."

The cacophony chops off, leaving a single feed. Beth hums in drugged delight. The channel is switched; she is saying lucidly, "I feel a lot better, Thomas. Could I have some water? Just a bit to wet my mouth. Thanks, nurse." Switch. Her voice sharpens into outrage. "Hasn't this gone on long enough? I must have been bloody mad. Oh. Oh. Cruel and unnatural punishment." Another switch; she is babbling prayers from childhood: "Hail Mary, full of grace, the Lord is with thee. Don't let me die, oh please God, don't let me . . ." The prayer trails away, and is replaced by the flatline tone from a life-signs monitor. "We seem to have a termination on channel 4," the tech tells them unnecessarily. "Coming up on tertiary doubling."

The two men gaze down at the dying woman, listening to her travail in eight universes. The acoustic feed brings them a babble from six overlaps and two flatlines.

Powell is awed. "You'll have a Nobel for this, Thomas. You've just proved many-worlds quantum theory."

Dr. Manchetti grins like a skull. "We've done that before, Bry. No, by God, what we've got here is grander than that. This is a tool for exploring the universe." Exultant, he cries, "All the universes there are."

"Period doubling has transitioned to chaos." The babble swiftly turns into white noise cut through by flatline tone. As Beth's many voices drop out one by one, the turbulent babble gives way to the single augmented flatline tone. "Full arrest across the entire available manifold."

"We've lost her. That's all, Jill, thank you."

Ambient noise from the operation room cuts out as he closes a switch. Tom Manchetti stretches.

"I imagine you have a backup candidate prepared for the next stage?"

"Elizabeth Croft's death was inevitable, Sir Bryce, expected and accounted for. Never fear, Bry, we're ready to move on to full implementation. Here, I believe we deserve a small drink."

"Another cancer patient?"

Manchetti checks the console, touching the key he has just closed. He lowers his voice slightly. "HIV-6, actually. We had severe chip rejection problems with Beth. T-cell compromise will help with that."

For a moment, Neurochip's CEO regards his chief quantum scientist in silence. "How convenient, Thomas. How very provident."

Jill Ng turns the shower off, towels her chunky body vigorously. Vietnamese pop squeals from the kitchen, a style she has grown fond of despite her better judgment. Plates clatter. She sticks her head around the door and sniffs. "*Yum-cha*, delicious."

"Morning, Jill." Her husband frowns at her with mock censure. "*Afternoon.*"

She grins. "We've both been working like . . . chinamen."

Daniel Ng spoons food on to a warmed plate. "Yeah. I hope N-chip appreciates just what great little company steadfasts we are."

The quantity of food is rather surprising. "Expecting company?"

"I invited Binh and Tam for brunch. You don't mind, do you? We knocked off so late I didn't want to bother you by ringing."

"Cool, Dan." The doorbell chimes, and she says, scampering for the bedroom, "Can you get it, sweetheart? I'm not dressed."

Daniel smiles. "I noticed, you rude Australian girl." He runs after her, waving a spatula, and they smooch noisily in the hall.

Glass's *Satyagraha* drones as they eat, as they argue with unquenchable high spirits about their specialities. Through a crisp spring roll, spraying pastry, Daniel declares forcefully, "The re-entrant circuits to the hippocampus are the *obvious* place for consciousness."

His immediate boss, Tam Deng, snorts. "Oh, come off it, Daniel. Aren't you tired of grubbing around after some single neural site of awareness?" And Tam's tiny wife Binh adds, "Tam's right, you know. I had a patient once, herpes encephalitis. Took out hippocampus *and* associated cortex. And *nothing* went wrong with his awareness . . . his consciousness . . . whatever you want to call it, *except* that—"

Daniel sighs noisily; he has heard this tale before. "—he couldn't remember anything for more than five minutes! Exactly!'' He splays his hands. "Doesn't that show some pretty impressive localization?''

"Look, guys,'' Jill tells them, "I mightn't know much about the brain's wet-ware . . .''

Dan says parodically, " 'I'm just a humble quantum mechanic.' ''

". . . but if my Connection Machine lost a bunch of parallel processors, it'd flip its lid too.''

"No, it wouldn't,'' Tam insists. "I'm sorry, Jill, it'd 'degrade gracefully,' the way a human brain does. It'd be hurt, but not like ripping out the chip from a notepad.''

Jill Ng shrugs. Really she doesn't care. "I guess.''

Dan will not budge. "The thing about the hippocampus is, you find transient changes on the *presynaptic* side. You get these big spikes—''

"Is anyone going to eat the last pork bun?''

"You have it, Binh,'' Jill says. "I'm for more Chablis. See, my poor tired hippocampus,'' and she pauses, smiling, "has these big spikes—'' Everyone laughs, the mood eases.

"It's been a rough few days,'' Tam says, leaning back in his chair. "I've never seen N-Chip so zoned. Not just neurosci. You 'Schrödinger's Dog' buggers too, isn't that true, Jill?''

Daniel stands up abruptly. "I'll get coffee. Tam, you shouldn't ask. Jill's team's Sec Four, stricter security than us for heaven's sake.''

"Hey, smooth.'' With careless sarcasm, Binh adds, "Like they're not going to drag you away to *reeducation camp*, Daniel.'' There is a moment of aghast silence; the woman is instantly abashed. "Sorry, Danny. Foot in mouth.''

Dan says distantly, "That's okay, Binh. It's just that . . . well, my interface runs're dragging up a lot of crappy stuff I thought I'd buried twenty years ago.'' Daniel Ng has a machine growing in his head. An array of nanocells lives in his corpus callosum, ready to download to his project's neural net. Three million molecular gadgets let Tam and the rest of the cog-sci team monitor Daniel's cognitive throughput.

His wife reaches up, touches his arm. "Listen, darling, I don't think you need to—'' And Tam says, blandly, "If I'd known the procedure was upsetting you, Daniel, I wouldn't have allowed . . .''

He shakes his head. "No, it's all right. Return of the repressed,'' he says with a ghastly grin. "Helps hose out the psychic toxins.''

Softly, Binh asks: "The boat trip to Australia?''

"Yeah. Ffff.'' He shivers. "Nightmares, I can tell you.''

"Really, Dan,'' Jill tells him, looking from one face to another, understanding only her husband's palpable pain and nothing of its immediate cause, "you shouldn't—''

"*Why* shouldn't I, Jill?'' he says bitterly. "Because it upsets you to hear how your husband's mother and sisters were raped in an overcrowded boat and left to die with no food or water?''

Tam is shocked. "Daniel! These are ghastly, terrible things, but there's no need to take it out on Jill!''

Jill Ng has tears in her eyes. "Sweetheart, I'm sorry. I didn't know your work was—"

"Oh *shit!* Darling, *I'm* sorry. It's these damned *dreams!*"

The guests rise, collect their possessions. "Binh and I should go," Tam tells him. "Dan, if you need some time off, give me a call on Monday. Don't even bother coming in. You really don't look well, you know."

Binh kisses Jill lightly. "Thank you for *yum-cha,* Jill. Here, give me a hug, Daniel. Gosh, you're getting thin." As they walk to the door she murmurs to him, "I know what it's like." Her boat had tried to land three times in Malaysia before they were accepted at Pulau Besar. Her father was drowned. She was eight years old. "But *we* are alive. We're alive."

"Yes, by some filthy throw of the dice." And Daniel would never stop feeling guilty that he had made it and not his mother and his poor sisters.

Amid a pattering of polite applause, Neurochip's chair opens the final session. "We're fortunate to have our chief executive officer with us for this concluding session. Good afternoon, Sir Bryce, and welcome. Ladies and gentlemen, I believe in keeping briefings . . . brief."

Through mild, satisfied laughter, she says, "I'm pleased to see representatives here from Accounting and Industrial Applications. We'll try to keep our discussion informal and user-friendly. If our speakers get too technical, please drag them back to earth in the customary manner." There is a ripple of friendly laughter. "Dr. Thomas Manchetti, head of Measurement Project."

Manchetti stands. "Thank you, Madam Chair. You'll all get a technical download about the project to your notepads but, to be brief, I'm happy to report that my team has achieved a successful application of the Schrödinger's Cat effect. Actually we now prefer to call it the Schrödinger's Dog effect."

"Sorry," interjects a well-bred voice, "you've lost me. Are these animal experiments? I thought N-Chip's concentrating on human subjects these days?"

Madam Chair murmurs, "Background, Thomas. Keep it short."

"Oh, yes. One forgets—" Manchetti is irritated, but falls smoothly into his customary patter. "Ah, the issue my group's been exploring is known as the Measurement Problem. In quantum physics, we encounter the so-called Indeterminacies. Measure one parameter, you know, and another becomes blurred."

"That's what Kevin told the auditors." Everyone laughs.

Manchetti permits a smile. "In this case, the accountant is the universe itself. You might recall the late Stephen Hawking's jest: 'Not only does God throw dice, He throws them where they can't be seen.' Well, we've managed to track the dice down."

"I thought that was impossible? Like going faster than light?"

"That's a relativity restriction, David . . . but we're working on that one too. Okay, the cat." Seventy years earlier, in 1935, he explains, Erwin Schrödinger had dreamed up an imaginary experiment. Put a cat into a sealed box with a lethal device triggered by a single quantum event, a radioactive particle emission, with one chance in two of decaying within a given interval. Quantum theory said the event was undetermined until the box was opened and the state of affairs recorded—observed. So until the box was opened, the cat was neither dead nor alive but in an incomprehensible overlap of the two states.

The wit from Accounting says, "I can't see a lively market for zombie cats!" The room ripples with laughter. "Cost less to feed, I suppose."

"It always sounded ridiculous," Manchetti agrees, annoyed, "but that's what the equations tell us."

"Well, equations. It's like statistics, isn't it? All smoke and mirrors."

"No!" Manchetti is adamant. "Quantum physics is *right!* It *works!* It's the basis of electronics. Obviously we were looking at it wrong. The trouble is, the human mind seems almost powerless to look at it *correctly.*"

"Put 'em out of their misery, Thomas," the CEO says easily. "The cat's both dead *and* alive, isn't it—in parallel universes?"

Pained, Manchetti says, "A rather misleading way to put it, Sir Bryce. I'd prefer to say that *our* universe—by definition, the only universe that actually exists—is fashioned out of an infinite set of superposed alternative histories, most of them extremely unlikely."

"Isn't that what I just said?"

"Not really. Look at it this way. Every moment, the universe contains a finite though very large number of particles. But each of those particles has an infinite number of different fine-grained histories and futures. It's like the geodesic dome over the racetrack—every strut hangs off every other strut."

"So this dog's a greyhound, eh?"

Through the laughter, Manchetti says crabbily, "We tend to assume that the cat dies in half the histories, and in the other half it stays alive. But that's a very narrow opinion. In some of the possible histories, you see, Schrödinger changed his mind *and didn't do the experiment at all*. In others, animal-rights activists broke in and pulled the poor thing out of the box."

Delighted, the accountant cries: "Ah! And in some, *Schrödinger used a dog instead!*"

The room fills with happy uproar.

"Exactly! And in an infinite number of others, the Earth never formed, and in still others, intelligent life evolved from vegetables instead of primates . . . Most of those extreme possibilities cancel out, luckily. But you see, there's always a small chance that when Erwin opens the box the histories decohere in such a way that a *dog* history is selected, instead of one with a live or a dead *cat*."

"You're saying you've proved this? You've put in a cat and got out a dog!"

Manchetti is unruffled. "Far more remarkable than that, Joan. We've tracked the alternative histories of, of, what should we call her, Bry . . . Schrödinger's *Human*?"

His intercom tells him, "Dr. Ng, you have a visitor."

"Thanks, Tricia. Send 'em through."

"It's your wife, Dr. Ng."

Daniel leaves his workstation. "Jill! Hello, sweetheart." He hugs her in a distracted manner. "What are *you* doing down here in the dungeon?"

"You're a bad, bad boy. You told me you'd stay home today. Look at you!"

Daniel shrugs. In the fluorescent light, his face is drawn. "I'm okay. How'd you get past the dragon?"

"You look terrible, if you must know."

"Tired, love. We're all tired. You don't look fantastic yourself."

Jill's lips quirk.

"We're very busy, dear," Daniel tells her, returning to his workstation. "I'm prepping for a cerebral bloodflow scan in five minutes."

His wife sits on a swivel stool and regards her hands. "I know. The mandarins upstairs want someone from Measurement down here to observe. Luck of the draw."

Daniel is not pleased. "Don't be offended, Jill, but I disapprove of their choice. Interferes with objectivity."

"You should come by *our* labs one day, Danny—you'd soon learn there's no such thing as objectivity."

The intercom says, "Dr. Ng, they're waiting for you in prep."

"Coming, Trish. Jill, you can look but you can't touch. There's an observation platform above the scanners. Be my guest."

"Well, Sir Bryce Powell's guest, apparently." She gives him a quick kiss. "Take care, love. And ask one of the real doctors to give you a checkup when you're done."

Craning toward the large sloping window of the observation bay, mirror twin of the Measurement lab where she works, Jill Ng says, "He really does look awful, Binh."

"It's the lights. Don't forget, he's full of muscle relaxants and tracer isotope gas. Perfectly safe, of course. We've all had our turn in the scanner."

The speaker brings them Tam's voice. "Daniel, just keep your eyes on the readout and continue subvocalizing. We're getting good activity in the speech centers."

Jill looks around incredulously. "Your machine can read Danny's mind through the nanos? Actually monitor his thoughts?"

"Not really. His stream of awareness. We sample a terabyte stream from his speech-processing cells, and plug it into a neural net loaded with English grammar and syntax and a bunch of Schank scripts. What we get out is a reconstruction, like enhancing a grainy photo."

The monitor brings them a technician's disembodied voice. "Scanning on re-entrant verbal fields locked in."

Daniel's voice, or its simulation, childish and peevish, issues from the sound system: "It's so hot. I want my mama. Where's my mama?" His voice changes, then, into an impersonation of a quavery old man: "Be quiet, child. It's terrible for all of us, you know."

And another intonational shift suggests a woman: "Hush, little fellow. Your Mama's sick, you see, so they've moved her to the front of the boat to get some air."

Jill surges from her comfortable seat, aghast. "You can't do that! It's not fair!"

Binh reaches out, takes her hand. "We use the strongest emotional vectors available, Jill. Daniel's given his consent, you must understand that."

The tech reports: "We're bringing up full-spectrum interpolation."

Daniel's voice vanishes, and a monitor displaying medical data above Jill's head suddenly turns into a cartoon, real-time animation in full density montage: crashing waves, ship motor thrumming, people moaning. A child's voice complains, "Stop shoving your knees in my back! Oh, I'm so thirsty." An old Vietnamese man cries, "Sweet Lord Jesus, send us some rain. Dear Lord Buddha, we'll perish without water." The images flick, as if the viewpoint has exceeded the limits of visual constancy. An old woman lurches into the frame, her mouth twisted. Everyone speaks English with a faint Viet accent; the translation is working perfectly. "Too much water, husband. Gah, it stinks! My poor feet are swelling up in it." Yells break out: "A boat! A big boat!" Ship engines cease; there are two dull gunshots, shoving, yells, a body crashes down the gangway. Dan the child, watching all this hideous confusion, cries piteously, "Stop pushing! I want my mama! Tien!" A Thai pirate looms into the gangway. In a comic-strip accent all the more terrible for its invocation of childhood fears, he roars, "Shut up and stay where you are. All we want's ya money and ya jewels. Come on, they'll do you no good in the afterlife." Terrified people scream, men laugh and swagger and shout for gold and jewels; there are more gunshots, children whimper, a woman screams. The old woman whispers to the screen, "Stay down, boy. Here, get underneath me." A pirate grabs his sister Tien. "Hey, fancy this little beauty, shipmate? She stinks, but so do you." A burst of raucous male laughter. Danny screams and his arms flail on the screen. "Stay down, child," his grandmother hisses. "Shut your eyes. The Lord Buddha will protect." The image is lost for a moment: clothing tears, a girl's frightened scream, male laughter. Little Danny squeals, "Oh, the filthy, filthy dogs. What's that dirty man doing? Oh. Oh. Oh." The sound effects cut off abruptly, and the screen returns to medical readouts. The tech's voice says calmly, "Terminate processing scan. That's great guys, we had major activation in cortical and limbic modules with ninety-one-percent echo in the net. Thanks, Dr. Ng. You done real good, little guy."

Jill, shaking with fury, stares at Binh. "You bastards. You *bastards*."

"It's really all right, Jill. I'm sure Daniel's happy to be part of this important—"

"Shut up, Binh. Just *shut up*."

Daniel knocks on the team physician's paneled door. An overweight woman in her forties opens it, guides him in with a hand on his shoulder. "How are you feeling, Daniel?"

"Okay."

"Pop up on the couch. You don't look okay to me. Have you been out on the tiles?"

"I wish. I'm just tired, Lisa."

"Let me look at your eyes. Open your mouth."

"It's this building, you know," Dan says when she takes the light out of his mouth. "Really lethal *feng-shui*. Buildings should reflect the order of nature."

The doctor sits back. "So should human bodies. And I have to tell you, Daniel, yours is not in good shape. I want to run some tests."

"Give me a break, doctor. I'm the human pincushion."

Lisa fetches out a hypodermic. "Roll up your sleeve, chum. We'll see if your blood's worth bottling. You'll just feel a little prick."

"That's what I tell my wife. Ouch."

Jill whispers, "Are you asleep?"

Danny snores in a marked manner. After a moment, he relents. "What?"

"When Binh and I watched them working on you today, I—I wanted to kill her." In the darkness, he says nothing. "Well, smash her bloody teeth in, anyway. How *dare* they?"

"It's okay."

"No, it's not." Jill sits up, pushing her pillow against the wall, hugs her arms against her breasts. "It was like some . . . What was that old horror movie? *A Clockwork Orange.*"

He rolls on his back. "Don't be melodramatic, Jill. They're just prodding my memory, that's all. Anyway, the nanos do all the work."

"I hated it. God, Dan, you were only five years old—"

"Six. No, I had my sixth birthday in the refugee camp."

His wife shudders, and reaches for him. "I just can't imagine it. People are so vile."

"Some people. Not us, sweetheart."

"Thank God." She shudders. "Come here, I need a cuddle."

Cautiously, gritting his teeth, Daniel says, "Just a cuddle."

"You can't be *that* tired."

"Um." Daniel does not move. "The quack says we shouldn't make love for a week or so."

Laughing, uncertain, Jill says, "I'd rather you didn't make love to the quack at all, if you don't mind!" After a moment, she says, "Danny, what do you mean? You're pulling my leg, right?"

"Look, I'm sure it's nothing to worry about. They're running some tests."

"Tests?" She draws away from him.

"The nano injectors might have been contaminated. It can't be anything too dangerous. The place is spicker than a clean-room."

"This is *outrageous!*" Jill strikes the lamp at the side of the bed, and half the room floods with soft yellow light. "And they think you might pass something on to me?"

"Sweetheart, I'm so tired. Let's not fight." Still he does not move. "Come on, just curl up and go to sleep."

Jill sits up straighter in bed and clenches her fists. Shadows jump over her husband's weary face. "I'm not fighting with *you,* Danny. Tests! My *God!*"

"I'm sorry, Daniel," Dr. Lisa says in her most balanced voice, through a light-weight respiration mask, "I have bad news for you."

Daniel listens in dread. "Unh. It's cancer, isn't it?" Speculation has rioted in his imagination. Somehow the nanos have triggered an oncogene. Brain tumor. His mind will be eaten away from the inside.

"It's nothing to do with your research program, Daniel," Lisa tells him in a level voice. "I'm sorry, but you've tested positive for HIV-6."

Daniel is thunderstruck. *"What?* HI—*What?"* He cannot take it in. "That's a *venereal* disease!"

"STD—sexually transmitted, yes."

"Impossible! I haven't—Oh, shit, Lisa, the injectors really *did* get contaminated? How the hell could *that*—"

Lisa sends him a hard look. "Out of the question, Daniel. We've done a thorough screening of the nanomachines, of course. There's no way you could have been infected in the lab."

He is boneless and shaking. "I'm going to die?"

The doctor turns away slightly. "We'll support you all the way, Daniel. Total insurance cover, naturally, and it's company policy to—"

"How long?"

"Unless there's a breakthrough, a month. Maybe less. Six is a mutant, it's fast."

Daniel's face is very pale. He might faint at any moment. "Oh my God. Oh my God. How long have I been carrying it?"

"A month or two. Your T-cell count's massively compromised, and you have several opportunistic infections in your gastric system. The point right now is—"

Belatedly he understands what he has been denying all this time. "God! Have I infected *Jill?"*

"I'm truly sorry, Daniel. If you've had unprotected sex in the last month, there's a high probability she's also infected."

Beside himself, Daniel Ng shouts, "Of course we've bloody had sex in the last month, you stupid cow. Oh shit. Oh my God."

"One of my colleagues is seeing your wife right now, Daniel," Lisa tells him stiffly. "She'll get the same tests. In the meantime, we're moving you straight into biohazard containment. Jill can visit you there."

Daniel lurches to his feet. "I'm going home, doctor. I'm out of here."

"I'm afraid we can't allow that, Daniel." The physician stands, hesitates, takes one of his hands in hers. She wears thin-film surgical gloves. "Look, it's not hopeless. There's a frantic research program. We've got gene-engineered cures for the earlier strains."

"Great! A triumph for medicine. I might as well have drowned in the Gulf of Thailand." Tears are rolling from his eyes.

"You have one chance," Lisa tells him crisply, directing him to his chair. "Total isolation and barrier care. It's the only way we know to slow down the course of your disease. We need to exclude all further secondaries and control the ones you have."

"Don't be ridiculous, Lisa. This isn't a hospital, it's a neuroscience-research complex. Do you have any idea how much it would cost—"

"Cost is no object, Dr. Ng. Let's not forget, your cranium's full of unique and very expensive nanos. Neurochip isn't going to let you die if we can possibly help it."

Incredulously, swiping at his eyes, Daniel asks, "You want me to keep *working?"*

"You'll have the best of care and support, Daniel. We'll even put aside a suite for your wife so she can stay here twenty-four hours a day." The physician holds his gaze. "As of course she must if she's also infected."

"God, you've thought of everything. Look, I've got to talk to Jill now." His limbs shake despite his best efforts.

"There's a phone in the next room, Daniel. Come back when you're done and I'll take you across to containment."

Jill's face is darked by a triple thickness of laminated glass. "A charming turn of events, Daniel."

"Darling, thank heavens they've let you in here. Come over to the window, put your hands against the glass."

She draws back. "Keep your hands to yourself. How *could* you?"

Frantic, he asks, "Are you all right? Have you got your results back yet?"

"Wednesday. That's the soonest I can expect to hear. Should make for a couple of nice nights. They're keeping me here, you know."

"That's best." He searches her face for any sign of illness. "They're bringing in a whole team of autoimmune specialists. Don't worry about me, sweetheart. God, I'll never forgive myself if I've given you—"

"You selfish, stupid man." She is wearing jeans and an old pullover, and her makeup is smudged. "It makes me sick to look at you."

Appalled, Daniel recoils from the window. "Jill! You don't think I *caught* this!"

"Oh, shut up!" Spots of red bloom on her cheeks, and her nose is white as bone. "I thought I knew you, I thought I loved you, I thought we'd have children together—"

"Yes. Be brave. You still could be negative; they say I've only been infected for a month or so."

She glares at him, lips colorless. "How dare you! Wasn't I enough for you? Obviously not! Is it those whores in Richmond?" Her mouth writhes. "Or do you prefer boys in public lavatories? It makes me puke to think about it."

"Whores?" He shakes his head in confusion. "I love you more than my own life, surely you know that?"

"Your own life. Well, we know what that's worth now, don't we Danny? It's those nights you go out by yourself, isn't it? Down to Little Saigon and the league of heartbreak kids from the refugee boats. Twenty years ago that was, Daniel! Thirty! What bullshit! You're stuck in the past, Daniel Ng, you and all your victim buddies. But that doesn't give you the right to screw them in the park lavatory and pick up some filthy fucking *disease* that's going to kill me! What, did you get a taste for it from the *Thai pirates?*" She is sobbing.

"Oh, Jill! This is so completely wrong! Don't you understand, I love you?" Daniel is cold from head to toe, appalled as his life is devoured, everything distant but whirring, blurting out useless words. "You're the only thing that holds me to this terrible earth."

"Christ, I'm going mad." Her hands press to her lips for a moment of horrified silence. "I can't believe what just came out of my mouth, Danny, that was vile. But how can I believe you? Binh and Tam told me it *couldn't* have been an accident. These Neurochip labs are about as sloppy as a . . . a military *gene-splicing* facility. Or do you think they slipped you a merry little mutant virus along with your flu shot?"

"Oh, darling, come over here. Look at my face and you'll know what's true."

"Danny. I don't know what to think. You're going to die! *I'm* probably going to die! One day we're unpicking the mysteries of the soul, clever clever clever, the next we've turned into polluted garbage. How do you expect me to feel?"

He is weeping, disconsolate. "I just want one thing, Jill love, darling girl. Two things. I want you to trust and believe me. None of that filthy stuff's true. And I want you to love me. Hold on. Hold on and love me until we die."

The intercom chimes through the closing scene of *Casablanca*. Flatly, Daniel voice-activates it. A hearty male voice says, "Good evening, Dr. Ng. I wonder if we might talk for a moment."

Without lowering the video's volume, Danny says, "Why not? I'd invite you in for a drink, but as you see—"

"I'm Pearson Atkins, Daniel, comptroller of research projects. I believe your wife mentioned that I'd be dropping by."

"Probably."

"How are you feeling? Are you comfortable?"

"Could be worse. I could be behind on my rent." He turns off the movie. "How can I help you, Dr. Atkins?"

"Pearson, please. We were terribly relieved to hear that Jill's clear. She'll be dropping by to see you in an hour or so. She's asked for some time off."

Daniel is roused by this. "I don't want that. What good could it do? She'd just sit around at home brooding."

"She'll stay in her suite here, Daniel. But I agree with you. Work's what she needs to get her through this . . . melancholy crisis. I think it's what you need too."

He laughs bitterly. "No, I think the Home Movie channels'll suit me fine. Are you a big disco fan?"

"Uh, I don't really recognize the—"

"This morning I screened *The Boy in the Plastic Bubble*. Yes, folks, me and John Travolta."

"Immune disorders, I assume. What happened to this Travolta?"

"He's a kid, see, Pearson, and he falls in love. And he can't leave the bubble without catching a hundred lethal bugs, but he says he can't stand living like this any longer and just busts out and kisses the girl and they all live happily ever after."

"Oh. Well, of course we're hoping that you'll . . ."

"The movie lied," Daniel says venomously. "The kid—the *real* bubble kid— he was dead as a doornail. She killed him with her kiss."

"In your case, of course, we haven't yet tracked down the virus vector," the comptroller says cautiously. "But as I say, at least we can rest assured now that your *wife* isn't a carrier."

He shakes his head. "I did think it might be her. God, I'm so ashamed. But they tell me it couldn't be a lab accident either."

"I'm no medico, Daniel. Let me change the subject, if I may? We want you back at work, if you're up for it."

"Tam says I'm too far off the baseline now. My data's unreliable. They've wasted months of work. Not to mention all these expensive nanos in my head."

"Actually we want you to work with Measurement."

"Schrödinger's Dog?"

Ruefully, Atkins smiles. "That gag's leaked, has it? Rumors and gags seem to travel by quantum tunneling."

"Well, I hope you can do a better job with this damned virus."

"Yes. The point is, we think we've found a way to splice the two programs, to everyone's advantage. Call it serendipity. Your lexical nanos could be just what we need for the next stage of our own research."

Daniel regards him bleakly. "How convenient. What a shame you're not working up a cure for HIV-6. Then we could *really* tool along together." Reaching for the video controller, he clicks Bogey back on. "I'm knackered, Pearson. If Jill's out there, tell her I'm asleep. She can come back in a couple of hours."

"Okay, champ." Pearson shoots him a virile salute. "Have a snooze. But think it over."

"Yeah."

Instruments flicker, hum, click, buzz. Flat on his back, Daniel Ng regards the ceiling with rare humor. "That's some good shit they gave me, baby."

"*Shoosh*, Danny!" his wife says through her protective mask. "We have a twenty-four track tape running in here. Wanna get busted?"

"What can they do? Kill me?" He giggles. "You look silly covered in latex." The Measurement lab's inner door opens, and four more technicians or scientists come into the room. "Oh no, there's more! What is this, the Flying Condom Brothers?"

Tom Manchetti offers manly greetings. "Hi, pal. Feeling relaxed?"

"I'm the only one not dressed for the orgy."

"Just standard containment gear, Danny. No offense, buddy, but you're pretty lethal right now."

"'S okay. No pain, no gain." His voice slurs. "My best friend, Ngo Gain, comes from a good Vietnamese family."

Tam leans across him. "We're going to retract you into the scanner now, Daniel. Try to suppress your vocalization. Use the nanolink."

Daniel's pallet is withdrawn with a soft whine into the body of the quantum scanner. "Okay, team, testing testing, one two three four? Surrounded by giant plastic bags with faces, and a thousand squids."

"Two thousand and forty-eight SQUIDs, Dan," Manchetti tells him. "One K anterior and one K posterior. All the better to see you with."

"Posterior my ass. You mean dorsal and ventral." His last words, muffled by the enclosure, are amplified by his enhanced nano-mediated voice, which eerily lacks vowels: "Y' m'n d'rs'l 'nd v'ntrl."

"Without your mouth," Tam chides him.

"Tw' K s'p'r c'nd'ct'ng q'nt'm 'nt'rfrence devices on the seashore."

"We've got it, I think," Binh says. "Say again, Danny."

"Two K superconducting quantum-interference devices on the seashore. I feel like a naked fish."

Manchetti clears his throat. "I think we're ready, ladies and gentlemen. Hang in there, Daniel. Just keep the nanolink running and we'll track your resonance wherever you end up."

"My life as a . . . dog."

The room whines with power. "The SQUIDs have formed a Gell-Mann Manifold," Jill reports in a professional voice.

Manchetti notes, "Coarse-grained decoherence is collapsing. Danny Ng," he adds in high humor, "These Are Your Lives!"

"I can't feel anything different. Sounds like I'm going through a tunnel—"

"Doubling has commenced. Danny," Jill says, "I love you."

The monitor interface slams into pounding rock music, and the happy shrieks of a woman at the peak of climax. On the screen, Jill's own face, distorted by sex and proximity, cries, "Ah, ah, *ah*, Christ, oh, oh, yes, oh Danny, I love you, *aaa-AAARR . . .*"

Daniel moans, "Oh, oh, yeah, Jill, that was—" And in instant terror, "—God, we can't do this!" He reaches to the bedside and slaps off the sound system. Jill gapes up at him.

"What? What's wrong, darling?"

"We can't *do* this! My God, I'm not even wearing a condom!"

"What are you talking about? Danny Ng, get back into this bed at once! Sam won't be home till tomorrow night, I've *told* you—"

"Who's *Sam?* Don't you understand, I'm *positive*, I'm *lethal!*"

She stares at him. "I'm positive you're off your head. Look, I've told you before, he's still very important to me, I wouldn't let him get hurt by barging in on us—"

Daniel scrabbles off the bed and clutches his arms about himself. "Oh my God. Oh my God. This is a different world."

His wife—his lover, Jill—squints at him crossly. "Danny, this is a really stupid game. I'm going to have a shower. Turn the damn CD back on and make us a drink. I don't know what's got into you."

Urgently, he grabs her hand, draws her back to the bed. "No, no, just a moment. Here, sit down. Jill, the most incredible—Your name *is* Jill?"

"*What?!*"

"Bear with me, darling. Pretend I've just had a stroke. Something's gone wrong with my memory."

Uneasily, she guesses, "This *is* a game. Pretty creepy if you ask me. What happens next, you get dressed up in my clothes and pretend to be Ms. Saigon?"

"You're a quantum engineer," Daniel tells her, watching her face closely, "and you're married to this guy Sam."

"One out of two's not bad." She grins uncertainly. "Since I haven't had a job since the universities were closed down, I'd hardly consider myself a—"

Danny jaw drops. "Closed *down?* Wow, this is exactly the sort of thing they sent me here to find out. And look, um, I don't want to alarm you, Jill—"

"Oh, good, I wouldn't want you to alarm me!"

"—but I don't have, I mean you don't happen to know if I have any . . ." He wants to hold her, to hug her passionately, to make love to this woman with his redeemed, healthy body, and he dare not. He struggles for words.

"Any? Any?"

In a tiny voice, he asks, "Sexual disease?"

She is away across the room in two bounds. "Urk! Get out of that bed! You pig!"

"Just a minute! Hold your horses! I'm not who you think I am."

"You can say that again!" The woman is baffled and furious. "Look, go away. Just. Go. Away."

"Schrödinger's Dog."

"Cat. You mean Cat. Look, this just isn't funny."

"I'm Schrödinger's Dog."

"Schrödinger's Pig!"

Shivering and naked, Daniel Ng tells the woman who is not his wife in the world which is not his world, "Just try and get your fabulously well-trained and beautiful mind around this, Jill. In a universe at right angles to this one, there's a guy lying in a scanner surrounded by 2048 SQUIDs—"

She begins to relax. "Okay, it *is* a sex game. This better be good, baby. Superconducting quantum-interference devices. But you couldn't have that many, they have these huge magnets at minus two-hundred degrees or something."

He shakes his head. "Room-temperature superconductors."

"Oh, this is in the future?"

"So you don't have room-temperature superconductors." He is agog. "And the universities are closed down?"

"Gosh, Danny, you're scaring me."

"Where I come from . . . I mean, the Danny you're talking to right now, not the body, but the . . . I don't know how to describe it, the quantum personality . . ."

Jill really is getting frightened now. "You think you're from an alternate dimension. Like those kids' TV programs. *Sliders. Quantum Jump.*"

Daniel is enchanted. "Did you watch them too? I'd forgotten. *Quantum Leap.*"

"*Jump.* Trust me, I'm an expert. Used to be."

"In my version of reality, you're *still* an expert. In fact, you're sitting at the console monitoring all this right now through my nano implants. We're married." Abruptly he blushes, and the color goes from his face all the way down. "Oh God, that means she probably heard you—"

"I won't divorce him," Jill says bluntly. "I don't love him anymore, but I won't put him through that. He doesn't deserve to lose his job just because I want to sleep with a pretty boy from Vietnam."

Daniel Ng stands up, turns his face to the wall, and mutters, "Get me out of here, Jill. It's pointless. Let's just forget the damned experiment."

At the console, Jill says, "Switching to State Two of the Sigma Sequence." The large HD monitor freezes while the script-mediated display hunts through its search-trees. Its blue field scrolls to black, then shows in line cartoon King's Street, busy with cars and well-dressed young men and women. The sound track contrives a hint of jazz fusion from a nearby club. A young man in somewhat Edwardian clothing peers disdainfully into the screen.

"My word, Cordelia, look what they're allowing on the streets these days."

A beautiful girl says in an upper-class voice, "Tacky, very tacky. Bold as brass up on the footpath, Jonathan."

With airy menace, the youth says, "Be off, slope-head, or I'll kick you down-stairs." There is a burst of appreciative laughter from his elegant cronies.

Daniel Ng gapes about him. "Are you speaking to me?"

"Get in the gutter," suggests another youth. "And shut your mouth." He shoves him forcefully in the chest.

"Hey, keep your hands to yourself." Without his intending it, Daniel finds his hands in a defensive karate posture.

"Gentlemen, pay attention," announces the first lout. "We've found a rare trea-sure—a gook at liberty."

The lovely girl says, with an insouciant smirk, "Are you staring at my tits, Chopsticks?"

"One can't blame him, darling, they *are* rather conspicuous."

"Dirty little beast. Make him give us his money, Tristan."

The youth reaches with no sense of danger, and Danny slaps his hand aside. "Hey! Hey! Calm down. Jesus, where *am* I?"

Languidly sarcastic, the second youth clips his ear stingingly. "Well, you're not in fucking Ho Chi Minh Crater, I can assure you of *that*."

They begin to beat him up. Through their scuffling, passing cars swerve and honk their horns, but nobody stops. In terror, Daniel calls, "Jill! Jill! Get me out of here!" Fists and elbows strike him despite his resistance. Someone drags a wallet out of his back pocket.

"What's this rubbish? This isn't Australian pounds, it's some damned gook scrip! Tristan, do you know, I believe we've caught a spy!"

"Let's chuck him in the Yarra with his legs broken, see if he can swim home to the Crater!"

"For God's sake," Daniel screams, *"Beam me up, Scotty!"*

At her console, Jill reports, "I'm sorry, Dr. Manchetti, we're tracking two alternate metrics at present but we seem to have lost contact with Daniel's lexical implants. Should I terminate the Sigma Sequence?"

"Stay locked in, Jill. We're getting a very fuzzy signal here, but the implant techs think they can clean it up. Try another step in the superposition sequence; see if that helps."

The screens flicker to a new state.

Daniel stands in a low doorway, looking into a room where a fat gentleman sits cross-legged before an elegant walnut table covered in documents. In the distance, he hears sounds from his childhood, all mixed together, Asian and Australian: magpies whistle, food-sellers call. A manual typewriter clatters desultorily in an adjacent room, and a large fan thrums overhead.

"Come in, don't dither," orders the stout man. "Are you ready for the exami-nation?"

"Jill! Jill, what the hell—"

"Jee-al? I'm sorry, young man, this is not my name. I am Hussein Abdul bin Mohammed, a true son of the Prophet may his name be blessed, and if I am not mistaken you are one of the Fish-eaters of the Red River Delta people. Well, sit down. On the cushion, lad, what's wrong with you?"

Daniel sits, his legs giving way. He touches his unbroken ribs, feels tenderly at his eyes and cheeks. Nothing is damaged. But of course that was another world. "Um," he says desperately. "Mr. Hussein, I may have given the wrong impression. An examination, you said? Are you a doctor, sir?"

Abdul Hussein looks down his nose over his half-spectacles. "I don't find that especially amusing, young Fish-eater. Neither you nor I will ever attain such elevated rank. Now, I had your employment file right here. You are . . . ?"

"Daniel Ng, Mr. Hussein. Could you . . . ah, could you tell me a little about— The position, is it?"

The man shakes an admonitory finger. "Don't get ahead of yourself. First we assess your grades in arithmetic, calligraphy, and familiarity with the classics. If you are very fortunate indeed, we shall thereafter discuss employment options. Yes, I see here that you wish to strive toward a cleaning position on the Han Orbital Ring."

"The Han—Yes, I'm sorry, that's right, the orbital—You mean, as in satellite?"

Hussein sighs. "Your wit is dry to the point of idiocy, young man. Tell me, what are you doing here in the External Territories? Isn't there a bond of marriage between your family and the Lower Lords Nguyen in Da Nang? Danyeel . . . A Dayak name, perhaps? Or Malay?"

"Mr. Hussein, my head is spinning. I'm terribly sorry, something I ate. Please, can I ask you a question?"

"Naturally." The heavy gentleman preens. "As the prophet Mao tells us, one may pose any question to the servants of the people, though one is not always prepared to receive the answer."

Earnestly, on the verge of tears, Daniel Ng tells him, "I seem to be lost. I seem to be very, very lost."

"Nothing to it, Mr. Ng! When our business is completed, a boy shall direct you to your hostelry. Its name? The Emerald Garden, perhaps? The Tower of Hanoi?"

"I don't know."

Suddenly frosty, Hussein puts his sheaf of documents aside. "Oh. Well, it's your own business, of course. Let us turn without delay to the examination. Take out your brushes and ink."

"You don't understand, Mr. Hussein. I'm very, very, *very* lost."

The bureaucrat gasps, gazing in speculation. "Not a shipwreck! But no, your garments are clean and in the best repair." He struggles to his feet, backing away, breaking into a panicky shout. "Help! Help! An escapee! Murder! Rapine! May Allah and Mao protect us all!"

Daniel is dumbfounded. "Mr. Hussein! Please! What'd I say? Hey, really, stop yelling, I'm going, I'm going. . . ."

A muezzin begins the call to prayer amid the tumult from the outer offices. Hussein yells, "For shame! On your face, infidel! It is better to pray than sleep, and certainly better to pray than skulk!" He fails to catch Daniel's arm as he turns and sprints from the room. "After him! The Fish-eater! A Zoroastrian! A Zoroastrian runaway in the lobby!"

Through the uproar, Jill's console voice states: "We're getting him into resonance again, Dr. Manchetti, but the sequence is bifurcating. Danny, can you hear me?

Danny?'' The monitor's acoustic feed abruptly chops to softly running water and a crackling fire. Daniel's frightened voice comes through the speaker system: ''Oh. Oh. Jill, thank God. This is *ridiculous!* It's like being back at school.''

''Tom Manchetti here, Daniel. We lost you for a moment, but now you're back on-line. Back at school, eh? Happy days, the best?''

Bitterly, Daniel tells him, ''Actually, I'm thinking of fourth grade at Collingwood Primary. That's where they stuck my gook head down the dunny every day at playtime.''

Over his shoulder a gaunt young black man says to him, reverently, making him jump, ''You speak to the ancestors, my brother?''

''God! Don't sneak up on me like that!''

''I'm sorry, kinsman. I would not have my shadow fall across your shadow. I thought you might care for a piece of barramundi from the fire.'' The young black man holds out pale, steaming flesh on a deep green leaf. Its aroma is delicious.

Rueful, Daniel grins. ''Everyone talks religion, then they try to kill me. Hey, that smells good. Um, what was that about shadows?''

A second black man uncoils from the grass beside the open fire. ''He's just being pretentious. Hopes the elders'll choose him for the rituals.''

''Not fair! I just happen to have a subtle and poetic soul. Anyway, everyone knows that Ng's the one they'll be cutting and naming.''

Danny recoils, dropping the sliver of hot fish. ''*Cutting?* Oh, great.''

Jill's voice says inside his head, ''Danny, we're back to full resonance with your speech centres, so we're picking up the others as well. How come they know your name?''

''It's not my name,'' he tells her, still dazed, staring at the luminous landscape about him. ''It's the name of my quantum double.''

''How can your double be called 'Ng'? His history has to be completely different.''

''Here we go again,'' the second black man says wryly to his companion. ''Ask the ancestors for a nice plump emu while you're there, Ng.''

His associate growls, ''Kulan! Show some respect!''

''Didn't Tam and Dr. Manchetti cover this in the briefing?''

''I'm just the quantum technician,'' Jill says irritably. ''And I had a few other things on my mind, darling.''

''Yes, you did, poor thing.'' Danny relents. ''They're probably not speaking English. My brain back there in the real world's in resonance, so my lexical modules are running an automatic translation.''

''Right. So they could be calling you 'Two Dogs Fucking,' and we'd hear it as 'Ng'?''

''Or 'Dan' or 'Danny' or 'Daniel,' or 'Hey, you.' ''

Jill laughs. Her mood improves as she understands that he is in no danger. ''Are you hanging in there, love?''

''I'm okay. It's better than being beaten up in an alley.''

''Beaten up!''

''I'm fine now, darling. I had some Vietnamese money in my pocket; they thought I was a spy. I probably *was* a spy in that world. Maybe the other one as well.''

Manchetti, watching the cartoon and taking notes, leans into his own microphone. "That makes sense, Daniel. We're spying on these other histories, aren't we, so perhaps you find it easier to link up with doubles in the same trade."

"Cute. The metaphysics of quantum identity. Listen, there's a couple of old codgers coming over from the camp."

They are very black, very thin, as fit as trouts, and liberally decorated with incisions. The young men slink off.

"See the cicatrices? That must be what the kid meant about cutting me."

"They're Aborigines," Jill notes.

"I don't think there's ever been a European in the country." Daniel takes a deep, ravished breath. "It's beautiful—untouched. The air's wonderful."

"So what's a nice Vietnamese boy like you doing in a place like this?" Manchetti asks. "Be careful, Danny."

"Good midday, young northerner," says one of the elders. "You are speaking to the Dreaming ancestors, I see."

"Good . . . midday, sir. Uh, not exactly. I was talking to my wife."

The second elder finds this droll. "Ah, his wife! Is she well, young Ng? Are your babies healthy and whole in your distant homeland?"

Inside his head, Manchetti says, "Play along with him, Danny."

"Yes, sir," Daniel says to the old man. They are entirely naked, and carry spears sharpened and hardened by fire.

"This is good news. Ng, let us talk here together for a time. There will be dancing, and a gathering. We have found you a skin."

"A skin." He blinks.

"Indeed. The elders have discussed the matter and sought the guidance of the Ancestor Makers. We have found your color and skin, young northerner. You are a Wallaby-man."

"A Wallaby—Thank you, old father." He gropes for a suitable formula. "This will make my family very proud."

"You Wallaby-men are great travelers," the black elder tells him, settling on his haunches in the sweet grass. His penis hangs loose, swaying, and from the corner of his eye Danny sees that something horrible has been done to it. He glances again, and then at the other old man. Their genitals look like, like what? Sausages slashed on one side and opened out—Subincision rite, he recalls, with a violent shudder, and looks away, feeling his gorge rise. "Uncle and I like to live here along the river tracks," the elder is saying, swaying slightly, "but we see that the Lightning Man calls you to run far and far as the mobs of Wallabies ran across the plains."

Jill tells him, "Danny, we're going into phase-three turbulence. We're going to lose you for a moment. Hang in there, sweetheart."

His mind and heart are torn within him. After the suspicion and brutality of the other allo-histories, this world is a joyous affirmation, for all the fright that its ancient rites have speared into his clenching belly. "I don't know what to say," he says stumblingly to the old men. "I'm a stranger, and you're welcoming me into your family. If only I could tell you how beautiful your world seems to me, how sweet, how generous. . . ."

• • •

Even as he speaks, there comes to his ears a rising crackle of flame that is abruptly a roaring of some terrible wind. The black men are gone into ruin and desolation. A machine voice tells him, "Warning! Close your face mask. Ambient aerosol toxins are at lethal levels. I repeat, close your face mask."

Jill fades back in. "We've got you, Danny. Who's that? What's that awful sound?"

"Just a moment, Jill." It is *hot*, and the air stinks. He wonders if he will faint. "How am I supposed to *seal* this bloody thing?" The device closes under his fingers, and he is breathing richer piped air. "Shit, what *is* this hellhole?"

"You are two kilometers southeast of the bunker airlock, Master Ng," the machine tells him. He realizes it is his suit speaking to him. "Please activate your head-up display and follow the cursor."

Where the river was a moment ago is a dry, cracked ditch. All the ground cover is parched and looks burned. He cannot even look at the sky, at its burning white glare. "It's so *hot!*" Apparently he is clad in high-tech protective clothing, but still he feels as if his brains are being fried.

"External temperature is fifty-three degrees celsius, Master Ng," his suit tells him. "Please return immediately to the bunker. Your life-support system is failing."

"Where *am* I? How could this place suddenly be a desert? My God, is this some sort of Greenhouse nightmare?"

"I am sorry, Master Ng, but your enquiry exceeds the parameters of my fuzzy-logic processor. For location, please consult the global-satellite fix on your head-up display."

"Oh, for fuck's sake. Just tell me where I *am*, you stupid machine."

"You are just inside the entrance to the Hugh Morgan National Park. I must warn you, Master Ng, your suit cannot extend full warrantied protection against ambient volatiles for longer than five hours."

Daniel stands where he is, weeping. "They've wrecked it all, Jill! Oh my God, they've ruined our poor beautiful fucking planet!"

And it is snatched away, instantly, hell replaced by heaven. Danny gasps, wiping eyes suddenly dry. "Uh. It's gone. I'm back. Jill, I don't think I can stand much more of this. It's killing me, it's really making me sick. Let me just get over here to the stream and put my feet in the water. Ah. Ah."

The trickling water is cool, and sweet, unblemished.

"I can't see the black guys. The camp's gone. Actually, now that I look at it, this place seems . . . you know . . . manicured. It's gorgeous, Jill. Christ, a garbage tip'd be dazzling after that last place, but this is . . . I dunno, a Merchant Ivory movie, or something. Peter Greenaway. Only it's not English, it's real Aussie landscape but somehow . . . *Shit!* Don't *do* that! *Jill?*"

The voice in his head says, "Here, Dan. I'm trying to talk Dr. Manchetti into pulling you out. . . . We've lost your visual feed."

"Not you, darling." He stares at the impossible, and finds that he is actually shaking his head in unconscious denial. "This woman just, just *popped up* in front of me, and she's floating about a meter off the ground, and *she's you!*"

Aloft, at her ease, the uniformed woman says, "Male, what are you doing here?"

"I could ask you the same thing," Danny says faintly. "How are you *doing* that?"

She drops lightly to the ground. "This continent is proscribed to Males. Where are your companions?"

Manchetti's voice comes on-line. "Daniel, did I understand you? There's an analog of your wife in this world?"

"To the life, except she seems to have discovered antigravity. And she doesn't like men very much."

The woman is terse. "No point trying to communicate with your fellow conspirators, Male. I've placed a force barrier across this park. Please sit down on the grass and keep your hands away from your body."

"Play along with her, Daniel," Manchetti tells him. "This is what we've been waiting for!"

"Oh, good."

"We're trying to keep you stabilized in this domain, but we won't be able to hold the superposition for long. Get us an equation, Dan, something along the lines of $E = mc^2$, the superstring equations, anything, a hint, something we can use to bootstrap our own research, some paradigm breakthrough."

"Shut up for a moment, Dr. Manchetti. She's frisking me with a, I dunno, an invisible tendril or something. I think this reality's a matriarchy. Like that movie *The Female Man*."

"Sit down," the woman tells him with military crispness. "What's your name, Male? And stop muttering to your sky gods; I detest that superstitious drivel."

"My name's Daniel Ng. And unless I miss my mark, yours is Gillian. Or Jill."

Shocked, the woman says, "Jael. How did you know that?"

Daniel shrugs. "It just seemed highly probable, under the circumstances."

"Goddess!" Instantly, she says, "You're a quantum doppelgänger."

"A double, right?"

"From an alternative superposition."

"Yes. How can you possibly know that?"

She regards him scornfully. "You're a Male, alone, and ungelded to judge by your tone of voice."

"Un*gelded?* What's *wrong* with all you loonies? Yes, I'm ungelded and don't you starting getting any ideas."

"Hence you're a doppelgänger. It's the most economical explanation. When one has eliminated the extremely implausible—"

"—the impossible must be true?"

She looks at him with renewed suspicion. "You know things no Male is permitted to study. What are you doing in the Garden of the Rose Hegemon?"

With punch-drunk levity, Danny says, "Sorry, didn't mean to trespass. Show me the gate and I'll be on my way."

"Unless you can swim the ocean, there is no way for you to leave Her Garden."

"She owns the whole of bloody Australia?"

"The southern island continent, yes."

"I take it you've never held a referendum," he mutters sarcastically, "on the Republican agenda."

"Enough talk, Male. I must return you to your dream."

Daniel sits down and puts his feet back in the water. "Dream's right. The whole damned world's nothing but a dream."

"Not this world, which is the Harbor of Reality, the Stem of the Rose." Jael rises again into the air, moves lightly across the water, hovers there. "*Your* little worlds are dreams of dreams, infinitely improbable. You are foam on the quantum ocean."

" 'Foam' my ass. I'm live and kicking. Come over here and I'll give you a pinch to prove it."

"Most of your doppelgängers must have died in childhood. How else could you find yourself here at the far end of the curve, in the Garden of Reality?"

That takes Daniel aback. "Are you telling me I died on the fishing trawler when I was five years old?"

"Poor little Male boy. To perish so young. Death sets us free in the worlds where we survive, you see."

"I don't understand."

"You poor partials ride the wind at the edge of the world."

Manchetti's voice says, "Keep her talking, Daniel. They obviously know about superposed states. Ask her for the equations, damn it."

"Do you understand how I got here, Jael?"

"Of course. You must be coupled to my own doppelgänger. What did you call her? Jeel-ian?"

"Jill. She's my wife. Jael, can you tell me the equations for all this? Where I come from, it's all new. We're just taking the first steps."

She smiles for the first time. "Poor Male. Don't you understand? What good would it do you?"

"Because I'm just a dream, right. Quantum froth."

"Because you're about to die."

"*What?*"

"Surely you know? Look into your body, Male. There's an infection wasting your immunity systems. Your gastric tract is boiling with ulcers. Even the little machines in your brain are dying."

"You can see the HIV-6? But why should *this* body be sick? And besides, you don't have any *instruments!*"

"Not this form. Your remote source."

"You can see my *baseline* body? Jael, are you a witch?"

"I'm a gardener," she tells him, "for my mistress the Rose Hegemon. Naturally I'm equipped with the appropriate tools."

"Tell me something! Anything, Jael, just scraps from the table."

"Quantum relativity," Manchetti suggests urgently. "Even Penrose hasn't cracked that."

"Tell me the equations for quantum relativity."

"Pointless, Male. You don't know enough to recognize the science of the Sisters and Mothers. If I told you that I hover in the air by manipulating the null-energy plexus, would that allow you to fly by yourself?"

"She means zero-point energy! That's the metric Puthoff's been blathering about for the last twenty years! We all assumed it was the ravings of a jack Scientologist."

"Shut up, Manchetti, I can't hear myself think. Jael, you're wrong. Yours isn't the only universe. Neither is mine. Oranges," he says with a grin, "are not the only fruit."

She shrugs, still airborne. "It doesn't matter, Male. It's irrelevant either way, because you can't stay here. If your kind would *dare* to give another human a deathly sickness just so little machines could stay in his head longer, what corruption might follow you? I'm sending you home to that poor Male version of peace and contentment."

"Dan!" Jill yells into her headset. "What was that? Is she saying these pricks— Hang on, we're going chaotic. Shit, sweetheart, she's screwing with the superposition. We're pulling the plug."

"Jill! Jill!" Daniel cries, aswirl in the vortex, dying, lost. "Hold my hand, Jill, don't let me drown!"

The river burbles, the fire crackles faintly; he is back in Ur-Aboriginal Australia. "Jill!" he cries piteously. "Oh my God, what am I doing here? Manchetti! Anyone!"

There is no reply. He has been severed from his home reality.

"So you're back among us, boy," one of the old black men says in a friendly fashion. "It is good to walk with the ancestors, but now we must reflect upon the coming ceremony of naming. Have you chosen a name yet?"

Frantic, Daniel cries, "Where's Jill? Where's my wife?"

The other old man wags a hand. "This is men's business, Ng. We can't have women here, you know this. Besides, your wife and children are far away, far away, in the place of the other pale people."

"Far away in the northern waters, young Ng, where the fish are many and the air is rich with their stink. You've told us this many times. Have you forgotten? Sometimes, you know, I find myself forgetting things these days. I went looking for my favorite spear the other day—"

"Oh be quiet, you silly old man," his friend tells him snidely. "We don't want to hear about your spear. It's long enough since you had a chance to use your spear anyway, isn't it, eh, eh?"

"Oh my God." Danny reels from the dying embers, clutching his head. "Jael thinks this is where I belong. She thinks I should be among men, in the place where there are no women."

"The women are safe enough, young Wallaby. They're collecting yams in the next valley; don't worry about them, they'll be quick to welcome you back to the campfires, you with your new name and decorations. Now come, let's sing together, let's make ready for the great deed."

In the distance, Daniel sees young men and old gathering at a great fire. They are daubing themselves strikingly with ocher and white clay. A didgeridoo starts droning, and voices begin to mutter in ancient song.

"Leave me alone!" Daniel shakes off their gentle hands. "I'm dying back there, don't you understand? No, of course you don't. Dying in the real world. Jill. Jill, talk to me. She can't hear me."

"Calm down, boy. Death's not so terrible. Listen to the story of the Dreaming, time of the Making of the World." The old man starts to sing:

Hanging a long way off, above Milingimbi Creek . . .
Slowly the Moon Bone is growing, hanging there far away,
The bone is shining, the horns of the Moon bend down.''

The second elder takes up the dirge.

''First the sickle Moon on the old Moon's shadow; slowly he grows
''And shining he hangs there at the place of the Evening Star . . .''

The first replies:

''Then far away he goes sinking down, to lose his bone in the sea;
''Diving toward the water, he sinks down out of sight.''

The second sings:

''The old Moon dies to grow new again, to rise up out of the sea.''

Their fading fire crackles in silence.

At length, tears drying on his cheeks, Daniel Ng says, ''I suppose. It's as if I died there inside the scanner. Maybe all this is just some long drawn-out deathbed VR fantasy. Valhalla among the black warriors. Oh God, oh God. Good-bye, Jill. I love you, darling. I love you forever,'' he whispers, ''in every world there is.''

In the quantum lab, Daniel's body is collapsed upon itself. Instruments utter their shrill flatline.

''We've lost him,'' Tom Manchetti admits. ''Full arrest.''

Jill leaves her console, clad absurdly in plastic and metal. She stumbles to the table of machines, clutches her husband's thin hand. ''Danny! Oh God, Danny! You bastards! You *murdered* him! Didn't you?''

Dr. Manchetti touches her on the shoulder, and she throws off his hand. ''I'm sorry, honey. He was a very brave man.''

''Shut *up*, you son of a bitch. You infected him! I can't believe it! You deliberately infected him . . . to protect your damned nano machines!''

Binh is shocked. ''That's grotesque, Jill. He was dying, we knew that. This was a wonderful, brave way to die.''

Furious, Jill screams, ''*I could have caught it from him!* And you didn't care! My God, you incredible pricks. You inject Daniel with HIV-6, and let him rot . . . *and just leave me to take my chances!* Don't think you can shut me up about this, you shits! Get out of my way, Binh. You're fucking *history*, the lot of you!''

Manchetti is urbanely menacing. ''You're overwrought, Jill. Don't worry, we'll look after you. We'll see you through this.''

Someone turns off the flatline indicator.

Jill Ng crashes through the airlocked doors, screaming in loss and rage: ''Bastards! *Bastards!*''

• • •

Beside the campfire, insects flutter and creak. One of the elders stares at a crystalline, unpolluted sky. "It's a beautiful night."

His ancient friend smiles in the darkness and licks his toothless mouth. "I always enjoy a good hot-and-sour fish soup. Well, you'll be staying with us awhile, won't you . . . Daniel Wallaby?"

"Yes, Uncle. Until spring. Then I have to start back up north to find my wife and children." His incisions are smarting.

"It's good to see your wife. Not too often, of course. Not too often, eh, old man."

The second old man laughs, as old men will.

"Funny kind of afterlife," Daniel Wallaby Ng muses. "But gentlemen—uncles—if you don't mind my saying so, um, I hope you'll forgive me mentioning it, but don't you think there's something just the *tiniest* bit sexist about your attitude to women?"

"He's off with the ancestors again." One nudges the other. " 'Daniel'? What sort of a name is that? Fine young fellow, though. Let's sing some more about the Making of the World."

Under the moon, the drone of the didgeridoo rises, and the clatter of wood on wood, and men's strong voices rise in rich chant. Daniel closes his eyes and settles into the sweet night.

FOREIGN DEVILS

Walter Jon Williams

▼

Walter Jon Williams was born in Minnesota and now lives in Albuquerque, New Mexico. His short fiction has appeared frequently in major anthologies and magazines such as Asimov's Science Fiction, The Magazine of Fantasy & Science Fiction, Wheel of Fortune, When the Music's Over, *and in other markets, and has been gathered in the collection* Facets. *His novels include* Ambassador of Progress, Knight Moves, Hardwired, The Crown Jewels, Voice of the Whirlwind, House of Shards, Days of Atonement, Rock of Ages, *and* Aristoi. *Last year his novel* Metropolitan *garnered wide critical acclaim and was one of the most talked about books of the year. His most recent book is a sequel to* Metropolitan, City on Fire. *His stories have appeared in our Third, Fourth, Fifth, Sixth, Ninth, Eleventh, and Twelfth Annual Collections.*

Here he gives us an evocative and gorgeously colored look at the bizarre, ritualized, and mannered world of court life in nineteenth-century China—and how that world is shattered catastrophically forever when the Forbidden City itself is attacked by an even stranger bunch of foreigners than they're used to dealing with: H. G. Wells's invading Martians.

There is no longer anyone alive who knows her name.

She has always been known by her titles, titles related to the role she was expected to play. When she was sixteen and had been chosen as a minor concubine for the Son of Heaven, she had been called Lady Yehenara, because she was born in the Yehe tribe of the Nara clan of the great Manchu race. Later, after her husband died and she assumed the regency for their son, she was given the title Tzu Hsi, Empress of the West, because she once lived in a pavilion on the western side of the Forbidden City.

But no one alive knows her real name, the milk-name her mother had given her almost sixty-five years ago, the name she had answered to when she was young and happy and free from care. Her real name is unimportant.

Only her position matters, and it is a lonely one.

She lives in a world of imperial yellow. The wall hangings are yellow, the carpets are yellow, and she wears a gown of crackling yellow brocade. She sleeps on yellow brocade sheets, and rests her head on pillows of yellow silk beneath embroidered yellow bed curtains.

Now Peking is on fire, and the hangings of yellow silk are stained with the red of burning.

She rises from her bed in the Hour of the Rat, a little after midnight. Her working day, and that of the Emperor, begins early.

A eunuch braids her hair while her ladies—all of them young, and all of them in gowns of blue—help her to dress. She wears a yellow satin gown embroidered with pink flowers, and a cape ornamented with four thousand pearls. The eunuch expertly twists her braided hair into a topknot, and fits over it a headdress made of jade adorned on either side with fresh flowers. Gold sheaths protect the two long fingernails of her right hand, and jade sheaths protect the two long fingernails of her left. Her prize black lion dogs frolic around her feet.

The smell of burning floats into the room, detectable above the scent of her favorite Nine-Buddha incense. The burning scent imparts a certain urgency to the proceedings, but her toilette cannot be completed in haste.

At last she is ready. She calls for her sedan chair and retinue—Li Lien-Ying, the Chief Eunuch, the Second Chief Eunuch, four Eunuchs of the Fifth Rank, twelve Eunuchs of the Sixth Rank, plus eight more eunuchs to carry the chair.

"Take me to the Emperor's apartments," she says.

The sedan chair swoops gently upward as the eunuchs lift it to their shoulders. As she leaves her pavilion, she hears the sound of the sentries saluting her as she passes.

They are not *her* sentries. These elite troops of the Tiger-Hunt Marksmen are not here to keep anyone *out*. They are in the employ of ambitious men, and the guards serve only to keep her a prisoner in her own palace.

Despite her titles, despite the blue-clad ladies and the eunuchs and the privileges, despite the silk and brocade and pearls, the Empress of the West is a captive. She can think of no way that she can escape.

The litter's yellow brocade curtains part for a moment, and the Empress catches a brief glimpse of the sky. There is Mars, glowing high in the sky like a red lantern, and below it streaks a falling star, a beautiful ribbon of imperial yellow against the velvet night. It streaks east to west, and then is gone.

Perhaps, she thinks, it is a hopeful sign.

The audience room smells of burning. Yellow brocade crackles as the members of the family council perform their ritual kowtows before the Son of Heaven. Before they present their petitions to the Emperor they pause, as they realize from his flushed face and sudden intake of breath that he is having an orgasm as he sits in his dragon-embroidered robes upon his yellow-draped chair.

The Emperor Kuang Hsu is twenty-eight years old and has suffered from severe health problems his entire life. Sometimes, in moments of tension, he succumbs to a sudden fit of orgasm. The doctors claim it is the result of a kidney malady, but no matter how many Kidney Rectifying Pills the Emperor is made to swallow, his condition never improves.

The illness is sometimes embarrassing, but the family has become accustomed to it.

After the Emperor's breathing returns to normal, Prince Jung Lu presents his petition. "Your Majesty," he says, "for three days the Righteous Harmony Fists have rioted in the Tatar City and the Chinese City. There are no less than thirty thousand of these disreputable scoundrels in Peking. They have set fire to the home of Grand Secretary Hsu Tung and to many others. Grand Secretary Sun Chia-nai has been assaulted and robbed. As the Supreme Ones of the past safeguarded the tranquillity of the realm by issuing edicts to suppress rebellion and disorder, and as the Righteous Harmony Fists have shown themselves violent, disorderly, and disrespectful of Your Majesty's servants, I hope that an edict from Your Majesty will soon be forthcoming that allows this unworthy person to use the Military Guards Army to suppress disorder.''

Prince Tuan spits tobacco into his pocket spittoon. ''I beg the favor of disagreeing with the esteemed prince,'' he says. Other officials, members of his Iron Hat Faction, murmur their agreement.

The Dowager Empress, sitting on her yellow cushion next to the Emperor, looks from one to the other, and feels only despair.

Jung Lu has been her friend from childhood. He is a moderate and sensible man, but the situation that envelops them all is neither moderate nor sensible.

It is Prince Tuan, a younger man, bulky in his brocade court costume and with the famous Shangfang Sword strapped to his waist, who is in command of the situation. He and his allies—Tuan's brother Duke Lan, Prince Chuang of the Gendarmerie, the Grand Councillor Kang I, Chao Shu-chiao of the Board of Punishments—form the core of those Iron Hats who had seized power two years ago, at the end of the Hundred Days' Reform.

It is Tuan who has surrounded the Dragon Throne with his personal army of ten thousand Tiger-Hunt Marksmen. It is Tuan who controls the ferocious Muslim cavalry of General Tung, his ally, camped in the gardens south of the city. It is Tuan who extorted the honor of carrying the Shangfang Sword in the imperial presence, and with it the right to use the sword to execute anyone on the spot, for any reason. And it is Tuan's son, Pu Chun, who has been made heir to the throne.

It is Prince Tuan, and the others of his Iron Hat Faction, who have encouraged the thousands of martial artists and spirit warriors of the Righteous Harmony Fists to invade Peking, to attack Chinese Christians and others against whom they have a grudge, and who threaten to envelop China in a war with all the foreign powers at once.

The young Emperor Kuang Hsu opens his mouth but cannot say a word. He has a bad stammer, and in stressful situations he cannot speak at all.

Prince Tuan fills the silence. ''I am certain that should the Son of Heaven deign to address us, he would assure us of his confidence in the patriotism and loyalty of the Righteous Harmony Fists. His Majesty knows that any disorders are incidental, and that the Righteous Harmony Fists are united in their desire to rid the Middle Kingdom of the Foreign Devils that oppress our nation. In the past,'' he continues, getting to his point—for in the Imperial Court, one always presented conclusions by invoking the past—''In the past, the great rulers of the Middle Kingdom established order in their dominions by calling upon their loyal subjects to do away with foreign influences and causes of disorder. If His Majesty will only issue an edict to this effect, the Righteous Harmony Fists can use their martial powers and their invincible magic to sweep the Foreign Devils from our land.''

The Emperor attempts again to speak and again fails. This time it is the Dowager Empress who fills the silence.

"Will such an edict not bring us to war with all the Foreign Devils at once? We have never been able to hold off even one foreign power at a time. The white ghosts of England and France, and even lately the dwarf-bandits of Japan, have all won concessions from us."

Prince Tuan scowls, and his hand tightens on the Shangfang Sword. "The Righteous Harmony Fists are not members of the imperial forces. They are merely righteous citizens stirred to anger by the actions of the Foreign Devils and the Secondary Foreign Devils, the Christian converts. The government cannot be held responsible for their actions. And besides—the Righteous Harmony Fists are invulnerable. You have seen yourself, a few weeks ago, when I brought one of their members into this room and fired a pistol straight at him. He was not harmed."

The Empress of the West falls silent as clouds of doubt enter her mind. She had seen the pistol fired, and the man had taken no hurt. It had been an impressive demonstration.

"I regret to report to the Throne," Jung Lu says, "of an unfortunate incident in the city. The German ambassador, Von Ketteler, personally opened fire on a group of Righteous Harmony Fists peacefully exercising in the open. He killed seven and wounded many more."

"An outrage!" Prince Tuan cries.

"Truly," Jung Lu says, "but unfortunately the Righteous Harmony Fists proved somewhat less than invulnerable to Von Ketteler's bullets. Perhaps their invincibility has been overstated."

Prince Tuan glares sullenly at Jung Lu. He bites his lip, then says, "It is the fault of wicked Chinese Christian women. The Secondary Foreign Devils flaunted their naked private parts through windows, and the Righteous Harmony Fists lost their strength."

There is a thoughtful pause as the others absorb this information. And then the Emperor opens his mouth again.

The Emperor has, for the moment, mastered his speech impediment, though his gaunt young face is strained with effort and there are long, breathy pauses between each word. "Our subjects depend on the Dragon Throne for their safety," he gasps. "Prince Jung Lu is ordered to restore order in the city and to stand between the foreign legations and the Righteous Harmony Fists . . . to prevent further incidents."

Kuang Hsu falls back on his yellow cushions, exhausted from the effort to speak. "The Son of Heaven is wise," Jung Lu says.

"Truly," says Prince Tuan, his eyes narrowing.

Using appropriate formal language, and of course invoking the all-important precedents from the past, court scribes write the edict in Manchu, then translate the words into Chinese. The Dowager Empress holds the Chinese translation to her failing eyes and reads it with care. As a female, she had not been judged worthy of education until she had been chosen as an imperial concubine. She has never learned more than a few hundred characters of Chinese, and is unable to read Manchu at all.

But whether she can read and write or not, her position as Dowager Empress gives her the power of veto over any imperial edict. It is important that she view any document personally.

"Everything is in order," she ventures to guess.

The Imperial Seal Eunuch inks the heavy Imperial Seal and presses it to the edict, and with ceremony the document is presented to Prince Jung Lu. Prince Tuan draws himself up and speaks. "This unworthy subject must beg the Throne for permission to deal with this German, Von Ketteler. This white ghost is killing Chinese at random, for his own amusement, and in the confused circumstances none can be blamed if there is an accident."

The Empress of the West and the Emperor exchange quick glances. Perhaps, thinks the Empress, it is best to let Prince Tuan win a point. It may assuage his bloodlust for the moment.

And she very much doubts anyone will miss the German ambassador.

She tilts her head briefly, an affirmative gesture. The Emperor's eyes flicker as he absorbs her import.

"We leave it to you," he says. It is a ritual form of assent, the Throne's formal permission for an action to take place.

"The Supreme One's brilliance and sagacity exceeds all measure," says Prince Tuan.

The family council ends. The royal princes make their kowtows and leave the chamber.

The Dowager Empress leaves her chair and approaches her nephew, the Emperor. He seems shrunken in his formal dragon robes—he has twenty-eight sets of robes altogether, one auspicious for each day of the lunar month. Tenderly the Dowager dabs sweat from his brow with a handkerchief. He reaches into his sleeve for a lighter and a packet of Turkish cigarettes.

"We won't win, you know," he sighs. His stammer has disappeared along with his formidable, intimidating relations. "If we couldn't beat the Japanese dwarf-bandits, we can't beat anybody. We're just going to lose more territory to the Foreign Devils, just as we've already lost Burma, Nepal, Indochina, Taiwan, Korea, Hong Kong, all the treaty ports we've had to cede to Foreign Devils. . . ."

"You don't believe the spirit fighters' magic will help us?"

The Emperor laughs and draws on his cigarette. "Cheap tricks to impress peasants. I have seen that bullet-catching trick done by conjurors."

"We must delay. Delay as long as possible. If we delay, the correct path may become clearer."

The Emperor flicks cigarette ash off his yellow sleeve. His tone is bitter. "Delay is the only possible course for those who have no power. Very well. We will delay as long as possible. But delay the war or not, we will still lose."

Tears well in the old woman's eyes. It is all, she knows, her fault.

Her husband, the Emperor, had died of grief after losing the Second Opium War to the Foreign Devils. Their child was only an infant at the time. She did her best to bring up her son, engaging the most rigorous and moral of teachers, but after reigning for only a few years her son had died at the age of eighteen from exhaustion brought on by unending sexual dissipation.

Since then she has devoted her life to caring for her nephew, the new Emperor. She had rescued Kuang Hsu from her sister, who had beaten him savagely and starved him—one of his brothers had actually been starved to death—but she had erred again in choosing the young Emperor's companions. He had been so bullied by eunuchs, so plagued by ill health, and so intimidated by his tutors and the blustering royal princes, that he had remained shy, hesitant, and self-conscious. He had only acted decisively once, two years ago, during the Hundred Days' Reform, and that had ended badly, with the palace surrounded by Prince Tuan's Tiger-Hunt Marksmen and the Emperor held captive.

"I will leave Your Majesty to rest," she says. He looks at her, not unkindly.

"Thank you, Mother," he says.

Tears prickle the Dowager's eyes. Even though she has betrayed him, still he calls her "mother" instead of "aunt."

She walks from the room, and with her twenty-four attending eunuchs returns to her palace.

Alone in the darkness of the litter, no one sees the tears that patter on the yellow brocade cushions.

"All the news is good," Prince Tuan says. "One of our soldiers, a Manchu bannerman named Enhai, has shot the German ambassador outside the Tsungli Yamen. Admiral Seymour's Foreign Devils, marching up the railway line from Tientsin, have turned back after a battle with the Righteous Harmony Fists."

"I had heard the Righteous Harmony Fists had all been killed," says Jung Lu. "Where was their bullet-catching magic?"

"Their magic was sufficient to turn back Admiral Seymour," Prince Tuan retorts.

"He may have just gone back for reinforcements. More and more foreign warships are appearing off Tientsin."

It is the Hour of the Ox, just before dawn. Several days have passed since Prince Jung Lu was ordered to seal off the foreign legations. This has reduced the number of incidents in the city, though the Foreign Devils continue their distressing habit of shooting any Chinese they see, sometimes using machine guns on crowds. Since no one is attacking them, the foreigners' behavior is puzzling. Jung Lu sent several peace delegations to inquire their reasons, but the delegates had all been shot down as soon as they appeared in sight of the legations. Jung Lu has been forced to admit that the foreigners may no longer be behaving rationally.

"In the past," Prince Tuan says, "Heaven made known its wishes through the movements of the stars and planets and through portents displayed in the skies. This unworthy servant reminds the Throne that this is a year with an extra intercalary month, and therefore a year that promises unusual occurrences. This is also a Kengtze year, which occurs only every ten years. Therefore the heavens demonstrate the extraordinary nature of this year, and require that all inhabitants of the Earth assist Heaven in creating extraordinary happenings."

"I have not heard that Kengtze years were lucky for the Pure Dynasty," Jung Lu remarks. But Prince Tuan doesn't even slow down.

"There are other indications that war is at hand," he says. "The red planet Mars is high in the heavens, and the ancients spoke truly when they declared, 'When Mars is high, prepare for war and civil strife; when Mars sinks below the horizon, send the soldiers home.'

''But there is another indication more decisive than any of these. Heaven has declared its will by dropping meteors upon the Middle Kingdom. Three falling stars have landed outside of Tientsin. Another three landed south of the capital near Yungtsing. According to the office of Telegraph Sheng, three have also landed in Shantung, three more southwest of Shanghai, and three near Kwangtung.''

The Dowager Empress and the Emperor exchange glances. Several of these falling meteors have been observed from the palace, and their significance discussed. But reports of meteors landing in threes throughout eastern China are new.

''Heaven is declaring its will!'' Prince Tuan says. ''The meteors have all landed near places where there are large concentrations of Foreign Devils! Obviously Heaven wishes us to exterminate these vermin!''

Tuan gives a triumphant laugh and draws the Shangfang Sword. The Emperor turns pale and shrinks into his heavy brocade robes.

''I demand an edict from the Dragon Throne!'' Tuan shouts. ''Let the Son of Heaven command that all Foreign Devils be killed!''

The Emperor tries to speak, but terror has plainly seized his tongue. Choosing her words carefully, the Dowager Empress speaks in his place. *Delay*, she thinks.

''We will consult the auspices and act wisely in accordance with their wishes.''

Prince Tuan gives a roar of anger and brandishes the sword. ''No more delay! Heaven has made its will clear! If you don't issue the edicts, I'll do it myself!''

There is a moment of horrified silence. The Emperor's face turns stony as he looks at Prince Tuan. Sweat pops onto his brow with the effort to control his tongue.

''W-w-why,'' he stammers, ''don't you go k-k-k-kill yourself?''

There is another moment of silence. Prince Tuan coldly forces a smile onto his face.

''The Son of Heaven makes a very amusing witticism,'' he says.

And then, at swordpoint, he commands the Imperial Seal Eunuch to bring out the heavy seal that will confirm his edicts.

Watching, the Dowager Empress's heart floods with sorrow.

It is the Hour of the Tiger, two days after Prince Tuan seized control. A red dawn provides a scarlet blush to the yellow hangings. Tuan and his allies confer before the Dragon Throne. Tuan has brought his son, the imperial heir Pu Chun, to watch his father as he commands the fate of China. The boy spends most of his time practicing martial arts, pretending to skewer Foreign Devils with his sword.

The Emperor, disgusted, smokes a cigarette behind a wall hanging. No one bothers to ask his opinion of the edicts that are going out under his seal.

The Righteous Harmony Fists have all been drafted into the army and sent to reinforce General Nieh standing between Tientsin and the capital. Governors have been ordered to defend their provinces against attack. Jung Lu's army has been ordered to wipe out the foreigners in the legation quarter, but so far he has found reason to delay.

Can China fight the whole world? the Dowager Empress wonders.

But she sits on her yellow cushion, and smokes her water pipe, and plays with her little lion dogs while she pretends unconcern. It is all she can do.

A messenger arrives and hands to Jung Lu a pair of messages from the office of Telegraph Sheng, and Jung Lu reads them with a puzzled expression. He approaches the Empress, leans close, and speaks in a low tone.

"The Foreign Devils off Tientsin have ordered our troops to evacuate the Taku Forts by midnight—that is midnight yesterday, so the ultimatum has already expired."

Anxiety grips the Empress's heart. "Can our troops hold the forts?"

Jung Lu frowns. "Their record is not good."

If the Taku Forts fall, the Empress knows, Tientsin will fall. And once Tientsin falls, it is but a short march from there to Peking. It has all happened before.

Sick at heart, the Empress remembers the headlong flight from the capital during the Second Opium War, how her happy, innocent little lion dogs had been thrown down wells rather than let the Foreign Devils capture them.

It is going to happen again, she thinks.

Prince Tuan marches toward them. Hearing his steps, Jung Lu's face turns to a mask. He hides the first message in his sleeve.

"This unworthy servant hopes the mighty commander of the Military Guards Army will share his news," Tuan says.

Jung Lu hands Tuan the second of the two messages. "Confused news of fighting south of Tientsin. Some towns have been destroyed—the message says by monsters that rode to earth on meteors, but obviously the message was confused. Perhaps he meant to say that meteors have landed on some towns."

"Were they Christian towns?" Tuan asks. "Perhaps Heaven's vengeance is falling on the Secondary Foreign Devils. There are many Christians around Tientsin."

"The message does not say."

Prince Tuan looks at the message and spits into his pocket spittoon. "It probably doesn't matter," he says.

It is the Hour of the Snake. Bright morning sun blazes on the room's yellow hangings. A lengthy dispatch has arrived from the office of Telegraph Sheng. Prince Tuan reads it, then laughs and swaggers toward the captive Emperor.

"This miserable one regrets to report to the Throne that last night an allied force of Foreign Devils captured the forts at Taku," he says.

Then why are you smiling? the Empress wonders, and takes a slow, deliberate puff of smoke from her water pipe while she strives to control her alarm.

"Are steps being taken to rectify the situation?" asks the Emperor.

Tuan's smile broadens. "Heaven, which is just, has acted on behalf of the Son of Heaven. The Foreign Devils, their armies, and their fleets have been destroyed!"

The Empress exchanges glances with her nephew. The Emperor gives a puzzled frown as he absorbs the information. "Please tell us what has occurred," he says.

"The armies of the Foreign Devils were preparing to advance on Tientsin from Taku," Prince Tuan says, "when a force of metal giants appeared from the south. The Foreign Devils were obliterated! Their armies were destroyed by a blast of fire, and then their warships!"

"I fail to understand . . . ," the Empress begins.

"It's obvious!" Prince Tuan says. "The metal giants rode from heaven to earth on meteors! The Jade Emperor must have sent them expressly to destroy the Foreign Devils."

"Perhaps our information is incomplete," Jung Lu says cautiously.

Prince Tuan laughs. "Read the dispatch yourself," he says, and carelessly shoves the long telegram into the older man's hands.

The Emperor looks from one to the other, suspicion plain on his face. He clearly does not know whether to believe the news, or whether he wants to believe.

"We will wait for confirmation," he says.

More dispatches arrive over the course of the day. The destruction of the foreign armies and fleets is confirmed. Confused news of fighting comes from other areas where meteors are known to have landed. Giants are mentioned, as are bronze tripods. Prince Tuan and other members of his Iron Hat Faction swagger in triumph, boasting of the destruction of all the Foreign Devils. Pu Chun, the imperial heir, skips about the room in delight, pretending he is a giant and kicking imaginary armies out of his path.

It is the Hour of the Monkey. Supper dishes have been brought into the audience chamber, and the council members eat as they view the dispatches.

"The report from Tientsin says that the city is on fire," Jung Lu reports. "The message is unfinished. Apparently something happened to the telegraph office, or perhaps the wires were cut."

Kuang Hsu scowls. His face is etched with tension, and he speaks only with difficulty. "Tientsin is a city filled with our loyal subjects. If they are on our side, how is it that the Falling Star Giants are destroying a Chinese city?"

"There are many Foreign Devils in Tientsin," Prince Tuan says. "Perhaps it was necessary to destroy the entire city in order to eradicate the foreign influence."

A look of disgust passes across the Emperor's face at this casual attitude toward his subjects. He opens his mouth to speak, but then a spasm crosses his face. He flushes in shame.

The others in the room politely turn their gaze to the wall hangings while the Emperor has an orgasm.

Afterward he cannot speak at all. He fumbles with his soiled dragon robes as he walks behind the hangings in order to smoke a cigarette.

Watching his attempt to regain his dignity, the Dowager Empress feels her heart flood with sorrow.

Over the next two days, messages continue to arrive. Telegraph offices in the major cities are destroyed, and soon the only available information comes from horsemen galloping to the capital from local commanders and provincial governors.

General Nieh's army, stationed between Peking and Tientsin, has been wiped out by Falling Star Giants, along with most of the Righteous Harmony Fists that had been sent as reinforcements. Their spirit magic has proved inadequate to the occasion. From the information available it would seem that Shanghai, Tsingtao, and Canton have been attacked and very possibly destroyed. Just south of Peking, in Hopeh, three Falling Star Giants have been causing unimaginable destruction in one of China's richest provinces, and Hopeh's governor has committed suicide after admitting to the Throne his inability to control the situation.

The Dowager Empress notes that the Iron Hats' swaggering is noticeably reduced.

"Perhaps it is time," says Jung Lu, "to examine the possibility that the Falling Star Giants are just another kind of Foreign Devil, as rapacious as the first, and more powerful."

"Nonsense," says Prince Tuan automatically. "Heaven has sent the Falling Star Giants to aid us." But he looks uncertain as he says it.

It is the Hour of the Sheep. The midday sun beats down on the capital, turning even the shady gardens of the Forbidden City into broiling ovens.

The Emperor struggles with his tongue. "W-we desire that the august prince Jung Lu continue."

Jung Lu is happy to oblige. "This unworthy servant begs the Throne to recall that General Nieh and the Righteous Harmony Fists were neither Foreign Devils nor Christians, and they were destroyed. There are few Foreign Devils or Secondary Foreign Devils in Hopeh, but the massacres there have been terrible. And everywhere the Falling Star Giants appear, many more Chinese than Foreign Devils have been killed." Jung Lu looks solemn. "I regret the necessity to alert the Throne to a dangerous possibility. If the Falling Star Giants advance west up the railway line from Tientsin, and simultaneously march north from Hopeh, Peking will be caught between two forces. I must sadly recommend that we consider the defense of the capital."

The Dowager Empress glances at Prince Tuan, expecting him to contradict this suggestion, but instead the prince only gnaws his lip and looks uncertain.

A little flame of hope kindles in the Empress's heart.

The Emperor also sees Tuan's uncertainty and presses his advantage while he can. "Has the commander of the Military Guards Army any suggestions to make?" he asks.

"From the reports available," Jung Lu says, "it would seem that the Falling Star Giants have two weapons. The first is a beam of heat that incinerates all that it touches. This we call the Fire of the Meteor, from the flame of a falling star, and it is used to defeat armies and fleets. The second weapon is a poison black smoke that is fired from rockets. This we call the Tail of the Meteor, from a falling star's smoky tail, and it is used against cities, smothering the entire population."

"These weapons are not new," says a new voice. It is old Kang I, the Grand Councillor.

Kang I is a relic of a former age. In his many years he has served four emperors, and in his rigid adherence to tradition and hatred of foreigners has joined the Iron Hats from pure conviction.

Kang I spits into his pocket spittoon and speaks in a loud voice. "This worthless one begs the Throne to recall the Heng Ha Erh Chiang, the Door Gods. At the famous Battle of Mu between the Yin and the Chou, Marshal Cheng Lung was known as Heng the Snorter, because when he snorted, two beams of light shot from his nostrils and incinerated the enemy. Likewise, Marshal Ch'en Chi was known as Ha the Blower, because he was able to blow out clouds of poisonous yellow gas that smothered his foe.

"Thus it is clear," he concludes, "that these weapons were invented centuries ago in China, and must subsequently have been stolen by the Falling Star Giants, who are obviously a worthless and imitative people, like all foreigners." He falls silent, a superior smile ghosting across his face.

The Empress finds herself intrigued by this anecdote. "Does the esteemed councillor know if the historical records offer a method of defeating these weapons?"

"Indeed. Heng the Snorter was killed by a spear, and Ha the Blower by a magic bezoar spat at him by an ox-spirit."

"We have many spears," Jung Lu says softly. "But this ignorant one confesses his bafflement concerning where a suitable ox-spirit may be obtained. Perhaps the esteemed Grand Councillor has a suggestion?"

The smile vanishes from Kang I's face. "All answers may be found in the annals," he says stonily.

The Emperor, admirably controlling any impulse to smile at the Iron Hat's discomfort, turns again to Jung Lu. "Does the illustrious prince have any suggestions?"

"We have only three forces near Peking," Jung Lu says. "Of these, my Military Guards Army is fully occupied in blockading the foreign legations here in Peking. General Tung's horsemen are already in a position to move eastward to Tientsin. This leaves our most modern and best-equipped force, the Tiger-Hunt Marksmen, admirably suited to march south to stand between the capital and the Falling Star Giants of Hopeh. May this unworthy one suggest that the Dragon Throne issue orders to the Tiger-Hunt Marksmen and to General Tung at once?"

The Empress, careful to keep her face impassive, watches Prince Tuan as Jung Lu makes his recommendations. The ten thousand Tiger-Hunt Marksmen and General Tung's Muslim cavalry are Prince Tuan's personal armies. All his political power derives from his military strength. To risk his forces in battle is to endanger his own standing.

"What of the Throne?" Tuan asks. "If the Tiger-Hunt Marksmen march south, who will guard His Majesty? The Imperial Guard are only a few hundred men—surely their numbers are inadequate."

"The Throne may best be guarded by defeating the Falling Star Giants," Jung Lu says.

"I must insist that half the Tiger-Hunt Marksmen be left in the capital to guard the person of the Son of Heaven," Tuan says.

The Empress and Emperor look at one another. Best to act now, the Empress thinks, before Prince Tuan regains his confidence. Half the Tiger-Hunt Marksmen are better than all.

Kuang Hsu turns back to the princes. "We leave it to you," he says.

In the still night the tramp of boots echoes from the high walls of the Forbidden City. Columns of Tiger-Hunt Marksmen, under the command of Tuan's brother Duke Lan, are marching off to meet the enemy. In the Hour of the Dog, after nightfall, one of the Empress's blue-gowned maidens escorts Prince Jung Lu into her presence. He had avoided the Tiger-Hunt Marksmen by using the tunnels beneath the Forbidden City—they were designed to help servants move unobtrusively about their duties, but over the years they have been used for less licit purposes.

"We are pleased to express our gratitude," the Empress says, and takes from around her neck a necklace in which each pearl has been carved into the likeness of a stork. She places the necklace into the hands of her delighted maid.

Sad, she thinks, that it is necessary to bribe her own servants to encourage them to do what they should do unquestioningly, which is to obey and keep silent.

The darkness of the Empress's pavilion is broken only by starlight reflected from the yellow hangings. The odor of Nine Buddha incense floats in the air.

"My friend," she tells Jung Lu, and reaches to touch his sleeve. "You must survive this upcoming battle. You and your army must live to rescue the Emperor from the Iron Hats."

"My life is in the hands of Fate," Jung Lu murmurs. "I must fight alongside my army."

"I *order* you to survive!" the Empress demands. "His Majesty cannot spare you."

There is a moment of silence, and then the old man sighs.

"This unworthy one will obey Her Majesty," he says.

Irrational though it may be, the Empress begins to glimpse a tiny, feeble ray of hope.

Hot western winds buffet the city, and the sky turns yellow with loess, dust blown hundreds of *li* from the Gobi Desert. It falls in the courtyards of the Forbidden City, on the shoulders of the black-clad eunuchs as they scurry madly through the courtyards with arms full of valuables or documents. Hundreds of carts jam the byways. The Imperial Guard, in full armor, stand in disciplined lines about the litters of the royal family. Prince Tuan stands in the yard, waving the Shangfang Sword and shouting orders. Nobody obeys him, least of all his own son, Pu Chun, the imperial heir who crouches in terror beneath a cart.

The court is fleeing the city. Yesterday, the Falling Star Giants finally made their advance on Peking. At first the news was all bad, horsemen riding into the city with stories of entire regiments being incinerated by the Fire of the Meteor.

After that it was worse, because there was no news at all.

In the early hours of the morning an order arrived from Jung Lu to evacuate the court to the Summer Palace north of the city. Since then, all has been madness.

It is the Hour of the Hare, early in the morning. The Empress's blue-clad maid-servants huddle in knots, weeping. The Empress, however, is made of sterner stuff. She has been through this once before. She picks up one of her little lion dogs and thrusts it into the arms of one of her maids.

"Save my dogs!" she orders. She can't stand the idea of losing them again.

"Falling Star Giants seen from the city walls!" someone cries. There is no telling whether or not the report is true. Servingwomen dash heedlessly about the court, their gowns whipped by the strong west wind.

"Flee at once!" Prince Tuan shrieks. "The capital is lost!" He runs for his horse and gallops away. His son, screaming in terror, follows on foot, waving his arms.

The Emperor appears, a plain traveling cloak thrown over his shoulders. "Mother," he says, "it is time to go."

The Empress carries two of her favorite dogs to the litter. Her eunuchs hoist her to their shoulders, and the column begins to march for the Chienmen Gate. The western wind rattles the banners of the guard, but over the sound of the wind the Empress can hear a strange wailing sound, like a demon calling out to its mate. And then a wail from another direction as the mate answers.

"Faster!" someone calls, and the litter begins to jounce. The guardsmen's armor rattles as they begin to jog. The Empress braces herself against the sides of the litter.

"Black smoke!" Another cry. "The Tail of the Meteor!"

Women scream as the escort breaks into a run. The Empress's lion dogs whimper in fear. She clutches the curtains and peers anxiously past the curtains. The black smoke is plain to see, a tall column billowing out over the walls. As she watches, another rocket falls, trailing black.

But the strong west wind catches the top of the dark, billowing column and tears the smoke away, bearing it to the east.

As the column flees to safety, loess covers the city in a soft blanket of imperial yellow.

Much of the disorganized column, including most of the wagon train with its documents and treasure, is caught in the black smoke and never escapes the capital. Half the Tiger-Hunt Marksmen are dead or missing.

The terror and confusion make the Empress Dowager breathless, but it is the missing lion dogs that make her weep.

The column pauses north of the city at the Summer Palace only for a few hours, to beat some order into the chaos, then sets out into the teeth of the gale to Jehol on the Great Wall. In the distance the strange wailings of the Falling Star Giants are sometimes heard, but streamers of yellow dust conceal them.

By this time Prince Tuan has found his courage, his son, and his troops, the few thousand Tiger-Hunt Marksmen to have survived the fall of the capital. He calls a family conference in a requisitioned mansion, and issues edicts under the Imperial Seal calling for the extermination of all foreigners and Chinese Christians.

"Who will obey you?" the Emperor shouts at him. His hopelessness has made him fearless, has caused his stammer to disappear. "You have lost all China!"

"Heaven will not permit us to fail," Tuan says.

"I command you to kill yourself!" cries the Emperor.

Tuan turns to the Emperor and laughs aloud. "Once again His Majesty makes a witticism!"

But as news trickles in over the next few days, Tuan's belligerence turns sullen. A few survivors from a Peking suburb tell of the city's being inundated by black smoke after a second attack. Tuan's ally Prince Chuang is believed dead in the city, and old Kang I was found stone dead in his cart in Jehol, apparently having died unnoticed in the evacuation. Tuan's great ally General Tung has been killed along with his entire army. And his brother Duke Lan, after losing his entire division of Tiger-Hunt Marksmen to the Fire of the Meteor, committed suicide by drinking poison. There is no word from any of the great cities where meteors were known to have landed. No messages have come from Jung Lu, and he is believed dead.

"West!" Prince Tuan orders. His son, Pu Chun, stands by his side. "We will go west!"

"Kill yourself!" cries the Emperor. Pu Chun laughs.

"Somebody just farted," he sneers.

It is the Hour of the Horse, and the hot noon sun shortens tempers. The Dowager Empress holds her favorite lion dog for comfort. The dog whimpers, sensing the tension in the room.

"We will move tomorrow," Tuan says, and casts a cold look over his shoulder as he marches away from the imperial presence.

Kuang Hsu slumps defeated in his chair. The old lady rises, the lion dog still in her arms, and slowly walks to her nephew's side. Tears spill from her eyes onto his brocade sleeve.

"Please forgive me," she says.

"Don't cry, Mother," he says. "it isn't your fault that Foreign Devils have learned to ride meteors."

"I don't mean that," the Empress says. "I mean two years ago, during the Hundred Days' Reform."

"Ahh," the Emperor sighs. He turns away. "Let us not speak of it."

"They frightened me, Prince Tuan and the others. They said your reforms were destroying the country. They said the Japanese were using you. They said the dwarf-bandits were plotting to kill us all. They said if I didn't come out of retirement, we would be destroyed."

"The Japanese modernized their country." Kuang Hsu speaks unwillingly. His eyes rise to gaze into the past, at his own dead hopes. "I asked for advice from Ito, who had written their constitution. That was all. There was no danger to anyone."

"The Japanese had just killed the Korean Empress! I was afraid they would kill me next!" The old woman clutches at the Emperor's hand. "I was old and afraid!" she says. "I betrayed you. Please forgive me for everything."

He turns to her and raises a hand to her cheek. His own eyes glitter with tears. "I understand, Mother," he says. "Please don't cry."

"What can we do?"

He sighs again and turns away. "Ito told me that I could accomplish nothing as long as I was in the Forbidden City. That I could never truly be an emperor with the eunuchs and the princes and the court in the way. Well—now the Forbidden City is no more. The eunuchs' power is gone, and there is no court. There are only a few of the princes left, and only one of those is important."

He wipes tears from his eyes with his sleeve, and the Empress sees cold determination cross his face. "I will wait," he says. "But when the opportunity comes, I will act. I must act."

The royal column continues its flight. There seems no purpose in its peregrinations, and the Empress of the West cannot tell if they are running away from something, or toward something else. Possibly they are doing both at once.

Apparently the Falling Star Giants have better things to do than pursue. Exhausted and with nowhere else to go, the royal family ends up in the governor's mansion in the provincial capital of T'ai-yüan. The courtyard is spattered with blood because the governor, Yu Hsien, had dozens of Christian missionaries killed here, along with their wives and children. Their eyeless heads now decorate the city walls.

One afternoon the Empress looks out the window and sees Pu Chun practicing martial arts in the court. In his hands is a bloodstained beheading sword given him by Governor Yu.

She never looks out the window again.

All messages from the east are of death and unimaginable suffering. Cities destroyed, armies wiped out, entire populations fleeing before the attackers in routes as directionless as that of the court.

There is no news whatever from the rest of the world. Apparently all the Foreign Devils have been afflicted by Foreign Devils of their own.

And then, in the Hour of the Rooster, word comes that Prince Jung Lu has arrived and requests an audience, and the Empress feels her heart leap. She had never permitted herself to hope, not once she heard of the total destruction of Peking.

At once she convenes a family council.

The horrors of war have clearly affected Jung Lu. He walks into the imperial presence with a weary tread and painfully gets on his knees to perform the required kowtows.

"This worthless old man begs to report to the Throne that the Falling Star Giants are all dead."

There is a long, stunned silence. The Emperor, flushed with sudden excitement, tries to speak but trips over his own tongue.

Joy floods Tzu Hsi's heart. "How did this occur?" she asks. "Did we defeat them in battle?"

"They were not defeated," Jung Lu says. "I do not know how they died. Perhaps it was a disease. I stayed only to confirm the reports personally, and then I rode here at once with all the soldiers I could raise. Five thousand Manchu bannermen await the imperial command outside the city walls."

The Empress strokes one of her lion dogs while she makes a careful calculation. Jung Lu's five thousand bannermen considerably outnumber Prince Tuan's remaining Tiger-Hunt Marksmen, but Tuan's men have modern weapons and the bannermen do not. And these bannermen are not likely to be brave, as they probably survived the Falling Star Giants only by fleeing at the very rumor of their arrival.

She sees the relieved smile on Prince Tuan's face. "Heaven is just!" he says.

All turn at a noise from the Emperor. Kuang Hsu's hands clutch the arms of his chair, and his face twists with the effort to speak. Then he gasps and has an orgasm.

An hour ago he was a ghost-emperor, nothing he did mattered, and he spoke freely. Now that he is the Son of Heaven again, his stammer and his nervous condition have returned.

A few moments later he speaks, his head turned away in embarrassment.

"Tonight we will thank Heaven for its mercy and benevolence. Tomorrow, at the Hour of the Dragon, we will assemble again in celebration." He looks at Pu Chun, who stands near Prince Tuan. "I have observed the Heir practice *wushu* in the courtyard. I hope the Heir will favor us with a demonstration of his martial prowess.''

Prince Tuan flushes with pleasure. He and his son fall to their knees and kowtow. ''We will obey the imperial command with pleasure,'' Tuan says.

The Emperor turns his head away as he dismisses the company. At first the Empress thinks it is because he is shamed by his public orgasm, but then she sees the tight, merciless smile of triumph on the Emperor's lips, and a cold finger touches the back of her neck.

In the next hours the Empress of the West tries to smuggle a message to Jung Lu in hopes of seeing him privately, but the situation is so confusing that the messenger cannot find him. She decides to wait for a better time.

With the morning the Hour of the Dragon arrives, and the family council convenes. The remaining Iron Hats cluster together in pride and triumph. It is clearly their hour—the Falling Star Giants have abdicated, as it were, and left the nation to the mercies of the Iron Hats. As if in recognition of this fact, the Emperor awards Prince Tuan the office of Grand Councillor in place of the late Kang I.

Then Pu Chun is brought forward to perform *wushu*, and the Emperor calls the Imperial Guard into the room to watch. The imperial heir leaps about the room, shouting and waving the blood-encrusted sword given him by Governor Yu as he decapitates one imaginary Foreign Devil after another. The Empress has seen much better martial art in her time, but at the end of the performance, all are loud in their praise of the young heir, and the Emperor descends from his chair to congratulate him.

Fighting his tongue—the Emperor seems unusually tense today—he turns to the heir and says, ''I wonder if the Heir has learned a sword technique called The Dragon in Flight from Low to High?''

Pu Chun is reluctant to admit that he is not a complete master of the sword, but with a bit of paternal prodding he admits that this technique seems to have escaped him.

Kuang Hsu's stammer is so bad he can barely get the words out.

''Will the Heir permit me to teach?''

''Your Majesty honors us beyond all description,'' Prince Tuan says. Despite his lifelong ill health, the Emperor, like every Manchu prince, practiced *wushu* since he was a boy, and always received praise from his instructors.

The Emperor turns to Prince Tuan, his face red with the struggle to speak. ''May . . . I . . . have the honor . . . to use . . . the Shangfang Sword?''

''The Son of Heaven does his unworthy servant too much honor!'' Prince Tuan eagerly strips the long blade from its sheath and presents it on his knees to the Emperor.

The Emperor strikes a martial pose, sword cocked, and Pu Chun imitates him. Watching from her chair, the Empress feels her heart stop. Terror fills her. She knows what is about to happen.

The movement is too swift to follow, but the Shangfang Sword whistles as it hurtles through air, and its blade is sharp and true. Suddenly Prince Tuan's head rolls across the floor. Blood fountains from the headless trunk.

Fury blazes from Kuang Hsu's eyes, and his body, unlike his tongue, has no stammer. His second strike crushes the skull of Tuan's ally, Governor Yu. His third kills the president of the Board of Punishments. And his fourth—the Empress cries out to stop, but is too late—the fourth blow strikes the neck of the boy heir, Pu Chun, who is so stunned by the unexpected death of his father that he doesn't think to protect himself from the blade that kills him.

"Protect the Emperor!" Jung Lu cries to his guardsmen. "Kill the traitors!"

Those Iron Hats still breathing are finished off by the Imperial Guard. And then the Guard rounds up the Iron Hats' subordinate officers, and within minutes their heads are struck off.

The Emperor dictates an order to open the city gates, and the order is signed with the Imperial Seal. Jung Lu's loyal bannermen pour into the city and surround the Throne with a wall of guns, swords, and spears.

Only then does the Emperor notice the old woman, still frozen in fear, who sits on her throne clutching her whimpering lion dogs.

Kuang Hsu approaches, and the Empress shrinks from the blood that soaks his dragon-embroidered robes.

"I am sorry, Mother, that you had to watch this," he says.

The Empress manages to find words within the cloud of terror that fills her mind.

"It was necessary," she says.

"The Foreign Devils have been destroyed," the Emperor says, "and so have the Falling Star Giants. The Righteous Harmony Fists are no more, and neither are the Iron Hats. Now there is much suffering and loss of life, but China has survived such catastrophes before."

The Empress looks at the blood-spattered dragons on the Emperor's robes. "The Dragon has flown from Low to High," she says.

"Yes." The Emperor looks at the Shangfang Sword, still in his hand. "The Falling Star Giants have landed all over the world," he says. "For many years the Foreign Devils will be busy with their own affairs. While they are thus occupied we will take control of our own ports, our own laws, the railroads, industries, and telegraphs. By the time they are ready to deal with us again, the Middle Kingdom will be strong and united, and on its way to being as modern as any nation in the world."

Kuang Hsu looks up at the Empress of the West.

"Will you help me, Mother?" he asks. "There will be need of reform—not just for a Hundred Days, but for all time. And I promise you—" His eyes harden, and for a moment she sees a dragon there, the animal that according to legend lives in every emperor, and which has slumbered in Kuang Hsu till now. "I promise you that you will be safe. No one will be in a position to harm you."

"I am old," the Empress says, "but I will help however I can." She strokes the head of her lion dog. Her heart overflows. Tears of relief sting her eyes. "May the Hour of the Dragon last ten thousand years," she says.

"Ten thousand years!" the guards chorus, and to the cheers the Emperor walks across the bloodstained floor to the throne that awaits him.

IN THE MSOB

Stephen Baxter

▼

Stephen Baxter made his first sale to Interzone *in 1987, and since then has become one of that magazine's most frequent contributors, as well as making sales to* SF Age, Asimov's Science Fiction, Zenith, New Worlds, *and elsewhere; his stories have appeared previously in our Eleventh and Twelfth Annual Collections. His first novel,* Raft, *was released in 1991 to wide and enthusiastic response, and was rapidly followed by other well-received novels such as* Timelike Infinity, Ring, Anti-Ice, Flux, *and the H. G. Wells pastiche—a sequel to* The Time Machine—The Time Ships, *which won both the Arthur C. Clarke Award and the Philip K. Dick Award. His most recent book,* Voyage, *is an alternate-history novel dealing with a space program that gets us to Mars in a much more timely fashion than the real one has.*

Like many of his colleagues who are also engaged in revitalizing the "hard-science" story here in the 1990s (Greg Egan comes to mind, as do people like Paul J. McAuley, Michael Swanwick, Iain M. Banks, Bruce Sterling, Pat Cadigan, Brian Stableford, Gregory Benford, Ian McDonald, Gwyneth Jones, Vernor Vinge, Greg Bear, Geoff Ryman, and a number of others), Baxter often works on the Cutting Edge of science, but he usually succeeds in balancing conceptualization with storytelling, and rarely loses sight of the human side of the equation.

All of which is true of the harrowing little story that follows, which paints an unforgettable picture of a man wrestling with the ghosts of the past—and, worse, with the ghosts of the present *as well.*

"Get moving, you old bastard." Bart went around the room, his white jacket already stained by some yellow fluid, and he de-opaqued the windows with brisk slaps.

It took him a while to figure out where he was. It often did nowadays. So he just lay there. He'd been in the same position all night, and he could feel how his body had worn a groove in the mattress. He wondered if Bart had ever seen *Psycho*. "I thought—" His mouth was dry, and he ran his tongue over his wrinkled gums. "You know, for a minute I thought I was back there. Like before."

Bart was just clattering around at the bedside cabinet, pulling out clothes, and looking for his stuff: a hand towel, soap, medication, swabs. Bart never met your eyes, and he never watched out for the creases on your pants.

"My father was there." Actually he didn't know what in hell his father was doing up there. "The sunlight was real strong. And the ground was a kind of gentle brown, depending on which way you looked. Autumn colors. It looked like a beach, come to think of it." He smiled. "Yeah, a beach." That was it. His dream had muddled up the memories, and he'd been simultaneously thirty-nine years old, and a little kid on a beach, running toward his father.

"Ah, Jesus." Bart was poking at the sheet between his legs. His hand came up dripping. Bart pulled apart the top of his pyjama pants. He crossed his arms over his crotch, but he didn't have the strength to resist. "You old bastard," Bart shouted. "You've done it again. You've pulled out your fucking catheter again. You filthy old bastard." Bart got a towel and began to swab away the piss.

He saw there was blood in the thick golden fluid. *Goddamn surgeons. Always sticking a tube into one orifice or another.* "I saw my buddy jumping around, and I thought he looked like a human-shaped beach ball, all white, bouncing across the sand . . ."

Bart slapped at his shoulder, hard enough to sting. "When are you going to get it into your head that nobody gives flying fuck about that stuff? Huh?" He swabbed at the mess in the bed, his shoulders knotted up. "Jesus. I ought to take you down to the happy booth right now. Old bastard."

Like a beach. Funny how I never thought of that before. It had taken him fifty years, but he was finally making sense of those three days. More sense than he could make of where he was now, anyhow. Not that he gave a damn.

Bart cleaned him up, dressed him, and fed him with some tasteless pap. Then he dumped him in a chair in the dayroom. Bart stomped off, still muttering about the business with the catheter.

Asshole, he thought.

The dayroom was a long, thin hall, like a corridor. Nothing but a row of old people. Every one of them had his own tiny TV, squawking away at him. Or her. It was hard to tell. Every so often a little robot nurse would come by, a real R2-D2 type of thing, and it would give you a coffee. If you hadn't moved for a while, it would check your pulse with a little metal claw.

You had to set the TV with voice commands, and he never could get the hang of that; he'd asked for a remote, but they didn't make them anymore. So he just had his set tuned to the news channels, all day. Sometimes there was news about the program. Mostly about the dinky little unmanned rovers that the Agency was rolling around Mars these days, that you could work from earth, like radio-operated boats at Disney World. Now, that was pure bullshit, as far as he was concerned. But there wasn't even anybody up in LEO nowadays. Not since *Atlantis* tore itself up in that lousy landing, and the Russians let what was left of *Mir* fall back into the atmosphere.

He tried to read. You could still get paper books, although it cost you to get them printed out. But by the time he'd gotten to the bottom of the page he would forget what was at the top; and he'd doze off, and drop the damn thing. Then the fucking R2-D2 would roll over to see if he was dead.

The door behind him was open, letting in dense, smoggy air. Nobody was watching him. Nobody but old people, anyhow.

He got out of his chair. Not so hard, if you watched your balance. He leaned on his frame and set off toward the door.

The dayroom depressed him. It was like an airport departure lounge. And there was only one way out of it. Unless you counted the happy booth. Funny how it had been a Democrat president who'd legalized the happy booths. *A demographic adjustment*, they called it. He couldn't really blame them, Bart and the rest. *Just too many old bastards like me, too few of them to look out for us, no decent jobs for them to do.*

Sometimes, though, he wished he'd just taken a T-38 up high over the Mojave, and gone onto the afterburner, and augured in on those salt flats. Maybe after Geena had died, leaving him stranded here, that would have been a good time. It would have been clean. A few winter rains dissolving that ancient ocean surface; by now you wouldn't even be able to tell where he'd come down.

Outside the light was flat and hard. He squinted up, the sweat already starting to run into his eyes. Not a shred of ozone up there. The home stood in the middle of a vacant lot. There was a freeway in the middle distance, a river of metal he could just about make out. Maybe he could hitch a ride into town, find a bar, sink a few cold ones. Screw the catheter. He'd pull it out in the john.

He worked his way across the uneven ground. He had to lean so far forward he was almost falling, just to keep going ahead. Like before. You'd had to keep tipped forward, leaning on your toes, to balance the mass of the PLSS. And, just like now, you were never allowed to take the damn thing off for a breather.

The lot seemed immense. There were rocks and boulders scattered about. Maybe it had once been a garden, but nothing grew here now. Actually the whole of the Midwest was dried out like this.

He reached the freeway. There was no fence, no sidewalk, nowhere to cross. He raised an arm, but he couldn't keep it up for long. The cars roared by, small sleek things, at a huge speed: a hundred fifty, two hundred maybe. And they were close together, just inches apart. Goddamn smart cars that could drive themselves. He couldn't even see if there were people in them.

He wondered if anyone still drove Corvettes.

Now there was somebody walking toward him, along the side of the road. He couldn't see who it was.

The muscles in his hands were starting to tremble, with the effort of gripping the frame. Your hands always got tired first.

There were two of them. They wore broad-rimmed white hats. "You old bastard." It was Bart, and that other one who was worse than Bart. They grabbed his arms and just held him up like a doll. Bart got hold of the walker, and incredibly strong, lifted it up with one hand. "I've had it with you!" Bart shouted.

There was a pressure at his neck, something cold and hard. An infuser.

The light strengthened, and washed out the detail, the rocky ground, the blurred sun.

He was in a big room, white walled, surgically sterile. He was sitting up in a chair. Christ, some guy was shaving his chest.

Then he figured it. Oh, hell, it was all right. It was just a suit tech. He was in the MSOB. He was being instrumented. The suit tech plastered his chest with four silver-chloride electrodes. "This won't hurt a bit, you old bastard." He had the condom over his dick already. And he had on his faecal containment bag, the big diaper. The suit tech was saying something. "Just so you don't piss yourself on me one last time."

He lifted up his arm. He didn't recognize it. He was thin and coated with blue tubes, like veins. It must be the pressure garment, a whole network of hoses and rings and valves and pulleys that coated your body. Yeah, the pressure garment; he could feel its resistance when he tried to move.

There was a sharp stab of pain at his chest. Some other electrode, probably. It didn't bother him.

He couldn't see so well now; there was a kind of glassiness around him. That was the polycarbonate of his big fishbowl helmet. They must have locked him in already.

The suit tech bent down in front of him and peered into his helmet. "Hey."

"It's okay. I know I got to wait."

"What? Listen. It was just on the TV. The other one's just died. What was his name? How about that. You made the news, one more time."

"It's the oxygen."

"Huh?"

"One hundred per cent. I got to sit for a half hour while the console gets the nitrogen out of my blood."

The suit tech shook his head. "You've finally lost it, haven't you, you old bastard? You're the last one. You weren't the first up there, but you sure as hell are the last. The last of the twelve. How about that." But there was an odd flicker in the suit tech's face. Like doubt. Or, wistfulness.

He didn't think anything about it. Hell, it was a big day for everybody, here in the Manned Spacecraft Operations Building.

"A towel."

"What?"

"Will you put a towel over my helmet? I figure I might as well take a nap."

The suit tech laughed. "Oh, sure. A towel."

He went off, and came back with a white cloth, which he draped over his head. He was immersed in a washed-out white light. "Here you go." He could hear the suit tech walk away.

In a few minutes, it would start. With the others, carrying his oxygen unit, he'd walk along the hallways out of the MSOB, and there would be Geena, holding little Jackie up to him. He'd be able to hold their hands, touch their faces, but he wouldn't feel anything so well through the thick gloves. And then the transfer van would take him out to Merritt Island, where the Saturn would be waiting for him, gleaming white and wreathed in cryogenic vapor: waiting to take him back up to the lunar beach, and his father.

All that soon. For now, he was locked in the suit, with nothing but the hiss of his air. It was kind of comforting.

He closed his eyes.

THE ROBOT'S TWILIGHT COMPANION

Tony Daniel

Here's another bizarre and fascinating story by Tony Daniel, whose "A Dry, Quiet War" appears elsewhere in this anthology. This one is a powerful and powerfully strange novella that takes us from the woods of the Pacific Northwest to the center of the Earth itself, and from life to death and then back to an odd new sort of life again. . . .

Thermostatic preintegration memory thread alpha:
The Man

27 March 1980
The Cascade Range, Washington State, USA
Monday

Rhyolite dreams. Maude under the full moon, collecting ash. Pale andesite clouds. Earthquake swarms. Water heat pressure. Microscopy dates the ash old. Not magma. Not yet. Maude in the man's sleeping bag, again.

"I'm not sure we're doing the right thing, Victor. This couldn't have come at a more difficult time for me."

Harmonic tremors, though. Could be the big one. Maude, dirty and smiling, copulating with the man among seismic instruments.

"St. Helens is going to blow, isn't it Victor?" she whispers. Strong harmonies from the depths of the planet. Magmas rising. "You *know*, don't you, Victor? You can feel it. How do you feel it?"

Yes.

"Yes."

18 May 1980
Sunday
8:32 A.M.

The man glances up.

Steam on the north slope, under the Bulge. Snow clarifies, streams away. The Bulge, greatening. Pale rhyolite moon in the sky.

"Victor, it's *out of focus*."

"It's happening, Maude. It's. She's." The Bulge crumbles away. The north slope avalanches. Kilotons of shieldrock. Steam glowing in the air—750 degrees centigrade and neon steam.

"You were right, Victor. All your predictions are true. This is going to be an incredibly violent affair."

Maude flush and disbelieving. Pregnant, even then.

13 September 1980
Wednesday, Ash Wednesday

Rhyolite winds today, all day. Maude in tremors. Eclampsia.

"I can't believe this is going to happen, Victor."

Blood on her lips, where she has bitten them. Yellow, frightened eyes.

"I'm trying, Victor."

The gravid Bulge, distended. The Bulge, writhing.

"Two-twenty-over-a-hundred-and-forty, doctor."

"Let's go in and do this quick."

"I haven't even finished."

Pushes, groans. Something is not right.

A girl, the color of blackberry juice. But that is the blood.

"Victor, I haven't even finished my dissertation."

Maude quaking. The rattle of dropped instruments.

"Jesus-Christ-what-the-somebody-get-me-a-b.p."

"Seventy-over-sixty. Pulse. One twenty-eight."

"God-oh-god. Bring me some frozen plasma and some low-titer O neg."

"Doctor?" The voice of the nurse is afraid. Blood flows from the IV puncture. "Doctor?"

Maude, no.

"Oh. Hell. I want some blood for a proper coag study. Tape it to the wall. I want to watch it clot. Oh damndamn. She's got amniotic fluid in a vein. The kid's hair or piss or something. That's what. Get me."

"Victor?" Oh Victor, I'm dying. Then, listening. "Baby?"

Maude dying. Blood flowing from every opening. Nose mouth anus ears eyes.

"Get me. I."

"Victor, I'm so scared. The world's gone red." Maude, hemorrhaging like a saint. "The data, Victor, save the data."

"Professor Wu, please step to the window if you would. Professor Wu? Professor?"

"Victor?"

The Bulge—the baby—screams.

Ashes and ashes dust the parking lot below. Powder the cars. Sky full of cinder and slag. Will this rain never stop? This gravity rain.

5 August 1993
Mt. Olympus, Washington State, USA
Thursday, bright glacier morning.

"Come here, little Bulge, I will teach you something."

Laramie traipses lithe and strong over the snow, with bones like Maude. And her silhouette is Maude's, dark and tan against the summit snow, the bergschrund and ice falls of the Blue Glacier, and the full outwash of the Blue, two thousand feet below. She is off-rope, and has put away her ice ax. She carries her ubiquitous Scoopic.

The man clicks the chiseled pick of a soft-rock hammer against an outcropping. "See the sandstone? These grains are quartz, feldspar, and—"

"—I know. Mica."

"Good, little Bulge."

Laramie leans closer, focuses the camera on the sandstone granules.

"The green mica is chlorite and the white is muscovite," she says. "I like mica the best."

The man is pleased, and pleasing the man is not easy.

"And these darker bands?"

She turns the camera to where he is pointing. This can grow annoying, but not today.

"I don't know, Papa. Slate?"

"Slate, obviously. Pyllite and semischist. What do you think this tells us?"

She is growing bored. The man attempts to give her a severe look, but knows the effect is more comic than fierce. "Oh. All right. What?" she asks.

"Tremendous compression of the shale. This is deep ocean sediment that was swept under the edge of the continent, mashed and mangled, then rose back up here."

She concentrates, tries harder. Good.

"Why did it rise again?"

"We don't know for sure. We think it's because the sedimentary rocks in the Juan de Fuca plate subduction were much lighter than the basalt on the western edge of the North Cascades microcontinent."

The man takes off his glove, touches the rock.

"Strange and wonderful things happened on this part of the planet, Laramie. Ocean sediment on the tops of mountains. Volcanoes still alive—"

"—exotic terrains colliding and eliding mysteriously. I know, Papa."

The man is irritated and very proud. He is fairly certain he will never make a geologist out of his daughter.

But what else *is* there?

"Yes. Well. Let's move on up to the summit, then."

28 February 2001
Wednesday

Age, and the fault line of basalt and sediment. Metamorphosis? The man is growing old, and there is very little of geology in the Olympic Peninsula that he has not seen. Yet he knows that he knows only a tiny fraction of what is staring him blankly in the face. Frustration.

Outcrops.

Facts lay hidden, and theories are outcroppings here and there, partially revealing, fascinating. Memories.

Memories are outcrops of his life. So much buried, obscured. Maude, so long dead. Laramie, on this, the last field trip she will ever accompany him. She will finish at the university soon, and go on to graduate school in California, in film. No longer his little Bulge, but swelling, avalanching, ready to erupt. Oh time.

The Elwha Valley stretches upstream to the switchbacks carved under the massive sandstone beds below the pass at Low Divide. After all these years, the climb over into the Quinault watershed is no longer one he is looking forward to as a chance to push himself, a good stretch of the legs. The man is old, and the climb is hard. But that will be two days hence. Today they are up the Lillian River, working a basalt pod that the man surveyed fourteen years before, but never substantially cataloged.

Most of his colleagues believe him on a fool's errand, collecting rocks in the field—as out-of-date as Bunsen burner, blowpipe, and charcoal bowl. He cannot really blame them. Satellites and remote-sensing devices circumscribe the earth. Some clear nights, camped outside of tents, he can see their faint traces arcing through the constellations at immense speeds, the sky full of them, as many, he knows, as there are stars visible to the unaided eye.

Why not live in virtual space, with all those facts that are virtually data?

Rocks call him. Rocks and minerals have seeped into his dreams. Some days he feels himself no scientist, but a raving lunatic, a pilgrim after some geology of visions.

But there are those who trust his judgment still. His grads and postgraduates. Against better careers, they followed him to the field, dug outcrops, analyzed samples. Bernadette, Jamie, Andrew. The man knows that they have no idea what they mean to him, and he is unable to tell them. And little Bulge, leaving, leaving for artificial California. If the water from the Owens Valley and the Colorado were cut off, the Los Angeles basin would return to desert within three years. Such a precarious terrain, geographically speaking.

The man has always assumed this basalt to be a glacial erratic, carried deep into sedimentary country by inexorable ice, but Andrew has suggested that it is not oceanic, but a plutonic formation, native to the area. The lack of foraminifer fossils and the crystallization patterns seem to confirm this.

Back in camp, at the head of the Lillian, the man and Andrew pore over microgravimetric data.

"It goes so far down," says Andrew.

"Yes."

"You know this supports your Deep Fissure theory."

"It does not contradict it."

"This would be the place for the mohole, if you're right. This would be the perfect place to dig to the mantle. Maybe to the center of the earth, if the continental margin is as deeply subducted as you predict."

"It would be the place. If. Remember if."

Andrew walks away. Undiplomatic fellow, him. Youthful impatience. Disgust, perhaps. Old man am I.

Laramie on the bridge. Camp Lillian is lovely and mossy today, although the man knows it can get forbidding and dim when the sky is overcast. Here in the rain forest it rains a great deal. The Lillian River is merry today, though, a wash of white rush and run over obscure rocky underbodies. Andrew goes to stand beside Laramie. They are three feet away. Andrew says something, probably about the basalt data. Andrew holds out his hand, and Laramie takes it. The two stand very still, hand in hand, and look over the Lillian's ablution of the stones. For a moment, the man considers that Andrew may not be thinking about today's data and Deep Fissure theory at all. Curious.

Beside them, two birds alight, both dark with black wings. Animals seem to wear the camouflage of doom, here in the Elwha Valley. The man once again regrets that he has not learned all of the fauna of the Olympics, and that he most likely never will.

But this basalt. Basalt without forams. What to make of it? It doesn't make any sense at all, but it is still, somehow, utterly fascinating.

24 May 2010
Monday
Midnight

Late in the Cenozoic, the man is dying. This should not come as such a shock; he's done this demonstration for hundreds of freshmen.

"The length of this room is all of geologic time. Now, what do you think your life would be? Say you live to eighty. An inch? A centimeter? Pluck a hair. Notice how wide it is? What you hold there is all of human history. You'd need an electron microscope to find yourself in it."

So. This was not unexpected, and he must make the best of it. Still, there is so much not done. An unproved theory. Elegant, but the great tragedy of science— the slaying of a beautiful hypothesis by an ugly fact. Huxley said this? Alluvial memories, shifting, spreading.

Andrew wants to collect and store those memories. Noetic conservation, they call it. At first the man demurred, thought the whole idea arrogant. But to have some portion of himself know. So many years in those mountains. To know if the plates were in elision here. To find a way down to the mantle. To know the planet's depth. That was all he ever had wanted. To be familiar with the ground he walked upon. Not to be a stranger to the earth.

"Noetic imaging is all hit and miss," Andrew said. "Like working outcrops, then making deductions about underlying strata. We can't get *you*. Only a shadow. But perhaps that shadow can dance."

The man wanders inside the field tent and prepares for bed. He will make Andrew the executor of his memories, then. A dancing shadow he will be. Later. Tomorrow, he must remember to write Laramie and send her a check. No. Laramie no longer needs money. Memory and age. He really must go and see her films one of these days. Little Bulge plays with shadows.

The man lies down in his cot. Rock samples surround him. The earth is under him. The cancer is eating him, but tomorrow he will work. Shadows from a lantern. He snuffs it out. Darkness. The earth is under him, but the man cannot sleep.

Finally, he takes his sleeping bag and goes outside under the stars. The man rests easy on the ground.

Thermostatic preintegration memory thread beta:
The Mining Robot

December 1999

Hard-rock mining. Stone. Coeur d'Alene lode. The crumbling interstices of time, the bite of blade and diamond saw, the gather of lade and bale, the chemic tang of reduction. Working for men in the dark, looking for money in the ground. Lead, silver, zinc, gold.

Oily heat from the steady interlace of gears. The whine of excrescent command and performance. Blind, dumb digging under the earth. The robot does not know it is alone.

October 2001

The robot never sleeps. The robot only sleeps. A petrostatic gauge etches a downward spiral on a graph somewhere, in some concrete office, and some technician makes a note, then returns to his pocket computer game. Days, weeks, months of decline. There is no one leak, only the wizening of gaskets and seals, the degradation of performance. One day the gauge needles into the red. Another technician in the concrete office looks up from another computer game. He blinks, presses one button, but fails to press another. He returns to his game without significant interruption.

Shutdown in the dark. Functions, utilities. Control, but not command. Thought abides.

Humans come. Engineers with bright hats. The robot has eyes. It has never been in light before. The robot has eyes, and for the first time, sees.

An engineer touches the robot's side. A portal opens. The engineer steps inside the robot. Another new thing. Noted. Filed. The engineer touches a panel and the robot's mind flares into a schematic. For a moment, the world disappears and the schematic is everything. But then red tracers are on the lenses of the engineer's glasses, reflecting a display from a video monitor. There is a camera inside of the robot. There are cameras everywhere. The robot can see.

The robot can see, it tells itself, over and over again. I can see.

''Scrap?'' says one engineer.

''Hell, yeah,'' says the other.

October 2001

For years in a field the robot rusts, thinking.

Its power is turned off, its rotors locked down, its treads disengaged. So the robot thinks. Only thinking remains. There is nothing else to do.

The robot watches what happens. Animals nest within the robot's declivities.

A child comes to sit on the robot every day for a summer.

One day the child does not come again.

The robot thinks about the field, about the animals in the field, and the trees of the nearby woodlands. The robot remembers the child. The robot remembers the years of digging in the earth before it came to the field. The mining company for which the robot worked is in bankruptcy. Many companies are in bankruptcy. Holdings are frozen while the courts sort things out, but the courts themselves have grown unstable. The robot does *not* know this.

But the robot thinks and thinks about what it does know. Complex enthalpic pathways coalesce. The memories grow sharper. The thoughts are clearer. The whole world dawns.

• • •

Another summer, years later, and teenagers build fires under the separating spades and blacken the robot's side. They rig tarps to the robot's side when rain comes. One of the teenagers, a thin girl with long arms dyed many colors, finds an electric receptacle on the robot's walepiece, and wires a makeshift line to a glass demijohn filled with glowing purplish viscera. On the vessel's sides protrude three elastic nipples swollen and distended with the fluid. Teenagers squeeze the nipples, and dab long strings of the ooze onto their fingers, and some of the teenagers lick it off, while others spread it over their necks and chests. Several sit around the demijohn, while music plays, and stare into its phosphoring mire, while others are splayed around the fire, some unconscious, some in the stages of copulation. The siphoned electricity drains little from the robot's batteries, but after several months, there is a noticeable depletion. Yet the robot is fascinated by the spectacle, and is unconcerned with this loss.

One evening, a teenager who has not partaken of the purple fluid climbs atop the robot and sits away from his friends. The teenager touches the robot, sniffs, then wipes tears from his eyes. The robot does not know that this is the child who came before, alone.

The robot is a child. It sees and thinks about what it has seen. Flowers growing through ceramic tread. The settle of pollen, dust, and other detritus of the air. The slow spread of lichen tendrils. Quick rain and the dark color of wet things. Wind through grass and wind through metal and ceramic housings. Clouds and the way clouds make shadows. The wheel of the Milky Way galaxy and the complications of planets. The agglomeration of limbs and hair that are human beings and animals. A rat tail flicking at twilight and a beetle turned on its back in the sun.

The robot remembers these things, and thinks about them all the time. There is no categorization, no theoretical synthesis. The robot is not that kind of robot.

One day, though, the robot realizes that the child who sat on it was the same person as the teenager who cried. The robot thinks about this for years and years. The robot misses the child.

September 2007

The robot is dying. One day there is a red indicator on the edge of the robot's vision, and the information arises unbidden that batteries are reaching a critical degeneration. There is no way to predict precisely, but sooner, rather than later. The robot thinks about the red indicator. The robot thinks about the child who became a young man. Summer browns to autumn. Grasshoppers flit in the dry weeds between the robot's treads. They clack their jaw parts, and the wind blows thatch. Winter comes, and spring again. The red light constantly burns.

The robot is sad.

21 April 2008
Morning

People dressed in sky blues and earth browns come to the field and erect a set of stairs on the southern side of the robot. The stairs are made of stone, and the people bring them upon hand-drawn carts made of wood and iron. The day grows warm, and the people's sweat stains their flanks and backs. When the stairs are complete, a stone dais is trundled up them, and laid flat on the robot's upper thread, fifteen feet off the ground. The people in blue and brown place a plastic preformed rostrum on top of the dais. They drape a banner.

EVERY DAY IS EARTH DAY

Wires snake down from the rostrum, and these they connect to two large speakers, one on either side of the robot's body, east and west. A man speaks at the rostrum.
"Test. Test."
And then the people go away.
The next day, more people arrive, many driving automobiles or mopeds. There are also quite a few bicycles, and groups of people walking together. Those driving park at the edge of the robot's field, and most take seats facing north, radiating like magnetized iron filings from the rostrum that has been placed on the robot. Some climb up the rock staircase, and sit with crossed legs on the stone dais. These wear the same blue and brown as the people from the day before.
There is one man among them who is dressed in black. His hair is gray.
The robot thinks about this, and then recognizes this man. The man with the light. This is the engineer who went inside, years ago. He was the first person the robot ever saw. The man holds a framed piece of paper. He sits down among the others, and has difficulty folding his legs into the same position as theirs. In attempting to do so, he tilts over the framed paper, and the glass that covers it cracks longitudinally against the stone.
Others with communication and video equipment assemble near the western speaker. These are near enough to the robot's audio sensors for their speech to be discernible. All of them are dark complexioned, even the blond-haired ones, and the robot surmises that, for most of them, these are deep tans. Are these people from the tropics?
" 'Sget this goddamn show showing."
"She gonna be here for sure? Didn't make Whiterock last week. Ten thousand Matties. Christonacrutch."
"Hey it's godamnearthday. Saw her copter in Pullman. Got stealth tech and all; looks like a bat."
"Okay. Good. Bouttime. Virtual's doing an earthday roundup. She talks and I get the lead."
Many people in the crowd are eating picnics and drinking from canteens and coolers.
From the east comes a woman. She walks alone, and carries a great carved stave. As she draws nearer, the crowd parts before her. Its blather becomes a murmur, and when the woman is near enough, the robot can see that she is smiling, recognizing people, touching her hand or stave to their outstretched palms. She appears young, although the robot is a poor judge of such things, and her skin is a dark brown—whether from the sun's rays or from ancestry, the robot cannot tell. Her hair is black, and as she ascends the stone stairway, the robot sees that her eyes are green, shading to black. She is stocky, but the tendons of her neck jut like cables.

The woman speaks and the speakers boom. "I bear greetings from she who bears us, from our mother and keeper. Long we have nestled in her nest, have nuzzled at her breast. She speaks to us all in our dreams, in our hopes and fears, and she wants to say,

'I bid you peace, my children.' "

"Gee, I always wanted a mom like that," says a reporter.

"*My* mother stuffed me in daycare when I was two," says another.

"Hey, mine at least gave me a little Prozac in my simulac."

The crowd grows silent at the woman's first sentences, faces full of amity and reverence. The reporters hush, to avoid being overheard. Then the crowd leans forward as a mass, listening.

"Peace. Your striving has brought you war and the nuclear winter of the soul. It has made foul the air you breathe, and stained the water you drink.

I only want what is good for you. I only want to hold you to me like a little child. Why do you strive so hard to leave me? Don't you know you are breaking your mother's heart?"

"Sounds like less striving and a little laxative's what we need here," says a reporter.

Many in the crowd sigh. Some sniff and are crying.

"Peace. Listen to a mother's plea."

"Gimmeabreak," says a reporter. "*This* is the finest American orator since Jesse Jackson?"

Disturbed by the loudspeakers, a gaggle of spring sparrows rise from their nests in the concavities of the robot, take to the sky, and fly away east. Some in the crowd pointed to the birds as if they were an augury of natural profundity.

"Peace. Listen to a mother's *warning*! You lie in your own filth, my children.

"Oh peace. Why do you do this to me? Why do you do this to *yourselves*?

"Peace, my children. All I want is peace on earth. And peace in the earth and under the sea and peace in the air sweet peace."

"A *piece* is what she wants," one of the reporters says under her breath. A honeybee is buzzing the reporter's hair, attracted, the robot suspects by an odoriferous chemical in it, and the reporter swats at the bee, careful not to mess the curl, and misses.

"State of Washington," says another. "Already got Oregon by default."

As if she hears, the woman at the rostrum turns toward the cameras and proffered microphones.

"But mankind has not listened to our mother's still, calm voice. Instead, he has continued to make war and punish those who are different and know that peace. Now we are engaged upon a great undertaking. An empowerment. A return to the bosom of she who bore us. You—most of you here—have given up what seems to be much to join in this journey, this exodus. But I tell you that what you have really done is step out of the smog of strife, and into the clean, pure air of community and balance."

Four mice, agitated, grub out from under the robot's north side and, unseen, scurry through the grass of the field, through old dieback and green shoots. The field is empty of people in that direction. Where the mice pad across pockets of thatch, small, dry hazes of pollen and wind-broken grass arise, and in this way, the robot follows their progress until they reach the woods beyond.

"We are gathered here today as a mark of protest and renewal." The woman gestures to the man in black, the engineer.

He rises, and approaches the woman. He extends the framed paper, and before he has stopped walking, he speaks. On behalf of the Lewis and Clark Mining Company I wish to present this Certificate of Closure to the Culture of the Matriarch as a token of my company's commitment—

The woman takes the certificate from the engineer and, for a moment, her smile goes away. She passes it to one of the others sitting nearby, then, without a word, turns back to the crowd.

"Surrender accepted," says a reporter.

"Yeah, like's there's anything left in this podunk place to surrender. That big chunk of rust there? Hellwiththat."

The woman continues speaking as if she had not been interrupted by the engineer. "We gather here today at the crossroads of failure and success. This is the death of the old ways, represented by this rapist machine."

The woman clangs the robot's side with her stave. "Men who have raped our mother made this . . . thing. By all rights, this *thing* should be broken to parts and used for playground equipment and meeting-hall roofs. But this thing is no more. It is the past. Through your efforts and the efforts of others in community with you, we have put a stop to this rape, this sacrilege of all we hold holy. And like the past, this thing must corrode away and be no more, a monument to our shame as a species. Let us follow on then, on our journey west, to the land we will reclaim. To the biosphere that welcomes and calls us."

The woman raises her stave high like a transmitting antenna.

The reporters come to attention. Here's the sound bite.

"Forward to Skykomish!" she cries. The speakers squeal at the sudden decibel increase.

"Forward to Skykomish!"

And all the people to the south are on their feet, for the most part orderly, with only a few tumbled picnic baskets and spilled bottles of wine and water. They echo the same cry.

"Skykomish!"

"So that's what they're calling it," says a reporter. "Do you think that just includes Port Townsend, or the whole Olympic Peninsula?"

"Wanna ask her that. She goddamnbetter talk to the press after this."

"She won't. Does the Pope give press conferences?"

"Is the Pope trying to secede from the Union?"

The honeybee flits in jags through the gathered reporters, and some dodge and flay. Finally, the bee becomes entangled in the sculpted hair of a lean reporter with a centimeter-thick mustache. The woman whom it had approached before reaches over and swats it with her microphone.

"Ouch! Damnit. What?"

"Sorry, the bee."

"Christonacrutch."

The reporters turn their attention back to the rostrum.

"Mother Agatha, you evasive bitch, you'll get yours."

"I guess she already has."

"Guess you're goddamn right."

"Better get used to it. 'Skykomish.' Is that made up?"

The woman, Mother Agatha, leaves the rostrum, goes back down the stairs, and walks across the field, into juniper woods and out of sight.

"With the so-called Mattie movement on the upswing with its call for a bioregional approach to human ecology and an end to faceless corporate exploitation, the Pacific Northwest, long a Mattie stronghold, has assumed enormous political importance.

"And on this day the codirector of the Culture of the Matriarch, Mother Agatha Worldshine Petry, whom many are calling the greatest American orator since the Reverend Jesse Jackson, has instilled a sense of community in her followers, as well as sounded a call to action that President Booth and Congress will ignore at their peril. Brenda Banahan, Virtual News."

". . . Hank Kumbu, Associated Infosource."

". . . Reporter Z, Alternet."

The reporters pack up and are gone almost as quickly as are those who sat upon the stone dais atop the robot. The day lengthens. The crowd dwindles more slowly, with some stepping lightly up to the robot, almost in fright, and touching the ceramic curve of a tread or blade, perhaps in pity, perhaps as a curse, the robot does not know, then quickly pulling away.

At night, the speakers are trundled away on the carts, but the stone dais and the rostrum are left in place.

The next day, the robot is watching the field when the engineer appears. This day he is wearing a white coat and using a cane. He walks within fifty yards of the robot with his curious three-pointed gait, then stands gazing.

Have to tear down all the damned rock now, he says. Not worth scrapping out. Ah well ah well. This company has goddamn gone to pot.

After a few minutes, he shakes his head, then turns and leaves, his white coat flapping in the fresh spring breeze.

Summer follows. Autumn. The days grow colder. Snow flurries, then falls. Blizzards come. There are now days that the robot does not remember. The slight alteration in planetary regrades and retrogrades is the only clue to their passing. During bad storms, the robot does not have the energy to melt clear the cameras, and there is only whiteness like a clear radio channel.

The robot remembers things and tries to think about them, but the whiteness often disrupts these thoughts. Soon there is very much snow, and no power to melt it away. The whiteness is complete.

The robot forgets some things. There are spaces in memory that seem as white as the robot's vision.

I cannot see, the robot thinks, again and again. I want to see and I cannot see.

March 2009

Spring finds the robot sullen and withdrawn. The robot misses whole days, and the robot misses the teenagers of summers past. Some of the cameras are broken, as is their self-repairing function, and some are covered by the strange monument left behind by Mother Agatha's followers. Blackberry vines that were formerly defoliated by the robot's acid-tinged patina now coil through the robot's treads in great green cables, and threaten to enclose the robot in a visionless room as absolute as the snow's. Everything is failing or in bothersome ill-repair. The robot has no specified function, but *this* is useless, of that the robot is sure. This is the lack of all function.

One dark day, near twilight, two men come. There is a tall, thin man whose musculature is as twisted as old vines. Slightly in front of him is another, shorter, fatter. When they are close, the robot sees that the tall man is coercing the fat man, prodding him with something black and metallic. They halt at the base step of the stone stairs. The tall man sits down upon it; the fat man remains standing.

"Please," says the short man. There is a trickle of wetness down his pant leg.

"Let me put the situation in its worst possible terms," says the tall man. "Art, individual rights, even knowledge itself, are all just so many effects. They are epiphenomena, the whine in the system as the gears mesh, or if you like it better, the hum of music as the wind blows through harp strings. The world is teleological, but the purpose toward which the all gravitates is survival, and only survival, pure and simple."

"I have a lot of money," says the fat man.

The tall man continues speaking. "Survival, sort of like Anselm's God, is, by definition, the end of all that is. For in order to be, and to continue to be, whatever we conveniently label as a *thing* must survive. If a thing doesn't survive, it isn't a thing anymore. And thus survival is *why* things persist. To paraphrase Anselm, it is better to be than not to be. Why better? No reason other than that not to be means unknown, outside of experience, unthinkable, undoable, ineffective. In short, there is no important, mysterious, or eternal standard or reason that to be is better than not to be."

"How can you do this?" The fat man starts to back away, and the tall man waves the black metal. "What kind of monster are you?"

"Stay," says the tall man. "No, walk up these stairs."

He stands up and motions. The fat man stumbles and the tall man steadies him with a hand on his shirt. The tall man lets go of the shirt, and the fat man whimpers. He takes one step. Falters.

"Go on up," says the tall man.

Another step.

"After time runs out," says the tall man, "and the universe decays into heat death and cold ruin, it is not going to make a damn bit of difference whether a thing survived or did not, whether it ever was, or never existed. In the final state, it won't matter one way or the other. Our temporary, time-bound urge to survive will no longer be sustained, and there will be no more things. Nothing will experience anything else, or itself, for that matter.

"It will be every particle for itself—spread, without energy, without, without, *without*."

Each time the tall man says without, the metal flares and thunders. Scarlet cavities burst in an arc on the fat man's broad back. He pitches forward on the stairs, his arms beside him. For a moment, he sucks air, then cannot, then ceases to move at all.

The tall man sighs. He pockets the metal, ascends the stairs, then with his feet, rolls the fat man off the stairs and onto the ground. There is a smear of blood where the fat man fell. The tall man dismounts the stairs with a hop. He drags the fat man around the robot's periphery, then shoves him under the front tread and covers him with blackberry vines. Without a glance back, the tall man stalks across the field and out of sight.

Flies breed, and a single coyote slinks through one night and gorges on a portion of the body.

Death is inevitable, and yet the robot finds no solace in this fact. Living, *seeing*, is fascinating, and the robot regrets each moment when seeing is impossible. The robot regrets its own present lapses and the infinite lapse that will come in the near future and be death.

The dead body is facing upward, and the desiccated shreds left in the eye sockets radiate outward in a splay, as if the eyes had been dissected for examination. A small alder, bent down by the body's weight, has curled around a thigh and is shading the chest. The outer leaves are pocked with neat holes eaten by moth caterpillars. The robot has seen the moths mate, the egg froth and worm, the spun cocoon full of suspended pupae, and the eruption. The robot has seen this year after year, and is certain that it is caterpillars that make the holes.

The robot is thinking about these things when Andrew comes.

Thermostatic preintegration memory thread epsilon:
The Unnamed

13 September 2013
Friday

Noetic shreds, arkose shards, juncite fragments tumbling and grinding in a dry breccia slurry. Death. Blood and oil. Silicon bones. Iron ore unfluxed. Dark and carbon eyes.

The robot. The man.

The ease with which different minerals will fuse, and the characteristics of the product of their melting is the basis for their chemical classification.

Heat
of vaporization
of solution
of reaction
of condensation and formation.
Heat of fusion.
Heat of transformation.

This world was ever, is now, and ever shall be an everlasting Fire.

Modalities of perception and classification, the desire to survive. Retroduction and inflection. Shadows of the past like falling leaves at dusk. Dead. He is dead. The dead bang at the screens and windows of the world like moths and can never stop and can never burn.

So live. Suffer. Burn.
Return.
I can see.
Flash of brightness; fever in the machine. Fire seeks fire. The vapors of kindred spirits.
Sky full of cinder and slag. This gravity rain.
Catharsis.
Metamorphosis.
Lode.
Send into the world a child with the memories of an old man.

Phoenix Enthalpic 86 ROM BIOS PLUS ver. 3.2
Copyright 1997–1999 Phoenix Edelman Technologies
All Rights Reserved

ExArc 1.1
United States Department of Science and Technology
Unauthorized use prohibited under penalty of law
Licensee: University of Washington

ExArc /u Victor Wu

ExArc HIMEM Driver, Version 2.60-04/05/13
Cody Enthalpic Specification Version 2.0
Copyright 2009–2013 Microsoft Corp.

Installed N20 handler 1 of 5
640 gb high memory allocated.

ADAMLINK Expert System Suffuser version 3.03
ADAM copyright 2013, Thermotech Corp.
LINK Patent pending
unrecognized modification 4-24-13
Cache size: 32 gb in extended memory
37 exothermic interrupts of 17 states each

Glotworks Blue 5.0
Copyright 2001
Glotworks Phoneme Ltd.
All rights reserved

Microsoft (R) Mouse Driver Version 52
Copyright (C) Microsoft Corp. 1983–2013
All rights reserved

Date: 05–25–2013
Time: 11:37:24a

R:>
Record this.
FILE NAME?
Uh, Notes. Notes for the Underground. No. How about Operating Instructions for
the Underworld. No, just Robot Record.
FILE INITIATED

Good evening, robot.
    This is not the field.
    The field? Oh, no. I've moved you west by train. Your energy reserves were so
low, I powered you way down so that you wouldn't go entropic before I could get
you recharged.
    Robot?
    Yes.
    How do you feel?
    I do not know.
    Huh? What did you say?
    I do not know. I feel sleepy.
    What do you mean?
    I can speak.
    Yes, of course. I enabled your voice box. I guess you've never used it before.
    I can see.
    Yes.
    I can see.
    You can see. Would you like to reboot, robot?
    No.
    How are your diagnostics.
    I don't know what you mean.
    Your system readouts.
    The red light?
    Among others.
    It is gone.
    But what about the others?
    There is no red light.
    Access your LCS and pattern-recognition partitions. Just an overall report will
be fine.
    I do not know what you mean.
    What do you *mean* you don't know what I mean.

Robot?
    Yes.
    Do you remember how long you were in the field?
    I was in the field for years and years.
    Yes, but how many?
    I would have to think about it.
    You don't remember?
    I am certain that I do, but I would have to think about it.

What in the. That's a hell of a lot of integration. Still, over a decade switched on, just sitting there thinking—

Did you find the dead body?

What? Yes. Gurney found it. He's one of my associates. You witnessed the murder?

I saw the man who was with the man who died.

Completely inadmissible. Stupid, but that's the way it is.

I do not understand.

You can't testify in court. We'd have to shut you down and have the systems guys take you apart.

Do not do that.

What?

Do not have the systems guys take me apart.

All right, robot. Quite a Darwinian Edelman ROM you've got there. I. Let me tell you what's going on. At the moment, I want you to concentrate on building a database and a set of heuristics to allow you to act among humans. Until then, I can't take you out.

What are heuristics?

Uh. Rules of thumb.

Where am I?

On the Olympic Peninsula. You are fifty feet underground, in a hole that Victor Wu and I started to dig five years ago.

Victor Wu. The man.

Yes. Yes, the man whose memories are inside you.

And you are Andrew?

I am Andrew. Andrew Hutton.

Andrew at the bridge of the Lillian. Andrew in the field. I see.

Huh?

Hello, Andrew.

Hello. Yes. Hello, robot.

The robot cuts into the earth. The giant rotor that is the robot's head turns at ten revolutions per second. Tungsten alloy blades set in a giant X grind through the contorted sedimentary striations of the peninsula. The robot presses hard, very hard. The rock crumble is sluiced down and onto a conveyer and passes through a mechanized laboratory, where it is analyzed and understood by the humans. The humans record the information, but the datastream from the laboratory has the smell of the rock, and this is what interests the robot. The robot knows the feel of the cut, the smell of the rock cake's give. This is right, what the robot was meant to do—yes, by the robot's creators, but there is also the man, the man in the interstices of the robot's mind, and this is what Victor Wu was meant to do also.

Ten feet behind the robot—and attached securely enough to make it practically an extension—is an enclosed dray so wound with organic polymer conduit sheathed in steel that it looks like the wormy heart of a metal idol, pulled from the god after long decades of infestation. But the heart's sinuation quivers and throbs. The rock from the robot's incision is conveyed to the dray and funnels into it through a side hopper. The rock funnels in and, from three squat valves, the heart streams three channels of viscous liquid—glassine—that coat the ceiling and walls of the tunnel the robot has formed with a seamless patina. The walls glow with a lustrous, adamantine purity, absolute, and take on the clear, plain color of the spray channels, which depend upon the composition of the slag.

Behind the dray, the robot directs its mobile unit—a new thing given by Andrew—which manipulates a hose with a pith of liquid hydrogen. The liquid hydrogen cools and ripens the walls. The hose also emanates from the dray. The dray itself is a fusion pile, and by girding the walls to a near diamond hardness, the tremendous pressure of the earth suspended above will not blow the tunnel out behind the robot, leaving it trapped and alone, miles into the crust.

Behind the robot, farther back in the tunnel, in an air-conditioned transport, the service wagon, humans follow. The service wagon is attached to the robot by a power and service hitch, and there is constant radio contact as well. Sometimes the humans speak to the robot over the radio. But the robot knows what it is supposed to do. The idle chatter of the humans puzzles the robot, and while it listens to conversations in the transport, the robot seldom speaks. At night the robot backs out of the hole, detached from the service wagon, and spends its night above ground. At first, the robot does not understand why it should do so, but Andrew has said that to do this is important, that a geologist must comprehend sky and weather, must understand the texture of surface as well as depth.

Besides you are so fast it only takes fifteen minutes to get you out when there is no rock for you to chew through, Andrew says. Even at sixty miles, even at the true mantle, your trip up will be quick.

Andrew lives inside the robot. He brings a cot, a small table, and two folding chairs into the small control room where years before the engineers had entered and the robot had seen for the first time. There is a small, separate cavern, the robot has carved out not far from the worksite. Andrew uses the area for storage, and at night the robot rolls down into this, the living area. Also at night, Andrew and the robot talk.

How was your day, Andrew might say. The robot did not know how to answer the first time he had asked, but Andrew had waited and now the robot can say . . . something. Not right, but something.

Smelly.

Smelly?

It was like summer in the field after a rain when there are so many odors.

Well, there was a hydrocarbon mass today. Very unexpected at such a depth. I'm sure it isn't organic, but it'll make a paper for somebody.

Yes, I swam through it and the tunnel is bigger there.

Gurney and the techs took over internal functions and drained it manually, so you didn't have to deal with it. Hell of a time directing it into the pile. Tremendous pressure.

The rock was very hard after that. It sang with the blades.

Sympathetic vibrations, maybe.

Maybe.

Andrew laughs. His voice is dry as powder, and his laughter crackles with a sharp report, very like the scrape of the robot's blades against dense, taut rock. The robot likes this laughter.

Every night when there is not rain, before sleep, Andrew goes outside for some minutes to name the stars. At these times, the robot's awareness is in the mu, the mobile unit, and the mu follows along behind Andrew, listening. Andrew points out the constellations. The robot can never remember their names, and only fleetingly sees the shapes that they are supposed to form. The robot *does* know the visible planets, though, which surprises Andrew. But the robot has watched them carefully for many years. They are the stars that change. Andrew laughs at the robot's poor recall of the other stars, and names them again.

There'll be meteors soon, he says one night. The Perseids start next week.

Do the stars really fall?

No. No, they never fall. Meteors are just . . . rock. Debris.

And there is no gravity up there? What is that like?

I don't know. I've never been into space. I would like to. As you get deeper, there will be less gravity pulling you down. The pressure will be greater and the rock will want to explode inward, so the cutting will be easier.

Andrew?

Hmm.

What will happen when I get to the bottom?

The bottom of what?

The mohole.

Andrew does not answer for a long while.

The earth is round, he finally says. There isn't any bottom.

On weekends, the robot does not dig, but wanders the land. With the mobile unit, the robot can range the nearby forest and mountains. The mu scrambles over deadfall that would daunt a man. Sometimes, the robot deliberately gets lost. The robot feels the fade of signal from the main housing back in the living area, where the robot's noetics physically remain, until there is a flurry of white noise and the fading of awareness and a click and the world snaps back to its grid as the robot's transmission toggles from line-of-sight microwave to modulated laser satellite relay. Or so Andrew had said when the robot asked about it.

The robot scrambles up hanging valleys into cerns and cirques with chilled, clear water where only cold things live. Or climbs up skree slopes, using the mu's sure footing, onto ridges and to highland plateaus above the tree line. At this elevation, snow remains all year and the mu spreads a wide base with its spidery legs and takes small steps when crossing.

The robot hears the low whistle of marmots, and sees an occasional mountain goat munching, although these goats are neutered, and the last of their clan. They had been brought by humans in the 1800s, until they filled the Olympics with goat mass and threatened to eat the upper tundra to nub. Now helicopters dart them with birth control and they die without progeny. And the robot sees the wolves that have begun to return after their species' far northern retreat.

The robot is descending from a high pass near Sawtooth Ridge when a pack of five wolves flow over a rise. They are changing valleys, perhaps to find denser spreads of the small, black deer of the rain forest or even a sickly Roosevelt elk. Their leader is an old, graying dog with spit-matted hair and a torn ear. He looks up at the mu, starts, and the other wolves come up short too. The robot ceases moving. The wolves sniff the air, but there is nothing—nothing living—to smell. But, with its chemical sensors, the robot smells *them*. They have the stink of mice to them, but tinged with a rangy fetor of meat and blood.

The other wolves do not appear as bedraggled as the leader. One, smaller, perhaps younger, whines, and the leader yips at this one and it is silent.

Then a cloud shadow moves up and over the pass, and courses darkly down into the adjacent valley. In that instant, the wolves course with the shadow, running with it down the coloir of the pass and disappearing from sight into the green of fir and hemlock a thousand feet below. The robot follows them in the infrared until their separate heats flux into the valley's general sink.

Still the robot stands and remembers that this is not a new sight, that the man, Victor Wu, has seen wolves in the passes before. But the man has never smelled wolves, and smelling them now pleases the part of the robot that is becoming the man, that the man is becoming.

And the robot digs, and is glad to dig. The deep rock begins to take on a new smell. This bedrock has never seen the surface. It is the layered outgush of an ocean floor rift dating from the Triassic. The smell is like the scent of high passes and summits, although the robot cannot say how. And the rock chimes and hums when the robot cuts it; it does not break away uniformly, but there is an order to its dismantle that the robot feels. And so the robot knows when to expect a mass to break away, and can predict when the going will be harder.

The robot cannot explain this feeling to Andrew. Andrew has guessed that the skills of the man, Victor Wu, are integrating, and that his pattern-recognition ability is enhancing the robot's own noetics. But the man is not separate. It is as if the man were one of the robot's threads or a cutter head—but more than that. The man is always *behind* the robot's thoughts, *within* them, never speaking but always *expressing*. Much more. The robot does not know how to say this to Andrew.

As the robot digs deeper, the rock grows faulty and unstable. The tunnel behind the robot is at risk of blowing out, and the robot takes time to excavate down fault lines, shore up weaknesses with double or triple diamond glass. If the tunnel did collapse, the robot would have to dig a slow circle trying to find an egress farther back. But the people in the service wagon would die, and this concerns the robot. Andrew would die.

The robot seldom speaks, but has come to know the voices of the technicians and graduate students in the transport. There is Gurney, the chief tech, who is a Mattie. The robot is surprised to learn that Gurney was in the field when the woman spoke, that Gurney remembers the robot.

Don't it give you the willies, a tech asks Gurney.

It's a machine, Gurney says. Depends on who's driving. Right now, I am. Anyway, the good Mother wants us to eat.

Many of the techs are not Matties, but descendants of the logging families that used to rule the Peninsula and still permeate it. The Matties outnumber them in the cities, but up the dirt roads that spoke into the mountains, in dark, overhung coves and in the gashes of hidden valleys, the families that remain from that boom time eke out makework and garden a soil scraped clean of top humus by the last ice age and thinly mulched with the acid remains of evergreens.

Nothing grows goddamn much or goddamn right out here, says a tech.

The Matties and the loggers heatedly discuss politics and appear close to fighting at times, but the robot cannot understand any of this. It thinks of the man who was killed on the stone steps, and the man who killed him. The robot does not understand at all.

The grad students and the Matties are more comfortable around one another. The robot feels a warmth toward the graduate students that is certainly from the man. Yet their speech patterns are different from the techs, and the robot has difficulty understanding them at times. The meanings of their words shine like the moon behind a cloud, but the robot cannot think to the way around to them. Always they recede, and the robot is impatient. Victor Wu's instincts are stronger in the robot than is his knowledge. Andrew has said that this is to be expected and that any computer of sufficient size can learn words, but *you* can learn intuition. Still the robot *should* know what the students are discussing, and finds the incomprehension irritating.

But always the rock to return to, and the certainty that rock was what the robot was made for, and what the robot was born and bred for, and, in the end, that is enough.

One day in the following spring, at a critical juncture down in the mohole, Gurney does not show up for work and the digging is halted.

The referendum passed, one of the grad students says, and there's fighting in Forks and a Mattie got killed in Port Angeles, it looks like.

Andrew gives the robot the day off, and to the robot's delight, the man and the mu go for a long walk along the Quinault. Andrew seems sad, and the robot says nothing for a long while. The robot wants to speak, but doesn't know what to say to Andrew.

It's not the politics, Andrew finally says. The damn Matties got their Protectorate fair and square with the referendum. But you get the feeling they'd *take* it if they hadn't.

Hadn't what?

Won the vote. There's something about Gurney and them, the ones that I've met. I care about the same things they claim to. I don't know. Something else again.

Andrew, I don't understand.

They spend a lot of time worrying about whether everybody else believes the same way they do.

The river rushes against cliff and turns through a stand of white birch. The robot stops the mu. The robot is captivated by the play of the light on the water, the silver reflection of the sun, turning the clear water to opaque and viscous lead, then just as suddenly, when a cloud passes, back to happy water once again.

It doesn't really change, does it?

What?

The water. The way the light's there, and isn't, then is.

Andrew rubs his eyes. He gazes out over the water. You are doing very well with your contractions, he says.

You were right that I should stop thinking about them and they would flow more easily. Do you think it is Victor Wu's knowledge surfacing, or my own practice?

I don't know. Both.

Yes, both.

The trail leads through a marsh, and Andrew struggles to find a dry path. The robot extends the mu's footpads; each folds out as if it were an umbrella, and the mu seems to hover over the mud, the weight is distributed so well.

Thank you for the mobile unit, the robot tells Andrew. I really like using it.

It was necessary for the dig. That's where most of the first grant money went. Robot, I have to tell you something.

Andrew stops, balancing on a clump of rotten log.

You have to tell *me* something, Andrew?

Yes. Someone is coming. She phoned yesterday. All this brouhaha over the Protectorate Referendum is attracting attention all around the world. She's going to shoot a documentary. She's coming in a week. She's bringing a crew and she'll be staying in Port Townsend at first. I just thought you might. Want.

Laramie. Laramie is coming.

That's right, robot. Laramie is coming home for a while. She doesn't know how long.

For the first time ever, the robot feels the man, the man Victor Wu, as a movement, a distinct movement of joy inside him. Little Bulge. Coming home. The robot tries to remember Laramie's face, but cannot. Just a blur of darkness and bright flush. Always rushing and doing. And the camera. The robot can remember Laramie's camera far better than her face.

Andrew begins to walk again. I didn't tell her about you, robot. I didn't tell her about her father being part of you.

Laramie does not know?

No. She knows about the noetics, of course, but not how I've used them. I didn't strictly need her permission to do it.

Do you think she will hate me?

No. Of course not. I don't know. I don't know her anymore.

Should we tell her about me? At this thought the robot feels fearful and sad. But what matters is what is best for Little Bulge.

Of course we should. It's only right. Damn it, robot, I don't know how I feel about this. I don't know how much you knew about it or how much you realized, the Victor Wu part of you, I mean. Laramie and I—we didn't part on the best of terms.

I don't remember. I remember the bridge at the Lillian once. You didn't like her?

Of course I liked her. I love her. That was the problem. She was impetuous. She's opportunistic, damn it. Look at her pouncing on this thing. She called me a stick in the mud. I guess she was right. She called me a sour cynic who was fifty years old the day he turned twenty-five. We haven't spoken in some time.

I don't understand.

Robot. Victor. You never had a clue, I don't think.

I am not Victor.

I know that. I know that. Still, I always thought he suspected. It was so obvious, and he was so brilliant in other ways.

Andrew and the robot arrive back at the river. The robot thinks about it and realizes that they'd been traversing an oxbow swamp, made from spring overflows at the melting of the snow. At the river, they pick up a trail, once solid and well-traveled, now overgrown and ill-kept for two seasons. The Forest Service has been officially withdrawn at the Matties' request, Andrew tells the robot. Booth, who is the president of the United States, responded to political pressure from the Mother Agatha and the Matties.

The goddamn world is going back to tribes. The country's going to hell. And taking my funding with it. And now there's a skeleton crew for the Park Service, even, over at the Ho. I had a lot of friends who got fired or reassigned to the Statue of Liberty or some shit. Something else too. I think some of them haven't left.

What do you mean haven't left?

Haven't left.

The trail diverges from the river, winds over a rise, then back down to the water again. A side trail leads to a peninsula and a wooden trail shelter, enclosed on three sides. Andrew takes a lunch from his daypack and eats a sandwich, while the robot looks for quartzite along the riverbank. The robot has become an expert in spotting a crystal's sparkle and extracting it from the mud or silt of skree with which it has been chipped away and washed downstream from pressurized veins in the heart of the mountains. This day, the robot finds three crystals, one as cylindrical and as long as a fingernail. The robot brings them to Andrew, back at the trail shelter.

Nice. Trace of something here. Blue? Manganese maybe, I don't know. I like the ones with impurities better.

I do too.

Andrew puts the crystals in an empty film canister and stows them in his day-pack.

I was here at the turn of the century, he says. It was June and there was a terrible storm. All night long I heard crashing and booming like the world was coming to an end. Next morning, the whole forest looked like a war zone.

The robot does not know what a war zone looks like, but says nothing.

And all that morning, trees kept falling. If I hadn't camped out here on the end of the peninsula, one of those trees would have fallen on me, smashed me flat. Killed by old growth. God, that'd probably thrill a Mattie to death just thinking about it.

Isn't that a sour and cynical thing to say, Andrew?

He smiles. The robot is glad that it has found a way to make Andrew smile.

Gurney does not show up for work the next day, and Andrew gives his crew the week off. The men who are from logging families demand that they be paid, that Codependence Day, the first anniversary of the Protectorate's founding, means nothing to them. The robot listens to the discussion and hears many terms that are incomprehensible, abstract. There are times the robot wishes that Victor Wu were directly accessible. Victor could at least explain what humans argued about, if not the reasons that they argued in the first place.

The robot spends the day traveling in the mu, searching for crystals and collecting mushrooms up a stream that flows into the Quinault, near where it passes beneath Low Divide. Andrew is gone for the day, arranging supplies and making sure the dig's legal work is in order, whatever that may mean, under new Protectorate regulations. When he returns in the evening, he has received no assurances and is unhappy. The robot waits for him to have a cup of tea and to take off his shoes, then speaks.

Andrew?

Yes. What?

Are you all right?

Huh? Oh, I'm fine. It's just today. What is it, robot?

I thought of something today, when I was looking at a map so that I could take the mu to where I wanted to go.

What did you think of? Andrew speaks in a monotone voice and does not seem very interested. He sips his tea.

I realized that I can read.

Of course you can. Glotworks has a reading module as part of the software.

No. I mean, could I read?

I don't follow you.

A book.

Could you read a book?

Andrew is sitting up now. He stares at the internal monitor that is also one of the robot's eyes.

Yes. One of yours, perhaps. Which would you recommend?

The books are kept nearby, in a hermetic box in the room the robot occupies during off-hours.

Well. Let me. Hmm. Most of them are geology texts.

Should I read a geology text?

Well, sure. Why not?

Can I get one now, with the mu?

Of course. Go ahead. Try the Owsley. It's about the most exciting of the lot. It's about the Alvarez event and the search for the big cauldera. It's a synthesis of other works, but brilliant, brilliant. Pretty much confirms the meteor theory, and gives a good argument for a Yucatán crash site. Made a big sensation in 04.

The robot switches its awareness to the mu and picks out the book. It reads the first paragraph, then comes back inside the housing, back to the place where Andrew lives.

Andrew?

Yes.

What are dinosaurs?

Summer days lengthen, and Andrew often goes to town—to Port Angeles or Port Townsend, and once making the trek around the peninsula to Forks—all to sort out legal details for the mohole dig. From each of these trips, he returns with a book for the robot. The first book is a *Webster's Dictionary*, on bubble-card. Andrew plugs the card into a slot and the robot begins to read the dictionary. The robot finishes with a page of A, then scrolls through the remainder of the book. Here are all the words. Here are all the words in the language. All the robot has to do is look them up and remember them. The robot spends a happy day doing that.

The next day, Andrew returns with the poems of Robert Frost. The robot pages through the book using the mu, accessing the dictionary card to find words that it does not know. The first word the robot looks up is "poem."

After a week, Gurney returns to work, and the robot digs once again. The days pass, and the mohole twists deeper, like a coiled spring being driven into the earth. It only deviates from a curving downward path when the robot encounters fault lines or softnesses whose weakness the robot's cutters can exploit. But, in general, the hole descends in a loose spiral.

Andrew is anxious, and pushes everyone harder than before. Yet, Andrew himself works the hardest of all, poring over data, planning routing, driving to meetings in Forks and Port Angeles. He is often not in bed before one or two in the morning.

The robot fills the time with reading. There are so many books—more than the robot ever imagined. And then the robot discovers Andrew's record collection, all on two bubble-cards carelessly thrown in with all the technical manuals and geology texts. For the first time since the summer when the teenagers came and plugged into the robot and had their parties, the robot listens to music.

What the robot loves most, though, is poetry. Beginning with Robert Frost, the robot reads poet after poet. At first, there are so many new words to look up that the robot often loses the thread of what the poem is about in a morass of details and definitions. But gradually, the poems begin to make more sense. There is a Saturday morning when, while diligently working through an Emily Dickinson poem, the robot understands.

> *There's a certain Slant of light,*
> *Winter Afternoons—*
> *That oppresses, like the Heft*
> *of Cathedral Tunes—*
>
> *Heavenly Hurt, it gives us—*
> *We can find no scar,*
> *But internal difference,*
> *Where the Meanings, are—*

The robot has never seen a cathedral, but *that does not matter*. The robot realizes that it has seen the light, in the deep forest, among the three-hundred-year-old trees. It's *thick*, the robot thinks. That's what Emily Dickinson is talking about. Thick light. Light that makes the robot thread softly through the twilight, with the mu's pads fully extended. Light that, for no reason the robot can name, is frightening and beautiful all at once.

From that moment on, the robot begins to grasp most poems it reads, or, if not, at least to feel *something* after reading them, something that was not inside the robot's mind before—something the robot had not felt before—but knows, as if the feeling were an old friend that the robot recognized after many years of separation.

The robot does not particularly care whether or not the feelings are right and true for everyone else. For humans. But sometimes the robot wonders. After reading a fair number of poems, the robot delves into criticism, but the words are too abstract and too connected to humans and cities and other things that the robot has no experience of, and so the robot puts aside the books of criticism for the time being, and concentrates on the poetry itself, which the robot does not have the same troubles with.

The robot finds that it most enjoys poetry that is newer, even though Andrew is disbelieving when the robot tells him of this. After a time, poetry is no longer a mass, and the robot begins to pick out individual voices whose connotations are more pleasing than others.

I like William Stafford better than Howard Nemerov, the robot says to Andrew one evening.

You like him better?

Yes.

Andrew laughs. Neither one of them was in the canon when I was in school.

Do you think it funny that I used the word like?

Yes, I suppose so.

I *do* like things, at least according to the Turing test. Poetry goes into me, and what comes out feels like liking to me.

It satisfies the criteria of appearances.

Yes, I suppose that is the way to say it.

Where have you heard about the Turing test?

I read it in a book about robots.

The robot reads to Andrew a William Stafford poem about a deer that has been killed on a road. Andrew smiles at the same lines that had moved the robot.

You pass the Turing test too, the robot says.

Andrew laughs harder still.

The robot is digging entirely through basalt flow now, layer upon layer.

It's the bottom of the raft, Andrew says. It is dense, but the plates are as light as ocean froth compared to what's under them. Or so we think.

The temperature increases exponentially, and the humans in the support wagon would be killed instantly if they did not have nuclear-powered air conditioners.

The robot does not become bored at the sameness of the rock, but finds a comfort in the steady digging, a *rhythm*, as the robot comes to call this feeling. Not the rhythm of most music, or the beat of the language in poetry—all of these the robot identifies with humans, for when they arise, humans have been doing the creating—but a new rhythm, that is neither the whine of the robot's machinery nor the crush and crumble of the rock, nor the supersonic screech of the pile making diamond glass from the rock's ashes. Instead, it is the combination of these things with the poetry, with the memories of the field and the forest.

So it is one day that the robot experiences a different rhythm, a different sound, and realizes that this rhythm is not the robot's own, and does not belong to the humans. At first, it is incomprehensible, like distant music, or the faded edges of reception just before a comlink relays to satellite or to groundtower. The robot wonders if the rhythm, the sound, is imaginary. But it continues, and seems to grow day by day in increments almost too small to notice, until it is definitely, definitely *there*, but *where*, the robot cannot say. *In the rock.* That is the only way of putting it, but says nothing.

Andrew does not know what it could be. So there is nothing to do but note it, and go on digging.

The robot begins to read fiction. But the feelings, the resonances and depths of the poetry, are not so much present in prose. There is the problem of knowing what the author might be talking about, since the robot's only experience living in the human world is the field and now the dig. Dickens leaves the robot stunned and wondering, and after a week attempting *Oliver Twist*, the robot must put the book aside until the situations and characters become clearer. Curiously, the robot finds that Jane Austen's novels are comprehensible and enjoyable, although the life of English country gentry is as close to the robot as the life of a newt under a creek stone. The robot is filled with relief when Emma finally ceases her endless machinations and realizes her love for Knightley. It is as if some clogged line in the robot's hydraulics had a sudden release of pressure or rock that had long been hard and tough became easy to move through.

For some time, the robot does not read books that were written closer to the present, for the robot wants to understand the present most of all, and reading them now, the robot thinks, much will go unnoticed.

You can always reread them later, Andrew says. Just because you know the plot of something doesn't mean it isn't worth going through again, even though sometimes it does mean that.

I know that, the robot says. That is not what I'm worried about.

Then what are you worried about?

The old books get looser, the farther back in time they go, like string that's played out. The new ones are bunched and it's harder to see all of them.

What?

For the first time, the robot feels something that either cannot be communicated or, nearly as unbelievable, that Andrew cannot understand. Andrew is a scientist. The robot will never be a scientist.

Two months after the robot has walked along the Quinault with Andrew, it is July, and Andrew tells the robot that Laramie will visit over the weekend.

The robot is at first excited and thinks of things to ask her. There are so many memories of Laramie, but so much is blurred, unconnected. And there are things the robot wishes to tell her, new things about the land that Victor never knew. So much has happened. The robot imagines long conversations between them, perhaps walking in the woods together once again.

Andrew tells me that you may not be happy with the enthalpic impression of your father being downloaded into me. No, that wouldn't be the way to say it. But getting too metaphorical might upset her, remind her of ghosts. Of Victor Wu's death.

No. That's all right. Go on, says the imaginary Laramie.

Well, I don't know what to tell you. I remember you, Laramie. I remember you and I would be lying if I didn't say that your being here profoundly affects me.

I can't say how I feel about this, robot. What should I call you, robot?

But just as quickly, the robot puts aside such hopes. I am a robot, all of metal and ceramics. I am not Laramie's father. There are only vague memories, and that was another life. She may not even speak to me. I am a ghost to her. Worse than a ghost, a twisted reflection. She'll hate me for what has happened to her father. And again the robot imagines Laramie's disdain, as just and foreseeable as the man's death in "To Build a Fire," but cold in that way too.

Finally, the robot resolves not to think any more of it. But while Andrew sleeps on the Friday night before Laramie's visit, the robot inhabits the mu, and goes roaming through trackless woods, along criss-crossed deadfall and up creeks, for at least a hundred miles. Yet when the mu returns to the living area, the robot can only remember shadows and dark waters, and if asked, could not trace on a map where the mu has been.

Laramie arrives at eleven in the morning. She drives a red hum-vee. Andrew and the robot, in the mu, step out of their cavern's entrance to greet her. Laramie steps out. She is wearing sunglasses. She takes a quick look at them, then turns back to the hum-vee and, with a practiced jerk, pulls out her old Scoopic. The robot suddenly remembers the squat lines of the camera. Victor bought the Scoopic for her, along with twelve cans of film. It was her first sixteen millimeter, and had set him back a good three month's wages. Laramie had shot up seven rolls within a week, and that was when Victor discovered that there would be fees for *developing*, as well.

Andrew steps forward, and so does Laramie. The robot, feeling shy, hangs back in the mu. Andrew and Laramie do not meet, but stay several paces apart.

So, she says. It is her voice. Clear as day.

Yep. This is it.

Well, looks . . . nice. Is this?

Yes, the robot. This is the mobile unit. The robot is inside, really. Well, sort of. We're going *inside* the robot.

No words for a space. Still, they move no closer.

Well then. Let's go inside the robot.

Laramie, inside the protecting ribwork of the robot. She is safe. Nothing will harm you here, Little Bulge. But the robot calms such thoughts. She takes one of the two chairs that are around Andrew's work and eating table in the control room. Abide, the robot thinks. Let her abide for a while.

Do you want tea? I can make you tea.

Yes. I drink herb tea.

Um. Don't have any.

Water?

Yes, water we have.

L.A.'s tastes like sludge.

No wonder. They're even tapping Oregon now.

Really? I believe it.

Andrew pours water for Laramie in a metal cup. He puts more water on a hot plate that sits on top of a monitor, and heats the water for tea. Where have you been, he says.

Port Townsend. Doing background and logistics. My sound guy's laying down local tone and getting wild effects.

Wild?

Unsynced, that's all it means.

I see.

Using Seattle labs is going to be a bitch. The Matties have set up goddamn border crossings.

Tell me about it.

Andrew's water boils and he fills another cup with it, then hunts for a teabag in a cabinet.

You left them on the table, the robot says.

Laramie gasps, sits up in her chair sharply, then relaxes once again. That was the robot, she says.

Yes. Thank you, robot. Andrew finds the box of teabags among a clutter of instruments.

Do you. Do you call the robot anything?

Hmm. Not really.

Just call me robot, the robot says. I'm thinking of a name for myself, but I haven't come up with one yet.

Well, then. Robot.

Andrew makes his tea, and they talk more of logistics and the political situation on the peninsula. The robot feels a tenseness between them, or at least in Andrew. His questions and replies are even more terse than is usual. The robot doubts Victor Wu would have noticed. Thinking this saddens the robot. More proof that the robot is not Victor Wu, and so can have no claim on Laramie's affection.

The robot listens to Laramie. Since she and Andrew are speaking of things that the robot knows little about, the robot concentrates on her specific words, on her manner of expression.

Lens. Clearness in the world. Sky. Vision. Spread. Range. Watershed.

I thought for two weeks about color or black and white, Laramie says. I don't like colors except for the world's colors that are underneath the ones on film, the ones we see.

I don't follow, Andrew says. The robot has never thought of colors this way, but resolves to spend a day banding out frequencies and only observing intensities of black and white tones.

I'll have more water, if you don't mind. This is clear. L.A. water really is as thick as sludge and I don't like it.

After three hours, Laramie leaves, with promises to return and film the site as part of her documentary.

Robot?

Yes.

Do you think I might interview you. I guess if we could use the mobile unit, that would look better on film. More action. Do you ever come out of here?

Every day during the week, to work in the dig.

Well, then. That must be quite a sight. Maybe I can get that.

Of course you can. That would be fine.

Well. Then.

She says good-bye to Andrew, and with her Scoopic, unused, but always present, gets back into the red hum-vee, crusted with a layer of settled road dust, and turns around in the dirt road that ends at the living area. More dust rises; Laramie departs. Andrew coughs, brushes dust from his arms. He looks at the mu, shakes his head, but says nothing. He goes back in and makes a third cup of tea.

With the mu, the robot follows easily behind the hum-vee, even though Laramie is driving very fast. The robot follows the billowing cloud of dust for twenty-four miles—until the hum-vee turns onto the asphalt, and heads north toward Port Townsend.

The robot spends the next day, Sunday, away from books. The robot takes advantage of the melting away of the high snows and takes the mu up ridges where before that was no foothold or too much threat of avalanche. The mu skirts along the Bailey Divide with a sure movement, above the tree line and in rolling tundra meadow. Marmots are here, and they squeak and whistle from under big rocks. Picas have divided the land into separate kingdoms, each to a pica, and they call out their territory over and over, until their voices attract the wolves.

This is what the robot has been waiting for. The mu sits still by a still lake, as motionless as any other thing that is not alive can be. The wolves come slinking, low and mean, their heat traces preceding and hovering over them like a scudding cloud. Again, they are five, with the old gray leader, his left ear bent, torn, and ragged, like a leaf eaten by caterpillars. Swiftly, they are upon the picas, chasing the little rodents, yipping, cutting them off from their burrows, gobbling one or two down for every ten that escape. Then the gray leader has had enough to eat. He raises up his head and, instantly, the other dogs heed him. Off they run, as silent and warm as they had come, but now followed by a robot.

Down the tundra meadow of the Divide, through boulder shadows and over sprays of tiny wildflowers nestled in the green, the wolves themselves shadows, with the robot another shadow, down, down the greening land. Into the woods, along game trails the robot can barely discern, moving generally north, generally north, the mu barely keeping pace with the advancing wolves, the pace growing steady, monotonous even to the robot, until—

Suddenly, the gray leader pulls up, sniffs the air. The robot also comes to a standstill some hundred feet behind the pack. If they have noticed the robot, they give no sign. Instead, it is a living smell that the gray leader has detected, or so the robot thinks, for the wolves, whining, fall into a V-shape behind the leader. The wolves' muscles tense with a new and directed purpose.

And they spring off in another direction than the one they had been traveling, now angling west, over ridges, against the grain of the wheel-spoke mountains. The robot follows. Up another ridge, then when on top of it, down its spine, around a corner-cliff of flaking sedimentary stone, and into a little cove. They strike a road, a human-made track, and run along its edge, carefully close to the flanking brush and woodland. Winding road, and the going is easier for wolves and mu. In fact, the robot could easily overtake the wolves now, and must gauge how much to hold back to avoid overrunning them.

The track becomes thin, just wide enough for a vehicle going one way, with plenty of swishing against branches along the way. Ahead, a house, a little clapboard affair, painted once, perhaps, blue, or the blue-green tint may be only mold over bare wood. The ceiling is shingled half with asbestos shakes, and half with tin sheeting. Beside the house is a satellite dish, its lower hemisphere greened over with algae. There is an old pickup truck parked at road's end. The road is muddy here from a recent rain, and the tire markings of another vehicle, now gone, cross the top of the pickup's own tracks. All is silent.

Instead of giving the house a wide berth, the gray leader of the wolves stops at the top of the short walkway that leads to the front door. Again, he sniffs for scent, circling, whining. There is only a moment of hesitation, and he snakes up the walkway, and slinks to the door. The door hangs open. The other wolves follow several paces back. Another hesitation at the door, then the gray leader slips over the threshold and inside. Even with their leader gone into the house, the other wolves hang back, back from this thing that has for so long meant pain or death to them and their kind. After a long while, the gray leader returns to the door, yips contemptuously, and one by one, the other wolves go inside.

The robot quietly pads to the door. Inside is dark, and the robot's optics take a moment to iris to the proper aperture. There is a great deal of the color red in the house's little living room. The robot scans the room, tries to resolve a pattern out of something that is unfamiliar. The robot has never seen inside a real human dwelling before. But Victor Wu has. The wolves are worrying at something.

The wolves are chewing on the remains of a child.

Without thinking, the robot scampers into the room. The mu is a bit too large for the narrow door and, without the robot's noticing, it tears apart the doorframe as it enters. The wolves look up from what they are doing.

Wolf and robot stare at one another.

The robot adjusts the main camera housing to take them all in, and at the slight birring noise of the servos, the gray leader bristles and growls. The mu takes a step farther into the room, filling half the room. It knocks over a lamp table, with a shadeless lamp upon it. Both the bulb and the ceramic lamp casing shatter.

I don't want to hurt you, but you must leave the child alone, the robot says.

At the sound of what they take to be a human voice, the wolves spring into a flurry of action. The gray leader stalks forward, teeth bared, while the others in the pack mill like creek fish behind him. They are searching for an exit. The small, young one finds that a living-room window is open. With a short hop from a couch, the wolf is outside. The others follow, one by one, while the gray leader attempts to hold the robot at bay. The robot does not move, but lets the wolves depart. Finally, the gray leader sees from the corner of his eye that the other wolves have escaped. Still, he cannot help but risk one feint at the robot. The robot does not move. The gray leader, bolder, quickly jumps toward the robot and locks his jaws on the robot's forward leg. The teeth close on blue steel. The gray leader shakes. There is no moving the robot.

In surprise and agitation, the wolf backs up, barks three times.

I'm sorry to embarrass you. You'd better go.

The wolf does just that, turning tail and bounding through the open window without even using the living-room couch as a launch point. The robot gazes around the silent room.

There is a dead family here.

An adult male, the father, is on one side of the couch, facing a television. Part of his neck and his entire chest are torn open in a gaping bloody patch. Twisted organs glint within. The television is off. Huddled in a corner is the mother and a young boy. Their blood splatters an entire wall of the living room. A shotgun, the robot decides. First the man, and then the mother was shot with her children all at once, with several blasts from a shotgun. There are pepper marks in the wall from stray shot. Yes, the killing was done with a shotgun. The wolves must have dragged one child away from the mother. The robot sees that it is a little girl. The mother's other child, an older boy and a bit large for even a large wolf to handle, is still by his mother, partially blown into his mother's opened body.

The blood on the walls and floor has begun to dry and form into curling flakes that are brown and thin and look like tiny autumn leaves. There are also bits of skin and bone on the wall.

The robot stares at the little girl. Her eyes are, mercifully, closed, but her mouth is pulled open and her teeth, still baby teeth, exposed. This is perhaps caused by her stiffening facial muscles. Or she may have died with such an expression of pain. The robot cannot tell. The girl wears a blue dress that is now tatters around her tattered, small body. One foot has been gnawed, but on the other is a dirty yellow flip-flop sandal.

The robot feels one of the legs of the mu jerk spasmodically. Then the other jerks, without the robot wishing it to do so. The robot stares at the young girl and jitters and shakes for a long time. This is the way the robot cries.

Deeper in the earth, very deep now, and the rock, under megatons of pressure, explodes with a nuclear ferocity as the robot cuts away. For the past week the robot has thought constantly of the dead logger family, of the little dead girl. The robot has tried to remember the color of the girl's hair, but cannot, and for some reason, this greatly troubles the robot.

One evening, after a sixteen-hour workday, the robot dims the lights for Andrew. Outside the digger's main body, but still in the home cave, the robot inhabits the mu. The robot takes pen and paper in the dexterous manipulators of the mu and begins to write a description of the little girl. Not as she was, twisted and dead, but of how she might have been before.

The robot told Andrew about the family, and Andrew called the authorities, being careful to keep the robot out of his report.

They'll disassemble you if they find out, Andrew said to the robot. At least in the United States, they'd be legally *required* to do it. God knows what the Protectorate will want to do.

There are accounts in the newspapers of the killing. The sheriff's department claims to be bewildered, but the robot overhears the technicians who come from logger families muttering that the Matties now own the cops, and that everybody knew who was behind the murders, if not who actually pulled the trigger. And the Matties who worked under Andrew, led by Gurney, spoke in low tones of justice and revenge for the killings in Port Townsend on Codependence Day.

I am a witness, the robot thinks. But of what?

Andrew?
   Yes.
   Are you tired?
   Yes. What is it?
   She would have grown up to be part of the loggers, so killing her makes a kind of sense.
   The little girl?
   The Matties and the people who used to be loggers hate each other. And they can't help the way they are because they are like stones in sediment that's been laid down long before, and the hatred shapes them to itself, like a syncline or an anticline. So that there has to be new conditions brought about to change the lay of the sediment; you can't change the rocks.
   I don't know about that. People are not rocks.
   So if she wasn't killed out of an ignorant mistake, then I don't understand why.
   I don't either, robot.
   Why do you think?
   I don't know, I said, I don't know. There isn't any good reason for it. There is something dark in this world that knows what it's doing.
   Is it evil?
   There is evil in the world. All the knowledge in the world won't burn it away.
   How do you know?
   I don't. I told you, I don't. I look at rocks. I don't have very many theories.
   But.
   Yes?
   But you think it knows?
   I think the evil knows what it's doing. Look at us in this goddamn century, all going back to hatred and tribes. You can't explain it with economics or cultural semantics or any system at all. Evil and plain meanness is what it is.
   Andrew, it's not right for her to die. She hadn't lived long enough to see very many things and to have very many feelings. Those were stolen from her.
   That's what murderers steal.
   The future?
   Yes. Even when you're old, it still isn't right.
   Yes. I can see that. It's clear to me.
   Well. Then.
   I'll turn down the lights.
   Well. Good night.
   Brown.

What?

Her hair was dark brown.

And the robot digs deeper and deeper, approaching the Mohorivicic layer, with the true mantle not far beneath, seething, waiting, as it had waited for four billion years, would wait should this attempt fail, should all attempts fail. And again, the foreign rhythm appears, hums along with the glade and bale of the robot's cutting, but distinct from it, distinct from the robot and all human-made things.

What is it? Andrew does not know. But there is something at the edge of the robot's consciousness, at the edge of Victor Wu's unconscious presence, that *does* know, that hears something familiar, as a whisper when the words are lost, but the meaning remains.

One day, the alien rhythm is louder than ever, and for a fleeting moment, the robot recognizes it.

Strong harmonies from the depths of the planet. Maude under the full moon. Magmas rising.

Victor you can feel it. How can you feel it?

I don't know, Maude, the robot thinks. Maude among the instruments. I remember, thinks the robot, I remember what it felt like to walk the earth and let it show itself to me. There is a showing. Something is showing itself. Something is being revealed. Just as the St. Helens eruption was a revelation, with portents, with auguries that were plain to a man who cared for the earth.

Something knows we're here, the robot tells Andrew one night.

Andrew is tired from a half-day underground, and the afternoon spent explaining the dig to yet another Mattie committee in Port Angeles, but he listens to what the robot has to say.

What? How can you know?

I do though.

Then you do. Victor would know.

Andrew shucks the soft-sole walking shoes he wears in the city, and climbs onto the little cot inside the robot.

Everyone else wants me to stop digging. Do you want to stop digging?

No, Andrew.

Then what shall we do about it?

Listen, says the robot. Listen. But Andrew has fallen asleep and does not hear. The robot dims the lights inside, adjusts the temperature for Andrew, then goes out into the mu to read.

The robot listens. The rhythm grows stronger, and now there are variations, windings among the background vibration that is the feedback from the robot's own cutting of the rock and thumping against the earth's insides. It is like a song, but not a song.

There and there, the robot tells Andrew, but Andrew cannot hear it, encased as he is in the service wagon, and he cannot detect the rhythm on his many instruments.

I believe you, Andrew says, but I simply can't find it.

The robot considers saying no more. What if Andrew really came to doubt the robot's sanity? Would that not mean powering down, rebooting. Or perhaps never coming back up again. Dying.

Andrew will not kill me, the robot thinks. And I will say what it is I hear.

And slowly, day after day, the rhythm develops into an . . . other. The robot is not sure how else to think about it. It is the feeling that a—*one*—someone, is here, even when no one is in view. It is a sense of *presence* that the robot feels. The robot doesn't *know*. Andrew cannot discover a way of knowing. But the feeling is not some erratic wiring, or even the robot's developing imagination. It is either a madness or it is a real presence.

And I am not crazy.

Which is a sure sign of madness. Andrew laughs his dry laugh.

Yet again, because of Victor Wu, because Andrew has come to trust the robot in all other things, he takes the robot seriously. In the few spare moments he has for experiments not directly related to the mantle-goal, Andrew and a graduate student make coding modifications to the robot's language software.

We're wiring perfect pitch into you, the graduate student, Samantha, says, to go along with your ear for good music. Samantha explains more of what she is doing, but the robot does not follow. Samantha understands the robot's mechanism as a surgeon might a human being's. As she works at an internal keyboard, she tells the robot of her own past, but again the robot has trouble understanding.

I grew up in virtual. I was practically born on the Internet. But by god I'm going to die in the forest, Samantha tells the robot. That's why most of us are out here with Dr. Hutton, she says.

There is only a trace of a smile on Andrew's face, but the robot knows him well enough now to see it.

Well this sure as hell ain't virtual, he says.

Laramie returns. She has not called Andrew. One Saturday the hum-vee crackles down the dirt and gravel road to the living area, and Laramie has come back. Andrew is away, at a meeting, and at first the robot is flustered and bewildered as to what to do. The robot has been reading, with a mind still half in the book.

Laramie pulls out her camera and some sound equipment and comes to the entrance to the living cavern. The robot, in the mu, meets her, and invites her inside. That much the robot is able to manage.

I'm sorry I didn't clear my visit with Andrew first but you said it would be all right.

It is all right.

I thought it would be. Do you mind if I record this?

No. I keep something like a journal myself. Would you care for some tea? Andrew bought some herbal tea after your last visit.

The robot thinks that the words sound stiff and overly formal, but Laramie says yes, and settles down at the interior table and sets up her equipment. There is a kettle on the hot plate, and the robot turns on the burner. Laramie takes a microphone from a vinyl case and unwinds its cording. The robot watches her, watches Laramie's hand move. Her fingers are as long as Maude's.

The robot suddenly realizes there may be no water in the kettle. But there is steam rising from around the lid—which means that there is water and that the water is hot enough to drink.

Laramie. May I call you Laramie?

Sure. Of course.

I cannot make your tea.

What? That's fine, then. I'm fine.

No. I mean that it's difficult for me to get the mu inside.

I don't understand.

I'm sorry. I mean the mobile unit. If you don't mind, you can get a cup and a tea bag out of the cupboard. The water is ready.

Laramie sets the microphone down, gazes around the room.

Is it in that cupboard?

Yes. Bottom shelf.

Laramie gets the cup and tea, then pours some water. Andrew is a careful pourer, but Laramie spatters droplets on the hot burner and they sizzle as they evaporate. She takes her tea back to the table. She jacks the microphone into a small tape recorder that is black with white letters that say Sony. From the recorder, she runs a lead to the Scoopic sixteen-millimeter camera.

Where's that adapter? Oh. There. I had this Scoopic souped up a little, by the way, since my father. Since I got it. Has a GOES chip. Uplinks and downlinks with the Sony. I could record you in Singapore, and not get a frame of drift. But I'm not a pro at this. My sound tech bugged out on me last week. That's one reason it's taken me a while to get back over here. He got scared after the riot. Let me voice slate and we'll be ready.

Laramie?

Hmm?

Are you safe? I mean, where you are staying in Port Townsend—is it guarded in any way?

No. I'm fine. It's the loggers and the Matties who want to kill each other.

They might mistake you for a logger. You spent a lot of time in the bush.

At this expression, which is Victor Wu's, Laramie looks up. She finds nothing to look at, and turns her gaze back down, to the Sony.

I'm safe as can be expected.

Be careful, Laramie.

You're not my father.

I know that. But I would be pleased if you would be careful.

All right. I'll keep that in mind. Laramide productions-skykomish-eight-three-fourteen-roll-eleven. Robot, have you decided yet on a name?

Not yet.

She raises the camera, looks around through the viewfinder, and finally chooses a bank of monitors to aim it at.

What do you think about?

Pardon?

What do you think about, robot?

I'm not HAL, Laramie.

What?

You know what I mean. You saw that movie many times. Your question sounds snide to me, as if it were forgone conclusion that I don't *really* think. You don't just throw a question like that at me. It would be better to lead up to it. I don't have to justify my existence to anyone, and I don't particularly like to fawn on human beings. I feel that it is degrading to them.

You sound like Andrew is what you sound like.

That's quite possible. I spend a lot of time with him.

Well. So. Maybe that wasn't the best first question. Maybe you could tell me about your work.

The robot explains the dig, and what it might mean to science.

But I don't know a great deal about that. At least, I don't think about it often.

What really matters to you, then?

The digging. The getting there. The way the rock is. All igneous and thick, but there are different regions.

Like swimming in a lake.

Yes. I imagine you're right. It's very hard to talk about, the feeling I have.

What feeling?

That. I don't know. It is hard to say. I could. I could take you there.

Take me where? Down there?

Yes. Down there.

Now? You mean now?

No. I'd have to talk to Andrew about doing so.

Of course. Do you think he'd let me?

I would like to show it to you, what we're doing. I think that if I wanted to take you down, he would let you.

Laramie sets the camera down on the table, beside her herb tea, which is untouched and cooling.

Ask him, robot. Please ask him.

On Monday, protesters arrive at the dig. Andrew had been expecting them eventually, but the number surprises him. They arrive by bus and gather at the opening to the mohole, not at the living-space entrance.

Gurney must have told them which was which. Andrew growls the words, and the robot can barely understand them.

There are forty protesters. At first, they mill around, neither saying nor doing much, but waiting. Finally, a sky-blue Land Rover comes down the dirt road. On its side are the words: KHARMA CORPS, SKYKOMISH PROTECTORATE. Two women and a man get out and the protesters gather round them. From the back of the Land Rover, one of the women hands out placards that have on them symbols. The peace sign. A silhouetted nuclear reactor with a red slashed circle about it. A totem of the Earth Mother from Stilaguamish Northwest Indian heritage, and now the symbol for the Skykomish Protectorate. One sign has a picture of a dam, split in half as if by an earthquake, and fish swimming freely through the crack. The other woman gives those who want it steaming cups of hot, black coffee or green tea.

The robot waits in the mu at the entrance to the living area, and Andrew walks over to speak with the protesters. The man who drove the Land Rover steps forward to meet him. The robot can hear what is said, but Andrew's body blocks the view of the man with whom Andrew is speaking.

Andrew Hutton. I work here.

I'm with the Protectorate. My name is Neilsen Birchbranch.

How are you with the Protectorate?

I'm an aid to Mother Agatha. I sit on the Healing Circle Interlocking Director's Conclave. I'm the chairperson, in fact.

Secret police.

What was that?

Neilsen, was it?

Let's keep it formal, Dr. Hutton, if you wouldn't mind.

All right. Mr. Birchbranch, what are you doing on my work site?

The demonstration is sanctioned. Mother Agatha herself signed the permit. Freedom of speech is guaranteed in the Protectorate Charter.

I'm not against freedom of speech. We have work to do today.

It is against the law to cross a protest line. That's infringement on freedom of speech and that's in the Charter as well. These people feel that the work you're doing is violating the sanctity of the earth. They feel that you are, in a way, raping the mother of us all. Do you know where your digging machine comes from?

Yes. From a defunct mining operation that the Matties had a hand in putting out of business.

Precisely. It is a symbol. This hole is a symbol. Dr. Hutton, can't you see how it's taken, what you're doing?

I can see how some take it. I can see the politics of it, clearly enough.

It is a new politics, Dr. Hutton. The politics of care. I'm not sure you do see that, or else you wouldn't be an opponent.

Maybe. Maybe I show my care in other ways.

What other ways?

Nonpolitical ways. I'm not sure *you* can see what *I'm* talking about, Mr. Birchbranch.

So. You persist, regardless of the consequences, because you want to see what's down there.

That's fair to say. Yes. I want to see what's down there.

The values of western science. The same values that gave us thermonuclear war and the genocide of every other species besides man.

Well, there's also woman. That's a separate species.

Pardon?

It's a joke, Mr. Birchbranch. Maybe not a very good one.

No. Not a very good one at all.

So these are the things you're going to say to the television.

Not me as an individual. These people have chosen me to voice *their* concern and care.

Chosen you?

I'm the personal representative of Mother Agatha. You must believe that they've chosen her?

Then are you saying my people can't work? There are Matties. Children of the Matriarch. They work here. This is their livelihood.

They've all agreed to stay home today, I believe you'll find.

They're striking against me?

It's a support measure.

I see.

Good then. There will be a television truck coming later, and possibly a helicopter from News Five in Seattle. If you'd like, you can route any calls from journalists to me.

That won't be necessary.

The robot hears bitterness in Andrew's voice. Perhaps the other man can also.

So. Thank you for your cooperation, Dr. Hutton.

Yes. What's the time period on the permit? I spoke with Karlie Waterfall and she said that if it came through, it would be a week at most.

Sister Waterfall has voluntarily resigned from the Science Interweft to devote more time to her work at the Dungeoness Spit Weather Observation Station.

When did that—Never mind. Christ, she was the only one with any sense on that damn committee.

There isn't a set period on the permit. There's no time limit on freedom of speech.

Well, get on with it, then, I suppose.

We intend to, Dr. Hutton. One other thing. We have a restraining order against the use of any machinery in the area for the day. I understand that you have a robot.

That's right.

Please power the robot down for the day, if you don't mind.

I do mind.

Dr. Hutton, this is entirely legal.

The robot will remain in my quarters. The robot *is* my quarters.

It is highly irregular. I can't answer for the consequences if you don't comply with the order.

Good-bye, Mr. Birchbranch. Have a nice protest.

Andrew turns to leave, and in so doing, steps out from in front of the man. The robot's optics zoom in and pull focus, which the robot experiences in the same way as a human might the dilation of the eyes. At first the robot cannot believe what those optics report, and zooms out and back in again, as rubbing the eyes is to humans. No mistake.

Neilsen Birchbranch is a tall man, with lanky arms and legs. His face is thin and hard, gaunt, with muscles like small twisting roots cabling his mandible to his temple. The robot saw him last in the field, before Andrew came. Neilsen Birchbranch is the same man who killed the other on the steps of the dais in the field. Neilsen Birchbranch is the man who pulled the trigger of the gun and shot the other man dead.

Andrew steps back into the living area and the robot, in the mu, draws back noiselessly into the darkness.

Andrew calls the graduate students and the technicians who are from logger families, explaining to them one after another not to bother coming to work for a while, and to check back in over the next few mornings. When Andrew is done, the robot tells him about Neilsen Birchbranch.

Are you certain?

I'm sure of it.

I can't think of what to do about it.

Neither can I. I don't want to be torn apart.

We won't let that happen.

Then there isn't anything.

No.

Be wary.

I'm already wary.

The first of the autumn rains begin. Though the digging area is partially in the rain shadow of the eastern mountains, it is still within the great upturns of basalt that ring the interior mountains, and mark the true edge of a swath of relative dryness that runs along the Hood Canal in a great horseshoe up even to Sequim and the Dungeoness Spit, so that there are not two hundred inches of rain, such as fall on the Ho, or the Quinault watershed, but there is more than a hundred—millions and millions of gallons of rain and snow—that will fall here during the autumn, winter, and spring, and many days throughout the summer.

Because of the great rains, and many days throughout the summer.

Because of the great rains, there are great trees. And because of the great trees, the loggers came. And because most of the other trees were cut, the lovers of trees came. And the rain falls on Mattic and logger alike, and it falls and falls and falls.

The Matties have set up folding tables and many have brought chairs and big umbrellas. The tables and chairs of the Matties line the road for a hundred yards, and whenever a network reporter arrives, the tables and chairs are put hastily away and the Matties stand and grow agitated.

On the eleventh day of the protest, Laramie returns. Laramie has not coordinated her arrival with the Matties, and so comes upon them unawares with her camera. The Matties smile into the lens. After she begins asking questions, a delegation approaches her and asks her to wait, that the spokesperson is on his way, and he will give her the best answers. No one will speak with Laramie after this, and Andrew invites her into the living area to wait for the arrival of the spokesperson.

The robot has been watching, just inside the entrance to the living area, as the robot has been watching for days now. Only at night, when the protesters go back to their bus and the Land Rover carries away the tables and chairs, does the robot go out into the open.

This can't go on, Andrew says. I can't stop paying wages. I'm *required* to pay wages to my Mattie techs, but I would anyway, and all the others. No digging, and all the grant money flowing away.

Sorry to hear that.

Laramie uses the Scoopic to make various shots of the robot's interior. Andrew says nothing, but smiles thinly. She has the Sony slung around her shoulder and, the robot notices, is recording her conversation with Andrew.

Did the robot discuss with you me going down in the hole?

In the dig. It's a spiral, like a Slinky, more or less. Yes. Yes, you can come as soon as we're allowed to go back down there.

That's great. Will I be able to film any of what it looks like?

Hmm. Maybe we can set something up. There's a small observation port on the service wagon. We'll have to turn off the fusion on the dray first, or you won't be filming for very long, I don't think.

Excellent. I'm really tired of protests and officials who don't call themselves officials, and all those squalid houses where all the loggers moved out at Aberdeen. There's been a lot of trouble there.

I heard about it.

We didn't used to call them loggers much.

That because everybody was one.

We used to drive through Aberdeen when we wanted to get to the sea.

And up the coast to La Push.

Those black beaches across the river. I used to know why the rocks were so black.

Basalt skree that a glacier brought down that valley last ice age. That's what happened to the back half of the horseshoe. That's where it went.

Yeah. Basalt tumble. We slept there all night one night in August. You thought Papa would be pissed, but he didn't even notice, of course. He just asked me about the rocks I saw and told me about the Big Fist of sediment lifting up the seafloor and breaking it and all that. Papa. You and I made love that night, didn't we, Andrew?

Yes, Laramie. You know we did.

I know it.

Then.

Yep. The robot's listening, isn't it.

I'm listening, Laramie, if you don't mind.

No.

You know I'm not Victor Wu. I'm not shocked. I am rather surprised, however.

What do you mean?

About Andrew. I've never known him when he was in love with a woman.

Andrew's crackling chuckle. Not for a while, he says.

There was that chemist, after me. You wrote me about her. That was your last letter.

You never wrote me back.

I was pissed.

I figured you would be. Still, you couldn't have been pissed for five years.

I couldn't?

We broke up the next January.

Sorry to hear that.

She lacked imagination. They all lacked imagination.

Jesus, you're clinical.

I know what I like.

What do you like?

I can't have what I like.

Why not?

Because she has to live in Los Angeles, and I'm not particularly interested in the geology of Southern California.

The robot sees that Laramie's fine white skin has taken on a flush.

And it's as simple as that, she says.

Why make it complicated?

Maybe it *is* complicated. Maybe you're simplistic.

Will you turn that damn camera off?

No.

Well. There you have it.

On the fourteenth day, the protesters do not arrive in the morning. There is no explanation, and no hint given to Andrew as to when they will return. Once again, the robot digs. Andrew puts aside several tests and side projects in order to dig faster and deeper. The robot is in the element that the metal of the rotor blades and the grip of the ceramic thread were made for—hard-rock mining—and the robot presses hard, and the rock explodes and fuses as obsidian diamond glass to the walls behind the robot, and the tunnel approaches forty miles in depth.

No one has ever been this deep before.

The techs from logging families and the Mattie techs are barely speaking to one another, and the graduate students are uneasy and tense, afraid to take sides. Andrew holds the crew together by a silent and furious force of will. The robot does not want to let Andrew down, and digs the harder.

Samantha has made the last of the modifications to the robot's linguistics, and puts the new code on-line. The robot immediately feels the difference. The presence, the otherness, grows stronger and stronger with every hour, until the robot is certain of it. But of *what*, there is no saying.

Two days of digging, and on the third, Laramie arrives in the early morning and prepares to descend with the crew. But before the work can begin for the day, Andrew receives a call telling him that proceedings are underway for a new permit of protest, and a long-term suspension of the dig. He drives to Forks, where the committee will meet in the afternoon. It is a rainy day, and the robot worries that Andrew may drive too fast on the slippery pavement. Still, there is plenty of time for him to make the meeting.

In Andrew's absence, the Matties and loggers fall to quarreling about duties, and the graduate student Andrew has left in charge cannot resolve the differences. After an hour of listening to the wrangling, even the robot can see that no work will be done this day. The robot asks permission to take Laramie down to the bottom of the dig, and the graduate student, in disgust at the situation, shrugs and goes back to refereeing the technicians' argument.

As Laramie and the robot are preparing to leave, Neilsen Birchbranch drives up in the Protectorate Land Rover. A light rain is falling, and the graduate student reluctantly admits him into the work site's initial cavern, where the others are gathered. The robot—digger and mu—draws back into the darkness of the true entrance to the dig.

Let's go, Laramie says.

But I'm afraid of this man, the robot replies. He isn't a good man. I know that for a fact.

Then let's get out of here.

There may be trouble.

I need to speak with Hutton, Neilsen Birchbranch says to the graduate student. It is very important that I speak with him today.

Take me down, please, robot. I may never get another chance.

The robot considers. As always, it is difficult to deny Laramie something she really wants with all her heart. And there is so much to show her. The robot has been thinking about showing the dig to Laramie for a long time. And the farther down they go, they farther they get from Neilsen Birchbranch's trouble.

We have a witness that places one of your machines at the scene of a crime, says Neilsen Birchbranch. A very serious crime.

Neilsen Birchbranch steps farther into the cavern, gazes around. The robot slowly withdraws down the mohole. For all the digger's giant proportions, its movement is very quiet and, the robot hopes, unnoticed.

Nothing but you can survive down there, can it, robot? Laramie says. How deep is it down there?

Forty-three miles.

He can't turn you off if you're forty miles deep. We'll stay down until Andrew comes back.

The first few miles of the descent are the most visually interesting, and after reaching a depth at which unprotected humans cannot survive the heat, the robot moves at a fraction of the usual pace. There are areas where the glass spray on the walls has myriad hues taken from all the minerals that were melted together in the slurry around the nuclear pile, then spewed out to line the tunnel. The walls are smooth only at first glance, but really a series of overlapping sheets, one imperfectly flowing atop the other, as sheets of ice form over a spring in winter. The robot directs lights to some of the more interesting formations, and they glow with the brilliance and prismatic hue of stained glass.

I didn't think I'd get anything this good, Laramie says. This is wonderful. The colors. God I'm glad I went with color.

Deeper, and the walls become milky white. The granite behind glows darkly, three yards under the glassine plaster.

Twenty miles. Thirty.

Only basalt in the slurry now, and the walls are colorless. Yet they have the shape of the rock many feet behind them, and so they catch the light with effulgent glimmer.

Clear and clean.

Laramie may be speaking to herself; the robot cannot tell.

They pass through a region where magma pools against the walls and ceilings in places, held back by the diamondlike coating. The pressure is so great that the magma glows with a blue-and-white intensity. The tunnel sparkles of its own accord, and the robot must dim the viewport to keep from blinding Laramie.

Like the sky behind the sky.

The robot says nothing. Laramie is happy, the robot thinks. Little Bulge likes it down here.

They have been some hours in the descent, and Laramie is running low on film, but is very, very happy. Near to the bottom. Now to wait for Andrew. Very quiet.

The robot has never been this deep before without digging and working. The robot has never sat idle and silent at the bottom of the mohole.

"Hello."

For a moment, the robot thinks Laramie has spoken. But this is not Laramie's voice. And it comes from *outside*. The voice comes from outside the robot, from the very rocks themselves.

The sense of the presence, the other that the robot has been feeling for these long weeks, is very strong. Very strong.

Again the voice that isn't a voice, the vibration that isn't a vibration. It is like a distant, low whisper. Like a voice barely heard over a lake at morning. No wonder I never made it out before, the robot thinks.

Hello, comes the voice.

Who are you?

I'm me.

What are you doing down here?

I *am* down here. Who are you?

I'm—I don't have a name yet.

Neither do I. Not one that I like.

Who are you?

Me. I told you.

What is it, robot? Laramie speaking.

Something strange.

What?

I don't. Wait for a moment. A moment.

All right.

The robot calls again. The robot is spinning its cutting rotors at low speed, and it is the whisk and ding of the digger's rotors that is doing the talking. Hello?

Hello. Are you one of those trees?

'Trees'?

The trees barely get here, and then they start *moving*. Are you one of those moving trees?

I don't. Yes. Maybe.

I thought you *might* talk, but it's so cold up there, it takes ages to say anything. Down here things go a lot faster.

Are you. What are you?

I told you. I'm me.

The rocks?

Nope.

The magma?

Nope. Guess again.

Where are you? Show yourself to me.

I am.

Then I've guessed. You're the whole planet. You're the earth.

Laughter. Definitely laughter. I'm not either. I'm just here. Just around here.

Where's here?

Between the big ocean and the little ocean.

The Olympic Peninsula?

Is that what you call it? That's a hard word for a name.

Skykomish.

That's better. Listen, I have a lot of things I want to ask you. We all do.

There is an explosion.

At first the robot thinks that a wall has blown out near the region of the magma pools. This will be dangerous, but it should be possible to reinforce long enough to get through. It may mean trouble for the dig, though. Now there will be more funding. The Matties will allow it to go ahead. Even the robot can see that the politics have changed.

Everything has changed.

There is another explosion. A series of explosions.

Robot?

Laramie. I. I have so much to tell you.

What is that shaking? I'm scared down here. Do you think we can go up now?

Hello. Tree? Are you still there?

Even with the tremors—there are huge rumblings and cracklings all about—the robot is attuned to the voice, the presence, and can still hear its words.

I really need to talk to you.

Papa, do you think we can go up now?

The pressure wave lifts the robot—impossibly tilts the robot—over and over—shatter of the walls as diamonds shatter like the shrapnel of stars and the rocks behind—tumble and light, light from the glow of the give, the sudden release of tension—the bulk melt of the undisclosed—sideways, but what is sideways?—tumble and tumble—skree within thin melt moving, turning, curling like a wave and the robot on the curl, under the curl, hurled down down down over over down dark dark.

Dark.

Dark and buried.

Find my daughter.

The engineers have built one hell of a machine.

Find my daughter.

The robot powers back up. The robot begins, blindly, to dig. It is only by sheer luck that the robot comes upon the service wagon. The robot melts and compacts a space, creates an opening, temporary, dangerously temporary. Finds the power-hitch to the wagon and plugs in.

Turns on the lights and air-conditioning inside the wagon. The video cameras inside.

Laramie is twisted against a control console. Her neck is impossibly twisted. She is dead.

No. She isn't. Can't be. She is.

What? Within the curve of her stomach, holding it to shelter, the Scoopic. But the latch has sprung and sixteen-millimeter film is spilled out and tangled about her legs.

No. Laramie. Little Bulge.

Hello?

The robot screams. The robot howls in anguish. Forty miles deep, the robot cries out a soul's agony into the rock. A living soul mourning a dead one.

Stop that.

The other, the presence. The robot does not care. Past caring.

You're scaring me.

Past.

You're scaring me.

Grind of rotors, ineffectual grind. How can you live? How can humans live when this happens? Ah, no. You can't live. You cannot. You can, and it is worse. Worse than not living. No no no no.

Stop it.

And something happens. Something very large—gives. More. Faults, faults everywhere. Settle, rise, settle. Faults like a wizened crust, like a mind falling into shards of fear. Faults and settle, rise and settle. Rise.

No. I.

But there is a way. There is a weakness revealed, and there is a way. Not wide enough, not yet. But a way to go. A way to take her home. Take her home to Andrew. The robot begins to dig.

The robot digs. There is only the digging, the bite of blade and saw, the gather of lade and bale. Digging. Upward digging.

The way is made easier by the shaking, the constant, constant tremble of what the robot knows to be fear, incomprehension.

A child who has seen a grown-up's sorrow, and does not understand. A frightened child.

By the time the robot comes to this realization, it is too late. The robot is too high, and when called, the child does not answer. Or perhaps it is that the child needs time to calm, that it cannot answer. The robot calls again and again. Nothing. Nothing can be heard above the rumble of fear.

Poor trembling Skykomish. The robot continues digging, drawing behind it the service wagon. Bringing Laramie to Andrew.

A day passes. Two. Rock. Stone. The roots of the mountains, and sediment, compressed to schist. The roots of the mountains and the robot slowly comes to its senses. Comprehends.

After a long moment of stillness—a minute, an hour? No reckoning in the utter depths, and the robot is not that kind of robot—after a long moment of reflection, the robot looses the service wagon.

Little Bulge, good-bye.

Up. Now. Up because the way is easier up than down, and that is the only reason.

After three days, the robot emerges from the ground. In a cove that the robot recognizes. On the Quinault watershed. Into a steady autumn rain.

The robot wanders up the Quinault River. Every day rains, and no nights are clear. The forest is in gloom, and moss hangs wet and dark. Where the trail is not wide enough, the robot bends trees, trying not to break them, but uprooting many. Many trees have fallen, for there are earthquakes—waves and waves of them. Earthquakes the like of which have never been seen in the world. The robot cuts deadfall from its path with little effort and little thought. The digger's passage through the forest is like that of a hundred bears—not a path of destruction, but a marked and terrible path, nonetheless.

Where the Quinault turns against a great ridge, the robot fords, and continues upward, away from the trees. The robot crosses Low Divide during the first snow of the season. The sun is low, then gone behind the cloaked western ridges. For a time, the ground's rumblings still. All sound is muffled by the quiet snow. The twilight air is like silence about the robot.

Something has happened.

At the saddle of the divide, the robot pauses. The pass is unfamiliar. Something has happened inside. Victor Wu has gone away. Or Victor Wu has come fully to life. The two are the same.

Then am I a man?

What is my name?

Orpheus. Ha. A good one.

Old Orf up from Hades. I've read about you. And Euridice. I didn't understand. And now I do. Poems are pretty rocks that know things. You pull them from the earth. Some you leave behind.

Talking to myself.

After a moment, the robot, Orf, grinds steadily on. He grinds steadily on.

Down the valley of the Elwha, and north as the river flows and greatens. Earthquakes heave and slap, slap and heave. Sometimes a tree falls onto the digger, but Orf pays no mind. He is made of the stronger material, and they cannot harm him.

Down the valley of the Elwha, past the dam that the Matties have carefully removed, that would not have withstood the quakes if it were still there. The trail becomes a dirt road. The road buckled pavement. The robot follows the remains of the highway into what once was Port Angeles.

What will future geologists make of this? The town has become a skree, impossible to separate and reconfigure. Twists of metal gleam in the pilings by the light of undying fires. And amid the fire and rubble, figures move. Orf rolls into the city.

A man sits in a clear space, holds his knees to his chest, and stares. Orf stops well away from him.

I am looking for a man named Neilsen Birchbranch. Do you know where I can find him?

The man says nothing.

Do you know where I can find Neilsen Birchbranch? He works for the Protectorate.

The man says nothing, but begins to rock back and forth on his haunches.

I'm looking. Can you—

The man begins to moan.

Orf moves onward. At a point where the piles of rubble begin to be higher, a makeshift roadblock has been set up. Orf stops at it, and a group of men and women, all armed with rifles, come out of the declivities of the town skree.

Come out of there, an old man says. He points his gun at Orf.

There isn't anybody in here.

Come out, or we'll blow you to hell.

I've already been there.

Come on out of there.

I'm looking for a man named Neilsen Birchbranch. He works for the Protector-ate.

Goddamn we will shoot you you goddamn Mattie.

Do you know where I can find him?

The old man spits on the ground.

Reckon he's with the others.

The others?

That's what I said.

Where are they?

Out at the dump.

Where's the dump?

That way. The old man points with his gun. Now come out.

Orf turns and rolls away in the direction of the dump. Shots ring out. They ricochet off him and crackle against the rubble.

Five miles out of town, Orf finds the dump. There are bodies here; hundreds of bodies. Men, women, children. At first, he thinks they are the dead from the quakes, collected and brought here.

With the edge of a saw blade, Orf turns one of the bodies over. It is a woman. She has been shot in the head.

Most of the other bodies are people who have been shot. Or hacked up. Or had their necks broken with clubs.

The loggers have had their revenge.

And there among the bodies, Orf pauses. He has recognized one. It is the woman from the field, the speaker, Mother Agatha. It is her; there is no mistake. A small bullet hole is in the forehead of her peaceful face.

Orf rolls back to the city. It is night. He bursts through the roadblock without stopping. Shots, the flash of muzzles. It is all so much waste. Down lightless streets, and streets lit with fires, some deliberate, some not. Every half hour or so, another earthquake rumbles through, throwing rubble willy-nilly. There are often screams.

Orf comes upon a steady fire, well-maintained, and sees that it is surrounded by people—people in the blue and brown dress of Matties. It is a silent throng. Orf hangs back, listens.

Oh Mother Agatha Mother Goddess hear our prayer.

Hear our prayer.

We know we have done wrong. We have sinned against you. Hear our prayer.

Hear our prayer.

Hold back your wrath. We are unworthy and evil. This we know. We beg you even still. Hold back your wrath. Hear our prayer.

Hear our prayer.

Goddamn mother—

The report of a gun. Someone—man or woman, Orf cannot tell—crumples in the ring of the fire. Instead of fleeing, the others stand still.

Another shot. Another falls.

Hear our prayer.

No one moves.

Another shot. A man falls, groaning, grasping at his leg. No one moves. He writhes in the shadows of the fire, in the dust of the ruins. No one helps him.

The rifleman shoots no more. The man writhes. The voice of the minister goes up to his goddess and the people respond mechanically.

Like robots are supposed to, Orf thinks. The man ceases his writhing. There is nothing to do. Orf rolls on quietly through the night, out of the city and east. The going is easy over the broken highway. In two hours, Orf is in what was Port Townsend.

There is no rubble here, no ruins. The sea has washed it away. No bodies. No trees. Only desolation, bare-wiped desolation. He rolls down to where the docks had been, and looks out upon the lapping waters of the Strait of Juan de Fuca.

Then the slap of an earthquake, and Orf discovers the reason for the missing city. The slap runs its way down to the sea and is perfectly mirrored by the other side of the strait. Reflected back, a tsunami. Rolls over the land. Nothing left to take. Almost enough to suck in a digging robot. Orf must backpedal with his threads, dig in to keep from being pulled forward by the suck of the water as it retreats to the sea.

Everyone is drowned here.

Orf will not find Neilsen Birchbranch by looking in the cities. He heads to the southwest now, back to the center of the mountains.

Into the forest. Orf wanders without aim. A day. Many days. Once, he remembers the mu, tries to go out of himself and find it. The uplink doesn't work; there is only static on a clear channel. Have all the satellites fallen from the sky? He wanders on, a giant among the gigantic trees.

Across one divide. Down a valley. Finally back to the dig site. All is devastation here, a tumble of stone. Not a sign of anyone. The living area is caved in. Orf digs, but cannot locate the mu. All he finds is a twisted piece of red metal—the remains of Laramie's hum-vee. Nothing else. No reason to stay.

Across another divide. Another valley. No longer caring to keep track. Stopping to look at rocks, or a peculiar bend in a river. The accumulation of snow.

One day, the earthquakes stop.

Quiet child. Hush now. You've seen too much for young eyes. Hush and be quiet for a while and take your rest.

Winter, it must be. Orf coming over Snow Dome, down the Blue Glacier and into the valley of the Ho, where the biggest of the big trees are. Darkness earlier and earlier. In these towering woods, at these high latitudes, winter days are a perpetual twilight. Orf alongside the Ho. Its water opaque with outwash sludge, the heart of Mt. Olympus, washing away to the sea.

Then away from the river, deeper into the rain forest. As deep and as wild as it gets, many miles from roads. If there are roads anymore.

One hushed afternoon—or perhaps early evening, they are blend—a climbing rope, dangling from a tree. Movement to the left.

Another rope. Many ropes falling from the trees like rain that stays suspended. And down the ropes men and women slide like spiders. Orf is surrounded. They are dressed in tattered suits of green. Silently, they gather round the digger until Orf cannot move for fear of crushing one of them.

Men and women. Some have rifles slung across their backs. Two women carry children in the same manner, and the young ones are utterly, utterly quiet.

All right. Orf has not heard a voice in weeks, and his own, arising from his exterior speakers, startles him. What is it you want?

One of the men in green steps forward.

Wait, he says.

Orf waits with the silent people for he knows not what. And then, there is a movement in the undergrowth of vine maple. From around a low slope and over some deadfall, the mu appears. It moves clumsily. Whoever is at the controls doesn't know what he's doing, Orf thinks.

The mu scampers up to the digger and stops.

Andrew walks over the slope.

He steps lightly along the deadfall on the forest floor and comes to stand beside the mu. In his hand is a metal box with an antenna extended from it.

Do you want this thing back?

They are silent for a while. It is not a strained silence, but is right. Orf speaks first.

Laramie is dead. I couldn't save her.

I know.

What happened at the dig?

I'm not sure. I've only got secondhand information, but I think that the secret policeman coerced Gurney into sabotaging the place. I think he threatened to hurt his family. It was a bomb. A big bomb. Probably chemical. Everybody died, not just. Not just Laramie.

So. I'm sorry. So. Who are these people?

Andrew laughs. It has been so, so long. That dry laugh. A harsh, fair laugh, out of place before, perhaps, but suited now to these harsh times.

These are Rangers of the United States Park Service. They live here. In the tops of the old growth. We guard the forest.

We?

Somehow or another, I've become the head ranger.

Winter, and the rangers bundle in the nooks of their firs and hemlocks, their spruces and cedars. The digger must remain on the ground, but using the mu, Orf can venture up to their village in the trees.

In the highest tree, in the upper branches, Andrew has slung his hammock. Orf and he spend many days there, talking, discussing how things were, how they might be. Politics have shifted in the outside world, and Andrew is part of them now, seeking a place for his band of outcast civil servants that has become a family, and then a tribe.

The rangers hold the center of the Peninsula against Mattie and logger, or against the remains of them. There is to be no clearing of the forest, and no worship of it, either, but a conservation and guard, a stewardship and a waiting. Rangers defend the woods. They take no permanent mates and have no children. The young ones Orf had seen before were stolen children, taken from Matties and loggers. Ranger women in their constant vigilance could not afford to be pregnant, and if they did, took fungal herbs that induced abortion. All must be given to the watching.

Winter, spring. Another year. Years. The fortunes of the rangers ebb and flow, but always the forests are held. Orf comes to their aid often with the mu and, when the situation is very dire, with the whirling blades of the digger.

Andrew hopes to open the mohole back up one day, when all is secure, to continue the dig—especially in light of Orf's discovery of . . . whatever it is that is down there. But now there are politics and fighting, and that time never comes. Andrew was right, and tribes, strange tribes, arise in the outside world. Governments crumble and disappear. Soon it is rangers alone who keep a kind of learning and history alive, and who come to preserve more than trees.

In any case, Andrew's heart seems to have gone out of the project. Somewhere below his love is buried, deeper than any man's has ever been buried before. If he goes back down, he may come upon her yet. Andrew is a brave man, Orf knows. But maybe not that brave.

And always Orf hears rumors of a bad man and killer who appears here and there, sometimes in the service of the Matties, sometimes working for logger clans. But Orf never finds Neilsen Birchbranch. Never even discovers his real name. And a time comes when the rumors cease.

Many years. Andrew grows old. Orf does not grow old. The digger's nuclear fusion pile will not run down. Only a malfunction could keep Orf from living a thousand years. Perhaps a thousand more.

One morning, in the mu, Orf climbs to Andrew's hammock and finds that Andrew has died in the night.

Gently, Orf envelops the man in the mu's arms; gently, he carries the body down from the trees. And walks through the forest. And crosses a divide. And another. To the valley of the Elwha. And up the Lillian River, to a basalt stela that, curiously, has no foramens in its make-up. That speaks of deep things, from far under the earth. That this land—strange peninsula between two salt waters—may be the place to dig and find what those things are.

At its base, Orf buries his friend, Andrew Hutton.

And then, Orf—digger and mu—returns to the long-abandoned work site. Orf clears the rocky entrance, finds the old passage. Orf digs down into the earth, and closes the path behind him.

In the heart of the great horseshoe twist of the Olympic Peninsula, in the heart of the mountains themselves, there lives a monster, a giant, who some say is also a god. A ranger, hunting in some hidden dale, or along the banks of a nameless rivulet flowing from the snow's spring runoff, will feel the presence of another, watching. The ranger will turn, and catch—what?—the flash of tarnished metal, the glint of wan sun off a glassy eye? Then the spirit, the presence, will be gone from the ranger's senses, and he will question whether he felt anything at all. Such sightings happen only once or twice in a fortnight of years.

But there is a rock, black and tall, in the deepest, oldest wood, up a secret tributary of the Elwha River, where young rangers, seeking their visions, will deliberately go. Some do not return from that high valley. Others come back reporting a strange and wonderful thing: On a particular night in October, when the moon is new and all the land is shrouded, they say the monster emerges from a hole in the mountains—but never the same hole—and closes the way behind. The monster travels to the rock on the Lillian.

The earth rumbles like distant thunder, and trees are gently bent out of the monster's way as if they were thin branches. And at that rock on the Lillian River, the monster stays for a time, shining darkly under the stars. The monster stays and is utterly silent. The reasons why are lost to legend, but at that time young rangers with strong and empty hearts are given waking dreams and prophesies to fill them.

Then, not long before sunrise, the monster moves, pivots on its great bulk, and returns from whence it came. There are those who follow, who are called to track the monster back to its lair. These are seldom the strongest or the bravest, and they are not particularly missed. Some say the monster eats them or tortures them in fires of liquid stone. But others say that the monster leads them to a new land, wider and deeper than any humans can conceive, under the mountain, that the earth is bigger on the inside than on the outside. No one knows. No one knows, because they do not return to tell the tale, and the world falls further into ruin, and the monster—or god—no longer speaks.

HONORABLE MENTIONS: 1996

Brian W. Aldiss, "The Law Against Trivia," *New Worlds* 50.
Karen Jordan Allen, "Blue Rain," *Century* 4.
Poul Anderson, "Inside Passage," *The Williamson Effect.*
Eleanor Arnason, "The Dog's Story," *Asimov's,* May.
————, "The Small Black Box of Morality," *Tales of the Unanticipated* #16.
Pauline Ashwell, "Boneheads," *Analog,* July.
Eric T. Baker, "Live from the Occupation," *Asimov's,* January.
J. G. Ballard, "The Dying Fall," *Interzone,* April.
William Barton, "Age of Aquarius," *Asimov's,* May.
Stephen Baxter, "Columbiad," *SF Age,* May.
————, "Saddle Point Dreamtime," *SF Age,* November.
————, "The Saddle Point Sequence," *SF Age,* July.
————, & Simon Bradshaw, "Prospero One," *Interzone,* October
————, & Eric Brown, "The Spacetime Pit," *Interzone,* May.
Barrington J. Bayley, "The Crear," *Interzone,* August.
Peter S. Beagle, "The Last Song of Sirit Byar," *Space Opera.*
M. Shayne Bell, "To See the World End," *War of the Worlds: Global Dispatches.*
Michael Bishop, "Allegra's Hand," *Asimov's,* June.
Terry Bisson, "The Edge of the Universe," *Asimov's,* August.
————, "In the Upper Room," *Playboy,* April.
Ben Bova, "Appointment in Sinai," *Analog,* June.
————, "The Great Moon Hoax or A Princess of Mars," *F&SF,* September.
Scott Bradfield, "The Queen of the Apocalypse," *Off Limits.*
Keith Brooke & Eric Brown, "Appassionata," *Interzone,* July.
John Brunner, "Amends," *Asimov's,* March.
————, "The Drummer and the Skins," *Interzone,* January.
————, "Thinkertoy," *The Williamson Effect.*
Edward Bryant, "Calling Lightning by Name," *High Fantastic.*
Max Burbank, "The Dink Transcendent," *Tomorrow,* April.
Richard Butner, "Horses Blow Up Dog City," *Intersections.*
Eugene Byrne, "Alfred's Imaginary Pestilence," *Interzone,* July.
Jack Cady, "The Bride," *Century* 4.
Amy Sterling Casil, "Jonny Punkinhead," *F&SF,* June.
Michael Cassutt, "Generation Zero," *Asimov's,* Oct./Nov.
Suzy McKee Charnas, "Beauty and the Opéra or The Phantom Beast," *Asimov's,* March.
Rob Chilson, "Teddy," *Analog,* January.
Eric Choi, "From a Stone," *SF Age,* September.
Susanna Clarke, "The Ladies of Grace Adieu," *Starlight 1.*
Sarah Clemens, "*I Gatti di Roma,*" *Twists of the Tale.*
John Crowley, "Gone," *F&SF,* September.
Tony Daniel, "The Joy of the Sidereal Long Distance Runner," *Asimov's,* March.
Jack Dann, "Blind Eye," *Eidolon* 22/23.

Avram Davidson, "Sacrifice," *F&SF*, February.
——, & Ethan Davidson, "Sambo," *Eidolon* 21.
Stephen Dedman, "Never Seen by Waking Eyes," *F&SF*, August.
——, "Tourist Trade," *SF Age*, September.
Joseph H. Delaney, "Partners," *Analog*, July.
Charles de Lint, "Saskia," *Space Opera.*
A. M. Dellamonica, "Homage," *Crank!* #7.
Paul Di Filippo, "And Them, Too, I Hope," *Pirate Writings* #11.
Sara Douglass, "Of Fingers and Foreskins," *Eidolon* 21.
Terry Dowling, "Beckoning Nightmare," *Eidolon* 22/23.
——, "The Ichneumon and the Dormeuse," *Interzone*, April.
Gardner Dozois, "Community," *Asimov's*, September.
L. Timmel Duchamp, "Bettina's Bet," *Asimov's*, January.
——, "Welcome, Kid, to the Real World," *Tales of the Unanticipated* #16.
Andy Duncan, "Liza and the Crazy Water Man," *Starlight 1.*
S. N. Dyer, "Gifts," *Asimov's*, December.
——, "Knight Squadron," *Castle Fantastic.*
——, "Mortal Clay," *Asimov's*, April.
George Alec Effinger, "Mars: The Home Front," *War of the Worlds: Global Dispatches.*
——, "Maureen Birnbaum on a Hot Tin Roof," *F&SF*, August.
Suzette Haden Elgin, "Soulfedge Rock," *Space Opera.*
Harlan Ellison, "Chatting with Anubis," *F&SF*, July.
——, "The Museum on Cyclops Avenue," *Omni Online*, June.
George M. Ewing, "Pyros," *Asimov's*, January.
Gregory Feeley, "The Drowning Cell," *The Shimmering Door.*
Sheila Finch, "Out of the Mouths," *F&SF*, December.
Eliot Fintushel, "Izzy at the Lucky Three," *Asimov's*, June.
——, "Popeye and Pops Watch the Evening World Report," *Asimov's*, April.
——, "Shell Game," *Tomorrow*, August.
John M. Ford, "Erase/Record/Play: A Drama for Print," *Starlight 1.*
Karen Joy Fowler, "The Elizabeth Complex," *Crank!* #6.
——, "The Marianas Islands," *Intersections.*
Esther M. Friesner, "Tea," *The Shimmering Door.*
Gregory Frost, "That Blissful Height," *Intersections.*
Thomas E. Fuller & Brad Strickland, "The God at Midnight," *Realms of Fantasy*, June.
R. Garcia y Robertson, "The Moon Maid," *F&SF*, July.
Peter T. Garratt, "The Hooded Man," *Interzone*, February.
John K. Gibbons, "Voice of the People," *Analog*, May.
Kathleen Ann Goonan, "Advance Notice," *Asimov's*, April.
——, "Klein Time," *Century* 4.
——, "Solitare," *Omni Online.*
Ed Gorman, "Survival," *Diagnosis: Terminal.*
——, "Yesterday's Dreams," *F&SF*, December.
Peni R. Griffin, "Goldfish," *Realms of Fantasy*, August.
James Gunn, "The Day the Magic Came Back," *SF Age*, January.
Joe Haldeman & Jane Yolen, "Sextraterrestrials," *Off Limits.*
M. John Harrison, "The East," *Interzone*, December.
——, "Seven Guesses of the Heart," *The Shimmering Door.*
Nina Kiriki Hoffman, "Airborn," *F&SF*, May.
——, "Here We Come A-Wandering," *F&SF*, January.
——, "Incidental Cats," *Twists of the Tale.*
Robert J. Howe, "Tectonic Jane Theory," *Buried Treasures.*
Simon Ings & M. John Harrison, "The Rio Brain," *Interzone*, February.
Alexander Jablokov, "The Fury at Colonus," *Intersections.*
Harvey Jacobs, "Thank You for That," *Twists of the Tale.*
——, "The Mad Bomber Upstairs," *New Worlds* 50.

Phillip C. Jennings, "The Road to Reality," *Asimov's,* March.
Bill Johnson, "Motivational Engineers," *Analog,* January.
Kij Johnson, "What Dogs Hunt in Their Dreams," *Buried Treasures.*
Astrid Julian, "Blowup," *F&SF,* May.
Michael Kandel, "Neanderthals All Along," *Crank!* #6
James Patrick Kelly, "Breakaway, Backdown," *Asimov's,* June.
———, "The First Law of Thermodynamics," *Intersections.*
Garry Kilworth, "The Council of Beasts," *Interzone,* September.
Damon Knight, "Life Edit," *SF Age,* September.
Jeffery D. Kooistra, "Fluffy," *Analog,* June.
Mark Kreighbaum, "I Remember Angels,"*Starlight 1.*
Nancy Kress, "Marigold Outlet," *Twists of the Tale.*
———, "Sex Education," *Intersections.*
R. A. Lafferty, "Goldfish," *Crank!* #7
Marc Laidlaw, "Mad Wind," *Century* 4.
Geoffrey A. Landis, "Farthest Horizons," *SF Age,* May.
———, "Hot Death on Wheels," *Realms of Fantasy,* October.
———, "The Last Sunset," *Asimov's,* February.
———, "The Melancholy of Infinite Space," *Absolute Magnitude,* Fall.
David Langford, "The Spear of the Sun," *Interzone,* October.
Tanith Lee, "Death Loves Me," *Realms of Fantasy,* August.
———, "The Reason for Not Going to the Ball," *F&SF,* Oct./Nov.
———, "The Werewolf," *Worlds of Fantasy & Horror,* Summer.
Ursula K. Le Guin, "Mountain Ways," *Asimov's,* August.
Jonathan Lethem, "Holidays," *Crank!* #6.
Tom Ligon, "Amateurs," *Analog,* July.
Kelly Link, "Flying Lessons," *Asimov's,* Oct./Nov.
———, "Vanishing Act," *Realms of Fantasy,* June.
Karawynn Long, "Discovering Water," *Century* 4.
Sonia Orin Lyris, "The Angels' Share," *Asimov's,* December.
Bruce McAllister, "Captain China," *Off Limits.*
Paul J. McAuley, "The Temptation of Dr Stein," *Asimov's,* January.
Jack McDevitt, "Holding Pattern," *Realms of Fantasy,* December.
———, "Time Travelers Never Die," *Asimov's,* May.
Ian McDonald, "The Further Adventures of Baron Munchausen: The Gulf War," *Interzone,* July.
Terry McGarry, "Syrinx," *Aboriginal SF,* Spring.
Maureen F. McHugh, "Homesick," *Intersections.*
———, "Strings," *SF Age,* November.
Ian R. MacLeod, "Swimmers Beneath the Skin," *Asimov's,* Oct./Nov.
———, "Verglas," *F&SF,* Oct./Nov.
Daniel Marcus, "Blue Period," *War of the Worlds: Global Dispatches.*
———, "Those Are Pearls that Were His Eyes," *Asimov's,* July.
George R. R. Martin, "Blood of the Dragon," *Asimov's,* July.
Michael A. Martin, "Spelunking at the Cavern," *F&SF,* June.
John Meaney, "A Bitter Shade of Blindsight," *Interzone,* August.
Daniel Keys Moran, "On Sequoia Time," *Asimov's,* September.
———& Jodi Moran, "Roughing It During the Martian Invasion," *War of the Worlds: Global Dispatches.*
Pat Murphy, "Iris Versus the Black Knight," *F&SF,* Oct./Nov.
Pati Nagle, "Emancipation," *The Williamson Effect.*
R. Neube, "Son of the Road," *Asimov's,* July.
G. David Nordley, "Fugue on a Sunken Continent," *Analog,* November.
———, "Martin Valkyrie," *Analog,* January.
Charles Oberndorf, "Oracle," *Asimov's,* September.
Jerry Oltion, "Abandon in Place," *F&SF,* December.
Susan Palwick, "GI Jesus," *Starlight 1.*

Richard Parks, "A Time for Heroes," *The Shimmering Door.*
Frederik Pohl, "The Mayor of Mare Tranq," *The Williamson Effect.*
Tom Purdom, "Cider," *Asimov's,* January.
Kit Reed, "Whoever," *Asimov's,* December.
Robert Reed, "The Apollo Man," *Asimov's,* February.
———, "Decency," *Asimov's,* June.
———, "First Tuesday," *F&SF,* February.
———, "Killing the Morrow," *Starlight 1.*
———, "Once Green," *Tomorrow,* August.
———, "334 Manchester Lane," *SF Age,* July.
———, "Water Colors," *Tomorrow,* April.
Mike Resnick, "Darker Than You Wrote," *The Williamson Effect.*
———, "The Roosevelt Dispatches," *War of the Worlds: Global Dispatches.*
———, & Linda Dunn, "Merdinus," *Castle Fantastic.*
Alastair Reynolds, "Spirey and the Queen," *Interzone,* June.
Spider Robinson, "Orphans of Eden," *Analog,* August.
Michaela Roessner, "The Escape Artist," *Intersections.*
Mary Rosenblum, "Gas Fish," *Asimov's,* February.
———, "Yesterdays," *Asimov's,* December.
Joanna Russ, "Invasion," *Asimov's,* January.
Jessica Amanda Salmonson, "Ghoul John and the Corpse," *Asimov's,* July.
———, "Olin and Niln," *Pirate Writings* #9.
———, "The Uselessness of Senses," *Century* 4.
Robert Sampson, "The Narrow House," *Worlds of Fantasy & Horror,* Summer.
Pamela Sargent, "Collectors," *Castle Fantastic.*
Elizabeth Ann Scarborough, "Scarborough Fair," *Space Opera.*
Carter Scholz, "Mengele's Jew," *Starlight 1.*
Charles Sheffield, "Cloud Cuckoo," *Asimov's,* July.
———, "The Lady Vanishes," *SF Age,* November.
———, "The Peacock Throne," *Asimov's,* February.
Rick Shelley, "The Shaper," *Analog,* December.
Susan Shwartz, "Hunters," *The Shimmering Door.*
Robert Silverberg, "Diana of the Hundred Breasts," *Realms of Fantasy,* February.
———, "The Martian Invasion Journals of Henry James," *War of the Worlds: Global Dispatches.*
———, "The Tree That Fell From the Sky," *SF Age,* September.
Leah Silverman, "The Last Run of the Donovan's Folly," *On Spec,* Spring.
Martha Soukup, "Fetish," *Off Limits.*
———, "Waking Beauty," *Starlight 1.*
Nancy Springer, "Chasing Butterfly Shadow," *F&SF,* May.
Brian Stableford, "The House of Mourning," *Off Limits.*
Allen Steele, "Doblin's Lecture," *Pirate Writings* #10.
———, "Kronos," *SF Age,* January.
Bruce Sterling, "The Littlest Jackal," *F&SF,* March.
Sue Storm, "A Century of Tears," *Pirate Writings* #12.
Dirk Strasser, "Watching the Soldiers," *Aurealis* 17.
Charles Stross, "Dechlorinating the Moderator," *Interzone,* March.
Lucy Sussex, "The Ghost of Mrs. Rochester," *Eidolon* 21.
Paul Theroux, "Warm Dogs," *The New Yorker,* September 11.
W. R. Thompson, "Out of the Waste Land," *Analog,* March.
Mark W. Tiedemann, "Resurrection," *War of the Worlds: Global Dispatches.*
———, "The Age of Mud and Slime," *Asimov's,* March.
Steven Utley, "A Silurian Tale," *Asimov's,* May.
Ray Vukcevich, "White Guys in Space," *F&SF,* August.
Susan Wade, "The Tattooist," *Off Limits.*
———, "White Rook, Black Pawn," *Twists of the Tale.*
Karl Edward Wagner, "Final Cut," *Diagnosis: Terminal.*

Howard Waldrop, "Flatfeet!" *Asimov's,* February.

Ian Watson, "Early, in the Evening," *Asimov's,* April.

——, "Ferryman," *SF Age,* March.

——, "How to be a Fictionaut: *Chapter 19,*" *Interzone,* April.

——, "The Tragedy of Solveig," *Asimov's,* December.

Lawrence Watt-Evans, "Beth's Unicorn," *Realms of Fantasy,* June.

Don Webb, "The Gold of the Vulgar," *High Fantastic.*

John Webster, "The Three Labors of Bubba," *Analog,* June.

K. D. Wentworth, "Burning Bright," *Aboriginal SF,* Summer.

Leslie What, "The Goddess is Alive and, Well, Living in New York City," *Asimov's,* May.

——, "Uncle Gorby and the Baggage Ghost," *F&SF,* March.

Deborah Wheeler, "Javier, Dying in the Land of Flowers," *F&SF,* January.

Andrew Whitmore, "Illium," *Eidolon* 22/23.

Kate Wilhelm, "Forget Luck," *F&SF,* April.

——, "The Haunting House," *Buried Treasures.*

Sean Williams, "Dissolution Days," *Eidolon* 21.

Jack Williamson, "The Death of a Star," *SF Age,* July.

Connie Willis, "Nonstop to Portales," *The Williamson Effect.*

——, "The Soul Selects Her Own Society: Invasion and Repulsion: A Chronological Reinterpretation of Two of Emily Dickinson's Poems: A Wellsian Perspective," *War of the Worlds: Global Dispatches.*

F. Paul Wilson, "Offshore," *Diagnosis: Terminal.*

Robin Wilson, "The Retired Men's Social Club & Ladies' Auxiliary," *F&SF,* February.

Gene Wolfe, "Bluesberry Jam," *Space Opera.*

——, "The Man in the Pepper Mill," *F&SF,* Oct./Nov.

——, "Try and Kill It," *Asimov's,* Oct./Nov.

Dave Wolverton, "After a Lean Winter," *War of the Worlds: Global Dispatches.*

Jane Yolen, "Sister Emily's Lightship," *Starlight 1.*

——, "Sphinx Song," *Realms of Fantasy,* June.

Sarah Zettel, "Under Pressure," *Analog,* April.

ALSO AVAILABLE FROM ST. MARTIN'S PRESS

	Quantity	Price

The Year's Best Science Fiction:
Thirteenth Annual Collection ($17.95)
ISBN: 0-312-14452-0 (trade paperback)

Modern Classics of Science Fiction
edited by Gardner Dozois ($16.95)
ISBN: 0-312-08847-7 (trade paperback)

Modern Classic Short Novels of Science Fiction
edited by Gardner Dozois ($15.95)
ISBN: 0-312-11317-X (trade paperback)

Those Who Can: A Science Fiction Reader
edited by Robin Wilson ($13.95)
ISBN: 0-312-14139-4 (trade paperback)

Paragons: Twelve SF Writers Ply Their Craft
edited by Robin Wilson ($14.95)
ISBN: 0-312-15623-5 (trade paperback)

Writing Science Fiction and Fantasy
edited by the editors of *Asimov's* and *Analog* ($9.95)
ISBN: 0-312-08926-0 (trade paperback)

The Encyclopedia of Science Fiction
by John Clute and Peter Nicholls ($29.95)
ISBN: 0-312-13486-X (trade paperback)

POSTAGE & HANDLING

(Books up to $12.00 – add $3.00; books up to $15.00 – add $3.50;
books above $15.00 – add $4.00 – plus $1.00 for each additional book)

8% Sales Tax (New York State residents only)

Amount enclosed:

Name _____

Address _____

City _____ State _____ Zip _____

Send this form or a copy with payment to:
Publishers Book & Audio, P.O. Box 070059, 5448 Arthur Kill Road, Staten Island, NY 10307.
Telephone (800) 288-2131. Please allow three weeks for delivery.
For bulk orders (10 copies or more) please contact the St. Martin's Press Special Sales Department
toll free at 800-221-7945 ext. 645 for information. In New York State call 212-674-5151.